To Mario

Patrick Bentley

Lovely to meet you!

Cover design by Sansa Arshad.
arshadsana645@gmail.com or find her on Fiverr.

Took the apple from the tree
Then she told me it would set me free
Like a fool I took her hand
Said she'd take me to the Promised land
But I found when I was there
There was nothing
And all the promises she made meant nothing.

Christy Dignam. Aslan.

INTRODUCTION

The year was 2010 when I first came up with the idea to write Dark Line.

The idea was to present first-hand accounts of the dangerous world of cocaine, ecstasy and other drugs that had taken a firm grip of the social life. Basing the book locally in Fingal proved getting the message across even harder. When confronted with the question why I based it in real pubs, estates, and clubs almost aimlessly and recklessly I expressed that in my opinion I really believed everyone was thinking the same. That drugs are now becoming a huge danger to the next generation of young people. We need to say it's everywhere. In every class of society. Working class, middle class, upper class. Some folks with influence deliberately set out to blacklist the supporting of this book on the grounds of where it was based. But regardless, the battle went on and the book went on to save the lives and futures of many young people, and helped to inform parents with an insight in the world of drug use.

That was its intended aim.

Some years later I did a deeper study on the drugs culture and its growing effects and the power of the hold it was having on our generation of young people. It was being normalised at this time. If you weren't taking a line with a drink at the weekend, there was something wrong with you. "Hey, it's like drinking a cup of coffee," one 17-year-old told me. "I don't know what all the fuss is about."

Due to the volume of people being caught in possession of drugs, there was talk coming out about making it not an offence. Everything was making it seem almost okay to do drugs. The message from the health services was: *Just be careful.* This points to how big it had become. When I studied it, I found that up to 90% of young folk between the ages of 13 to 25 were taking something. People high up in social care were able to tell me the growing problem of mental health was hugely down to drugs like cocaine as well as the grass young people were smoking, which, when brought into a lab, was found to have very harmful additional chemicals added to enhance the effects and make it more addictive and destructive on many an underdeveloped young mind.

Over and above all that, the study of the history of drugs involves another more chilling warning and extremely dangerous side-effect to users: the spiritual danger. A danger literally unknown or completely rejected by most people. But certainly, more than a suggestion to the storyline of *Dark Line.*

In the Book of Revelation, Chapter 22, Verse 15, it talks about the practice of magic arts or sorcery. When you translate the word 'sorcery' from the Greek you find the word *pharmakeia*, from which we get the word 'pharmacy'. The understanding is if you mix potions to get a desired effect that will take you and your senses out of the here and now outside the normal feelings of life, you are in fact opening a doorway into the supernatural. Anyone on cocaine has entered another level of consciousness. The level of confidence increases the level of awareness, where our sex drive is taken to unnatural levels.

The fall-out never noted is the dangerous side effects seen in society – an increase in violent attacks and deaths and stabbings and murders. Families ruined and relationships destroyed. Jobs and careers lost. Mental Health issues on the up, with huge increases in depression and suicides.

It's my firmly-held opinion that everything drugs is trying to create is a form of paradise. We all want to be content, at peace, feeling self-confident within the normal everyday life. We all crave it, but don't know where else to find it. Religion in all its forms certainly doesn't reach it and if folk are honest, they find all this totally boring as an experience. But what isn't boring is a real tangible relationship with the living God who created you for himself. But our sin blocks the pathway to God completely. Christ has intercepted your punishment and paid for it, at no cost to you. On the cross it was paid in full. When a person sees this and commits to Christ from the heart, it then brings that person directly into the very presence of God, who from there forward creates a real sense of the paradise we crave for individually.

We find certain things fall into place as a result.

Death has no more fear attached to it. We are certain of Heaven because our sins were paid for by Christ.

Our life is changing for the better. It won't be easy, or some bed of roses. But you can be certain it will be real and it will make you into a person you will be grateful for in the years ahead.

That I promise.

But because Jesus lives forever, his priesthood lasts forever. Therefore he is able, once and forever, to save those who come to God through him because he always lives to intercede for them (Hebrews, 7: 24, 25).

Hope you get something from this book.
Patrick Bentley

CONTENTS

DARKLINE

Chapter One

This is the Life

The knock on my bedroom door.

'Lisa, your taxi's after pulling up!'

'Ok, Ma, tell him I'm on my way down.'

I pick up a rolled note and bend down to the CD cover on my dressing table. I snort three lines of coke. Running my finger across the plastic to remove any bits left, I rub the traces across my gums. I pick up the half-finished bottle of Miller beer and knock it back as I grab my jacket, keys and bag.

I look in the mirror one last time to make sure there are no tell-tale traces around my nose. Then I'm off down the stairs.

'Ma, I'm off! I love you. Come here, and give me a hug. I love you, you know that, don't you?'

'Of course I do. Lisa – you sound tipsy already. How many drinks did you have while you were getting ready?'

'Just one, Ma. Bye!'

'Have you got your keys?'

'Yeah, yeah, got keys . . .'

I'm gone.

The taxi door opens and Cara, my best friend since school, jumps out.

'You can sit in the middle. I hate it. It hurts my ass!'

Typical Cara. Always calls it like it is. I hug her and jump in beside Ruth, our other great friend from secondary school. It was Holy Faith De La Salle. We all get on so well – 'No Secrets Club' is what we call the bond we share. Nothing happens in our lives that we don't share with one another.

Ruth with her long red hair made into a lovely ponytail had been nicknamed Foxy back in her school days.

Cara on the other hand wears her light brown hair cut short like mine. Her natural tanned skin and dark brown eyes makes her a real eye-catcher for all the guys.

We're all twenty-three years of age and life could not be better for us. We all have great jobs. Cara is a nurse. Ruth works part time in Bank of Ireland. And me? I'm a primary school teacher. I've lived in Skerries all my life, moved into Kelly's Bay Drive five years ago, after my father died. I'm the only child in our family and my mother thought a two-bedroom apartment would be a sensible move, as the four-bedroom house was just too big for two people. I never saw the sense in Dad buying that big house for just the three of us; Ma said that they had planned for more kids but never had them.

The taxi pulls up outside the Blue Ocean, overlooking the harbour. There's a lovely view to take in over a few drinks at any time of the year. It's December and you just want to get inside out of the cold and enjoy it in comfort.

Closing the taxi door, Cara bends over and whispers in my ear.

'What you think of the new batch?, I'm flying Lisa. Bloody rocket fuel!'

'I took a few lines, and a couple of bottles of Miller to wash it down. Some of the best coke we've had in ages.'

'I told you it would be. John told me it's going to be like this all over the Christmas.'

Ruth pushes her head between us.

'Em, are we going into Blue or just standing here till we turn bloody blue with the cold?'

Laughing, we push our way into the bar.

'Three bottles of Miller? I'll get this round,' said Cara. 'You got the taxi, Lisa, and anyway, I owe you one from Nealon's last week.'

'This is some buzz!' said Ruth. She checked no one else could hear her and dropped her voice. 'I'm flying from that stuff! I must have had four or five lines and a couple of cans. Sure it's only the start.'

'John texted me,' says Cara. 'He's bringing a few E's with him. He'll be down around 10:30.'

'I think Orla and Carl have some as well. They're out with each other in Balbriggan. Just got a text saying *See you all at The Life*'.

The Life is a well-known nightclub looking out on Balbriggan harbour. We've all practically lived in the place at the weekends since we were eighteen.

Before we've finished our first bottle of Miller, John comes in, smiling as always, hugging everybody he meets as he walks towards us, with his curly light brown hair and thin pale face, wearing G-Star jeans and top as always. For a guy who hardly ever touches the stuff, he certainly looks well out of it tonight. He grabs Cara and kisses her.

'Oh no, not you two again!' I said. 'Stop, will ye!'

'You want a kiss as well?'

'Nah, you're alright, John.'

They have been dating four years on and off, kind of rocky, but most of the time they get on great. Ruth's in a relationship with Steve who's twenty-nine. They're dating three years. A bit stormy at times, but he's dead on and we all get on so well as a gang.

As the night goes on, Steve joins us along with Frank, who's dating another girl, Anne. They hang out with us as well. She's lovely, very funny – when she's out of the head.

You may be wondering if I have a boyfriend too. Well, I had – for four years. Ron. How I loved Ron . . . until I found out that he was going to parties, taking coke and sleeping with girls behind my back. That was the end of him.

I date guys all the time. One guy, Brian, we seem to always end up together after nightclubs. He's got his apartment just round the corner from where I live in Kelly's Bay. Not so far to go in the mornings to get home. I suppose I don't really trust men anymore, not to open up my life to them, anyway. I think after four years with the one-and-only Ron that was enough for me as far as true love is concerned. I'm out to enjoy life to the full, and it's working great at the moment for me. So why change anything?

With everyone drinking, Ruth dropped an 'E' into my hand.

'I got a half one down,' said Steve. 'They're great, so take my other half and we'll all come up together and head down to The Life and dance the night away.'

With a mouthful of beer, down went the E tablet. John smiles as he watches me take it.

'Go easy, Lisa. They're strong.'

We all laugh and talk as we wait for a couple of taxis to take us to The Life. I can feel the heat, the buzz of the E starting to race slowly up my body. It's amazing. I look into Ruth's face and it told its own story. Same look, same wavelength. You can almost read each other's thoughts when you're on E. It's like a circle comes down around everyone that's on it and you sense you're all together. In a lovely place called paradise, I just feel I love the world. Even people I don't like seem like people I want to go and put my arms around and be best mates with. It's amazing.

Minutes before the taxi comes, we all drink the last of our drinks slowly. I look out to the path outside Blue. A passing glance from a guy I only know to see, David Salle. He stares at us all. His electric blue eyes stop onto mine for a split second, but it seems longer in my head.

'What's the creep looking at?' says John, looking at me.

'What's the story with him, John?'

'He's a loner who went a bit off the wall over a girl in Rush. Come on, here's the taxi!'

We all jump in. The driver, looking in the mirror, asks us where to.

'The Life – in Balbriggan.'

I can see David Salle as the taxi pulls around by the public toilets. I look into his eyes and feel a chill.

'What's the fool looking at?' Ruth snaps.

'There's a look in his eyes . . .' I say.

'Yeah! He's mad!' laughs John. 'Some girl broke if off and he's never been right in the head since. He stays in or walks his dog on the beach. What a loser!'

I look into Cara's eyes as we drive the road to The Life, telling her I love her, and Ruth too. What super friends to have. Everyone is talking over each other's conversations. It feels surreal. The buzz from the E is getting stronger by the moment. All I want to do is dance and let out everything I'm feeling inside. I can't get out of the taxi fast enough. Feeling like a superstar, walking on air!

I grab Ruth and give her a hug.

'I love you, Ruth!'

'You're flying!' she laughs.

Once in the doors, it's just a sea of bodies, wall to wall. The sounds of the music sending a deeper rush up my body. John goes to get drinks as we head to the dance floor. Everyone we meet on the way is flying. Everyone smiles, sweat running down their faces. Ruth grabs Steve and starts kissing him as they take off dancing. Cara, Anne and Frank all lock together under the sounds of the music. The E has taken its full effect and I feel so invincible, like everyone else must. Two arms wraps around me. It's Orla and Carl.

'Hi there, Lisa!'

I reach out and hug them both.

'Some buzz in this place, Orla!'

'Yeah, we're just in. Heading up to the bar, John's up there with a few heads. Thought we'd surprise you . . . Hey, I saw Brian when I came in. He asked if you were here.'

'Ah, if you see him, tell him I'll see him at some stage.'

'Ok, you go back dancing and we'll see you later.'

As I turn back to the amazing flashing of the lights and the pumping music, my eyes take in the beauty of the sight. A crowded floor of people, all with their arms above their heads as if all reaching for something unseen above. Maybe reaching for that buzz higher than the one we were all experiencing. It's amazing how you can bond so closely on a dance floor with everyone who's on E and coke. It's like having some kind of code between you. One look and you know you're on the same wavelength. Amazing!

I can feel the perspiration running down my face so I look at Ruth and shout, 'I'm going for a drink!'

She follows, pulling Steve by the hand behind her.

'Get our drinks, Ruth, and head out to the smoke room,' Steve says, pulling away. 'I've got to take a leak.'

When we get to John and Cara, he has the bottles of beer on a small table just off to the left of the bar. Cara gives me the eye to go to the toilets. Locking the door, she takes out a bag of coke.

'Here, let's get a couple of lines up real fast.'

She had it cut down already so we just pour it out. Cara had a €20 note rolled and a small bit of tape holding it tight. We're in and out in a couple of minutes.

'That's the way to do it!' she says with a smile. 'The bouncers watch everything very closely, so you can't be spending ten minutes in the loos nowadays.'

When we get back, John says,

'Hey Lisa, there's Emma Ryan from Rush. We were just talking about you.'

'Who's Emma Ryan?'

'She's the ex-girlfriend of that weirdo David, the one who gave you the weird look outside the Blue Ocean tonight.'

'He didn't give me a weird look, John. It was just a look, nothing strange.'

Emma walks over with a guy. You could tell they were well out of it. She bends over to invite us out to the smoke room. We all need a smoke. Ruth and Steve are already out there so we all pick up our drinks and head out for a fag. The moment we arrive, she turns to me.

'John tells me my ex was giving you all strange looks. He's an oddball, Lisa.'

'Well, he didn't give us a strange look, just kind of searching, if you know what I mean. What happened between you both?'

Emma drags on a fag and takes a mouthful from her drink before telling me a bit about it.

'We started dating a few years ago. He was grand, but I was more into going out to pubs and clubs than he was. I got fed up and dumped him after just over a year. Then he started stalking me with texts and calls and following me. Then on my birthday in the Coast Inn, I had started dating Mark. That's him talking to John and your mates. Anyway, during the party David came in drunk to talk to me, causing a big row. The door guys got him and threw him out. Mark told him to stay away or he'd kick his head in. Thankfully that was the end of it. He's a weirdo, Lisa.'

'When did this all happen with the party?'

'March this year. I blocked him off my Facebook and that was the end of it.'

'Wow, that's crazy, Emma. So you're happy with Mark?'

'Yeah, he's cool.'

'Small world – 'cause he knows John really well. We've seen you around but never got to meet you. You're all sound. The minute I met you, I liked you.'

'You've got great mates too, Lisa. I know Cara a small bit through John.'

'Well, there you are. Now *we're* mates, Emma!'

'That's so sound. Have you got a fella, Lisa?'

'Nah, I . . . I gave up on love a year ago. I've dated a few guys in college, but nothing too deep. I don't really trust men, Emma. I've loads of guys that are friends. But love? Well it's a bit of a myth in my books to be honest. Are you in love with Mark?'

'Only when he does what I tell him, ha, ha!'

'Sounds like you have him in his place, Emma!'

Ruth breaks in on our conversation.

'I'm heading off to the bar. You want a drink, girls?'

'Yeah, here, take some money and bring me back a couple of bottles.'

When she goes I ask Emma if she'd like a line of coke. She pulls out a bag and says,

'Here, follow me to the loo. Try a couple of lines of this stuff. Mark gets his from John, I'm sure you all do as well.'

'Yeah, and it's always great stuff, Emma. I'll follow you in. Just get John or someone to watch our drinks.'

After a couple more lines and a few more dances, everyone is flying out of their heads. I can see Brian watching me dancing and he gives me that *See you later* look.

Before I know it, we are all crowded into three or four taxis heading back to Brian's house. As we walk in, there are about twenty people there all talking, drinking and snorting coke off the tables and cd covers. I hear Cara's voice as I walk by the kitchen.

'Hey, Lisa, come here!' She bends over and gives me a big hug. 'I love you. You know that, don't you?'

'Yeah, yeah. I love you too.'

'You're the best mate anyone could ever have.'

'What about us?'

Orla and Ruth come over, opening another bottle of beer.

'Look, we all love each other,' says Orla. 'Always have, always will. What do you think of the new batch of coke?'

'The best in ages!' says Cara. 'John's going to make sure he gets the same for the Christmas in case a bad batch comes along, so get your orders in today!'

I turn to John and tell him to make sure he boxes off enough to cover the run up to Christmas and the whole holiday period. The rest of the gang agree.

'Yes, Teacher. Count it done. I'll have it all a few days before Christmas and I'll buzz you. Everyone who's got an order in will be looked after. There's always E's around, so you don't need to bother ordering them.'

'Ah, I think I'm going to stick to just taking the coke from now on, John.'

'So, what's your plans for this year?' Cara asks me.

'Well, I'm taking a week off before the school closes down for the break so I can get all my shopping done early. Can't wait. Then there's your Stephen's Night Party when your parents are away. I love that night! It's always the best party.'

'Big four-bedroom house, loads of beer and great music. Bring it on, girls – legend!'

John calls us over.

'Here, Lisa, take a couple of lines of this, then pass it on to Ruth.'

With coke going around and all the beer you wanted, it's a super night.

*

I wake up around 1:30pm. Brian is still asleep beside me. The house is silent, no music, just a dead sound. I'm naked. So is he. The hangover is so bad, it's as if a fear travels up from the very pit of my soul and attacks all my thoughts and feelings and overtakes me with a horrible sense of anxiety and fear. I always wake like that from a night of coke and beer. I crawl out of bed and get dressed fast, hoping no one will open the door thinking it's the loo and see me naked.

'See you, Brian, I'm off home.' I bend over and kiss the side of his face.

'Mmm? Ok, see ya. Lisa. Yeah – Lisa.'

I go into the loo and try to wash to look half normal before my mother sees me. Going down the stairs, I see Ruth and Steve still up chatting in the sitting room.

'Have you guys not slept yet?'

By the look of them, they've been up talking all night.

'Hey, Lisa!' slurs Ruth. 'Give us both a hug before you go!'

'Yeah, sure. You both okay?'

Steve tries to talk but his jaw is unable to open.

'We love you!' Ruth whispers.

'Text me later, okay? And get some sleep. See you both soon.'

As I make my way out the door, I feel like shit. The hangover is really taking hold. I make my way home and go straight to bed for a few more hours' much needed sleep.

'Ma, it's just me. Call me later, okay? Just home, going to get an extra sleep in. Wake me for dinner later.'

'Okay, Lisa. Around 6:30.'

That's one thing I love about her: she's concerned, but never critical or judgemental.

I crash onto the bed, trying to undress again. The night before flashes over and over in my mind. The coke, the drink, the music, sleeping with Brian . . . As always, it seems as if a film is playing out, we're all superstars for one night only. I feel so crap. I turn over on my side and pull the covers over my head. Now it's dark and I feel so alone, so empty inside. I start to shake like I'm frightened of something. All I want is to fall asleep and wake up feeling normal again. My mind won't shut down. All the faces from the dance floor in The Life keep flashing over and over and over in my head. Just as I'm finally falling into a sleep, David Salle's eyes from outside the Blue Ocean club flash across my mind. Strange as it may seem, knowing he's such a weirdo, it's his eyes alone in the end that helps to comfort me as I fall into a deep sleep . . .

Chapter Two

The Girl in the Mirror

'Lisa, wake up. I've been calling you for the last half hour. It's 6pm. Your dinner will be ready in half an hour.'

'Yeah, yeah, Ma. I'm getting up now.'

'There's hot water if you want to take a shower.'

Closing the bathroom door after the struggle to drag myself out of the bed, I look in the mirror. The sight is awful. I look crap, like I've lost a stone in my face alone. Hate this feeling, the day after a coke session. I feel I'll never be normal again. And there's always that feeling with it, that voice inside giving out to you for what you got up to the night before. What's that all about? I don't know. After a shower and clean clothes I feel that bit normal again.

My phone rings. It's Cara.

'Hi, Cara, how are you? I'm dying. What time did you leave Brian's? I don't remember seeing you go.'

'I'm grand, Lisa. A bit hung over, to say the least. Mad night – paying for it today. We had to leave around 6:30am as John got calls to drop a few bags over to a party in the Grove, so we went on home to his house and crashed out. We were up around 2pm, dying a death but got dinner down. Not easy, but feel half normal.'

'Shit, I'm only going to eat my dinner now, don't think I can face food.'

'Ah, get it down you, Lisa. You'll feel grand after it. How did you get on with Brian? I never said goodbye to you 'cause you were bet into a kiss with him in the hallway, so I kept going.'

'Ah, you know yourself! I ended up staying the night with him again. It suits me fine, Cara. No strings. We have an understanding between us. Ah, maybe one day I'll meet Mr Right, who knows? Anyway, how's the rest of the gang? Ruth and Steve were still up when I was leaving at 1:30pm, the heads on them both funny.'

'I haven't heard from them, Lisa. I'd say they're still asleep. Anne and Frank went home same time as us. What do you think of The Life?'

'Ah, it was great, Cara. The place was rocking as always, some buzz.'

'I saw Ron, your ex, there. Did you see him?'

'Ron? No, no. I never saw him. Just as well, I suppose . . . Ah, I'm well over that creep, Cara.'

'Would you not try to start up a steady line with Brian then, Lisa?'

'Ah, no. It's not like that. I'm not looking for anything long term.

Just a bit of fun, if you know what I mean. Maybe down the road things could get a bit more serious, but as I tell everyone, I'm fine with it the way it is and so is Brian. Listen, my mother's calling me for dinner. Maybe I'll catch you on Facebook later on, ok? Take care. Love you, Cara. Bye.'

'Bye, Lisa.'

Trying to eat dinner was a job and a half but I got it down. Ma looks at me from over the Sunday paper.

'Where did you stay last night?'

'Stayed in Brian Crawford's – around the corner. Bit of a party after The Life disco.'

'You look like you drank too much.'

'Nah, I'm grand, Ma. We had a few bottles back in the house – nothing too crazy.'

'So, are you dating Brian? You seem to stay around there a good bit.'

'Nothing too serious, Ma. Anyway, what's in the Sunday papers? Any good news to tell the world?'

If she knew I was just changing the subject, she never let on.

'Papers don't print good stories, Lisa. It's all bad. You'd wonder why we want to run to the shops and buy them. There's a big story about that killing on Friday in Blanchardstown.'

'Really? Never heard that.'

'Yeah. A young lad, twenty-two years of age, shot in a pub. All drugs and greed, Lisa. It's so evil. God, I can't imagine what his poor mother must be going through. It says here he was shot twice in the head and face. It doesn't bear thinking about. How does a twenty-two-year-old get mixed up in all that? God, life has so changed from the days of me and your father, God be good to him. We were so innocent, Lisa. You'd be read the riot act if you took a drink before you were eighteen.'

'Ah, the world is so different today. You have to live in the times, Ma.'

As she went off to wash up and I went on Facebook, I kept thinking, *What if she ever found out what everyone gets up to around here at the weekend!* Ah well, what she doesn't know won't hurt her, I suppose.

I always keep my coke well hidden in my room, and anyway she never goes near my things other than to take out the washing.

I logged onto Facebook and the first thing that caught my eye was a friend request from Emma Ryan from the night before. So I quickly accepted it and then saw a private mail as well from her:

Hi Lisa. Great meeting you last night. You're so sound, can't believe we never got talking until now. Hope you're not too hung over. I'm dying. lol. My boyfriend Mark thinks you're so sound also. Glad I was able to warn you about David my ex, weirdo! Hope we meet again over the Christmas time. You take care. Your friend Emma.

Ruth came online saying she was dying, but not as bad as earlier.

That coke is some of the best ever, Lisa. Did John tell you he's making sure to keep us some for Christmas?

Yeah, I was standing beside you when you were talking to him. Where is your head?

How's Steve?

He's not as bad as he was. I'm so looking forward to bed. I've work tomorrow at the bank.

Orla came online asking to meet up midweek for a coffee and asking did I enjoy The Life.

Yeah it was a blast, Orla. Can't wait for next week as I've three days off teaching, which brings me into the holidays. I've a full week off free to shop and get all sorted for Christmas. This is my first year teaching five-year-olds, so the break will do me wonders.

Orla asked me how much coke had I after the weekend.

I've about half a bag, but I'm getting another before next weekend, then I've ordered an ounce to keep me going over the Christmas and New Year. I blew all mine in Brian's last night, but Carl is getting sorted with more Friday.

Is there any way you could drop me a bit when we meet for a coffee coz I'm going out Thursday night to Swords? I'll give you back some over the weekend when Carl gets ours.

Yeah sure Orla. That's no problem.

Ah you're a legend Lisa. Thanks.

After I put up a post about the night before being a super night and rambled down a few people's posts I went to log off, but the nosey side to my nature got the better of me and I logged onto David Salle's Facepage. He had everything nearly private bar his photos – only one, and a small bit of info stating that he was twenty-five years old, loves walking, watching films and reading. The photo was of him walking his dog. I had to zoom in to get a closer look at his face. It was as if those electric blue eyes of his were looking straight at me. *He's cute for a weirdo,* was all I could think of as I logged off for the night.

When Thursday came round I met Orla and gave her half the bag of coke and took what was left before heading out to meet Cara and Ruth in Tommy's, a well-known pub in Skerries.

All Cara could talk about was Christmas shopping and the parties we were all invited to, not to mention the big one we always had in her house every Stephen's Night, as her parents invariably went away on holidays for a few nights, leaving the house free. Her brother never stayed in that night so Cara had a fantastic party each year. Each year it got better and it was the highlight of the Christmas for us all. Last year there was a packed house, and with it being on a private acre of land we didn't have to worry about neighbours ringing the cops about the loud music.

'You know,' said Cara, 'John and I are getting closer lately. Something changed between us, not sure what it is, but it's great. We used to row a bit, but that's starting to go from our relationship.'

'That's great to hear,' Ruth said, smiling. 'Steve and I have our moments, but I love him to bits.'

'Girls,' I said, 'don't start asking me about Brian 'cause you both know it's just a casual relationship and I'm fed up people asking me about it.'

'Ok, Lisa. Ok.'

'No problem.'

I let out a sigh.

'I texted him today but got no reply.'

They both smiled at my short-lived determination not to discuss him.

'What did you say to him?'

'I just said I enjoyed Saturday night, hoped to see him at the weekend. We're good friends as well, girls, so I don't want to ruin the buzz we have. I like being single for now. I'm so enjoying life without the complications I had in the past. You know, I'm so thrilled for anyone who's in love like you pair are. It gives me a glimmer of hope for the future!'

The door in Tommy's opened and in came Anne for a last drink. She plonked herself down beside us, her long, auburn ringlets giving off that freshly-shampooed look.

'Sorry I'm late, girls. Talking to Frank on the phone for over an hour.'

'Another couple in love,' I said, laughing.

'Ah, sometimes I wish I could kill him. Men! Huh! They never understand women's feelings. Stay single for as long as you can, Lisa, that's my advice.'

With that my phone beeps, a text back from Brian.

Yeah enjoyed the other night, hope to be out the weekend, might see you at the Life. Brian x

It seemed rather cold for a guy I was sleeping with for the past six months, but that was our agreement from the start – no strings. Yet for some reason it sort of hurt me, and the thought did cross my mind: was I actually falling for Brian? Had I got other feelings for him other than sexual?

Cara broke across my train of thought.

'Are you ok, Lisa? You look like you're miles away.'

'Nah, I'm grand, Cara.'

'So, where are we going after here?' said Anne. 'Back to my house? I've a few bottles. Has anyone any coke left from the weekend?'

'Shh!' hissed Cara. 'Not so loud!'

'Shit,' I said, 'I took the last few lines before I came out and gave the rest to Orla.'

'Don't worry, I've a good bit,' said Cara, 'and Ruth has a half bag, so we're sorted.'

We spent the next few hours drinking and snorting a few lines, laughing and talking about everything. It was one of those girlie nights where you just felt how good it was to have such great friends whom you trusted and loved and respected. The bond we shared was magic, and since Anne got to know us all she'd become a big part of the gang.

*

Got home about 3:30am, which was bad, as I had one more day teaching before I was off for the holidays. I went into the bathroom to brush my teeth and I looked at my face in the mirror. My pupils were huge from the coke. I stood there just wondering could I see something about myself that I didn't know – trying to freak myself out would be a better way of putting it. I had such confidence in myself and it was made stronger by the fact that so many guys had told me how good-looking I was. I wasn't big-headed about it, but I loved to hear guys say, *You're beautiful, Lisa.* I ran my fingers through my short blonde hair. I don't know what they call it, but I guess I was checking out my looks to reassure myself that I was a good-looking girl, that people liked me because I was dead on to hang around with. Yeah.

I think everyone does this when they're on their own in the bathroom or in front of a dressing table mirror. But it was my eyes that interested me most, as they say they are the windows of the soul. You can tell so much by looking into a person's eyes – are they fake or are they hiding something from you? I bent over and kissed the mirror and said *Goodnight Lisa, I love you, see you in the morning,* laughing to myself. If anyone saw me they would lock me up in a nut house.

I woke up with the alarm going off to another awful sense of fear that hit me from the pit of my soul all the way up my body.

'Oh, shit, it can't be 7:30!'

I dragged myself out and into the shower. I plastered the makeup on to take the coke hangover away and did my best to get my breakfast down. *Oh, thank God this is my last day.* I drank a boost drink in the car as I drove to Swords. I got through the day until the bell went at 2pm. A teachers' meeting for an hour. *God, if they had any idea of my lifestyle I'd be out on my ear, no questions asked, no second chances, no chance of a teaching job ever again.* 3pm and I was driving home, music blasting in the car. Free for three long weeks.

True, the Principal was none too pleased with my taking my three course days just before Christmas.

'*Three* Course Days, Miss Webb?' she had moaned, tapping her bony fingers on her desk diary. '*Now?* Well, it's a little inconvenient, to say the least, and will not look good on your cv for future employment. The class will have to be split up, of course, and it's so upsetting for Junior Infants to have all this chopping and changing. I . . . I feel I have to tell you that some of the parents are beginning to talk about you and have been on to me about . . . certain matters.'

Bitch.

I drove to Euro Spar in Skerries to grab a coffee to give me an extra boost. I went up to the counter to pay and turned around to see Brian standing there in the queue.

'Hi, Brian. How are you?'

'Grand, Lisa.'

It felt a bit strange this time seeing him, I don't know why. The last time I saw him was in his bed, just the week before. He grabbed a coffee and we chatted.

'What's your plan for the weekend? You never texted me back last night.'

'Eh . . . sorry. Yeah, we're going out on a mad one as it's my holidays from today until the 7th of January.'

'That's a bit early to be off – even for a teacher, Lisa?'

'Yeah, I know. I did a week-long course during the summer, so now I'm entitled to three days leave.'

'Very clever, Lisa, you'll have loads of time to get your Christmas shopping done. Fair play.'

I kept sort of looking into his eyes to see if there was some kind of spark there as he talked, or a sense that there may be something deeper happening between us other than sex with a night of drink and coke, but no, nothing. I told myself, *Look, Lisa, you both talked about this and agreed it was no strings attached.*

After a few minutes of small talk I said I'd got to get home, I'd probably see him at the weekend.

'Yeah, sure. Take care. Catch ya then.'

I got into the car and looked one last time as he went back into the shop. He was cute with dark eyes and dark hair and I knew a good few girls had their eyes on him, but look, neither of us was ready for anything long term.

A part of me was still not over opening my heart to Ron only to find out he was sleeping around behind my back. That really hurt me. I was so into him, he was the bloody love of my life. It took me ages to get my head around it. I wanted to forgive him but the trust was gone, and once that's gone it's over in my books. Trust can't be reborn and you're left thinking was there ever real love on his side? If there was he would never have done what he did, and what's worse, I knew he had done it behind another girl's back too because she told me, so it wasn't just me or one mistake. He was still doing it, I bet.

When I got home, Ma was watching tv so I slept for a couple of hours and woke up at 7pm to a number of texts from the girls and two missed calls from Cara. A few of them were going out but I texted them saying I was staying in as I was wrecked from the night before. I rang Cara back. She wanted to know if I wanted John to put a bag of coke to one side for me.

'Yeah, make sure it's the biggest bag and it's still *on the rock*. Tell him I said that, Cara. Are you planning on going out?'

'Nah, we're staying in and watching a dvd. He has to make a few calls to a few heads. His phone's ringing non-stop since today. He promises to turn it off at 9pm. I'll drop around in the afternoon with your bag. Will you be home?'

'Yeah, around 2pm onwards, drop in. Can't wait till tomorrow night.'

'Yeah, you're so lucky to be on your holidays until the New Year. I'm still working up until a few days before Christmas, but have loads of time off over the Christmas. So, anything strange happen to you since last night, Lisa?'

'Bar being hung over, everything's great. Bring on tomorrow night!'

'I think Emma Ryan and Mark, her boyfriend, are coming out with us. Is that ok with you, Lisa?'

'Yeah, they're a lovely couple to hang around and talk with. Listen, Cara, I've got to go. I've hardly had any food and I'm going to order a takeout and sit with Ma for the night.'

'Ok, Lisa, take care. See you tomorrow after 2pm.'

'Enjoy your romantic night with John. Bye.'

Got into my pjs and crashed on the sofa next to Ma. She was all on for a takeout. We never really cooked on a Friday as she did part-time work three times a week so we'd leave Fridays open for takeouts. Most Friday nights I would be out but on nights like this we'd watch a dvd or a film on Sky together.

For some reason as we ate our takeout I kept thinking of Brian. I felt like my feelings were starting to get deeper, and a part of me wanted us to start dating rather than just sleeping together when we met. Maybe it was getting to me that all my friends were in steady relationships apart from me. I turned to Ma and just out of the blue I asked her about her relationship with my father.

'Was Dad your first love, Ma?' I asked her. 'How did you know he was Mr Right? Did you know the minute you met him? Was there someone else before he came along?'

She looked somewhat taken aback that I'd ask her such personal questions, as I'd never done so before. She smiled with that searching look in her eyes. I'm sure she sensed I was in a place of confusion about my own search for the right guy in my private life.

'There were people I dated before I met your Dad. I was in a five-year relationship with a guy called Sean from Rush, but he went to work in London and we just drifted apart. I was hurt for a long time, but time is a great healer. I did love him, Lisa.

'Then I met your Dad – in a disco. Across a dance floor I could see someone watching me. When the slow set came on he walked towards me and asked for a dance. My heart was melting with nerves. The first thing I noticed was his soft voice. Then, that look in his eyes. He had lovely eyes. I didn't even answer him about the dance. I just walked into his arms and stayed locked away in his heart until . . . well, until five years ago when he died in my arms in our sitting room . . .'

I remembered it clearly. The heart attack. The tv still on. *Match of the Day.* The half-finished Irish Times crossword still clutched in his hand.

'We had our rows and our ups and downs, Lisa. Everyone does. Don't think because you find love that it's all romance seven days a week. Life is not like that, but there was a kind of magic about our lives when we were together. A look across the room from your Dad would send my heart spinning. All the years until he took his last breath that never went away.'

I squeezed her hand gently.

'I think you're asking me this 'cause you're looking for advice, Lisa. The best advice I can give is that you will meet the right man, and when you do, everything will be different. The way he looks at you, the touch, it will feel so right in every way.

'That guy Ron you dated – I never liked him. But you had to find that out for yourself. I had seen from the start he was a taker, Lisa. There's a lot of them out there who will take, take, take until there's nothing left to take.

'They know nothing about love. They spend all their time making sure they stay in control of everything. But you can't do that and love someone, in the real sense of the word. People like to control, because it means there's no danger of them ever being hurt. They're afraid of real love, so they just let the other person become vulnerable while they stay the same. It's all very deceiving and hidden. You need to be so careful, pet.

'Am I explaining this right? To put it another way, if you set out to control the relationships you are in and tell yourself when you get to a certain age you'll pick the right person and then settle down with them, you'll find it doesn't work that way, and you'll most probably end up with the wrong person. That's what happens to those who play games. You'll get hurt along the way in all this. Sure who doesn't? But don't close your heart just because someone hurts you.'

God how come I never knew all this! What planet has my head been on?

'Love is a funny thing, Lisa. It seems to have a mind of its own. If you play games with it you'll lose it forever. It seems to withdraw from people who play games and guide those who don't to one day find the right person. That's the way I always have seen it since I was a young girl in 5th year, dreaming in the classroom.'

I tried not to show it in front of Ma but I was so moved a couple of times as she spoke I felt a tear in my eye. I had never known she knew all this or that she and Dad had loved each other so much. She told me that I had everything going for me in life –

'You have your friends, a great job, family life. Plus, you have money saved to buy your own home one day. You just need to wait and everything will fall into place for you.'

It was like a jigsaw was put into place that night. I thanked Ma, and there I was again looking in the mirror before bed, a different picture, a look in my eyes that was different from the night before. Tears ran down my face. I am sure that some of them were for my Dad, some were for my Ma whom I never was really there for, through her heartbreak of losing him. I was eighteen and far too into myself. *A bit of a taker, is that what I really am?*

Last night I stared into the mirror, coked out of my head, smiling. Tonight I'm crying. What will tomorrow bring?

Chapter Three

Life on the Line

I sleep in until eleven, and wake up still thinking about what Ma told me about her love for Dad and staying true to my own heart. But it's not long until my mind is stormed with thoughts of going out later that night. The same excitement always grips me when I know I'm going to be taking coke again. The excitement stays in my stomach and builds as the hours tick by. I toy with the feeling all day and it keeps me in top form no matter what else happens. It's as if I'm on coke before I even get a line into me.

What kind of coke will it be? Will the deal be *on the rock* or will it be broken down and mixed? I'm sure other people who do coke feel like me. The minute I touch it, my hands start to shake as I break down the lumps, thinning out lines as fine as I can get them . . . Those first couple of lines hitting the back of the throat, the taste, the warm sensation rushing up your body . . . Then I'm texting my mates and telling them I love them . . . music going . . . bottle of beer on the dressing table . . . getting showered and dressed, thinking I'm the greatest person alive.

Only four years ago, when I entered Teacher Training College, I hadn't had as much as a joint. With medical examinations and interviews, not to mention being watched daily for the merest whiff of scandal, I stayed clean for almost a year. But then, at a late-night party in the house of one of Cara's friends, I snorted my first line. A week later I tried it again and never looked back. Of course, I still had to be careful. It wasn't just the authorities who would take a dim view. The other students would probably blow the whistle if they ever found out. I can't imagine life now, going out without a line of coke, maybe dropping the odd Ecstasy for late-night clubbing. Most weekends, just coke and beer though . . .

I get up and get breakfast with Ma and head out to buy something nice in the Pavilions Shopping Centre in Swords. I'm getting texts and calls from Ruth about what the plan for meeting up tonight will be. We're all to go to Emma Ryan's house for a beer, then off on a pub crawl in Skerries and on to Life. Maybe a party afterwards . . . That's nearly always the case.

I ring Cara to tell her I'm running a bit late and to call around at 3 pm. I pick up a few girlie Christmas gifts and am back home by 2:30. Ma has dinner on but all I want now is to get into the new top I've bought and hit the nightlife.

The doorbell rings. It's Cara.

'Hi, Mrs Webb!' she says as Ma answers the door.

'She's in her room, Cara, go on up.'

She comes up the stairs and knocks on my door.

'It's open, dummy! I saw you pulling up. Whatcha think of my new top for tonight? Picked it up in T K Maxx for €30. Was 90!'

'Ah, it's lovely. Suits your hair. You'll look stunning in that later.'

'So, show me,' I whisper. 'Did you get the coke?'

'Yeah,' she says, locking the door behind her.

She pulls out the €100 bag.

'It's still *on the rock* and it's off the stuff from last week. It's a lovely bag. John always looks after the gang. He told me to tell you he'll have the ounce for the Christmas and New Year a week on Monday. I think it's €1,000.'

'That's great. Brian's buying some of it from me, sort of going halves. Well, he's getting €300 worth, maybe €400. It's a long Christmas, Cara! Give us a look at the bag.'

I feel the bag. It's rock hard. I smile and hand her two €50.

'It's great having John. Sure we'd be ripped off for sure if we went to half the dealers around this place. So, we're going to Emma Ryan's house in Rush. Who planned that, Cara?'

'John did. He's to go there to drop a few bags, so Emma asked if we wanted to come as she has a free house. Her parents are away for the night. She has beer in so you won't have to bring anything but yourself. I'll pick you up in a taxi at 8pm with Ruth, and I think Anne's probably coming with us.'

'Sounds like a plan. I'm tempted to take a line of this to try it out, but if I do I won't be able to stop and I've to get my dinner yet . . .'

'No, no, Lisa – don't touch it. Get your dinner, and if you want I'll come around for 7pm and we'll take a few lines together before we head to Rush.'

Cara leaves and I half eat my dinner. The excitement is getting so much. I wash my hair and get my clothes ready so I have time before she comes to have a few lines.

'I'm off up to get ready, Ma, taking a can of Bud with me! Will you send Cara up when she gets here? Should be around 7.'

'Don't forget to take your keys with you when you're heading out. That's if you plan on coming home!'

Ma gives me that disapproving look again.

She knows I'm always in safe company and stay mostly in local pubs and clubs. I lock my bedroom door and take a cd out along with my ATM card. I have a small, sharp blade at the side of my make-up bag, taped down one side. You'd hardly know what it was if you saw it. It looks like a small nail file.

I cut down and slice the lump into two parts and then into four. I can feel the perspiration starting to run as my heart races faster. My hands get damp and sticky. With a couple of fine lines ready, I take them up my nose, throwing my head back to get the lines well into each nostril. A couple of seconds later, I feel it hit my whole body in a wave from my head down to my toes. That unstoppable feeling just leaves me hungry for the next line, which I start cutting down and getting ready five minutes later.

The music sounds ten times more amazing after a few lines, which is all part of the buzz. A mouthful from the can of Bud and another line . . . *Welcome to life on the line* as Ruth always says when we're snorting together.

I'm dressed and finishing my make-up as Cara knocks. As I open the door, her eyes tell me she's taken a few lines herself. She's hugging me and telling me she loves me.

'What do you think of the coke?' she asks.

'Ah, Cara, it's super. He's really getting great stuff all the time. Fair play to him, he's sound. Stay here and I'll go down and get you a can of Bud.'

Ma is still sitting, watching TV. I go in and give her a hug and tell her how much I enjoyed our talk the night before.

'I love you, Ma.'

She sighs, returning the hug.

'How much have you had to drink, Lisa? You sound drunk already. Take it easy, you haven't even gone out to the pub yet.'

'I'm grand, Ma, just in top form. I'm bringing a can up to Cara. See you before I go.'

Cara has a couple of lines out and ready when I get back up to her. With another couple of lines and a can, we burn the ears off each other.

'How did your romantic night with John go?'

'Ah, it was great. He told me he has a fantastic present for me for Christmas. I think it's a new laptop, 'cause I told him last week mine's acting up.'

'Ah, he must love you! That's great. Listen, I'm . . . I'm thinking of asking Brian about . . . you know, going a bit further. Starting a real relationship. What do you think?'

'I told you weeks ago to ask him! You don't remember, do you?'

'Mmm. Must've been at a party, was it?'

'Yeah, at Orla's house.'

'Well? Do you think I should?'

'Yeah, ask him. You can't just sleep with him forever, you know!'

'Yeah, I think I will say something. I'm starting to think I'm falling for him. Like, I know I said it's just casual, but I think my feelings are growing stronger the past couple of weeks or so.'

'At least you'll know where you stand, Lisa. Go for it.'

'I'd say *he'll* go for it.'

'Be great to have the whole gang dating. Mega, Lisa!'

'It's such a great gang. We're so lucky to have each other, Cara. The bond is getting stronger between us all. Don't you think so?'

'Defo. We're all getting closer as time passes. We have the unbreakable bond, Lisa.'

'Ah, we're out of our heads on this coke. Next I'll be asking you for a kiss!'

I laugh.

'Feck! What time is it? I told Ruth we'd pick her up in a taxi at 8pm to go to Rush.'

'It's 7:45. Text her and say 8:30, then we can do another few lines and chat.'

'Ok, I'll text her, you make up a couple of lines . . . Take mine. John gave me that bag so it's free. Him and Steve are meeting us in Emma's. I'm pretty sure Frank and Anne might be going up with them.'

I pick up the rolled note and take another couple of lines. Then Cara does the same.

'Ah, it's going to be a great night, Cara! What pub we going to first?'

'I'd say we'll end up in the Blue Ocean club. We'll see what the gang say. I don't care once there's beer and music. Listen, we'd better ring a taxi or we'll be here at midnight out of our heads with everyone ringing us.'

'You ring, I'll tell my mother I'm going and get my bits together.'

'Ruth's just texted. She's all ready. She says, *I bet you two are having a few lines without me lol.*'

I hug my mother as the taxi pulls up outside.

'Love you, Ma.'

This time she doesn't quite return the hug. She just pats my back as I hug her.

'Love you too, Lisa. Take care, girls. Have fun.'

'Bye, Mrs Webb. See you soon!'

We pick Ruth up. We just know she has a few lines in her.

Joe, the taxi driver, looks in the mirror.

'Where to, girls?'

'Rush, Joe. Down to South Shore Road.'

Joe knows us all well enough from picking us up over the years. He's always sound, always slagging us about everything, but wouldn't go too far.

'Oh, if only I was 21 again, girls! I've missed everything. I'd be on a mission to hang out with you lot. You're always happy and having fun.'

'You should come out with us some night,' Ruth said.

'You're jokin' me! I'm 57. One Saturday night with you girls and I'd be in the grave by Tuesday!'

'You're not that old, Joe. We'd take good care of you.'

'Yeah, yeah. That's what I'm afraid of . . . Here we are. That's €12. Have a good night, girls. I'm sure I'll see y'all at some stage in the night.'

We run into Emma's. The door's open and the music's on. Anne, Frank, John, Orla and Carl and a few of Emma's friends give us a hug. There's a real sense that everyone is on the same wavelength, the perfect way to start what's going to be a super night. Mark, Emma's boyfriend, comes in from the kitchen clutching a load of bottles of beer in both hands.

'Come and get them, girls! I can't hold onto them forever.'

You couldn't beat the buzz! We're in the house of a girl we hardly know, yet feel we're invited in like we're family. I sit, stuck into a chat with Emma, from the minute we get a bottle of beer handed to us. Mark gives me a hug. He'd certainly overdone the Lynx deodorant tonight.

'It's great to have you all over,' he says. 'It's so great to start to get to know you.'

'Ah, thanks,' says Ruth. 'You're so nice to ask John to ask us over when you hardly even know us.'

'Anyone who's a mate to John is a mate to us. That's the way we see it.'

Cara comes over, carefully holding a CD cover with six lines of coke.

'Here, take a couple, then pass it to Emma and Mark.'

Steve comes over.

'You're getting greedy with those lines, girls.'

Steve, with his smiles and jokes, kept the buzz going while I bent over to tell Ruth to take some of my coke, make a few lines. Cara's been giving me hers and I've hardly touched mine all night.

We chat to some of Emma's friends whom we only know to see but who turn out to be all great to chat with. The music mixes with everyone locked in deep conversation about everything and anything. I feel this has to be the best buzz ever to start off my three weeks' holidays.

'Ah, we'll definitely come back to this house,' I shout to John and Cara, 'It's legend!'

I look at the clock on the mantelpiece: it's 10:15. I tell Ruth we'd better ring for taxis. Emma turns the music down.

'Everyone, we're heading to the pub in Skerries, so a few taxis are needed. Will somebody ring them?'

I take another couple of lines before we hit the road. The taxi is a blur, everyone talking and laughing in the back.

We pull up outside the pub and within minutes we are all inside flying and drinking beer. Emma comes in last.

'I just put all the bottles in the wheelie bin. Cover up the evidence, yeah?'

I put my arm around her.

'Emma, you know I think we're going to be the best of friends. We have so much in common.'

'We even like the same music!' she shouts into my ear.

'I knew the moment we met last week that you were so sound. Cara says you're the life and soul of the party.'

'Did she say that? Really?'

'Cara's been my best friend since we were kids. You'll fit in so well, Emma, with this gang. And Mark's so sound . . .'

'Ah, we so love each other, Lisa.'

'How did you meet him?'

'Last January we were out in Tommy's for a meal with a few friends and he was with his buddies at the bar and we just got talking. I told him I was being stalked by that David Salle guy, and we just talked away. Then that weekend I was out with the girls and I met him again and we started dating. He works in the airport with one of his friends, Terry Cullen.'

'I know Terry, Emma, just to see.'

'He'll be meeting us later down at The Life, if we ever make it that far!'

I down the last mouthful from my bottle of Bud as we all start leaving for the Blue Ocean. I get into the last taxi with Ruth and Anne, and one of Emma's mates, Chris. When we walk into Blue the atmosphere is great, until we get to the bar. I know from Emma and John's faces something is amiss.

'What's up?'

I look for Cara who is standing with Orla and Carl.

'What's going on? Will someone tell me?'

'Ah, it's nothing, Lisa,' John said.

'Have a look over into the corner, over my left shoulder. Don't make it look like you're looking.'

I order a beer and glance over, and there sitting in the corner is David Salle with what turns out to be his sister and her boyfriend. I turn back to the gang.

'What's the big bloody deal? I think you lot are paranoid.'

'I know, Lisa, but Emma gets freaked out when he's around.'

I turn to Emma.

'Are you okay?'

'Yeah, yeah, it's just he gives me the creeps when I see him, Lisa. He kept looking over when we walked in.'

'Look, you're with your buddies now – don't let him bother you. You were on a great buzz and you're letting him ruin it.'

After a few minutes, everyone settles back into the buzz. I keep near Emma and get her back on the wavelength we were on before we left the last pub.

'I'm grand now, Lisa.'

Mark bends over her shoulder.

'I'll break his neck if he looks over one more time.'

'Ah stop, Mark. That's what he wants, to freak everyone out.'

From the corner of one of the pillars at the bar, I have the best view to peep around. I see David stuck into a very intense conversation with his sister. Her fella seems engrossed, listening to him explain whatever he's saying. He crooks his finger in our direction like he's saying something about the gang. I turn to Emma.

'Listen, what was your man David like before it all went wrong? Like, was he always the weirdo?'

The whole expression on Emma's face changed dramatically.

' Are you okay with me asking you about it?'

'Nah, you're grand. He seemed okay at first, like I tell everyone. Then he became a control freak. That's all there is, Lisa. Why are you asking me?'

'I'm just curious.'

'He's a creep. That's all you need to know, Lisa.'

I bend back to have one last look at them but as I do, I come right into David Salle's eye line. He's looking straight at me. His sister and her boyfriend have gone into the smoke room. I look away as fast as possible.

'Shit! I think he saw me.'

'You're playing with fire, Lisa.'

Ruth is standing right behind me, watching me.

'You don't want Hannibal Lecter inside your head, do you now, Lisa? Oh shit, he's looking right at you. You're going to be his next victim. You were warned, but now it's too late!'

'Ah, shut up, Ruth! Come on outside. We'll go up towards the harbour. I'm dying for a line.'

I grab John to come with us. We stand for a fag near the small ice cream shop as I take out a Euro coin. We all take turns to get a couple of lines, Even John, this time.

'I thought you didn't touch the stuff, John, as a rule?'

'Rules are made to be broken, Teacher. You should know that.'

'Hmm. Anyway, I owe you that. You're always sharing yours with us.'

'That's no problem. I take care of my mates, Lisa. You're all like . . . family to me at this stage.'

Family.

As he says that I have a fleeting image of Al Pacino in The Godfather.

'Ah, that's cool,' I say, bending over to hug him.

We step out of the cold back into the pub. Last drinks are being bought before we head to the nightclub. Everyone is buzzing off each other and we start ringing for taxis. Just before we do, I see Brian at the other side of the bar. I catch his eye – *See you later.* He winks at me

– *Yeah, later, Lisa.* As we head to the main door, I take another last look over to where David Salle has been sitting. I keep looking as I can only see his sister with her boyfriend. I'm not watching where I'm walking and walk straight into someone coming the other way.

'Oh, sorry, I'm sorry!' I say frantically.

I look up. It's David Salle.

'Shit, em, sorry!' I say again.

'You're okay. It's okay.'

He keeps going.

'You stupid fool!' says Ruth, laughing her head off. 'He's in your head forever now, Lisa. That's it, you're a goner!'

'Aw, shut up, will you!'

We pull up outside The Life in four taxis. Before I can catch my breath, I'm walking, coked out of my head, into a sea of sound and dancing people. The atmosphere is truly electric and as always, everyone is on that same wonderful wavelength. Before long, after we drink a beer we're on the floor dancing. The whole gang is locked together like one big happy family, dancing our hearts out to the music. I feel so in tune with everyone, and so, it seems, do they. Ruth grabs me and asks me to go out for a fag in the smoke room.

Brian is there so I call him over. I grab him and give him a real 'eat your face off' kiss.

'So, what's the story?'

'Listen, I want to ask you something.'

'Yeah? What?'

'Well, do you think we should be . . . dating rather than just doing what we're doing?'

'Like . . . going out as boyfriend and girlfriend?'

'Yeah, something like that. What do you think?'

'Ah, Lisa, to be honest, I'm not into dating like that at all. I sort of told you this before, I thought we went over all this. You're fantastic and great-looking and everything, but I'm just . . . not that type.'

I'm taken aback but hide it well in the moment.

'Ah, yeah, sure, you're right, Brian. Who wants ties at our age? You're dead right.'

'Are you okay with this?'

'Yeah, cool. That's sound.'

'Listen, Brian. John's giving me that coke on Monday week. Do you still want some?'

'Yeah, defo. Do you want to go 50/50? Half is well enough for the both of us.'

'Yeah, that sounds okay.'

Ruth comes over and we chat away, pulling on a fag. I hide my feelings well, which is easy when you're on coke. Though I'm hurt that Brian isn't interested in dating, I won't let it spoil the night. We take over the dance floor and it's the most amazing night ever.

*

We find ourselves back in John's house for a party. The kitchen table is filled with lines of coke as I step into a corner to chat to Cara.

'I asked Brian about the relationship thing. He said he wanted it to remain the way it is. I was a bit sick about it, but it's cool.'

'So, what are you going to do?'

'Ah, I'm not sleeping with him again. I texted him in the taxi and said that part's over.'

'You're dead right, Lisa. There's loads of guys mad to date you. Loads watching you and trying to chat you up.'

'Yeah, yeah, but I don't trust any of them. I've closed a big part of me down since Ron. It's grand just sleeping with someone and going home, but then again I feel crap the next day. Then I start to want to open up and date Brian, and look what happened tonight! You know, I had this big talk with my mother, and she told me to be real and true to my own heart and to wait. So that's what I intend to do. She had real love with my Dad. You don't find that today, Cara. I know you and John have love but the way my mother explains it, it was different in the old days . . . Ah, I'm out of my head! Am I, Cara?'

'No, no, you're grand, Lisa. You'll find Mr Right one day soon. Look at you – you have everything going for you.'

'That's what my mother says. And you're all dead right. I'm going to enjoy life to the full. Whatever happens will happen. But for now, let's make this the best Christmas ever!'

'Yeah, bring it on!' shouts Ruth, who joins our chat along with Emma and Orla.

'Hey, why don't you and Mark come to the party Stephen's Night?' asks Cara.

'Ah, we'd love to! You sure it's okay, Cara?'

'Yeah, we'd love to have you both there. You're part of the gang now!'

With that sorted, we party on until 7 or 8 the next morning. John shouts to me and Ruth as we're heading out the door –

'Don't forget, we're all going out next Saturday to celebrate Orla's birthday. Meeting here for a drink first. Nobody forget.'

As it turned out, we wouldn't forget. Ever.

Chapter Four

Love is in the Air

I woke up around 3pm with that awful fear mixed with an empty, hollow feeling, both racing up from the pit of my stomach. Words can't do it justice, to be honest. It's what we call the Horrors, which is like a horror film being played inside your soul. Only you never see the film, but you feel the sense of dread being acted out.

There's nowhere to hide from it. You try to fold over and cover yourself under your duvet for some kind of comfort, but you never succeed in finding any.

My mind flashes back as it always does to the night before. All that seemed so beautiful, all the confidence and the self-esteem, all the chats with everyone you meet that seemed so fearless and powerful – it now all seems a million miles away from the place I now find myself. I seemed to have everything in my control. In the palm of my hand I held the world. But now the struggle is on to try and lift yourself out of a dark hangover, which can take up to a couple of days.

There were a few texts from the girls, all dying, but saying they had a great night. I can't say that in the middle of this kind of hangover I was looking forward to next week's party night out for Orla. But hangovers do go, and the moment you feel half normal again, it's *Roll on the Weekend.*

That's life for all of us. And knowing I was off work helped me cope with the Sunday blues this time round.

Ma cooked a lovely dinner as always and I watched a dvd and later in the evening I went on Facebook to catch up on the news from the weekend. Everyone was posting how great it was, with most admitting to be well hung over.

I got a few mails from the girls saying what they were buying Orla for her birthday. I logged onto YouTube and started listening to slow songs with my headphones turned up full. Those songs only make me sad and dream of being in love, plus they're always about people breaking up and being hurt. What's that all about? What's the point of singing about such awful moments of sadness? The fact that people like me would sit staring at a wall for hours, listening to them, daydreaming about being in the kind of love you only see in movies, made me feel I was to be pitied more than anything else.

Emma came online and suggested I add one of her mates to my friend list, which I did. His name was Ian Carter from Rush. He had been out with us the night before, but I never got a moment to chat with him. He was cute, if I remember rightly.

I went onto his page to check him out. Tall, dark and handsome-ish. Even with those glasses. Not bad at all, I thought. Before I could think another thought he came online to chat.

Sorry I never got to talk with you last night, Lisa. The night was over before I had a chance to even say hello. Ian

My first thought was *Emma's trying to fix me up here.* Which was the bloody truth, but he was so sound to chat online with, and with Brian out of my life, something was telling me not to hold back and to open the door, even if it's just for a wee bit of friendship.

As I flowed along chatting to Ian about everything from last night to anything at all, Brian came online asking about the coke I was splitting with him. I told him Monday week as John was giving it to me then. He started asking me why I pulled the plug on our meet-ups. I started getting annoyed and just said I'm not into that kind of relationship anymore.

I'm looking for a real relationship, Brian, which you're not prepared to commit yourself to.

I'm not into long-term relationships, Lisa. That's just the way I am right now. Maybe down the road things could change.

I could feel my blood boiling.

Down the road you go, Brian, but not with me as your sideshow. Now, look. I'll have your coke next Monday and leave it at that. Just don't ask me anymore about you and me. There's no you and me. There never was. It was just sex after a load of coke.

Ok, ok, Lisa. I get the message. But we're still mates, yeah?

Yeah, sure. But that's it, Brian. Nothing else.

He went offline and I got back to Ian. The chat went on for over an hour before I got fed up and gave him my phone number.

Ring me. Can't talk right now on this Facebook chatline. It's just for smalltalk, Ian.

His voice! That deep, manly voice that just makes us women melt.

As the talk continued, it turned out Ian was only after breaking up with a girl in the summer after a couple of years. He was 24 and worked in CIE main office. As we talked, I went through his photos on Facebook. Saw a couple with his ex-girlfriend.

'You don't look like a couple, Ian.'

'No? Why do you say that? We got on great.'

'So what happened?'

'Ah, we just drifted apart and she moved to Wexford. No big deal, Lisa. Life goes on.'

We talked for ages till he asked me would I be at the get-together in Tommy's Bar Thursday.

'Think there's a bit of a drink-up for Orla, your friend. I just heard there was, so I'm heading down with Emma and Mark.'

'Yeah, that's cool. We always meet up on a mid-week night.'

'Think I remember someone saying something about a surprise thing for Orla, then a full-swing party Saturday? But it had gone out of my mind.'

'Yeah, sure, that's great. So I'll meet you for a drink and chat Thursday, Ian.'

'Sound, Lisa. Great chatting with you.'

As I hung up the phone I had a great sense of hope that I had clicked with someone I really liked. There was something about this guy. Just had a feeling. Ah, it's a woman's thing, I suppose.

My phone rang some time later. It was Emma, laughing.

'Well, what do you think of our Ian? He was talking about you a lot last night and rang me today about you. He's so sound, Lisa. How did you get on? He just rang me to say he loves talking to you.'

'Emma, he's fine. So funny as well – and a nice bit of stuff. Yeah. Where was he hiding last night? I can't remember seeing much of him. Was he dancing on the floor with us? Was he with us all night?'

'No, he was just with us on and off. He kept watching you dancing. So – I heard you're meeting him for a drink Thursday. Legend, Lisa! That's so cool.'

'Couldn't leave you out there single on your own. Ha, ha, ha.'

'That's our gang complete for Christmas, yeah?'

'Ah, don't be jumping ahead of yourself there, Emma. I had one chat with him on the phone and you have me marrying the guy. Slow up!'

'I'm telling you, Lisa. He's the one for you. I know a match when I see one. You'll have the greatest time chatting to him Thursday. Listen, have to run. Mark calling back. He's gone to pick up a dvd in Xtra-vision. We'll see you Thursday.'

'Ok, Emma. Say hi to Mark for me. And thanks for putting me in touch with Ian. I've got a strong feeling about this guy. Bring it on. Ha, ha, ha.'

'Just play the game, Lisa. See how it pans out.'

Hanging up the phone, I saw Ruth coming online.

Heard there's romance in the air. True or false?

Ah here. Who's spreading this? You can't have heard that fast.

Emma told John and Cara that Ian was way into you and he was going to ask you out. So tell me, tell me. Are you meeting him?

Yeah, Thursday in Tommy's.

What about Brian?

Ah, that's over, Ruth. I told him that's it.

About time. Knew that would never go any further. He's a user, Lisa. Says he doesn't want to commit. But that's just so he can date whoever he wants. He's a nice guy but wouldn't trust him at all. So – what do you think of Ian?

He's very cute and we hit it off. So can't wait for Thursday.

Never know, Lisa. This could be Mr Right. Ha ha ha.

I logged off Facebook and fell back on the bed. Love songs still ringing in my ears. Amazing how different they sound when you're dating someone rather than being alone. It's like they take on a new meaning and every one of them sounds like they're about the new guy in your life. How mad is that!

*

I slept soundly and woke, still thinking of Ian. *Ah, here, get a grip, girl. You're running way ahead of yourself.* But that was me, I suppose. Always searching for the love of my life. And everyone you meet and date, some part of your heart tells you, this is it. This is the guy you're searching for. And with me it turns out to be just another case of being used and hurt.

But this Ian guy had a different ring to him. I was sure of it.

By the time Thursday came, the days seemed to have dragged out like weeks. Cara and Anne rang to wish me the best, but to be honest that just made me more nervous than I already was. God, I felt like a bloody teenager all over again. Butterflies dancing around inside as I got ready to head out. *Just be yourself, Lisa. No need for all this extra crap you're putting on your face.* I got a bottle of Bud and had a good few lines of coke left over. So I got stuck into them. I must be taking everyone else's when I'm out as I still had half of my bag left . . .

After four lines, all the confidence returns and I felt unstoppable inside. I looked in the mirror. My pupils were razor sharp and lit up, like I was plugged into the mains.

A sense of *Bring it on* rushed across my mind. I was ready for anything now. Cara and Orla rang to pick me up as they were coming down together. Ma was gone out with her sister Rose and I had the place to myself so I was free to put the music up full blast.

The phone was ringing. It was Cara.

'Eh, we're outside, Lisa. We've been ringing your bell for ages. Are you ready?'

With the last line up my nose I was out the door and walking into the pub within a couple of short minutes. Ruth, Emma and Mark were the first I saw when I pushed open the door.

Laughing, Cara whispered in my ear,

'Ian's over at the bar with John.'

I just went over to the gang at the table and got Cara to go to the bar. Everyone seemed to be flying, so the mood was super, everyone straight into chatting. I handed Orla a card out of my bag and gave her a hug.

'Happy Birthday!'

'Ah, thanks. You could have waited till Saturday night. You have enough on your mind tonight. Ha, ha, ha.'

'Ah, it's just a card. I bought you something. I'll give it to you at the weekend.'

What was keeping Cara? I turned to the bar. Ian was standing right behind me.

'Hi, Lisa. Here's your beer. Cara gave it to me to bring over.'

That voice. Even deeper – deeper, and more reassuring – than it was on the phone. Our eyes met for the first time. I could see right away he was well out of it, so that settled us into a lovely, warm flow, *in the zone,* as we call it. We talked like we had known each other for years. He made me laugh.

'I think we met in another lifetime, only we're wearing different clothes this time. Yep, I'm sure I was wearing that dress last time!'

'Yeah? And what was I wearing?'

'Oh, nothing but a smile – and Chanel No. 5.'

'And what happened between us in our last lives then, Ian?'

'Ah, it was bloody awful. You fell off a cliff and died but screamed, "See you in the next life!" So here we are. At least you kept your word.'

'Are you sure it wasn't you that pushed me over the cliff? Men have this habit of doing that with me. And I break so bloody easy.'

'Nah, I jumped after you.'

'Yeah? I know you an hour, and already you've given your life for me! Not a bad start to the night, what? Let's hope we keep this buzz going.'

Before long the whole gang was stuck into a chat as the drinks flowed. I couldn't keep my eyes off Ian, and he felt the same towards me.

Ruth called me into the loo.

'So – what's the story? You both look amazing together. This is Mr Right, I'm telling you, Lisa! He's so sound. We're all heading back to John's for a drink and a few lines. Never know where you'll end up!'

'He's a hunk, Ruth. A *nice* hunk. We just seemed to click. I'm not jumping into it, just taking it easy, no rushing it this time.'

'Yeah, you're right. Take it one step at a time.'

Before I knew it we were back in John's house, taking a few lines, and I found myself in the hall with Ian.

'Hey, you two! Slow down! There's people watching!'

I stopped kissing Ian and turned to see Cara and Ruth coming down the stairs.

'It's getting a bit hot in this hall!' said Cara.

'Yeah,' laughed Ruth. 'You'd think you pair were dating years!'

It didn't go any further after that.

*

'I've an early start in the morning,' said Ian, as he put on his jacket. 'Look, I'll see you Saturday, Lisa.'

'Yeah, that's cool,' I said, grabbing one last kiss as the taxi pulled up outside.

'You're so wonderful, Lisa. I'm so glad I met you.'

'Likewise, Ian. You take care. Text me tomorrow, won't you?'

'Course I will.'

As he walked towards the taxi he turned back.

'So – are we dating? Ha, ha, ha. "You better not be fooling me, Harry!" That's a Jim Carrey line, you know.'

'Yeah, yeah, I know. See you soon, Ian!'

All I knew, as the taxi pulled away, was that this was the real deal. I'd found someone so cool, so funny – and a great kisser to top it all. I took a deep breath and rejoined the rest inside.

'Well!' laughed Cara. 'Would you just look at her face! You're smitten, Lisa!'

'I knew you'd click,' said Emma, coming in from the kitchen, holding a cd cover with a few lines of coke. 'Welcome to the Couples Gang, Lisa. Here – take a line of this to celebrate your new-found love.'

'Ah, he's gorgeous, Emma. You're a star, linking us up together.'

'I knew you'd suit each other, Lisa. Well – that's my Christmas present out of the way!'

Everyone was so glad for me, knowing what had happened with Ron. And all of them kind of knew my relationship with Brian was going nowhere.

I walked home alone around 4am as John's house is only a 20-minute walk from Kelly's Bay. I felt like I was floating along, thinking about Ian.

Later, as I struggled to get asleep, I remembered the moments chatting with him, the long, endless kiss in the hallway, and I wondered how life could get any better than this . . . A part of me didn't want it to end with just a kiss, but I knew I had to take things slowly this time round. But it's very hard to do that when you're coked out of your head. And that was part of the problem with coke, it had me sleeping with Brian for so long.

I wanted this to be different, a real relationship with all the trimmings – hanging out, going to the cinema, getting a takeout and crashing on the sofa for the night with a dvd. Just normal things like taking a walk around the Head of Skerries in the summer sun, holding hands. That's what I craved more than anything else in life – real love.

I've never been lucky like the rest of the gang with relationships. Something always goes wrong, horribly wrong. Even as far back as teenage love. But as I drifted off into a deep sleep I felt my time had come. Even though I'd only just met Ian I knew this was different in every way.

*

I woke up at 12 noon on Friday with my phone ringing. It was Ruth.

'Did I wake you, Lisa?'

'Nah, you're grand, Ruth.'

'Listen – Ian rang Emma this morning saying he thinks you're beautiful. Thought I'd ring you with that little bit of news. Ah, it's fantastic, Lisa!'

'Did he really say that?'

'Yeah, you know me. First with the news. Bet you can't wait for tomorrow night to come! Oh, bring it on! Ha, ha, ha!'

'Oh, I'm dying, Ruth. Ring me back later. I'm half asleep still.'

'Ok. Drop around later when you get your head sorted. Bye.'

After a quick shower I lay back on the bed and nodded off.

*

'Ah, Lisa! You're still not up, and it's half two in the afternoon!'

'Yeah, Ma. Bit hungover.'

'You need to take it easy with the drinking, Lisa. I'm worried about you.'

'Ah, Ma. Don't start.'

'Here. Have this tea and toast, at least.'

'Ok, Ma. Thanks, Ma.'

I drove around to Ruth's, where she and Steve were drinking coffee.

'How come you pair are not at work?'

'We both took the day off to make it a long weekend.'

Steve worked in landscaping, but with the downturn work was not easy to come by. So he had more time on his hands now. He was the quiet one of the gang, always in the background. But when he did speak, you'd always listen and get a great laugh.

The three of us chatted away about everything, but mostly about Ian. They didn't know him well at all, so they were no real help.

'Just take it slowly,' Steve said, smiling. 'You got hurt before, so don't rush into anything. I think you look too hard for this relationship that you want, and then there's a part of you that's far too trusting. I'm saying that as your friend, Lisa. This is Dr Phil. That'll be €20, please.'

The three of us burst out laughing.

'I know, Steve,' I said. 'You're right. But Ian is so gorgeous, in every way. Everyone who met him says it. Didn't they, Ruth?'

'Yeah, I must say he impressed me. Go for it, girl. What a Christmas this is turning out to be!'

'Right. I'm off shopping. Are you pair coming? We have to find something really nice to wear for tomorrow night's big party for Orla.'

'Big party for you, more like it!' said Ruth, laughing.

'Well, it's a double reason to party. Yeah!'

'Come on. We'll drive in Steve's car to the Pavilions. There's a sale in TK Maxx.'

I suppose the truth is everything became tunnel vision from here on in my day with Ruth and Steve. I was on this big high that no one could take me off.

It's every girl's dream to have a great job, great friends, great home life – and to top it all, to find real love. I'd searched for years through so much disappointment and now I felt I had everything a human heart would wish for. To say I was looking forward to Saturday night would be an understatement. This was it. I saw it almost unfold before me like a film with the most perfect and most exciting ending a girl could wish for. A fairytale unfolding. That's the way I saw my life that Friday afternoon. To top the day off, Ian started texting me the moment he got off work and rang me that evening as well. We chatted for a couple of hours non-stop.

I fell asleep with his face the last image floating around in my head.

Chapter Five

Dark Side of the White Line

My eyes opened on Saturday, 19th of December, 2011. My very first thought was of Ian, closely followed by the exciting prospect of Orla's party, knowing we'd all be taking coke. This was my night. I just couldn't wait for the day to pass so I could see Ian again. I pulled open the curtains and saw the layer of white frost that still lay fresh across the path, road and grass outside our top-floor apartment. What a beautiful sight to behold on such a special day in my life. I got dressed and made my way down to eat breakfast.

'You're up early,' said Ma, pouring me a cup of tea.

'Ah, yeah, Ma. Big day ahead. Orla's birthday party in John's house. Well . . . that's not all. I think I met Mr Right! He's gorgeous, Ma. Amazing. I know we just met, but I'm telling you, there's that magic about him. You know the magic you told me about when you met Dad? Well, it's like that.'

'God, that all happened a bit fast,' she said, that concerned look in her face again. 'Are you sure this is as deep as you're saying? I don't want you getting hurt again. And what about Brian around the corner? I thought you were sort of seeing him?'

'Nah, that's over. It wasn't anything like this, Ma.'

'Well, I hope you're right. It won't be long till you find out if this is what you say it is. Just be careful, pet, won't you?'

A text on my phone. Orla.

Listen I've to drop around to you today. Have a lovely bit of coke for you. I owe you it from last week.

Yeah, drop around. I've your birthday present here wrapped and all.

'What? Yeah, yeah. Of course, Ma.'

'Well, you look certain, so you have my best wishes.'

Another text.

Hi Lisa. Looking forward to seeing you tonight. It's going to be a savage party. Ian xxx

Hi Ian. Yeah, looking forward to seeing you there. Lisa x

Orla arrived some time later.

'It's only a flying visit, so I can't stay long. I've got to get my hair done and meet Carl for lunch. He's taking me to Stoops for a seafood meal.'

Stoop Your Head, a pub on the harbour road, was famous for its seafood.

I gave her her present and told her not to open it till she got home.

The bag of coke she gave me was more than what I gave her. Plus it was still *on the rock.*

'Ah, Orla, thanks so much.'

'Look, I got a big bag off John for my birthday. And anyway, you were so good to me in the past.'

She checked her watch.

'Listen, Lisa. I've got to go. Best of luck with the Big Date tonight with Ian. It's going to be a mega party!'

*

The day raced on. With my clothes laid out on the bed, hair washed, shower over, I was drinking a can of Bud and opening the bag of coke. I placed the lump on my Coldplay cd cover. I put on my make-up, then a few lines went racing up my nose, hitting me fast. *Shit, that's lovely stuff,* I thought.

Everyone was texting and ringing me. *Best of luck on your Big Date.* Etc., etc.

Ruth rang.

'I'm heading to John's now, Lisa. Are you ready?'

'I'll be there in half an hour.'

I sat in front of the mirror to get the final touches done. Getting ready on coke can be mental. You lose track of time and start taking another line. Then another. Before you know it, you're dancing and getting lost in the music. I felt so good inside as I rang a taxi. He was there within minutes. I grabbed my bits and headed for the door.

'See you, Ma. I'm out of here.'

'Come here – give me a hug.'

This time she actually held me in her hug longer than usual, as if she was reluctant to let me go.

'Love you so much.'

'Bye.'

My heart was racing so fast from the coke and the expectation of meeting Ian – our first real, official date. The taxi pulled up outside John's. I could see in the front window that there were a good few heads already there. I walked in the door. It was like it was my birthday party. Well, that's how I felt inside. Cara and Ruth met me.

'You look so great, Lisa,' said Ruth, handing me a bottle of Bud.

'Yeah,' laughed Cara. 'You'll blow Ian's mind when he sees you!'

'Is he here?'

'Yeah – in the sitting room.'

I took a mouthful of the Bud and walked in. There he was, with John, Steve and Mark. He turned round and smiled.

'Wow!' he said, giving me a strong hug. 'You look stunning, Lisa.' Then he kissed me on the lips.

Good God, I thought. *This is some start to the night.* I went a bit red in the face as everyone was looking at the two of us.

'Eh,' I said to them, 'you'd swear you never saw someone kiss! Will you lot get a life!'

We settled down into the party, with lines of coke and bottles of beer in plentiful supply. Everyone was in top form as always. I was deep in conversation with Ian when Ruth came over.

'Em, can we have Lisa for five minutes, Ian?'

She dragged me into the hall.

'Well? Tell me. How's it going? You seem to be hitting it off so well.'

'Ah, Ruth. You're mad. It's going great. He's so down to earth.'

'I bet you end up sleeping together tonight!'

'Shut up, will ya! I'm taking this slowly. That's the best way to go about it. Let's see where the night takes us. Yeah?'

Cara, Orla and Anne came down the hall looking for the same bit of news.

'I'm not saying another word, girls. Now, someone get me another bottle of Bud.'

After a few more lines of coke, we were all in taxis heading down to The Life Nightclub. On the way, the gang I was with burst into *Happy Birthday, Dear Orla* in the back seat.

We rolled in the doors of The Life, laughing our heads off. Ian held on to me as we gave our coats in at the cloakroom. Before I could catch my breath, I was on the dance floor, dancing with him, kissing the face off him. I looked around at the rest of the gang. They were all flying. This was the greatest night of my life, by far. Nothing could touch the high I was experiencing. The cocktail of coke and beer flooded through my body, from my head to my toes and back again. We danced like superstars. I lost track of time as we went from dancing on the floor to dancing at the bar. Everyone we met was on the same wavelength, hugging each other, smiling and enjoying every moment as the speakers throbbed, blasting out the best of music, the music we all loved.

The gang got a bit split up as some went out for a smoke. Others went talking to other friends. I found myself with just Ruth, Cara and Orla to the side of the dance floor, as no drinks are allowed on the dance floor itself. We were giving it loads to the sounds. To my right on the floor Frank, Steve and John were all with their mates, dancing their hearts out.

Then – in a split second, everything seemed to go in slow motion . . . My body seemed to be losing all power . . . The music seemed to die to the point that I couldn't hear it at all . . . My mind couldn't take in what was happening . . . Or wouldn't take it in . . . I wasn't sure what to do . . . I thought I was im-ag-in-ing it all . . . I looked at the girls . . . They seemed to be smiling and still in top form . . . My head seemed to take ages to move as I turned it right to face the dance floor where Steve and the gang were dancing . . .

My eyes stopped on John . . . There, standing right beside him, kind of attached to him or even a part of him, was this dark grey figure . . . I opened my mouth to scream . . . But I was frozen with the most terrifying fear imaginable that no human words could ever describe . . . I turned away, and looked back again . . . It was still there . . .

I just lost all control and as I did I could feel all the feelings in my body returning. I dropped the bottle of beer and it smashed on the floor. The next thing I remember was the look on the faces of Ruth and Cara – a look that changed from happiness to concern, shock and fear.

Are you ok?

My God!

Are you ok, Lisa?

I could hear the music full blast again.

My God, are you all right?

You look like you're going to be sick.

I couldn't talk. I was still stricken with fear and a sense of shock. I could see a bouncer coming towards us, a look of concern on his face as he spoke into his clip-on mic. Next thing I remember was the girls taking me by both arms into the loo. The bouncer came up behind us.

Is everything ok, girls? Is she ok?

Yeah, yeah, she's grand, Liam. Just feeling a bit sick. Everything's ok.

Cara held me up to the wall.

Are you ok, Lisa? Are you ok?

I could hear Ruth.

What happened to you? What happened? You were in top form. God, you just freaked out for nothing.

'I'm grand, girls. I'm grand now. Don't know what happened to me out there. My God, I just thought I saw something . . . It was so strange . . .'

'Like what?' asked Orla.

'I'm not sure.'

'You must be having hallucinations, Lisa. You'll be ok. Happens now and again. You're going to be ok. It must be the mixture of the coke and the drink and all the excitement.' 'Come on,' said Ruth. 'Let's rock this party again! You're going to be ok. Look, you look great. Come on!'

I took a mouthful of water from the cold tap and tried to click back into the lovely buzz I was on. I looked into the mirror to try and reassure myself it was all just a bad moment but something seemed strange about my eyes, they didn't look like mine!!

We made our way back out of the loo. The bouncer was standing outside.

'Is everything ok, Lisa?'

'Yeah, yeah, it's cool. I just felt a bit sick.'

'Come on,' said Ruth. 'Let's rock the dance floor with the gang!'

'Yeah, sure. I'm just going to get a fresh bottle of Bud. I'll follow you in a minute.'

As I walked unsteadily to the bar, everything started to go strange again. An awful fear rose up inside me. I thought I could hear a sinister voice saying,

It's all fake, Lisa. Everything is fake. Nothing is real.

I tried to fight away the feelings but I couldn't. I looked around – in slow motion.

Faces . . . That's all I could see . . . Disfigured faces . . . People's jaws slumped down to one side, grinding their teeth – one of the effects of E and coke . . . People's eyes looked abnormal . . . A girl gave me a smile as she passed by, but I knew it wasn't real . . . Nothing was real . . . I tried again to snap out of the nightmare and back into the happy buzz, but I couldn't . . . I felt so scared and so alone . . . When I got to the bar and asked for a drink I became so paranoid as I stumbled over the simple words . . .

Here you go, Lisa. Are you ok?

Yeah, yeah, I'm fine, thanks.

I turned around, keeping my back to the end of the bar. I looked out at the sea of people all dancing, all hugging each other. I could see all my buddies, all smiling and having a great time. As I stayed locked away in what seemed like another world to theirs, I was so afraid in case I saw that dark figure again.

I couldn't see Ian. I needed him. I needed him to hold me. My eyes searched for him but he wasn't with the gang on the dance floor. I looked up to the left where there was a big pillar off in the corner of the club. And there he was, my Ian, talking up close to a girl. He sneaked a look from behind the pillar out across the dance floor, with his hands all over her! He gave her a full passionate kiss on the lips before pulling away.

Oh my God, this can't be happening to me again!

I looked around as the place started to dim . . . I couldn't hear the music . . . Again, everything went back in slow motion . . . I wanted to scream but I was gripped by some unknown fear . . . My eyes seemed to be the only part of my body that could move . . . A voice screamed in my head:

It's all illusions, Lisa. Everything you have is nothing but an illusion.

I looked back at the dance floor, where Ian had now rejoined the gang as if nothing had happened . . . I looked straight at John, and again and felt I could see something like a dark grey figure standing next to him. . .

O my God!! Someone please help me. What's happening to me?

I looked away in terror . . .

'Lisa! Lisa! Are you ok, Lisa? Lisa?'

I turned as the feelings rushed back into my body . . . The bottle of Bud went smashing to the floor again . . . I just wanted to run and run till I was far away from this place . . .

The voice calling my name was that of Liam, the bouncer. I pushed him to try to get past so I could get out of this nightmarish place. Before I could think I went crashing to the floor.

Liam, along with Jonathan, the other bouncer, picked me up. They took me to a side room next door to the cloakroom. I was kicking at them and screaming,

*Get away from me, you f**king assholes; get your hands off me.*

'Calm down, Lisa! Everything's ok. You're safe now. No one's going to hurt you now. We're only helping you.'

I started to come round and found myself sitting on a chair in a small office room.

'Lisa, listen to me now,' said Liam. 'Did you take something tonight? We're not going to say anything. We just need to make sure you're ok.'

'You're going to be ok,' said Jonathan, handing me a glass of water. 'What did you take?'

'I'd say you just had a bad experience,' offered Liam. 'But it's ok now. Everything's ok.'

I started to come slowly back to myself.

'I took coke and some drink and . . .'

'When you say *coke* do you mean . . . ?'

I could feel the tears welling up. I just broke down in floods. It was like a deep, deep pain in my heart, screaming through the rest of my body. I just lost it.

'Oh, God! No one loves me! No one, Liam! Everyone just uses me. No one cares about me. What am I going to do?'

He put his arm around me.

'It's ok, Lisa. It's going to be ok. Everything's going to be ok.'

Next minute I was at the front side door, puking my guts up and crying at the same time. Flashes of all I had seen inside raced across my mind. Inside I was screaming with fear.

Please, someone, help me!

'Please, Liam. Ring me a taxi. Please, I want to go home to my Ma.'

'Ok, ok. One on the way. Are you sure you're ok? Do you want us to ring someone to come for you?'

'God, no. Just get my jacket. Thanks for helping me. I'll be ok.'

The taxi pulls up. I can't get in fast enough, slamming the door. It's Joe.

'Ah, hi, Lisa. You're going home early! Where's the rest of the gang?'

My head slumps back, my mouth open, trying to take in some air to ease the ongoing sense of fear and dread still gripping every part of my heart and mind.

'Just drive, Joe. Just . . . take me home.'

The taxi pulls away from The Life, but I know my life will never be the same again.

Chapter Six

Ma, Please Listen

The taxi speeds along the Skerries road, Joe saying nothing, just glancing in the mirror anxiously. When we get to the Ladystairs, halfway to Skerries, I begin to feel sick again.

'Joe, stop the car,' I groan. 'Stop. I'm going to be sick.'

He quickly pulls over to the side of the road. I get out and puke my ring up again and again.

'Get it all up, Lisa.'

I continue to heave and dry retch for what seems like ages.

'Sorry, Joe.'

'You're grand. You're grand.'

I slump back into the car and keep the window open till I get home. I think Joe knows not to ask me anything. I step out slowly and fumble in my bag for my purse.

'Go on inside, Lisa. Pay me next time you see me, love.'

He speeds off into the night.

I couldn't gather my thoughts. Too much was racing across my mind – flashes of what I saw, what I felt, seeing Ian touch and give that girl a sly kiss. *The dirty creep. The two-faced shithead.*

I turned the key slowly, not wanting to wake Ma. Then my bloody phone went off, Ruth's name flashing on the screen. I let it ring out and put it on Silent. I dragged myself up the stairs to my room, closing the door quietly behind me. I fell on the bed, my whole body trembling. I was so confused. Nothing like this had ever happened to me before. Yes, I'd got sick loads of times, but this was so frightening, I was scared that I'd never be normal again.

I could see the light on my phone flashing again. I just could not face talking to anyone. How was I going to explain this to anybody? I tried to convince myself it was just a really bad buzz, as shit like this happens to people all the time. But deep down I could hear something like a voice say otherwise. I could feel a cold chill that made no sense to me, like something dark had touched my soul. It left me riddled with fear, a fear that left me knowing I would never touch coke again. Even to see it would freak me out . . .

Then I jumped up off my bed. I realised I still had a good bit of it left over. I looked a sight. I opened my bag very slowly and gingerly, as if there was a bomb in it. Carefully, I took out the coke, went into the bathroom and emptied it into the loo. My hands were shaking as I pressed down on the lever and flushed it all away. The water settled in the toilet bowl. Clean, clear, still.

I raised my head, and once again found myself staring at myself in the mirror. Good God, there was sick on my top. My face was sunken in, my cheekbones sticking out. I looked more like an alien than a human. Like a zombie. Mascara and make-up streaking down my face from crying. My eyes – I was afraid to look at them for long. A sense of shame. Maybe I was starting to wake up to the full horror of who I really was. I looked again. I looked like someone who had seen a ghost. God, maybe I had.

I washed my face, brushed my teeth and climbed into bed, pulling the covers over me.

My phone flashed again, weaker this time. *28 missed calls.* Voice Messages. Texts. One from Ian.

Where are you Lisa? Looking everywhere for you. Xxx

My hands shaking with anger, I texted him back.

NEVER text me again you 2-faced creep. I saw you kiss and touch that girl in The Life. Take my number out of your phone right now. Never ring or text me again!!!!

I listened to just one voicemail from Cara, asking where the hell I was, to answer my bloody phone, that they were all heading back to John's now.

3:15am. The very thought of seeing anyone, let alone talking to anyone, seemed unbearable, but I had to try to make one phonecall just to let them know I was ok.

I rang Ruth. She answered right away.

'Where are you, Lisa? We're all looking for you!'

I could hear all the laughing, all the loud voices.

'Everyone's outside The Life trying to get taxis.'

'Hi, Ruth. Look, it's . . .'

'Ian's here, looking for you. What's going on?'

'Em, I just . . . I just got a bad drink and came home early. I'm home in bed. Listen, I saw that creep Ian kiss a girl behind the pillar in The Life, he had his hands all over her, Ruth. I texted him and told him to piss off.'

'What? He kissed who?! You're bloody joking me, Lisa. He's here, looking to talk to you!'

'Tell him to piss off, Ruth. Ok?'

'Are you sure, Lisa? Maybe it was just a messing kiss – you know, with a friend?'

'No, Ruth. He was looking around to make sure nobody was watching him. Look, I'm going.'

I started getting upset again.

'Shit, Lisa. You're crying. Come to the party. We can talk here.'

'Look, I'm sick, Ruth. And please don't tell anyone what I just told you till tomorrow, ok? I don't want everyone ringing me. Bye, Ruth.'

I turned the phone off and wrapped myself in the covers. I snuggled up, trying to comfort myself. But I just cried and cried. I felt so empty inside. There was nowhere I could escape to from the awful pain, a pain that seemed to be playing with me as if I was under its full control.

Voices screamed inside my head.

You're going to lose everyone, everything. You always lose, Lisa.

Flashes of myself on the coke in pubs and parties and clubs, looking so happy, so in control. So much the centre of the show. Seemed now like something I wished I could get away from. At that moment it all looked fake, a string of moments that were only illusions, that had me fooled for years.

I saw myself under the covers of my bed, split into two persons: the great, super-confident, sexy dancer who had life all figured out under the spell of a drug; then the other girl, me, now crying my heart out, alone with nothing or nobody to help me.

As the pain got worse, I just lost all control. I could hear the words in my head:

You're a fake. A fake, Lisa. Go to the party! Get a line of coke into you! Come on, you're missing it all! Missing the buzz!

I snapped. I jumped out of bed and ran into my mother's bedroom. She could hear me crying as I came out of my room. She was already up, looking still half asleep, but her face in shock at what she now saw in her daughter's face.

I grabbed her.

'Oh, God, Ma! Please, please hold me!'

She held me tight, as tight as she could.

'Lisa, Lisa! What's wrong, pet? My God, what's happened to you?'

'Just hold me, Ma, please! Please, just hold me!'

I clung to her like a child, my body trembling in her arms. I held her as close as I could as inside I screamed out for some form of comfort from the pain I was experiencing.

At that moment, I felt like I was actually going to die. That's the only way I can explain it. I don't remember much after that. Everything just went blank.

*

I awoke about 11am. As I slowly opened my eyes I realised I was in my mother's bed. Her arms were still wrapped around me. I drifted back into a deep sleep.

*

The smell of rashers and eggs woke me up. 2pm. I could hear Ma downstairs, moving round the kitchen.

'Lisa! Lisa? I've a late breakfast ready. Up you get now!'

I slowly crawled out of bed, still feeling the effects of what I hoped was a bad dream. But I was fully aware that everything I experienced was in fact all horribly true.

After a shower to wash away something of the night before, I made my way downstairs. Still very much hung over, I thought, *God, what is Ma thinking, the state she saw me in last night?*

'Well, Lisa,' she said, placing the fry-up in front of me. 'You don't have to explain anything to me, 'cause I know exactly what happened to you last night.'

I gulped a mouthful of tea.

'You do?'

'Yes, it all went wrong with that guy you were to meet. I just knew it couldn't all be that great that soon. Come here!'

She leaned over and hugged me.

I sighed, cutting up the rasher on my plate.

'My God, Lisa. I don't think I've ever seen you so upset and broken-hearted. It was frightening to see you like that. You cried yourself to sleep!'

Before she said another word, I just knew I had to come clean and tell her everything. But I was scared. How would she take the news of her daughter being on drugs? I knew deep down that I'd never touch drugs again, so I had to be truthful. I'd being lying to her for three years about my whole life, and I felt shit about it now.

'Well, Ma. It's like this. For some time now I've . . .'

The doorbell rang. I jumped.

'Ma, if that's any of the girls, tell them . . . tell them I'm gone for a walk. Please! I can't face anyone right now.'

She looked at me with that searching look of hers. The doorbell rang again.

'Ok, Lisa. Ok.'

It was Cara.

'Hello, Mrs Webb. Is Lisa home?'

'No, no. She's . . . she's gone for a walk, Cara. A long walk.'

She was never a good liar.

'Is she? She has her phone off. I've been trying to contact her all morning.'

'Yes, well, maybe if you drop back later.'

'Ok, Mrs Webb. Tell her I called. Bye.'

Ma returned, looking concerned. She sat down at the table.

'Lisa – what's going on? Are you telling me everything?'

I looked into her eyes, then down at my barely-touched breakfast. I left down my knife and fork, took a mouthful of tea and cleared my throat.

'Ma,' I said, 'if I tell you, will you please listen to everything I have to say and not start shouting at me? I so need you to listen to me, Ma, and to stand by me.'

'Oh, no,' she said, standing up and crossing to the window. 'I know. You're pregnant. That's it. Isn't it?'

It was almost too funny for words.

'No, no, Ma! I'm not. I'm not having a baby.'

In an odd sort of way, I kind of wished that's all it was – that I was having a baby.

'Will you sit down and listen to me? I need your help, Ma.'

I could feel my tears welling up again. She sat on the edge of her chair.

'What is it, then, Lisa? You know I'll stand by you no matter what. Just be honest with me.'

'Ok, Ma.'

I took a deep breath and bowed my head, unable to look her straight in the eye.

'Ma . . . I've been . . . I've been taking . . . drugs.'

Drugs.

The word just hung in the air.

'What? Drugs?'

She looked at me in horror and disbelief.

'Don't tell me. Drugs? Lisa, please. Not bloody drugs!'

'Listen, Ma . . .'

She's now up off the chair, her voice becoming louder and angrier by the second.

'Not you, Lisa! What drugs? Tell me!'

'Ma, please, calm down. You said you'd listen to me. Please!'

'What drugs, Lisa? Tell me!'

'Coke, Ma. Ok. Coke. I've been taking coke for over three years now.'

'Coke? You mean . . . *cocaine?* Oh my God! That's a hard drug, isn't it? What . . .?'

With tears streaming down my face, I shout,

'It's over, Ma. I promise. That's why I'm telling you this now. I've stopped doing it since last night.'

'Last night? Just like that? Lisa, people don't just give it up after three years just like that. I can't believe my girl's on drugs. And three years! How did you hide it for three years?'

'Ma, sit down.'

'I won't sit down. And you a teacher! Of five-year-old kids! You're supposed to be an example to everybody in the community. Suppose the parents found out the teacher of their children was a drug addict!'

'Oh, Ma! Stop, will you. I'm not a . . .'

'I can't believe it. I mean, you had everything given to you in life. I thought you were happy, with all the love in the world your father and

I gave you. So why turn to drugs, Lisa?'

'Ma, it's nothing to do with upbringing. Is that what you think? Do you think you have to live in the Grove to be on drugs?'

'How dare you say that! I know plenty of fine, respectable people who live in the Grove, they're not all junkies, you know.'

'Ma – I'm not saying that. It's just . . . it's everywhere. People are taking coke right across the board. From the best families in this town to the worst. These days it's just like . . . having a drink. They now go hand in hand. Nearly everyone I know is taking it.'

'You mean to tell me that nearly all the teachers in the school take cocaine!'

'Ah, no, Ma! I'm talking about . . . my friends.'

'Your *friends?* Some friends! Huh, well, maybe you're mixing with the wrong kind . . . My God you don't mean to tell me that Cara and Ruth . . . ?'

'Yes, Ma, they're all on it. And please, I'm trusting you. You can't say a word about this to their families. Promise me, Ma.'

'I won't. I won't. I just . . . I just can't understand why. Tell me – where did you get the drugs?'

'Ma, if I tell you that, you have to promise not to tell a soul.'

'I won't. You have my word.'

I took a deep breath.

'Ok. I got them from John. John Noonan.'

'What? John? Cara's boyfriend? Oh my God! I always thought he was such a lovely, nice boy.'

'He is, Ma. He is.'

'He's a bloody drug dealer, Lisa. That's what he is. You're hanging around with a drug dealer.'

I felt I was getting nowhere.

'No, Ma. It's not like that. We didn't want to go to dealers, so John started going. He just gets it for his mates. He's not . . . he's not a drug dealer.'

I realised how foolish I was sounding.

'If he's making money out of it, then, in my books, he's a drug dealer! My God, Lisa. I can't believe all this. How could I be so blind! So stupid! I need a fresh cup of tea.'

She got up to put the kettle on.

'Here, Ma,' I said, feebly. 'Let me make it.'

She turned around, looking like she was about to start crying.

'Lisa – don't tell me you took drugs in this flat. Did you? Not under my roof?'

That was it. I just couldn't take any more.

'Stop, Ma. Just stop. I'm in a living nightmare. I feel like I'm losing my whole life. Please – I need your help, your support. I've nowhere to turn to, Ma. I'm so sorry about all of this, and I promise I'll make it up to you somehow. But I need you to please listen, to stand by me. Will you do that for me? I'll never ask you for anything ever again.'

She just stood there, staring straight at me, with tears streaming down her face. After a couple of minutes she sat down, reached over and held my hand.

'Ok,' she said, her voice shaking, but strong. 'Ok. You're my daughter. And I know you need me to listen. So I will. But promise me you'll tell me everything. And promise me you'll never take drugs again.'

I grasped both her hands in mine.

'I won't, Ma. I promise.'

The words hung in the air between us.

'So tell me – how can you be so sure you won't take drugs again? You just stopped last night. And what happened that made you decide to stop?'

She tore some kitchen roll off its holder and we both wiped our eyes.

'I had this awful experience last night, Ma. It was so frightening. One minute I was feeling great, the next, everything seemed like a horror film. I had to leave The Life Nightclub, and that's why I came home early and came into you, crying.'

I felt embarrassed about the next detail, but wanted to tell her anyway.

'And to make matters worse, I saw my new boyfriend – Ian, the fella I was telling you I was crazy about – I saw him kissing a girl on the sly. Anyway, I got rid of any coke I had left. I flushed it down the toilet. Yes, here in this apartment. And that's it, Ma. Now all I'm asking from you is to learn to trust me again. And I promise I'll never touch drugs again. Will you do that for me?'

It took Ma a minute or so to take it all in. Then she patted my hand, just like she used to when I was a toddler.

'Ok, Lisa. I'm going to stand by you. But it will take me a while to trust you again. Have you told the girls all this?'

'No, Ma. But I will. I have to take it step by step.'

She stood up, straightening her back, as if a burden hadn't yet been lifted off her shoulders.

'Have you thought how you're going to cope being around them if they're all still taking drugs? Won't you be tempted to try it again?'

She looked into my eyes, looking for some reassurance.

'Ma – after last night, there is no way on God's earth I would ever put a line of that stuff up my nose again. It won't be easy for them to understand why. But don't worry – I'll handle that part. Just please don't say a word to any of them or their parents. Sure you won't?'

'I won't, Lisa. Once I have your word you won't take it.'

'You have my word, Ma.'

'God, Lisa. Have you any idea how dangerous it all is?'

I looked into her eyes, noticing for the first time how tired they were.

'No, Ma. I never knew. But I do now.'

'Thanks for telling me everything, Lisa.'

I hugged her and we left it at that.

'Now,' she said, patting my back and breaking away from the hug, 'Where's that cup of tea you promised me?'

*

Later, I turned my phone back on. Oh my God. Fifty-eight texts and voicemails.

You were missed so much at the party. I love you so much. Hope you're better soon. Rock on next weekend. Ruth xxx

On and on it went. Texts and voicemails from all the gang, all at early hours of the morning. All out of their brains.

We love you.

Rock on Christmas.

Sorry to hear about Ian. Don't worry. You'll find Mr Right. Orla xxx

On it went.

Texts from Cara at 5:30am:

Love you, love you, love you.

And from Emma:

So sorry about what Ian did. He said to say he was sorry. Give him another chance. We miss u. We're all at John's. Hope to see u soon. I love u. Emma xxxx

Everybody who texted was from the party after The Life the night before. I could see through it all. None of it was real. It's just the bloody coke. Why in God's name did I never see all this before! And why was I the only one out of the gang that this happened to last night? Why just me? I couldn't take it all in. It's like I was blind. I thought everything was real when I was on coke. My mind was racing as I read text after text. All the same! Just like the texts I sent when I was on the coke. Loving everyone. Everything amazing.

How was I going to tell Cara, Ruth and the gang? How was I going to cope being on the outside looking in at them all on coke, knowing what I knew now?

I felt I was now alone. I was even afraid to meet them. My mind went into overdrive. How would I replace the buzz I got from drugs?

I felt like I was sinking with fear, fear of what my future would now be on the opposite side of the line.

Chapter Seven

The Outsider

The doorbell rang again. I ran out to the landing to give Ma the sign *I'm still not home.* It was Cara again, with John this time.

'Sorry, Cara. She's still not back.'

I tiptoed back to my room and turned my phone off again. The floorboard creaked under my foot. I held my breath. Cara seemed to pause before responding,

'Ok, Mrs Webb. Tell her to ring me when she gets back.'

'Goodbye, Mrs Webb. Sorry for troubling you!' chimed in John, as if butter wouldn't melt in his mouth.

I waited till I heard the car drive off before coming halfway down the stairs.

'Thanks, Ma. God, I just can't face anyone right now. What am I like, hiding from my friends like this!'

I came down the last few steps and sat with Ma at the kitchen table.

'It's not going to be easy, Lisa,' she sighed, stroking my hair. 'You just have to face them and tell them straight out that you're not doing drugs again. But you're going to be ok. I'm standing by you.'

She gave my hand an encouraging squeeze.

'God, I could have given that John lad a kick you-know-where, the two-faced criminal! But, no. I bit my lip and tried to look all smiles. I held it together for *you*, Lisa.'

'Thanks, Ma. You did great.' I kissed her on the cheek. 'It'll all pan out in the end.'

Saying that, my mind raced as to how I was going to hang out with them in parties and clubs while they were all out of their heads. It felt overwhelming, just thinking about it, let alone being in the situation itself.

Ma put her arm around me.

'You're deep in thought, aren't you? Are you going to be all right?'

'Yeah, yeah,' I sighed. 'I just can't see how I can be around all that way of life and pretend to be *in the zone* with them.'

Ma made that disapproving *tsk* sound with her teeth which summed up what she thought of the phrase *in the zone*. I felt foolish for using it.

'Are you sure you're going to be strong enough to say no, to resist the temptation?' she asked, looking at me straight between the eyes.

'Yeah, Ma,' I answered, looking out the window. 'I just need . . . I need a few days, on my own, away from everyone, to think this thing through. So if anyone rings or calls, tell them I'm not home. I'm going to put it on Facebook that I'm not going to be around for the rest of the week. It'll give me time to gather my thoughts.'

'That's a great idea, Lisa,' she said, half-heartedly, not sounding totally convinced that I was being ruthless enough. 'You take all the time in the world to think about whatever you need to sort out. And I'm here for you, anytime you need to talk. You hear me?'

We enjoyed a lovely dinner together, and afterwards I logged onto Facebook. I stayed offline as I wrote my post about not being around till the weekend. There were quite a few private messages from all the gang, plus,

Sorry about what I did. Forgive me. Xxx

I blocked him off my friends' list straightaway.

I had one from Anne's boyfriend, Frank. He wouldn't know me all that well, but he's sound. At five foot six he's called Shorty. He works with a lorry-building firm and does DJ some weekends.

Are you ok Lisa? Heard you got a bad drink in the Life. Bummer. Missed you in John's last night. Ring me or Anne if you want to chat. X

All the other messages were the girls wanting to meet up, and saying *Roll on the weekend!*

Emma sent me a long message saying how sorry she was over Ian, saying she wanted to meet to explain everything to me.

Yeah, right.

I just logged off and lay on the bed. I was overcome with a sense of shame as I looked back over the past few years. The guys I slept with on coke at parties. The relationship I had with Brian – it wasn't just him using me, but I was using him as well.

It just hit me that I had let myself down. I'd let my mother down. I was letting my pupils down – no teacher, especially a teacher of junior infants – can give one hundred per cent when she's been spaced out of her head the night before. To put it mildly, I was endangering my career.

But that's what drugs do. They take you high, so high you don't know what you're doing. And it was so hard to take it all in.

Where was the sense of values I knew I once had? Had even that been sacrificed along the way?

Where was the girl that had always wanted real romance? Years back, till I was about nineteen, that's all I had ever dreamed about – being in love. But I lost all that in empty-hearted relationships. There was always that side to me that just wanted what was real. No games . . . Just to be me . . . Just to be with a guy that was real, that wanted the same close feelings I wanted. But that nineteen-year-old dream was lost the night I started to take coke – and date Ron. My God – I've lost years over all this! It's like a different person took over my body. . .

As I lay there, I could feel a sense of fear. How was I going to get back to me? Maybe I never will! How would I replace the buzz I got off coke? God, I never thought about this like this when I was on it. I thought the buzz would go on forever.

I sensed I could hear a small voice inside me saying,

You've got to beat this thing from the inside out, Lisa. From the inside out!

Screaming across that voice was a cold sinister voice, laughing at me.

You're going to lose all your friends! You're going to lose everything you've ever loved!

It sounded like an awful battle had begun to rage in the loneliness of my mind. Apart from my mother, I felt I had no one to turn to. Everyone I hung out with took coke. No one would or could understand me. I felt hollow inside my heart, like I had nothing or nobody left. I grappled with all the facts of last night at The Life. I couldn't think of anything else. How could my life turn on its head in a split second like it was not normal? Nothing seemed normal to me.

Inside, I just wanted to grab something warm. A memory of a past event when I was eighteen, smiling and simply a happy-go-lucky girl. But everything I saw was a fading picture, like my life died when I got into coke. And now I was nothing but an empty shell. Back, but lost forever. That's how it felt as the hours ticked by that Sunday evening.

A gentle knock on my bedroom door.

'Are you ok, Lisa? Do you need anything, pet?'

'Come in, Ma.'

She looked at me with a look of sadness and pity.

'You look lost.'

'Ah, I'll be ok, Ma,' I struggled. 'I'm going to beat this thing. From the inside out, as the saying goes. You just watch me.'

'Well, I'm off to bed, pet. If you need me, I'm right next door. Night, love.'

'Night, Ma. Em, thanks for standing by me in all this. You've been –'

'Shh! The New Year will bring new hopes, new dreams. Just you wait and see.'

I drifted off into a deep sleep, into a deep, exhausting and vivid dream. I was falling, falling, falling into a dark, terrifying abyss. Endlessly, endlessly falling. Nothing or no one to hold on to. And the moment before I hit the ground, I woke up.

In a pool of sweat. Gasping. Trembling.

I always try to stay awake after a dream like that in case I fall back into it. Stay awake. Stay alert. Don't fall asleep . . . Don't fall . . . Don't . . .

Ringing. A ringing sound. A phone ringing. My phone ringing. Ringing. Ringing.

John.

Shit.

'H-hello?'

'Hi, Lisa! How's the head? Heard you got a dodgy drink in The Life. You poor thing. Listen – will you be around later today? I have your ounce of coke boxed off here for you! Can we meet at some stage? I need to offload as much as I can today and tomorrow.'

Shit.

'Listen, John. I . . . I don't need any.'

'What do you mean, Lisa? This is your order for the Christmas and the New Year. You ordered it, Teach. Remember?'

His voice started to get louder.

'Lisa! Stop doing my head in! I've twenty-five f**kin' ounces in front of me and I've to go down the list of orders and offload them as soon as I can. I told you Monday. You said you'd pick it up today . . . Hello? Lisa? Are you still there?'

'Yeah, yeah. Look – em . . . Brian wants half my ounce, so buzz him and he'll take half of it.'

'And what about the other half? You're havin' me on here, Lisa! You always get an order here every Christmas, so what the f**k is goin' on?'

'I know, I know. But, look – I have some already and, em . . . so look. I just don't want any right now. Ok?'

'So what will I do? Will I box it off for you till the end of the week? Lisa? Hello? Are you ok?'

I just lay there on the bed, breathing heavily, the phone in my sweaty hand now hurting my ear.

'Shit, Lisa. You don't sound right to me. We called yesterday to your place and you were out, and your phone was off. Plus you posted on Facebook that you wouldn't be around till the weekend. I mean, what's going on, Lisa?'

'Look, nothing, John. I just don't want any coke, ok? Now I'm sure you can sell it to one of your mates. Look, I've got to go. My Ma is calling me. See you at the weekend. Bye.'

I hung up.

Shit – this is a never-ending nightmare.

John rang back but I wouldn't answer. He left a message.

Will you text me Brian's no. I don't think I have it.

I did, then turned my phone off.

I looked at the time – 12:30am. Shit. It can't be that late. I fell back on the bed. I've just got to tell them all I'm off taking the coke. What's the big deal, anyway? If everyone freaks out, that's their issue, not mine.

I thought about John's phonecall. He had twenty-five ounces to get rid of. We get ours cheap because we know him. I think he sells to others at €1,100 an ounce . . . Shit, that's over €25,000 worth of bloody coke! *€25,000!* How come I never copped on to that? And I thought all along he was just scoring for his mates. Come to think of it, he was always busy doing drops to this house and that house, meeting people I'd never even heard of. Maybe I was enjoying the buzz and was blinded to the reality. This was getting worse by the minute.

I turned on my phone just to check. Two missed calls, Cara and Brian.

Brian was asking what the story was with John giving him the half-ounce instead of me. Had I got an issue with him over our relationship?

Cara wanted to know why I wasn't buying my coke from John.

Oh, shit, I thought. *Would you all just piss off and leave me alone! I'm sick of all this crap!*

I turned my phone off and put it into the drawer of my bedside locker.

That's it. I'm not talking to anyone. Anyone. Till next weekend.

*

I spent the following day with my mother, just around the apartment, catching up on some reading, listening to music. I drove her to the Pavilions to do some shopping. As we went from shop to shop I was like a paranoid freak, looking around in case I saw someone I knew.

When we got home, we spent the afternoon just talking. She couldn't understand how she had never seen a single sign that I had been taking coke for so long 'right under my nose', as she put it. We both laughed at her unfortunate choice of phrase.

I explained that I started off slowly with it, just to try it, and that it was only in the last eighteen months that it had got way out of hand. I think when I broke up with Ron I became more hooked on it. Before that it was only the a few lines at parties and nightclubs. But then again, everyone I know started that way. We all ended up getting more and more into it.

'What's frightening is I don't know how I can fit in anymore. I feel like an outsider already. And I haven't even gone out with the gang yet.'

'How do you know, Lisa, that you won't be tempted to take it – just to fit in again?'

I kept reassuring her that I couldn't go back to that way of life, and while I was saying it, the awful horror of the experience kept flashing across my mind. I knew she would be worried the next time I went out. To be honest, so would I. Deep down in my subconscious I knew I was controlled by a fear of rejection, like most of us are. Being on coke gave me that sense that everyone loved me, I was the life and soul of the party. Take the coke and drink away, and what would I be like? It didn't bear thinking about. Even the thought of drinking made me feel ill. That's the impact Saturday night at The Life had on me. I was stricken with fear of something strange like that happening again, even if it was just the coke and not the drink. I felt it had catapulted me into another whole new world and frame of mind and I was not going back to *that person*, come what may.

*

The next morning, I got up early and went for a jog to clear my head. When I got home, Ma had breakfast ready.

'Wow,' she beamed, as I came in the door, panting. 'I haven't seen you up so early in ages! And jogging! It must be months since you went for a jog, Lisa.'

'I know, Ma,' I said, filling a glass of water from the tap. 'And that's just the start. I'm going to the gym later today.' I gulped down half the glass. '*And* I'm going for a jog every morning over the Christmas. You never know – I just may catch up with that girl in me that got lost.'

'The way you're going, you'll pass her out by the weekend! Here's your scrambled egg and toast, just the way you like them. And listen – don't go overdoing it, pet.'

*

We spent the day again laughing and joking. I so felt I wanted to redeem the time I had lost with my mother. And it felt so good, just the two of us, hanging out, just being there. I know it meant a lot to her too. You could see it in her face. We sat and read, then watched *Sleepless in Seattle* on tv, both pretending not to cry. Another day slipped by. Beautifully.

*

Wednesday morning. Across the bedroom, on the wall, was a framed photo I had seen a thousand times. Me on my fifteenth birthday, blowing out the candles on the cake. Standing over me, Ma and Dad. They were looking at each other and smiling, but it was Ma's smile in particular that caught my eye. For whatever reason, I'd never noticed it before – the love in her eyes for Dad. But that smile. I haven't seen it since Dad died. It's like it died with him. I sat up in bed for ages, just looking at that picture.

Ma is just fifty-two, yet she never dated or looked at another man since Dad passed. She's a good-looking woman, too, and goes out with Rose and her friends, but never crosses that line. Maybe she's still broken-hearted.

I went out for my jog, and halfway back I saw a car pull up. It was Ruth.

'Hey, you!' she shouted, rolling down the window. 'What's going on? Have you fallen off the bloody earth? Jump in for a second.'

Nervously, I sat in. Ruth switched off the ignition and sat back calmly in her seat, eyeballing me with that searching look. She lit a cigarette.

'Can somebody tell me what the hell is going on? 'Cause I'm lost, Lisa. Last time I saw you, you had that bad turn in The Life. And I haven't seen you since. That creep, Ian Carter! I cursed him from a height on the phone to Cara last night. I mean, everything was going so great at The Life. It was perfect! Then, since then, no one's seen you. Cara's saying you told John you don't want your Christmas coke. Your phone's off the hook. You leave a message on Facebook saying you won't be around or on the phone – see you all next week! I mean, it's not like you at all!'

I didn't really know where to start. Or even if I wanted to.

'Well, I was so hurt over Ian. I mean, I so liked him, Ruth. You saw that I opened my life again and let someone in. And he was just like the rest of them – a two-faced creep. If you had seen him, looking around to make sure no one saw him. Then, that kiss, l don't want to see That creep ever again. And tell Emma that from me.'

'Ok, ok,' she said, stubbing out the cigarette in the ashtray. 'You're dead right. I'm so sorry this happened to you, Lisa. I saw how you liked him. Ah, well, shit happens to us all. Yeah. So – you coming out to rock Saturday? We're all going to Tommy's. It's our get-together. We do it every year. Remember?'

I could feel my whole body tensing up.

'Em, I'll see, Ruth.'

She reached for another cigarette, but changed her mind.

''There's something you're not saying, Lisa. What is it? You don't seem yourself.'

'Look, Ruth. You saw what happened with Ian. I've had an awful week and I just need time, ok? I'm off home to get out of this tracksuit.'

As I reached for the door handle, I stared into Ruth's eyes. *God, I loved her so much. What a friend. But I was changed. Inside.*

Even as she switched on the engine, I wanted to climb in again and give her a full explanation, but I held back. I wasn't ready yet. Would I ever be? She drove off and I could see the sad, puzzled look in her eyes as she glanced in the rear view mirror.

I knew I had to make the effort to go out on Saturday to the get-together. But how would I handle it?

After my shower I looked again into the bathroom mirror. *You can't hide away, girl. You have to face the world.*

*

As Saturday approached I kept to myself, jogging, training in the gym, keeping out of sight of everyone as best I could.

I happened to see Orla one day. We were passing each other in our cars. We just waved and smiled.

But soon, in spite of my best intentions, I found myself turning on my phone. Again, umpteen texts and voicemails. All wondering was I ok.

We love you.

See you at weekend in Tommy's. It's going to be great.

On and on it went. Life will go on, that's for sure, with or without you. Isn't that a song? U2? Yeah.

I read all the texts, replied to some.

See you all later, girls.

Emma with more voicemails, saying how she felt it was her fault, and couldn't believe Ian did what he did.

But who cares? I thought. *It's history now.*

There I was, getting ready to go out. Ma looking in the bedroom door.

'Are you sure you're going to be ok, pet? Ring me later. I'll be worried.'

''I'll be ok, Ma. Yes, I'll ring you. Promise.'

I sat looking into my dressing table mirror, feeling so odd. A bottle of Bud that I still hadn't touched yet. Shower and hair done. I felt uneasy. Looking down at my cd covers that had all the scratch marks . . . This was so weird.

No coke. No other person to switch into like Wonder Woman. No dancing around my room. No, not even the music on. Just me, looking into a mirror, Alone.

And a girl looking back.

Never in my whole life did I feel so lost than at that moment.

The penny dropped, hard but slow. This was life without lines of coke.

I put on a small amount of make-up and just sat there, dressed and ready to go.

Chapter Eight

Facing into the Wind

A gentle tap on the door.

'Are you ok, Lisa? I don't hear the music on. That's not like you!'

'No, Ma, I'm grand. Just putting on some make-up. Come in.'

She came in and sat on the edge of the bed.

'You'll be ok out there, pet. I do trust you. It's just . . . you may be tempted. *They* may tempt you.'

'I'll be alright, Ma,' I said, turning round to face her. 'It's just strange knowing I'll be in their company, but not taking part in . . . in that aspect of the night. Look, I know you're worried, and that's understandable. But I'm going to ring you – and I'm coming home early, ok?'

She stroked my face gently with the back of her hand.

'You know what? Your face has filled out nicely in the past week. It has! You're looking better already!'

'Ah – that's just the make-up,' I said, glancing at the mirror.

'Ok, I'll leave you to get ready, love.'

She was just closing the door behind her when my phone rang. I took a deep breath.

'Hi, Cara.'

'Lisaaaaa!! Well – hello, stranger! So your phone *is* working after all!'

'Very funny. Look, I'm . . .'

'Oh, can't wait to see you later. We'll have to talk. A *long* chat – face to face. I'm worried about you. Oh, I love you, Lisa. I really, *really* do.'

'And I love you too, Cara. Look – we'll talk later, ok? Maybe over a drink in Tommy's?'

'Great! That's sound! Oh, listen – we're all heading to John's place for a drink first. Ruth's coming now to pick me up. Do you want us to pick you up?'

'Nah, you're grand, Cara. I've a few bits and pieces to sort out here before I head out. I'll meet you all at John's, ok?'

'Ok! Hey – did you get a line into you yet? I'm flying! Yeah, I took a couple, but they were very big ones!'

'Em . . . ok that's great. I'll see you in a bit, Cara!'

As I hung up, I knew this was it. Tonight was the night I'd have to come clean. They'd all be together in John's, so there'd never be a better time to tell them all. At the end of the day, it's not the end of the world . . .

My phone rang again. It was Ruth. I let it ring out. I just knew she'd be coked and buzzing and asking me down to John's as well.

I sat down one more time before calling a taxi. I bent over to check my mascara and lipstick.

Why all the make-up, Lisa?

That inner voice again.

Why hide your beauty?

Hide my beauty? I'd always been self-conscious regarding my appearance, but not excessively so. Most people, whether they admit it or not, try to make the most of their looks – and the right clothes, the right hairstyle and a little make-up can make all the difference. Maybe I'd never stopped to think about such things when I was on coke. Maybe I was just seeing a small glimpse of the real me under all the make-up. For years I'd hide behind the mask before going out to face the world. Flashes of what I used to be like – in my room, getting ready . . . music blasting . . . texting, ringing everyone . . . lines of coke, bottles of Bud . . . jumping around to the buzz . . . Replaced now by a lonely silence, where even the make-up on my face seemed out of place . . . a sense of no direction . . . and the prospect of meeting the gang without coke was awful beyond words. But I was not going to give in. Not ever. I knew it would be hard to try and click into their wavelength.

I heard the taxi pulling up.

Pull yourself together, I said, taking one last mouthful of beer, – *and just be yourself!*

'Ma,' I said, putting on my jacket downstairs, 'you know that picture of you, me and Dad – the one taken on my birthday?'

'Of course, love. Why?'

'Well . . . Nah, it would take too long. I'll talk to you again about it. Here – give us a hug!'

She held me close. Again, that patting, the tell-tale sign she was still concerned, and with reason.

'Just take care now, Lisa. Ok, pet?'

I could see her still standing at the door, watching the taxi till it disappeared from view.

John's place was a fine house in Skerries Rock. Cara told me he had got a great deal, buying it at just the right time, after the prices crashed in 2009. *Hmm. A smooth operator,* I thought, taking a deep breath and heading towards the front door. *John always lands on his feet.*

'Lisaaaaaa!! There you are!'

Orla and Ruth ran out from the hallway to hug me.

'You look great, Lisa!' said Orla.

'Come in, come in! Close the door!'

Ruth grabbed me by the arm and dragged me into the sitting room.

'Hey, people!' she announced, clinking two bottles of beer together. 'Look who I found wandering outside, Missing in Action for years! Sorry – what's your name again?'

There was a loud burst of laughter as Cara, Anne and Frank all turned to hug me.

'Ah, it's great to see my best friend in the flesh at last!' said Cara, throwing her arms around me and kissing me on the cheek.

'Em . . . sorry I'm late,' I mumbled.

'Here you go,' said Anne, opening a bottle of beer. 'Get that down you. Hey – I heard someone spiked your drink in The Life last week. Is that what happened? We were all so worried about you. Cara was saying you freaked out.'

'Yeah, yeah. Ah, it was a sad night, Anne. But, you know . . .'

Steve walked in. He bent over to kiss Ruth.

Sorry I'm late guys, pile up at the Ladystairs.'

In one of the corners of the room I could see John hunched over, his back to the rest of us. A chill went up my spine as he turned, holding a cd cover full of lines of coke. His eyes met mine. A flash in my mind of what I had seen that night in The Life. His coke-fuelled eyes showed me he was well out of it. *Not like him at all, I thought.*

'Well, here you go, Lisa,' he said, smiling. 'Welcome back from your week-long retreat. Sorry I was a bit off-hand with you on the phone the other day. I was under a bit of pressure. Here – take a few lines of this stuff. It's great!'

'Em . . . em . . . Nah, it's ok, John. You go ahead. I'm grand!'

'What? Take it! It's a freebie, Lisa. Go on!'

'No, John. I don't want it! Ok?'

The music stopped. Everyone stopped . . . and looked at me.

Cara broke the silence.

'Hey, what's up? Take a line, dummy! It's party time!'

The buzz of conversation resumed – 'Yeah! Party time!' – and the music restarted, louder than before.

'Em . . . I . . . *Hey!!* Can someone turn the music down? For just one minute? Thanks.'

I knew I had their undivided attention.

'Look – maybe it's time I told you all . . . something that needs to be said . . . to clear the air . . .'

'Good God. she's not pregnant, is she?' whispered Steve.

'Shhh!'

The expression on John's face changed dramatically. I looked at the others. Everyone looked freaked, which is never nice when you're on coke, when someone cuts across your buzz.

This was the moment. My hands were wet with sweat.

'Well, em . . . it's a kind of long story. But I'll keep it short. As you all know, I had a bad night at The Life, yeah, and went home early. Well, since then, I've made my mind up – to stop taking coke.'

The silence was even more intense.

'Ah, fair play to you,' said Steve. 'I thought it was something bad.

I admire you, Lisa. But I'm sure you'll soon be back on the straight and narrow – with a few lines over the Christmas!'

An uneasy laughter spread around.

'No, Steve,' I said, cutting through the giggles. 'No. I mean it. It's over. For good.'

'What do you mean?' said John, carefully placing the cd cover on the mantelpiece. 'You have one bad buzz and that's it? We all have bad experiences on coke and E. You're joking us. You *love* your line of coke. Plus, Teach – it's Christmas party time! Yeah!'

They all looked gobsmacked.

'Look, everyone, it's no big deal. We're all friends. Mates. A few bottles of beer will do me from now on.'

Cara kept glancing at John as if to say *Is this really happening?*

'Look, Lisa,' she said. 'We have to clear the air with you. We've all been talking about you. Nothing bad, mind. Just concerned at what happened with you, first with Brian, and now with Ian Carter.'

A murmur of agreement.

'We all know you had your heart set on Ian – and then you saw him kissing someone. But he says it was nothing, it wasn't what you think, and he wants to explain it all to you. That's why no one mentioned him when you came in. We know you were hurt and sort of hid yourself away to think things over.'

She nodded at Ruth.

'I know Ruth talked to you in the car the other day. So we all know things have been hard for you. But Lisa, you can't stop living! You *will* meet Mr Right one day. But you have to pull yourself together. It's Christmas, and you'd be mad if you let Ian ruin all this. We love you, Lisa!'

That triggered a wave of *Yeah, we love you, Lisa! Yeah!*

'Well! Thanks, everybody. I know you all love me – and I love you – but this has nothing to do with Ian or Brian – or even Ron. It's just *me. I've* had enough. Look – let's all get on with the night. I'll have a few beers, you can just . . . do your thing. Put the music back up! Enough said! Let's not waste the night on this subject, ok?'

'Sure, sure,' said Ruth. 'I can't understand it. I don't want to keep going on about it, but – just like that? How can someone give up coke overnight?'

'It happens,' said Orla. 'Ask Steve. He knows a few heads who just stopped over night. Some people just stop. Something happens to them. No big deal, guys!'

I'd told myself before I left home that at the end of the day these are my friends and I love and respect them, so I knew I had to make a big effort to act normal and just pretend there was no coke going around. I could sense from the vibe that Cara and John were more freaked out by all this. Ruth was too high on coke to take it all in, but she kept watching me all night.

By ten o'clock I'd had just two bottles of Bud. I drank them slowly. I suppose I was a bit nervous about getting drunk and ending up taking a line. No. I needed to stay well in control.

We left for Tommy's. All the way there, Ruth kept snuggling up to me, telling me again and again that she loved me. She loved me, loved me, loved me – and *admired* me.

As soon as we entered the porch area of the pub, the music and the voices of the crowd inside threw me off my stride, not that anyone would notice. I felt a *déjà vu* flashback to what I had experienced in The Life. For a second or two I just froze with fear.

'Hey, come on! Are you going to stand there all night or are you going in?'

It was John, coming behind me with Cara. He gently pushed me forward a few steps.

'You won't get a drink standing there doing Doorman,' she laughed.

'Hi, Cara. Yeah – this place is packed tonight.'

'Well, pack it even more. You both find where the gang are, and I'll get the drinks.'

As we made our way towards the back I couldn't help but notice how many people were well out of it.

Bloody hell, I'm becoming a coke detective. I've got to stop scrutinizing people and just enjoy the night.

We were lucky to get the last table. Before I could settle, Emma Ryan came in the door with Mark in tow. The minute she spotted me she was over like a shot.

'We need to chat, Lisa. I'm *so* sorry over what happened with Ian. He's never done anything like that before. He promised me – on his mother's grave.'

'Look, Emma,' I said, 'I'm just out to have a nice, relaxing night, not to hear about Ian Carter. Just drop it, will you? You don't have to explain anything to me on his behalf.'

'Yeah, yeah, I know all that. But look – come into the loo with me. Five minutes – that's all. I won't talk about Ian. Promise.'

I agreed. I was going in anyway. We inched our way across a sea of people. Good. No queue. Inside, two girls were touching up their make-up.

'How do I look?' asked the blondie one, plastered with fake tan from the toes up. 'What do you think?'

'You look great,' said the brunette, engrossed in making the most of her cleavage.

I tried to block them out by putting my back to the hairdryer and asking Emma to hurry up.

'Listen,' she said, 'I know you don't want to talk about it, and I won't. But we *have* to talk. Yeah? We get on so well, you and I. And

I know you don't want to hear this, but Ian's not like that. It was the coke. He was out of his brains.'

The two girls pretended not to be listening, but they were all ears.

'Look, I don't need to hear this, Emma. Ok? If he did it to me, he did it to others. I'm sick to death of guys saying, "Oh, it was the coke." I know what coke does, but he knew what he was at, Emma. He was looking around to make sure no one could see him. That's not someone out of their bloody brains. Look – I don't blame you, ok? It was just as well I saw it before I got way in over my head. Then what? Another Ron all over again? No thanks.'

At this point I was getting upset. I fumbled for a tissue to dry my eyes.

'Ok, ok, Lisa. I won't say another word. I'll tell you what. Let me make it up to you. Will you?'

'What? What do you mean?'

She waited till the two make-up girls left.

'Come on – follow me in here.' She started pulling me by the arm into one of the cubicles. 'You can have a few lines of my stuff.'

I stood my ground.

'Look! Stop, will you!' I hissed. 'Let me go! I've given up taking that.'

'Stop messing, Lisa! Come on!'

'I'm not joking, Emma. Ask the gang. I told them all earlier, back in John's. I'll never touch it again. Ever.'

'But why? I'm confused. Was it over Ian and that bad buzz you got in The Life? I don't get it!'

'Look, Emma. I just saw things that night on the coke. It was horrific. You have no idea.'

'We all get a bad buzz from drugs from time to time. But next day it's cool.'

'This was different. And it wasn't *cool* the next day. I don't think I'll ever be the same again after that experience. Look, I'm going back to the gang. We can talk outside.'

As we made our way back, we could see our friends leaning across the table to each other, engrossed in earnest conversation. But as soon as they saw us coming they stopped and sat back, picking up their drinks in one move. No prizes for guessing who they'd been talking about. This just wasn't working out, was it? I was all over the place now.

Emma asked me again, in front of everyone, what had happened to me in The Life.

'Get this, guys – Lisa just told me that she'll never do a line again! I mean – what's going on?'

'Yeah,' chimed in John. 'At least tell us. We'd all love to know the whole story.'

His eyes stared right through me, demanding an answer.

'There's nothing to say, except that that night I had a . . . a strange hallucination of some kind.'

'A hallucination?' said Cara. 'What exactly did you see?'

Everybody craned forward, not wanting to be left out. But there was no way I was going to give too many details now, not with John here, his eyes still fixed on mine.

'What I saw . . .'

They craned forward even more.

'What I saw, when I finally came out of the loo that night, was this: everything – *everyone* – was fake. Yes. Fake. It was all just an illusion. And we'd been conned into thinking that this was reality. Or I should say that I felt it was reality. People were smiling, oh yeah, but their smiles were insincere. The whole elation, that buzz, that good feeling? That was just a false euphoria, a coke-filled euphoria, nothing to do with real life. It was just that all these people – yes, I mean you guys, and me – were just out of their heads on cocaine. Yeah – cocaine.'

I let the words sink in. I knew I had gone too far. But I was on a roll.

'And all these people hugging each other? Give me a break! That's not love. That's not affection. It's not even friendship. It's just cocaine. That night in The Life, my eyes were finally opened to it all. I felt like someone who had been hooked, tricked into it. I felt alone. So alone.'

I looked around at their faces, each with that *You know you're killing the buzz with all this preachy stuff* look. And even though John was still staring at me, I took a deep breath and decided to go for it.

'I saw a strange figure that night,' I continued, 'and this mysterious guy, whoever he was, it was like he knew *I knew*, and he just laughed at me. It was like a horror film, only worse. I got sick, fainted and ended up at home in bits.'

I was saying all this as if I was just talking to my mother, but I was with the gang in Tommy's, and despite the fact that they were all quiet, I knew they were still high as kites. They looked so uncomfortable, looking at each other, hoping I had finished, but not knowing what to say.

'Yeah, yeah,' said Steve, breaking the silence.

Everybody turned to him, hoping for one of his jokes to lighten the moment.

'Yeah, Lisa, that sounds pretty weird alright. But listen, I think you're super. And fair play to you for giving it up.'

He raised his half-finished pint of Guinness in a toasting gesture towards me and drained it in one go. No punchline this time? He winked at me, affirming his approval. Then belched. The rest of them sniggered, trying their best to hide their discomfort, but failing miserably. I felt I just wanted to leave, to go home. *I don't fit in here anymore.*

'Oh, shit!' said Emma. 'Look who's coming in the door. I think he's coming over here!'

'Who?' I said, straining to see across the crowd. 'David Salle?'

'No, Ian Carter!'

Before I could catch my breath he was in front of me.

'Listen, Lisa,' he said, that deep voice of his re-entering my life, 'I know you don't want to talk to me. But I'm here to beg you to forgive me. I'm so sorry. Ok? There. I've said it.'

I got up, pulling on my jacket.

'Listen, I'm going home, guys. I've had enough of this. I should never have come out. Sorry for wrecking the night and your buzz. Ok?'

'Hey! Don't go!' they chorused.

'Yes, Lisa. Please don't go,' said Ian, standing in front of me. 'Let's talk.'

'Leave her alone!' shouted Frank. 'She's going through enough at the minute.'

I turned to leave. My head was spinning. *Everything has gone wrong again.* I picked up my bottle of Bud for one last mouthful.

Ian grabbed me by my left arm.

'Don't go, Lisa,' he said. 'We can fix this!'

I looked right into his coke-fuelled eyes and something inside me just snapped. Without thinking, I went to slap him across the face, not realizing I was still holding the beer bottle. The bottle hit his forehead, bounced off and went flying towards the plate-glass mirror behind the bar. It shattered the mirror, an elegant ad for Paddy Whiskey, probably once a collector's item. *Not any more, it's not.*

'You f**king bitch!' he said, holding his head, blood running down between his fingers. 'Whatcha do that for?'

Everyone just froze, with their mouths open. It was like everything just stopped for a moment and I was moving in slow motion. I just needed to run. *Run. Get out and run. Don't stop. Don't ever stop.*

I could see Ruth coming towards me, presumably to offer her comfort, to cool me down. Emma was holding Ian, dabbing the blood with tissues from her handbag. The burly, self-important-looking doorman was coming towards us, with the livid-looking owner right behind him.

I walked calmly towards the door. Just inside sat the two make-up girls, their mouths open in disbelief. Even the fake-tan blonde looked pale. Once outside, I turned right, heading for the main street. Ruth's and Anne's voices were behind me, calling me back. I saw a taxi coming past AIB bank. I flagged it down and jumped in.

'Hi, Lisa. Where to? You're in a hurry.'

'Oh, Joe. Just drive me home. Go, go, go!'

He checked the mirror and we were off. I could see Ruth waving for the taxi to stop.

'Keep going, Joe. Don't stop!'

'Ok, ok! What's up? Isn't that Ruth waving?'

'Yeah, yeah. But keep going, Joe. Thanks.'

I took my phone out of my bag to switch it off, only to notice I'd had it on Silent since I was at John's, making my announcement. Seven missed calls from Ma. Oh, shit, I was supposed to ring her at ten. It was now 11:15. I jumped as the phone came alive in my hand. A call from Cara.

'Lisa! What's the story? Come back! My God, I never saw anyone hit anyone with a bottle! It's ok. He's just got a small cut to his eyebrow. You just missed his eye. Are you coming back?'

'No, no, Cara. I'm going home. I'm sorry, Cara. I keep messing everything up for everyone. I'm sorry. I'm really sorry!'

Call waiting. Ma.

'Cara, I have to cut you off. My mother's trying to get through.'

I switched over.

'Lisa? Where are you? Are you ok? You promised you'd ring. You said ten o'clock. I've been ringing and ringing, but you wouldn't answer. You're back taking that stuff, aren't you? I know you are! Where are you now, Lisa? Oh, Lisa, I can't . . .'

Ma crying on the phone. Ian's forehead burst open. My life with my friends falling apart.

So much for my dream of this being the best Christmas ever.

Chapter Nine

One small Christmas wish . . .

My mind went into meltdown as my phone kept ringing, stopping and ringing again. I felt like throwing the phone and myself out of the moving taxi as it sped along the Selskar Road towards Kelly's Bay.

'Where, Lisa?' said Joe, half turning his head. 'Here? Hey, Lisa, are you ok, love? What's wrong?'

'God, Joe. Everything. I'm . . . I'm in a mess. Thank God it's you picking me up. I'm sorry.'

'No need for apologies to me, Lisa. I'm just doing my job. I pass no judgement on anyone who sits in this car. I've seen it all, love.'

As he pulled up outside the apartment block, I half-tried to dry the tears from my face and gather my thoughts.

'I'll talk to you again, Joe. Here's what I owe you from a couple of weeks back.' I stepped out. 'Thanks again.'

He rolled down the window.

'Listen – for what it's worth, your best bet is to get out of the whole lot of it, Lisa. I'm doing this job twenty-three years, and in the past five I've seen things in the back of this car that shock even me. It's getting worse out there. No one cares anymore. All morals are gone out the window. It's a free-for-all, and it's all down to drugs. It's taken over everything, Lisa. If you're a clever girl, you'll sort yourself out and move on. You have so much to offer. And don't take this up the wrong way, but you're a lovely-looking girl. Don't waste it on this crack! Got to go. Take care.'

He drove off, rolling up the window as he went.

I turned to walk into my flat, only to see my aunt Rose's car parked a short distance away. My phone rang. Ma again.

'Yeah, yeah, Ma. I'm outside, just coming in.'

Before I could get the key out of my handbag, Ma opened the door. It was obvious that she had been crying.

'Oh, you're safe. Thank God. Come in. What on earth happened? You were crying. Why didn't you answer the phone, Lisa? Why?'

'Ma, I had it on Silent while I was telling my friends that I was off drugs. And I just forgot to switch it back on. I'm sorry, ok? God, what a nightmare!'

Ma closed the door behind me, taking my jacket.

'Listen, pet. Rose and Jim are here. And they . . . they know. They know.'

'They know? Know what, Ma?'

'Look, when I couldn't get you on the phone, I rang Rose in sheer desperation and broke down. They were already in bed, but they got up and came around as soon as they could, and . . . well, it all came out. I'm sorry. I know I promised you I'd say nothing. But you can trust them. They're family, at the end of the day.'

'You *what?* You told them about the drugs? Ma, for crying out loud! I'm under enough pressure as it is without bringing Rose and Jim into all this. I can't face them. I've been through a lot of sh– . . . I've been through an awful lot tonight, Ma, and everything is just getting worse. You won't believe . . .'

The sitting room door opened. Jim poked his head out.

'Everything ok, Mary? Hi, Lisa. Why don't we all come in and sit down! Mary, you get another cup of your best tea. Grand. Lisa, you come in here and sit down, pet.'

He winked at me, and I followed him in. Rose was sitting nervously on the edge of the couch, holding onto her handbag for dear life, not knowing which way to look. She always let Jim take charge of all the big issues and stayed in the background.

Jim looked straight at me, his rimless glasses perched on his long nose, his grey hair still spiky from being woken up in mid-sleep. No joke, but he was a dead ringer for Albert Einstein gone slightly wrong. He patted the back of the armchair for me with those long, thin fingers of his. Ma told me they used to call him 'Jim'll Fix It' – the name of a popular tv programme from years back. That was Jim – always wanting to fix the world's problems. He was so kind. A harmless gent – would do anything to help a soul. Because he worked with kids in the HSE he knew how to handle people. But this was a matter outside his domain, I'm afraid – or so I thought.

'Ok, Lisa. No one's here to add to your problem or put added pressure on you. Christmas is just a week away, and we're all here to help you in any way, to make sure you're ok and to be an added resource for you – someone you can turn to at any time.'

Ma came in, holding a tray of tea.

'Aah, grand. Let's all have a cup of Mary's best tea and have a little chat. What do you say?'

I looked at Ma, wanting to scream at her for putting me into this situation. I could feel my phone vibrate. More missed calls from the gang, no doubt.

Rose made herself busy with the milk and sugar for everyone, happy to be contributing in a practical way.

I sipped my tea self-consciously, not knowing what to say.

'Well, Lisa. If I could start? Grand. Your mother rang us tonight and was upset and told us you have . . . you know, you've been taking . . . drugs. Isn't that right, Mary?'

'Yes, that's right, Jim. I'm sorry, Lisa, but I panicked.'

Jim stayed positive.

'Well, now you're home, Lisa. And look at her, Mary! You can tell she hasn't gone back on the drugs. She's kept her word!'

He leaned closer, coming into my eyeline.

'Grand, Lisa. Now, no one wants to start going around the rest of the family, talking about this, making it out to be worse than it is. No one else needs be told the details of your personal life. Plus, it would be very dangerous if this got out. Your whole career as a teacher would be put in jeopardy. I've told Mary . . .' – he tapped the coffee table twice with his index finger – 'it *stops here.* Ok?'

'Ok,' I sighed, placing my cup back on the table.

Jim was just getting into his stride.

'Now your mother thinks that maybe you need to think about rehab. Now, before you say anything, I told her I don't think you need anything like that. Isn't that right, Mary?'

'Yes, yes, Jim. That's right. More tea, anyone?'

'All you need is support – people you know you can turn to at any time to talk, people who will listen. And that's all we're here to do. Not to *interfere* in your life, but to let you know we love you and want to do anything in our power to help. Not to crowd you in any way.'

He put his arm around me.

'Everything will be grand, Lisa. You wait and see. You're going to have the best Christmas ever. Wait and see.'

'We're behind you all the way,' said Rose, her brittle voice betraying her self-consciousness.

'Thanks, Rose,' my mother and I said, almost in unison.

'And you, Jim,' I added. God, it's a week to Christmas, and inside I wish I was dead.'

Jim nudged Rose and nodded towards the teapot. She was glad to pick it up and offer to replenish the cups.

'So, what's Santa bringing you this year? Anything nice? Here – I hope you remembered to post your letter in good time!'

'Of course I did! God, all I want is something *real* for a change. That's my small Christmas wish. Just something *real*. I'm sick of all the illusions I've been so accustomed to for so long.'

As I spoke, the tears began to well up.

'Ah God, that's all I do nowadays is cry. I tried so hard tonight, Ma. I went out and tried to fit in.'

Rose handed me a hanky.

'Thanks. I mean, these are all my friends. I love them all so much. And it killed me to look at them all taking that stuff. I just couldn't fit in. I felt so lost, like I was a different person, a stranger to them. What am I going to do, Ma? I feel so lost inside. In the pub, everywhere I looked, everyone was dressed to kill, fake tan. Everything seemed so unnatural to me. Everyone wanting to be noticed, to be admired. Everyone out of their heads on . . . on cocaine . . . or ecstasy. And outside I was like them, but inside all I want is to just be me. But who am I? I don't know, Ma. I'm so confused, so lost, so lonely. Everything is going away from me. But nothing is coming back. It's awful. I can't bear it for much longer. Where is the real world gone? *Real* things! Everything is painted over to look like something that's unreal. And I don't know why. I mean, Ma, why has all this happened just to me? How can I see all this, and nobody else can? Am I losing my mind?'

'You're not losing your mind,' said Jim. 'You're just getting everything off your chest. You're going to be fine. Trust me. Life is going to change for the better. You're just waking up to the nightmare of the world of drugs and all the insecure people that take it to feel good about themselves. The laugh. The buzz. I saw it all in one of my best mates brothers son a few years back. You remember David, don't you, Rose?'

Rose nodded.

'Ah, yes. Poor David. So young. What a waste. God be good to him.'

'I know I'm old school, Lisa,' continued Jim, 'but I've seen a few things in the past few years to do with drugs. You're a very brave girl to stand up and walk away. You may think you're losing everything, but you're not. You're just losing the illusions. Your friends will come around eventually – if they're true friends. In the meantime, you keep up the jogging – as Mary says you do! Get out and do a bit of Christmas shopping. And we'll be here the whole time if you need us. Ok?'

Ma came over and hugged me, wiping away her tears. Jim and Rose stood up and hugged me too.

'We all love you very much,' said Rose. 'Everything will turn out fine – you'll see.'

'Thanks, Rose. Thanks, all of you. Sorry for going on so long.'

'No, no. That's what we're here for, Lisa,' said Jim, putting on his coat. 'We'll leave you two to get some sleep. Here, Lisa, that's my phone number if you ever need me, day or night. And don't worry – this goes no further. My two lads won't hear a word of this. You can be sure of it.'

'Right,' said Ma. 'Look – the two of you go back and get your beauty sleep. Sorry for getting you out of bed. And thanks again for everything.'

When they left, I told Ma about the injury to Ian Carter.

'Ma, it was an accident. I thought I had put the bottle down. But it was still in my hand. He's ok. Bit of a cut to his eyebrow. But that's all I needed. I just ran out into a taxi. But look – at least they all know now I'm not taking drugs anymore. The news will spread like wildfire.'

'I'm proud of you, Lisa. It couldn't have been easy on your own, facing the whole group of them.'

'None of this is easy, Ma, but life must go on. I'm off to Pavilions first thing in the morning. A bit of shopping therapy. Will you come with me?'

'Just try and stop me!' she beamed, giving me the warmest of hugs.

Up in my room, I looked at my phone. Everyone at it again.

Don't worry. Ian's ok.

Are u ok?

We're all back in John's.

We luv u.

On and on it went.

I rang Ruth.

'Hi, listen. Em . . . I'm ok. Sorry for doing a runner. I just couldn't . . .'

'Look, Lisa. It's ok. That Ian Carter fool should never have come to Tommy's. Are you ok?'

'Yeah, yeah, grand. How's the party?'

'*Everyone's* here! Carl just arrived. He was doing a job with his dad. That's why he couldn't join us earlier. He's gobsmacked at the news you're off the coke. Everyone's talking about it. John said he'll give you a week. He bet us all you won't last the Christmas. He took a lot of coke tonight, Lisa. It's not like him. He was always just a few lines now and again. But he's flying.'

What could I say? I sighed audibly into the phone.

'Anyway, Lisa. Will you still be coming to all the parties over the Christmas?'

'Yeah, sure. But you can tell John he'll lose that bet. Listen. Tell the gang I send my love. I'll buzz you, ok?'

'Ok, Lisa. You take care. I love you.'

'I love you, Ruth. Always will.'

Alone in my room again I lay on my bed, phone off. I hugged my pillow. That sinister voice or feeling reminding me how lonely and empty my life now was. Flashes of all my friends up in John's, laughing, joking, drinking, snorting, having a great time. A place where I had always been the centre of the party. I felt as if that inner voice was speaking to me, invading my thoughts.

You can have it all back, Lisa. All this pain will go away, Lisa.

I put the pillow over my head and drifted into sleep, warm tears soaking the bedsheet.

*

'It's half ten, Lisa. Would you like some breakfast?'

'Well, I'm going for a jog first, Ma. Ok?'

'Alright, love. I'll have it ready for you when you come back.'

I ran down the road, gathering some speed before settling into a regular jog. That determined feeling rose up inside me. *I'm going to beat this thing from the inside out.* Laura Branigan's *Self Control*, a song I loved years ago but only heard once lately, came to mind –

I live among the creatures of the night
I haven't got the will to try and fight
Against a new tomorrow
So I guess I'll just believe it
That tomorrow never knows.

Heart racing with hope, I felt the fighter inside come alive. *Don't go looking past each day,* I thought. *Take it one step at a time.*

As I came in the front door, Ma had breakfast all ready.

'Thanks, Ma,' I gasped, downing a glass of water. 'This is really . . .' My phone vibrated and stirred on the table. '. . . really great.'

'Hi, Cara. I'm just in from my jog. How are you?'

'Great, Lisa. Listen – can we meet up sometime today?'

'Today? Well . . . I'm actually heading to the Pavilions, but how about later? After six?'

'Yeah, that's great. I'll drop over, if that's ok. I'm worried like hell about you. I explained everything to Tommy, and he said no one's in trouble about the broken mirror.'

I glanced at Ma, who was all set to dish out the breakfast.

'Listen, Cara. I'll take this upstairs. Hold on . . . I didn't hit Ian with the bottle on purpose! I just forgot I had the blooming thing in my hand. God - what a mess of a night.'

'Ah, it wasn't that bad. You missed the great craic back in John's. Everyone missed you. When's the old Lisa coming back? We all miss her. I miss her.'

'Look, I'll talk to you later. My Ma's just putting the breakfast on the table.'

'Ok. I'll be there around seven. See you.'

'See you. Love you. Bye.'

The ever-patient Ma placed the plate on the table.

'Wow, Ma,' I said. This looks lovely. Mmm. You can't beat Ma's fry-ups. Oh! And fried bread! Long time since I saw you doing fried bread. Are you trying to fatten me up there, Ma?'

'Just eat it, Lisa,' she said, her patience wearing just a little bit thin. 'And get a shower before you come down with a dose.'

'Of course, Ma. I was just . . . '

'So – are you still angry with me over telling Rose and Jim?'

'Nah, you're grand, Ma. It's a lot to ask anyone to carry a burden on their own. But rehab? That's a bit extreme, isn't it? Am I that bad?'

She didn't answer.

'It works for some people, Ma,' I continued, between forkfuls. 'But I'll win this battle, come what may. I'll find my Lost Little Girl. She can't have gone too far away, can she?'

She placed her hand on mine.

'Nice to see you smiling again, Lisa. That's my girl.'

I downed the last piece of rasher, leaving some of the fried bread on the plate.

'Mmm, I couldn't take another bite. Thanks for the breakfast, Ma. I'll be down in a few minutes. All set for the Pavilions then?'

'I . . . I might just give it a miss this time, pet. I'm feeling a bit tired.'

'Really? Aaw!'

I looked at her face, and the barely-touched fry on her plate. She looked tired alright. And, for the first time ever, I thought, older than her years.

*

I decided for once to leave the car and take the bus to Pavilions. I sat upstairs with my earphones on, listening to Gary Numan's *Jagged*. When I got off in Swords, my legs felt weak, my head light. But I took no notice and headed at a brisk pace to Pavilions, where I trekked from shop to shop. The place was packed with pre-Christmas shoppers. I couldn't help but notice so many couples, smiling, holding hands, arms around each other as they window shopped and picked out presents together.

I entered the lift which would take me to the ground floor and HMV record shop. The door opened and I just stood there for a moment before coming out. I felt uneasy, like I was being followed, or people were watching me. Images of me snorting lines of coke flashed into my consciousness. Parties I'd been at . . . things I'd got up to at them . . . Shoppers started to bump into me, looking strangely at me. *Watch where you're going!* a girl said to me. Or did she? Everything started to feel odd. My arms felt heavy. That same sinister voice inside, laughing at me. *Look at the state of you! All alone, losing everybody, losing your life. Cop on to yourself before it's too late!* Flashing images of long lines of coke and me bent over, snorting them up with that hungry, satisfied look in my eyes. I tried not to look, but yes, it *was* me.

I was crashing. The whole experience of coming off coke and all that was going on in my life, the breaking of relationships with my mates, came to a head in the middle of a bloody shopping mall. It felt like being in the Twilight Zone. A sense that I belonged nowhere. I could feel this awful pain coming up from deep within.

I ran to the toilet for the disabled – I knew it would be more private. I felt like I was running in slow motion. I closed the door behind me, my hands shaking, my body drenched in sweat. I bent down, burying my face in my hands. My life seemed to be slipping away, away from me. Everyone was drifting away. Everything I held dear, all my dreams crashed away. I had no control, no ability to do anything to help myself. I tried to scream, but the pain was buried too deep to come out.

I searched for a warm moment from my past in the hope that this would stop the pain and I'd feel normal again. But nothing. All I saw were shadows that turned to dark dust and blew away.

The panic attack left me trying to catch my breath. I sat down on the tiled floor, curling up in the corner of the cubicle. Over and over again through my mind raced the feeling, the temptation to take coke to cure this pain, to end this nightmare, once and for all. I remained there, crying, but never getting to the end of the pain.

I struggled to get my phone out. I texted Jim.

In disabled loo in Pavilions. In bad way. Please come and get me. Lisa.

Jim rang immediately.

'I'm on my way, Lisa. Just stay right there, pet.'

Half an hour later I was in the back of Jim's car, heading home.

'You're going to be ok, Lisa,' he said in that strong, comforting voice of his. 'You're safe now. We'll take good care of you.'

I felt a lot better as he pulled up outside my house.

'Listen – do you want me to come in, Lisa?'

'Nah, I'm grand, Jim. Sorry for dragging you out like this again. And thanks so much for being there today.'

He didn't need to say anymore. His warm hug said it all.

I told Ma everything that happened.

'But what's all this, Lisa? Please – help me to understand.'

'It's withdrawal symptoms, I'd say, Ma. Paranoia, panic attacks, the whole sense of fear that I'm losing every one of my friends. It's like I feel no one will ever love me again. Everything came crashing down on me.'

I glanced at the clock on the mantelpiece.

'Listen, Ma. Cara's coming around later. I'm going to text her, tell her I'm not well. I'm just not up to any of that right now. I'm going to lay low till Christmas Eve.'

'Rest up, yeah. Good idea. Then we'll have a Christmas no one will ever forget. How's that sound?'

She hugged me.

'I feel so sorry for you, pet. I wish I could do more to help you with all this you're going through. I feel . . . helpless!'

I hugged her even tighter.

'You're here for me, Ma. That's all that matters to me. Roll on Christmas. Yeah!'

After dinner I went up and lay on my bed. And, corny as it may seem, I sent out my Wish For Christmas. To beat this thing. To win the battle to find Me again. To be real. To feel real. For the pain inside to go away. To find real love. I was asking for a lot, I suppose.

As I sat down with Ma to eat my Christmas dinner in Jim and Rose's, little did I know that the strangest events were about to unfold.

Chapter Ten

The Pure Hit

I woke up on the morning of Christmas Eve feeling better than I'd felt in years. The only thing I can say that was still causing the pain was just that I felt lonely inside, all the time. I'd been on the phone to the girls and kept the chat just to Christmas talk – what they were buying their boyfriends, what they hoped to get. The subject of all the parties that were planned came up – most of which I had promised to attend. I lost my head with Orla on the phone when she suggested I do a few lines Christmas Night in John's and at the big Stephen's Night party in Cara's.

'No bloody way, Orla,' I said. 'Just don't go there.'

'Ok, ok, it's just everyone thinks you'd be better maybe cutting back on the coke rather than stopping altogether. I mean, it's just a bit of fun, Lisa.'

'Look,' I sighed, 'just a few bottles will do me. I'll be grand.'

It was after such phonecalls that I felt I was drifting even further from all my friends. I just wasn't in their circle like before. I used be the one that cracked them all up with the laughs, the joking. Now, the funny, outgoing girl was gone, and the prospect of losing touch with all those I loved frightened me deeply. I simply felt I had no future. It was as if there was a sign dangling in front of me: *Go back on the coke and everything will return to normal.*

I sat that morning wrapping Christmas presents. We all planned to meet around in John's to have a Christmas Eve drink and give gifts to each other. So I drove around in the late afternoon. As I pulled up outside, I saw Frank and Anne getting out of Frank's van. They both came over and hugged me.

'Great to see you, Lisa,' said Frank. 'The gang is not the same without you. Here – let me carry in those presents for you.'

'Ah, you're a gent, Frank. Thanks.'

'It's great to see you, Lisa,' said Anne. 'It's going to be a super Christmas.'

When he had walked ahead out of earshot, she added in a whisper,

'I can't wait to see what Frank got me!'

'Did you hint at anything?'

'Nah – a bottle of perfume and a couple of cds will do me. You know I'm not fussy.'

Cara opened the door to us.

'Come on in. It's so cold out there!'

She let the others through and grabbed me by the arm.

'Come here you,' she said. 'Give us a hug. I can't tell you how much I miss you, miss talking to you. It's not the same. Everyone says the same. John's getting you a beer.'

'Thanks, Cara. I can only drink the one, now – I'm driving. Listen – I miss you all so much. I just needed time to chill out, clear my head. I feel so much better the last few days. So – I'm back!'

She turned to the others.

'Hey! Ruth, Orla, John – did you hear that? Lisa says she's back! Legend!'

'Calm down,' I said. 'I just mean I'm . . . I'm in better form, clear-headed. I feel great today.'

Steve popped out from the sitting room with his bottle of Miller, slurring his version of a Paul Young song.

'Please hurry, come back
And stay for good this time
Why don't you . . . ?'

Ruth pulled him back in.

'Why don't you shut up, Steve! You're half shot already. Leave the girl alone!'

Everyone was in top form, and I turned a blind eye to the few lines that were going around. I felt more relaxed than at any other time since kicking the habit. *Maybe this will work out after all.*

After we gave out our Christmas presents, Cara had a quiet word with me.

'Listen, Lisa. You're ok, aren't you? I mean, we're still the one Gang, right? And you're coming to my house on Stephen's Night?'

'Of course I am. And of course I'm in your gang. We've been mates all our lives and nothing will ever change that. Not ever.'

We hugged, but as we broke away I noticed the trace of white on the side of her nose.

'There's just . . . a bit of coke there,' I said, almost touching it with my finger.

'Is there? Oh shit!'

She wiped it away with a tissue.

'We're all going easy,' she said. 'That's my last line. Long Christmas ahead!'

As I mingled among the rest, the lively chatter, the jokes and the bursts of laughter continued. Everyone was bubbly – except John, who seemed a bit cool with me. He kept watching me, but anytime I glanced at him he'd turn his head away. I took no notice. I was pretty sure that, even though I was in their company, some of them were still talking behind my back. And no doubt, the word *coke* was probably also being mentioned in the same conversations.

Before I knew it I was back home, feeling I'd at least made some progress in drawing myself back into the gang. I sat in that evening, texting the girls, and everyone seemed in great form, even though for some of them it was because they were out of it.

Emma Ryan rang me to wish me a Happy Christmas. Then, just as I expected, she was saying sorry over Ian again, that she'd chat to me at Cara's party Stephen's Night.

'It's ok, it's in the past, Emma. We'll have a laugh over it in Cara's, ok? Now enjoy your Christmas Day with Mark.'

I sat down with Ma, asking in my little-girl voice,

'Well, what you get me for Christmas, Ma? Tell me, tell me, tell me!'

'You'll have to wait till Santa comes,' she laughed. 'He must be on the way by now. It's after half ten. So – how did it go round in John's today?'

'Ah, not bad, Ma. Not bad at all. I'm a lot stronger around them than I thought I'd be. I just feel I may be getting close to them again.'

There was an uncomfortable pause. She cleared her throat before replying in that casual-sounding tone of hers which I knew by now was far from casual.

'And would you not . . . would you not look around now, Lisa? Maybe find a few nice, new girls to hang out with?'

'Maybe when I get back to teaching in the New Year, Ma. Maybe I'll widen my circle of friends. But it's grand. I know you think they're all junkies, but they're not. As I've told you before, almost everyone out there is taking coke nowadays.'

There was another uncomfortable pause, but Ma brushed it aside.

'You look great, Lisa,' she said, gulping down her misgivings.

'So much better than a couple of weeks ago. I'm very proud of you. I'm proud to have you as a daughter.'

'And I'm proud to have you as a mother. Happy Christmas, Ma. I'm off to bed before Santa comes. Night. Love you.'

'Love you too, pet. 'Night.'

*

Christmas Day dawned with lovely bright sunshine, but with frost on the roads. Lovely to see, next best thing to a White Christmas. The birds were singing. I sat up in bed, hoping my small Christmas wish would come true.

Wishful thinking, Lisa.

That sinister voice, that lonely feeling was still very much there. But today I'll put my best foot forward and enjoy the day with Ma, Jim, Rose and their boys.

Ma came out of her room as I opened my bedroom door.

'Hi, Sleepyhead,' she said. 'Well – let's not stand here. Let's see what Santa brought us!'

Like a pair of five-year-old kids, we raced down the stairs and into the sitting room. No waiting around, I pulled open the first lovingly-wrapped package. It contained a bottle of perfume.

'Ah Ma! 212 VIP! That's just new out. I remember now telling you I loved that smell. Mmm! Thank you!'

I opened the rest – two beautiful tops, just my style, and a couple of cds.

'Thanks, Ma,' I said, hugging her. 'I love them!'

She opened her present from me – three tickets to see her favourite band from years back, Duran Duran. The other two tickets were for Rose and Jim, who had always been fans too.

'You always said you'd love to see them, Ma. And now your chance has come. Simon le Bon! Wow, Ma. You'll just melt!'

'God, thanks, Lisa. I'm shocked. That's a surprise. Yes, I've always wanted to see them, but down the years, something always got in the way. Your dad was always a big fan too, though he never let on.'

With the mention and memory of Dad, we hugged each other again.

'I can't believe it. I'm going to see my pin-up man from the eighties. Wow! Oh, Lisa. I was mad about Simon le Bon. This is the best present ever!'

She stood up, placing the tickets on the mantelpiece.

'I'm going to make a light breakfast. And hey – why not put on a Duran Duran cd there – if you can find it.'

I flicked through the cd collection – many of the covers with tell-tale scratches – and came up with their Greatest Hits. I put it on, keeping the volume reasonably low for Christmas morning.

My phone rang. Cara. At 10:35am? *A bit early for her,* I thought.

'Hi, Lisa. I'm on my way around to you for a few minutes. Is that ok?'

'Are you on the phone and driving?' I asked.

'Yeah, yeah, I know.' Her voice was full of excitement. 'But I have to see you. Hold on. I'm just pulling up now.'

I heard the car outside.

'Ma, Cara's coming in, just for a minute. Don't know what's up, but she sounds so different on the phone.'

'Cara? Now? Here, she can't see me like this.' She started up the stairs. 'I'll be down in a minute.'

I checked myself in the hallway mirror. *I'll do.* And opened the door. Cara's face was beaming. I'd never seen her like this in my life.

'Come in, come in,' I said. 'What's up? Did you win the lotto or something?'

Ma came halfway down the stairs, wondering what all the fuss was about.

'Hello, Mrs Webb. Oh, Lisa. I couldn't wait till later. I had to come around to tell you in person. I'm *so* excited!'

'About what? What is it, Cara?'

'Remember I told you I thought John was getting me a laptop for Christmas?'

'Yeah, I remember.'

'Well, he called up with it – one of the best and most expensive money can buy.'

'Right. Well, that's great, Cara. I'm so happy for you. Come here and give us a hug.'

'No, no. That's not it, Lisa. There's more. When I opened it, he said, "That's not the real present." I looked up and he was holding a small wrapped present. Lisa – it was an engagement ring! Look!'

She held out her hand, showing me the ring.

'And then he asked me to marry him!'

'What? Let me see. My God, Cara. It's so beautiful. Wow! I can't believe it.'

'We got engaged on Christmas Day. We even set a date, for July next year. Can you believe it, Lisa! I'm getting married! My dream has always been to get married. I'm so happy!'

'My God, Cara. Come here and give us a hug. I'm so happy for you. I know you're both mad about each other.'

Ma came down the last few steps of the stairs.

'Come here, pet,' she said, not exactly over the moon. She hugged Cara. 'Let's see the ring. Mmm. My God, that must have cost an arm and a leg. An arm *and* a leg.'

She sneaked me just the slightest of glances, but I got her point. As Cara and I hugged again, Ma continued.

'Well, what a Christmas this has turned out to be for you, Cara. For you and what's-his-name again?'

'John.'

'Ah, yes. John. How could I forget. John.'

I glared. *Alright, Ma. You made your point. How about that light breakfast you mentioned?*

She turned towards the kitchen.

'That's not all, Lisa!' continued Cara.

Ma stopped at the kitchen door, her hand on the doorknob.

'He's hired a chef to do the food at my party tomorrow night! *And* he's got Frank to do D.J. It's going to be our engagement party! He's invited loads more people to it. He's been planning all this for weeks – just for me! My life is going to be complete at last!'

Ma went into the kitchen, closing the door behind her.

'It's all you ever wanted, Cara,' I said, ' – to marry the right guy. I'm so happy to see you this happy. How about a cup of tea?'

'No, thanks. I can't. I gotta fly. I just had to tell you first. Will you make it round to John's later for a drink?'

'Em, I dunno. I don't really want to leave my mother all alone on

Christmas night. But I may drop around, just for an hour. Look, you go and enjoy all of this moment, Cara. I've never seen you look so happy. I mean, have you looked in a mirror? You're beaming. You'd better text the gang. My God, they'll all be around to you. Your poor ma will never get the Christmas Dinner up!'

We hugged.

'Ring me later, Cara, won't you? Rock on tomorrow night!'

I went into the kitchen, where Ma had the juice, tea and toast all out on the table.

'I'm saying nothing, Lisa. It's Christmas Day. But don't tell me that Johnny fella can lay golden eggs now.'

'Sorry?'

'Come on. Breakfast is ready, pet.'

'Thanks, Ma. Ah, did you see her? She's so happy. Imagine – she's getting married in July!'

To be honest, I felt a bit put out that it wasn't me who was marrying Mr Right. But yes, deep down I was happy for Cara.

My phone was hopping for the next couple of hours. All the gang were ringing me with the 'news'. Everyone was over the moon for Cara, and couldn't wait for the party in her house the following night.

I even had to turn off my phone eventually, as I couldn't get a thing done when trying to get ready to go to Jim and Rose's for dinner.

As we drove to their house in Balbriggan, Ma told me I looked stunning.

'You don't look half bad yourself, Ma.'

Traffic was light on the road, as most families were already settling down to their traditional Christmas Dinner together. I just knew that Ma and I were thinking the same thing – it won't be the same without Dad. I took my hand off the steering wheel briefly and gave her hand a squeeze. *She knew.*

'That photo in my room of the three of us,' I reminded Ma.

'Ah yes, yes. What memories.'

'What a smile you had that day! Captured forever in that simple photo. You know, Ma – I hope this is not the wrong time to bring it up, Christmas Day, of all days. But I don't think you've ever smiled like that since.'

There was a long pause as I waited on the deserted street for the pedestrian lights to change.

'Do you think you'll ever date again? Like, I'm sure you have a fan club – with your looks!'

I glanced over. She just looked straight ahead and smiled. I just knew she'd heard all this before. The lights changed and I drove on.

'I haven't lost my smile, Lisa. I just don't have a man like your dad to make me smile the way he did. And yes, if you must know, *nosey*, I've had a few men ask me out. But all in good time. All in good time.'

As I pulled up in the quiet cul-de-sac and switched off the engine, Rose was already opening the door, beaming.

'Great to see you both,' she gushed, stepping out to open the garden gate. Jim wasn't far behind her. Hugs all round. Genuine hugs that meant so much.

When we got inside, they picked up a big parcel from beside the Christmas tree.

'This is for you, Lisa,' Jim announced.

'What?' I said, embarrassed. 'I just got you something small. What's this?'

'Open it!' beamed Rose, nudging Jim.

I pulled off the lovingly-folded wrapping paper. Inside was a complete outfit of the latest in jogging gear – tracksuit, runners, t-shirt, shorts, socks, the lot. Top quality. Must have cost a small fortune. I was speechless.

'We got all your sizes from Mary,' said Rose.

Ma nodded, admitting her collusion.

'Yes,' Jim elaborated. 'We thought your old gear was a bit outdated, so we thought this would encourage you in your jogging and gym workout.'

'God, thanks so much,' I said. 'I don't know what to say! Believe it or not, I was going to buy all this after Christmas. You're so thoughtful. Thanks again, both of you!'

I hugged them both.

'Oh, I've already given Ma your Christmas present. It's . . . You show them, Ma.'

'Oh, yes. Of course.'

She reached into her handbag and took out the little modest brown envelope and handed it over to Rose.

'Two tickets,' said Rose, intrigued, 'for . . .'

'Duran Duran!' said Jim. 'Are they still on the go? Well, whaddya know! That'll bring us back to our coortin' days, what, Rose?'

'I hope you'll enjoy it,' I said. 'All three of you.'

Ma waved her ticket too.

'Well, that'll be a great night,' said Jim. 'I wonder if I can still do my hair in that Simon le Bon look?'

We all laughed.

'Now,' said Rose, carefully placing the tickets behind the clock on the mantelpiece. 'Who'd like a quiet glass of wine before Paul and Darren come back and join us for dinner?'

It was one of those really warm Christmas family days. Everyone in great chat. Dinner lovely, as always.

'I couldn't manage another mouthful,' said Ma, turning down a second helping of Rose's famous plum pudding. 'I'll need a crane to lift me home!'

Jim and Rose said nothing about *you know what.* They just sat and told stories about their early days dating. Their sons Paul and Darren kept asking me embarrassing questions and slagging me about some of the stories they'd heard about me years ago from Ma and Rose.

We got home around seven, with me a little tipsy from the wine. I turned on my phone. Emma had left a voicemail saying she was looking forward to tomorrow. It was like a broken record at this stage.

I rang Cara. She was still on Cloud Nine.

'Are you coming round to John's?' she asked. 'Just a few coming, as everyone wants to save themselves for tomorrow evening's big one.'

That was my way out, I thought.

'Ah, I'd love to, Cara, but Ma's on her own. I couldn't just leave her. But rock on tomorrow, yeah? Can't wait. Plus, I'm bushed. I already drank a lot of wine.'

Everyone seemed on good terms with me, and giving up coke for now anyway didn't seem an issue that came between us.

Ma and I made sandwiches from leftover turkey that Rose insisted on giving us. We got into our pjs and crashed on the sofa to watch the Christmas Night movies. It was clear we were getting closer since I came off the coke. I'd become more settled in myself, and as well as that, I was giving her more 'quality time' instead of being out at the all-night parties. They had really taken over my life – had become my life, in fact.

Later, when Ma went to bed, I went on Facebook for a couple of hours. Everyone was buzzing about Cara and John's big plans.

At 12:30am I crawled into bed and slept like a log for once, waking up around 9:30am. Before breakfast I took in a jog – in my new jogging gear, of course. I lazed around the apartment for a few hours then, playing music, half-watching tv, tidying up my room.

The countdown to the party was on. Phone ringing. Texts. Everyone on a big high. Ma was going out with Jim and Rose, so before she left she didn't say much regarding being careful tonight at the party.

The house felt strangely quiet after she left. That strange lonely feeling came up inside me as I started to get ready. So many people would be on coke, I knew, and me on the outside looking in, trying to act normal and fit in.

I rang a taxi, but not before the phone went hopping. Everyone already at the party, well out of it, wondering where I was.

I jumped into the taxi, and said very little to the driver, though he was doing his best to be chatty.

'Larry – yeah, that's me. Happy as Larry! Ha, ha, ha!'

Cara lived two miles outside Skerries, in a place called the Black Hills. We stopped at the gateway to see the whole house lit up with Christmas lights and a big sign up across the front of the main doors:

Welcome to Cara's & John's Engagement Party!

The music was blasting through the walls. I could actually feel the vibrations inside the taxi.

'Thanks, Harry,' I said, placing the tenner into his hand.

'It's Larry, actually,' he chuckled. 'You're not the first one to make that mistake. My God, this looks like one hell of a party!'

'Yeah – should be a great night,' I said, nervously closing the taxi door. 'Thanks . . . Larry.'

As I walked up the long driveway, I could see through the main window that the place was packed – even more than last year. The door was open, and the first person I met was Annie who was talking to Orla. Both of them were already out of it. Before I had a chance to hug them both, Ruth, together with Gail and Niamh, two of Cara's mates, came by with Steve trailing behind.

'Anyone for a chicken curry and the key to the jacks for the night?', joked Steve.

The aroma of the food was mouth-watering. The chef, complete with white hat, was in his element, mixing, stirring, tasting. If he heard Steve's joke, he didn't let on.

'My God, this is the business, isn't it?' I repeated as I hugged each of the gang.

I looked over to the d.j.'s deck. Frank was giving it loads, totally lost in the music. John was standing shouting into his ear, probably telling him what to play next.

Ruth handed me a bottle of Bud.

'So tell me, Lisa. How did your Christmas Day go? I stayed in with my parents.' She rolled her eyes to heaven and shrugged her shoulders.

'Ah, I had a great day, actually. Ma and I went over to my auntie's house for the Christmas Dinner.'

'Oh? Sounds a bit more interesting than my day, anyway.'

'Em . . . have you seen Cara?'

'Cara? She's in the back sitting room, going around showing off her ring to the world. Legend!'

'I better go in and . . .'

She came out just at that moment.

'Ah, there you are! Come here to me!'

She threw her arms around me.

'I *love* you!' came those oh-so familiar words again.

We stood with our backs to the music deck.

'Well – are you going to . . .?'

The music drowned out what she was saying.

'Sorry?'

'I said, are you going to take one or two lines to celebrate the big occasion?'

'No, you're grand, Cara,' I said, calmly. 'Just a bottle will do.'

An embarrassing pause, despite the pulsating music. Over at the fireplace, John and a few of the guests were chopping up lines of coke on cd covers. I became edgy, my hands sweaty. All of a sudden I felt panicky, and that feeling I got in The Life nightclub returned once again.

'Hey!' said Cara, pulling me back to earth. 'Who's your man who just walked in the door?'

'Who?' I asked, turning to look.

'The guy with the blue hoodie, curly short hair. A hunk. He's looking over this way!'

She was right. He was a hunk, but not in a swaggering, cocky way.

'I don't know, Cara. How would I know? It's your party. You should know him.'

'Shit, Lisa. He's coming over to us. This may be your lucky night. He's looking straight at you!'

'Hi, girls,' he said, in a warm, reassuring voice. He looked straight into my eyes. 'Hi, Lisa.'

He knows me, somehow. From somewhere.

'Sorry – do I know you?'

'No, no! Em . . . it's just that you're standing in front of the cans of beer, so . . .'

'Oh, sorry. Here. What do you want? Bud? Miller? Heineken? There's everything you want here.'

'Just a can of Heineken, thanks.'

'Well,' said Cara. 'I'll leave you two to talk. I'm off over to John for a top-up.' She winked at me. 'Sorry,' she said to the new arrival, 'I didn't catch your name?'

'Oh, it's Jason. Jason Bailey.'

'Ok . . . Jason. I'm Cara. Well, help yourself to food. See you later.'

He sipped his Heineken.

'So – you're Lisa.'

'Yes, but . . . how do you know me? I've never seen you before. Who invited you to the party?'

'I invited myself,' he said, not missing a beat. 'No one asked me out, so I gate-crashed this party. Couldn't stay in all alone another Stephen's Night. So here I am.'

Another sip of beer.

'So – are you not getting a few lines into you? Or are you still off it?'

I looked at him, puzzled.

'I'm . . . I'm still . . . I'm still off it. But how did you know I was off it?'

I looked right into his eyes, searching for a clue as to who this guy was. He was strange, to say the least.

'Ah, news travels fast in the drugs world.'

'Well, are you into it – taking coke?'

My throat was dry, so I took a good mouthful of beer to steady myself. I could see Cara and a few of the girls eyeing us up. Ruth gave me a thumbs-up sign. John was still looking at me, still with that searching, untrusting VIP look about him.

'Listen, Lisa,' said Jason, leaning closer to me. 'The music's very loud. Do you want to come out to the back garden for a bit of fresh air? We can talk there.'

'Yeah, why not!'

We slowly made our way out, me grabbing another Bud to bring with me. Steve brushed against me, giving me that *You're made up!* look as I closed the back door behind us.

The garden was enormous, with its own gazebo, probably used by smokers. We stepped inside, and I noticed it had its own heating system, perfect for cold nights such as this. All I could hear from the house was the music and voices competing with each other, but it seemed so quiet and serene out here, just me alone with this good-looking stranger. For once, I felt relaxed.

'Now,' he continued, a gentle smile playing around his lips, 'to answer your question: no, I don't take coke, or any drugs for that matter. I only have the odd bottle of beer, like at Christmas time or on Paddy's Day.'

'So – why did you gatecrash a party like this, where everyone's on coke or E? Don't you feel a bit strange, a bit out of place here?'

'Do you, Lisa? Do you feel strange, out of place here? You don't take drugs anymore, right?'

'Right – but these are all my friends, Jason. I've a reason for being here. You dont.'

'Maybe I do. Maybe. . . I just came to see you.'

'Me? Yeah, right!', I laughed.

'What if I told you I came all this way just to talk to you, and for no other reason?'

'Wait – this is a joke, isn't it? The gang in there put you up to it, didn't they? They wanted to cheer me up so they got you to talk to me. Something along those lines? Am I right?'

'No, you're wrong, Lisa.'

I felt a bit nervous.

'Look – maybe it's time we went back inside.'

'Ok,' he said. 'You go on ahead. I'm staying here.'

I stopped and looked into his eyes, so sincere-looking, so honest. *Just like Ron's*, I thought. *Just like Ian's.*

'Why should I trust you, a complete stranger? And why would you want to talk to me? For what? What's the reason?'

'Look, Lisa,' he said, 'I know people hurt you in the past. I know that. All I'm asking is for you to trust me . . . for like, ten seconds.'

'Are you having a laugh? Ten seconds! I mean, what can happen in ten seconds? You're so weird, you know that, Jason? Are you sure you're not taking drugs?'

'Well,' he continued, calm as ever, 'you have to trust your instinct. Just this once, forget everyone who hurt and used you. That's all I'm asking for – ten seconds. I promise you from my heart you'll be ok.'

'Who are you?' I laughed. 'You're crazy, right? Do you know how strange you sound? Hah! Well, at least someone's given me a good laugh this Christmas. I'm very amused, I admit that. A bit nervous, too. But hey! It's Christmas, and I'm smiling!'

I took another swig of the beer.

'So tell me, what's this strange ten-second thing? Show me. I'm all yours!'

'It's simple,' he said. 'I'll stand back about four feet from you. All you do is close your eyes. In your mind, count to ten. That's it.'

'You're joking me! That's it? Ok, ok, I'm doing it. Yeah.'

I closed my eyes and slowly counted backwards, trying not to laugh. As I counted back, I got to six, when suddenly I felt something race up my nose, sending a rush of something so warm that invaded every part of my body, my heart, everything. My head went light. I could feel my legs turn to jelly. Everything went from under me. I opened my eyes to find Jason catching me before I hit the ground.

'You're ok, you're ok. I got you.'

I was too dazed, too confused to even try to talk. I felt like I'd been hit by lightning on the inside.

'Listen,' he said. 'Let's get you back inside. You're grand, I promise you'll be ok, Lisa.'

I tried to talk.

'What was . . . ?' I mumbled. 'My God, what did you . . . ?

He pushed open the back door. The girls came over.

'Are you ok, Lisa?'

'What's going on?'

'Get her a chair, Cara,' said Jason. 'She's fine. She just fainted. I'll get her a glass of water. You girls help her onto the chair.'

John and Steve came out of the kitchen, holding two plates of curry and rice.

'What's going on?' asked John. 'Hey, Frank! Lower the music down a bit.'

I started to come round slowly.

'Wow! What the hell was that?'

Many of the guests were now crowding round, asking what had happened and was I ok.

'I'm fine, I'm ok, everybody.'

'Where's that glass of water?'

'Where's Jason?'

'He's gone. He left a couple of minutes ago.'

'What? Gone?', I asked. 'What do you mean *gone*?'

John's face changed. He put his plate down.

'Tell us what happened, Lisa,' he said. 'You look out of it to me. Who was that guy, anyway? Who invited him here?'

He was getting more and more agitated.

'I don't know,' said Cara. 'I never saw him till tonight. I thought *you* must have invited him.'

'Me?' said John, through gritted teeth. 'And why the hell would I invite a complete stranger! Ok, so tell us, Lisa. What's going on? What did he say? What happened out in the garden to you?'

'Well,' I smiled weakly, 'he was actually really nice. We talked, and then he asked me to close my eyes and count to ten. I know, I know, it sounds strange, but all of a sudden it was as if I breathed deeply through my nose and I was overwhelmed, flooded by this . . . this . . . warm sensation. It was just amazing.'

'Ok, ok, I get it,' exhaled John. 'So you were out in the garden, taking coke with your new man. The two of yiz, on the sly. I thought you told us you were off the coke?'

'It was not coke, John, ok?' I shouted.

I could feel my temper starting to go.

'He was standing four feet away from me, for crying out load. He couldn't have given me coke!'

'Four feet away? But eh . . . how would you know if your eyes were closed? I told you before, Cara. I told all of yiz, she's playing games with the lot of us. Just look at you! You're out of your head! We can all see it!'

At this point, everybody was looking on, and listening.

'Hold on a minute,' said John, getting louder and more aggressive as he got into his stride. 'Ok, Frank! Off! Turn off the music.'

He waited for the silence.

'I know what's going on,' he hissed. 'She's buying coke off someone else! A new dealer!'

Cara's face filled with rage. Everyone looked at me as if I had committed murder.

'Don't be ridic . . .' I started to say.

'*That's* why you stopped buying off me, 'cause you're getting it off that f**ker Jason whatever-his-name-is. And on the night of our engagement party you bring him onto my patch, into this party! Into Cara's own home! I knew all along there was something odd about this. I told yiz all – no way can someone like you kick coke overnight!'

'Don't shout at me!' I fired back at him. 'I know it was nothing like coke that happened to me out the back. Don't you dare accuse me of taking coke on the sly with a new dealer. How dare you! Who do you think you are, anyway?'

The crowd were really quiet now.

'You go out to the garden,' John snapped back, 'and come in *flying*, saying something went up your bloody nose? Do you think we're all fools, Lisa? You got some bloody pure coke. Yeah – a real pure hit. We buy coke mixed a bit, but it's still great white. But you wanted better stuff. So you went to a new dealer – a dealer with a purer form of coke!'

'How could you do this to me and John?' sobbed Cara. 'This was meant to be the party to celebrate our engagement. You bloody planned this, you bitch, 'cause you're jealous 'cause you can't hold down a relationship and all your mates can! All these games – saying you're off coke, and then bringing a dealer into *my* home! You sneaky little bitch!'

John put his arm around her as her sobs became worse.

'Listen to me,' I pleaded. 'You have this all wrong. I'm not back on coke. I . . . I . . .'

I started to feel like a fool.

'Look, this is meant to be a party, said Steve, 'not a bloody funeral! Put the music back on and let's get this party going again! Yeah!'

'No, no, Steve. It's ok. I'm going. I'm not even supposed to be here if people think I'm playing games. Well, I'm sorry, but this party is over for me. I'm going home.'

I pulled myself off the chair, picked up my coat and started to leave.

'Hold on a minute,' said John, grabbing me roughly by the arm. 'I want to know where this dealer came from. Who is this creep?'

'Get your hands off me!' I shouted, pulling my arm free. I walked straight out the door. Ruth and Annie followed me just a few steps down the driveway.

''Hey, Lisa,' they said, half-heartedly, 'Come back. We'll sort it out.'

I kept going, the crisp night air on the tears streaming down my face. *Oh my God, I can't take this all in. What's happening to me?*

I made my way down the long Black Hills in the dark and then out onto the coast road leading back to Skerries.

What now?

Chapter Eleven

Running Out of Road

The very thought of trying to walk the dangerous, unlit road to Skerries with no footpaths would be reckless, but then again, being killed would instantly put me out of all this pain, once and for all. I rang a taxi.

I had just hung up when another taxi came towards the railway bridge where I was standing. I saw Carl in the backseat, rolling down the window.

'Lisa – what the hell are you doing, standing here in the dark? Are you crying? Hold on.'

He jumped out and paid the driver.

'Go on, Paul. I'm fine here.'

The taxi did a u-turn and drove off.

'What the hell is going on, Lisa? I'm just reading a text here from Orla saying you're back on the coke and that you caused a big row at Cara's party.'

'Oh, Carl. You know me a long time. I didn't start any row. And I'm not on the coke again. My God, I can't believe what's happened to me. I thought I was getting things sorted out finally. Then all this crap started.'

Carl offered me a cigarette before lighting up one for himself.

'No thanks. Some guy I'd never seen before in my life chats me up. I'd already told myself, never trust a man again. Just half an hour – no, fifteen minutes – with some weirdo, and I'm back in a worse dark place than ever before. My God, when is this nightmare going to stop? I'm at breaking point.'

Carl put his arms around me.

'Look – my God, you're trembling. Come up to the party and we'll sort it out. I don't know what's going on, but we'll talk to Cara and John and things will calm down. What do you say?'

'No, no. I'm never going into a situation or a party with them ever again. It's over, Carl. That John lad is off his head. I can't take anymore!'

I pulled away from Carl and continued on my way.

'Come back! You can't walk the road. You'll be killed.'

But I kept going. A couple of minutes later the taxi I'd called pulled up behind me. It was Larry, with Carl beside him in the front passenger seat.

'Get the hell in, Lisa. You'll be knocked down!'

He reached behind and opened the back door.

'Get in.'

Reluctantly, I sat in and just kept my head turned away, staring out the window.

'Look, I'll just drop you home and then go on up to the party.'

In the rearview mirror I caught Larry's eye. He wasn't so happy now, and had that *I don't want to know* look.

'Look, Carl, you're going to hear all kinds of stories up there. But guess what? I don't care anymore. My head's melted. Let everyone reject me. That's it. I've had enough.'

Within minutes I was standing outside my flat, an empty flat. Stephen's Night, ten pm. Alone again. I turned back to the open window of the taxi, Carl looking at me. *Nothing will ever be the same again. I truly have become the outsider.*

'Bye, Carl.'

Once inside, I closed the front door and slid down to my knees like a helpless child, shaking from the cold, from crying, from fear, from feeling the worst sense of abandonment one could ever feel.

My phone went off. I jumped, back to reality. It was Emma. I cleared my throat, swallowed and took a deep breath. *Must sound composed.*

'Hi, Emma.'

'Hi, Lisa. I'm in the loo in Cara's house. Just got here ten minutes ago with Mark. What's going on? The party's dead. Everyone's upset. Cara's going mad. People are saying you're back on the coke, that you brought a new dealer to the party with 100% pure white. That you were kissing him in the back garden after taking coke with him behind everyone's back! What's going on? And John! John is cursing you from a height.'

I tried to defend myself. But my bottom lip was trembling from the crying, from the cold, from the state I was in.

'Listen, Emma. I . . . I don't care anymore, ok? *I* know the truth. *I* know I never took coke tonight. Listen, I'm going, ok?'

'Hold on, listen. Ruth's here. Wants to talk to you for a second.'

'Listen, Lisa. I saw you. You were out of your head when you came in from the garden. Stop this! I mean, you couldn't even stand. Who cares if you're back on the coke again and getting better stuff off your dealer! But why did you do it in Cara's house? On her and John's big night? Sneaking around, playing games with all our heads for weeks! It's freaky what you've been doing!'

'Listen, Ruth. I'm hanging up. Goodbye.'

I rang Ma just to tell her I was home safely and was fine. I put on my best voice, not wanting to upset her on her night out with Rose and Jim.

'What? I . . . I can't hear you all that well with the music, pet. You're home? Already? It's very early! Is everything ok?'

'Yes, fine, absolutely fine. Agh – I just wasn't enjoying it, Ma. I'm just going to watch tv now for a while. You enjoy the night, ok? See you tomorrow.'

'Ok . . . Love you . . . Bye.'

I couldn't tell if I'd put her mind at rest. She knew me too well. I pulled myself up off the floor. My phone rang again.

'Hi, Carl.'

'Lisa! Shit! Everyone's giving me a different story to the one you gave me. They said you told them you were out in the back garden with a dealer and came in out of your brains. I don't know what to think . . .'

'Don't think, Carl. Goodnight!'

I hung up and switched off for the night. In the loo, I leaned over to the mirror, straining to look up my nose to see if, by any chance, there were any traces of coke there. Nothing. Not that I could see, anyway. God, they now had me thinking maybe that weirdo did somehow spike me with coke. How stupid could I be, going out the back with Mr Trusting Eyes! My God. In the matter of five minutes I had been sucked into another nasty trap. My life was torn apart and I went along with it all.

I racked my brains to retrace the sequence of events, but none of it made a bit of sense to me. The more I replayed the film in my head, the creepier it all seemed. The same old faces, high as kites. The strange encounter with Jason. The collapse. Then smart-arsed John, making a complete fool out of me and loving every second of it. All he's worried about is losing money, the money he got from me for years, the little creep.

I got into my pyjamas and just sat on my bed. Everyone out enjoying themselves, me in the empty flat, alone and deeply hurt again. A real, awful sense that I'd run out of road – a pure sense of total desperation, that's all I felt. A hollow feeling, like you're sinking down inside, nothing to grip on to. Just crying, hoping the pain will ease. But if anything, it was getting worse. God, we were all so close, got on so well up to just a few weeks ago.

I let out a deep sigh and opened my laptop to go on Facebook – my last resort for a source of comfort to block out the pain of rejection. But to my horror, the first post I saw on the news feed wall was from Cara on her phone:

Amazing what people will do to try and wreck the best night of my life! Jealousy is an awful thing!

I raced past it, not wanting to see the replies. There was no way anyone was going to go for my story. I mean, I said I felt something go up my *nose*. I could have chosen a different word. I was all over the place. It was crazy, so crazy. I felt like it was a kind of bloody conspiracy hanging over me.

I lay back on the bed and slipped into a deep, uneasy sleep. When I awoke I had no idea of the time. I checked it on the laptop: *5:09am*.

A bad dream? No, that sinking feeling told me I was back in the real world and everything was just the same. I started to close the laptop but something – *that voice again?* – told me to keep it on.

I switched on my phone. *Ok, here we go again. Brace yourself.* Texts from the party-goers.

Why did you try to wreck Cara and John's night?

Well, we're all so happy for Cara and John.

The party's going great!

It's not Cara's fault you can't hold onto a man.

Etc., etc.

The only one who didn't text was Steve. I just stopped reading them and hit the delete button.

Delete all?

Yes.

I lay back on the bed in tears. After a short while I sat bolt upright, as I could feel myself losing my breath. *Oh God, I can't breathe. Oh God, a panic attack.* I ran downstairs and opened the backdoor. I stepped outside and gulped the cool, early-morning air into my lungs. After a few minutes of deep breathing I could feel myself coming round. I stood there in my pyjamas, shivering in the frosty air. *My God, what a state to find yourself in.*

*

Back in Cara's, everyone was back partying away full on, music banging, everyone up dancing, drinking, taking more lines of coke, removing any thought of the event with Lisa earlier in the night. John was taking line after line, selling a few €100 bags to a few new heads that came to the party, picking up a cd with a few lines and a fresh bottle of Bud.

'Just have to make a phonecall, Cara. I'll be back in ten minutes.'

Putting the cd cover down on the table, he rang James O'Connor who, he knew, would be at a party himself. James had been John's coke supplier for the past four years and they got on well, businesswise.

'Hi, James. It's John.'

'I can see that, man. Your name came up, ye fool. Ha! How's the big party going? How come I never got an invite? Am I not good enough for youse yuppies out in Skerries?'

'You know you could come anytime. It was you who made the rule – never to be seen together around my parts. To keep it strictly business. That's what you said, James.'

'Ok, ok! take it easy, man! You sound freaked. Hey – you're missing a great party up here in Finglas, man. Why don't you drive over? There should be no cops around the back roads at this hour on Stephen's

Night.'

'Listen, James. I'm after running into a bit of a problem. That's why I'm ringing you.'

'. . . Yeah? Go on.'

'I think there's someone moving in on our patch. I had this bird buying a lot of coke off me for years, then stopped, out of the blue. Tonight she brought this guy to our party, both of them on top-of-the-range coke – not mixed at all. He was selling it to *her!*'

'Let me get this straight. . . This little scumbag comes into your bird's house, and starts selling coke? You're joking me! What does he look like?'

'About thirty-odd, hoodie, light, short, curly hair. Said his name was Bailey. Jason Bailey.'

'I'll stop you there, our lad. I'll ring you back in a bit.'

John stayed out the back, taking a couple of lines and a mouthful of beer, puffing on a fag.

James rang back.

'Yeah, I rang Darryl. We know about this little f**ker. But couldn't find out what he was up to or who he's working for. He showed up in a few places, and after that, strange shit happened. Few heads never bought coke again off our lads. We couldn't be sure till now, till you confirmed it for us that he *is* selling coke, the bollix. Listen, our lad – don't you worry. Darryl's the boss and he'll track down the f**ker's address in a few days. Don't you worry. It'll be sorted, once and for all. So you won't have any more problems.'

'Cool. Can't have this going on on my patch.'

'Shit, no way. He must be working for a southside gang, yeah?'

'Well, just a word in his ear, so. Warn him off, like. That's all that's needed, James.'

'Look, John. I don't want to say too much over the phone, yeah? I said too much already. You go back to your bird and enjoy the buzz, our lad. I'll give you a shout in a day or two. Do you need a drop sent down?'

'Em . . . I've a few ounces left, but they're already ordered to sell. And with New Year's Eve next week I'll need a fairly big drop. Plus, I've money here I owe you. So send down one of your lads or drop down yourself, yeah?'

'Right. My bird's calling me.'

He hung up.

John returned back into the house and called Cara aside.

'Listen, I rang someone and found out your man Jason Bailey is a coke dealer who's been moving in on other patches. So Lisa was lying through her teeth. I knew it, but wanted to confirm it for sure.'

'God, John. The little bitch! That's it. I'm ringing her.'

She took out her phone.

'Don't. Don't. It's nearly 5am. Once we know the truth now, that's all that matters.'

'I don't care. I'm ringing her.'

'Well, go out the back so and make your call.'

*

I locked the backdoor and came back upstairs into the warmth of my bedroom. My phone again. Cara. *Shit, here we go again.*

'Hi, Cara.'

'Don't "hi" me! I can't believe after all the years we hung out together that you turned into the lying little bitch you are. John's just off the phone and we found out your new friend is a coke dealer who's trying to move in on John's patch. And you're taking coke off him behind all our backs. How could you lie to us all, bringing that creep into my party, starting a big row on the biggest night of my life? If you didn't want John's coke anymore you should have just said so. But no. You went around for weeks, hiding, lying and playing mind games with all your mates' heads!'

'Listen – you have it all wrong, Cara. It's . . .'

'Shut up, Lisa. Don't tell me I'm wrong. We all know the truth. You have changed so much so fast. You're jealous, Lisa. Admit it. Just 'cause we're all happy in relationships and you can't find someone like John. Tell the bloody truth.'

'Hold on, will you! Let me talk!' I said, shaking, trying not to scream abuse down the phone. 'I'm off the coke since that night in The Life. I don't know what happened tonight. I'm still confused. It's all so strange. But if you don't believe me that I've quit drugs, ask my mother. I told her everything.'

There was a pause.

'What do you mean, you told her everything?'

I'd gone too far. I knew it.

'Does she know we're all taking coke? Don't tell me you told her about me and the gang. Don't tell me that, Lisa! That was a sworn promise in our gang, remember?'

'Look, I'm sorry, but I told her everything. It just all came out. I can't lie to my Ma. Look, she won't say a word. She promised.'

'Listen now, Lisa. Don't tell me you told her about my John getting us the coke.'

'Em . . . I'm sorry, ok? Yeah, I told her everything. I'm sorry, Cara.'

'Did you tell her about your new dealer? I bet not! Oh, no! You can get lost for good, Lisa. It's over now. Hear me? Over! John is going to go mad. Don't ever ring or try to contact any of us ever again, you two-faced bitch!'

She hung up.

I was in shock. *Why, oh God, why did I have to open my mouth and tell her all that?*

Five minutes later, my phone rang again. John. I turned it onto Silent. Texts started coming through as well, everyone cracking up over me breaking the code of silence we had always agreed to keep. *Never, never tell any family members about any of this.*

Yes, I had broken the big rule. As far as the rest were concerned, this was the last straw. Weeks ago I had thought things couldn't get worse, but they had. Nothing would ever be the same again. Ever.

I sat on the bed, broken in spirit, as broken as any human could be. I stared helplessly into my Facebook screen, unable to make out the words because of the tears in my eyes. Slowly I reached for *Log out* but in a split second I had clear vision and the only thing I could see through my blurred vision was *Tommy's Special Event, 30th December.*

God, Tommy's – yeah. I've got to go down and see him over what I did, even offer to pay for the mirror I broke.

I logged onto the event: *40 people attending, €3 a drink*. I flicked down through the names till I came to one name staring back at me like it was lit up in flashing lights: *David Salle*. I smiled when I thought back to the night he went by the Blue Ocean and gave us all the strange look, then stopped and just stared at me, like a stalker would.

I pressed onto his Facebook wall and sat, staring at his profile picture. The thought came from nowhere: *Why don't you send a friend request. I dare you! No, I can't. Why not? What have you got to lose? You lost everyone tonight. I dare you!*

Nervously, I hovered over the *Send* button. *Will I or won't I? You're mad if you do, Lisa. You'll start an even bigger war. Things are bad enough . . . To hell with it. Nothing can get any worse than this.*

I pressed *Send.*

Oh shit. Maybe I shouldn't. It's too late now. It's sent. That was a bad, bad idea. I'm playing with fire.

I was taking a very big risk. *I could be bringing another weirdo into my life! Should I say it was a mistake?*

I closed my laptop and lay down. I was wiped out emotionally, so, so tired. I passed out.

*

'Wake up, Sleepyhead! It's 11:30. I've coffee and toast on. Can't face a fry, Lisa. I've a sore head from last night. That Jim lad – I'll kill him. He talked me into going to the Rugby Club to an 80s Night, Rose and her friends were with us. Oh, Lisa. I made a show of myself! Up dancing with Jim to Guess Who, Girls on Film, Duran Duran. I thought I was a young one again. That Jim lad's some mover for his age. Rose laughed her head off. Oh, I'm paying for it today, Lisa. My legs are so sore.'

I crawled out of bed.

'So glad you got out and enjoyed yourself, Ma,' I said, trying to smile and look happy for her.

'Are you alright, pet?' she said, looking closely at me. 'My God! Did you see your eyes? What happened, love?'

'Em . . . I know, Ma. I was crying a lot last night. I'll tell you when I feel more up to it.'

'No, no, if you were crying, tell me about it. God, I forgot – you were home early last night. Something happened, didn't it?'

'Ah, don't worry, Ma. It's grand. You were right, you know. I can't hang out with that crowd anymore. It was a nightmare. I'm grand. Promise!'

'But your eyes, Lisa. Your eyes.'

'What about them?'

'I don't know. They look . . . different. Have a look in the mirror. Maybe it's just me – after a few drinks back in Jim's at 3am.'

I went into the loo and felt a strange sensation pulsing through my heart. I looked in the mirror.

'Nothing different, Ma.'

But I looked again. There *was* something different.

'Maybe I'm having a nervous breakdown, Ma!'

'Don't be talking nonsense! I'll make the toast and pour you out some cornflakes. I think I'll lie down myself for an hour or two after that.'

'Why don't you, Ma! I'll clean up and get the dinner ready. Nothing too fancy.'

'Oh, that'll be great, Lisa. You're a pet.'

I walked back into my room, trying not to think about last night. *What's the point? I'm all cried out. Can't be a tear left inside me after that whole episode.*

I switched on my laptop and went onto Facebook to see what the news was on the party. I went to go to Cara's page but soon realised she had blocked me off her list, as had John, Ruth, Annie.

The sickening sense of rejection began to grip me, but just as I was logging off, two red lights came on. One a private message. I switched to the first, then to the private message. Both posts were from David Salle.

Chapter Twelve

Coffee at Olive

I pulled back. The first mail was David Salle's accepting me as a friend. The second was the private message from him which I was uneasy about opening. God, I'd sent it in desperation. What about what Emma had told me about this guy? That seemed to be far from my mind while I was in the state I was in last night. My judgement was out the window, along with just about everything else.

I opened the private message.

'Lisa – your cornflakes are ready, toast half-burnt. Don't know what I'm doing down here!'

I hurried down to the kitchen.

'Bowl of cornflakes will do me, Ma.'

I came back up, trying not to spill the cornflakes and coffee at each step. I munched the cornflakes, milk running down my chin. I was glad there was no camera on me.

Hi, Lisa. Thanks for asking me to be added to your friends list. But I am somewhat puzzled as to why. If I remember rightly, you hang about with my ex, Emma Ryan, and a few people who refuse to talk to me over our split-up. Are you sure you have the right David Salle?

That voice again: *Don't open this door. Don't go there. You'll cause all-out war. He'll be stalking you next.*

What will I do? Ah, crap. I can't stop now. What else can go wrong for me? He's just a Facebook mate. What's wrong with that?

Hi, David. No, it's not a mistake, me asking you to be my friend. As for Emma and the gang, I don't hang out with them anymore. None of them talk to me.

I sent it, then skipped down to get a fresh cup of coffee.

'You're very jumpy,' said Ma. 'What are you up to?'

'It's the strong coffee you made, Ma,' I said as I strode up the stairs.

Another mail.

What? I'm baffled. I saw you all out together only a few weeks ago. You looked a very close-knit bunch. What happened? You don't have to go into it if it's too personal.

Now what do I say? Do I tell him it's because I've given up taking coke? If I remember rightly, Emma told me David did coke for three years, then kicked the habit. So he would have known for sure we were all out of our heads the night he saw us.

I mailed him, hoping it would not be stepping over the line again. I told him I'd given up coke and that all hell broke loose over it. I wrote,

I hope I'm not bothering you, landing all this on you, a person I don't even know. But I feel very lost, to be honest.

After I hit the *Send* button, I just sat there, wondering had I done the wrong thing again. Five minutes passed. Ten minutes. No reply.

Ma was tapping on the door.

'I'm off to bed for a few hours, love. Will you be ok? And when I wake up, I want you to tell me everything that happened last night.'

'Ok, Ma. Enjoy your sleep. I'll call you later.'

Twenty minutes. Nothing.

Ah, I went too far. Shit. I should never have . . .

The red light came on. I spluttered my coffee, almost spilling it over the keys.

Lisa, can you meet me at Olive coffee shop at 3pm?

What? Meet him? That's a bit serious. Olive at 3pm? Just like that? I can't just go down and meet David Salle in a coffee shop in the middle of Skerries in broad daylight. What can I say? What will I say?

Another mail coming in from him.

I'm not great at talking on Facebook to be honest, so can you meet me today for coffee? Would love to hear your story. P.S. Well done getting off the drugs. Brave girl.

Oh, just go for it. It's just a chat. What are you going to do – hang around the flat all day, depressed and crying . . .? Ok, Ok.

I take a deep breath and mail him.

Ok. Thanks for your comment about kicking the coke. I'll see you then at 3. Thanks for your time.

There was no going back. Meeting David Salle in Olive! *Someone is going to see us. But then again, it's none of anyone's business who I talk to, right? Everyone has left me out in the cold.*

I raced round the apartment, cleaning it from top to bottom. I peeled the potatoes and cut up the carrots and let them steep. A quick check that I had done everything I could for now, and I jumped into the shower. By 2:30 I was in front of the mirror again.

Now don't go overdoing it with the make-up, Lisa.

My heart was racing like crazy. Well – it beats lying on my bed, hugging my pillow, feeling sorry for myself any day of the week.

My bedside clock showed *2:48.*

Shit, I can't do this. I can't. What about the things Emma told me? I can't bring more hassle and worry onto Ma.

2:57.

I sat on the bed, my mind racing a million miles an hour.

Ah, crap. I'm going.

Out the door. Car speeding off out of Kelly's Bay, down the Dublin Road, past the Community Centre. I parked outside Nealon's pub and walked up the Garda Station lane, my hands sweaty, looking at my phone: *3:07.* I turned at the top of the lane onto Strand Street. Only a few yards away from Olive, my legs going to jelly under me. That voice again – *Turn back, turn back.* As I came to the outdoor seating area, I scanned the tables for David, feeling a bit of a fool.

I can't see him. I'm getting out of here.

Just as I was turning to leave, someone tapped me from behind. A young, fresh-faced girl.

'Hi, you're Lisa?'

'Yes.'

'Hi. I'm Carol, David's sister.'

Those electric blue eyes. I should have known.

'Oh, right . . .'

'Yeah. David's just getting a parking ticket for my car. I drove him down. I was coming into Skerries anyway to pick up a few bits and pieces in Gerry's supermarket. What coffee would you like?'

'Oh, em . . . a latte would be great. Thanks.'

'He should be here any minute. Always late! I'll get the coffee, you grab a table.'

There was only one free table left in the outdoor area, right under the heater. I pulled out a chair and spotted David crossing from the far side of the street.

Oh my God. I'm making a mess of this, amn't I? What am I doing here? Too late. He's here.

The closer he got, the clearer I could see those captivating blue eyes of his.

'Hi, Lisa,' he said, giving me a disarming peck on the cheek.

I just gulped. *Wow. Wasn't expecting that.*

'David.'

'Take a seat. Not too cold out here? Or maybe you'd prefer inside?'

'No, this is fine.'

'Great. Sorry for being late. The first parking meter wouldn't take any money. Hope you're not waiting long?'

'No, no. I just came.'

He nodded at his sister through the window.

'So – you've met Carol. Hope you don't mind her joining us for a quick coffee? She'll be heading off soon.'

'No, not at all.'

'She was dying to meet you when I told her a little about you. Hope you don't mind.'

'No, no. I don't mind.' *How much has he told her?* I glanced around as casually as I could to see if there was anyone I knew in the café – or even passing by, as we were on full view.

'So – you told me your friends distanced themselves from you over you giving up the . . .'

He glanced around, then dropped his voice.

'*. . . the you-know-what.*'

'Yeah – it's been a nightmare. Listen, thanks for coming to meet me.'

'It's ok. I'm glad to be here to help in any way I can. You're so brave, giving up that way of life. It takes a lot, Lisa. What made you stop? Do you mind me asking you?'

'No, no, you're grand. I just went to The Life Nightclub a few weeks ago and we were all . . . well-coked out of it. Then I went through a . . . a really bad experience. It was awful.'

Carol came out and placed the tray of coffees on the table.

'Ok, sorry for the delay. They're under-staffed today. That's why I'm your waitress! Now, there's the latte for you, Lisa.'

'Thanks, Carol. How much do I owe you?'

'No, you're fine. It's on me.'

'You don't mind Carol being here when we're having our chat, do you? She knows a lot about all this from my years of taking the stuff.'

Carol smiled, her kindness and compassion showing through.

'No, no. That's grand with me.'

David leaned closer to her.

'Lisa was just saying she had a very bad experience on coke, and that convinced her to give it up.'

'Yes,' I said, now comfortable about confiding in them both. 'It was so strange. I mean, in the club that night I was dancing away, in great form – or so I thought. Then – bang! I lost it.'

David put down his coffee and leaned forward, resting his chin on the palm of his hand, giving me his full attention. Carol sipped her coffee and sat back on her chair.

I recounted for them the sequence of events, as I remembered them: coming out of the loo, seeing for the first time that everything was fake; hearing the strange voice telling me that I was fake, that nothing was real; seeing all the faces in the crowd, twisted and distorted from drugs; how I fainted, then got violently sick and ended up back home totally distraught, crying helplessly; and finally, how I got rid of my coke down the toilet and never touched it since.

'And I never will again,' I concluded, taking another sip from my latte.

There was a respectful silence as they both waited.

Carol put down her cup.

'My God, that sounds awful. You poor thing. It sounds like a nightmare.'

David never moved. He continued to stare into my eyes, searching, searching, trying to make sense of what I had told him. When he realised he was making me slightly uncomfortable, he shook himself out of his trance and blinked.

'Sorry, sorry.' He sipped his coffee. 'Just . . . can I just go back a bit? The voice you heard, telling you . . . Is that all it said?'

'Yes. It seemed to be mocking me, laughing at me. Saying everything is fake, I was fake. Then, to top it all, there was this guy I was with, a guy I had just met, whom I trusted. And I saw him kissing another girl on the sly. I was so shocked, so disappointed. Ah, my mind's been in turmoil ever since.'

'And what about your mates, your close circle of friends? How did they react?'

'They just drifted away, one by one, when I stopped. I just didn't seem to fit in anymore. I tried – but all I could see was the illusions in and around the whole world of drugs. It was as if someone had taken a blindfold off me. But everyone else still had theirs on, and was unaware of it. I told my mother everything – eventually. She's been a great support, I have to say. But I just feel like I'm losing everything. I went out with 'the gang', as I call them, since, but it got worse. They all blocked me off their Facebook because I told my mother they were on drugs and that our dealer was John Noonan.'

David and Carol glanced at each other at the mention of the name.

'I mean, I love them all, but it's over. I'm on my own now.'

I could feel the tears coming again. I took a sip of the latte, which was now cold.

'Hey, it's ok,' said Carol, putting her arm around me. 'Look – you have us. We'll stand by you, ok? It's going to be ok. You've been through a nightmare. David – will you get a hanky out of my bag, please?'

'Yeah, sure. Sorry.'

I glanced around self-consciously.

'No one's looking, Lisa,' she continued. 'God help you. And what a time for all this to happen – at Christmas.'

I wiped away my tears. David leaned forward again, resting his chin on his cupped hands.

'You're an inspiration, Lisa,' he said, emphasising each word with a shake of his head. 'I know it's been very hard for you to stand up for yourself and risk losing all your friends rather than go back on drugs. Have you any idea what a powerful testimony of who you are that is?'

'Look,' said Carol, standing up, 'I'll leave you both to chat. I've bits to do. I'll be back for you in half an hour, David. That ok?'

She bent over and hugged me.

'I'm here for you, Lisa. Don't think you have no mates. You have two new ones already!'

'Thanks, Carol. Thanks very much.'

She headed off across the street.

'God, she's such a lovely girl, David.'

'Yeah. Great sister. Lousy waitress, though.'

We both burst out laughing, drawing a few puzzled looks from the other patrons.

'Yeah, Carol's the best sister on Planet Earth. I'd be lost without her.' He drained his coffee and produced a pack of cigarettes from his pocket. 'Do you mind?'

'No, no, go ahead.'

'My only vice,' he said, lighting the cigarette. He took an ashtray from a neighbouring table, now empty. The smell of the match and the first puff of smoke drifted pleasantly towards me. 'So – what made you mail me, Lisa? I thought Emma, my ex, would have blacklisted me to you.' His smile indicated he was joking.

'I don't know, David. Really. I don't know why I . . . Maybe I'm so lost. I don't know what I'm doing. And yeah, Emma did tell me a thing or two, but. . .

'What did she say?' he laughed. 'That I'm a stalker?'

'Yeah, yeah, something like that.' It was time to change the angle. 'Do you want to tell me your side of the story?'

'God, Lisa. Where do I start?' He dragged on his cigarette, inhaled deeply and exhaled, releasing his memories with the long plume of smoke. 'I met Emma, a year-and-a-half ago now, fell deeply in love, and thought she felt the same. I mean, we got on great at first, but she started getting more and more into the coke, whereas I hadn't taken any since 2006. I, like you, tried to turn a blind eye, but we started to end up at parties, with her high as a kite and me sticking to a couple of beers, everyone else all coked up and me cold sober – relatively, anyway. I tried to talk to her about the danger, but she ignored me. Then we started to drift apart. She started going to parties on her own, I'd go home at twelve midnight. Next I heard she was going out with Mark Murphy.'

He flicked the ash from the cigarette dismissively, his action matching the mood of what he was saying.

'I put it to her. She said she never did. But look – they're together now. So what does that tell you?'

'Wow,' I said, 'that's not what she told me. She told me she never knew Mark till you two broke up.'

He stubbed out the cigarette and pushed the ashtray away.

'She tries to tell different people different stories,' he sighed. 'But look – it's in the past now.'

'So what happened at her party? She said you caused a big row, that you kept stalking her.'

'No, no,' he said, reaching automatically for the cigarette pack again. 'What happened was, I kept texting her and ringing her to say I loved her. Then I was actually at home the night of the party. I mean . . .'

He picked a fresh cigarette from the pack and twirled it between his fingers. I could see the upset in his eyes.

'I mean, there I was on my own, at home. 160 people invited to her 22nd birthday party. I mean, it was no big deal – it's not as if it was her 21st or anything like that. But between her dad and Mark and her friends, what was supposed to be just a few people round for drinks turned into a major party.'

He lit the cigarette, but didn't seem to be enjoying it.

'I know, I know, it was none of my business. True. But I would have given the whole world just to sit there beside her. I was the one who loved her, and yet I got no invite. I suppose just sitting at home alone, drinking a few cans, feeling sorry for myself got to me.'

He stubbed out the cigarette after only a few pulls.

'Against my better judgement, I suppose, I just went round to talk to her about my feelings. *And yes*, to warn her about the drugs. But . . . agh! I made a big mess of it. I admit that now, in hindsight. I went in, tried to say something, but she turned it into a big drama, like I came down to wreck her party. Before I knew it, two bouncers threw me out. That was it!'

He looked at me in the eye, but this time I thought there was an element of shame or embarrassment in his normally calm, cool demeanour.

'I know it was just down to the fact that I loved her, Lisa. Nothing else. I'd never do a thing to harm her. She knew that. But I suppose that's life. You want to meet someone and well, you know, fifty-fifty, you love them, they love you. No games. God, Lisa. I hate all the games people play with each others' hearts and lives.'

He glanced at his watch, then across the street.

'The next thing that happened was a bit disturbing. I had sent her a number of texts during this time, and she started going round, showing them to everyone, out of context, of course, making me out to be crazy. But hey, it's in the past, as I said. In the past year I just opted out of the whole circus. And guess what? I don't miss it, Lisa! The whole so-called Social Life – it's just drugs and games. Not for me!'

Through the window I caught the eye of the girl behind the counter. I indicated that we wanted the same again. She nodded and smiled.

'Anyway,' continued David, 'I'm sorry. I'm rambling on here. I came round to listen to *you*.'

'No, no, I'm glad you told me all this because, to be honest, Emma made me think it was all *you*.'

'Really? And you still came down to meet me, thinking I was a weird stalker. I love it! That's just legend!' he laughed.

'I can't believe it. You mean to say she lied about the whole thing!'

'Ah, don't worry, Lisa. It's in the past.'

The girl arrived with the two coffees.

'Sorry about earlier,' she said. 'We were run off our feet.'

'No problem,' I said, giving her a fiver, and indicating she keep the change.

'Oh, thank you,' she said, briskly clearing away the old cups and replacing the ashtray with a fresh one.

'So, David,' how do you feel about her now?'

'God, I don't know. I mean, I went in over my head, you could say. I was mad about her. I did everything for her. But when I look back I see I got very little in return, to be honest. Put me off love forever. I was in bits over the break-up.'

'God, it's strange hearing a guy talking about loving someone like you just did.'

'It's real life, Lisa. Why should anyone not feel free to talk about their feelings? They're real, and a big part of life.'

'Yeah, yeah, but you just don't hear many people, particularly guys, express it like that.'

'So tell me,' he said, a mischievous glint in his eye, 'Who was the guy who kissed the girl behind your back?'

'Well, I had only started dating him a week. He was from Rush, His name was Ian Carter. Emma persuaded him to invite me out.'

'Ian Carter? Ah, I know him from the time I was with Emma. They say he can't stay with a girl five minutes. He was dating a girl, but she moved to Wexford. Lovely girl. He messed her up big time.'

'What? He told me they just drifted apart.'

'No, there was more to it than that,' he said, lighting up cigarette number three. 'Emma should never have put you in touch with him. My God, I'm glad I'm out of all this. It's just crazy out there.'

'So, can I ask you about why *you* gave up drugs?'

Just as I spoke, Carol came back, laden with groceries.

'Hi, you pair,' she said, cheery as ever.

'Hi, Carol,' I smiled.

'Did you get everything you wanted?' asked David.

'Oh, yes. And more. As usual. How are you now, Lisa?' she said, sitting down, a look of concern on her face.

'I'm grand now, thanks,' I said, nodding towards David. 'Another coffee, Carol?'

'No, I'm fine. Listen, Lisa,' she said. 'Where do you drink at weekends?'

I hesitated.

'Mostly in Tommy's, I suppose.'

'Aah, *that's* how I saw your name! David, you're down to go there the day before New Year's Eve.'

She turned to me.

'Did David tell you why he's picked that night to go out? Tell her, David!'

He looked a bit embarrassed.

'Ah, it's because I hate New Year's Eve. I know, I know, it's supposed to be the best night of the year. Everyone loves everyone. For One Night Only! People hugging other people even though they hate their guts. Oh then, next day, it's back to the Real World. Nobody talking. It's just all so fake, so false. I'm not saying everyone is like that, but most are. All this countdown business – *10, 9, 8, 7, 6 . . . Yippeee!* Not for me. I hate it. Give me the real world any day. Whatever that is!'

He laughed as he reached for another cigarette.

'Be warned now, Lisa,' said Carol, smiling as she put her arm round her brother. 'Our David is what I call an Analyst. He leaves no stone unturned. He must study everything till he finds out the truth. Isn't that right, David?'

'No, it's not. There's a lot of crap out there that's not worth five seconds of my time, or anyone else's. You have to be careful you don't end up thinking there's truth in everything. If you do, you end up going around listening to every new idea, and end up with a head full of crap. Pick out what's interesting to you, something that most people shy away from because maybe they have set lives: go to school, get a job, go to the pub, take up a sport, find a girl, get married, have kids, buy a house, buy a car, go on holidays, get old, say a prayer, then die. Anything outside that, most people have no time for. And maybe it's easier to be like that. That's a lot in itself to handle. Me – I just like to dig a bit deeper.'

Carol winked at me. 'Em, Lisa. That's why David has only forty-eight friends on Facebook!'

'Hey, forty-*nine*! Lisa's my friend now.'

'So, really,' I said, pushing away my empty latte cup. 'Why did you kick drugs? I mean, what made you stop?'

There was an awkward silence. Carol's face dropped. David became uncomfortable, stubbing out his half-finished cigarette.

'Sorry, Lisa,' he said. 'That's a long story. I'll tell you again some other time, if you don't mind. I will tell you. But not here. Not here.'

It was time for me to be embarrassed, though I didn't really know why.

'I hope I didn't put a dampener on the nice atmosphere. Sorry if I did.'

'No, no, Lisa. You have every right to ask me that. You told me your story, I should tell you mine. But it's such a . . . a long story, but I'll tell you next time. Ok?'

'Ok. Cool. But can I just tell you one other thing that happened since I came off drugs? Something weird! Maybe you, being the Analyst you are, may be able to explain this, because it's really doing my head in.'

'Fire away. Tell me.'

So I told them both about my encounter with Jason Bailey – every detail, including the aftermath.

David just stared at me, as did Carol.

'My God,' she said, 'I never heard anything like that before. Over to you, Doctor David.'

'Thanks, Carol. Whew! This might sound like a silly question, but .

. . did you check your nose?'

'Yes, I did, but nothing. I felt a right fool, looking into the mirror.'

'You said he told you to close your eyes and he stood four feet away. But if your eyes were closed, how did you *know* how far away he was, and if he stayed there?'

'I know, I know. That's what everyone else said. I just *knew*.'

'Well,' said David, 'I don't mean to be like the others, Lisa. I'm just trying to understand. He must have spiked you with something. He must have. There's quite a few weirdoes going around to these parties, Lisa. Mad stuff going on. Just put it behind you.'

'Yeah, I suppose you're right.'

Carol cut in. 'Another possibility just crossed my mind. Maybe this guy did hypnosis on you. I mean, with the whole countdown of numbers, isn't that the way they do it, like?'

'Good God! I never thought of that, maybe that's it. What do you think, David?'

There was a pause, everyone deep in thought, before David clicked his fingers.

'I'll tell you what, I'll Google a few sites on the net, see if I can come up with some explanation. But look – don't worry. You're off drugs now. Do you know what? I remember the last time I saw you, over in the Blue Ocean, and I can tell you, you look a million times better now!'

His eyes looked into mine with that reassuring look, the look that said *Everything will be ok*. Carol too looked so supportive. She reached over and lightly grasped my hand.

'You're heading for greater and better things, Lisa. Wait and see!'

'Listen,' said David, picking up Carol's groceries. 'We've got to go. Our dad's health is not the best. We both nurse him.'

'Oh, I'm sorry.'

'Ah, he took a stroke three years ago. A bad one. Listen, I'm just curious. What do you work at, may I ask?'

'Em, I'm a teacher. Just started. My first year.' *Headline: Junior Infant Teacher is Drug Addict.*

'A teacher? That's great,' said David, standing up. I noticed for the first time how tall he was.

'So,' said Carol, 'would you like to come up for dinner tomorrow, or do you have other plans? It'll just be David, me and Richie – he's the guy I'm marrying next year. We'd love to have you round. Be a chance to get to know you a bit better. Isn't that right, David?'

'Yeah, it'd be great if you could make it. Carol's a super cook. Lousy waitress, of course . . .'

'What . . .?' said Carol, as we laughed at our private joke.

'Sure, why not! Are you sure, now? I don't want to be a bother to you.'

'Not at all. Let's say . . . 3pm?'

'3pm. How could I forget.'

'You know where the house is? Just near the Rugby Club, four houses away on the left. Green door. My Skoda will be parked outside.'

'Cool. Can't wait.'

Carol hugged me, and I found myself facing out towards the traffic. A car slowed down in front of the café. The people inside were breaking their necks to look out, even rolling down the windows to get a better view. I looked closer. *Oh crap*. John, Cara, Ruth. Eyes nearly popping out of their sockets. John almost crashed into the car in front of him. He slammed on the brakes. They all watched as David bent over and gave me a lovely warm hug.

'See you tomorrow at three. Great meeting you, Lisa. You're sound.'

'Come on, you!' said Carol, grabbing his arm. 'We have a dinner to make for Dad. Bye, Lisa!'

I stood there as they walked away, feeling great that I'd met such wonderful people. I walked out onto the footpath, a renewed sense of confidence and purpose in my stride. Out of the corner of my eye I could see the gang sitting there in the stationary car, the driver behind them beeping at them to *move your bloody car!*

Looking straight ahead, I smiled – just a little, private smile – and kept going.

Chapter Thirteen

A Worthless Power

I drove off towards Balbriggan, smiling. Can't go home just yet. God, I have not smiled like this in so long.

But God, don't get me wrong. I had my walls well built up, and the awful side effects of the past few weeks were still red raw on the inside. But a smile is a smile, so I'll take it, thank you very much.

I diverted first to Red Island, pulling up in the car park facing the sea close to the children's new playground. My mind was so clear for the first time in years. It seemed the talk with David and Carol was just the tonic I needed to pull myself up from the dark pit I'd been lost in for weeks. I was so thankful that I had followed my instincts and had got it right for once.

I switched off the engine but kept the radio playing. Within minutes I found I had to turn off the radio as that strange feeling I'd felt this morning in the bathroom came rushing through me again, like a burst of butterflies inside, but this time it was getting, stronger. It kept racing across my heart, warm waves touching me, bringing tears to my eyes.

I sat there thinking, *What is this? Can my life get any stranger?*

Maybe it's my lost girl inside, coming back to life again. It felt so deep but lovely and if it was me coming back to my full self, well, what can I say? Bring it on!

I raced home to tell Ma the whole story of my day, plus the strange events of last night in Cara's house. She was very supportive of my linking up with people like David and Carol.

'You need people who truly care about you – and they do sound like caring people,' she said.

We sat down to a lovely dinner. She couldn't get her head around the story of what happened in Cara's back garden with Jason Bailey.

'Hmm. There are too many weirdoes going around those parties, Lisa. Maybe it was a sign for you at last to pull away from that way of life. Sounds like that guy spiked you, or whatever the word is. It wouldn't surprise me if they planned it all.'

'No, Ma, I don't think . . .'

'Look, love. You go to that dinner tomorrow with David and Carol. It's doing you good – I can see it in you already.'

'I will, Ma,' I reassured her. 'They're a great pair to be around. Very supportive. Funny as well.'

*

After dinner I went on Facebook. But as I was logging on, my phone rang. *Number Withheld.*

'Hello?'

'Hi, Lisa. It's Emma.'

'Hi, Emma.'

'So – what's your game?'

'Game? What game?'

'You know! Cara rang me. Said she saw you at Olive with my David and his sister.'

'*Your* David? Em, you don't even talk to him anymore. Plus, you have blacklisted the guy. You told me you can't stand even the merest sight of him. So what the hell are you doing, ringing me, saying, *My David?* Get a grip! It's none of your business if I sit drinking a hundred cups of coffee with David or Carol or anyone else for that matter!'

'Yeah? So how did you get talking to him? More games, yeah? Is there any end to it, Lisa? You're doing all this to get back at me and the gang. It's so plain to see. Everyone can see what you're playing at. What's he been saying about me?'

'None of your business, Emma. You have no right ringing me asking me questions about someone who's been out of your life a year now. You and David are history. Not only that, but it seems you were also lying to me and to everyone about the way you broke up.'

'What do you mean? What did he tell you?'

'You lied to me about not knowing Mark till after you broke up with David. You were seeing him at parties all the time.'

'I was not! I knew Mark a while, but we never dated.'

'But you told me you never met him till one day in Tommy's. You're full of it, Emma. So tell me, why are you ringing me? Just because I had a coffee with your ex! You treated him awfully. Making up weird stories that he was stalking you. Blacklisting his name round the town. I mean, was it not enough for you to hurt him? But then you had to go and nearly push him over the edge. Seems you wanted the best of both worlds, Emma. And you got what you wanted. So please don't ring me again about him or for any other reason.'

'You fancy him! Is that it, Lisa? You're both weirdoes, you suit each other!'

'Bye, Emma.'

I hung up. She tried to ring me back, but I wouldn't answer. She left a voicemail.

'Everyone knows you're playing mind games, Lisa. The whole gang are on to you!'

None of them was there when I went down into the pits. Not even Steve, who I thought would have rang. But I just felt, *enough is enough, I'm not taking this kind of crap anymore. Time to move forward to wherever this new road takes me.*

My car pulled into David's driveway next day, at 3pm. On the passenger seat was an apple pie my Ma had made. I turned off the ignition and took a deep breath, apprehensive at the thought of eating in front of people I hardly knew. But I was sure I'd settle down and everything would be grand.

David opened the front door. His hair was cut short at the sides and spiked at the top with gel and he was dressed in denim jeans and a short-sleeved t-shirt.

'Come on in, Lisa,' he shouted, 'It's freezing!'

'I'm coming,' I said. 'Of course you're freezing, you mad thing! You're only wearing a t-shirt!'

'I'm still dressing. Saw you pulling up from my bedroom, so I legged it down. Carol's getting dinner.'

When he closed the door he hugged me warmly. I could smell the Lacoste cologne.

'Great to see you again, Lisa. Can I put up your jacket?'

'Sure, just let me take my phone out of the top pocket.'

As I pulled out the phone, a small note fell from my pocket onto the floor. I picked it up, but before I could read it, Carol came up the hall from the kitchen.

'Lisa!' she gushed, throwing her arms around me. 'Come on down. I've a glass of red wine poured for you. Hope you like it. There's white if you prefer.'

'Thanks, Carol. Red is fine.'

'Oh, David,' she said. 'You're so helpful, taking Lisa's jacket. Wow! Don't strain yourself. Ah, no, Lisa. He's really been very helpful. Up all afternoon, listening to Coldplay.'

'That's just a lie! I set the table and . . . and . . . took Wilson for a walk.'

'Who's Wilson?' I asked. 'Your dog?'

'Hold on. I'll introduce you. Wilson! Wilson!' he shouted up the stairs. 'Here, boy!'

This small crazy dog scampered down the stairs and into the hall, half of one of his ears missing.

'Sit, sit, Wilson,' said David, patting the dog. 'We found him on Donabate Beach, half dead. We nursed him back to health. Another dog had ripped his ear off. The vet told us there were teeth marks all over him.'

'Tell him why we called him Wilson!' laughed Carol.

'Ah, stop, Carol. It was her idea, Lisa. Just because I don't have that many friends and spend far too much of my time alone, she called him Wilson, after the ball in the Tom Hanks movie, *Castaway*. Did you ever see it? Tom Hanks is stranded on this island and makes friends with this football, and calls it Wilson. So Carol here thinks I live on my own little island and Wilson's my only mate. Funny or what!'

'Did you have to tell Lisa that story!' said David, smiling.

'I love it,' I said. 'That's a great story. So you're a bit of a loner, David?'

'No, no. I have a few friends. I used to have many more, mind, but we lost touch after we moved here seven years ago and Dad got sick. And then, of course, when Emma and I broke up, I suppose we lost touch with a lot of mutual friends. But sure, I'm happy. Isn't that right, Wilson?'

Wilson barked.

'His way of agreeing, I suppose. Right. Let's move into the kitchen, shall we? Wilson – stay. Stay!'

'Listen,' I said, 'my mother baked this for you. It's a homemade apple tart.'

'Ah, you shouldn't have gone to all that trouble.'

'Ah, I wanted to bring something. Anyway, it was my Ma. She baked it. I just watched.'

'Hope you like roast beef,' said Carol, opening the oven door.

'Oh, anything will do me, Carol. I'm not a bit fussy. Thanks very much for asking me over. It means a lot to me. You've both saved my Christmas from all but going down the drain. I loved talking with you yesterday. Felt like a big weight came off my shoulders.'

'Ah, that's great to hear, isn't it?' said David. 'Yeah. That's what we want. We want to be friends and help you in any way we can. As well as that – you're . . . normal!'

We all laughed.

'Must be ten years since I met a real, normal person.'

'Oh, I don't know about being normal, David. But I'm slowly returning to it, I hope.'

'Here,' said Carol. 'There's your glass of wine. I think we'll dish up this dinner before Dad wakes up from his afternoon nap.'

She glanced at the kitchen clock.

'Richie's running late, so it's just the three of us, I'm afraid.'

I sipped the wine, savouring the mellow taste.

''Mmm. Nice. So – where do both of you work?'

'I work in Boots Chemists three days a week,' said Carol. 'David does three days a week in a sports centre in Balbriggan. Very fit-minded, is our David!'

'Yeah,' he grinned. 'I just show them what to do, then sit down and read the paper. Great job!'

'We both have to take turns helping Dad. So that's why we both cut our hours to three days. We have Home Help coming in every day as well for a few hours.'

'Yeah,' David sighed. 'He depends on us a lot. Our ma passed away some years ago. I was only fourteen at the time.'

He glanced towards Carol as if to say, *Ok, I know. Not really the time to be bringing up such sad memories.*

'I'm so sorry about your ma. My dad is dead five years now, so I know the feelings that come with such a loss.'

I swirled the wine round the glass and placed it back on the table.

'Anyway,' I said, as brightly as I could, 'so you're getting married next year! How long have you and Richie been dating?'

'Since we were both fifteen. We were what you might call teen sweethearts. He's my only one love. He used to carry my bag from school every day. He dropped into my heart, I dropped into his. We closed the door and have lived there ever since.'

'Wow,' I said, taking another sip. 'So romantic. And so rare.'

'Oh,' said David, 'she's so blessed. Both of them are. How come we all can't have it that easy? Just jump into my heartbeat forever, close the door and *Yippee! Away we go!* Wouldn't it be so cool? But oh, no. The rest of us get drawn into a web. Then hurt, rejected. Big ten-inch blade rammed into your soul. *Take that, and that and that!* Twisting the blade to make sure you'll never recover from the pain! But our Carol? She's the luckiest woman alive!'

'Stop, David,' said Carol. 'You're putting me off my roast beef!'

'Speaking of roast beef,' I said, 'your cooking is great, Carol. The roast is so tender.'

'Thanks, Lisa. So tell me – if it's ok asking – have you ever been in a long-term relationship?'

Carol stared at me, hoping she wasn't asking the wrong questions at the wrong time.

'Nah, you're grand, Carol,' I said, taking another sip of courage from the glass. 'I've no problem talking about past relationships. I had a couple. But would you call it love? Real love? Like what you and Richie seem to have? Don't think so. I was with a guy for four years. Ron was his name. I thought he was my perfect match. I worshipped the ground he walked on. Did everything for him. Then found out he was doing the dirt behind my back for a year. It was awful. I . . .'

David interrupted.

'Tell me about it! They draw you in, then rip you apart!'

'David,' whispered Carol. 'Let her finish.'

'Sorry.'

'I mean,' I continued, 'when I look back now I ask, did he ever love me at all? I suppose when you're so close to someone you can't see the wood for the trees. Maybe you don't want to see the truth, that you're really in this on your own.'

David chipped in again.

'Sorry, Lisa. Sorry, Carol. But these people don't have a clue about love to begin with. You put your heart and soul into them, but get nothing in return.'

'Ok, ok, David,' said Carol. 'Why don't you go and cut up Mrs Webb's apple pie. And whip the cream. Yeah.'

There was an awkward silence as David stood up.

'Can I take your plates with me?'

'Yeah, sure,' she said. 'I'm all done. Are you, Lisa?'

'Yeah, yeah. I've just room left for some of Ma's dessert.'

When David left the room, Carol closed the door.

'Listen, Lisa,' she whispered, 'I'm sorry. I really am. I don't know if David told you the story about Emma?'

'. . . Yeah, he told me most of it, I think.'

'Well, he's far from over it. Believe me, that girl hurt him so badly. He says it's in the past, but once someone brings up being hurt, he flies off the handle. He's a lot better than he was, mind you. If only you saw him six months ago. He was all over the place. I still think he's got feelings for her. don't ask me why. She never gave a damn about him, played him for a fool. I never got on with her from Day One. Saw right through her games. But you couldn't tell David that. He thought she was Miss Perfect.'

She glanced towards the door.

'What killed me, Lisa, is this: I know David has a heart of gold. Wouldn't hurt a fly. It was awful for him, with Dad sick and picking up the pieces after Emma dumped him.'

'God, that's awful. Was he ever tempted to go back on the coke after the split?'

'Oh, God, no, Lisa. Not for a second. But that's a long story. I'll leave it to David to tell you about it when you're up to it, when the time is right. It's an unusual story, Lisa.'

'Apple pie and cream!' announced David, carrying the tray back into the room. 'I'll need a workout after this.'

He gave each of us a portion.

'Sorry for being so negative. I know there are so many people who wouldn't dream of playing games with people's lives.'

He stared at me with those gentle blue eyes of his and didn't let go. I didn't know where to look.

'Cream?'

'Sorry? Oh, yes. Just a little bit on the side.'

He smiled.

'So, have you heard from any of your mates since yesterday?'

'No,' I sighed. 'And I don't think I ever will, either. I saw three of them just after you left Olive. They were in a car. They looked so hung over from the coke and drink at Cara's party the night before. God, those awful hangovers after the coke. I used to hate them.'

'Tell me about it!' he said, tucking into his own apple tart. 'God, I used to be a party animal. Thought I was a superstar. Had an answer to everything. Full of confidence. Line after line.'

He put down his fork.

'Greed, Lisa. That's what it was. That's what I became – a greedy little fool. Never had enough. All judgement goes out the window when you take too much. Can't judge how high you are, so you just keep taking it.'

He dabbed some cream onto his next forkful.

'My God, the things I did and said on coke. The things I texted! The phonecalls. Thinking everyone was feeling what I was feeling. But at the time, *Ah, it's the buzz!* Isn't that what we all said? We laugh at the warnings. The danger. *There's nothing wrong with a few lines. And a few more lines. I'm well in control. What's the harm in it? Sure we're all at it!*

'That's the mindset, and Lisa, it doesn't surprise me you couldn't fit back in with your mates. It's another world. I mean that in the truest sense of the word. *It's another world.*'

I placed my plate on the coffee table.

'I know what you mean, David. I lived for a line. I loved the buzz and saw nothing wrong. And, to be honest, it gave me, well, what I thought was a wonderful freedom. I lived for that buzz. But now . . . well . . . I feel . . . fooled. Tricked. By something with a mind of its own.'

'I know. I know that feeling. Anyhow, who wants another slice of that apple pie? Tell your mother she knows her apple pies. This is the best I've tasted in years. Carol?'

'No, David, you're grand. I'll go. Stay where you are. Anyone for another slice?'

'Oh, bring it in,' he laughed. 'Why not? I'll fit it in somehow!'

He rubbed his tummy.

When Carol left, I moved closer to David, looking into his eyes.

'You know, it's the next day, the morning after, that really got to me. That awful sense of . . . fear. Did you ever feel that?'

Our eyes locked.

'Eh, yeah. I know it well, Lisa,' he said, turning his head away. 'Too well. It's the worst feeling ever. Carol is lost listening to this. She never took drugs. Ever. Talking about the next day, well, you have to have been through it all to understand. I'm really glad we met you.'

There was another one of those silent moments when we just sat, looking into each other's eyes. He flicked a piece of pastry from the table into the fireplace.

'I think Carol really digs you. She thinks you're so . . . real, so down-to-earth. What age are you again?'

'Twenty-three. Well, nearly twenty-four. In March.'

'Carol's twenty-nine. My big sister. She hasn't that many friends around this area. I think you two would get on great.'

'Sure. I'd love to be mates with her. I need a top-up in that area of my life!'

Carol came back in and beamed a lovely smile. She put the pie down and came over and hugged me, without a word.

For a couple of hours more we just sat and talked, joking and laughing, David smoking, of course. And as the evening went on I felt that wonderful bond of friendship gelling the three of us together.

*

Meanwhile, back in John's house, Cara was making dinner when John's phone rang. It was James O'Connor again.

'Hi, John. Listen. That information you gave me about Jason Bailey – yeah. The little scumbag, selling coke over in your bird's party! It's been sorted. You won't have any more problems. So forget about it. Right?'

'Ok. What's happening about it? Did you find him and warn him off?'

'Look – you don't need to know how we deal with scumbags like him. It's been sorted. We know his address. Listen. I'll be sending one of the lads out tomorrow around 7pm to drop off a batch and pick up cash. Will you be there?'

'Yeah. 7pm. Be great. Thanks, James.'

*

Around 6:30pm a white van pulled up outside a flat in a housing estate in Swords. Three men stepped out – James O'Connor, Rob O'Hara and Mickey Mulligan. They looked around, making sure no one was eyeballing them. Rob walked up to Number 15, closely followed by James. Mickey pulled open the side door of the van. James knocked once. The door opened. A guy in a striped shirt stood there. Jason Bailey.

'Yeah? What do you – ?'

Rob pulled a gun from his pocket and struck Jason across the head, stunning him. Mick put a black bag over his head.

'Open your mouth,' said Rob, 'and I'll shoot you in the f**king head, you scumbag!'

They dragged him to the van and shoved him in the side door.

'Drive, Mickey. Drive. Go!'

The van revved up and drove away, its tyres screeching.

Jason struggled and tried to speak.

'Don't you move or I'll shoot you myself!' James shouted into his ear.

'So – where are we going, James?' said Mickey, glancing in the rearview mirror.

'The old barn, where do you bloody think. Darryl's meeting us there.'

They drove down an old dirt road, switching off the lights.

'Get him out. Get him out!'

Holding him by both arms, they dragged him into the barn, pulling off the black bag that was over his head.

He gasped for breath, covered in sweat. Standing in front of him was eighteen-stone gang leader, Darryl Casey. James and Rob stood each side of him. Mickey stood at the entrance.

'Ok. I'll make this real easy for you, Jason Bailey. That's your name, isn't it? Dragging me out here, away from my wife and kids. I've one question. Give me the answer and you can go. Who are you dealing coke for on my patch? Don't lie to me now. You were out selling a few nights ago in the Skerries area. Don't mess with me. Just tell me which gang from the Southside you're working with.'

Jason said nothing.

'You're selling a pure form of coke. We got word the other night. Now you're starting to get on my f**king nerves!'

'I never sold anyone coke in my life. I don't know what you're talking about.'

'Aah – a little smartarse! Is that what we have on our hands!' he said, smiling at the others. 'Do you realise who I am? Do you realise I have the power to release you or kill you?'

'You have no power, mate,' said Jason, without a hint of fear in his voice. 'And any power you think you have is worthless, Darryl. That is your name, isn't it?'

The other guys looked at each other.

'You have money,' continued Jason. 'You have cars, a big house. You have coke.'

He points at the guys.

'You have your men. But no, you've never known real power. And a day will come, trust me, when you're going to be on your own deathbed. Moments from death, gasping for breath, everything going away from you. Everything you ever held dear, all of it slipping away. At that moment you will realise you never had any real power. You just fooled yourself into thinking you had. But as you gasp your last breath of life, you'll see it was a worthless power! Nothing in it at all. And I'm afraid, that won't be the end of it.'

Jason raised his hand pointing to the rest of the gang members.

'Something dark will be awaiting you, all of you, and that's only the beginning!!!'

The rage in Darryl's face said it all. He just completely lost his head. 'Shoot him! Shoot the f**ker, James!'

'But . . . but . . .' said James, waving the gun away from Jason. 'You said we have to find out!'

'Give me the f**king gun!' shouted Darryl, grabbing it from James's hand, his body racing with coke-fuelled rage. He pointed it at Jason, just five feet away.

'No one talks to me like that!'

A shot rang out, hitting Jason on the side of the head. A gush of blood burst out of the neat round hole in his temple, sending his body turning back towards Darryl. Another shot followed, hitting him on the side of the face just under his right eye. A third shot rang out, hitting him in the chest, sending his body turning full circle before hitting the ground. Dark red blood oozed out of the three gaping wounds. Jason's body jerked and twitched on the ground, his legs kicking as the life ebbed out of him.

Darryl was breathing heavily, the sweat dripping down his body.

'Jaysus. The little scumbag! Talking to me like that! Did you hear him, James? Did you hear what he said to me! James – you drive. Drive back with me. You pair – wrap this fool up and bury him in the woods on the way up to the Wicklow Mountains. The usual place. You know it. Yeah. Make sure he's not found for a few years. We don't want a bloody feud on our hands for the New Year.'

Rob and Mickey wrapped his body in plastic and bundled him into the van. They took a spade from the back of the barn and drove off.

Darryl and James drove off in James's car. For a few minutes they said nothing. Then Darryl punched the dashboard in a fury.

'That scumbag! He'll be talking back to the dead tonight. No one – I mean *no one* – ever talks to me like that!'

He punched the dashboard again.

'Easy, Darryl,' said James, looking at the marks on his dashboard. 'He won't be selling any more coke. Here – have a fag. Cool off, mate. It's over now. Cheeky little f**ker.'

*

Meanwhile, back in David and Carol's house, Richie arrived.

'Hi, all!' he said, bending over to kiss Carol. 'Missed you.'

'Eh, you saw her a few hours ago,' said David.

I just smiled. You could feel the bond between them. Pure magic.

'So,' he said, taking off his glasses and wiping them, 'this is Lisa. How do you do? That kiss has me all fogged up!'

Carol brought him his re-heated dinner from the kitchen.

'Oh, thanks, love. I'm so hungry after pulling pints all day.

David and Carol told me you were beautiful, Lisa. And they were right.'

I blushed.

'Ah, it's the make-up, Richie. Just the make-up.'

'You *are* beautiful!' came Carol's voice from the kitchen.

David, not knowing where to look, said nothing.

'Enough, enough, thank you!' I said.

'Well, it's great to meet you, Lisa. You'll be sick of us before long. We're all a bit crazy, Carol did tell you. Didn't you, Carol?'

'No, Richie, I told her you're the looney around here. We're all sane. Or are we?'

My phone rang. It was Ma.

'Sorry, guys, have to take this.'

I pulled the phone out of my pocket, pulling with it the note that was with it. I held it half open as I talked to Ma.

'They all loved your apple tart, Ma. I'll be home soon.'

As I put the phone down on the table I opened the note fully. The writing was blurry.

'What's this?' I said, trying to make it out.

'What's what, Lisa?' said David, all three of them looking at me.

'Are you ok?' asked Carol, concerned.

'How did this note get into my pocket? Can you make that out?'

I handed the note to David.

'Yeah, yeah. It reads

G27 Hope we'll see each other again. Sorry for leaving in such a hurry. Jason Bailey x'

Chapter Fourteen

The White Plague

Jason Bailey. That's the guy from Cara's party. The bloody weirdo. What does G27 mean? What does the note mean? He must have put it in on the way out.

'I'm so lost,' said Richie, looking around at the rest of us.

'Oh, we'll explain it all to you later, pet,' said Carol. 'Just eat your dinner.'

David stared at the note.

'Well, G27 is a room number, isn't it?'

'You took the words right out of my mouth,' mumbled Richie, through a mouthful of food. 'That's a room at a hotel, or it could be a safe deposit box at AIB Bank, for all you know.'

'Yeah,' David chuckled. 'There wouldn't be much in AIB after the big cleanout – maybe just an IOU note!'

'God, I'm puzzled,' said Carol, looking at me strangely. 'Why would he put a note in your pocket?'

'You know,' said David, holding the note in both hands, 'it may be the name of some new drug that he spiked you with, or as Carol suggested maybe it's the name of some strange form of hypnosis, God only knows. All I know, Lisa, is that very weird people show up at drug parties. I've met my share of oddballs down through the years.'

He folded the note and held it up.

'I'll tell you what. Leave this with me. I'll do everything I can to find out if there's anything to uncover. I wouldn't let it wreck my head. The main thing is, *you* know, plus, *we* know you're off all that crap. Ok?'

'Yeah, you're right,' I agreed. 'Yeah. You keep it.'

'Oh, leave it to David!' said Carol. 'He'll pull an answer from under some stone. You can bet your life on it, Lisa. Sherlock Holmes wouldn't get a look in at him!'

'So, anyway, I better get going. I told Ma I'd spend some time with her tonight. Maybe watch a dvd. Listen – thank you so much for asking me over. It was a lovely meal and I had a lovely time chatting to you all. You're a breath of fresh air to me.'

'It's been great having you, Lisa,' said Carol, standing up. 'Here. Take my phone number, put it in your phone.'

' Yeah, sure and you take mine.'

'You can have mine too – that's if you want,' said David, sounding a bit self-conscious.

'Yeah, give me yours, David,' I said, smiling reassuringly. 'Of course.'

I put my jacket on, though to be honest, I wanted to stay. I loved these people's company, and couldn't help but feel that I might never hang out with the gang again once I went out of their company.

As Carol walked me to the door, she said,

'Why don't you come to Tommy's tomorrow night with us? I could do with your company again. Can you make it?'

'Yeah, sure,' I jumped. 'Would love to go. Be great!'

She hugged me.

'You know, it's great getting to know you. I hope we can get to know each other better. I'd like that.'

'Me too,' I beamed. 'You're a great family.'

'Oh, I think I hear Dad. He's awake. Back to work. No rest for the wicked!'

As I closed my car door I looked back at the house. David was at the front sitting room window, waving and giving me one of his smiles.

As I drove down Skerries Main Street I realised that I needed to clear the air with Tommy, especially as I was going there the following night with Carol and David. I parked in a side street and walked through the doors of Tommy's Bar, feeling somewhat nervous. I asked Sharon, the bar girl, if Tommy was about.

'He's in the back in his office. Will I get him, or do you want to just go back and knock on his door? He won't mind.'

I tapped gently on the office door.

'Come in. Door's open.'

I slowly opened it, feeling somewhat embarrassed.

'Ah, Lisa, come in,' he said, looking up from a mountain of paperwork on his desk. 'Sit down. Excuse the mess. How have you been?'

For a man whose mirror I had broken, he was disarmingly polite.

'I'm . . . I'm grand, Tommy.'

'Can I get you a coffee or something?'

'No, thanks. I . . . I just came by to offer my apology for what happened that night with Ian Carter, as well as the bottle breaking the mirror behind the bar. I just tried to slap him to let me go, but forgot the bottle was still in my hand. I know it's no excuse, so I'm very sorry about it all.'

'Well, that's great that you came down of your own accord to apologise. It's not like you at all to act in such a way. Not since I first met you some years ago have I seen you lose the head in such a manner.'

I clicked open my handbag.

'I want to pay for the mirror.'

He held up his hand.

'Look, it's ok this time, Lisa. Just please – don't let it happen again. I've customers to think about and if I was to let everyone bounce bottles off each others' heads, the pub would end up like John D.'s Pub – or, as they nicknamed it, John E.'s. Plus, you have to remember, if that bottle had hit another customer, I'd be in trouble along with you. But, saying all that, you don't have to pay for the mirror. It's in the past, but no more rows, Lisa. Ok?'

'Ok, thanks. I've just been going through a very bad few weeks and, well, it's all sorted now, thank God. Personal stuff, Tommy.'

'Well, ok. Great to hear whatever you went through is behind you. Will we see you at the New Year's Party as usual?'

'Nah, not this year. But I'm coming down tomorrow night with a few friends.'

'Hmm. Cara and the girls, yeah?', he sighed.

'No, no. They're new mates. David Salle and his sister Carol. And her boyfriend Richie.'

He looked relieved.

'Ah, yeah. Lovely people. I know Carol well. Lovely person. She eats here a lot at weekends.'

He glanced at his watch.

'Ok. So we'll see you tomorrow. Thanks for coming down. Great seeing you looking better as well.'

'Thanks, Tommy. Are you sure you won't take something to pay for the mirror?'

'No, no, it's grand. It's in the past, Lisa. See you tomorrow.'

When I sat back in my car something just prompted me to ring Ian Carter. I took a deep breath and dialled the number. It rang and rang. *Was this such a good idea?* Just before I hung up, he answered.

'Hi, Lisa.'

'Hi, Ian. Listen, this is just a call to say I'm sorry for hitting you with the bottle that night. I thought I'd put the bottle down.' *God, I'm sounding like a broken record.*

'Ah, it's cool, Lisa. No worries. I've had worse done to me! Thanks for the call. So – would you like to meet for a chat sometime?'

'No, it's ok, Ian. Thanks anyway.'

A traffic warden was making his way down the street, checking each parked car for parking tickets. I had none. I turned on the ignition.

'Ok. Sure I'm sure I'll see you over the New Year at some stage, yeah?'

'Yeah, sure. Gotta go. Take care, Ian.'

'You too. Happy New Year, Lisa!'

'Same to you, Ian. Bye.'

I drove home feeling better for having sorted out that issue. After pulling up in my driveway, I sat in the car reflecting on the day I'd spent with David and Carol. What a lifesaver it had been finding people like them at such a time as this.

I turned off the engine and opened the door to step out, when that warm feeling came racing across my heart again I put it all down to returning to the real me from being on the coke. Nothing else made sense as to what it was, but it was mysterious to say the least.

I sat with Ma for the evening.

'Well, Lisa. Tell me before we watch the film. What's David like?'

She had that smile in her eyes. I had to laugh.

'Ah, it's nothing like you're thinking, Ma. We're just mates, just good friends. Anyway, he's still hung up on a girl.'

'Well, what does he look like? Is he a hunk or what? Tell me!' she laughed.

'He's really good-looking. He has lovely eyes that I find hard to look back at. You'd think he could read your mind. *And* he has a lovely personality.'

'Is that a spark I see in your eyes, Lisa?'

'No, Ma, no. Ok – the film. What film is on tonight?'

'Well, *Castaway* is on at 9 o'clock. Have you seen it?'

'Oh yes, with Tom Hanks. Yeah, I've seen it,' I laughed.

'What's so funny, pet?'

'Nothing, Ma. How about one of those 80s films you love to watch? *Children of a Lesser God* with William Hurt. That's one you always talk about.'

'Oh, yeah, put it on. It's been years since I watched it. Your dad loved that one. He loved the ending. Used to hide the tear in his eye or get up and yawn and pretend that was the cause of the tears. I'd say nothing, of course.'

'Sounds lovely, Ma. Sitting together watching a romantic film. I can just imagine the pair of you.'

My phone beeped with a text. It was David.

Carol's going to work tomorrow at 3pm. Would you be free to meet me? There's something I need to tell you in full about why I gave up taking coke. I feel you have told me everything about your reasons and it's only right I tell you my story. David.

I texted back.

Sure. Where do you want to meet? Would Olive be ok again? You know their coffee is the best on the planet.

Can't be in Olive, Lisa. It has to be my house. Dad will be asleep. It will be just you and me. It will take a while to explain the whole story to you.

Ok. Your house at 3. I'll bring some of Olive's coffee and some of their yummy homemade buns. How's that sound?

Latte for me! That's great. Look forward to seeing you Lisa. Night. David.

I couldn't help but feel that there was something strange about it all. The secrecy surrounding his reason for kicking coke had been odd from day one. Most people come out and just say why they gave up drugs, but David's story seemed almost as if it was sealed away from the whole world. The look in his eyes when it came up. Even Carol's reaction. I must say I was becoming very intrigued.

After another lovely night's sleep I woke up and went jogging. The weather was so cold, but I beat the elements once again. I cleaned the house for Ma, did some shopping for her, then, before I knew it I was pulling up in David's driveway with the lattes and buns from Olive.

I could see David at the window, looking somewhat nervous, rubbing the side of one of his arms with his other hand.

He opened the door slowly and quietly.

'Don't want to wake Dad,' he whispered, his eyes still as warm as yesterday. God, inside I was just dying to know what this story entailed. He bent over and hugged me gently, almost knocking the coffees out of my hand.

'Crap! Sorry, Lisa. Come into the sitting room.'

I followed him, conscious of not making any unnecessary noise.

'Why are we being so quiet today, and yesterday we were all chatting loudly, if I remember rightly?'

'I know,' he said, still in a hushed tone. 'But yesterday, if Dad woke up, both Carol and I were here. If he wakes up, it's just me till Carol gets home. She's due back around 6pm.'

He quaffed a mouthful of latte, then looked me straight in the eye.

'My grandmother left this house to my dad. When we moved in, we came across a stairway leading from the hallway down to a kind of basement. It had been put in years ago by our granddad. The only one in the street, I think. Just one big room. He stored wine there, amongst other things. But after we moved in I had this idea of turning it into a gym. But the lack of ventilation put paid to that. Then, other things happened in my life which led me to use it for a totally different purpose. If I'm going to explain the whole story, I'll have to bring you down. Is that ok with you?'

'Well, ok. Lead the way!' I said, feeling a mixture of intrigue and nervousness.

He led me down the dark, unlit stairway. *Hell, I hope he hasn't got ten dead bodies down here!*

At the bottom of the steps he unlocked the door and pushed it open.

'Mind that last step, Lisa,' he said.

He turned on the spotlights in the ceiling. Yes, indeed. It was quite a big room. On one wall, from one end of the room to the other, were large noticeboards displaying what seemed like newspaper cuttings. There were arrows pointing from one clipping to another, with handwritten comments beside each item. There was one small table to the right of the basement, with two chairs. And that was it.

My eyes fixed on a small framed picture on the table. It was a photo of a young lad. I looked across at David. He too was staring at the picture, saying nothing. He looked like he was trying to hide been upset.

'Who's that in the photo?' I asked, trying to sound casual. 'He looks like someone I've seen somewhere before.'

David pulled out the couple of chairs.

'Here, sit down, Lisa. Maybe I should start at the beginning,' he sighed, as we both sat down. 'It was a cold, December morning back in 2006. I had been at an all-nighter of coke and drink with some mates from that time. I was coming home in a taxi, flying out of my head, still waffling away like 90 to the taxi guy.'

I could now see a different side to David. It was like he had left the other side of his nature at the top of the stairs and was now beginning to open up his heart and share a new side of his life to me. It was like a veil fell from him. I can't explain it any other way. His voice was deadly serious.

'It was just after 12 o'clock midday. I know that, because the taxi guy had his radio on, and he asked me to hush for a second as he tried to listen to what was being said on the 98fm news. All I could make out was they were talking about a gangland shooting of some kind, which I didn't give a damn about. All I wanted was to keep talking about the party I'd been at, so I took no notice. I got home and tricked around for an hour, smoking a couple of joints of grass to try and mellow out from the coke. Just before I went to bed to catch up on some sleep I put on the tv. RTE News was on. Well, it was all about that gangland shooting.'

David picked up the framed photograph.

'That photo,' he sighed, 'is of a kid by the name of Anthony Campbell, a twenty-year-old apprentice plumber who just happened to be in Martin "Marlo" Hyland's house that December morning. A couple of hit-men came to the house to shoot Hyland. They shot this young innocent kid in the head, just because he had seen both their faces and might identify them.

'I sat there, Lisa, with a joint in my mouth, coked up to the eyes, staring in disbelief at the tv. God, I'd heard about gangland killings. We all had. But something happened to me, I can't explain it. It was as if something gave way, deep inside me. In disgust, I stubbed out the unfinished joint in the ashtray. A chill ran right through me. I felt I had that young man's blood on my hands. Like somehow I was involved, because I had bought the coke. We all had. I felt that anyone who takes this drug was aiding and abetting his murder. If none of us ever bought coke, that kid would still be alive today. I know only too well that nobody else taking coke would see it that way. But it's how I felt personally.

'I remember I stood up, turned off the tv, stumbled to the bathroom and got sick. Violently sick. It was horrible – beyond words. I got a bag of coke I'd hidden on top of the wardrobe and flushed it down the loo. As I watched it disappear I vowed I'd never touch drugs again from that moment onwards. And I never have.'

He paused for effect, letting me absorb the details. I smiled at him in admiration and empathy.

'I've never told anyone that story – just Carol, Richie and now you. I never even told Emma, 'cause, well, she was still taking coke, so she wouldn't have listened to me, would she!'

I kept looking at David. You could see a tear in his eye as he placed the photo of the unfortunate Anthony Campbell back on the table and held his emotions in check.

'So that's your story, David?' I said. 'That's why you stopped taking coke? It's so different to my story. Plus, it's the most unusual reason. I mean, God, how many people do you think stopped taking drugs over that poor kid's murder? Most people just never link snorting coke themselves to such events as that. I know I never blinked an eyelid at any of the bloodshed surrounding drugs in this country.'

'Well, Lisa,' he said, shifting the photo slightly, 'that's just the start of it.'

He stood up and reached for a dimmer switch on the wall. He turned up the spotlights to the max so I could clearly see all the newspaper clippings. I stood up and stepped closer to get a better look. At the top, handwritten in block capitals with a black felt marker, was the word DARKLINE. One clipping after another showed photos of gangland members – some shot, some still at large. Household names and faces I knew from tv and newspaper reports down the years.

'After I stopped taking the coke that day young Campbell was murdered, I watched all the outpouring of grief, of anger, of real rage on tv and in the papers. My God – his mother, Lisa! I'll never forget seeing her, heartbroken. It did something to me. For days I was haunted by her face, and then, the face of her young son. I mean, I was twenty at the time, same age. My mates thought I was losing the plot because I kept asking them how they felt about his death. "Life goes on, David!" That's all they had to say. "Nothing to do with us. We're only taking a few lines and having the buzz."

'When I told them I was off the coke for good, they drifted away from me – just like your mates did. I was left very much alone. And from then onwards, without thinking too much about it, I was drawn into wanting to study the whole drug culture. The whole bloody history. I think the fact that someone would shoot dead an innocent child in cold blood sparked off the beginning of my realisation that there was something much darker behind the world of drugs than the vast majority of people out there comprehended. I started to cut out these newspaper clippings and keep them down here. Just in a folder at first, but then I started to stick them on noticeboards, and the display just got bigger and bigger till it became what you see in front of you.

'Have you ever heard of Paul Williams, Lisa?' he asked.

'Yeah, yeah, I know him,' I said. 'The guy who writes all the books and reports about gangland.'

'Yeah, that's him.'

'I read that book of his, *The Untouchables.*'

'Well, I sat and watched him on tv as he pulled those gangland drug murderers apart, using all the worst words he could muster – *new breed of thugs, scum of the earth*. On and on he went, ripping them apart, right down to the bone. He's a very intelligent man, I suppose brave, as well. I've read all his books. He knows everything there is to know about this subject and the empire it's become. He knows everyone who's involved. I mean, I'm small fish next to him, Lisa. And the information he gathers, I mean, it's endless! They wage war on front line on tv against very dangerous people, but one angle, one line of thought none of them took – Williams and every other reporter right down the line – was the one I ended up taking.'

He paused for effect.

'Which is?' I offered.

'One word all the journalists and commentators used more than any other is a simple word – the word *Evil*. And Paul Williams was no exception. Me being the type I am, I studied everyone who wrote about gangland drug crime. That was my starting point. I wanted to see how many of them could really define this word *Evil*. It wasn't long before I realised none of them could. Not one. It's like they say *Evil* but then stop. No real explanation is ever put forward. Everything stops with them, right there, which I suppose is expected. Who wants to attempt to unravel something as dark as this kind of thing.

'So, well, I took it upon myself to try and uncover the origin, I suppose, of the evil behind the whole gangland empire in Ireland. Am I mad or what. My God, what a task to take on by yourself, in a spooky basement of your own home. Creepy stuff. And me with little or no experience of what the hell I was supposed to be even looking for. But I pressed on, even as I battled my own withdrawal demons after years being enslaved to that vicious addiction. I'd be down here late in the evenings looking for the ultimate truth. No stone left unturned, cutting out paper clippings, interesting printouts, write-ups, photographs – you name it, Trying to form my own picture bit by bit, slowly beginning to understand the true nature of it all.'

He touched my hand lightly.

'Are you ok? I hope I'm not boring you?'

'Not in the least,' I assured him. 'My God, I so admire your passion, your all-out dedication. When all your friends turned a blind eye, you took yourself away from taking coke and devoted yourself to this single-minded idea. It must have taken you to some very dark corners, putting all your brain power into trying to uncover the truth in such a murky underworld as you've described.'

'You could say that, I suppose,' he nodded.

I pointed to his wall display.

'Has Carol ever seen this? Or Richie? Have they ever been down here?'

'Just Carol, she's seen it. She lasted thirty seconds! I can still hear her skipping up those stairs. "Far too much information, David," she said to me. "I mean, I love you to bits, but this is too much for me. Sorry!" Ah, it comes up now and again. But God, I don't blame her. Would you? I mean, it's not called DARKLINE for nothing. This is the stuff of nightmares. Trying to unveil, to uncover the meaning of Evil. Trying to dabble in the world of the unseen forces behind all of what you see on this wall.'

David was now standing up, and he bent down level with my eyeline.

'I hope this is not frightening you. If it is, just tell me. I wouldn't be offended in any way.'

'No, no. I don't know why, but I'm not afraid, David. Carry on, Professor!' I said, smiling.

'Great. You do know if I'm right in my findings, then this country's moving into something so terrifying beyond anything anyone can comprehend.'

I fidgeted in my seat, not knowing why. Then it dawned on me – the room was quite airless. David picked up on that immediately.

'I know – it's a bit stuffy down here. One of the problems of building a basement without planning permission, I suppose.'

'David, if what you feel is right in your heart about this whole subject, that's all that matters right now. We're all too small to change the whole world's views. But at least you're trying to understand something which is one of the biggest issues in Ireland today. So carry on. Explain more to me.'

'Ok, thanks. . . em, I'll go through this without going into all the details, or we'll be here till next Christmas. Just a short review of some of the main facts as they unfolded.

'Most of the drug trade has its main roots in Larry Dunne's gang back in the late 70s, early 80s. It's widely accepted that Dunne and his brothers were the first to import the drug heroin (smack) onto the streets of the working class in the inner city of Dublin, destroying many families in the process. But looking closely at the drug heroin – it's brown in colour, you have to put needles into your body, it's a very downer buzz. Most addicts just nod off to sleep in the end. It's got Death written all over it. To the masses of people it's just not appealing. People fear it. They know – one hit, you're hooked.

'I knew, even looking that far back, that this drug would never captivate the wider section of society into its deadly net. And I was right. When the Dunne Gang came to an end in the 80s, Larry Dunne left us with his chilling and dark prophecy that worse would follow in his steps – a prophecy that would soon be fulfilled.

'If you skip down to the new craze drug, ecstasy – in the early 90s, when it came, out, guess which drug was coming up behind it? Coke. Following behind, riding on the back of another part of the whole illusion, the Celtic Tiger. The whole thing, when you stand back and fix your eyes on the unseen, it almost seems like a horrible, evil mind-set, planning out its deadly game.

'Going back to the ecstasy. Most people just drank and smoked hash up to this point. But now all the young people were drawn into this new drug. Even the music had changed to suit the buzz from the drug. Behind the drug trade you had people like Martin 'The Viper' Foley. And maybe the one everyone won't forget, John Gilligan and his gang, who pumped the whole of Ireland with drugs on his watch.

'Now for the first time we have a drug that can kill you, but unlike heroin, no needles, just a tablet. Down the throat and away you go. Dancing out of your brains for the night.

'So now the new net was pulling all classes of people in – people from families without any real upbringing issues, well-to-do people – all being drawn into what seemed a harmless enough drug. But, as I said, you watch behind all this and, bit by bit, the coke was replacing ecstasy for many people, creeping slowly into people's lives.

'Which brings me to my theory, that I believe there is something unseen, something with a certain mindset, involved in all of this. If you watch Gilligan, It was no secret that he was taking coke himself and began to become reckless. The more he took, the more it started to change him. A darker, more sinister person began to emerge. He became paranoid about everything. And the threat upon him by one journalist, Veronica Guerin, led him to snap. Or something dark made him snap. Take your pick. So on the 26th June 1996 Gilligan's gang fired five shots into her at point blank range with a powerful magnum handgun.

'All hell broke loose. Suddenly, everyone awoke from their comas. They brought in the Criminal Assets Bureau (the CAB). They brought down Gilligan and his gang and jailed the lot of them. The Government put a lid on it all. Evil had been put to bed. And when people look back, most see it as a great victory, a landmark in the fight against the drug underworld bosses.

'But when you look closer it's not! Most felt the war against drugs was to a large degree being won. And while people like Paul Williams were making a small fortune on their writings and books a greater, more sinister story of evil was about to unfold.

'This other event is the real landmark, a proof to me in this study anyway that you're not just dealing with human powers.'

'Go on, tell me,' I said, trying to hide the fact I was now becoming a little nervous of the route we were on.

'A more ruthless story came to life when the new drug dealers, Declan Gavin and his then best mate Brian Rattigan took over the drug scene. Only eighteen years of age, yet they masterminded the drugs trade, with coke becoming the main drug, while ecstasy fell back to second place. When they both became big-timers, there was a split over a raid in a hotel in which Gavin was supervising, himself and members of the gang were bagging coke for sale, and the cops got wind of it. From there on, after Gavin was arrested (but not charged, as he was in the next room, not in the room where the coke was being bagged). Rattigan became paranoid that Gavin was ratting to the cops, and they went their separate ways.

'In August 2001, outside the Abrekebabra Restaurant on the Crumlin Road, Gavin was spotted by a couple of members of Rattigan's gang. In no time at all, Rattigan himself drove to the spot, coked up to the eyes, and – allegedly – drove a large knife into Gavin's heart, killing him in front of a dozen or so people. That knife going into Declan Gavin's heart opened up a new world of evil never seen before in the history of organised crime.

Crime writer Mick McCaffrey in his book *Cocaine Wars* called the events of that night, *The Curse*.

'After Gavin's murder, all hell did indeed break loose. Fifteen violent young gang members were murdered in what's commonly known as the Crumlin/Drimnagh Feud. Gavin's right-hand man, Freddie Thompson on one side, Rattigan on the other. Now killing each other off. Guns out, really for the first time.

'Now you have the papers and Paul Williams all back on the bandwagon, scratching their heads, not confused at the outward effects it's having on so many young lives, but confused that there seems to be a deeper manifestation of Evil now controlling the new gangs, which left the authorities bewildered on all sides. The word hangs in the air but again no one can define it . . .

'Ah, I could be here all night till next year, going through it all. The Westies Gang. Shane Coates. Stephen Sugg. The same again. Pure evil at work, Williams said. Both killed in 2004. The list goes on, and will continue to go on. But one thing I was certain of is now only one drug was pushed to the forefront which was always the goal from the start – coke. Bloody coke. Not like the deadly drug heroin. No, no. This is a white powdered drug with such words to embellish it as *Pure. White*. A drug you can control over a few pints with your mates at the weekend.

'As you can see, I spent a lot of time down here, trying not just to watch the movements of any of these gang members, but trying to learn the mindset of evil that was advancing, using these people like pawns, with the objective to rope more and more victims into its dark web. It's like a bloody plague, the White Plague, spreading out its wings across Ireland, drawing more and more people in. If I'm right, Lisa, if there is an unseen evil behind it, then it has a set goal'.

'Which is what?'

There was a silence. As I ran my eyes slowly across David's noticeboards, a strange chill raced across my heart. I sat back in the chair but remained as calm as I could. Something in what he was saying seemed to now match the look in the faces of the gang members. It was so scary in that moment to try and imagine, what if all this is true?

'Lisa – it's after the next generation of kids, the youth coming through at this moment in time, and from what I hear it's already getting them. It's at work right now, and once it succeeds you'll end up with something like hell on earth, even worse.'

'So what are you going to do with all this information, David?' I asked. 'You've put so much time into studying it. But for what?'

'Nothing, Lisa,' he said, sitting down again. 'What can you do? I never did this to prove a point to anyone. I did it to find out for myself. Nobody out there gives a damn about this kind of thing. Anyway, I gave up a while back because for some reason I'm missing something here. Some part of the jigsaw is missing. Something I can't see. Maybe I'll never fully understand it all.'

'Ok,' I said. 'So let me ask you, just to make sure I understand what you're saying overall. You did all this study because you believe that behind all this crazy drug culture and gangland murders is some kind of living, unseen being of some kind that's instigating everyone to do . . . what? To ultimately destroy as many people as possible. Yeah?'

'Yes, that's what I'm saying. . . You know, when I was in the middle of this study, I went and interviewed a few cops. Well, I just said I was doing research into gangland crime. I really wanted to know what their frontline experience was.

'One cop pulled me to one side and told me to my face that he knew for a fact that he was dealing with something non-human. He said, "Anyone, don't care who they are, if they take just one line of that stuff, they're putting themselves into the control of something very sinister, that will in most cases take years, but in the end it will pay everyone back in some awful, dark way. It could be just a removal of what's real, an altering of one's personality. I've seen it all," he told me. "The awful increase in vicious violence outside nightclubs, people coming out crazy, fuelled up to the gills with coke, and going from being all happy to running a blade into some guy."

'So you see, Lisa, it's not just me. It's cops who see it. I never saw anything with my own eyes, but well . . . I wasn't going to tell you this, but one night I was down here about two years ago and – well don't laugh – but I swear, Lisa, it freaked my head out. I was standing facing the noticeboard like I'm standing now, and all of a sudden I felt someone was in the bloody room watching me, this awful manifestation, like someone passing by me. I froze on the spot. I never saw anything with my two eyes, but something was there, I'd swear it.'

'That's so scary, David. So scary, God! Hold on a minute. I just got this awful feeling. Just like the night in The Life Nightclub when I had that bad experience. I saw something really awful. But I never talked about it or told anyone. I put it down to a bad hallucination. But it was so real.'

'What? Tell me,' he said, trying to pull the words out of me. 'What did you see?'

'I was dancing away in great form. Then I looked out onto the dancefloor. And God, this awful-looking thing was . . . standing next to John Noonan . . .'

David sat down again pulling his chair closer to me, his face having changed dramatically.

'And what did it look like?'

'Awful, David. I screamed and went into a panic. It was a dark, grey colour. The colour of . . . My God, come to think, it had no colour, not that I could describe, anyway. I remember it had a strange, formless kind of face. God, David, I couldn't really describe it to anyone.'

'And that's all you saw?'

'Isn't that enough, David?'

'No, no. That's not what I mean. You never saw other strange things. Just that?'

'No. Everything went strange after that. But that was the only thing I saw.'

'So what was it, what was it doing with John?'

'I don't know. He was dancing away in great form with all his mates, oblivious to it all. It looked like it was trying to attach itself to him, or become part of him, then it moved slowly around the whole gang. Oh God. It creeps me out, just thinking of it, David.'

'My God, that's so strange, Lisa. I've been studying all this for some time now, and then we met, and it turns out you may have seen the real thing with your own eyes. For some reason I don't believe what you saw was a hallucination. And you have seen it for a reason.'

'God I don't know, but maybe we were supposed to link up to confirm that what you studied is fact, not fiction.'

'So – you believe all this?' he asked, somewhat assured that he was no longer alone with all his information.

'Yeah, I think it's true. In fact, it makes more sense than anything else I've ever heard. My God, David, what were we involved in taking that drug?'

'I don't know, Lisa,' he said. 'But going back to what you saw in The Life – you have to ask why your man John and that gang and no one else? Isn't he the one that's dealing the coke to the whole gang?'

'Yeah. I thought he was just dealing to a few of his mates, but over time he spread out to anyone who was looking. God, I'm so blessed to be out of all this. I ask myself *Why me?* all the time. Like, why did this only happen to me and not to the rest of the gang?'

'That's something I can't tell you, Lisa. But you're out. You're safe. And I can see a different girl to the girl peeping at me from behind the pillar in the Blue Ocean.'

I think David knew it was time to lighten the atmosphere, and fast.

'You . . . you saw me?'

'How could I not! I was watching the whole lot of you all night. Maybe I bumped into you on purpose when you were leaving!' he laughed.

'You miss nothing, do you!'

'No, I'm serious. You do look different.'

'I do? In what way?' *God, I hope I'm not blushing.*

'Your face was thinner, I think. But it's filling out now quite nicely. Plus, that look people have who take coke – that look has gone from your eyes.'

We both looked into each other's eyes for a moment in silence. There was a connection between us. There we were, in an airless basement, surrounded by a rogues' gallery from Ireland's drug trade, the only innocent picture that of young Anthony Campbell. Under his picture was a quote from a reporter at the time of the killing:

He was not in the wrong place at the wrong time.
They made it the wrong place at the wrong time.

Chapter Fifteen

A Dead Son Rising

We went back upstairs, glad to be out of the heavy atmosphere of the basement. It felt good to breathe the fresher air of the sitting room, with natural daylight coming in through the bay window, as we continued to talk about David's findings. Like me, he seemed more at ease now that we weren't close up to the faces of so many gangland members.

He went on to talk about the side effects coke has on people's lives, and how the unseen world weaves its dark spell like a deadly web of deceitfulness, leading ordinary people astray, too often to a tragic end.

My own story, culminating in the episode in The Life, was beginning to make sense. Seeing the parallels between my experience and what David had to say, I could see the missing parts of the jigsaw falling into place. Although, in a strange way, deep down, I didn't *want* to believe it.

David asked all kinds of questions about that dark night in The Life. His interest now seemed renewed. He kept jotting down notes, like he was working for Crimewatch – standing up, sitting down, tapping his middle finger on his bottom lip. His mind was racing with his new-found information. He seemed so certain of what he was doing, what he was heading into, there was a sparkle in his eye which suggested he was closing in that bit further on completing his project.

'It's great to have you on board, Lisa,' he said, rewarding himself by lighting up his first cigarette. He exhaled, reaching over to the mantelpiece for the ashtray. 'I know I can trust you as well.'

'But don't you find it a bit frightening, David? I mean, we don't really know what we're dealing with here, do we? Should we be opening doors into such a dangerous, unpredictable world as this? I mean – is it safe, what we're doing?'

He took another drag from his cigarette, inhaled and blew out a long plume of smoke.

'God, I know what you mean. But once we keep our findings to ourselves, everything will be ok. Who's going to care in the slightest, anyway? People out there don't give a damn about this sort of thing.'

'It's not *people* I'm worried about, David. It's . . . well, it's the *unseen world* aspect of all this. Are we not tampering with something that could harm us in some way?'

He stubbed out his cigarette and sighed, looking at me straight in the eye.

'I never really thought of it like that, Lisa. I mean, if something was going to harm us, it would have done it well by now. I just have a strong feeling that my findings and what you saw are somehow linked to a bigger picture. And our paths were destined to cross so that we would pursue this together. I just know that ever since I started this I've been missing a big piece of the jigsaw. Right from the start I had this feeling. That's why I stopped in the end, because I couldn't make it out. But maybe two heads are better than one.

'If you want out, I'll understand. I just don't think this is an accident. I want to reopen the whole study with both of us – together!'

I hesitated, then took a deep breath before replying.

'Ok – but only if . . . only if we're being extra careful.'

He placed his hand gently on mine, giving me that smile of his.

'You know, Lisa, I'm grateful for your input. You never know – we could both end up writing a book about our findings one day. How cool would that be! Maybe even outsell Paul Williams!'

We both laughed, but our laughter was cut short by a feeble, wheezy shout from the back of the house.

'David – is that you? I need help to get out of this bed.'

'Ok, Dad. Coming. I won't be a minute.'

He stood up.

'Sorry, Lisa. Oh, just to tell you, he's got Alzheimer's as well as his stroke.'

'You're grand. Take your time. Is there anything I can do?'

'No, you're fine. I won't be long.'

About two minutes later, he wheeled his very thin, frail dad into the sitting room.

'Ah, it's Emma! She's back, David!'

'That's not Emma, Dad.'

He mouthed *Sorry* to me.

'Ah, it is! Give me my glasses. I told you she'd be back!'

'It's Lisa, Dad. Lisa.'

'Lisa? Lisa who?'

'Lisa Webb, Dad.'

'Hold on till I get my glasses.'

'They're on you, Dad. Sorry, Lisa.'

'No, you're grand,' I said, standing up. 'Hello, Mr Salle. It's lovely to meet you at last. I'm Lisa Webb, a friend of David's.'

'Oh, David, she's lovely. When are you getting married?'

We both giggled.

'Dad, we're just friends. We're not getting married.'

He rolled his eyes to heaven and shrugged his shoulders, urging me to take no notice.

'Well, hello, Lisa. My God, she's lovely, David. Well done! She's nicer than Emma, you know. Come here to me, Emma – or, sorry – Lisa! Let me hold your hand. My God, David, she has the face of an angel!

Am I dead and gone to Heaven? Where's your mother, David?'

'Mother's with God, Dad! But she's watching you all the time.'

David winked at me.

'So behave yourself around Lisa, do you hear me!'

'Well, you're very welcome to my home, Lisa. I hope you and David are happy together.'

'Ok, ok, Dad. Let's get your dinner ready and get the tv on. The news is on in a few minutes. Here, I'll put it on for you.'

He picked up the remote control.

'I can put it on myself,' said Mr Salle, grabbing the remote control from David's hand. 'I'm not disabled, you know.'

'Ok, ok, Dad. You put it on.'

His dad turned away, facing the tv. He went very quiet, just staring at the screen.

We went back to gather my bag and put the takeout coffee cups into the bin.

'I better get going, David. Dinner will be ready soon.'

We stepped back into the sitting room and I went over and gave Mr Salle a peck on the cheek.

'It's lovely to have met you, Mr Salle.'

'It's Tim, Lisa. Call me Tim.'

He grasped my hand, tapping it with his fingertips.

'You're an angel!'

'Thanks, Tim.'

He looked back at the tv.

'Nothing but bad news on the News nowadays,' he sighed.

David did a double-take.

'Raise that up a bit, Dad. Sounds like gangland stuff again.'

The female newscaster was in full flow.

' . . . and for the very latest we go over to our Crime Correspondent, Paul Reynolds.'

'The grim discovery was made of what's believed to be that of the body of a man in his twenties. The body was discovered this morning by a local man out with his dog. Here behind me, in a woodland area of the Dublin / Wicklow Mountains, he came across a patch of ground that had been disturbed. He notified the local Gardaí, and the area has since been sealed off pending the arrival of the forensic team and the State Pathologist. Gardaí have not named the man as yet, but have said the man was shot a number of times and that this has all the hallmarks of another gangland murder. This is Paul Reynolds, Roundwood, County Wicklow.'

'How strange, Lisa,' said David, turning down the volume, 'we were only talking about gangland crime – and now another murder takes place.'

'Yeah,' I said, 'I wonder who it is this time. Well, Mr Salle – or Tim

– I'm off. Hope to see you soon. Take care.'

'Come back soon, Lisa.'

'I will, Tim,' I said, smiling.

He raised the volume again and changed channel.

David and I went out into the hallway.

'God, he's such a lovely man, David. I'm sure he's so proud of you.'

'Yeah – sorry about the "Emma" thing.'

'Not at all. I understand.'

David took my jacket off the hook on the wall.

'Here. Let me put it on for you . . . Turn around . . .'

'Oh, thanks.'

'There you go.'

'You're a gent.'

I turned back around, not realising how close he was to me. Our faces were just inches apart, our smiles, our eyes meeting. A warm, close encounter. We both stopped for a moment and held our breath. For the first time we gazed into each other's eyes in a way that was almost intimate. I got lost as I delved into his blue, piercing eyes. My gaze dropped down to his lips, then back up to those blue eyes again. My heart started to race. Images flashed through my mind – unwanted images – of Ron, of Ian and others. Users. I exhaled.

'Hey – you ok there?' he said, straightening the collar of my jacket. 'There you go!'

He dropped his head slightly to one side and, my God, he looked back into my eyes like he knew everything I was feeling.

'Ok – so it's Tommy's tonight, yeah? 8:30pm?'

He drew me into a hug, closer than previous hugs. My face was against the side of his neck. *God, the lovely smell of Lacoste again.*

I reversed awkwardly and self-consciously out of his driveway, aware of him standing at the hall door, waving. I selected first gear and drove off, with one wave of my hand.

Deep breath.

What happened just there in the hallway? What happened for the whole afternoon? Flashes from the wall display. Guys coming out of court, sneering, two fingers up to the camera, to the country. The look in their eyes. Pure hate. No shame. No remorse. Pure evil looking at you through human eyes. And that moment at the door with David. That look in his eyes. His mouth. His lips. The feeling inside. Hey, he's still in love with Emma! So stop losing the run of yourself with such thoughts! You'll mess up a great friendship . . .

I pulled into my own driveway, turned off the ignition and sat there, blinking.

Deep breath.

Ma opened the door, smiling at me.

'Well, well, well! Would you look at the glow off you! Come on in. Dinner's ready.'

I had only one mouthful and she started.

''You're spending a lot of time over in David's, I see.'

'Now, now, Ma. Just eat your dinner. We're just friends, nothing else.'

'Mmm. Is that Lacoste I smell, Lisa? Or am I imagining things?'

'Oh, will you stop, Ma,' I laughed. 'He gave me a hug when I was leaving. No big deal. Come on – eat your dinner. I've to get a shower. I'm heading to Tommy's with Carol . . . and yes, David.'

*

Meanwhile, over in John Noonan's house, Mickey arrived to drop down a fresh supply of coke and pick up cash that was owed.

'Alright, Johnny boy?' he said, glancing shiftily around. 'You alone?'

'Yeah, yeah,' said John. 'Come on in. Close that door. You want a bottle of beer?'

'Yeah, just the one. Don't want to be pulled over for drunk driving with a ball of cash and coke.'

John gave him the beer. Mickey took a swig.

'Thanks. Jays, you look well out of it. Thought you only took the odd few lines?'

'Ah, it's Christmas, Mickey. Time to break out for a change and enjoy life. Plus, I got engaged to Cara, so we're making this into one big party this time. I'll stop in the New Year. I've a wedding to sort out. I'll be up to my bloody eyes with the arrangements.'

'Well, you only get married once. Unless you're from Hollywood. Here – do you want a line of this new stuff I got in today? It's different to what I've given you before. I'll have this new white for you next week.'

Mickey pulled a bag out of his top jacket pocket.

'Wait till you try this, Johnny. This is real rocket fuel. Best I've ever had myself. Sit down. Give us a cd cover fast.'

He broke a lump off, chopping the bits down with his ATM card.

'Right. Try it.'

John rolled up a €20 note and snorted two lines through it up his nose.

'Well?' laughed Mickey. 'Whaddya think?'

'F**k sake, Mickey! Wow!!'

'Told ye! Good, isn't it? Best ever. That's just a taster. I'll be dropping a full batch of it down to you next week.'

'It's f**king lethal, mate!' John gasped, laughing.

'I couldn't bring it down this week. Had to get rid of the last of the old batch, which is what I gave you. It's great as well, but nothing like this new stuff. I'm surprised at how good it is myself, lad. Make sure you box off a good lump for yourself when you get it. Be years before you get it like that again.'

'Wow, that's some buzz, man!' said John, dropping his head back on the sofa. 'That's the best I've ever had. *Ever!*'

Mickey finished off his beer and placed the bottle on the table.

'So listen,' John continued, slurring his words. 'James was saying your man, Bailey . . . the guy selling the coke out this way at Cara's house . . . it's going to be sorted, yeah?'

Mickey sat back, taking off his hat, his bald head shining under the spotlights in the sitting room.

'Listen now, John,' said Mickey. 'Don't ever bring his name up to anyone ever again. It's been sorted. You hear me now? It's over. Sorted. You never talked to anyone about him, did ye? I mean, does your bird know?'

'No, no one knows a thing. I tell my bird nothing, Mickey.'

'Did anyone see . . . ? Like, do you think anyone would remember him being at your party? Like, you did talk to him on his own, to get offside, out of your house, like?'

'Em . . . em . . . yeah. I talked to him and the girl he was selling the coke to. Nobody else saw anything. They were all out of their heads.'

'That's cool. That's cool. So, did you warn him off?'

'Look, John. You don't need to know anything. It's sorted, ok? End of story'

'Did you beat him up? Tell me, will ye!'

Mickey looked into John's eyes.

'Don't ever ask me again. Don't mention his name to anyone ever again. Are you listening to me now?'

The look in Mickey's eyes said it all. End of subject.

'Ok, ok. That's it. I won't ask again, Mickey. It's cool.'

'Right, I'm off,' said Mickey, putting his hat back on. 'I'll be down next week with the new batch. The head on ye, Johnny! Look at your eyes – after just two lines! Take it easy on that stuff. You'll get lost on it, like most people I know. Look – here's a taster off this week's batch.'

He broke off a lump.

'Take this as a happy engagement present. There's enough there for you and your bird for a week if you go easy. But don't share it with anyone. It's for you only, you hear me? You'll have your mates wrecking your head wanting this off you all the time. Make sure you mix next week's down that bit more. You'll make a killing on it.'

'Thanks. That's great, Mickey. Fair play to ye. You're sound. Come here, give us a hug. You're the best mate I ever had.'

'Will you get lost, Johnny! Hugs? I don't want a hug off you. You're out of your head on that white. Ha! Get a grip. A hug? Ha, ha! Good luck. I'm out of here.'

Cara dropped in around 8pm, after Mickey left. John had taken a couple more lines of the good stuff.

'Hi, sweetheart!' he said, grabbing her in the hallway and kissing her passionately. 'How's my bride-to-be? Sit down. I've something for you to taste.'

'My God! You're very romantic tonight. You're out of it! Did you have a line before I came?'

'Yeah, yeah. I want you to try it. It's a brand new batch. Here. See what you think.'

She bent down and snorted two lines, one up each nostril.

'Oh, what a day in work! Glad I'm off till Tuesday. Here – get me a bottle of beer there, like the good husband you are.'

John went to the fridge in the kitchen. While he was opening the bottle of beer, Cara called out.

'Oh my God, John! That coke! Wow! Where did you get it?'

'Aha! Told you it was good. You can't tell the gang we have it, ok? It's just a little lump for you and me. I've to give out last week's batch to the gang. Next week I'm boxing off a big deal of this. It's going to be years before we see stuff like this again. Yeah – I've never taken coke like it. I've only taken a few lines now and again, which was great. But this is unreal, Cara!'

'Yeah. I've never felt so out of it on a couple of lines. Don't worry. I'll say nothing to the gang – promise. You go easy on it now. You're getting very greedy for it this Christmas. Come here!'

She grabbed him and kissed him full on the mouth.

'I can't wait to marry you, John Noonan! You're the best guy on God's earth. You know that, don't you?'

'I am?'

'Yeah. Course you are! We were destined to meet and fall in love.'

'Now is that you or the coke talking?'

'Both, I think! Come on – let's have another drink and a couple of lines before we head down to the gang in Tommy's.'

*

I sat in front of my dressing table mirror, with 98fm playing on the bedside radio. That song *Yellow* came on. *Bet David likes that song, seeing as he's a big Coldplay fan.*

My phone buzzed. A text – from David!

Thanks for listening to me today. Can't tell you what it means to me. You're a legend, Lisa Webb. David x

I texted back.

Great to have my mind opened to such deep truths. You've put so much into this, one day it will do a lot of good. I'm sure of that. See you in Tommy's in half an hour. P.S. Do you like that song Yellow by your band Coldplay?

It's my favourite song! x

I got the taxi down with Joe. I noticed he wasn't his usual, talkative self. He kept glancing at me in the mirror, more than he would normally. As I was getting out, he rolled down the window and smiled.

'You don't mind me saying, but are you sure you're the same Lisa Webb from a few weeks back – getting sick at the Ladystairs? My God, I've never seen such a change in a person, and in such a short space of time. Whatever you're doing, keep it up, Lisa!'

He rolled up the window and sped off before I could get the words out of my mouth to thank him. I continued to walk the short distance towards Tommy's and heard my name being called from behind me.

'Lisa! Lisa!'

I turned to see Brian Crawford running up the pathway, waving a small gift bag.

'Lisa, wait!'

He came up close. I had to step back as he bent to try and kiss me.

'Listen – I rang you a couple of times, but no answer. How have you been?'

'I'm grand, Brian. And you?'

'I'm doing great!'

I could see he was on the coke.

'My God, you look great, Lisa. So listen – is it true you're dating some guy? Emma's ex? David What's-his-name?'

'No, I'm not. Any more questions?'

'No, no. Just asking. Listen – here's a present. I saw on Facebook you were coming down to Tommy's so I wanted to give you your Christmas present. So – is it true you're off the coke?'

'Yes. I'm off it for good.'

'So what happened?'

Here we go again.

'Ah, it's a long story, Brian. But bottom line, I'm off it for good. And I've never felt better in my whole life.'

'So ok, ok. That's great news. So listen – I wanted to ask you something. You remember our last chat in The Life. You asked me about dating. A steady line, like? Well, I was thinking of you, and to be honest, I've really missed you. We had something great going on. So, like, would you still be interested in it? Dating, like?'

Oh. My. God. How could I have slept with a guy like this – a guy I now knew just wasn't my type, under normal circumstances? I blushed with embarrassment as the memories of sleeping with him flashed through my mind. Deep down at that moment I felt a sense of shame. He was a harmless guy. Sound. Wouldn't harm anyone. But now, with a clear head, not a clouded, coke-fuelled head, I could see he was just nothing near my type of guy.

He bent closer.

'Well – are you on for dating, Lisa?'

I leaned back slightly.

'Look – I can't. Things have changed so much.'

'Like what, Lisa? It's just a couple of weeks or so ago.'

'Well – *I've* changed. And I can't date you, Brian. I'm sorry. Do you want the present back?'

'No, no. It's for *you*. God, you have changed so much. You don't even look like Lisa, the Lisa I knew . . . Ok, ok. So any chance of a late Christmas kiss? Or an early New Year's kiss? Or even have a drink with me?'

He put his arm around me.

'No, you're ok, Brian. Thanks, but no.'

Just then a taxi pulled up. I looked to see who was getting out. It was David. He walked over.

'Hi. Sorry – am I interrupting you both?'

'No, no,' I said, moving towards him. 'This is Brian Crawford, a mate of mine. This is David Salle.'

'Hi, David. Are you the David Salle who once dated . . . ? Ah, doesn't matter. Anyhow, lovely to meet you. I was just heading in to meet my mates. See you again, Lisa.'

Brian quickly hugged me and walked off into Tommy's.

'I'm sorry about that, David,' I said, embarrassed.

'You don't have to apologise to me, Lisa. He's your friend. Come on, I'll get you a beer. Carol's on her way with Richie.'

We picked a nice corner seat, just off to the left of the pub. I could see Brian eyeballing us every few minutes.

'So – where did you get the present?' asked David as we settled into our seats.

'Brian, the guy outside. We used to date when I was into the coke. You know how it is. My judgement was off at the time. Don't get me wrong – he's sound, but not my type in the real world, when off the coke, if you know what I mean.'

'Yeah, I know what you mean. I dated girls at parties on coke. Jamie – my mate at the time – used to tell me that he rang his granny a number of times on coke and asked her out on a date!'

'Ha, ha! That's funny!'

'So tell me something, Lisa. Who is your ideal man? What kind of guy is your type?'

He smiled that smirk of his as he waited for my reply. Once again, he held me with his piercing blue eyes.

What a loaded question!

'Like . . . what do you mean? What do I like in a guy? Yeah?'

I took a mouthful of beer.

Oh God, where's this going?

'Well, I suppose for me, anyway, the first thing that attracts me to a bloke is, believe it or not, his eyes.'

Oh, damn. I'm saying this to the guy with the most striking blue eyes in Dublin.

'But, having said that, I've got it wrong in the past in that respect.'

'Next is trust. If you can't trust a guy, there's no point to the relationship. Alongside that, he has to be fun to hang out with. I suppose looks play a part, but it wouldn't be a priority with me. It's what's inside that counts at the end of the day. Don't you think?'

My throat was dry. Another swig.

'Yeah. I'd agree.'

'So – what about you? What's your type of girl?'

Before he had a chance to reply the doors opened and in came Carol and Richie. The moment was lost. For the time being, anyway.

'Well, well, Lisa,' said Carol, throwing her arms around me. 'I heard our David took you down to his chamber of horrors today. I did tell him to hold off till the New Year. Fair play to you. He tells me you lasted longer down there than I did. Are you ok?'

'I'm grand, Carol. Didn't bother me as much as I thought it would.'

'Look, Richie. Will you get the drinks, pet? Another bottle of Bud for Lisa.'

We all sat around the table, holding our bottles. David raised his and gestured for attention.

'Ok. Seeing as we're not going to be bringing in the New Year, I now propose a toast. Here's to New Friendships!'

'New Friendships!' we chorused, clicking our bottles together and raising them high.

Just then the doors opened and in walked John, Cara, Ruth, Steve and Emma. They stopped in their tracks and stared at us. Behind the bar, Tommy picked up the vibe straightaway. He caught my eye and gave me that unmistakeable look that said *No trouble, Lisa!*

John stared at me with a look that cut me in two. My God, they looked well out of it. Maybe I just noticed it more now, having been off it for some time. Cara avoided eye contact, keeping her head turned away. Emma nearly broke her neck trying to look over Ruth's shoulder at us. There was a strong look of disbelief in her eyes. They all drifted towards their usual table and ordered their drinks.

'You ok, Lisa?' said Carol, grasping my shoulder. 'If you want us to leave, we can go to the Blue Ocean.'

'No, it's fine, Carol. Thanks all the same. Life goes on! It's just sad, really, that everything ended up the way it did.'

'It's so strange, don't you think?' said David. 'After all we looked at today concerning coke, and after all you told me about your experience – and then to come face to face with it in such a raw form as this!'

'Yeah, I know.'

'You know, a thought just crossed my mind about your mates, Lisa. It's a bit scary, but the . . .'

'Ah, David, please!' interrupted Carol. 'We're out for a relaxing drink. Let's not start down this morbid road, talking about drugs again. I'm sure Lisa wants a break from it all after today!'

'No, it's grand, Carol,' I reassured her. 'Really. Did David not tell you we're going to study the drug culture in detail?'

'You're *what?*' she said, darting a withering look at David. '*Study?* What . . . what's there to study? People take drugs! That's life. There's nothing else to say about it! Tell them, Richie, will you?'

'Calm down, Carol,' he said, not used to being the centre of attention. 'Look – you know David's into all this . . . this *unseen* side of it. Maybe it'll help some kids somewhere down the road to see the awful danger behind it all.'

Richie pulled Carol's chair closer, putting his arms around her to reassure her.

'I don't understand any of it, David,' said Carol. 'I thought you had put this whole matter behind you. Now you're dragging Lisa into it.'

David looked around, searching the faces of all present. Then he faced Carol.

'Look, sis,' he said. 'Lisa wants to be part of this. She has a story that links into my findings.'

'Story? What story?'

'Well, I'll give you the edited version.'

I told all present about my experience in The Life.

'Ah, no offence, Lisa!' said Carol when I had finished. 'But you were on drugs that night. What you think you saw could have been a hallucination. People see crazy things when they're under the influence. Isn't that right, Richie?'

'So I'm told,' he said, shrugging his shoulders. 'I don't know much, love. I've never taken drugs, but if what Lisa saw was in any way real, it may mean something.'

'For God's sake!' said Carol. 'Like what?'

'I don't know. Like maybe, some kind of warning?'

I looked over at David with his elbow on the table and his head resting in his hand.

'Believe it or not, that's the thought that crossed my mind before Carol cut across me. Tommy! Another round of drinks, when you're ready!'

'I'll get this one, David,' I said. 'You keep talking. I want to hear about this warning.'

I went up to the bar and ordered the drinks. I could see my old gang still sizing us up, especially Emma, who never took her eyes off us. While I waited for the drinks, I took a trip to the loo.

'Well, well! If it's not Paul Daniels! Full of new tricks.'

It was John. He had followed me in, stopping me in the passageway outside both loos. Before I could reply, I found myself surrounded by

Cara and Emma and John.

'So – how's the big love affair?'

It was Cara, spitting venom.

'Word has it you're doing a line with David Salle. Not a line of *coke* – a *dating* line!' she sniggered.

She stepped closer, adding to the sense of intimidation.

'So – are you going to say sorry about the things you've done? The games you're playing with Emma's ex to try and get back at us, not to mention bringing the drug dealer to my party!'

I took a deep breath.

'Look – why don't . . . ?'

The door swung open and I could see Tommy coming in our direction. Emma and Cara ducked into the Ladies, leaving me alone with John.

He leaned closer to me and whispered in my ear.

'Oh yeah. I had your little coke friend sorted out!'

He pushed open the door into the bar and was gone.

Tommy came in.

'Everything ok in here, Lisa? You ok?'

'Yeah, yeah. Just a small chat. Nothing wrong, Tommy.'

'Your drinks are on the counter. I'll bring them over.'

I turned and went back towards the table, past Ruth and Steve, who looked uneasy with all the tension in the air. Orla and Carl looked somewhat the same. There was a sense that they were fed up with what was happening.

Just as I approached the table, for no reason I stopped dead in my tracks. A sudden surge of energy raced through me, coming from the very centre of my heart. It was like the previous experiences I'd had, but this time it was even more overpowering. No one, I think, noticed anything, only that I was now stopped in mid-floor, looking somewhat overwhelmed. I wondered if the inner turbulence I was experiencing was manifesting itself visibly to some degree in my facial expression.

I began to snap out of it – whatever it was – and saw David standing up to let me get by him. He looked concerned.

'You ok there, Lisa? What did they say to you? Did they upset you? I'll have a word with them if you want.'

'No, no, you're grand. It's nothing like that. It's this . . . this strange feeling I keep getting. It's so weird, like . . .'

David put his arm around me.

'Come on, sit down. Don't mind them.'

But I felt a strong urge come over me to face up to Cara once and for all. I turned back towards the loo.

'I won't be a minute, David. Here.' I handed him €20 from my purse. 'You pay for the drinks.'

As I pushed open the door into the Ladies, Emma and Cara were coming out, sniffing and rubbing their hands across their noses. I let the door swing shut and stood between it and them.

'Now you listen to me, Cara,' I began.

Emma squared up to me.

'Get out of our . . .'

'Not a word from you, Emma! This is between Cara and me. Please leave now. I want to talk to Cara alone.'

'Go on, Emma,' said Cara. 'I'll be out in a second.'

Emma went off, still sniffing and rubbing her nose.

I stood there, fearless.

'How long do we know each other, Cara? Since we were kids. Never once in all that time have I ever attempted to play games with you and your feelings. My God, don't you know me at all, Cara? We did everything together, and in the space of a couple of weeks you think I've turned into your greatest enemy? Come on! You know me better than that. This is not a game I'm playing, Cara. I swear to you on my father's grave – something happened to me in The Life that night, and since then I'm a different person. Everything's changing faster than I can keep up with – and it's all *good!* I can't for the life of me explain the events that happened at the party in your house. But I promise you I did not go there to play a game, or bring a coke dealer. I never saw that guy in my life till that night. And I haven't seen him since.'

Cara looked stunned, unable to gather her thoughts. Being well coked out of it maybe contributed to the way she just stood and listened to me.

'I love you, Cara. I've always loved you. You're my best friend. Look at me – do I look like I'm doing coke right now?'

In spite of my best efforts, I started to sob. Tears streamed down my face. I moved in closer to her, and she stepped away, her back to the wall.

'Em . . . so how do you account for the state you were in? I mean, the story you told about something going up your nose?'

'Yeah, maybe he spiked me. I don't know, Cara. But I wasn't out there doing lines of coke!'

'So what about dating David Salle, a day after this all happened?'

I just had to laugh.

'We became *mates! Friends! Pals!* That's all! Like I'm mates with his sister Carol. I can't convince you, and I'm not going to keep trying. Time will prove I'm not lying to you!'

I put my hand out, placing it on her arm.

'I love you, Cara. I'm thrilled to bits you and John are getting married.'

She turned her head, dropping her gaze to the floor.

'Look at me!' I pleaded. 'Look at me, Cara. I love you. I really do!'

The door burst open. Ruth and Orla.

'What the hell is going on?'

'Nothing,' I said, 'I was just leaving.'

I turned, wiping the tears away, and walked back to the table.

'What's happening?' asked David.

'You're crying!' said Carol, putting her arm around me. 'What did they say? Did they upset you?'

'No, no, it's ok, I promise. I just needed to talk to Cara face to face and sort out a certain issue, and I got upset.'

'My God, Lisa – your eyes, your whole face, when you pulled away to go back into the loo . . .'

I took a big mouthful of my bottle of beer.

'Well, it's pretty obvious I didn't plan any of this. Something keeps happening to me inside. It's been happening a while. I keep putting it down to coming back to myself after the coke. But I'm not so sure anymore. I'm . . . I'm changing. But it's too fast. I'm changing too fast . . . How about you, David? How long after you came off the coke did it take you to change?'

'God – I don't remember. Couple of years, give or take.'

'Couple of years? It's a few weeks, and things keep happening to me – like tonight. And yesterday it happened too.'

'Explain what it feels like,' said Carol.

'I can't explain it. I mean . . . don't laugh, but it feels like . . . like butterflies . . . only stronger. God, maybe I'm going around the twist. Am I?'

The loo door opened and Cara, Ruth and Orla came out and went back to their seats. They looked shell shocked. Everyone at their table went back to chatting and laughing – except Cara. I could see John trying to snap her back into their zone, into their buzz. But she kept looking over in our direction.

'Listen – I feel I've messed up our get-together. Sorry.'

'No, no, not at all,' said Carol, pulling me closer to her reassuringly. 'We love you, Lisa! We're buddies! Remember?'

I glanced over and caught Cara's eye.

'They keep saying I planned all this – like meeting you all is a game to get back at them. As if I would! You know I never planned any of this. It just happened. Fate, I suppose. I'm just so thankful I have you three people. I love you all!'

'And we love you too!' they chorused.

'Listen, David,' I said, suddenly remembering. 'What were you going to tell me before I went to the loo?'

'Oh, that? Maybe it's better to leave that for another time.'

'No, no, tell me. I want to hear it.'

Carol dropped her head.

'Go on. I've three beers in me now. Let's have it, brother!'

There was a hush of expectation.

'Ok,' he said. 'I have this feeling that what you saw that night in The Life was some kind of warning. Maybe something along the lines of an omen. But whatever it was I think your mates – your so-called mates –are in some kind of awful danger. A real and present danger, as they say. Maybe not all of them. But some definitely are.'

He looked me straight in the eye.
'Someone . . . definitely is.'

Chapter Sixteen

A Tear Between Years

We all left Tommy's after another beer. In one last glance in the direction of my old mates I saw Cara still looking out of sorts from our face to face encounter in the loo.

Deep down, I knew I had done and said the right thing. I knew I wasn't playing games and I needed to bring that home to Cara above anyone else. I still missed her hugely – and the friendship we had shared down the years. There was a time when drugs weren't a part of our lives, and now I could see how it had played its part not only in destroying our friendship, but in changing Cara – and all of my friends. There was a time when we all lived clean, healthy lives, doing harmless things like going to the cinema, spending nights in, watching television, going for pleasant walks or, on special occasions, going out for a meal. But all of that slowly went by the wayside and was replaced by a preoccupation with coke, drink, nightclubs, parties and – in my own case, anyway – dead-end relationships.

Overshadowing my thoughts was David's idea that something dreadful was about to befall the gang – or someone in the gang. The more I thought about it the more I was convinced that he was right – someone was in real, imminent danger. But who? And was it that person alone who was in danger?

Somehow I had to find a way to warn them. I knew that, out of all of them, Cara would at least listen to me. Everyone else, particularly John, would just laugh in my face if I said anything. But I could reach Cara, I felt, or at least *try* to reach her. And who knows? Maybe if she took heed of my warning, it might just lead to John, Ruth and the rest coming to their senses before it was all too late.

After stopping off at the chipper, we went back to David and Carol's house, where Tim, their dad, was being taken care of by his own younger sister, Rachel. We walked into the sitting room just as she was getting him ready to bring him to his bedroom in the back.

'Ah! If it's not our Emma, bringing me home fish and chips! What a lovely smell! You can't beat the smell of chips, soaked in vinegar. Yummy!'

'Now, now, Dad,' said Carol. 'It's too late for you to be eating chips.'

'Ah, give him a few,' I said. 'Won't harm him at all.'

I brought a chip up near his mouth, gently bringing his hand up to hold it himself.

'And it's *Lisa*, Tim. Not Emma.'

'Aah, you're such a thoughtful girl, Lisa,' he said, smiling warmly.

He bit half the chip, then mumbled as he chewed,

'Very thoughtful.'

'Ok, Tim,' his sister Rachel chimed in. 'Time to go. Way past your bedtime.'

She started to turn his wheelchair out of the room. His eyes never left mine, like he sensed a bond was being formed.

'I'll be seeing you tomorrow, Mr Salle – or *Tim*. I'll make you chips myself the next chance we get.'

Till he left for his bedroom, he continued staring at me, as if he saw something about me I myself was unaware of.

'Oh, I think he's taken a shine to you, Lisa!' said David, emerging from the kitchen with glasses of 7up and plates for the food. 'He kept talking about you today over dinner. You're his angel!'

'Ah, he's lovely,' I said, helping with the plates. 'So gentle, too. He misses your mother. I can see it in his eyes.'

'Broke his heart when she passed away,' said Carol, distributing the food onto the plates. I could see the sad memory in her face.

'He's so blessed to have you both by his side. So many people would put their parents into a home if they were that ill. Fair play to the two of you!'

I smiled at them with a sense of pride, almost as if they were my own family and I was privileged to be associated with them.

'Ah, thanks, Lisa,' said Carol. 'But we'd never dream of putting him into a home. Isn't that right, David?'

'God, no. No way. He's a pain in the bum at times, but we love him deeply. I'd die if anything ever happened to him. When Ma died, all our lives came apart for a number of years. We knew Ma would want us to take care of him at home. Plus, he'd die within one week in one of those homes. He'd give up. Wouldn't he, Carol?'

'Oh, for sure. He loves being around his family. The rest of his family – like his brother, for instance – never really come round anymore to see him. Very sad.'

He tried to open a sachet of tomato ketchup with his teeth, and it squirted onto his white shirt.

'Damn! I hate that!', he said, embarrassed as he wiped the ketchup in vain with a tissue.

'Ah, it'll wash out,' said Carol. 'Here – take it off. I'll put it into a white wash.'

He stood up, pulling his shirt off over his head, his t-shirt coming off with it. I blushed and kept just eating my chips, trying to look anywhere but at his half naked body. He quickly put his t-shirt back on, still self-conscious but with that smile again on his face.

'Come on, guys,' he said, turning our attention to the food. 'Let's eat this before it gets cold.'

We all settled down into eating and chatting away. Richie asked me was I interested in sports or music.

'Hate football, Richie,' I told him. 'Can't understand all this Man United and Liverpool stuff. Hate the thing with the fans. It's so over the top. I love bike racing, mind you.'

'Really?' he said, sounding surprised.

'Oh, yeah. I mean, when you see road races up North – my God, that's what you call Real Heroes of Sport. Not little girls running around a pitch after a football and getting £200,000 a week. Nah – give me six bikes together, speeding past you neck and neck at 180mph. Makes all other sports look like ballroom dancing, don't you think?'

'I love it!' laughed David. 'You're right, Lisa. I'm not a bike fan, but football is a load of rubbish.'

'I like it,' said Richie. 'I love following Liverpool. I know they're vastly overpaid, but it's still a great sport, in my opinion.'

'Ah, they're just ganging up on you, Richie,' said Carol.

'So, what about music, Lisa?' asked David. 'What are your favourite bands?'

'Em, well, there's Foo Fighters . . . Coldplay . . . and Gary Numan.'

'Gary who? Oh, yeah. They guy who sang *Cars*. Thought he died years ago in the 80s. Ha! He was a bit of a weirdo! But Coldplay are great. Nice one, Lisa.'

'David, stop!' said Carol. 'Gary Numan's a legend.'

'Thanks, Carol,' I said.

We talked and laughed till 2am. I rang a taxi. Carol walked me out after we all hugged each other.

'So what are your plans for New Year's Eve?' I asked.

'Ah, Richie has to work, so I'm staying put to watch a dvd. What about yourself?'

'Not sure. My Ma always goes to my Uncle Jim's, so I'll see what the story is tomorrow.'

We hugged again, like sisters.

'You take care, Lisa. I love you.'

I smiled at her.

'I love you too, Carol.'

Lying in bed before I dropped off to sleep, I was aware that my thoughts were transfixed on David. Feelings were stirring in my heart, but not without a certain amount of fear of wrecking a great friendship. There was also a sense of *what if I get hurt again?* God, I couldn't bear to have that happen all over again. *Stay safe, Lisa,* was my last thought as I slipped into a deep sleep.

After an invigorating early morning jog next day, I showered and dressed. When I came down I saw that Uncle Jim had dropped in and was now half way through breakfast.

'Well, well,' he said, standing up to hug me, 'if it's not Lisa Webb, looking better than I've ever seen her!'

'Ah, thanks, Jim. Nice to see you. How are you?'

We all sat down. As Ma served out the breakfast she smiled at Jim with that look that said *I told you she was looking great!*

'And what has you in this neck of the woods?' I asked.

'Well, I dropped around just to see how things are going with you, and see if there's anything you need.'

'Nah, everything's great. Thanks, Jim.'

'So, eh, have there been any temptations with the . . . well, you know what I mean? Your Ma said you're doing great, better than we all expected, Lisa.'

'What I mean is . . .'

He pushed his plate away and took a last mouthful from his mug of tea.

'I'll come right to it. Everyone who comes off any kind of drugs always has awful struggles, and many get tempted to go back. Have you been going through any of those symptoms of late?'

Ma had that searching, anxious look on her face as she stopped midway through cutting into her rasher, awaiting my reply.

'No,' I said. 'I had, as you know, that awful experience in the Pavilions Shopping Centre, and of course, withdrawal symptoms. But tempted to go back? No, not at all. I know many do, but I've seen the awful side to coke, and I couldn't be happier to be away from it all. And as a bonus, I've met some really fantastic new friends.'

'Yeah, yeah,' Mary was saying, That's great news. I'm so thankful to God things are going so well. To be honest, Lisa, there were a few times I expected you to relapse. Don't get me wrong – I trusted you. But drugs can be a nightmare to kick after you've been hooked in for years! But what can I say? Just look at you! You look like a different person. Full of life. You look so happy!'

'Everyone's saying that, Jim – that I look so different. I *feel* so different – inside, I mean.'

Jim stared at me, as did Ma. Shaking his head as if he was coming out of a trance, he said,

'I don't get it, Lisa.'

'You don't get what?'

'You seem so happy in such a short space of time.'

'Well, I did go through a nightmare, Jim. I cried myself to sleep many a night. It's just lately things are getting together.'

'Oh, Jim,' said Ma, giving his arm a nudge, 'I think there's romance in the air!'

'Ma, stop! Don't listen to her, Jim! I've got a guy, David, as a friend. Nothing else.'

'Well, Mary,' said Jim, 'if she's found romance, it's working. Let her run free!'

He glanced at his watch, pushed his chair back, and stood up.

'I'm off. I'll see you later, Mary. What are your plans for New Year's Eve countdown?'

'Ah, I'll probably just sit in and read. Watch tv, maybe.'

'Come around to our place! There's a group staying in to bring in the New Year.'

'Thanks, Jim, but no. It's not a big deal. It's just a new year. No big deal really.'

'You can't sit in alone.'

'Ha, look, if I get lonely, I'll drop around to you all. How's that?'

'Ok. But make sure you do, now.'

That evening, Ma did decide to go after all. She hugged me as she told me to make sure to come down if I got bored. As the taxi took her away, she waved at me, still looking a bit worried at the idea of me staying in alone on such a night.

I curled up on the sofa, all set to watch an old black-and-white movie on the tv. I couldn't help feeling a bit distracted, and found it hard to concentrate on the corny storyline. The clock ticked on towards 10pm.

A text came in. David.

Well – what you up to? David x

Just sitting in. And you? x

Nothing. Going to take a New Year's walk. Want to come? x

Em, let me think. Bloody right – sounds good to me. On my way. Give me 20 mins. x

In only ten minutes I was pulling into his driveway. Carol opened the door.

'Ah, Lisa!' she laughed. 'You may pack your bags and come and move in with us!'

She threw her arms around me.

'You know, Lisa, you're the best thing that's happened to me this year!'

'Ah, that's so nice to hear. Same here,' I said, smiling.

I could hear Wilson barking excitedly as he ran up the hall.

'Well, well! Happy New Year, Wilson!' I said.

David was standing in the sitting room, putting on his jacket.

'Well,' I said, 'this is some way to bring in the New Year – going for a walk around Skerries with you and your crazy one-eared dog!'

He laughed. 'Tell me about it! It's odd alright. At least we'll have no hangover tomorrow, which, it's safe to say, can't be said about the rest of Ireland.'

'Wrap up well, you two,' said Carol, handing me her gloves. 'You'll need them, Lisa. It's cold out there tonight.'

Before we knew it, we had reached the main street in Skerries, passing packed pubs with people singing, and past houses full of people partying the night away.

'It's a strange feeling, isn't it, Lisa? Like, everyone's partying, and we're the only ones I imagine doing this.'

'Yeah,' I said, pulling up my collar against the cold. 'It's a bit surreal. I mean, this time last year I was in John's house, coked up to my eyes. It just seems like a different world to the world I now find myself in tonight. Hard to believe, to be honest.'

David let out a sigh.

'I remember the first Christmas and New Year off the drugs. It was very lonely, to be honest. I think I spent New Year's Eve in that basement, doing my research.'

'What was your best New Year? Don't tell me it was down the basement!'

'No, no. The best? Em . . .'

That smile of his again.

'Ask me that after twelve o'clock!'

We both laughed.

'And you? What was your best?'

'Well . . . em, I'll have to pass on that one!'

A few revellers passed us, heading for the pub.

'So listen, David,' I continued. 'Going back to last night. What do *you* go for in a relationship?'

'Ah, I knew you'd come back to that. Em, let me think . . . Well, the first is, believe it or not, the same as yours. I go for the eyes first.'

'No way! You're just saying that because I said it!'

'No, I'm serious. Like, I've always been amazed at a girl's eyes. They do everything for me. But like you, I've got that wrong in the past. Second, I'd have to go for personality.'

'Ah, you're the same as me. I bet trust is next as well.'

'No, you said trust was your number 2. Remember?'

'Then I think everything else falls into place. Doesn't it? But here's a question for you, Lisa. What's the most important thing about a relationship?'

We now found ourselves around the Head in the dark at the bathing slip called The Captain's, standing next to the wide open sea. Just the stars looking down us, watching our every move. Well, that's how I felt, anyway. Wilson just sat there, looking out at the lapping waves.

'What's the most important? Well, I suppose, trust. Yeah, trust. It has to be trust. What do you think?'

David sat up on one of the cold stones that formed part of the wall and lit up a cigarette, taking a deep drag.

'This is my last fag, by the way. I'm giving them up for the New Year.'

'Yeah? You're joking!'

'No. There's the box, and the lighter as well!'

He threw them both into the dark sea. Wilson perked up, springing to his feet, but David stroked him.

'Stay, boy. Stay.'

Another drag on the cigarette.

'Make the most of it, so.'

'I will.'

'So? Tell me!'

'What? Oh, yeah. Well, I think it's . . . love. *Real* love. If you have real love, then trust will follow. When you're in love for real, you don't have to worry about trust. That's always been my take on it.'

'So, have you ever felt that? Well, I know you have with Emma. But had you ever felt it before Emma?'

'Ah, I've been very close to girls in the past. But I wonder, Lisa. Like, I know how close I was to them, but how close were they to me? I gave so much, but never seemed to get much in return. But that's life, I suppose. The older you get, the more you learn. I thought I had it – real love – with Emma, I admit that. But that's yesterday's news. But what about you?'

For the first time since we set out, he looked straight into my eyes. I could see him clearly, even in the dark. The moon gave enough light to see his eyes, his disarming, irresistible eyes.

'I really don't know anymore, David. I thought I knew about love when I was with Ron. But looking back, it was all a game. Nothing was real. Like, it wasn't love on *his* part, that's for sure. Like, inside I've got a picture of what it should look like to be really in love, what it should feel like. But I can't say I've ever had it so real, where it felt like there was nothing in between me and the other person. No games going on. But you know something, David? For the first time in my whole life, I don't know why I feel so happy, so complete inside my heart. And I don't know why, maybe it's because I don't take drugs. But as I said last night, I don't know! Maybe I'm not supposed to know. Maybe being happy should not be questioned, but just *lived*.'

David kept looking at me, absorbing my every word.

'That's a lovely way of putting it, Lisa. You look so happy. Like you said, you look *complete*.'

He took a last drag from his cigarette and flicked the butt into the darkness.

'That's it – last fag!' he smiled.

He exhaled the smoke with a sense of finality.

'Well done! So proud of you, David Salle!'

He climbed down off the cold stone wall.

'You know, there's one other part of a relationship that is very important, Lisa. And I'm not sure if you ever experienced it. In fact, I'm nearly certain, from getting to know you the past week or so, that you may never have felt this.'

'Yeah? Like, what? Tell me.'

'In the relationships you were in, as you said, it was all *you*. Am I right? *You* put everything into it.'

'Yeah, I suppose, yeah. And . . .'

'Well, you know what time it is?'

'Time? No. What?'

'It's 11:30. Thirty minutes to 2012!'

'Yeah? So? Big deal!' I laughed. 'Tell me what it is I've never experienced – before I throw you into the sea!'

'I don't think you've ever experienced . . . being kissed!'

'Kissed? You're joking me! I've had a million kisses, David,' I protested, trying not to blush. 'You're messing with my head!'

'No, I'm not. You kissed loads, yeah. But have you ever experienced being *really* kissed?'

'I'm not sure what you're getting at.'

'Well, like, as you said yourself, you never had a relationship where there was nothing, no obstacle, between you and the guy. No hidden agenda. No games. You never had just you and him . . . bare souls next to each other, face to face with only true feelings passing from you to him and likewise, from him to you.'

My mouth dropped open – or so it felt.

'My God! I never heard it put like that, but, like, no one gets to have something like that nowadays. It's unheard of, David.'

My heart started to feel strange, my words tripping over themselves.

'How do . . . how do you know all this, anyway?'

'I think, deep down, we all know this, Lisa. I'm just saying it to you.'

'Ok. So what! I've never been kissed, because no one's ever met me as full on as I was trying to meet them . . . God! Does that make sense?'

David stood up. I glanced at my watch. 11:40. His eyes looked even more amazing than ever.

I started to tremble inside as he was only feet away from me. Our eyes met, locked in a sense with this incredible feeling that I'd never felt in my life before.

11:50.

I was waiting for him to say something else, but deep inside there was nothing else to say. We were passing beyond words into feelings, the ones he just told me about. Nothing in between. No fear. *My God, this can't be happening!* The feeling was so strong. My whole body shivered, trying to cope.

David gently lifted up his hand and warmly slipped it around my shoulder. His fingers stroked the back of my neck, sending a shiver of emotion right through me. Our faces started to close in towards each other. My bottom lip dropped open, as did his. His other hand came around my waist and pressed against my back, pulling me closer. Our mouths, our lips came within an inch of touching . . . and stopped.

In all my life I had felt nothing like this. Our eyes were still transfixed. It was by far the closest I had ever felt to anyone in my life.

With both our lips almost touching, David breathed what seemed like warm air, but it was more than that. The air seemed to be mixed with some kind of feelings from deep inside. I could feel it go down my throat and touch a part of me inside. Instinctively I responded and feelings raced back up, sending the same wave of feelings back into David's mouth. Both our bodies trembled. My eyes closed and opened again as the feeling got more intense.

David's top lip softly touched my bottom lip. I let out a deep, deep sigh. He just held it there, then slid it slowly across and back. I was so lost. Before I could gather my thoughts, he moved to my top lip, touching it in the same way. For what seemed like forever, the sensation passed back and forth between us. As the slow kiss picked up pace, our mouths and lips triggered deeper feelings with each movement! With each touch. . .

I held his face in my hands as he ran his fingers through my hair. Just when I thought it couldn't get any better, he grasped my face with my mouth open and sent this overwhelming feeling from somewhere deep inside his own being down into mine.

My head fell back with the sheer force of sensation, and I burst into tears. He held me close, as close as anyone could hold another human being.

'Oh, my God, David!' I cried as we stood, suspended between the years. A tear fell from my cheek I could feel it leave my face and somehow magically David saw it and reached out and it fell into his hand . . . *Wow!* I thought.

Up over Skerries, over our heads, the sky lit up as the fireworks burst into a brilliant explosion of dazzling colour and sound, bringing in the New Year.

We held each other so tight. It was the moment of moments in my life. My first true close encounter with a person, nothing in between. David was so right. Up till now I'd never been kissed, not in the true sense.

Our bodies trembled from the closeness. I couldn't imagine another couple experiencing a passing between years of the nature as we just had.

He slowly brought his eyes into line with mine. I thought I could see a tear in his eye.

'Happy New Year, Lisa Webb!'

'Happy New Year to you, David Salle!'

Don't even try to ask me how I got home that night. I don't remember. All I remember is driving down through Skerries around 2am after a cup of tea and a chat with Carol and Richie. Carol couldn't keep her eyes off the pair of us, but said nothing.

The streets were full of people drunk, some out of it, shouting and singing. I had already texted Ma, so she knew I was ok.

I hit the pillow and passed out in the most wonderful sleep I ever had in my life.

I woke the next morning around 11am. *My God! Was I dreaming it all?* I knew Ma had stayed in Jim's, so I went for a long New Year's Day jog. My heart and mind racing with the memories of the kiss from David last night. I could still taste him on my lips.

After a shower and breakfast I took a walk in what turned out to be a lovely, sunny afternoon, down into the town of Skerries, floating on Cloud Nine. I put my hand into my pocket for my phone, only to realise I had it on Silent since last night. Two missed calls from Ma, and eighteen from David. I smiled.

Just as I put it back, it rang. It was David.

'Hi, David. Sorry. My phone was on Silent.'

'Hi, Lisa. Where are you?'

His voice sounded anxious.

'I'm down the street, out for a walk. Are you ok? You sound different.'

'Are you near a shop, Lisa?'

'Yeah – I'm just outside Gerry's Supermarket. Why?'

'Go inside and take a look at the headlines of the Star newspaper and tell me what you see.'

Keeping my phone on, I walked in quickly and went straight to the newspaper stand. A picture of a young man was on the front of the Star – and every other Irish paper.

Those eyes . . . That face . . .

My mouth dropped open.

'My God, David. That's Jason. Jason Bailey. The guy from the . . .'

It read:

Well-known youth leader shot dead. Full-scale Garda investigation under way.

Chapter Seventeen

High Risk

I could hear David's voice dying away.

'Hold on, David,' I said. 'I'm trying to read it.'

I went on to the next paper, trying to absorb all the information. I went from walking on Cloud Nine to feeling sick inside. My mind raced back to John in Tommy's two nights before. I could still hear that whisper,

We sorted out your little coke dealer!

'Are you there, Lisa?' came David's voice, still on the line.

'Yeah, sorry, David. My God, David – they've killed him! It says here he was a youth leader who helped young people with drug issues, and was well respected and widely known in the inner city. He only moved to Swords six months ago. Oh, David, I . . .'

'Stay there, Lisa. I'm on my way. We'll take a drive. Don't talk to anyone till I get there. You hear me, Lisa?'

The whole thing made no sense. What about when the two of us were in the garden? What did he do to me? The papers said he never took drugs. I could still see those soft eyes of his. I could still hear that soft voice. Nothing added up. Now – murdered by someone. John's face flashed across my mind again and again as, still shocked and stunned, I started to walk out of the shop with the paper in my hand.

'Are you paying for that paper, love?' the shop owner called after me, his voice breaking across my trance.

'God, sorry!' I said. 'I'm half asleep! Here you are.'

I paid him and left, just as David pulled up in his car. He leaned over and opened the passenger door for me.

'Jump in, Lisa. There's two cars behind me.'

I got in, placing the paper across my lap.

'Are you ok?' said David, glancing anxiously at me, before indicating and pulling out again.

'I think so,' I said, putting on my safety belt. 'Thanks.'

As he drove along I couldn't help but feel that there was an unmistakeable sense of safety, of serenity in the confines of his car. Yet I was still ill at ease.

'This is so weird, David. To think that the guy who put the note in my pocket just a matter of days ago is now dead – murdered! And I know who did it!'

'Ok, ok, calm down, Lisa. We don't know all the facts – not yet, anyway.'

'*I* know, David!' I said. 'It was John bloody Noonan! He's involved. He said it to me the other night in Tommy's, that they had "sorted out" Jason Bailey!'

David pulled into the car park around the Head, only yards away from The Captain's where we had kissed into the New Year. Only a half an hour ago I had been floating, dreaming as I looked again at the exact spot where we had hugged and kissed. I glanced across at him now. He was totally engrossed as he avidly read the account in the paper. I felt caught between two worlds – the amazing closeness to David on the one hand and on the other, the nightmarish realisation that a man had lost his life violently and that, like it or not, I was involved in it, right smack in the middle.

'Well, David? What do you think?'

He heaved a sigh and rubbed his fingers slowly across his mouth. *He'd just love a cigarette right now!* I thought.

'My God, Lisa,' he said. 'Only two nights ago I said that one or more of your friends were in danger of some kind. And today, we wake up to *this?* How odd is that, Lisa! I read that note he left in your pocket, over and over again. To me, it just makes no sense. And to think he was murdered right after his chat with you. Everything is so surreal. My own story involved the death five years ago of an innocent kid. Then I met you, and your story clicks in with my own study. Now another innocent man is dead. I can't get my head around it, Lisa. It's crazy!'

'Cara rang me that same night,' I said, 'saying they knew who this guy was who was in the garden with me. They had him shot because they thought he was selling me coke. That's it, David. Can't you see it?'

His fingertips brushed across his lips again.

'There's a phone number in the paper for anyone with information to ring the Gardaí in Swords or Santry.'

He put the paper down and looked straight into my eyes.

'Listen, now, Lisa. These are very dangerous people. The risks are far too high. They'd come after you and have you shot dead if you started making calls. We need to calm down here. You hear me? We can't be 100% sure that the papers are right. They're saying he never took drugs or sold them or was in any trouble with the law. But we don't know for sure, do we? John has some very dangerous heads behind him, if you go mouthing off or making threats. Believe me, they won't sit back and do nothing. Do you understand me, Lisa? Lisa – look at me! Do you hear me now? We can't say a single word about this to anyone.'

I slumped back in the seat, realising how right he was. But I didn't want to admit it.

'Yes, David, but I feel like it's my fault. If that guy never came to Cara's party and talked to me, he'd still be alive today. Like, I can't make it all out. What in God's name was he doing there? What really did happen to me that night? What did *he* do to me, David? God, thinking back, he seemed so nice, so kind, so soft-spoken – not anything like a coke dealer. Something about the whole sequence of events just doesn't add up.'

'Look, Lisa, he said, 'I know quite a few coke dealers who are otherwise sound people. Yes, they're dealing coke, but only as a sideline, to make some cash. We know next to nothing about this Jason Bailey guy.'

I looked away.

'If what the papers are saying is true, that he wasn't involved in drugs, then the question still remains: why did he get me to close my eyes? And what did he do to me for those few seconds when my eyes were closed?'

'I don't know, Lisa. I'm as much in the dark as you are about that aspect of it all. But look, we have the note, and it's got to mean something. I promise you, if it's the last thing I do, I'll get to the bottom of all this for you, ok?'

'Ok. Thanks, David,' I said, patting his hand. 'Oh, my God – his poor family. It said he was shot twice in the head. He's got one sister a year younger. What must they be going through right now? His mother and father are devastated, it said.'

I folded the paper and dropped it behind us on the back seat.

'Look, I won't say a word to anyone. You're right. It's far too risky. But the least I can do is to go to his funeral, which is tomorrow in Rathmines. Then I'm going to pick a time to meet John and Cara. Don't worry – I'm not going to make any threats about talking to the cops.'

'My God, Lisa,' he sighed. 'What a start to the New Year!'

'Tell me about it!'

I glanced out to the right, down to the spot where we stood, wrapped around each other the night before, the pictures still so real, feelings so new, the moment my head dropped to one side, a tear falling into David's open hand as we crossed into a New Year, a New Life, awoken inside by a single kiss! I never wanted to lose the taste left on my lips, and the romantic way he held me so close.

'Are you ok, Lisa?' said David, breaking across my thoughts.

'Yeah, yeah,' I said, turning to look him in the eyes. He seemed yet again on another wavelength, with everything that had taken place, which made me feel somewhat guilty for drifting away when we were face to face with a murder that involved me to some extent.

We drove back to my apartment. David came in for a coffee, and we chatted away about everything to do with Jason's murder. Nothing came up about the night before. Inside, I just had to leave it alone, to put it down as a New Year's kiss between friends, and move on with the events that were now unfolding.

*

John woke up. Cara was standing beside the bed in her dressing gown, handing him a mug of coffee.

'There you go, sleepyhead!'

'My God, what time is it?'

She glanced at the alarm clock.

'12:52. I've breakfast on.'

'God, I couldn't look at food. Must have been 5am when we got back from Annie's house.'

'Yeah. You were up singing. Do you remember?"

He slurped his coffee.

'No way!' he spluttered, laughing. 'Oh, shit! It's all coming back to me now! Where's my phone? I put it on Silent when I got home.'

Cara picked it off the floor.

'Here.'

'Shit! 32 missed calls from James! That's very strange. Better ring him and see what this madman wants.'

Another slurp of coffee.

'All right, James? Happy New Year! Sorry I missed your . . .'

'Don't F**kin' Happy New Year me, you stupid little b**tard!'

"What? Calm down! What's up? What's . . . ?'

'Who's there with you? Get them out of the house! I'm on me way down to ye *now!* Put on the news, you little fool!'

He hung up.

'What's wrong?' asked Cara. 'What's happening? You look freaked.'

He put down the coffee.

'I don't know. Put on the tv. *The news!* Fast, Cara!'

The news came on. A photo of Jason Bailey.

". . . was found shot dead. He was a 30-year-old youth leader, and was well liked. Gardaí say that a major investigation is underway. In other news, the . . .'

Cara turned it off. Her face was a deathly pale – as was John's.

'That's your man, isn't it? Your man from my party – the coke dealer! Isn't it? What's going on, John?'

He got out of bed and started pulling on his clothes.

'Gimme a minute. Shit! My God, Cara. Get dressed and go to your ma's. James is on his way down here. Don't say a word to anyone. Just go, pet. *Fast!*'

'Youth leader? What's that about? He was a coke dealer, John. Who killed him? What's going on, John? *Tell me!*'

'I've no idea. I swear, Cara. Just go. Please. I'll ring you after James leaves. Hurry, love.'

'Ok,' she said, as she whipped off her dressing gown and started to dress. 'Ring me the minute he leaves. I love you.'

'Love you too. Go. *Go*!'

John snorted a couple of lines of coke to try and clear his head before meeting James. He sat back, lighting up a fag, his hands shaking as he held the remote control and read the news details on ceefax.

He jumped at the sound of the doorbell.

He slowly opened the door, but James shoved it in, sending John flying back down the hall. Mickey Mulligan followed behind as James slammed the door closed.

His face said it all. Pure rage. Mickey just stood back, saying nothing, not showing any emotion.

'Is there anyone else here?' said James, pushing his way into the sitting room, looking around for any signs of life.

'What's going on, James?' said John. 'I just seen the news. What the hell did you guys do?'

James turned round, grabbed John by the shirt, pushing him up against the wall, sending a framed photo crashing to the floor.

'Have you any f**kin' idea the shite you just brought down on us? I've spent all last night and today trying to stop Darryl coming down here and ripping your heart out for what you've done!'

'For what? Let me go! You're hurting me!'

'Don't say a word, or I swear I'll kill you myself, right here and now. You hear me? You little fool!'

He flung John down onto the sofa.

'You rang me, Stephen's Night, yeah? Filling my head with a load of crap about a guy selling pure coke out this way. My God, I should never have listened to you. You were out of your face on coke, paranoid to bits. You never took more than a few lines up till Christmas. Now you're out of your f**kin' head every day, losing the run of yourself. You swore to me this guy Bailey was dealing coke at your bird's house.'

'But he *was*, James!,' said John, getting to his feet. 'He *was!*'

'Shut your hole, John! Don't interrupt me again. Sit down and don't say another word till I ask you, or I'll smash your face to bits! We took you on your word and went and looked into this Bailey guy again. We found he was seemingly always around coke heads. But you made out he was dealing. You swore blind on the phone to me.'

'But he *was*, James! Listen – do you want a bottle of beer or something? Coffee?'

'Is he trying to wind me up, Mickey? Bailey is a youth leader, never touched a drug in his life. He's helped loads to kick drugs. We picked him up to give him a fright – like, to see who he was dealing for. But the little asshole got cheeky. And, well – he's dead now!'

'*Whaaat?* My God! But I told you just to warn the guy off! Not kill him! I'm sorry, but I don't want any part of it. No way, James! No way. Sorry, but this has nothing to do with me. I'm just into the coke selling end of things.'

He put a cigarette between his lips and flicked his lighter. Before the flame could make contact, James punched him in the face, sending cigarette and lighter flying across the room.

'Nothing to do with *you?'* he roared. ''I'll kill you, you little asshole! You're the one who got us into this big mess! You hear me now? You're up to your skinny neck in all of this!'

John put his hands up to try and protect his face. Mickey gave James a look that said *Keep it down a bit*.

James lowered his voice, speaking through gritted teeth.

'I asked you were you 100% sure he was selling on your patch. You said yes. It was your words that got us to act. You confirmed it. It's your mess, not ours. You hear me? Your mess, Johnny Boy. Our business – everything – is under threat over your stupid mistake.'

John grabbed a paper towel from the kitchen to wipe away the blood running down his face.

'Look – calm down, will you! It'll blow over.'

'Blow over? Can you believe what he's saying, Mickey? Blow over! Are you f**kin kidding me? There's cops all over Swords. We had to move coke and cash out of houses all last night in case the raids started coming. And my bet is they will. You just don't get it, do you? This isn't a drug dealer who's been murdered. This is a well-respected youth leader. The outcry is only starting. They're stopping cars. They're going from house to house. Top cops have been called in. *Blow over?* Wake up, you fool, you! This is one serious mess you landed us all in. And you have the cheek to say it's nothing to do with you? Tell him, Mickey, before I kill him altogether, the fool!'

James sat down, opening his jacket.

'It's not safe to move coke. There's road blocks everywhere, even one today as we came out this way.'

'Ok, James,' said Mickey, giving him the eye. 'Take it easy. I'll take over.'

James nodded, letting out a heavy sigh.

'Give us one of your fags first,' said Mickey, 'and a line of that coke on the cd.'

He bent down and snorted a couple of lines and sat back, dragging on his fag.

'Right. Here's the story. Don't for a second think this is going to go away easily. It won't! When you started buying coke off us you became part of a gang. So get rid of this idea that you can just step away and leave us to mop up your mess. Ain't gonna happen!'

He dragged on his fag, flicking the ash across into the fireplace.

'Now this is important. Who else knows? Your bird? Any of your mates? Now don't mess with me, John! We need to fill in all the holes – and fast!'

'No one knows a thing, lads. I swear. My bird knows nothing.'

'Everyone tells their birds secrets, John. Don't take me for a fool!'

'All she knows is, I sell coke. I never tell her names.'

'But she was at the party. So were your mates. They'd remember the whole incident. They would have seen this Bailey lad.'

'No. No one remembers it. I just threw him out. Everyone was coked and drunk. The party was full on. No one saw anything that would lead them to think today I had anything to do with this. Cara wouldn't know about calls I made to you lads about this or anything else. And even if she did she'd never breathe a word. But I'm telling you – none of them knows a thing!'

'So that's it? No one knows? That could earmark you. You never told a soul!'

John put his head down. There was a moment of silence. Then he whispered.

'Oh, shit.'

'Oh, shit, what?' said James. 'Out with it! Oh, shit, what?'

'There's . . . there's one person who does know. The girl. The girl who was with your man Bailey that night. I thought you guys maybe just beat him up or warned him off. So I . . . I seen the girl a couple of nights ago. And well, I had a few on me and I . . . well, I told her something along the lines of *We sorted out your little coke dealer.* Sorry, lads. I never dreamt he was dead. Lisa! That's her name. Lisa Something . . .'

James looked at Mickey.

'Well, that's it, Mickey. She's going to know the minute she sees the news today that John's involved. How stupid can someone be! He gets coked out of his thick head and then mouths off the whole story to a girl!'

'Calm down, James,' said John. 'No cops have busted in a door. It's hearsay. She may be too scared to tell anyone.'

'Let's hope you're right – for all our sakes. Is there something wrong with you? Telling a bloody girl! You know it won't be local cops that you'll be dealing with. This'll be the top boys. He won't be able to hold it together, Mickey.'

'Lads! Not on my life would I open my mouth. You know me, James. You know me better than that.'

'Come on, Mickey, said James, nodding towards the door. 'That's all for now. You stay out of sight and off that coke. You hear me? If you get pulled, I don't have to tell you what will happen if you rat any of us up! If it dies down a bit, Mickey will drop down with a batch of white next week.'

When they left, John rang Cara.

'Ok. They've gone. Can't talk on the phone. Just get back here as soon as you can.'

He washed the blood from his face and cleaned up the room to make it look like nothing had happened. A few minutes later Cara pulled up in the driveway. John opened the hall door.

'What happened?' she asked, getting out of the car.

John put his finger to his lips and motioned her inside.

'I can't believe it or understand it, Cara. You're not supposed to know a thing. But they killed the guy. You're not supposed to know any of this, ok? Something just went wrong, and they're 100% certain he never touched drugs. He helped people to kick drugs. My bloody head's melted, Cara! They're going mad over this with me, 'cause I made the phonecall that night, telling them he was selling coke in your home. But I don't understand it. You saw Lisa with your own eyes. She was on coke. She said something went up her nose. I mean, it had to be drugs – coke!'

'My God, John! Murder? This is so serious. A man is dead. And God! It's linked to you! We have to stop. Right now, John. You have to stop selling the coke, and get out of all this. You hear me, John? It's time to stop dealing!'

'I can't just stop, Cara. It doesn't work that way. You can't just walk away. I wish I could. But you think this gang will let me do that, knowing it was me who got them into this whole mess? Plus – Lisa is going to know today that I'm involved. I said we "sorted him out", but the lads told me it was sorted. I thought they meant a few digs, or a warning. God! Do you think she'll go to the cops?'

'You told *Lisa?* When?'

'In Tommy's, at the loo the other night. I was on that new coke. Shit!'

'My God, John. What are we going to do?'

'Lisa won't open her mouth. She'll be afraid. If she does, I'll say it's a load of crap. No one else heard me say it.'

'Do you think any of the gang will remember anything from the party?'

'I'm sure they will. But look, all they'll remember is just that he was at the party and then left. Plus, I was never out of Skerries for the whole Christmas. Look, my plan was always just to sell the coke for a few more years, make enough to keep us good for the future. But I'm getting another lad to sell for me. I've a guy in Balbriggan, but one more runner will free me up to spend time with you when we get married. Ok?'

'I don't know, John. You're getting in way over your head. You started out just selling it to a few of your mates. Now look – you're selling it to the whole Fingal area. It's all got too deep. I'm frightened, John. Please – you have to find a way out now!'

'Look, love. I can't. If I tell them I'm out, they'll think it's over the murder. They won't have it that I'm telling you. Cara, you don't know these heads. We'll just have to sit it out, take it easy. Yeah? Don't go out that much. It'll die down. I promise!'

*

I went back with David to his house before Ma came home. We sat as Carol, helped by Richie, made up the New Year's Day dinner. They were both still in shock from the awful events that led to Jason's murder. They advised me to do nothing, as the danger would be great.

'They'd kill your whole family,' said Carol. 'You don't know what you're dealing with, Lisa.'

David held the note from Jason in his two hands, reading, re-reading and scrutinising it for some clue.

'This G27 has to mean something,' he said. 'Like, we can now safely say he didn't give you drugs that night. Well, let's wait and see what unfolds later in the news. Nothing is certain, is it?'

'You know,' said Richie, 'this whole story is getting crazier by the minute. I mean, who would have thought it: a guy puts a strange note into a girl's pocket and then, two days later, he ends up dead. It's like a bloody movie you'd see!'

'Listen, Lisa,' said Carol, coming out of the kitchen, 'David's working in the morning, but I'll take you to Rathmines to attend his funeral. Are you sure you really want to attend it?'

'Yeah, it's something I just have to do. Something tells me I just have to go and be there and pay my respects. I know nothing is clear about what really happened in that garden that night. But deep down I know drugs were not involved. I just have to be there.'

'Ok, I'll take you.'

'Thanks so much, Carol. I'd hate to go on my own.'

I rang Ma, who was still in Jim's, to let her know I was staying for dinner in David's, and I'd be late home.

*

That evening, James and Mickey pulled up outside Darryl's house. The front door opened. His wife stood there, holding their two-year-old baby girl in her arms. Darryl popped his head out, looking over her shoulder.

'Take the kids into the sitting room, Emily. Come into the back kitchen, lads. Close the door – it's freezing out there. Grab a can of Heineken and sit down. Now – where's Rob? I told him and Jess to be here.'

James lit up a fag.

'They're both moving cash and coke to safer houses, just in case a raid goes down.'

'Right. Right. Before I start, I've said enough last night and today to you, James. But Mickey, how the hell did you not bury the body like

I told you? A simple job and you both ballsed it up.'

'Darryl, it was mad dark that night. All we had was a couple of flashlamps. I was sure we done a great job of burying the fool. We wanted to pick a remote part of the forest, but we must have picked the wrong spot in the end. We . . .'

'That's enough! I'm sick to death of bullshit excuses. I keep going over it in my head. James – the night you came to me with this problem, I told you to just leave it alone for a while, till after Christmas. But no! You kept pushing it and pushing it because it was your patch he was supposed to be dealing on. We moved too fast on this. I should have gone on my own instinct. So anyway, what did you find out off John, this fool of yours?'

'He's a mess, Darryl. All over the place. But he won't open his mouth if he's pulled. The only problem is . . . this girl that was at his bird's party Stephen's Night. The fool mouthed off to her in a pub a couple of nights ago that he had sorted the guy out! He told me he thought we just hit him or warned him off.'

Darryl put both hands up over his face.

'What sort of f**kin' fool is he, James? This is the guy you swore by as being the best!'

'Look, he's the best at selling coke. But, well, he's not great at much else, it seems! He's been sorting coke a lot over the past few weeks, which he's never done before. He's become reckless, to be honest, and it's led to him being paranoid, and then this big mess. Isn't that right, Mickey?'

'Yeah, yeah. The last time I dropped to him he was well out of his face, which was never like him. But he said he's staying off it for the New Year. He's due to get married in June, I think.'

'Do youse pair realise I shot someone, based on the information from that idiot? Do yiz?'

'Look, Darryl,' said James, 'let's be honest here. And don't get defensive when I say this, ok? But on the night this happened, well, we were only supposed to have words, frighten him off, like, not f**kin' *kill him!*'

Darryl stared into the flickering flames in the fireplace.

'We went over this last night, James. You heard the way he spoke to me. I don't take crap from anyone, don't care who he is. And that weirdo talked down to me. To *me!* No one does that to Darryl Casey.'

Everyone went silent. The only noise was the faint crackling of the coal burning in the fire, and the gulp of Mickey taking a mouthful from his can of beer.

'Ok. So let's look at it again. It's down to this: two people can link this back to us, John and this girl, Lisa. Right, well, I'm not taking any chances of going down for this, and I'm sure you both feel the same. Right? So the only way I'm going to sleep right again is . . . if we take out John.'

There was another tense silence.

'We take him out. Nobody can finger us. *No one.*'

Mickey stared at the floor. James lit up another fag.

'Look, Darryl. I know he's messed everything up. But he's covering a wide area for us. Plus – *another* shooting, so soon after the last one?'

'Look, lads. He's a weak link. If he's lifted, he could break. He's not like us. He's never been inside a cop shop in his life. He's too soft, James. He's in this just for the money. I'm telling you, he'll crack under pressure. The cops won't stop on this one till they bring someone down for it. This has Veronica Guerin written all over it. The public outcry is growing as we sit here talking. And it's just the start. If we whack John it won't matter about the girl. Once John's dead, it's over!'

'I see what you mean,' said Mickey, handing the ashtray to James. 'But is it not better to hit the girl? Once she's out, nobody can trace it back to John, and it's case over.'

James nodded his head in agreement.

'Mickey – am I right? John is very valuable to us. He's stretching out further into other areas. If we take him out, we'll lose. We'll lose a lot of cash. Think, Darryl! It'd take forever to replace him out that way. I know for sure he wouldn't rat us up if he gets pulled. He knows he'd be a Dead Man Walking if he does.'

Darryl was tapping his fingers on his forehead, deep in thought.

'What do you think, Darryl?'

Darryl let out a long sigh.

'I'm thinking: shut . . . the f**k . . . *up!* Let me *think!*'

They held their breath, waiting for his decision.

'Ok. We won't jump the gun this early. We'll sit tight and see what unfolds. There's no point hitting her at this stage. We don't know if she's told people. If we do find out that she has, then we take her out. We'll be in a worse mess than we're in already. You say she was a mate of John and his bird, yeah?'

'Yeah, they were all close mates,' said Mickey, flicking his cigarette into the fire and downing the last of his can of beer.

Ok we'll sit and wait. See if she contacts John about it. Maybe she remembers nothing of what John said. We'll see. But no more mistakes, lads. Yiz hear me? No more f**kin' mistakes!'

Chapter Eighteen

Right Place, Wrong Time

I got home late to find Ma gone to bed. I'd made my mind up not to say anything about Jason. I hoped she wouldn't remember the name when she read the reports in the newspapers. I awoke early and left a note on the kitchen table to say I was off for the day with Carol and I'd be back around teatime.

As I drove with Carol towards Rathmines, that strange butterfly feeling came sweeping across my heart again. Whatever it was, it held me together for what lay ahead at Jason's funeral. Carol kept reassuring me how none of this was in any way my fault. Her support made such a difference, as I was filled with so many mixed emotions and thoughts about Jason's untimely death. What if I had never gone to Cara's party that night? He'd still be alive today. Above everything else, I wanted to understand the events of that night so I could make sense of what he was doing there. How did he know me? And above all, what exactly did he do to me in those few seconds when my eyes were closed?

We parked the car a short distance from the church, with a good fifteen minutes to spare. A chilling feeling crept over me as I watched the crowds starting to gather – so many young people, already in tears.

The hearse slowly came into view. My heart sank. That sick feeling kicked in again. The sides of the street leading to the church were now lined with people, the crowds growing. We made our way forward and stood near the main doors of the church, so we had a full view of the sad events as they unfolded.

A black car carrying Jason's family pulled up behind the hearse. His mother and sister got out first, dressed in black, being held up by relatives, holding each other, sobbing their hearts out. The scene was unbearable to watch. The father limped out of the car, a small, grey-haired man, thin and frail looking, dressed in his black suit, determined to be strong for the sake of his family. Six young men lifted the coffin, draped with a Liverpool flag, out of the hearse. Under the guidance of the undertaker, they hoisted it onto their shoulders, and carried it into the church. I glanced at Carol and saw that she too had tears streaming down her face.

'My God, Lisa,' she whispered, handing me a tissue from her bag, 'this is heartbreaking.'

I was so glad that I had come.

We were lucky to get seats midway up the aisle. They had installed loudspeakers out the front for the hundreds who stood outside in the cold morning air.

I glanced discreetly around at the mourners, wondering if I could recognise any of them. Some of the faces looked vaguely familiar, but I couldn't put a name on any of them.

The microphone crackled, startling me.

'Good morning, my brothers and sisters,' said the Minister.

'Good morning.'

'Just over a year ago, Jason spoke to me in private. We talked about the growing problem of drug abuse in Dublin and in Ireland generally. He said, though it was his first priority to try to lead as many people out of the web of drugs, his main focus was to continue to study the nature of the drug culture. He told me he always had a very unsettling, disturbing feeling that something darker and far more sinister lay at the heart of the problem of cocaine, something from the unseen world? I wasn't sure what he meant, and said something along the lines of *Ah, do your best and be careful. At the end of the day it's a growing social problem, linked to peer pressure. You can only do your best, Jason.*

'His face changed and he looked somewhat disappointed at my remark. He said, "Bill, I'm sorry, but I've studied this issue for years. And the more I understand, the more I see it's not just a social issue. The social aspect is just a side effect. I'm telling you, Bill, unless we grasp this nettle and take action now, we're going to be facing a nightmare no one will be able to stop."

'That seemed to be his growing fear. As to what he meant, I was never really sure. But we all know it was leading him further and further into risky situations. And I shared his concern. But no one thought for a second it would lead to his untimely death. We all thought at first it was a case of mistaken identity, that no one would hurt someone who just went around schools and local youth clubs, trying to help kids with drug issues.

'But yes, someone out there took a dislike to him and his work. And may God forgive them for taking out such a bright light in such a violent manner. May God look down on his family and all those who loved him, and give them a sense of peace, a sense of healing at this sad time.'

Carol and I glanced at each other. All I could think of was David and his basement, his own research.

The service went on. The six young men who carried his coffin were all ex-addicts who had been weaned off drugs at different times by Jason. Two of them spoke from the pulpit, sharing with us how Jason had helped them. One of them, Paul, broke down halfway through his speech and couldn't continue.

The thought that Carol and I were the only ones in the church with information about this murder began to unsettle me no end. I felt we should leave now. We had paid our respects. It was time to go. It was getting far too upsetting. But as I reached down to pick up my handbag, the Minister spoke again.

'Lastly, Mr Bailey has asked to say a few words.'

I stopped in my tracks and sat back, as did Carol. The place went into a deeper silence. *How can he find the strength to speak in public on such an occasion as this?*

He limped up to the pulpit, helped by a younger man, a member of his family, I presume. He spoke without notes, his dignity showing through his broken voice.

'I'd like firstly to thank all of you for your support, your cards, your flowers – and most of all, your love. Your prayers. Thank you . . . so much.'

He bent forward, holding himself up with the support of the pulpit.

'Sorry – em, this isn't easy. Bear with me. I loved Jason so much. He was my son, my only son. He did so much for other people, and someone took him away from me. Someone took my boy away . . .'

He broke and had to be helped back to his seat. I snapped. I couldn't bear this. John's face flashed before me. I grabbed my handbag, almost pushing Carol back on the seat.

'I can't breathe, Carol! I have to get out now. My God, the pain in that man's face.'

I left her stumbling to catch up with me as I pushed my way through the people crammed at the back of the church. *I shouldn't be here!*

As soon as I got outside, I started half-running down the steps, the people still staring at me, mystified.

'Lisa, wait!' called Carol after me.

I stopped just outside the gates. I could still hear the Minister's voice over the loudspeakers. Carol grabbed me.

'Hey, are you ok? Come here.' She held me close. 'It's ok.'

'Are you ok?' came a male voice from behind us.

We both turned to find a tall, well-built guy in his 30s, with short, brown hair, dressed in a grey suit, looking intently at us both.

'I saw you running out of the church just now. Are you ok?'

'Yeah, I think so. Yeah, it's just so awful, so sad. His poor father. My God.'

I tried to catch my breath.

'I know,' he said, 'it's heartbreaking. You must have been close to Jason. Lisa, isn't that your name? I heard your friend here call after you.'

'Yeah, I'm Lisa. This is Carol. No, no. We don't know him at all, really.'

'Where are you from? Are you both friends?'

'Yeah, we are. My name's Carol Salle. This is Lisa Webb. We're from Skerries.'

'Skerries? That's out past Swords, right? So what brought you all the way out to his funeral if you didn't know Jason?'

I looked straight at him, his eyes searching me for an answer.

'Em . . . sorry, but who are *you*, by the way?'

Carol looked more uncomfortable by the second.

'Yeah, who are you? You never gave us your name.'

'You never asked! My name's Jack Magee. I work for the Special Branch.'

I swallowed, hoping he didn't notice.

He looked me straight in the eye, paused, then said,

'Maybe we'll talk again. Sorry for your loss.'

Then he coolly walked away, rejoining two other tall men, presumably colleagues from the Special Branch. He said something to them under his breath, and they glanced in our direction before all three of them turned their backs on us.

'Let's get out of here, Carol,' I whispered. 'Now!'

I turned one last time to look at Jack, and caught his eye. Unblinking, he held my gaze for what was just a couple of seconds, but felt like an eternity.

'Come on, Lisa!' said Carol. 'Let's just go home and forget we ever came here. There's nothing we can do to bring Jason back.'

When we got into the car and closed the doors, we both let out a sigh of relief.

'My God,' she continued. 'That detective put the creeps up me. He made me feel like he knew *we* knew something.'

'I know, I know.'

We drove back to Skerries and went to a restaurant for lunch, both trying to put aside the awful moments of seeing Jason's family torn apart with grief. But images of his father crying at the end crowded our thoughts as we talked late into the afternoon.

There was nothing we could do. Carol was right. David was right. What could we do? I wished we hadn't met that Jack Magee character. I just felt that it didn't make sense that two girls would run from a funeral, upset and crying, and then state that they never knew the deceased. I felt that Jack Magee saw inside me, that I was hiding something. He was no fool. He knew part of the jigsaw just did not fit.

I had my first day back teaching the next morning, so I needed to clear my thoughts of all of this as best I could. But there was yet more drama awaiting me when we drove back to Carol's house so that she could take over from Rachel from looking after Tim.

Just as Rachel was leaving, David arrived in the door. I told him about the events of the morning.

'My God, Lisa! A detective! You didn't tell him anything, did you?'

'No, but he seemed to sense something. He's not working for the Special Branch for nothing. They're bloody well-trained to pick up on things, even the smallest things.'

'I'll never forget the hurt in Mr Bailey's face, David. It crushed me to watch it, knowing I knew something about it.'

'Lisa – what you know is hearsay. Nothing else. John said something to you. It's your word against his. And listen to me – as I've told you, his gang would shoot you down five minutes after you talked to any cops. Don't forget that.'

'I won't,' I said, looking into those blue eyes of his. 'I won't, David.'

'Listen, maybe with everything that's happened, this is not the time to tell you this, but . . .'

'. . . But what? Tell me what! I'm able for anything after the events of the last couple of days. Tell me.'

'Well, I was in work today and, with nothing to do, I went on Facebook, only to find Emma had unblocked me and asked me to be her friend again. She sent me this long, private mail.'

'Did you let her be your friend again?'

'Yeah. I mean, after reading her message, I had to at least be nice. That's me. I don't hold grudges, Lisa. Never have. I don't believe in being bitter.'

'So what did the message say? You don't have to tell me if it's private.'

I could feel the apprehension and my walls closing in around my insides. Something spelt Danger. An uncomfortable feeling set in very fast. *This can't be happening. Not now. Not again!*

'Well, she just wants to be friends again, and apologised for all she had put me through. Said she was off the coke since New Year's Eve, and just needed a friend who would understand what it was like.'

'Ok . . . Well, that's grand that she's off the coke . . . a few days.'

I tried to hide it, but this was not something I wanted to hear.

Carol walked in from tending to her father.

'Did I hear Emma's name being mentioned?'

'Yeah – David's back in touch with her.'

'*What?* Are you joking me?'

She banged her empty coffee cup on the table.

'My God, David!'

'Listen, Carol,' he said. 'I can explain.'

As he spelt it out, Carol stood there with her arms folded, shaking her head in disbelief.

'Oh, how odd! So, does her fella – what's-his-name – know all this?'

'Well, it's all off between them. She broke it off sometime over the Christmas. She wants to get a clear break from drugs and get her life sorted out. She said she couldn't do that while going out with Mark, as *he* wouldn't stop taking it. So it's over.'

David swirled the remainder of the coffee in his mug.

'I know what you're both thinking – that I'm a fool, after all she did. But look – are we not supposed to forgive and forget and move on? It sounds like she's really trying to get her act together for once and for all. We have to be there for anyone who needs help from drugs. Yeah?'

I scrabbled for words to try and sound supportive.

But Carol just blew her top.

'Would you just cop on to yourself, David! I don't for one second fall for this crap! Just like that, she's off drugs and single? Give me a break! It's a game, David! I can see through her. I always have.'

She looked over at me to see how it was affecting me. But I kept my feelings hidden. The truth is, I was hurt. It had been a crazy few weeks, a crazy couple of days. A lot had happened to me, too much too soon. Now this! I knew David and I were close, but now it was beginning to dawn on me that maybe I was going to end up losing him as a friend, with Emma back in the picture!

David stood up.

'Girls, look – she said sorry. It's no big deal. It's not like she's coming over for dinner or anything. I told her I'd be there, advise her. That's it. Ok? Nothing else! Will you stop looking at me like that, Carol!'

'Like what?'

'Like I'm doing something foolish. I'd never fully trust her. But if I can be of some help, I think that's ok. Isn't that right, Lisa?'

I suppose he had a point. And we were just being selfish about it all. I loved our little gang of four. And after what Emma had done to David, I was concerned that he was getting mixed up with her again.

'So, are you meeting her – or just talking on the phone?' asked Carol, picking up her mug and bringing it back to the kitchen.

'Look – I replied to her mail, saying I'd meet her – for a coffee. That's it. Thursday. If I can give her advice, great. We should all be thankful she's off the coke, Carol.'

'Yeah,' said Carol, 'I suppose you have a point. But to be honest, I don't think this is a good time for all this to happen. So much has taken place. A young man is dead, David. And in case you have forgotten, *we* have what may be the only information about his death. Plus, we have his note. I think we've enough on our plate without Emma Ryan downloading her issues at this time. It's just the wrong time, David.'

I sat there trying to look detached, but deep down I was in agreement with Carol.

'Look,' said David, 'I'll have one chat with her. That's it. Just one. I'll tell her I'm very busy, but maybe another time down the road I'll chat to her again. I'll give her some advice, recommending she stay clear of any parties or friends who are taking coke. Ok?'

'It's your life, David,' I found myself saying. 'We can't tell you how to live it. But just be careful this time. Ok?'

'Ok.'

Once again, those blue eyes of his reassured me. It was as if they were saying, *Don't worry, Lisa. It's going to be ok.*

A half hour later I left for home, hugging them both and planting a kiss on the side of Tim's face as he watched tv.

'See you all soon.'

'Best of luck with your first day back to school!' shouted David, smiling and waving from the door as I pulled out from the driveway.

I got home and said very little to Ma about the day, getting stuck in instead into preparing my lessons for next morning. I don't think she picked up on anything, though it was difficult for me not to reveal my emotional response to what I had seen: Mr Bailey's face at the pulpit; his wife and daughter crying as they stepped out of the car; not to mention that Special Branch guy looking at me straight in the eye. And now David back in touch with Emma! So much for one person to try and take in. I suppose Christmas was over and real life was about to kick in. Five days a week working. Welcome to the real world, Lisa!

I fell into a deep sleep some time before midnight.

I saw Jason Bailey's face, his kind eyes.

I heard his voice, his gentle voice.

And then, a light – a dark light – shone on me while another light – a bright light – shone on him.

He said, *It's time to switch around, Lisa. Watch.*

The dark light went onto him and the bright light switched to me.

I opened my eyes.

I couldn't move.

Someone was in my room.

Some *thing* was in my room.

A dense, dark presence seemed to surround my face.

I tried to move my hands, but couldn't.

I was gripped with fear – I'd never sensed such a fear in my life.

I tried to scream out.

But my mouth wouldn't open.

A voice whispered, *I'm going to kill you!*

I jumped up.

I realised it was all just a dream.

A bad nightmare.

And I was only really waking up now.

The sweat on the bed.

I reached over and switched on the light.

For a few seconds I felt there was an evil presence in the room with me.

I prayed to God, just a few words, to please take it away.

Everything went back to normal. And I sat there, so afraid.

It's just a dream, Lisa. There's nothing there! Your mind's being working overtime!

I lay there for a while, thinking things over, and eventually, fell back to sleep.

My first day back to school was amazing. I felt so different to the girl who used to come in, trying to hide her coke hangover. I was so grateful for a second chance at doing what I loved, without playing such a dangerous game with my whole career as a teacher.

I really noticed in every way the difference in how I ran my whole class. My interaction with the kids was far more patient, and I was sharper in spotting all the kids' needs, and giving them individual attention. I also felt more at ease in the staffroom, chatting with the other teachers about their school work and holidays. Even the Principal engaged me in pleasant conversation.

I got a text from Carol, asking me how I was, and could we meet Thursday for lunch.

David texted me from work.

Hi Lisa. Pick up Star newspaper on way home. 2 page write up on Jason. X

I read it over dinner. Ma kept watching me with those suspicious eyes of hers.

'Is everything ok, Lisa?' she asked. 'You've been a little on the quiet side the past day or so.'

'Sorry?' I said, looking up from the two-page spread. 'No, no, I'm grand. Just getting back into the swing of school. Did you read about this murder – the youth leader?'

I tried to hide my face, back in the paper, waiting to see did she remember Jason's name from what I told her. But all she said was,

'Terrible story. Saw it on the news last night and heard it on the radio again today. There's a programme on tonight about it at 9:30 on RTE, appealing to the public to come forward with any information.'

I texted David and Carol to let them know about the programme. Carol rang me when I was up in my room changing into my pjs. She told me how she had had it out with David after I had left the day before, warning him to be extra careful, and to make sure not to give anything away about what we knew about Jason Bailey's death.

'I'm so angry with him, Lisa. And I don't trust that Emma one. Don't you think it's all a bit of a coincidence that after seeing us all out together, she turns up with this big story and wants to be best of friends, after all that's happened? David's too bloody soft, Lisa. That's been his downfall in the past. He's just getting over what she did to him.'

'Do you think there's a chance they might start back up with their relationship?'

'Oh God! Don't even say that, Lisa! I'd kill him if he came home and told me something like that. She can't be trusted. He knows that. But how about you, Lisa? How are you with all this? I hope you don't think it will wreck our close friendships?'

'Well, no. Of course not.'

'Never, Lisa. Never. You're family to us now. I'll keep a close eye on David. Don't worry.'

'Ok. I'm off downstairs to watch this programme. See you at four tomorrow in the Blue Ocean. Night, Carol. Thanks for the call. Love you!'

'Love you too!'

I stood in silence in my room. My mind drifted back to New Year's Eve and that amazing kiss, a kiss that touched me deeply, much more than all the experiences of past relationships put together. And yet the experience was now being overshadowed by Jason's murder, and even by Emma's coming back on the scene.

I went downstairs and turned on the tv, while Ma busied herself with the ironing. As the presenter opened the programme with a description of the last sightings of Jason prior to his disappearance, a cold chill ran through me. A handful of people who had known Jason well were interviewed, and all confessed to being still in shock that anyone would want him dead. The presenter read out a statement from Mr Bailey, who was unable to appear on the programme.

'I always stood by my son – and his work, helping others with drug issues. I did feel at times there was a small risk in the work he did, but nothing to be overly concerned about. But when he came to me and said he was moving to live alone in the Swords area, away from all his friends, I was anxious. I saw a different Jason. He seemed relentless in wanting to help people on the northside, but never explained to me why there.

'Then, only a few weeks ago, he told me that his findings about the drug culture had led him to a very deep and unexpected and dark conclusion – which seemed to change him as a person altogether. He seemed distracted – alarmed would be a better word. And I'm convinced that whatever it was he found, played a part in his death in the end.

'The last time I saw him and talked to him was Christmas Day. He said to me, "Dad, my life will never be the same. If my findings are correct, this country of ours is descending into a very dark place, but I know something that's starting to unfold that may stop it." He smiled.

'I asked him to explain, but he said, "Long story, Dad! Next time."

'But there never was a next time. I never saw him alive again. We went through his writings, but he had never written notes on his findings. We're in the dark, you could say, but I know someone out there knows who his killers are. Someone knows something.'

Curled up on the sofa, I tightened my grip on the cushion and gulped down my apprehension.

The presenter paused before announcing that the last word would be from one of the detectives leading the investigation.

My mouth dropped open as the camera swung right and showed the Special Branch man we'd met at the funeral.

'Inspector Jack Magee, do you have any leads in this case you can tell us about?'

'We're looking into a few leads at present,' he said, his voice entering my life again. 'But I can't say anything further at this point in time as it might jeopardise the ongoing investigation. We do have a strong team on this case and we'll stop at nothing till we track down those responsible for this senseless murder of a well-loved young man.'

He addressed that last sentence at the camera, and I felt that he was looking straight through me.

My phone rang. I nearly jumped out of my skin. *Carol.*

'Did you watch it? My God, the Garda at the end! My nerves are shot, Lisa!'

'I know. I couldn't believe it. He's leading the investigation.'

'Wait a minute. David wants a word.'

David took the phone off her.

'Hi, Lisa. Are you ok?'

'Yeah, yeah. A bit freaked, mind you. What did you think of his father's statement?'

'Well, it sounded like Jason was also studying the drug culture, along the same lines as myself.'

'Yeah. I meant to tell you that the Minister at the funeral was saying Jason knew that there was something dark and sinister at the heart of this problem.'

'Wow! So he knew stuff we knew. How strange is that, Lisa! Listen – I've to help Dad do a few things. How about the two of us meeting over the weekend for a chat?'

'Yeah, sure,' I said, trying not to sound too excited.

'Ok. I'll text you or ring you. And don't forget – say nothing to anyone. Ok? Take care, Lisa. Bye.'

'Bye. Oh – tell Carol I'll see her tomorrow at 4pm.'

That night I fell into what seemed like another awful nightmare. I couldn't see anyone in the dream, just this awful dark presence that seemed to follow me persistently, no matter how much I ran and ran to get away from it.

I woke up, drenched in sweat, and in the dark I could have actually sworn there was something – or someone – in the room.

Next day after school, when I met Carol in the Blue Ocean, I told her about the dreams I'd been having.

'They're spooking me a bit, to be honest, Carol.'

She put her arm around me and gave me that reassuring smile of hers.

'Listen, Lisa. It's all this stuff you and David talk about. Plus the stress of the last few days. It's playing on your mind when you go to bed. Don't worry about it. It'll pass, pet.'

We ordered another latte and chatted away about more light-hearted girlie matters.

*

Over in Olive Café, David sat at an outdoor table, waiting for Emma to arrive. He stirred the sugar in his coffee, as the cigarette smoke wafting from a nearby diner tantalised his cravings. Emma pulled up in her car, smartly dressed with newly-cut short hair and full of smiles as she came into his view.

'Hi, Emma,' he said, pulling out a chair for her. 'You look great. What can I get you?'

He hoped he wasn't blushing. Or, if he was, that she didn't notice.

'Latte will do. Thanks. You look great yourself. Thanks so much for meeting me.'

'It's ok.' He signalled through the window for the waiter to bring one latte.

'So. Well – God, it's been a while, Emma.'

'Yeah. It has all right.'

There was an awkward silence, just a few seconds. Emma reached into her handbag.

'Do you mind if I smoke?'

'No, not at all.'

She offered him one.

'No, thanks. I'd *love* one, believe me! But no. Not since New Year's Day.'

She lit up, inhaling deeply, and blew the smoke away from the table, but it drifted back towards David, like an old memory.

The latte arrived.

'Thanks,' said David. 'On my tab.'

'Oh, thanks,' said Emma.

She sipped from the creamy surface.

'Mmm.'

'So,' he said, dropping his voice to a hush. 'Great to hear you're off the you-know-what. Well done. Great news.'

'Yeah, well, if I had listened to you a year ago, I'd have saved myself a lot of pain. But I just had to find out for myself, I suppose. You know, I just can't seem to forgive myself for things I did in the past when I was on the you-know-what. I was so mean to you.'

'Well, I wouldn't say that, but . . .'

'No, I was. I *was* mean to you, David. I know I mailed you and said sorry, but now I really am sorry I treated you so badly. Do you think you can ever forgive me?'

He gazed into those eyes that had held him in a trance many a night over the time they spent together.

'Em, yeah, as far as I'm concerned, it's over. It's in the past. I do forgive you, Emma. I never hold grudges. Never.'

She took another pull from her cigarette.

'You know what happened, don't you, David? Like, I've just realised it lately *why* we broke up.'

He looked around and saw that thankfully no one was sitting within earshot of them now.

'Well, tell me if you want,' he said. 'I always felt you got sick of me, and part of it was down to the fact that I wasn't into the coke buzz, and clubbing and so on.'

'No, no, that's not it,' she said, stubbing out her cigarette in the ashtray. 'Deep down I knew you loved me. But I was afraid of the kind of love you had to give. I'd never felt anything like it before in my life. So I ran, pushed you away, closed you out. I kept taking the coke and in the end I got lost in that world. But over time, I realised, looking back, what we once had, how real it was. I mean, you have to admit we were great together.'

'Well, I suppose . . .'

'You did everything you could to try to get me to love myself, to get me off the coke. And today what you see is the New Me, and it's all down to you, David, and I just want to thank you face to face.'

She leaned over and hugged him.

'You're a life-saver, David Salle!'

'Well, thanks. That's so kind of you to say.'

He tried to hide it, but he was shocked at the change in her. Everything about her was different. Even her looks. You could see she meant what she said.

They laughed and joked about the old times, as they called them, and put aside the negative ending to their relationship.

She took another sip from her latte and lit a second cigarette.

'So, anyway, how about you? How's Carol? And your father – Tim?'

'They're both doing great. You know, Dad has his moments, but health-wise, he's doing great.'

'And I see Lisa's hanging out with you and Carol. Well, it was great she got off the coke as well. Fair play to her.'

There was a silence. Emma tapped the cigarette on the edge of the ashtray.

'So, are you . . . are you dating each other? You don't mind me asking?'

'No, no, you're grand,' he said, smiling. 'No, we're just good friends, as they say, Emma. Good friends. We all get on great.'

'Mmm. Ok. Sounds all good.'

They lost track of time as they chatted on about anything and everything till the owner came out to say,

'It's nearly six o'clock. We're just closing. Sorry.'

David walked Emma to her car.

'So – can we stay in touch?' she said, turning to stand close to him. 'I'd like to meet you again – as a friend, like.'

'Yeah, sure,' he said. 'You have my number. Buzz me and we'll meet again. It's great to see you looking so good.'

Their eyes locked, that look from past days. Emma turned away, opened the door of her car, then turned back, reaching up and hugging him close. He returned the hug. She kissed him on the cheek, whispering,

'You look good, David.'

Just at that moment, I drove by with Carol beside me. Both of us caught sight of David and Emma, hugging closely.

Chapter Nineteen

In-Between Love

I pulled awkwardly into the driveway, almost clipping Carol's parked car.

'Shit – that was close. Sorry.'

I turned off the engine. We both sat there in silence, just for a moment.

'What a strange sight,' sighed Carol, opening her seat belt. 'Unexpected – to say the least. Where in God's name is that lad's head? It's as if nothing ever happened in the past. All smiles and hugs. Forgive me for saying it, Lisa, but what a idiot he can be from time to time.'

I sat there, just staring blankly into the dark evening.

'What? . . . Yeah, strange all right,' I said, trying to hide the real disappointment I was feeling. 'Sure, look, Carol. It's David. He just wants to help people. That's him all over. He's a giver. He's doing what he's best at. Look what he did for me – in just a couple of weeks.'

In the reflection of the windscreen I could see that Carol was looking directly at me, as if she was trying to pick her moment to bring up something about David and me.

'Look,' I said, switching on the ignition, 'I've got to go, pet. I've a pile of stuff to get ready for school tomorrow.'

'Will you not come in for a cup of tea or coffee?'

'No, thanks, I drank enough in the Blue Ocean. I'll be awake all night. Sure I'll see you over the weekend. Yeah – ring me tomorrow. We'll make a plan for the weekend, if that suits you.'

'Ok,' said Carol, leaning over to hug me. 'Now listen – don't worry about this Emma one coming back on the scene. You hear me?'

I looked into her eyes, trying – but failing – to hide my feelings from her. I could tell she knew I was upset by the whole episode.

She stepped out and I reversed slowly out, only to see David walking towards the house. He waved me down, so I stopped and rolled down my window.

'Hey there!' he said cheerily, his eyes, beguiling as ever, looking into mine.

'Hi.'

'How have you been? Will we see you over the weekend?'

I tightened my grip on the steering wheel.

'Well, Carol and myself will be in touch, so we'll arrange something.'

I was trying to stop my mouth from trembling as I spoke.

'Did you . . . how did your . . . your meet-up go with . . . with

Emma?'

I even found it hard to say her name.

He dropped his eyes.

'Em . . . yeah. Great. She's doing well, off the coke. We talked a few things over. You know what I mean – about the past. Hope she stays off the stuff now. I really hope so. Another one saved from that horrible drug.'

'Yeah.'

My eyes were smarting and my throat was dry.

'Did she say anything about Jason? Or John? Or the gang?'

'No, nothing, thank God. I was waiting for something, but nothing came up. I would have stopped the conversation.'

He leaned closer.

'How have *you* been over the whole Jason thing?'

'Ah, a few nightmares. But getting there. I still feel so awful about him, and keep thinking about his poor family.'

'Hey, come here,' he said, bending down and leaning straight into the car, putting his arm around me. 'You stay strong, Lisa Webb. You hear me? I'm just a phone call away.'

'I will,' I said, forcing a smile. 'See you at the weekend. Bye, David.'

He stood there looking after me as I pulled off down the Skerries Road towards home.

A strange sensation raced up my insides. I began to quiver all over. Flashes of David holding Emma and smiling were followed by flashes of our own time together. Everything seemed to be racing a million miles an hour and something was about to give way. I had to pull myself together as I was driving the car. I could see myself laughing, smiling and joking with him. Ever present in those images were those irresistible eyes of his, smiling at me at every turn.

Ah, shit. What's really going on here? This is freaking my head out!

I pulled into my driveway, with the radio playing out the end of a song. In my mind's eye, everything switched to New Year's Eve. The slow walk. My God – that kiss. The feeling of being that close to someone. That can't be the end of it. Can it? I was reminded of conversations we had shared, and his statement of his love for Emma.

When I went inside, I threw my bag in the hallway and went upstairs to change.

'Hi, Lisa. Dinner's ready.'

'Thanks, Ma. Give me five minutes.'

I turned on my laptop and went onto Facebook, switching onto David's wall. A message – a short message – from Emma.

Hi, David. Thanks for meeting up today. So glad we cleared up a few things. You looked amazing. xxx

Oh great. That was all I needed to see. I went downstairs and half-ate my dinner, as Ma watched my every move from the corner of her eye, pretending to read the paper at the same time.

I could see the front page. The familiar photo of Jason, now known nationwide. Beside the photo it read:

No developments in murder case.

Jason's kind, gentle eyes brought me right back to that night we met. How did he know I had turned my back on drugs? Why did he travel from Swords just to see me? Why did he not just meet me for a coffee? Why come to a party? Why? I don't think I'll ever know the answers, will I?

Ma folded the paper and placed it on the table.

'Ok, out with it,' she said. 'What's bothering you, Lisa? You're not yourself the past day or so.'

'Ah, I'm grand, Ma. I'm grand.'

'No, you're not. Something's bothering you, and I'm starting to worry about you again, to be honest. How are your friends, David and his sister – what's her name?'

'Carol, Ma. And her boyfriend, Richie.'

I stood up and leaned against the work counter, staring into the gas fire.

'Well, I'm not back on the coke. That's one worry you don't have to be concerned about. It's just . . . it's . . . well . . . it's David. It's David.'

'Well, I sort of knew this was coming. But I wanted you tell me in your own good time.'

'Well, we're friends, and we hang out a lot. And, well, on New Year's Eve . . . well, I don't know . . . we got a bit close, to say the least . . . and, well, he kissed me. Yes, that's it. He kissed me. That's all. But it was far more than a kiss, like . . .'

I was trying not to sound stupid, but wasn't succeeding.

'Well, ok. He kissed you. That's no big deal. Sure you've kissed lots of guys since your teens. I know you, Lisa. You kiss a guy and come home all lovey-dovey, smiling, saying, "This is it! This is the one!"'

'Ma, stop. Just stop, ok? This is completely different.'

I could feel the tension rising up inside me as Ma continued talking.

'Look, pet. I know David's a lovely guy. But so were Ron and Ian. And what's-his-name, Ian Gannon from years back. You kissed them all and came home saying what you're saying right now.'

She smiled warmly at me as she took my hand in hers.

'You look too hard for love, sweetheart. I told you – you have to wait till it comes to *you*.'

'But Ma, you weren't there when David kissed me. You didn't feel what I felt.'

'Ok, ok. So what's happening? Are you dating? Explain it to me.'

'No, it was just a spur-of-the-moment kiss, like. It just happened. I don't know what's really happening. And now his ex-girlfriend is back in touch with him and I think he's still got feelings for her.'

'My God, Lisa, you can't get involved in that. That has hurt written all over it. I mean, one kiss and you're like this, all over the place.'

'Ma, don't say that. It was more than a kiss. Something . . . something passed between us, like something breathing from him to me, and then it passed out from me. Something like that. I can't explain it, but my God, I almost passed out from the feelings. I never felt that with any guy before. Never. It was like magic.'

'Ok, calm down, pet. Come here. You're shaking.'

She put her arms around me.

'You have to protect yourself from this, pet. I can't watch you get hurt again. Not now. You're at a very vulnerable stage in your life, coming off the drugs and losing Cara and the gang.'

I pulled frantically away, tears starting to roll down my face.

'I should have seen all this coming, shouldn't I? It's too late to protect myself. Protect from what, Ma? It's not like anything I've ever experienced before. I'm just seeing it all now, all the flashes of me and David since that night. It's so clear to me now. Every other relationship I was ever in was based on trying to find someone to love me, to come into my life and make me happy. God, I was so insecure. I thought, if I find this guy, he'll make me happy and we'll live happily ever after.'

'So, ok. What's different, Lisa?' she said, handing me a tissue from a box on the window. 'Here.'

'I don't want to be with David just for what I can get, feeling-wise. I want to be with him because of the love I have inside my heart for him. That's how I know this is the real thing. What am I going to do, Ma? I mean, I can't be with anyone else ever. It's him or no one.'

'My God, Lisa. You're falling apart over this.'

'No, I'm not. I *was* falling apart in other relationships, all wrapped up in my needs. But now for some reason I feel so complete inside, just being me. I don't want David to *make* me happy. I *am* happy, Ma.'

She let out a sigh.

'So – what's next? I mean, how does *he* feel? Did you ask him? And what about his ex-girlfriend?'

'No, I've said nothing. I mean, it's only now that this has really hit me. I'm in love with someone for real, for the first time in my life!'

'God, Lisa. Please don't let yourself get hurt again. Please. I don't want to sound off-putting, but don't you think you're running way ahead of yourself here? You don't even know anything about his feelings, and you're saying he's the love of your life!'

I sat down slowly, putting my arms around my body, staring into the gas fire again. My heart felt like it wanted to explode with the feelings I felt for him.

'What's it matter, Ma? *There are no rules in the Book of Love. You* told me that. Somehow love found me. I love him, Ma. I love him. I love him so much, Ma!'

I broke into floods of tears. She put her arms around me.

'Oh, Lisa, Lisa! What am I going to do with you this time!'

*

Cara and John sat in front of a warm fire, drinking freshly-brewed coffee. Cara stared into the flickering flames.

'You know,' she said, 'when all this blows over – that's if it ever does – I'm going to see Lisa.'

'What? *Lisa?* Why?'

'Because she was telling the truth. I knew it when she confronted me that night in Tommy's. I've known her all my life, and John – she was definitely telling me the truth.'

'But Cara – you seen her at that party. She was on coke. You seen her! Maybe that Bailey guy didn't give her drugs, but God, Cara – don't tell me you've been deceived by her!'

'Look –' she said, 'we've been over this a hundred times. I don't know what happened in that garden that night. There was no one there except Lisa and Jason Bailey. Now he's dead. If only we had believed her that night, none of this mess would have happened. I can't sleep right thinking about that poor guy, John. All this selling coke, taking coke, led to this. Ruth and Steve came round today when you were off with your dad working. Ruth asked about the Bailey guy, saying she had seen him somewhere before, but couldn't remember where. Steve said nothing, but I'd swear he knows.'

John stood up and placed his cup on the mantelpiece.

'Look, Cara. It's all going to blow over. If the cops knew anything they'd have called by now. I moved some cash and my mixing equipment over to Alan's house in Balbriggan. He sells out that way for me, so he'll be minding everything in case a raid goes down here.'

Cara buried her face in her hands.

'Cara, Cara! Look, everything is going to be fine. Trust me! We're getting married in July, right? I've already booked the Waterside Hotel in Donabate. Things are moving forward. You just need to trust that everything is going to pan out. It's just a . . .'

His phone rang. *James.* He went into the kitchen, closing the door over.

'Hiya, James. How's things?'

There was a pause.

'Are you alone?'

'Yeah, yeah. No one here. Why? What's up? Everything's great down here. I think everything's blowing over, to be honest.'

'Blowing over, my arse! Will you f**kin' wake up, you little fool! It's only bleedin' startin', you stupid eejit. Jess and Mickey got raided this morning. They're both being held in separate cop stations – one in

Store Street, the other in Santry. It's over the killing. They can be held up to 24 hours. Darryl's goin' mad, he is, climbin' the bleedin' walls.'

'Shit, James.'

'Did you move everything out of your house?'

'Yeah. Of course. I've nothing here.'

'This is only the start. I'll be in touch.'

He hung up.

'Em . . . Bye.'

'Who's on the phone?' shouted Cara. 'One of the gang again?'

John came back in, holding a can of beer.

'Shite. Two of the gang have been pulled. They're being questioned over the killing.'

'The killing? You mean the *murder.*'

'Yeah. Whatever.'

He opened the can of beer and took a deep swig.

'I was going to head out, but I was thinking we'll just sit in, have a few beers and a few lines. What do you think?'

'What if . . . what if one of them lads talks? My God, John! It's all going to come back to *you. Your* phone calls led to this. And no, I don't want lines of coke. God, John! You said you were knocking back on the coke after the Christmas. But if you ask me, you're taking more than ever!'

Another long swig.

'Look, Cara. I'm just stressed out of my mind right now. I need something. My head's melted over all this. I need some kind of . . . buzz. Come on – let's take a few lines. I hate doing it on my own.'

'You go ahead. Count me out.'

She stood up and headed out of the living room, slamming the door behind her.

'Where are you going?'

'I'm taking a shower.'

*

I cleaned up with Ma after the dinner. I used some kitchen roll to dab at my eyes.

'God, I look a mess after all that crying.'

'No, no, you don't, pet. You look grand. Look – it'll all sort itself out, I promise. You're stronger than you think.'

'I'm not stronger than my feelings, Ma.'

'God, you know, you remind me – well, your story reminds me – of a famous love song I was fond of back in the 80s.'

'Yeah? Which one?'

'*I Just Died in Your Arms.* A band called Cutting Crew. Before your time, I suppose.'

'No, can't say I ever heard it.'

'Why don't you look it up later on whatcha-call-it, YouTube, and have a listen. You'll love it.'

She smiled her special smile, that smile that said *I love you, Lisa, and that's why I'm concerned.*

I went up to my room and spent some time preparing next day's lessons. Then I turned on Facebook. David had replied to Emma's post on his wall.

Great seeing you today. Great chat. Stay in touch.

I took a deep breath and went onto YouTube to hear the song Ma had told me about. Seconds into it, my heart melted. *My God, that's like how I felt New Year's Eve.* The whole song rang all my bells. I played it over and over again. The guy singing it was cute as well. He sang it with so much passion. It sort of became my song, expressing how I felt inside for David.

My phone rang, clashing with the music. *Carol.*

'Hiya,' I said, turning down the volume on my laptop.

'Hi, Lisa. Just ringing to see how you're feeling after today.'

Deep down, I knew she knew I had feelings for David (she's a woman, right?)

'I'm grand, Carol. Grand. How's all with you and David?'

'Ah, I asked him lots of questions about his meet-up with Emma. He got pissed off with me for going on about it. He said she's doing great, and that we must all forgive and forget and help anyone coming off that stuff. Where's his head, Lisa? You can't trust that Emma one just like that, opening all doors as if she was an angel. She's up to something, I bet.'

'Ah, Carol. You just have to accept it. He's a grown man. You know as well as I do he has a heart for the people. He'll help everyone if he gets the chance.'

'Yeah, but he was different when he came back from talking with her. See if you notice it over the weekend. We're all going out Saturday. My dad's brother is taking him to stay with him. That's a bloody miracle! Must be after his will! Or trying to find out if he's in it!'

'So – where are we supposed to be going?'

'Tommy's, then the chipper, then home.'

'Great. I'll have to go for a longer jog on Sunday morning so!'

We chatted away for ages. She took my mind off all the serious issues that were unfolding in my personal life. She had me in stitches, laughing over little or nothing, ending the call by telling me how much she loved me. And in her voice you could tell she really meant it.

Next morning I was seated at my desk in my classroom, checking through my folder a good ten minutes before the children arrived. Just as I was sipping from my cup of coffee, the Principal popped her head in the door.

'Hi, Miss Webb,' she said. 'Can I have a quick word with you? I won't keep you.'

'Sure,' I said nervously, putting the coffee down with a slight sense of guilt.

She closed the door behind her and stood facing me. I glanced at her face, trying to ascertain what mood she was in. Was I in for a telling off again?

'Well, I won't keep you,' she repeated. 'I just want to say . . . how amazed I am at the whole change in you since the Christmas break. You seem to be a brand new person – not that there was anything wrong with you before. It's just you seem so much more . . . focused on your work. Even the other teachers have commented on it. Even your appearance has changed somewhat – for the better, of course. I can't quite put my finger on it, and maybe it's none of my business. But, as we teachers say, keep up the good work!'

'Well, thank you, Mrs Fitzgerald. I'll do my best.'

'It's Ethna. I think we can be of first name terms now. Oh, here come your first arrivals now. Right, Lisa. I'll leave you to it.'

I had an extra bounce in my step for the rest of the day, and relaxed into my work for the first time in months.

After school I drove over to the brand new shopping centre outside Balbriggan. I just felt like having a browse around some of the shops. I went into Eason's and spotted a particular book among the New Releases that reminded me of David. So I bought it for him, and when I got home I wrote a small message on the flyleaf and wrapped it up as a late Christmas present. Sounds a bit silly, I know, but I just wanted him to have this book from me.

I slept well Friday night and went jogging Saturday morning. I spent a few hours on class work in the afternoon, and all that day David was never far from my thoughts. As I finished my tea I kept looking at my phone on the table and thought about ringing him.

The phone came to life and vibrated against my saucer. My heart skipped a beat. David.

Looking forward to later. Hope everything ok with you. David x

Got you a small present today. See you later. I'll bring it with me. Lisa x

You shouldn't have! Thanx so much. x

Ma gave me her little speech about protecting myself.

'And don't forget to bring your keys.'

'I won't, Ma. You worry too much.'

The taxi pulled up outside.

'You look a knockout,' she said, beaming, as she kissed me on the side of the face. 'Enjoy yourself, love.'

Joe again.

'Well, well, well. If it's not the best-looking girl in Skerries!'

'Ah, Joe, stop, ye charmer, ye!'

My heart felt strange as we pulled up outside Tommy's. It was the prospect of meeting David there, knowing that I loved him. This changed everything. But I just had to keep it under wraps as best I could and just, well, be myself.

'Keep the change, Joe – and thanks for everything,' I said.

'Many thanks, Lisa. You take care now.'

When I stepped into Tommy's, the first person I saw at the bar was Carol. She spotted me, and pointed over to our usual seats. I looked over, and there was David, talking away to Richie. *My God, keep it together, girl.* As I approached them, his eyes met mine and he broke into a big smile.

'Lisa!'

He stood up and I walked straight into a hug from him. I held him close, my mouth inches away from his neck. The hug seemed to last ages. That song Ma told me about came to mind – *I Just Died in Your Arms.* It felt so perfect holding him, like we were made for each other.

'Well, well!' said Carol, handing me a drink. I pulled slowly away from David to hug her. 'Great to see you! Wow! You look extra fab. Doesn't she, David?'

She winked at me on the sly.

'Yeah, yeah,' said David, not knowing where to look.

Richie stood up and hugged me.

'Great to see you, Lisa. How have you been? Here, sit down. Take my chair. I'll sit next to Carol.'

'I'm grand. God, so much has happened. Where do we all start? School. Well, school's going great. The teachers are all saying I'm a different person from the girl who started last year. So that's good to hear.'

I glanced into David's eyes, trying to look and act normal, but I kept thinking I was giving it all away somehow. Then I remembered the book I'd bought him.

'Oh, here you are, David,' I said, taking the gift-wrapped package from my bag and handing it to him.

He smiled. Both Carol and Richie asked what it was.

'Ah, a late Christmas present. Just something small that I saw today. No big deal.'

David started to open it.

'You don't mind?'

'No, no. Go ahead.'

He pulled the wrapping paper off the book.

'Ah, *Badfellas*. Paul Williams' new book – the only one of his I haven't read. You're a star, Lisa. Very thoughtful of you.'

He opened it and read the message on the flyleaf aloud.

To David Salle.

I became your 49th friend on Facebook.

But you became my best friend in the whole world.

Thanks for everything you've done for me.

I'll never forget it.

Love Lisa xxx

There was a silence. His head stayed down. You could tell he was touched.

'Have a look,' I said, 'at whose photo is in it.'

I took the book from him and flicked through the pages till I came to the picture of young Anthony Campbell.

'Wow. Em . . . I'm so thankful for this, Lisa. Really. Thank you so much.'

He gave me a kiss – well, a peck on the cheek, really.

We spent the night chatting and telling stories, some funny, some sad. When we went back with our chips to David's house the talk turned to Jason Bailey's murder. I told them I was being extra careful, but I wasn't sitting back and forgetting that a man had lost his life just for taking a risk – for me.

'I'm planning to see Cara and John at some stage – maybe next week. I just have to pick the right time.'

By the time I stood up to leave, David had fallen asleep on the sofa.

'Well?' whispered Carol at the door. 'What do you think? Is he any different?'

'A bit, yeah. But it's to be expected. He has a lot on his mind.'

I looked over at him as he slept soundly, the book splayed open on his lap. If anything, my feelings for him had grown in the past few hours.

I hugged Carol and made arrangements to see her Monday night.

On the Monday morning I woke up at 6am, with those strange butterfly feelings fluttering disturbingly inside me – not the love feelings I had for David, but the ones that had been coming and going since the Christmas holidays. The last time I had felt this uneasy was the night I confronted Cara in the loo in Tommy's. I got up, showered and dressed, then tried to read for an hour. But the feeling wouldn't go away. *What is this? What is it?*

I got to class early and the day was going great. Then at the 12:30 break Ma rang me.

'Lisa, are you able to talk?'

'Yeah, sure. Are you ok?'

'Yeah. Yeah.'

There was a pause.

'Lisa, the Guards are after being here, looking to talk with you. They wouldn't tell me what it was all about. What's going on, Lisa?'

Chapter Twenty

Code of Silence

I sped home after school, all kinds of mixed thoughts racing across my mind.

What am I going to be asked by the Gardaí? What will I say? How can I get out of this without lying to them about what I knew about Jason's death? The fear deep inside would play havoc with me as soon as I opened my mouth.

God, I'll be shot. So will my mother.

The whole thing didn't bear thinking about.

I pulled into the driveway only to see Ma looking out the window, with worry written all over her face. I motioned with my hand – *Five minutes* – pointing to my phone.

I rang David.

'Hi, David. Did they call to see Carol?'

'No. Nobody called here. Are you ok? Calm down. It's just the police asking a few questions of everyone they saw at Jason's funeral. You may remember I had a bad feeling about both of you going there, but look, you have to stay with the plan. Stick to the Code of Silence. Say nothing about John. Nothing. You hear me?'

'Ah, crap, David. My head's melted. I've never even been questioned by the Guards. And this is the Special Branch – a task team who fight against criminal drug gangs. What am I going to say if they ask me how I know Jason?'

'Listen. You're running way ahead of yourself, Lisa. You don't know what they'll ask you. Remember – you didn't do anything wrong. You hear me?'

'I know that, David. But I'm withholding information about who did kill him. They'll see right through me that I'm hiding something. They're not fools, David. I'll fall to pieces in a room with them.'

'Lisa – stop. Stop. Take a deep breath. You're not on your own. We're all in this with you. If you want me to come as a support, I will. We're with you all the way. You hear me? You hear me, Lisa?'

'Thanks, David. You're great to have in moments such as this.'

'So listen. What did they say to your mother?'

'Nothing, really. Just asked for me. Left a card to ring them. Ma's in a bit of a state. I'll have to explain it all to her now. What else can I do? She knows something's up.'

'Ok. Where are you now?'

'I'm outside my apartment.'

'Ok. Go in and explain to her as best you can. But tell her she can't speak about any of this to a single soul. Sit her down. Be gentle and just go over the events again. She's your mother, at the end of the day. Everything's going to be ok. I'll drop up in an hour when Carol gets in. ok?'

'Ok, David. Thanks. You're a star. See you in a bit.'

The front door opened. Before I locked my car, the sight of Ma's face just added to my sense of guilt yet again. In a short space of time I'd brought more stress to bear on her. As if the whole drugs issue wasn't enough now I'd brought the bloody police to her door. Her words – *What's going on? I'm sick with worry all day.* Her voice filled with a sense of fear and alarm. I put my arms around her.

'It's ok, Ma. It's going to be ok.'

I don't know where I found the strength in that moment, but I stayed strong.

'Those plainclothes Guards came from Dublin Castle. One of them, a Jack Magee, showed me a badge. Some kind of task force team. Lisa, why would such people want to talk to you? God, don't tell me this has anything to do with your past with the drugs!'

'No, Ma, it's ok. Listen, it's nothing to do with my life of drugs.'

But deep inside I felt it had everything to do with it. If only I'd never touched drugs, then none of this nightmare would be unfolding.

'Listen. Sit down. I'll make you a nice mug of coffee and explain it all to you from the very start.'

With a hot mug of coffee I sat facing Ma and gathered my thoughts and told her everything about the Stephen's Night party, all the way up to Jason's murder. Before I said another word, Ma stopped me.

'Murder? What? You mean John had that chap in the news murdered? And all because he thought the poor man gave you drugs? And what did happen? I mean, I'm confused. What did this chap Jason give you in the garden? My God, Lisa. Murdered!'

'We don't know what exactly happened to me in the garden. And to be honest, we never will know, as Jason's gone. But I'm sure it wasn't drugs.'

'None of this makes sense, Lisa. My God! Murdered! They *murdered* him! Oh my God!'

'Look, Ma. We can't tell a soul. You hear? Not Jim or Rose. No one can know. If we do, these people John works for . . . Ma, they're dangerous people. If we went on record about this they would have me shot next day. They're ruthless people. You think they would sit back and let themselves go down for murder and do nothing? Ma – are you listening to me?'

I reached out to shake her gently, as she was staring into space.

'Ma – promise me on Dad's grave you won't breathe a word outside this door. Promise me!'

'My God. Ok, I won't. But Lisa – the police. What are you going to tell them? You can't lie. And how do they know you know something? How?'

So I told her about going to Jason's funeral and the guy walking up to me outside.

'He saw right through me, Ma. He must have had me checked out since – where I lived, where I worked and so on.'

I sat back on the chair, shaking my head.

'I've no idea how I'm going to handle meeting and talking to that policeman. But I've you to think about. I can't risk someone hurting you. I know even Jason wouldn't want me to risk all that.'

Ma sat back, picking up her mug slowly to take a mouthful, then stopping before it reached her mouth. She put it back on the table.

'I'm . . . I'm lost for words. I'm in shock. When's this all going to end, Lisa? When? I don't know what to think. A man's dead, and all because of drugs, f**king drugs. God forgive me.'

I started crying.

'Ma, I'm scared. I'm so scared. I'm so sorry. I thought everything was really starting to go so right in my life. Then all this happened. And everything has just started to become a never-ending nightmare. I'm so sorry, Ma. Please forgive me for bringing this trouble on you again.'

She leaned over.

'Come here. This part is not your fault. I know that deep down, pet.'

She held me tight, shaking her head.

'That John lad, dealing his drugs, then he gets a man killed. Oh Lisa. I wish your dear father was here. He'd know what to say. What do I . . .? I'm lost for words. Oh God. What must Jason's poor family be suffering right now?'

'Oh, Ma. You'd want to see his poor father – as well as his mother and sister. I'll never remove the pictures from my mind of their pain, the pain in Mr Bailey's face.'

'Ok, ok, love.'

Ma tried to console me, but I just couldn't stop crying.

'Calm down, pet. Everything will be ok.'

She rubbed her hand up and down my back.

The doorbell went. She stopped in mid-stroke.

'Oh crap,' I said. 'It's David. Can't let him see me in this mess.'

But what could I do? I was too late to run upstairs.

Ma opened the door.

'Hi Mrs Webb. I'm David. I told Lisa I'd be up.'

He put out his hand.

'It's so nice to meet you at last,' he said, smiling. He could see Ma's upset.

'Come in, David. It's great to meet you. Lisa's told me so much about you. Sorry if this isn't the best situation to meet you in, but . . .'

'You don't have to explain a thing to me, Mrs Webb. I understand. Believe me. I understand.'

'Come in. God, I'm leaving you standing in the cold. Lisa's in the back. And call me Mary.'

I could hear David coming through the hallway. I tried to wipe away all the marks from my face, the tell-tale signs I'd been crying, but failed miserably. A part of me now felt somewhat insecure, letting David see me in such a mess.

But he never batted an eyelid.

'Ah, Lisa, come here,' he said, bending down to pick me up off the chair. He held me close, his body locking into mine, his hair rubbing off the side of my face, my lips glancing off his soft ear. Tears began streaming down my face again – not tears of sorrow this time, but tears of love, of deep love for him. I never wanted this hug to end. Never. I was holding the love of my life, the only person I wanted to give my heart to. I wanted to pull his face around and kiss him full on the lips, like that last time.

I wanted to, but didn't dare.

I opened my eyes to see Ma staring at me, her back to the cooker. At that moment I knew that *she knew* for the first time how powerful, how real my love for David was.

David broke the silence.

'Ok, sit down,' he said, handing me a hanky. 'Hey. There you are.'

His eyes held mine.

'It's ok, Lisa. Everything's going to be ok.'

I searched his eyes, wondering did he sense or pick up on how I was feeling, other than the fact the Guards were looking for me over the murder.

Ma's voice came across the room.

'As you know all about this, David, we don't have to go into it all over again. But can't the police do something if they know someone's withholding information about a murder? Can't they hold people over things like that? And my God, Lisa! What about your job if it all comes out that you've been involved in drugs?'

'Mrs Webb . . . Mary.'

David stood up slowly, turning to face her.

'You have every right to be very upset over everything that's happened. But let's not jump away ahead of ourselves. Let's take this together, one step at a time. We don't know what the police already know about this murder. Maybe it's just a normal procedure for them to interview everyone that claims to have known Jason. And what does Lisa know? Only that she met him for fifteen minutes, and what John whispered to her – that he had this guy "sorted". That's all hearsay.

That's no real proof to convict anyone. John may never have actually been involved in the murder. Chances are he was at home all that day, so he'll have an alibi. So it's not worth risking both your lives by telling them all about John. That's my advice, Mrs Webb. It's too damn dangerous. You have to protect yourselves.'

Ma stared at him, then looked at me.

'You're right. You're both right. I'm just so nervous, so shocked that these people murdered that chap.'

'I know, Mrs Webb. It's awful beyond words. I feel awful myself. But we need to stand together. Get this interview out of the way and move on with our lives and hope the police can somehow nail all those who are responsible for this heinous crime.'

Ma broke the tense atmosphere.

'Ok. Enough said for one day on this subject. I'm worn out with it. I was just about to warm up this stew. Would you stay, David, and join us for a bowl?'

'Sure. I've never refused a bowl of mother-made stew in my life,' he smiled.

'Ok,' I said, standing up. 'I'm heading up to change and shower. Give me ten minutes.'

Up in my room I looked in the mirror at my teary eyes, my love-smitten eyes.

God, I still look a right mess. Will I ever stop crying?

Deep breath.

Ok, girl – you're going to get through this interview and move on with your life.

I sat down to put some eye-liner on.

Oh God, if you're up there, please don't leave me with all this love for this man, only to find out in the end he feels nothing and I'm alone with all this. Please don't do that to me. I couldn't bear to live like that, knowing I love him this much but can't give him my love.

That voice again.

Why don't you ask him straight out, Lisa?

No, no, it's not the right time. There's too much going on, with poor Jason's death, the dreaded interview coming up. I'll wait till the interview's over and then I'll pick my moment.

I looked one last time in the mirror. My mind raced over all the events of the past few weeks – on the coke, that creepy experience in The Life that had now somehow changed everything.

I'm off drugs forever. I'm so happy inside!

Bar when things like what happened to Jason came crashing into my mind and heart and tore me apart. But it can't have all been for nothing. Good had to follow this. I couldn't let it all end badly. It was up to me to fight, to keep fighting, come what may, and win this battle!

I came back down the stairs, feeling somewhat more together, into the warm sounds of Ma and David laughing their heads off as they ate their stew.

'He's a scream, Lisa!'

'I've just talked her into taking Dad out on a blind date. Don't think she bought into it, though.'

'Well, David,' I said, 'at least you brightened up the whole house.'

Ma smiled and gave me that *I so approve of this guy* look.

Wow, I thought, I never saw anyone so change Ma out of a stressful mood – not since Dad was alive.

I joined them at the table as we all ate the stew. David told us jokes to further lighten the dark pressures of the day. By the time he stood up to leave it was after 7:30pm, which left it too late to go back to his house with him to meet Carol. I had quite an amount of class work to prepare for the following day.

Ma stood up and gave him a hug.

'You're very welcome in this house anytime you want, David. Thanks for coming down and cheering us all up.'

'My pleasure. Thanks for the lovely stew. I'll definitely be back next time Lisa tells me you're dishing it up.'

He encouraged her not to worry at all about the upcoming interview as I walked him to the door. He checked his phone.

'Wow. 9 missed calls. I'll check them later.'

He looked into my eyes.

'Are you going to be ok, Lisa?', he said, placing his hand on my shoulder.

'Yeah, yeah. I feel much better, thanks. You're a star for coming up and talking to us both.'

He hugged me.

That melting feeling again.

'Ok. I'm off. Buzz me the minute you talk to that detective. And if you want me to go with you, I'll be there.'

I stood at the door as he got into his car, and I could see the blue glow of his phone as he made a call. With some misgiving, I closed the door and went back inside.

*

'Hi, Emma. I got a few missed calls from you. Sorry – I had my phone on silent. Is everything ok?'

'Ah, David – I had no one else to turn to. I hope I'm not bothering you, am I?'

'No, no. Fire away. What's up?'

'I had an awful weekend – people ringing me to come out. *Party on in a mate's house!* But all of them are still into the coke. I just didn't feel strong enough to go. It's just dawning on me how many of my mates do coke. I was so tempted to go, but I just stayed home and watched tv.'

'Well done, Emma. God, I know it's not easy. Those first few weeks can be very hard going. You probably feel that all your friends are out enjoying life while you're stranded on a lonely island. But you're not alone. You hear me? I'm very proud of you for not giving in. Can't have been easy. Listen – you have to stay clear of them all for now anyway. You're doing so well. Is there anything I can do to help?'

'Be great if you could meet me for a coffee sometime. The last chat helped me so much. And believe me, I do appreciate it so much. You're great at encouraging people.'

'That's no problem. How are you fixed for tomorrow at four at Olive?'

'Oh, that'll be great, David. You're a legend. Thanks so much.'

'It's ok. Listen, if you hit any more bad moments, don't be afraid to ring me. You hear? Don't feel you're alone in this battle. Listen – I've got to fly and help Carol with Dad. I'll see you tomorrow at four.'

*

'Well, Ma. What do you think?'

'My God, Lisa,' she said, her eyes beaming. 'He's lovely! Listen – I know now how much you love him.'

'Yeah,' I sighed. 'But does he love me? That's the part I don't know.'

'Well, I know he likes you a lot. But I couldn't be sure. I was watching the way he looked at you. There's a look there all right. Oh Lisa, I hope this all works out. I really do. He's a gem. He really is!'

'I feel much better about everything now. Not sure why, but I've a deep feeling everything is going to work out. We all just have to be strong and get this interview over and done with.'

I looked at her and it struck me then that she felt she was being left out of the picture.

'Look, Ma,' I said, grasping her hand, 'I promise I won't keep anything from you again about the drug situation. I just didn't want to stress you out with this. I would have told you when it had blown over. *Blown over!* God, does a man being killed ever blow over!'

'Oh, Lisa. We'll get through this. We always do.'

She looked up at a picture of Dad on the wall.

''If only your father was here! It's times like this I wish he was with us. He was so strong, no matter what. God bless him!'

I went up to my room to get stuck into schoolwork. Just as I put pen to paper, my phone rang. *Carol*. Her voice alarmed me.

'This detective that spoke to your mother, Lisa – David said it was the same guy we met outside the church. Crap, Lisa! What are you going to tell him? What are you going to say?'

By now I felt somehow stronger. Maybe it was the chat with myself, not to mention David's reassuring words.

'Look, Carol,' I said, calming her down. 'I can't explain it. I just know everything is going to be ok at the interview. I've just got to face this and get through it and then move on with life. What other choice do I have?'

'Would you like me to come with you? It's no problem. Are you allowed to bring someone?'

'I'm sure you are, but to be honest, this is something I feel I must face alone. Maybe deep down I feel Jason risked his life to come to me alone that night. So I want to face it that way too – on my own.'

'God, Lisa. You're so brave. If you change your mind I'm here with you all the way. So is David – and Richie.'

'Ah thanks. I know you all are. I'll buzz you after I ring them to see what date they fixed for the interview. Don't worry – I have a strong feeling everything is going to be fine, Carol.'

'Ok. I'm off to take care of Dad. I'll be thinking of you.'

*

Carol hung up and looked across the room at David sitting glued into the book Lisa had given him. Tim looked across.

'David – what are you reading? You haven't put that book down since you came in.'

'Ah, Dad, it's Paul Williams' s new book *Badfellas*. It's about criminal gangs.'

'Is Charlie Haughey and the rest of them cowboys in it!'

'No,' he laughed, 'but I suppose they should be, the lot of them.'

'You look tired, David.'

'You're right, Dad,' said Carol, looking concerned. 'You should get an early night.'

'Haven't been sleeping well at all, sis. All kinds of strange nightmares. I woke up a couple of times and could have sworn I felt a strange presence in the room with me. A bit scary, to be honest!'

He lowered his voice so Tim couldn't hear him.

'One of the dreams was awful. I could hear a voice, cold and sinister, screaming that it was going to kill Lisa. I woke up in a state.'

'That's very odd,' said Carol, 'Lisa's having bad nightmares as well. Almost the same as yours.'

'Well, don't go scaring her by telling her about mine. God knows, she has enough on her plate.'

'You don't think,' said Carol, sitting down close to David and dropping her voice to a whisper, 'you don't think this stuff you're both dabbling in has anything to do with the dark side to the drug underworld? I mean, it's spooky to open doors to unseen stuff, David. Are you listening to me? Stop reading that book for a second and look at me, will you? *David!* Put the book down!'

'What?'

'Like, listen to me. You have said all along that there's some kind of force of evil behind all this drug gangland crime. So how do you know you're not stirring some hornet's nest, something that could harm you both?'

'Carol, stop, will you! What are you saying – that some *thing* could come after us both?'

'Yeah, well, you heard Lisa's story about seeing something. And your whole study is about the unseen controlling all this. So yeah. What if what you're trying to expose doesn't *want* to be exposed and decides to come after you?'

'WooOOO! Boo!'

'Stop it, David! It's not funny!'

'Ah, Carol. Lighten up. I know there's something out there unseen and evil, but the idea that it would come after a couple of people like us! Are you joking me?'

'No, I'm not, David. I don't know. Since you linked up with Lisa your stories have linked up together. Something strange is happening. Even I'm starting to think you may be right about all this. When I went to Jason's funeral I too felt something strange. God, I hope I'm wrong. Will you promise me you'll be careful? Promise me.'

'Ok, sister. Come here. Give us a hug. Everything is going to be ok. Just a lot going on at the minute. Emma rang today. She's in a struggle to stay off the coke. I've to meet her tomorrow for a chat, to encourage her a bit. Now don't start preaching at me, ok?'

'I thought you were only meeting her the once, David? I'm saying nothing, but just . . .'

She bit her lip and stood up.

'Come on, Dad. I'll get your bed ready.'

'Ok, Carol. Night, David. Oh – is Bertie Ahern in that book?'

'Stop, Dad. No, he's not in it. It's drug gangs, Dad. Night, Dad.'

'Night, son.'

*

Next morning I braced myself before making that phonecall. My hands were sweating as I dialled the number on the card.

Ring, ring. Ring, ring.

Come on. Answer.

'Hello?'

'Hello. Can I speak to Jack Magee, please?'

'Speaking.'

'Em . . . Hello, Jack. I'm Lisa. Lisa Webb. You called to my house yesterday.'

'Ah, Lisa. Thanks for getting back to me so soon.'

His voice sounds so friendly, doesn't it?

'I hope we didn't startle your mother. She seemed a bit taken aback to answer her door to two plainclothes detectives.'

'No, no. She was ok. Just a bit worried – as I am, as to what you want to talk to me about.'

'Well, Lisa, I can't go into too much detail over the phone, I'm sure you can appreciate. But when can we meet for a chat? We're interviewing everyone who may have known Jason Bailey. It's just a part of our widespread investigation. Just a few routine inquiries – a very normal procedure, nothing to worry about.'

'But as I told you at the church, Jack, I didn't know Jason at all, really.'

'Listen, Lisa. I can't go any further on the phone. When will you be free for a chat?'

'Well, I'm free Thursday afternoon, anytime after three.'

'Thursday. Ok. Could you make your way to Swords Garda Station for . . . let's see . . . just checking my diary here . . . How's 3:45 sound?'

'Yeah – that's great. Would it be ok if I brought someone with me?'

'Yes, of course. If your mother wants to come, she can.'

'I was just checking. I . . . I think I'd actually prefer to come alone. So – are you close to catching who did this, Jack?'

There was a moment's silence.

'I'll talk to you Thursday, Lisa. We're very grateful for your willingness to come and meet us. Every little thing can be a help. Even the smallest detail could turn out to be the biggest clue to cracking a case. So we'll see you Thursday.'

Crap. Thursday. Swords Garda Station on my own. Maybe I should ask Carol to come.

That voice again.

This is something you must face alone, Lisa.

I texted Carol and David, then rang Ma to put her mind at rest. They all said the same thing. It's just a normal, routine police procedure.

Yeah.

*

David set out after work to meet Emma, only to see her pull up in her car just yards from his house.

'Jump in! A guy like you will only be kidnapped with a walk like that!' she laughed.

David sat in.

'So – Olive for coffee – yeah?'

'Tell you what, David. Why don't we just get the coffee to go and head off for a spin. Is that ok with you?'

'Yeah, sure. That's grand.'

After he picked up two lattes, they drove around to the head, parking in the car park with the car facing out to the sea.

'God, it's so lovely, isn't it? The sea . . . and the latte as well. Thanks for buying it. My shout next time.'

David took a sip.

'So – it was so good to hear how you stayed off the coke all weekend. You're a strong girl, Emma. Stronger than you give yourself credit for.'

'Mmm. It was hard sitting in, watching tv, knowing all my friends were all out enjoying themselves. Well – if you call that enjoying yourself! It's not real, is it?'

'No. You missed nothing, believe me. So – what did you watch, anyway? Not that it matters.'

'Would you believe, I watched that movie you and I watched together some time ago – *P.S. I Love You*. Remember?'

'Yeah. How could I forget! We fell asleep on your bed. I woke up and got dressed and landed home wearing one of your socks. Dad slagged me for days. I can still see him staring at me, laughing.'

She leaned over to the glove box and took out her handbag.

'Do you mind if I have a fag? I'll open the window and blow the smoke out.'

'No, no. Go ahead.'

He gulped down his re-awakened craving as she slowly pulled the cellophane off the new pack of John Player Blue, pulled out a perfectly-formed cigarette and placed it slowly between her glossy lips. She flicked her lighter and lit the cigarette.

David sighed.

'Ah, here. Just . . . give me one. Just the one.'

'God, are you sure I'm not putting temptation your way?'

'No, no! One won't hurt.'

He pulled one out. When she leaned over with her lighter to light his cigarette he could smell her perfume. It brought him back. He inhaled deeply and blew the smoke out slowly.

'Ah, that's better!' he said, feeling somewhat guilty.

Another mouthful of latte and another drag of the cigarette made it seem like heaven, if only for the few moments.

They chatted away, reminiscing about the good days in their time together.

'You know,' said Emma, stubbing out her cigarette in the ashtray, 'looking back with a clear head, it was the small things that made our time together – like getting a takeout from the chipper and crashing on the sofa in front of the tv. It's so sad for me, David, looking back at how the bloody coke even robbed us of that simple enjoyment.'

'That's what it does in the end, Emma. It steals everything slowly, strips you of everything bit by bit, till you're left with nothing. Nothing. May take a year, may take twenty years. But it will get everyone in the end. It plays with – deceives – everyone in different ways. Take an example. I knew this guy whose best friend took coke for a year. Then one night at a party – bang! Something happened to him. He's now strapped to a bed, in and out of some crazy coma, unable to do anything for himself. He'll be like that for the rest of his life. Then take a person who's doing it all the time for years with simply no side effects bar awful hangovers. But as they get older, weird, strange things start to happen to them. Something's been taken from them. They feel it – something stolen.'

'How come you know so much about it all?'

'Ah – another long story for another day – another latte!'

'You're so right about it. I feel a complete fool for getting into it.'

'You're not a fool, Emma. Don't say that. You made a mistake. We all did. But look at you now! You're off it and you look great! You're only . . . what . . . twenty-three years of age, girl. Your whole life is ahead of you. You make it sound like you're sixty-three. Everything is on the up for you now. Enjoy it!'

'Yeah. But look who I lost along the way. *You*. That's so hard to take right now. To be truthful, I need to ask you something.'

'Go ahead.'

She opened the cigarette pack again and offered him one. He shrugged and pulled one out. Again she lit up both cigarettes.

'This is hard for me, ok?' she said, blowing a plume of smoke out the window. 'But I've put a lot of thought into this and . . . well, I know I've made mistakes, big mistakes. I admit all of it. Plus, worst of all, I hurt *you* so badly. But deep down I know we had a super relationship before the drugs, as well you know. But there were real feelings on both sides, I think, and I know somewhere deep inside your heart you still have some feelings for me.'

There was a pause, during which she pulled on her cigarette again.

'Maybe just a small feeling, but look, if we gave it one more go, even for a trial period? I promise you, David, it won't be anything like before. With no drugs we can make it. If I thought we couldn't, I wouldn't dream of asking you. I know I still love you and it's real. You're the best thing that ever happened to me.

'Listen,' she continued, tears streaming down her face, 'you don't have to answer me now. Maybe have a think about it. What do you think?'

David arrived back in the house shortly after six o'clock. Carol looked up from tending to their father, cutting up the meat on his dinner plate. He took off his jacket and stood without a word, staring across at the tv set.

'Is that smoke I smell?' asked his father, breaking the silence.

'Yeah,' said David sheepishly. 'I had four fags today.'

'I thought you were off them, son?'

'Yes, Dad. I am. Just had a few with a coffee today. Don't worry – I'm not going back on them. Just a slip-up today.'

'So – how's Emma?' asked Carol, looking him right in the eye for any tell-tale signs of how the meeting really went.

'Went great,' said David, looking down at the dinner plate. 'Mmm. Gigot chops. She's doing great.'

He looked at her.

'Don't start at me, Carol. I'm in no mood for one of your lectures.'

'So – is that it, then? Is that your last meet-up with her?'

'Well, if you must know, I'm heading over on Friday to her house to see her parents. Haven't seen them since the break-up.'

'Oh, right. By the look on your face, David, you're not telling me everything. What's really going on here? You're not thinking of going back there, are you? Tell me you're not!'

'Look, don't start, Carol. I've enough going on in my life at the minute. I'm off down to the basement to study a bit more.'

'Well, listen to me,' said Carol, dropping Dad's fork out of her hand and following him as far as the door. 'Don't come to me when it all comes crashing down around you and she dumps you again. I won't be here. You hear me, David? Buy a bottle of *cop-on* the next time you're in Gerry's! They're only €1.99 a shot!'

The basement door slammed shut.

'What's going on, Carol?' asked Tim. 'Is David ok? He looks different today. Where's Linda? When's she coming up again? I miss her.'

Carol put both her arms around him.

'Oh, Dad, Dad. I don't know. I really don't. And it's *Lisa*. Her name is Lisa. Oh, God. Not this again. Poor David. I'm really worr –.'

She stopped in her tracks.

'Don't worry, Dad. He'll be fine. He'll come through this.'

She kissed the crown of his head.

'I promise.'

*

The gang members waited in silence in the living room of Darryl's house. Darryl walked in, slamming the kitchen door behind him. He glared at each and every one of them.

'Right. If yiz want a beer, get it out of the fridge.'

They looked sheepishly at each other. Then Jess went in and brought out six cans of Miller and left them on the table. A few of the gang took a can each and cracked them open.

'I called yiz all here for a meeting 'cause, as yiz know, Jess and Mickey got pulled. Their houses pulled apart. Mickey – you tell them.'

Mickey cleared his throat.

'Yeah. They held us for twenty-four hours, asking all the usual bullshit. That smart-mouth cop Magee is heading the whole thing. They have f**k-all to go on. f**k-all about the killing. I laughed at him, the fool!'

'Right,' said Darryl. 'So we know they have nothing. Not yet, anyway. But . . . *James!* Will you stop staring at the wall and wake up! I'm telling yiz all now – *wake the f**k up!* We're all under surveillance. I seen an unmarked car sitting outside my gaff all day yesterday. I'm bloody suffocating here! I can move F**k-all coke! Me business is falling apart right in front of me!'

He jabbed his finger across the room in the direction of James.

'And all because of your *dopey* little fool out in Skerries! I swear, James. He's after crippling me. If he ever stands in front of me, I'll F**kin' tear him apart, bit by bit, in front of yiz all! *I swear!*'

You could hear a pin drop.

'John Noonan?' said James, pulling deep on his fag and taking another swig from his beer. 'He's no mate of mine. No mate of mine. No way. He just sells for me, Darryl.'

'And what about that girl?' asked Darryl, slumping into a chair and lighting up another fag. 'What's the story with her?'

'Look – I'm doing a run out there Saturday. Don't worry. It'll be ok. I'm taking a mate's car. He needs a drop. I'll find out about the girl. Everything is cool – so far.'

'Well,' replied Darryl. 'Isn't it well for him! No hassle! The little gobshite!'

'Right,' said James, flicking his fag-end into the cold fireplace. 'That's it, Darryl. Is it?'

Darryl gritted his teeth and dropped his voice to a menacing level.

'*Is that it?* Are you trying to wind me up? Are yiz all thick in the head or wha'?'

Mickey cleared his throat again.

'Look, Darryl. I know that cop is going to make it hard for us all for a while. But it'll die down. It always does. And then we'll be in full swing again!'

Darryl stood up slowly, picked up a full can of beer and slammed it off the wall, leaving a dent and a foaming spray of beer which bubbled noisily through the silence that followed. Everybody's face dropped.

'*Back in full swing again?* Not one of yiz know why I called yiz all here, do yiz? Yiz think this is all about the cops watching us?'

'Calm down, Darryl,' said Mick, putting up both hands.

'Lads, wake up!' shouted Darryl. 'Don't yiz know the f**kin Bradley south-side gang are eyeballing all of this – our every move? I got tipped off today. Yiz all know they've been itching to move north with their boys. Now they see us under pressure, not being able to move our coke. They see an opening developing, a weakness, and while we're all sitting here scratching our arses, that gang are watching us and planning to take us all out and take over!'

He let that thought sink in. Then he pointed into the faces of each one in turn.

'Your lives are all in danger.'

He let that thought sink in too.

'If they take a couple of you lads down, added to the pressure of the cops on us, it's the end. Yiz hear me, lads? The end. It's over. Yiz have to watch your backs, day and night.'

He glared at each of them, one at a time.

'Now, for the last time, wake up! *Wake the f**k up!'*

Chapter Twenty One

The Branch Out

After a few encouraging words from Ma and a phonecall that afternoon from Carol, I was driving to meet Jack Magee in Swords Garda Station. As the miles of the journey clocked up, so did the sense of fear in the pit of my stomach. I uttered a small prayer to God asking for the strength to hold up in the interview and to be as truthful as I could when asked the odd difficult question.

It's just a routine interview, right? Nothing to worry about.

I parked the car yards from the station and took a deep breath. I fed €2 into the parking meter. *One hour – that should be long enough.* As I walked up the steps I heard a voice behind me.

'Hi Lisa.'

I turned around.

'Hello?'

'Lisa Webb? Hi, I'm Jack, Jack Magee. Remember?'

'Oh, yes. Hi.'

He shook hands with me and ushered me into a small hallway as he spoke on his mobile phone.

'Hi, Ray? Yeah, I'm here now. Can you come out and we'll all head into the back office? Ok.'

He slipped the phone back into his pocket.

'That was Ray Mellor. We work together on most cases. Is there anything I can get you? Coffee, tea, glass of water?'

'No, I'm grand, thanks.'

The door opened and out came a tall, black-haired guy, mid-thirties, thin-faced but well-built. He was carrying two folders. There was no smile, just a firm handshake. We walked together down the corridor and into a small side office which had chairs and tables. On one of the tables was a digital audio recorder. We all sat down and they opened their two folders, flicking through the pages and notes. I was feeling somewhat calmer than expected, which was a help.

Jack switched on the recorder.

'"It's January the 12th 2012. Time 3:38pm. Interview with Lisa Webb. Present: Jack Magee and Ray Mellor, Swords Garda Station."'

He looked at me.

'You don't mind, Lisa, but we do have to record all interviews in cases like this.'

'No, no. It's your job. Fire away.'

'Ok. Let's just start by asking you how well you knew the late Jason

Bailey, and when was the last time you spoke to him. In your own words. No hurry.'

He folded his arms and sat back. Ray was still flicking through his notes, looking up every few seconds as if to assure me he was giving everything his full attention.

'Well,' I said, 'to be honest, I didn't really know Jason at all. I only met the guy once in my life, and that was only for about ten or fifteen minutes.'

I went on to outline all the events of Stephen's Night leading up to what happened out in the back garden.

'And I never saw him again after that, till I saw his picture in the paper on New Year's Day – the day after he was found murdered.'

They both glanced at each other, then looked back at me, their eyes giving the strong impression they were not buying my story.

'And that's it?' said Jack, continuing to eyeball me. 'You went out to a garden at a party with Jason, a guy you'd never met before, something strange went down, he left and . . . what? That's it?'

He stood up, pushing his chair back noisily.

'Lisa, in case you're unaware, we are in the middle of a very serious murder investigation. And the last thing I need from you is lies!'

'I'm not lying, Jack. I swear. That's the truth.'

I could feel my body tensing up.

'That's the whole truth.'

'Ok. Let me explain some facts to you. We're leaving no stone unturned in our investigation. I've pulled certain gang members, gone through every detail, knocked on every door, interviewed everyone. And I mean *everyone*. I'm not at liberty to divulge any details to you, as you can understand, but I can tell you this: some of the people we spoke to say Jason was shot for helping a few drug addicts – which, to be honest, I don't buy into. Needless to say, we went through his place with a fine tooth comb, and one of the items of interest to us was, of course, his computer. So we hacked into it and found certain files. One of the files had a list, a list of names. And guess whose name was among them?'

'I haven't a clue!'

'Yours, Lisa! And some particulars about *you*. Like he knew you were a school teacher for one. That you lived in Skerries. Even down to personal facts like, that you took drugs. Does that surprise you?'

I sat speechless . . .

'Now when this list was discovered, it had details about other people that Jason had lined up to meet, but according to it you were the first contact. The others never had the chance to meet him. 'Cause after your little chat with him, someone violently took his life.

'And you sit there and say you never met the guy till Stephen's Night? Don't you think, Lisa, that this is just a little bit hard to fit into your neat little story?'

At this stage his voice had risen to the point where he was almost shouting.

'Ok, ok,' broke in Ray. 'Calm down, Jack. Calm down.'

I sat stunned.

'I don't understand what you're talking about, Jack. Why would Jason be so interested in me and have a file about me? And by the way, I gave up taking coke before Christmas. I . . . '

'No, no. I've no interest in that,' he said, as he sat back down and composed himself.

'Lisa – I've been on this task team fourteen years and I've never come across a more . . . baffling case, a more intriguing case than this. And believe me, I've seen pretty much everything, but this case is strange, to say the least. We also found other files which would indicate . . . well, if I didn't know how well-respected Jason was, after reading them I'd say he was nuts, to say the least. Get this: he was convinced that something in the *unseen world* was involved in the awful increase in everything that's going on in the drug world – the murders, the violence, everything that's been pushing the drug problem out of control. When a murder takes place I have to read everything, and believe me, what he wrote about was frightening, to put it mildly.'

'A load of crap, to be honest,' said Ray, looking up from his folder and half-smiling at his own choice of words.

'That's enough, Ray,' said Jack. 'Look, Lisa – I've seen enough evil in some people's activities over the years that would strongly support such a dark theory.'

I reached into my bag for my bottle of water and took a few mouthfuls. There was a pause for a few moments before Jack pulled a sheet of paper from his file.

'There's one other aspect to Jason's case which we can't unravel. Maybe it will mean something to you. In the file containing the list of names there is a written couple of dates – or codes – which only appear on that file. We've tried everything to break them, to find out what the numbers mean, but no joy.'

'Numbers? What numbers?'

'This one, for instance. Does *J2022* mean anything to you? Other than the date, 2022, which is the easy part.'

'No, means nothing to me.'

'How about this one?' Ray chimed in. '*G27*? Does that ring a bell?'

'*G27?* Oh yeah. I couldn't make out what it meant at the time – still can't – but the night of the party Jason left a note in my pocket and that was on it. He also wrote on it something like "Sorry I had to leave. See you soon."'

Jack picked up his file, put the page back in and stood up again.

'And where is this note now?'

'Well, I gave it to a friend of mine, David. David Salle. He himself has been studying all this dark, unseen side to drugs, especially cocaine. He's been studying it for a number of years now and holds the same views as Jason did.'

'David. David Salle?'

Jack nodded to Ray, who jotted down the name.

'Hmm. Another ex-druggie, I expect. Yeah?'

'Well, yes. But he . . . David . . . stopped five years ago.'

Jack closed his file and threw it on the table.

'Look, Lisa,' he shouted, his face becoming red again. 'What's going on here? I don't believe what I'm hearing! This Bailey character has been "studying" the gangland drugs crime for years – *like we haven't?* Then he goes on and on about the "evil, unseen force" behind it all! He's written dozens of files, with *your name* on one. He ends up dead, and on closer inspection we find, codes and numbers that – forgive me – don't mean jack shit to me!'

He turned to his colleague.

'But Ray – look at me. Here's the funny part. He puts one of them codes on a note and into the pocket of this girl – a girl he's never met before!'

He turned back to me.

'Not to mention the strange *up your nose* experience that happened in the middle of your romantic chat with him in the garden. Then it turns out that *another* guy, this David . . .'

'David Salle,' said Ray, checking his notes.

'This David Salle character is – guess what? – studying the same "unseen evil" behind the drugs scene! *And* you're hanging out with him! Is there anything else you'd like to add, Lisa, to this amazing cock-and-bull story? Is there?'

There was a pause – an endless pause, it seemed – as I picked up my bottle of water and took another mouthful. I surprised even myself by how calm I remained at such a heated moment.

'Yes, Jack. There is. There is another part to the story. I think this unseen thing that Jason was so concerned about, and which David spent time researching and following up, well . . . I think I may have actually seen it. For real, like.'

Ray sniggered under his breath.

'Over to you, Jack!' he chuckled, and went back to looking through his notes.

'Well?' said Jack, looking at me. 'Continue, Lisa. You saw what?'

'It was the last night I was on coke. I saw something too awful to explain – a creature of some kind. That's what freaked me out, and I gave up the coke after that. I saw this when I was on the dance floor with my friends. But no one else saw it, just me. Now it seems Jason Bailey had been studying this phenomenon all along and came to the same conclusion as me. And I'm convinced that all this is some kind of warning to people selling and taking coke. Something else, something really dire, is going to happen soon. I'm sure of it.'

Ray stood up while Jack never moved an inch, just sat staring into my eyes.

'What a pile of crap!' said Ray, throwing his hands out in despair. 'Oh, God, I've heard it all now! You were out of your head on drugs and you think you saw something from the unseen world? I'll tell you what I think – you young people are watching far too many of them supernatural, hocus-pocus films that are coming out now, like *Twilight* or *Harry Potter*. And you go out and take coke, and your minds start playing games in those messed-up heads of yours!'

'But what about Jason, Ray?' I asked, keeping my voice calm. 'He never took a drug in his life.'

There was a pause. Then Jack leaned across the table closer to me and spoke, his voice matching mine for calmness.

'Lisa. Who shot and killed Jason Bailey?'

His calmness and bluntness caught me off guard. I didn't know where to look. I could hear David's voice telling me *Don't say a word about John. They'll kill your mother. Not a word, Lisa. Not a word.* My throat went dry again and I gulped. I blinked under his stare. My bottom lip trembled. All the giveaway signs.

'Well? Who killed him, Lisa? Hmm?'

He banged his fist on the table and shouted.

'WHO??'

My heart skipped a beat.

'I . . . I don't know. I don't know who killed him.'

I couldn't look him straight in the eye anymore, so I looked down at the floor, thinking about taking my bottle of water out again. Despite my best efforts, a single tear rolled down my face.

'I don't know.'

'Lookit, Lisa,' said Ray. 'We're following a definite line of inquiry. We just need you to . . .'

But Jack cut across him disapprovingly.

'Ok, ok, Ray. Thanks. We'll leave it there for the moment,' he said, reaching towards the recorder. '"End of interview, 4:31pm." You can go, Lisa. But I'd like to talk to you again.'

He pulled out his diary and glanced through its pages.

'Mmm. Let me see. How about . . . Monday? No, Monday week? The 23rd? Let's say 5:30pm? Is that ok?'

'Yeah, yeah, great,' I said, standing up and grabbing my bag.

I took out my mobile phone and entered the details.

'Monday 23rd, 5:30. Ok, thanks.'

Ray held the door open for me, looking a bit sheepish after being cut short by Jack.

Jack shook hands with me.

'Ok, Lisa. The next interview is just a last couple of questions, just tidying up a few loose ends. Nothing heavy like today. I think we have almost everything we need from you. As you can imagine, we're just going to collate the information we've collected from various sources. But you don't have to worry your pretty little head about it. Thanks again for coming.'

'Bye, Jack. Bye, Ray.'

I walked briskly back to my car, conscious of the fact that they were probably still watching my movements. *Don't worry your pretty little head about it. Ugh!*

*

Jack kicked his chair over.

'What the hell was that about, Ray? *We're following a definite line of inquiry!* My God! Do you not remember Lesson 1 in Interview Techniques from Templemore? "Don't *give* information. *Get* information." For crying out loud!'

Ray slammed his folder down on the desk.

'What are you talking about, Jack? We bloody had her, and you pulled the plug! What's the story?'

'Ah Ray, she was so scared, which means she knows the killers. Ok? Now it's time to play them. Ring the media – tv, radio, papers, the lot – put the story out that we've done everything but have come up with nothing, that we're pulling the plug as we have other commitments elsewhere. We'll pull all the surveillance teams back, make it look like this is over. In that way the gangs will relax and start moving round again, thinking it's all water under the bridge. Have you got Jason's father's number there?'

'Yeah. It's here somewhere. Why?'

'Have a quiet word with him, will you? Explain to him that what he reads in the papers tomorrow is just part of our plan. Don't want him or his wife being upset anymore than they already are, do we?'

Ray let out a heavy sigh.

'I'm telling you, Ray,' Jack continued, 'we don't have to talk to anyone else. This girl is the key that will unlock this case. She knows, Ray. *She knows*. We'll crack it. My God, have you ever heard of a case like this in your life! What next? Go on, Ray. Make them calls fast.'

'Sure, Jack. Sure.'

*

I pulled up in our driveway, relieved that the worst was over. But I couldn't get my head around the fact that Jason seemed to know so many facts about me. And what about that extra code, *J2022?*

I rang David, looking forward to filling him in on how things went. But his phone rang out so I left him a voicemail. I was extra circumspect in what I said, knowing that the Guards just might be tapping my phone, and I didn't want any message to come back and haunt me.

Hi David. It's me. I just finished the interview a few minutes ago. It was grand, but a bit heavier than expected. All went well. No problems. Oh yes, they did mention some files they found on Jason´s computer which had information about me. That would be strange enough, but beside my name and others was a coded number – G27. Yes, the number on that note I gave you. And there was another : J2022. Does that mean anything to you? I've another interview with them on the 23rd. Give us a buzz when you can. Ok? Take care. See you. Bye.

Next up I rang Carol, who answered right away. I ran everything by her. She was so glad it all went so well and that it was all over. The part about Jason's computer files interested her no end.

'By the way, Carol, I rang David, but no answer. Is he working late?'

She sighed down the phone.

'No, no, he's not. Ah, I'm not talking to him anyway, Lisa. Last I saw of him, he was coming up from the basement here to get his laptop and bring it back down. We're not on speaking terms, you might say.'

'What's up? You both got on so well. What happened?'

'Well . . . I don't know if I should say . . .'

'Oh?'

'Ah, you know he met up with Emma again? Well, he's meeting her again tomorrow night.'

There was a pause. My heart sank.

'Lisa? Are you still there?'

'What's . . . what's going on, Carol?'

'Look, Lisa. How about going for a drink later on? Just a couple. Say Nealon's for 7:30? I need to talk to you. About David.'

'Ok,' I sighed. 'See you then. 7:30. Bye.'

Oh God, no. Not this. Not now. I can't be left holding all these feelings for him. What will I do if he goes back to her?

I went inside and filled Ma in on how the interview went. I didn't mention David.

'Oh, Lisa, I'm delighted that it's all over. Now – you're just in time for your dinner – lamb chops. Sit yourself down there now and I'll bring it in.'

I only picked at the meal as my mind – and heart – were elsewhere.

'Are you all right, Lisa? You keep looking at the clock. Are you going somewhere? Meeting David, by any chance?'

'Well, no, Ma. It's Carol. I'm meeting Carol for a drink in half an hour. Any chance you could drop me to Nealon's?'

As I changed and got ready I felt like I was in some kind of twilight zone. All I could think of was David. How could I deal with this? No phonecall back, even after today, knowing the ordeal I must have been going through. I was hurt – and understandably so.

Ma dropped me at the pub, and Carol was already there, having secured a little table by the open fire in the cosy snug.

'Listen, Lisa,' she began, as soon as our drinks had arrived, 'I've known for ages you had feelings for David. But I wanted to let it all happen as I expected it would. The night you both came home from your New Year's Eve walk – my God, you should have seen the look on both your faces. It was just beautiful. Myself and Richie picked up on it right away. You were both glowing. I was sure it wouldn't be long before you'd start dating.'

She paused to sip her glass of wine.

'And then Emma came back into the picture, and everything changed so fast. I mean, he's even back smoking. Did you know that?'

'No, I . . .'

'He's down in that bloody basement with that book you bought him for hours every day, smoking. And there's no ventilation down there. And he's meeting her again tomorrow night.'

'Oh. Really?'

My hand trembled as I topped up my drink, the beer foaming up over the rim of the glass.

'Look, Lisa. I'm sorry. You're my best friend, and this isn't going to stop us being mates, is it? And it hurts me to tell you all this.'

'No, no,' I said, letting out a deep sigh. 'It's just . . . it's just . . . Oh God, Carol, I think I love him. No, I *know* I do. I'm crazy about him.'

'Hey, come here.'

She put her arms around me.

'It's ok, Lisa. I'm here. It's ok. Look, this thing with Emma will fall apart, just like it did the last time. I bet my life on it. She's after drawing him into her web again. The bloody fool. He's so easy-going. He's always falling into traps like this. It's going to be ok. I promise you, Lisa. I promise.'

We sat there till closing time, chatting away about my feelings for David, as well as the interview with the Guards. I knew I could trust Carol, even so, David was her brother.

Despite having had three drinks, I found it hard to sleep that night. I tossed and turned, kept awake by niggling thoughts and feelings: the whole story of the night I gave up coke . . . how everything unfolded from that moment . . . the detailed information about me on Jason's files, not to mention the mysterious codes . . . and then of course, my feelings for David . . . how my heart was close to breaking at the prospect, the real fear of losing him, losing the one person I knew I truly loved . . .

In the blink of an eye, the alarm clock was buzzing: *7:30am*. It couldn't be! I checked my phone. It was. God. There was one unread message. Who? *David*. Wow.

Hi Lisa. Sorry I couldn't get back to you. Up to my eyes. I'll buzz you later. Glad to hear all went well with interview. David x

I had a jog, a shower and a light breakfast before picking up the phone and replying:

Ok. Lisa x

I felt slightly guilty sending such a brief reply to the man I loved. But deep inside I felt that *closing-up* feeling. *Soul protection* – maybe that's the best way of putting it.

In the car on the way to work I switched on the radio. It was that irritating dj again, full of himself as usual.

'And here's the theme song from *Loooooove Story*, yes, a loooooove song, especially for everyone out there who's in loooooove! Is that you? Maybe it is! Are you in *loooooove?'*

I hit the *off* button.

Give me a break.

At my lunch break my phone rang. *Carol*.

'Hold on, Carol.'

I stepped outside the staffroom.

'Hi.'

'Hi, Lisa. Just thought I'd tell you that I tried to stop David a couple of times for a chat, but all I got was, "Not now, not now! Too much going on!"'

'Ok, Carol. Thanks. Gotta go.'

After I hung up, something inside told me it was time to put the last move together – and ring Cara. I checked all round me to make sure there were no teachers – or kids – within earshot. A feeling of trepidation rippled through me as I dialled her number. As her phone rang I reminded myself not to say too much over the phone, just in case.

'Lisa, hi,' came her tentative voice on the other end.

'Hi, Cara. It's been a while, I know. I was wondering if I could meet up with you – and John – for a chat as soon as possible? I know this is a bit out of the blue, but it's important.'

'Ok. But what's it about? I'm not sure about John, if he'll agree to meet you, Lisa. You know yourself.'

There was a pause before she added:

'*I'd* meet you.'

'No, no. Tell John I have to see you both, and sooner rather than later. Look, Cara. A lot has happened. I think you know what this in relation to.'

'No. What?' said Cara, trying to sound normal.

The Principal teacher passed me on her way from her office to the staffroom. She nodded at me with a smile and went in.

'Cara, come on,' I whispered, moving further away from the door.

'I was interviewed only yesterday by the . . . by the Guards . . . about Jason Bailey. Surely you remember him from your party on Stephen's Night? Now come on. I need to meet you both for a private talk.'

There was a silence at the other end.

'The cops talked to *you?* Em, ok, look. I'll ring John and ring you back, ok?'

'No, just text. I've to go back into class.'

Oh shit. Have I said too much? I could just see Jack and Ray analysing every word of that conversation.

I left my phone on silent. Half an hour later it vibrated on my desk. The kids were all engrossed in their artwork so I glanced at it.

Ok Lisa Johns house 2nite 830 Cara.

The scene was set. I was going to have to face John, once and for all. I knew why he agreed to meet me – he knew only too well that Jason's death was something I could trace back to him. And I'm sure he wanted to hear first-hand what questions the police put to me, and, more importantly, what I had to say to them.

On the way home I picked up the Irish Times. *Dead end in Bailey murder case,* it stated. The other papers had the same story on their front pages. They all said that the team on the case had to withdraw in order to work on other outstanding cases. Everything seemed to point to a winding down in the investigation, and it sounded like there was no hope, no clue to the identity of the killers.

*

John arrived home and gave Cara a big hug.

'What's got into you?' she asked, breaking away from him. 'You do know Lisa will be here soon?'

'Yeah, yeah. So what! Who cares? She has nothing on me, love. Haven't you read the papers today? It's over! The cops have thrown in the towel in their hunt for the killers. So let's put it all behind us and get the rest of the wedding plans up and running.'

'Ok. Well, it's all very well for you, John, that the case is blown over. But what about the guy's family? Don't you care? Don't you feel anything for them? It's never going to blow over for them. Not tomorrow, not next year. Never!'

'Look, pet. I *do* feel for them. But look, you know I had no part in all that. I would never dream of going out and taking someone's life. Never. It was . . . it was them – the gang who done it.'

'Ok. So will you promise me something from here on? It's the only thing I'll ask of you.'

'Sure. What, pet?'

'Will you cut way back on the dealing? When this whole fuss dies down a bit more, go back to dealing, but just a few mates. I don't want to ever go through something as dark as this ever again. Plus, I want to have kids, which we agreed to. I don't want my kids growing up surrounded by all this.'

'Ok, love. You have my word.'

She hugged him.

'And one more thing – that you cut back to just the odd line yourself. The Christmas is over, John. Time to get back on track.'

'Ok. Look, Cara,' he said, pulling her closer into his arms, 'I love you with all my heart. And I'll never put us at this kind of risk ever again. Annie's having her birthday party next Friday night. I promise – that's my last session, ok? Promise!'

'You promise me, John? Last party?'

'Yeah, that's it. I'll go back to taking just a couple of lines before I go out to the pub. So we have a deal, yeah?'

He hugged her even tighter, kissing her.

'Ok, Cara. Let's leave this bad experience behind us and get this chat with Lisa out of the way and move on with our lives.'

*

I rang the doorbell and waited in the cold night air. I glanced around to make sure I wasn't being followed. The road was empty. Good. *Ok, Lisa. Hold your own, girl. Say what you came to say, then move on with your own life.*

Cara opened the door. She looked tense.

'Come in, Lisa,' she said, her voice sounding unsure, anxious. 'God, you look great.'

'Thanks, Cara. You don't look half bad yourself. Thanks for seeing me at such short notice.'

'John will be down in a sec. He's just in the loo. Can I get you a coffee or a beer or something?'

'A glass of water will be fine, thanks.'

I felt so relaxed. It must have been that I was getting used to all the tense situations I'd found myself in of late.

*

John bent over the window sill, firing a couple of lines up his nose. He threw his head back.

'Ah, lovely! Sorted now!'

His phone rang. *James.*

'Hi, James! What's the story? Did you read the papers today? Happy days! Yeah?'

'Yeah, yeah. Read the Star. A bit of good news at last. The cops have pulled back, which is great. We can start moving the coke more freely now.'

'How does Darryl feel about it?'

'Darryl? I dunno. It'll take a lot more than this to make him smile again. Anyway, I'll be dropping down to you Saturday with a batch of that good stuff. Have me money ready. I'll be in a hurry. How's 7:30 sound?'

*

John walked into the sitting room, cracking open a can of Miller as he did.

'Ah, Lisa!' he said, sitting down by the fire, glancing over at Cara to size up the mood. He took out a cigarette and lit it.

'You don't mind if I smoke, do you?' he said, with that smirky grin he'd never used with me when I'd been into the coke.

'It's your home, John. Fire away.'

I took a deep breath and got straight into my spiel.

'So – I was just explaining to Cara here before you came down that it's very clear that on Stephen's Night Jason Bailey was not coming onto your patch to deal coke. And no, I was *not* playing a game to wreck your engagement party. I think it's safe to say it was a big misunderstanding right from the start which led to calls being made to whoever your mates are who then went ahead and . . . well, killed that poor guy.'

Cara, ashen-faced, didn't know where to look. There was an awkward silence which was broken by John.

'Hold on a minute, Lisa. Something did go down in that garden. Something that left you out of your f**king bin. Yeah, anyone there with a bit of cop on could see you were spaced out of it. You were shouting about sorting something. Like, give us a break! We're not fools, Lisa. Admit it – you must've taken coke, or something, on the sly.'

'I took *nothing!*' I said, standing up and banging my glass of water on the table. 'I've been clean since that night in The Life. I don't have to explain myself to you or anyone. Everyone else knows I'm off it since that night. We'll never know what happened in the garden, will we? The only person who knows is now dead!'

'Yeah, yeah. But I had nothing to do with that, right? I made a call, but that's all. I'd *never* do something like that. It had nothing to do with me. I thought they'd just hit him or warn him off. I never imagined that they'd . . . well, I can't talk about it, ok? It's all in the past now. It's over. We all have to move on with our lives.'

'Yeah, yeah, John. We'll all move on. Just like that. But what about his broken-hearted family? Don't you ever think about them?'

'I do, Lisa!' Cara interjected, standing up and putting her arms around me. 'I do.'

She sounded genuinely distraught, like it had been troubling her deeply.

'I haven't slept right since it happened, to be honest. John'll tell you. I can't imagine what that family must be going through. It doesn't bear thinking about.'

John threw her a glance, then glared at me.

'So – what did the cops ask you? Why did they pull you in? I don't have to remind you what the boys will do to you if you start mouthing off. They are not to be messed with, you hear me?'

He threw his fag into the fireplace and slowly, menacingly crushed his empty beer can with one hand, staring at me throughout.

'Well, they didn't even mention your name,' I said, holding his stare. 'You've no need to worry there. The reason they wanted to interview me was because of a number of files Jason had on his computer. 0ne had a list of names, and mine was on it.'

'Ha! So yiz *did* know each other after all!' he snarled, lighting up another cigarette. 'Couple of freaks! Yeah!'

'John, that's enough!' said Cara, her eyes welling up with tears. 'None of this is funny. None of it! Just let Lisa say what she came to say, ok?'

'Go on, then. Say what you came to say.'

I drained my glass of water.

'I can't go into all of my reasons. I can't explain all of this. But listen.'

Cara motioned me to sit beside her on the sofa. I did. She looked intently at me. We waited as John got another beer from the kitchen, then stood at the fireplace, leaning on the mantelpiece.

'This Jason guy,' I continued. 'I didn't know him, or why he picked me and was studying me. We'll never know. But it seems the other files he had were all part of his study of the drug culture, his findings. And this is why I came here. But before I get to that, I have to tell you this: I'm sorry I told my mother everything – about us taking coke, I mean. I just broke down one day and let it all out. It doesn't mean I ratted on you – I didn't. And she would never speak a word to anyone anyway. She's my ma, and I trust her.'

Cara looked somewhat uncomfortable, John even more so.

'But Jason was convinced – and not only Jason, but another guy who has also studied the whole world of drugs – they're both absolutely convinced that you are all in danger. Great danger.'

The word hung in the air.

'Danger?' asked Cara, looking anxiously at John. 'In what way? What danger?'

'Well,' I said, 'you're going to find this hard to take in, but here goes. In the unseen world that surrounds us every day of our lives, there is evil – an evil spirit – or a kind of dark force – that manipulates the seen world and is behind the whole drug culture, especially coke. That's its main focus. Jason Bailey had this down to a tee. Others feel we're at a time in history when this dark, unseen force is about to inflict its greatest damage, its main objective being to take down the next generation, wipe them all out with this drug. I've a strong feeling that something awful is about to unfold within our own circle of friends. I've thought that since that night in The Life. I actually saw something, one of those . . . those evil beings. I know it sounds crazy. Yes, I know that. But I'm 100% convinced of what I saw.'

John jumped up and burst out laughing. He flicked his cigarette butt towards the fireplace but missed. Cara had to act immediately to prevent it burning the carpet.

'Gimme a break!' he roared.

His eyes turning dark with rage. He stormed over and leaned down to me, his face almost touching mine. I could smell his breath, a mixture of cigarettes and beer.

'You come up here to waste our time with this pile of *shit?'*

He spat that last word into my face.

Cara stood up.

'Don't you touch her, John! Don't you touch her, or I swear I'll . . .'

'You'll what?'

For a moment I knew I was witness to a real threat. And Cara looked as if this was something that was becoming all too familiar in her life. He sniggered and tousled her hair, then turned his attention back to me.

'You're mad, Lisa! Mad! There's some wire after coming loose in that stupid head of yours,' he said, tapping me on the forehead. 'I've never heard such crap in all my life! Is it them strange xbox games you play? Have they driven you mad? Wha'? You're a nutcase! You hear me? You're nuts! Cara – get her out of my house. *Now, Cara!* Before I do hit the crazy, f**king bitch! Get out! You hear me? *Get out!'*

'Don't worry. I'm going. But don't blame me when something does happen. My advice to you, John, is – stop now. Tell Ruth, Steve and the rest to stop too. The police are pulling me back for a second interview on Monday week. Don't be surprised if I do tell them the whole truth. Now, get your face out of mine.'

'Get out! Get her out, Cara! Get out, or I'll shoot you myself!'

He grabbed me by my coat collar.

'You'll be dead if you open that little f**kin' mouth of yours! I told you, Cara. She's no mate of ours. She's a crazy witch.'

He shoved me away.

'Ok, ok, John,' said Cara, tears beginning to stream down her face. 'Look, Lisa. Please go. Just go.'

As I made my way towards my car I could still hear John inside the house, laughing his head off and shouting after me.

'Watch out now you don't knock down a ghost on your way home! You stupid, crazy fool!'

Cara followed me to the car. I sat in and opened the window.

'I'm sorry, Lisa,' she said, the stress of her divided loyalties showing on her face. 'Please don't say anything to the police. I'm begging you. For me, Lisa. You know how much I . . . I love John.'

I could see in her tear filled eyes that she believed it was love. *But surely she knows the difference between love and fear?*

She dropped her voice, though he was well out of earshot.

'Can we meet up again? Can I ring you, go for a coffee? I know you never set out to cause all this. I know now. I miss you.'

I patted her hand.

'Oh, Cara. Where did it all go wrong? We were so close, then the coke came along. Now look, I know it's not your fault. I do want to meet you, but not . . . not with John. Sorry. It just won't work.'

'Ok. I'll ring you.'

I let out a deep sigh as I drove off.

I did the right thing, didn't I? I said what had to be said. Maybe I could have handled it better. But it's over now. Poor Cara, she looks like she's stressed out by it all. And John? He's getting worse as time passes. Paranoid. I just hope her marrying him won't turn out to be a big mistake.

*

'My God! Did you have to go on like that, John? You made a show of yourself – and me!'

'Ah, Cara, come on now! I've told you about her. But no, you wouldn't listen, would ye? Come on! *Evil spirits!* She's as mad as a f**king brush! I'm not sitting there listening to that shit talk!'

'Ok. Look. I'll chat to her on my own. Maybe it was a mistake bringing her here to the house. It was too soon after everything that's taken place.'

'Don't bring her here to this house ever again, Cara! Right? Her mind's not right. And I'd prefer if you kept her and those mental ideas of hers as far away from me as possible.'

'Ok. Point taken. It's over. Look - can we snuggle up at the fire here and watch a dvd? I picked up two today – half-price in HMV. Plus, I've started to make up the wedding list. So how about going through some names together? Tomorrow, maybe?'

'Yeah, sure. Come here. I love you, Cara. You hear me? I love you. And I can't wait to start our lives together as man and wife. You know – have a couple of kids, settle down . . .'

'Aah, how romantic! Yeah! Come here. Put on a film there. Which one do you want?'

'Couldn't care less. You choose.'

She looked at both dvd covers and started reading the blurbs on the back.

'Just one thing,' said John.

'Mmm?'

'Don't touch her or I swear I'll . . . what?'

'What?'

'That's what you said to me, in front of Lisa.'

'All I meant was . . .'

'Don't ever . . . ever . . . threaten me again. Ok, pet?'

He hugged her tight. Very tight.

Cara's throat went dry.

'Ok,' she murmured, gulping down her fear. She stared into the flames of the fire and pondered his words. She also pondered Lisa's strange insights and warnings to do with the dark forces of the unseen world.

*

I rang Carol. She supported what I said to John.

'Ok. Now step back, Lisa. You did all you can. Now walk away, pet.'

'Ok, I will. You're right. Thanks, Carol.'

'Anytime.'

There was a pause.

'Is there any news on . . . I was just wondering what's happening with David?'

Carol sighed.

'Lisa, he's lost about a stone in the past week. I swear. He looks pale. He's smoking away. Every time I try to talk to him, he says, "Sorry? What? Ask me again!" Then back he goes, down to his Basement of Horrors. I'm worried for him, Lisa. I really am.'

'God, that's . . .'

'He's off, all done up, to see *herself* again tonight. Last night, about 12:30am, Richie and I were in the sitting room. We heard him coming up from the basement. He made a coffee, said nothing, but stood beside us, staring into the fire. Just staring, in a trance, like, muttering something under his breath. Then he walked back out of the room as if we were invisible. It's not good, not good at all, Lisa. I'm sorry I haven't got better news for you. Maybe if *you* try ringing him?'

'Yeah, yeah,' I said, glad that she suggested it, not me. 'Maybe I should. God, what am I going to say, though!'

'Don't worry. You'll think of something. Gotta go. Bye, Lisa.'

As I hung up, this awful frightening feeling raced across my heart – the feeling that I was losing him – *losing David!* – forever.

When I got home I talked to Ma about the events of the day. She wasn't impressed that I had gone to John and Cara's on my own, but understood that I needed to bring my own closure to everything that had occurred.

'Just one word of warning, Lisa,' she said, grasping both my hands in hers. 'Look at me when I tell you this. *Look at me.* I want you to promise me never, ever to entertain that John character again. Will you do that? It's over now, pet. Over. Time to move on. If you can help Cara in some way – great. But stay well clear of that . . . that criminal.'

'Don't worry, Ma. I'll steer clear of him. I promise.'

She hugged me tight.

'I'm so relieved, pet. So that's the end of it.'

She planted a kiss on my cheek, like a seal of approval.

'So,' she smiled mischievously. 'Any word from David? Hmm?'

She looked me straight in the eye for any tell-tale signs that things might have turned around for me.

'No, no. Nothing. He's drifted further away, if anything.'

I put my head down, not wanting to bother her anymore after the worries she'd had to confront all week.

I went up to my room and texted Carol. She rang me and we had a long chat that lasted nearly an hour. She was so supportive, yet concerned about me – and David, of course. We arranged to meet Sunday for a coffee as she was off out on Saturday for a meal with Richie.

I sat on the bed for the next few hours, just thinking of David. The pain was so real, picturing him alone with Emma. I tried everything to push myself into a positive frame of mind, but failed.

I lay across the bed holding my pillow and closed my eyes, trying to banish my sad thoughts. If only I could turn back the clock. Imagine – no drugs, no gangland crime, no murder . . . no Emma . . . Imagine meeting him afresh, for the first time, no baggage, just a new start . . .

David was running towards me, shouting *Lisa, Lisa! I love you!* I smiled and called back to him, *I love you too!* He shouted again, *I love you so much! Run! Run!* His hands were waving as if he were trying to warn me. I turned around slowly and saw a motorbike pulling up with two guys dressed in black leather. The guy on the back jumped off and pulled a gun out of his jacket. All the time I could hear David screaming at me, *Run, Lisa! Run!* as the guy pointed the gun at me. I could see his dark, coke-filled eyes so clearly. I heard the echo as three shots rang out. I could feel them hit my body, shot after shot after shot. Dark red blood oozed from my chest, my shoulder, my head. I screamed, *No! No! Please!* I screamed and screamed and sat up in bed.

Ma ran into the room.

'Lisa! Are you ok? Are you all right, love?'

I sat there, dripping with sweat, trying to catch my breath.

'Shit, that seemed so real! Oh, sorry, Ma. Just an awful nightmare. But God, it felt so real!'

She held me tight.

'It's ok, Lisa. It's ok. Just a bad dream. You're safe now, pet. You're safe now.'

*

Saturday evening, James arrived to do his drop at John's.

'Come in, come in,' said John, nervously looking back out before closing the door.

'I'm in a hurry, John,' said James, pulling a large package from his jacket. 'So let's make this fast, yeah?'

'Yeah, sure. Listen, James. I've a couple of things to run past ye before you leg it. Is that ok?'

'Yeah, but hurry the f**k up. I'm taking the mot out.'

John lit up a fag, taking a deep, confident drag before blowing the smoke out.

'You remember about a year ago you kept going on about how Darryl always wanted to get something going in the Dundalk/ Drogheda areas but could never get the right openings?'

'Yeah?'

'Well, I've got it all sorted!'

'Yeah?'

'Yeah. I've six new heads who want to move coke into big areas. There'll be no hassle, as no one's controlling these places at the moment. It'll be big, James. Big! I'm branching out!' he said, smiling.

He took another drag from his cigarette.

'But not till July – after the wedding, right? Can't let the bird know anything or she'll go mad. But I'll be putting everything into place and we'll be ready to go in the summer.'

John dragged again on his smoke, enjoying every bit.

'Darryl will love that bit of news. Yeah?'

'Getting greedy there, John,' said James with a grin. 'The money's going to that little head of yours!' he laughed. 'I won't say anything to Darryl yet, as the very mention of your name puts him in the horrors for days. But yeah, this sounds good to me. Be a big move. You were always good at this sort of thing. Not much good at anything else, mind! But yeah, that's sound. Where's me cash now? I'm flying off.'

'Yeah, sure,' said John, opening a tin from the kitchen press and pulling out a wad of notes. 'It's all there.'

'Right. I'll be down next Saturday, around eight, yeah?'

'Yeah, cool. Listen. There's something else. This girl, Lisa – Lisa Webb? She dropped around yesterday, right? Off her head, James. She was pulled Thursday by the cops. She said nothing about us. But they're bringing her back Monday week and well . . . well, she threatened to talk, James.'

'Yeah?'

'Yeah. Gave me a load of mouth here yesterday, the bitch. She was off her head big time. The crap she came out with, saying we're all in some kind of danger! I don't like it, James. Not one bit.'

'Yeah . . . I was supposed to ask you tonight about her. What did you say her name was? Lisa what?'

'Webb. Lisa Webb. Yeah. A f**kin' schoolteacher, believe it or not. Small. Blonde. Good-looking bird.'

'Lisa Webb? Hmm. So she got pulled what? Thursday? That's not good. Not good at all. Darryl won't like this one bit. He'll go f**king mad again. Ah, shit. I'll buzz him later. Right, leave it with me. I'm gone. Bye.'

John closed the door with a smile.

Chapter Twenty Two

All Over Soon

James took the back road to Finglas, pulling in to get petrol.

'Fill her up, lad.'

'No problem, mate.'

I'm not your mate, lad.

He lit a cigarette and switched on his mobile, ignoring the clear signs that said *No Smoking* and *Turn off Mobile Phones*. He walked a few paces away, out of earshot of the young attendant.

'Darryl! James here.'

'Alright, James! Everything alright? Did you drop out to Skerries?'

'Yeah, yeah. On me way home now. Listen – the John lad has been putting a plan together to branch out into the Drogheda and Dundalk area in July. Now I know you don't want me bringing him up. But it's been something you always wanted to see happen, right? The fool's good at this kind of thing.'

'Yeah – but f**k-all good at anything else. Are you sure he's not bullshitting to get back into me good books?'

'No, no. He's just waiting to get his wedding out of the way first, then he's got six lads lined up, ready to go. It'll be big. I'd imagine we'll be branching out even further when we get things moving.'

'Fifty seven euros, mate.'

'Hey! I'm on the bleedin' phone! Do ye mind?'

'Sorry, mate.'

'*Wha'?* Who the f**k is there with you?'

'Relax, Darryl! I'm just getting petrol.'

'Right. Well, the fool better not be mouthing off or I'll go down and break his f**kin' neck with me bare hands. You hear me, James? I'm sick of him and all the crap he's after getting me into.'

'No, lookit. I'll work with him all the way and watch it closely. But listen – there's something else. And don't start shouting down the phone, right? It's this girl, Lisa. Lisa Webb, her full name is. A bleedin' schoolteacher, would you believe. Well, she . . .'

There was a loud, impatient honking of a horn. The driver in the car behind him signalled to him to move.

'Wait, Darryl. I've to move me car.'

He pulled over to the tyre-pumping bay. The attendant followed him and started washing his windscreen with a squeegee.

'Hey! Did I *ask* you to wash me windscr . . .? Ah here. How much for the petrol?'

'Fifty-seven euros, mate.'

He pushed three twenties into the young guy's hand.

'Keep the change, lad.'

'Hey, thanks, mate!'

'Darryl? Are you still there?'

'Yeah. If it's not too much trouble to drag you away from your boyfriend there.'

'Ha! No, but seriously. This Lisa Webb one, right? She got pulled Thursday. Then she shows up at John's house yesterday. Now she hasn't opened her mouth yet, but she made threats to John that she has to go back for a second interview with the cops Monday week. Get this, right? She warned John that we're all in danger. *In danger!* The bitch! My bet is she's going to open the can of worms. She's off her bleedin' head, Darryl, according to John.'

He threw the cigarette butt out the window.

'Ah shit, James. This is all I f**king need to hear right now. I bet it was Magee who interviewed her. Look. Ring Jess, will ye? And Mick. And drop round in the morning, say ten o'clock. Leave me to think. I'll sort something. I'm out with the wife right now. I don't want to say anymore on this f**kin' phone. Just bring the lads with ye. Bye.'

*

The atmosphere yet again was tense. Darryl, unshaven, held a mug of coffee while lighting up a fag. His wife was cleaning and washing up after the breakfast.

'Emily – I need to talk to the lads. Yeah – get the kids ready for shopping. I'll just be ten minutes.'

Emily smiled nervously as she glanced at all four gang members. With a look of quiet resignation she bowed her head and, without a word, walked out of the kitchen, closing the door behind her.

Darryl picked up the newspaper off the coffee table.

'Right. Friday's Evening Herald. See all this crap about cops pulling back? *Dead end in murder case?* It's all a pile of shit. Magee never gives up just like that. I sensed something wasn't right, so keep your guard up. Don't leave any cash or coke in your gaffs. Yiz hear me?'

Everyone grunted and nodded in agreement. Mickey pulled out his pack of Marlboros.

'Anyone want one?'

Jess reached out and helped himself.

James pulled out his own pack.

'I'll have a John Player Blue.'

They all lit up.

'Right,' continued Darryl. 'All this came out the day after Lisa Webb got pulled Thursday, as I'm sure James informed the lot of yiz.

So all of what yiz read since then is a cock-and-bull story. Smart arse cops again. I'm no fool!'

There was an uneasy shuffling of feet as all four took a deep drag of their cigarettes.

'Now James tells me we're branching out into the Drogheda and Dundalk areas – maybe further – in July. I'll run that by yiz all again.

'Now I don't have to tell yiz how I despise the very name of that fool, John from Skerries. But despite all that's happened, he's the one who's going to be spearheading this move. At the end of the day it's all about one thing – making money. Right? So there's just one little problem we need to sort out so we can all move on with our plans for the year ahead. And it's to sort out this Lisa Webb one. She's the one and only link back to us, connecting us with the murder. I want this closed off and fast. Are yiz all listening to me?'

'Yeah, yeah,' said Mick, standing up. 'I'm listening. But lookit, Darryl. I can't believe you're thinking what I *know* you're thinking. This will bring another load of crap onto us all.'

'Look, Mickey – will you sit down! She's the only one who can finger John, and that fool will fall apart under questioning. And you know what that means. It'll come back to my door before long. The little bitch is mouthing off, threatening to talk.'

'Yes, but *another* hit, Darryl? Crap, that'll bring more investigation, more of us being pulled. Do we really want that? We're just starting to get going again. Have you any idea the pressure it'll bring? We'll all be pulled *again!*'

'Listen, Mickey. Here. Give us one of your fags.'

James leaned over and lit it for him.

Darryl took a deep, hungry drag.

'Sit down, all of yiz. Sit down. No one in this gang is going to be involved in this. Right? In fact, all of yiz will make sure yiz are in the local pub that morning with rock solid alibis.'

He dropped his voice.

'I've already hired the best shooter to carry it out. Right? Yeah, he's the best. And we need the best to make sure it's clean and no mistakes.'

'Who is he?' asked Jess.

The rest glared at him.

'Only jokin'!' he laughed.

'Now listen to me, James. The hit is planned for this weekend. Yeah, that's right. Sunday the 22nd . Now I want you to go down to John with your drop next Saturday as usual. Stay awhile, small-talk the fool up. You know – blah, blah, blah. Just bring up about the girl. Get her address. Just ask him casual-like, like you're small-talking. Don't make it look like you're asking serious, important questions, like. Whatever you do, I don't want him to know a thing. He's just not able for this side of what we do.'

'No problem, Darryl,' said James, giving his full support to the plan. He saw that Mickey still looked unsettled, unsure, not happy. 'Look, Mickey, it's cool. It's the only way to end this nightmare, once and for all. She has a history of coke, so no one's going to give a shit once that comes out about her.'

Darryl took a deep drag, blowing the smoke towards Mick. He checked his mobile.

'Here, James. Here's a phone number. The minute you get the girl's address ring this number.'

James copied it onto his phone.

'Don't say a word. Don't ask anything. Just say your name – *James*. Give the address. Hang up. Delete the number from your phone and go home.'

Jess stubbed out his cigarette.

'Does this hit-man know what your one looks like?'

'Yeah – small, blonde, good-looking. Just don't mess this up on me, James, or it'll be your buddy John who'll be going down instead. One way or another, this ends next Sunday.'

'No mistakes, Darryl. Don't worry. I'll get the address. No worries.'

Jess stood up, putting on his jacket, letting out a laugh.

'Best plan we heard in a while. So Sunday I can tell my bird I've to be in the pub at 10am and stay for the match!'

'Who's playing, anyway?' asked Mick, putting his fags into his top jacket pocket.

'Man United, at half-twelve. Can't wait.'

'Right so. I suppose this will end it all for good, 'cause I'm getting one pain in my arse coming to these meetings, talking about this, not to mention being pulled over the Bailey killing. Sure maybe I'll join you, Jess, for the match? What about you, James?'

'Ah, sure why not? A few lines and a few beers, watching Man U getting shot to pieces by Arsenal!'

'Ha, ha, ha!' said Jess. 'I get it. The headlines – *Man Utd shot down by Gunners in Swords pub*. Yeah – I love it!'

Darryl cut him short with a look.

'Ok. Maybe not the best joke ever, but . . .'

'Right, that's it,' said Darryl. 'Yiz can all split. I've a wife to bring shopping.'

They all started moving out the door.

'Hey, James! Don't f**k this up, right? I've paid big money to end this. You hear me?'

'Sure thing, Darryl. Consider it done. Absolutely no mistakes on this one.'

*

After a long jog first thing on Sunday, I spent most of the morning cleaning up the apartment for Ma. I did some work for class on Monday, but everything I did seemed to be clouded with the nagging urge to pick up the phone and ring David. Every time the thought of him entered my mind it was always accompanied by a fleeting image, or a series of fleeting images, like a slideshow, showing his face. Sometimes he was smiling, sometimes serious, but always, always it was those amazing eyes of his which entranced me once again, sending a frisson of excitement through me. Again I wondered how his meet-up, *okay*, his *date*, with Emma had gone.

With a feeling of trepidation I picked up my phone to make the call. But right at that moment, a text came through. Cara.

Hi Lisa. Sorry again about John & big distance between us. Great Emma doing so well off the coke. Let's meet 4 coffee soon? Miss the way it was. Cara xxx

I took a deep breath and thought hard about my reply.

Hi Cara. Sorry but won't be meeting u again if John is with u. I forgive u, it's all in the past. Will be in touch for coffee some time down the road, but 1 on 1. Miss u 2. Lisa xxx

Message sent.

It was nice to be bringing closure to what had happened. Lying back on my bed, I couldn't help but put most of the blame on one thing: drugs.

I took up my phone again. Another deep breath. *Ok, here we go.* I rang David. It rang and rang, then rang out. After a pause I rang again. Still no answer. I felt a deep sense of rejection searing through me. I knew my love for him was so real, so deep, and yet here he was, closing me out of his life. The pain turned to panic, a frightening dread that was beginning to pull me apart. I had nowhere to hide.

Nowhere to hide. God, I've got to ring someone. I need to talk to someone. Maybe see what's happening on Facebook?

I rang Carol. The phone rang and rang. *God, not her too?*

'Hi, Lisa!'

'Carol!'

I nearly burst into tears with relief.

'How are things?'

'Oh, Carol. I'm . . . I'm all over the place. I just can't cope with these feelings. If anything, they're getting stronger. They're pulling me apart inside. I rang David, but no answer. I thought at least he'd be my friend. To be honest, the very thought of him back with Emma is killing me inside. Has he said anything to you? I hate landing all this on you, Carol, but I've no one else to turn to.'

I could hear a deep sigh from Carol.

'Oh, Lisa, Lisa. I'm so sorry. I'm really hurting with you, I swear. And you know you can ring me anytime. I'm your friend forever.

Please don't forget that, will you? You need me right now and I'm here for you. Never think otherwise.'

'Thanks, Carol. You're a star.'

'It's awful. It's not good news at all. And it kills me to say that. I never heard him come home Friday night, Lisa. I stayed awake till about one, but fell asleep. We saw very little of him yesterday' And this morning he looked awful – unshaven, puffing on a fag. His glow is gone. Had a coffee in his hand, heading back down to that godforsaken basement again.'

'God.'

'I tried to stop him and ask him had he been in contact with you at all, had he returned your calls. He just looked at me with those ghostly eyes and shook his head, looking confused, bewildered. Then he said,

'"Oh, look, Carol. There's so much going on right now. My head is just full of it."

'I had to bite my lip, Lisa, from saying, *Yeah, full of shit!* Then he went on to say:

'"What I've got to say to Lisa . . . well, I'm not sure yet, but I have to find a way of saying it. It may be too much for her right now to take on board."

'He said no more. Just turned and walked down those steps. That was it. I shouted at him,

'"Hey! When's the *old* David coming back?"

'But I don't think he heard me. He just closed the door. Richie is going to have a word with him later.'

'Oh, goodnight. That's it, Carol. He's back with her but doesn't want to hurt me by telling me to my face . . . Oh, no!'

'What?'

'I'm looking at his Facebook page right now. Have you seen it?'

'No, no. What's it say?'

'From 3am this morning: *How do you say goodbye to someone without hurting them?'*

'Oh, no. That's not good. Look, leave it till Richie has a word with him. You're not on your own, Lisa. You hear me? Richie may be a guy of few words, but he has another side to him, believe me. He'll give David a good talking to, plus a good kick up the backside. You wait and see. A good Size 9 kick back into the real world – that's exactly what he needs.'

I hung up and just lay there, re-reading the Facebook message. *How do you say goodbye to someone . . .?* That meant one thing, and one thing only. He's gone. *He's gone back to her. What's the use? It's over . . .*

During all this time, Ma kept to herself, never prying into my life. But it was heartening to know that she was still there for me, day or night.

When I met Carol later that day, she told me Richie went down to try and talk to David but found the basement door was locked. He went to knock, but then heard that Coldplay song *What If?* playing inside. And he swore he could hear David crying. So he left it for another time.

'He's a total mess, Lisa. But look – he'll come round in time. We just need to have more patience. We'll just stand back a bit. I appreciate it's very hard for you, but I know him better than anyone, and I've seen him go downhill before. He'll bounce back to his real self. Don't worry.'

Even with Carol by my side, even with Ma's ongoing support, everything started to become dark and strange. The past few weeks of turmoil had been enough to face without this latest development. After Carol left me that Sunday I found myself truly alone, the light darkening around me, tormented all the more by my unrequited love for David. I felt frightened, but never fully sure of what.

By Tuesday there was no news at all. Nothing.

That evening I spent a few hours preparing schoolwork for next day. As I was putting the books back in my bag I was overwhelmed once again by those strange, disquieting feelings. I had experienced them a few times in the past month – nothing to do with David – but this time they came at me stronger than ever, wave after wave. I couldn't move. I felt I was going to pass out. Or maybe I did, just for a moment. And in that moment I thought I heard a soft voice.

It will all be over soon, Lisa. All over soon.

I fell back on the bed, overpowered. I tried to stand up, but couldn't.

What the hell is happening to me? God! Maybe . . . should I get down to the doctor? Get a blood test? Maybe it's all the stress? Everything taking a toll on my body? My mind? I'm starting to hear voices now . . . Maybe I'm losing the plot altogether?

I tried to calm myself down by breathing deeply . . . deeply . . . deeply . . .

David was holding me so close whispering in my ear I love you Lisa God I love you so much his lips wet touching softly on mine his eyes were closed but then he opened them slowly my God they were a thousand times more crystal clear full of magic full of joy full of love that I knew was all for me yes for me yes for me yes

'Lisa? Are you all right, pet?'

Darkness. My own room. Alone.

'Yes, Ma. Thanks. I'm . . . I'm having an early night.'

'Goodnight, pet.'

'Night, Ma.'

I lay in the dark. An awful feeling, a cold feeling, rushed across my heart. My mind flooded with fear. I closed my eyes.

Nothing that a few nice lines of coke wouldn't sort out, Lisa. Get back in touch with your mates. David's gone, Lisa. Gone! Cara's dying to hang out with you. Go back. Go back! You're lost on your own, Lisa. Go back. Go back!

My alarm was buzzing. *7:30am*. It couldn't be! Exhausted, I crawled out of bed and stood under the shower for a full ten minutes, letting the hot water wash away those dreadful nightmares.

I'd rather die than ever go back to put myself under that evil spell again.

On my way home from work I dropped into Eurospar for a handful of groceries and the paper. At the meat counter I bumped into Steve and Ruth. There was an awkward silence.

'Hi, Lisa!' grinned Steve. 'Hey – what's the two best things about being a primary school teacher?'

'I don't know, Steve.'

'July and August! Ha, ha!'

'Oh yeah. Funny.'

Ruth looked everywhere but at me, trying to avoid eye contact.

'So – how have you been?' Steve continued, cheery as ever. 'Look – joking aside, it's lovely to see you. Isn't that right, Ruth?'

'Yeah, yeah. Hi, Lisa,' she said, relaxing a little. 'Good to see you.'

'Look, Cara told us you dropped around. Didn't go into it all, but said she's trying to clear the air and fix things up. Said a lot of what happened was down to simple misunderstandings. We all chatted, bar John. But sure, John is John! And well, the rest of us really miss you.'

'Yeah, a lot,' chimed in Ruth, her voice choking slightly.

She looked remorseful for closing me out of her life. I couldn't be certain, but that was the vibe I was getting from her.

'Look, Lisa,' she said, with a hint of her old smile, 'I'm glad we met you today. I know things got way out of hand at Christmas, but the gang have all said since then that they miss you, miss you a lot. It all went too far alright. The texts, blocking off Facebook. But look, you did break the Number One Rule by telling your mother about us all taking coke.'

'Listen, Ruth,' I said, 'Ok. It was wrong for me to tell her. But you forget something: half of Skerries and Balbriggan already *know* about us taking coke and Es. People are not stupid, you know. They have eyes in their heads, and word gets about. And when they're in the pubs and clubs and see the way we're carrying on, it's not exactly rocket science for them to work out that we're coked out of our heads! But don't worry about Ma – she won't breathe a word to anyone. And look, it's good we met today and cleared the air a bit. I gotta go.'

'Well,' said Ruth, 'I'm sorry about stuff I said and did. Yes, I did bad-mouth you behind your back to people in the gang. And I'm sorry. And to be honest, I do miss you, Lisa. Cara's always with John, and it's like a big part of my life is missing since you're gone. Everyone says the same. Don't they, Steve?'

'Yeah. Since Christmas blew over and the air has cleared, we all feel the same. Well, Cara was going to ask you . . .'

He glanced at Ruth, as if checking with her that it was ok to say this. She shrugged her shoulders.

'. . . but now that we're talking, we were going to ask you out just for a few hours this Friday night for Annie's birthday party. Now John won't be there till about . . .'

'Half-eleven,' suggested Ruth.

'. . . half-eleven at the earliest, so if you come along about eight till about half-ten or eleven? It would be an ice-breaker. Orla, Frank, the whole lot will be there and they'd love to see you. No one will bring up a thing. It's all in the past as far as they're concerned too.'

'Well, thanks. I do appreciate you asking me. I do still take the odd social drink, you know, but nothing else. About the coke, well, I do have a problem with that. Don't get me wrong, if anyone else wants to take it, that's their business, I'm not being judgemental at all. Me, of all people! It's just, well, I found out some chilling stuff about the drug that's very frightening, to put it mildly. So I just can't sit and relax around it. Not anymore.'

'Ah, Lisa!' said Steve. 'A few lines here and there is no harm. Come on! Lighten up! Come out Friday to Tommy's. We'll all be there, the whole gang. No one will be offering you any. I swear. And you can split before the John lad comes. Leave him to me. I'll bring him around in time. It's a New Year – new beginnings! We all go back too far to let this little row break us all up for good. What do you say?'

Ruth had a tear in her eye.

'Look,' I said. 'Leave it with me. Ok? It's great that everyone is putting this whole nightmare behind them. It's really great. But to be honest, it's me.'

I looked at Ruth, my best buddy for years, along with Cara.

'It's *me*. I've changed so much – inside. I can't even explain it. Not in a shop, anyway.'

Steve smiled.

'Defo not the place for something that deep. Unless we pull up a few chairs? But don't think the boss would approve.'

Ruth and I giggled. *Good old Steve.*

'No,' I said, 'don't think so. But I am different. And I'd love to meet up and share it with you both. With the gang, even. But maybe it's just not the right time. Maybe another time soon, yeah? I am thankful for your asking me out. But give me some more time to sort out some issues in my life. Ok?'

'Ok, sure, yeah,' said Ruth, nodding her head, looking relieved that we were making ground.

Steve leaned over and gave me a lovely, sincere hug. Then Ruth held me so close I knew in that moment that no matter what had happened I still loved these people so much. I could see Ruth trying to hold back the tears as Steve put his arm around her and they headed towards the checkouts.

Wow, that was strange, I thought, driving towards my apartment.

But would I . . . could I . . . go back to sitting in a pub, everyone around me on coke? Going to parties, everyone taking line after line? Even to see that drug, knowing what I know, that was the issue. It was nothing to do with the people taking it. It was what I knew about this bloody drug . . . the evil playing around with people's very souls. And it wouldn't be long before a line would be offered. Then there was John selling it to them all. How could I be around them before he came into the picture? No, no. I couldn't. I'd rather rot alone in my room than go back into that atmosphere. But maybe the best thing would be to meet them all for coffee and explain the situation? You never know. They may see the danger in the end. You never know . . .

'No way, Lisa! No way!' shouted my mother when I told her. 'Over my dead body! I don't want you anywhere near them in a pub. A café for coffee – no problem. But not in a pub with that . . . that *murderer* John Noonan. No way!'

She slammed the kitchen press door shut. I had never seen or heard her so angry in my whole life.

'You're right, Ma. I just thought I'd tell you, but you're so right. And I know that it's just that I'm a bit lonely. Carol works. She's got Richie. I'll just have to start searching for new friends. Someone out there must be looking for friendship. Yeah?'

By Thursday I felt worse. I rang Carol, who chatted with me for ages. She told me she hadn't seen much of David for the past few days. She asked me out – just the two of us, Saturday night for a meal and a drink. We agreed on 8:30pm.

On Friday evening I sat in after Ma and I ordered a Chinese takeaway. We were watching tv, waiting for the Friday Movie to come on.

'You know, Ma,' I said, 'I've got this strange feeling something's going to happen to me. But I'm not sure what.'

'Ah, Lisa,' she said, looking somewhat concerned and yet amused, 'you're only twenty-three years of age. You have your whole life ahead of you. Big things are ahead for my girl. Come here!'

She put her arm around me and I curled up into her like a five-year-old child.

The movie was *The Notebook,* and despite our misgivings, it captivated both of us. My thoughts, of course, were of David, wondering what he was doing tonight. I wondered how he was getting on with Emma. Hmm. *Emma.*

We both went to bed as soon as the movie ended, just before 1am. I turned my phone onto *Silent,* making sure I wouldn't be disturbed from my Saturday lie-in. With the theme music from the movie still in my head, I passed out into a peaceful sleep.

*

Saturday 10am. Darryl rang James.

'Don't forget: just ring and give the address. Then hang up. He'll be expecting your call between eight and nine. No bullshit, James. You hear me?'

'Yeah, yeah. Just ring, give the address, hang up. I hear ya.'

'Oh yeah. And Rob's back from Spain last night. Has he rung you yet?'

'No, not yet. Why?'

'I told him to join all you lot in the pub tomorrow. That'll cover the whole lot of yiz. Ring me when you get home tonight, right? Bye.'

*

I awoke sleepy-eyed. Trying to open my eyes was a struggle. I felt like I'd been in a coma. What a great sleep! With the curtains pulled closed the room was still quite dark. Then I thought I saw something flashing, like a light, in the darkness. I thought I was imagining it. But after rubbing the sleep from my eyes I could hear a gentle vibrating sound, and I realised it was my phone. I reached over to pick it up but it was too late. I rubbed my eyes again, holding the phone up close to see who was calling.

David. 6 missed calls.

I sat up and jumped out of bed. I checked the phone again.

1 voicemail.

My heart was racing like crazy. I was awake now.

Hi Lisa. It's David. Yeah, so sorry about not being in touch. I've been down in the basement flat out. The codes, Lisa. Jason Bailey's codes? I think I know what they mean. I think I know what happened in the garden Stephen's Night.

Chapter Twenty Three

The Unseen End

Shock and disbelief set in as, with hands shaking, I dialled David's number.

'David – it's Lisa. Just got your message. What's going on? Are you joking or what?'

'It's no joke, Lisa. I've been down in the basement partially day and night and I think I've cracked it. But I'm finding this hard to take in myself. I don't know what you're going to think of it. It's nothing close to what I thought it would be. Can you come down as soon as possible and I'll go through it with you?'

'I'm on my way!'

I hung up only to hear Ma calling.

'Lisa – your breakfast is on the table. Are you up, love?'

'Yeah, Ma. Thanks.'

I got dressed as fast as possible and raced down the stairs, my heart pumping with a mixture of excitement and expectation.

'I've got to run, Ma. I'm sorry. I've to go to David's. I'll explain everything when I get back.'

'He's asked you out! I can tell by the excitement in your eyes!'

'No, no. I wish!'

I put a couple of rashers and an egg between two slices of bread and downed the lot in a minute flat. I washed it down with a couple of mouthfuls of tea. Ma stared at me.

'What is it then, love? I've never seen you in this big a hurry!'

Before she could say another word I had my jacket on, my keys in my hand and was out the door. I drove way over the speed limit down the Selskar Road, turning onto the old Station Road.

My head was in a spin. How could David have cracked all this? Sure even the police couldn't crack it. Distracted, I took a right turn after the Little Theatre, driving the wrong way down a one-way street. I passed the well-known Ollie's Pub, getting a strange look from a couple of lads standing outside, smoking. They were wondering, no doubt, why I was driving the wrong way. Thankfully, no cars came in the opposite direction.

I turned right, and before I could catch my breath I was pulling into David's driveway, still in one piece. Richie opened the front door before I even had time to get out of the car. His face looked as puzzled as I was feeling inside. He said nothing, just shrugged his shoulders. I walked in, searching his face for any hint or sign of what was going on. But nothing.

Carol was standing over Tim, brushing his hair. She welcomed me with open arms.

'He won't tell any of us, Lisa. He wants to tell *you* everything first. I haven't got a clue! I swear! Thankfully, he looks a lot better, and is back to his old self.'

With Carol's words still ringing in the air, the basement door could be heard closing followed by the sound of David's footsteps as he hurried up the stairway out into the hallway and leading into the sitting room where we all stood now in silence.

His hair was cut short and he was clean-shaven, making him look quite different from the last time I had seen him.

My God, his eyes seem even brighter, with that extra sparkle. Wow!

'Oh yeah – he's off the fags again,' remarked Carol as she sat down on the sofa. 'Well, David,' she continued. 'Will you at least give us a clue as to what is going on? This is killing the lot of us!'

'You've cracked the codes,' I said. 'At least tell them that part.'

He looked at me and smiled.

'Yeah, Lisa's right,' he said. 'I think I've cracked the whole lot. But to be fair, it's best I explain this to Lisa in private first. If that's ok with the rest of you?'

'Ok,' said Carol, 'but hurry up!'

She really did look like her patience was running out fast.

'Mary Coleman rang me last night,' wheezed old Tim, his voice breaking across us. 'Great oul' chat we had!'

'Mary Coleman? From Bray?' asked Carol, glancing over at David.

'Yeah. Mary Coleman!'

'Dad – Mary passed away years ago, pet.'

She grasped his hand and smiled.

'Em, say hi to Lisa, Dad. Lisa? Remember?'

He stared at me in bewilderment.

'Sorry, I thought you were Emma Ryan.'

Carol bristled at the mention of her name.

'Where have you been?' he asked me. 'We've all missed you. Haven't we, David? Tell her.'

'Yes, yes, we have indeed,' said David, caressing his father's shoulder.

He winked at me.

'Shall we head down, Lisa? Would you like a coffee or tea to bring with you? I'm making a coffee for myself.'

'No, no. A glass of water will be fine.'

'I'll get it,' said Richie, relieved to have the opportunity of somehow getting involved and helping.

As he ran the cold tap and filled the glass I stood there, looking into David's eyes, searching for any hint of information of what awaited me below in the basement. But he just concentrated on topping up his coffee, then turned away, beckoning me with his hand to follow him.

Richie handed me the water.

'Best of luck, Lisa,' he said, looking as if he was lost for words.

Wilson the dog began to follow David down.

'No, Wilson,' said Carol. 'Stay.'

'No, he's ok,' said David. 'Here, boy!'

I walked slowly down those dark steps once again. My heart raced as I stepped on the last step and through the open basement door. David closed it gently behind me. My eyes glanced round the room, searching for clues. Anthony Campbell's photo still stood there on the small table. Just beyond another table holding David's laptop were all his write-ups and photos of the chilling history of drug gangland criminals. Everything he'd shown me the last time was still in place, but for the last two display boards to the right which were empty the last time I was here. There was also a stereo I hadn't seen before, as well as a handful of books. I could see write-ups that were new, but for the life of me couldn't make head or tail of their content. On one board there seemed to be what looked like a sketch of a sword at some kind of entrance to something.

What on earth has all this got to do with me and codes and Jason Bailey?

'Hey, Lisa,' said David, breaking across my train of thought. 'Please sit down. Relax.'

Before we started, David bent down to face me head on.

'I'm sorry I've been so out of touch with you. So much has happened, and all my time was spent trying to crack all of this.'

He smiled with that look that helped me see he was being sincere.

'It's ok, really,' I said, trying to hide what it meant to me, being this close to him, being alone again in the same very private room with the man I had dreamt about all week long. I don't know if I gave anything away, but if I did, he never blinked an eyelid or gave any sense he knew what I was feeling.

'Ok,' he said, smiling again, 'do you want the long version or the short version? Because we don't want to be down here for hours, do we?'

'Short version, please. Go for it! I can't wait to hear this. I'm dying to know.'

'Ok. But I'm of the strong opinion that no one outside this room will ever believe any of this. But that's not our problem, is it?'

He stood up and pointed towards the noticeboard he'd worked on for years.

'See all this? All the gangland members, all the mayhem caused by the war on drugs and how I felt convinced there was some form of real evil working to drag the problem into a deeper and darker place, pushing the one drug to the front, which is cocaine, making it more acceptable in society? The social drug, as they call it? Well, we don't have to go over all that. You know the story. But if you remember, I gave up the study because I felt I was missing something. I couldn't see the wood for the trees, so to speak. Then I met you, Lisa. You had given up coke because you said you saw something on the scale of what I was studying. But with naked eyes in a nightclub. A kind of evil being or demon of some kind. Then my interest in all of this was reawakened. Then, before we had time to catch our breath, the Jason Bailey note became part of it. Not to mention the experience you had with him in the garden. So now all three of our lives are linked together. Sadly, poor Jason lost his very life over all of this, God bless him. God, it's so awful.'

David bowed his head in silence. I felt I should say nothing. It was a moment we both had to think about this poor guy who was murdered, trying to unravel something, like we both had been doing.

It truly felt for the first time like a member of our circle of friends was dead.

David looked up, staring into my eyes. I let out a gentle sigh, trying to stay calm under his warm gaze.

'Where was I?' he asked, snapping back into his train of thought. 'Ok, Lisa, let's get down to the codes. The police couldn't break them, according to what Richie said when he filled me in last week. The reason I asked *him*, was that Carol and I had . . . had fallen out for a while at the time.'

I took a good mouthful of the cool water, so refreshing in that airless basement.

'On Jason's file, he had a list of names, yeah, and your name was among them, plus the codes. Not only that, but he seemed to know a lot about you. The question is: why you? And what was his interest in you about? And where was he getting his information? All very mysterious, don't you think?'

'Hmm. Just a little, David,' I agreed, resisting the temptation to just reach over and kiss him.

'The first code – G27 – took me days to break. And that was only by accident! You see, a couple of spotlights blew down here and I brought down a replacement lamp as I couldn't find any replacement bulbs. I placed it over the note on the table beside my laptop. I scrutinised the note and under the extra light I noticed that there seemed to be a dot between the *2* and the *7*. And on closer inspection it seemed, yes, I was right.

'From there I started to just add letters to the *G*, starting with *A* working my way down through the alphabet. I didn't get very cause when I got to *E* and Googled *Ge2.7*, well, to be honest with sa, what I found couldn't be further from what I was expecting

'So? What did you find? What does it all mean?'

'You're better off taking a look for yourself. Here.'

He pointed to the noticeboard.

'It's written on this section of the display.'

He sat down, took a sip from his mug of coffee and just stared at the floor, waited for my reaction. I stood up and walked over. There was a strange silence, like I was on my own, a deep wave of something so warm – that feeling again gently engulfing my heart as I read the quote:

Genesis 2.7

And the Lord God formed man from the dust of the earth and breathed into his nostrils the breath of life; and man became a living soul.

Everything went kind of blank as I tried to take in the statement.

'I don't get it, David. What are you trying to say here? That makes no sense to me whatsoever. What is it?'

My hands were shaking, my bottom lip trembling. My legs started to go.

David stood up, catching me in his arms as I stumbled back.

'Here, sit down. It's ok. It's ok. I'll explain. Here. Drink some water.'

He handed me the glass, his calmness removing my fear somewhat.

'Listen to me. Jason's code is a Bible verse, Lisa. And not only that. It goes back, as you can see, to the very beginning of time itself, the dawn of history. The second chapter of the Book of Genesis.'

'Yeah, but what's that got to do with me, David? What . . .?'

'Lisa, I think this has everything to do with you, and not only you, but me as well. Jason Bailey, the whole issue of all I've put together down here, the whole lot is linked all the way back to this statement. This is the very nerve, the heartbeat, the origin of the cocaine problem. And believe me, it's more frightening than anyone could ever imagine it to be. Maybe we'll never fully understand how, but Jason Bailey cracked wide open something that in my opinion has God written all over it.

I tried to take in most of what David was saying, but a lot of it was way over my head.

'I'm totally confused,' I confessed. 'Maybe Wilson here understands, but I don't. Explain it clearly, David. What on earth are you trying to say? Please!'

'Right. It's Stephen's Night. In walks Jason Bailey, a guy you never met before. Everyone's snorting coke. And remember, he could have just met you for a coffee, but for reasons unknown he's guided to a big drug party to meet you. Out in the garden, while you have your eyes closed, something like a breath blows into your nostrils, leaving everyone convinced you had taken a lovely bit of coke on the sly.'

I took a nervous breath. David, still bent down on one knee, kept close eye contact with me at all times as he talked.

'Are you saying what I'm thinking you're saying? That it was God out in that garden? Is that what you're trying to say, David?'

'Well, kind of. But not exactly. Let me explain more before I get to that part. You told me you kept feeling something strange happening to you, like a wave of feelings inside? You asked me in Tommy's how long it took *me* to recover from the coke. I said a couple of years. You felt you were changing too fast, too soon. You couldn't keep up with the speed of it. Can you remember the very first time you felt that happening to you?'

'It was . . . let me think. Yes, it was the morning after the party in Cara's house. It was my mother who noticed it first. She said my eyes looked different, and from then on it's been happening on and off. So – what do you think it is? Do you think it's to do with what happened to me that night with Jason?'

'I'll tell you what I did. I studied all of this inside and out. I left no stone unturned. And trust me this is all very new to me, I never imagined it would lead to this kind of conclusion. But you have to listen to this, because it's hard to take in. Then we'll see if it all fits, if it all makes some kind of sense.'

He squeezed my hand gently as he stood back up. Another swig from his coffee, then he pointed to the second noticeboard bearing the picture of the sword at a kind of entrance or opening.

'I'll go over all this in greater detail another time, Lisa. But here's the shortest version I can give you. *Genesis 2.7.* The breathing up the nostrils of the first human – I expect it means something so deep and personal that linked the unseen God with the human form of man, bringing with it a connection, a contentment, a wholeness, the way to transfer affection to the human soul and heart. Lovely thought, don't you think? A bit like Paradise, right?'

I still wasn't sure where he was heading, but a picture was forming inside, though I still couldn't see clearly. So I just nodded to him to continue.

'I don't have to go into it all, but as you read on in *Genesis* you find that this link, or line of communication, was broken and lost, and the human race found itself outside its rightful place of Paradise. It's like a third of what we were meant to enjoy was lost, leaving behind an awful void in the human heart and soul. Plus, in came this awful unseen realm of evil to make matters worse. Hence the story of the history of the world and its struggle to try in every way possible to get back into Paradise, a position we all feel we were meant to enjoy. Which leads me to the final part – this sword at the entrance, which you'll find in chapter 3 of *Genesis, verse 24*. Now what this does, believe it or not, is it wipes out all religions, all philosophies, yes, even drugs as simply man's attempts to regain Paradise. But none of them can do it, because this sword guards the way back. It says it's flashing back and forth to guard the way to the Tree of Life. No man, no religion, no drug can get you back in to retake what was lost!!

'Which now leads me to the last part of this, Jason Bailey's second code – *J2022*. Which is very closely linked to the first code. Before anyone has the right to return to Paradise, they must keep the Law of God completely which as we all know no one has, which leaves us all outside our rightful place. That's what this sword at the entrance stands for. It's symbolic. But!. . . according to my findings, one person, and only one person, broke back in, because he was perfect and kept the law. So he had every right to walk back in freely.'

'Em, who are we talking about now?'

'Christ Lisa, Christ! He had the right to go back into the unseen Paradise. But he chose to remove the sword at the entrance on our behalf by being struck by it on the cross. That's what happened. That's what killed him. That's what all that means. Which makes him and him alone the only one who can give us entry. He's like a by-pass, if you like.'

I sat staring at David.

'Ok. But what about the code? *J2022* – what does it mean?'

'It's another Bible verse. Taken from John *20.22*. After Christ died, Lisa, and rose again, we all remember hearing this don't we, in religion class? Yeah? But I don't ever remember this part been explained.

With that he breathed on them and said, "Receive the Spirit."

'Which means, if I have it right, he's given it back, the Paradise lost at the beginning of time, back to mankind, as in *Genesis 2.7*. And that's why I told you that night in the garden it wasn't exactly God who I thought did this to you. I think it may have been Christ himself, Lisa. It seems, from what I learned in a short space of time, everything points to him. He's been given the right to do it to any human being – he and he alone. It's personal. Religion has no part in any of this, if you ask me. Nothing or nobody can put this inside you but him. God's seal is on him to do this. He regained Paradise for us. That's it!'

David bent back down.

'There's loads more, but that's enough for one day. That's what those codes mean. And don't ask me how on earth Jason Bailey found all this out, I can only guess that God was behind all of it, Lisa. But one thing is very clear, something that was lost at the dawn of time, something of immense importance has been put back inside you, and it happened Stephen's Night in that garden. You have the real thing, Lisa. And half of Ireland – not to mention all your mates – are running around putting a pure white powder up their nostrils in the same way as in Genesis 2.7, trying to recapture Paradise. Isn't that why you and I took it? The better the coke, the better the sense of Paradise? Don't you see the irony of it all? How we were all fooled into thinking how wonderful it all was, only to wake up next morning to the awful fear, the horrors, the realisation that it was nothing but a counterfeit illusion, nothing in it at all but an awful sense of loss.'

The penny was dropping slowly. It was all starting to click into place, like a huge jigsaw coming together at last.

'Gosh, it's so true, we all feel deep down that we belong in such a place, snorting cocaine up our noses trying to recapture it. Using a bloody drug to try to get back in . . . How dangerous, how evil, how sick. Oh my God, David, the whole thing is . . . is. . . crazy. I'm, I'm lost for words!'

'You know, Lisa, there are people high up in universities and colleges, studying away at what they believe is now only the beginning of a true understanding of drug addiction, trying to find out what triggers it all off. Well, here's the only true answer if you ask me. People have no idea what they're fighting against in this cocaine epidemic sweeping across our country. The danger isn't just to our physical health, it's far worse. Anyway, enough said. I can see I've said far too much as it is.'

'I've one last question, David. Why . . . Why this list? Why was I picked out in such a personal way? Why all the lead up? Why was Jason led to me, and why to the Stephen's Night party? If he'd met me outside he'd still be alive today.'

'I can only guess it's the way God wanted things to happen. A big coke party, everyone snorting coke up their noses, trying to reach that place. He decides to turn up in a garden, like he did at the dawn of time, and give you the real thing, sending it up your nose. Why you? God, I don't know, Lisa. But you can bet your life this is not the end of it. It's the start of something very powerful. If you ask me, bottom line, I think he's moving to expose cocaine for what it is and what it's doing to people's lives – to allow people to finally see what's behind it all from his perspective, and as well as that he's exposing so-called religion if you ask me, for misleading people down the wrong road and further *away* from him rather than *to* him.

'Like, isn't it the plain, simple truth that religion is boring? But what you have is anything but boring. You don't need half a brain to see that.

'A very powerful thought crossed my mind while I came to the close of this study: if everyone across Ireland had what you have, could you imagine how it would change everything? Even the depression of the recession hanging over people's heads wouldn't seem so bad.

'Maybe that's it! Maybe God's going to move and start doing to thousands of people what he did with you. What a thought!'

'My God. What's my mother going to say? What's everyone going to think? David, this is bigger than I ever imagined!'

The reality started to kick in.

'Why did God touch my life?'

David put his strong arms around me, hugging me warmly as the tears began to stream down my face.

'It's all going to be ok, I promise. At least we know the truth. We'll go gently with Carol, Richie, your mother. It'll be ok.'

He held me even closer.

'I can feel it, you know, David, right now. It's so beautiful. It's like a wave of love, but you know you're only stepping softly into its never-ending deep ocean. There is no end to this love, there never will be!'

'Hey, listen. Why don't we get out of here and head for a walk on the beach! There's something else, something big I need to talk to you about.'

His eyes looked away, almost as if he were nervous.

'If you've had enough for one day, we can leave it for another time. It's no problem, but it is important.'

'No, no. I want to hear it. But yeah, let's get out of this basement.'

I sensed, as I tried to gather my thoughts, that this was his moment to break the news about Emma. His body language seemed to give that away. I dried my tears and felt light-headed as I stood up.

'Are you ok?' he asked, reaching out to help me up.

'Yeah, maybe it's just the basement. I'm not used to the lack of air, I suppose. Yeah, I'll be fine. Right, Wilson. Any questions?'

When we came back upstairs, Carol was sprawled out on the sofa fast asleep. Richie had gone to work, and Tim was asleep in his chair. She opened her eyes and took in the situation.

'Well,' she said, 'are you ok, pet? My God, your whole face is glowing. You've been crying as well.'

She gave David that *I hope you didn't upset her* look.

I hugged her.

'Listen, I've got to get some air. So we're taking a walk. I'll leave David to tell you his findings later. But be prepared, that's all I'm saying, Carol. Talk later.'

'Ok. Bye,' said Carol, looking even more puzzled.

David reached to Carol, pulling to give her a hug.

'Talk to you later, sis. Won't be long. Everything is ok. Promise.'

The fresh afternoon air hit both our faces with a cold, gentle breeze. Somehow the visible world looked even more amazing with the sun now breaking through.

Inside I felt a mixture of pure joy, but it was overshadowed by the nervous vibes coming from David as we strolled along. He seemed to want to lighten the mood by asking me about my visit to Cara's and John's, as if that were a light subject.

I explained the bones of it.

'Leave it at that, Lisa. Don't entertain that guy again,' he said, wagging his finger gently, but the look of concern for my welfare still apparent.

'No, no. That's it. I hope to see Cara before the wedding in July. Maybe get a chance to talk with her alone. The rest of the gang want to mend things. I bumped into Ruth and Steve as well. I'll meet them again at some stage, but not around all that coke. Maybe over a coffee. I still love them all very deeply. I've nothing against any one of them just because they take coke. It's the coke itself and what's behind it that I have issues with. And even more so now.'

'Yeah. Me too. I hope you can mend some of the friendships. I really do. It'd be good for you, and maybe you could help them see what you know now, what you have now.'

We came up to a spot on the beach just across from the well-known amusements arcade called Bob's Casino. Suddenly David stopped in his tracks and turned to face out to the sea.

I could feel it. Here we go.

'God, this isn't easy at all, is it?' he said. 'Em, I need to tell you something, Lisa . . . I'm not good at this, so . . .'

'It's ok,' I said, cutting across him. 'I know what it's about, David. It's ok, really.'

But inside it was killing me to admit it.

'Look,' I said. 'It's about Emma. Carol told me you're back dating and that you went on a dinner date up to her house a couple of Fridays ago. We all know, David. It's ok. You can tell me about it now.'

'Carol said that?' said David, turning round to face me.

But I couldn't look at him. I just couldn't. I didn't want him to see my pain. Then, to make matters worse, I just remembered in my rush that morning to fly up to him I had forgotten to put a shred of make-up on, not even a hint of eyeliner, nothing. Even my hair was uncombed.

Oh crap. I must look a total mess.

That thought was soon replaced by another.

Isn't this the way it should be? Your natural self, no facemask, nothing. Just my plain face. Wasn't that what I always wanted to be, just me? No hiding places. What you see is what you get.

'Carol said that? Yeah, yeah. I went up to Emma's. She wanted to tell her parents face to face about her coke issue, but was nervous as her Dad's very anti-drugs. So I went to support her. She wanted their support. It was hard, but she did it and thankfully her parents, both of them, are behind her one hundred per cent.

'Anyway, Lisa, part of what I wanted to talk about was, yes, about me and Emma. I don't know where to start. I'm not good at this, to be honest.'

'Just say it! Whatever it is, I'm still going to be your friend. I promise.'

I kept my head up this time, staring straight into those eyes of his.

'Out with it, David. You can tell me.'

'Ok, Lisa. Well, we met up a couple of times and sorted out our issues, laughed at some of the silly things we had got up to in our relationship. We got on as if nothing had gone bad between us. We were sitting over the head there in her car, laughing and chatting. I felt no anger at what she had done to me. It was gone. It was like we used to be, before it all went so wrong. Then . . . then she asked me to come back to pick up where we left off, like, asked me to have one more shot at making it work, promising me she'd never hurt me again. You could tell from the tears in her eyes she meant it. I knew she was truly sorry for all the hurt she had caused me. God, Lisa, I wasn't expecting it, to be honest. As her words hung in the air, I glanced out the window of the car to the very spot you and I kissed on New Year's Eve. Remember?'

'What? Of course . . . of course I *remember,*' I said, my voice trembling.

'Look, Lisa. All I could think about was that kiss. I know it sounds strange. I know. But something happened inside me when you and I were close that night, something so powerful. But before I had a chance to explain, to chat with you about it, I opened the paper next morning and there was Jason's murder. Then Emma got back in touch. Not to mention the codes, the police, trying to understand all of it. I got lost, sidetracked in it all. And suddenly I found myself sitting with Emma, her in tears, asking me back. It killed me to see her hurt. But I had to say no!! She wanted to know was there someone else. I wouldn't tell her, because I wanted to talk to you, explain to you that I've never felt with anyone what I feel for you. That kiss . . . my God! I've never felt feelings that strong come back at me from a girl.'

I tried to open my mouth to say something, but shock seemed to take over the whole moment. I slurred the word,

'What?'

David looked vulnerable, to say the least. He dropped his head, sensing he might be alone in his feelings. I went to say something but he put his hand up indicating he wanted to say more. So I backed off to let him continue.

'You know me, Lisa. I'm into a 50:50 relationship, no games, no hiding places. And I see all that in you. I think from the moment I first met you, something started to happen to me. Then, I became so afraid of the feelings. I was sitting down in the basement the other night listening to Coldplay. You know that song *What If?*

What if you should decide

That you don't want me there in your life?'

'Is that what you're afraid of, David?'

He put his hand behind his head, rubbing the back of his neck nervously.

'I'd just hate to feel so much for someone I know I love this much and to be left feeling it on my own again.'

I could see – or thought I could see – his eyes searching mine for the right response.

'Maybe, David, maybe you should have remembered the last line in that song:

You know that darkness always turns into light.'

I stood closer to him, a mere foot away, my eyes filling with tears (I know, I'm always crying). But this was so different.

I couldn't believe this was happening! My heart was ready to burst with feelings.

Stumbling over my words, I finely pulled myself together.

'You know something, David? The first time I heard that song, before I looked at the words, I thought one of the lines went:

That you don't want me there in your eyes . . .

'Corny, I know. See, that was always my fear since I was a teenager. That no one would want to feel the closeness I wanted. I believed it was part of me that would one day be matched perfectly to someone who wanted the same. The night you kissed me, that was it. I knew it was you. You or nobody. It was like two halves became one. And I've been feeling everything just like you have ever since. You'll never know what that kiss did to me. You blew me away, David Salle.'

He broke out in a smile, a kind of shy smile I'd never seen before. He put his hand out, pulling me gently closer, our faces inches apart, eyes interlocked . . .

'I just want *you*, Lisa. No one else. I love you so much. I'd never do anything to hurt you. I hope you know that. I've never felt this way for anyone . . . I'm . . . I'm in love, with you . . . I really am!'

'I love *you*, David. I can't believe this is happening. My God, I found you!'

There was a silence. No sound except the crashing of the waves as the tide receded.

Delicately, tentatively, our lips touched. I could taste him, taste his breath, tinged with the salty air. One of his hands held my face, the other holding the back of my head so gently, fingers running through my hair. I was lost again in one of those amazing, incredible kisses. The intimacy was surreal. We were . . . as one. It felt even stronger than the last time. As we kissed, all those locked-away feelings we both felt alone in opened up and flowed out. We held each other close, so close! David slowly pulled my face around, holding it gently in both hands.

O my God, the feelings I saw in his eyes! I just knew in that moment there was nothing in between us, no walls.

'Can you see me, Lisa? ' . . .

'Yeah, can you see me? ' . . .

'Yeah' . . .

We both smiled!

Then we laughed like a couple of teenagers as he chased me up the beach. We fell onto the sand and kissed and hugged and just sat, looking out to the sea – Shenick Island, Rockabill Lighthouse and, faintly visible in the distance, the Mountains of Mourne. They looked as if they were there just for us.

Later, when we got back to the house, Carol came out of the kitchen from cooking dinner. She looked into our faces. Then she glanced down and saw we were holding hands. She ran over, hugging us both.

'I can't believe it!' she beamed, tears welling up in her eyes. 'What's . . . what's going on? Sit down, tell me everything!'

*

Cara was putting the chips on.

'Will a quarter-pounder and chips do you, pet?' she shouted to John, who was in the sitting room watching tv. 'I've to be in work at four.'

'Yeah, yeah, thanks, love,' he said, dragging on his fag.

'Then you get some sleep, you hear me?'

'Yeah. One of the boys is coming at eight. So I'll wait up, play the Xbox, couple more beers, then crash out. What did you think of the party?'

'Great. Did you see Annie's face when Frank gave her the engagement ring? Wow, this wedding buzz is catching on, what?'

'Yeah, but he told me it'll be a few years yet, with the recession and all, they've to save up for it.'

'Some party! I'd a great buzz with Carl and Orla. Well, that's the last big party till the wedding. You hear me? Most of what we need is paid for. Which is great. I can't wait!'

'Be a blast, pet. Over one hundred and fifty people coming so far – and counting.'

'Right. Here you go. Get that down you. You look wrecked. Get an early night, you hear? I'm off. Come here.'

She leaned over and kissed him.

'I love you. I'll ring you about nine. Ok? Bye.'

'Bye. What time will you be home?'

'Around 4am. Keep my side warm.'

'I will. Love you.'

Cara drove off, with John watching and waving from the door.

After his dinner he pulled out a few cans of beer from the fridge, plus a fresh bag of coke. He broke down the lines, taking a few.

'Aah! That's it! Sound!'

Carl rang.

'You still up? You mad thing! Did you not go to bed yet?'

'Nah. I've a bit to do later. Going to wait to get that sorted. What did you think of the party?'

'Savage! I'm only up now. Dying a death. Listen – me ma's calling me for me dinner. I'll catch up with you midweek. Take care.'

John went on playing the Xbox with a few cans of beers and waited for 8pm till James came.

*

I stayed in David's for dinner. Carol kept hugging me.

'I can't believe it! You're dating David! I rang Richie. He's dying to see you both.'

I rang Ma with the news. She cried over the phone. By 7pm Carol had gone out to meet Richie. Tim was fast asleep in his chair again. I was all wrapped up on the sofa in David's arms. I could see he was exhausted.

'David?'

'Hmm?'

'Do you think Jason had this?'

'This what?'

'What happened to me on Stephen's Night.'

'Not a shadow of doubt about it, pet, he couldn't have been led to you without it. And I'd imagine he had little or no fear when those shots were fired at him. You know, it may be a good idea to visit his family soon and explain all this to them. What do you think?'

'Yeah, sure. I've an interview with the Guards on Monday. Can you imagine what they'd say about the codes? They'll think my cheese has definitely slid off my cracker!'

'If you want, I'll go with you.'

'Would you?'

'Yeah, defo. I want to be there with you.'

'Ah, thanks. You're better at explaining all this than me.'

'I've to explain it to Carol in the morning. Good grief – the poor girl!'

He snuggled even closer to me.

'This is so great, isn't it? It's like a dream . . .'

Within seconds he was in a deep, deep sleep.

I found myself staring into the fire, the flames making me sleepy. My mind flashed back to a moment at one of the coke parties about a year ago. Cara, John, Ruth, Steven, Frank, Orla and others all there. Lines of coke on cd covers. Bottles of beer. A joint of grass going round. Everyone talking at the same time, loudly, pumped up to the max. Music thumping. Everyone looking so happy, in control. I saw myself bending over, snorting lines off a cd cover. Wow. The picture stopped there and folded away, burning up in my thoughts . . .

Now . . . I was holding my soulmate. Off drugs forever. My career intact. And a love, a real love from God growing in my heart. A life of its own. A lovely peace. My eyes started to close . . .

Then a deep presence filled the room. The presence of God.

David stirred, then opened his eyes. He smiled at me.

'Do you feel that, Lisa? In the room, right now?'

We both smiled at each other.

Then he fell back asleep.

I held onto the moment. I felt so . . . so complete. Not perfect, but yes . . . complete.

It's not a subject one should write about. Words can't . . . It's too pure for words . . . I'm so happy! I can't wait. I can't wait for tomorrow.

I drifted off into a peaceful sleep . . . in David's arms . . .

I am the door. If anyone enters by me, he will be saved, and will go in and out and find pasture. The thief comes only to steal and kill and destroy. I came that they may have life, and have it more abundantly.

John: 10, 9-10

*

7:30pm. A couple more cans. Checks his watch. *James'll be here soon.* Bends down, taking another couple of lines. Lights up a fag. Rings Steve.

'Alright, Stevie! Whatcha think of the party?'

'Ah, crazy, John! Crazy! I'm dying. How are you? You were mad out of it last night! Whatcha up to?'

'Still going! Have business to attend to in half an hour. Then wind down. Will you be around tomorrow night? Cara wants to go through a few wedding things with a few of yiz. More to do with Ruth and the girls.'

'Yeah. We'll call over. How's 8pm sound?'

'Yeah, yeah. Right. Sound. See you then.'

John cleaned up after the dinner, racing around the house, getting cash counted for James.

8pm. He downed the end of a can of Miller. Couple more lines, then waited for the doorbell to sound. He washed his face to try and look half normal. Lit another fag and turned on the tv.

The doorbell went.

'Ah, how's it going, James! What's the crack? Come in.'

He checked around outside before closing the door.

James strolled into the sitting room, pulling down his hoodie.

'What the f**k are you playing at, John? Did you look in the mirror at the head on ye? We're all supposed to be keeping a watchful eye, not getting blasted out of our heads!'

'That's the last party till the wedding, James.'

'Yeah? I hope so, for your bleedin' sake. Now, another thing before we get down to business. What the f**k are you at, texting me at 5:30 this morning?'

'What? Did I? What did it say?'

'I'll read it for ye, ye fool.

Hi James. Best coke ever. Your d best mate ever. Luv u john.

'You woke me bird up with that text! Don't *ever* text me out of your head about coke. You hear me? Do you hear me?'

'Yeah. Shit. Sorry, James. I was mad out of it at the party. That won't happen again.'

'What time did the party go on till? Or is it still going?'

'It stopped at twelve o'clock – today. But sure I knew you'd be coming, so I stayed up. Are you staying for a beer with me?'

'Yeah, yeah. I'll stay . . .' James checked his watch. '. . . half an hour. Yeah, get me a can. Sit down and we'll chat.'

John got the beer from the kitchen and cracked it open.

'There you go, mate. Get that down ye.'

'Thanks.'

John pointed to the coke on the cd cover.

'Do you mind if I . . .?'

'Hey, it's your house, your coke, your party. Here – give us a line of it.'

James bent down and snorted a couple of long lines.

'Aaah! Some stuff that! The best. Yeah! Listen – how did you pull off sorting out this Drogheda/Dundalk deal? You kept that very hush-hush.'

John lit up a fag.

'You want one?'

'Yeah. Why not!'

John blew out a long plume of smoke.

'Ah, a few Skerries heads who still buy from me moved out that way. Then they wanted to set up. And as me ma used to say, *Down there for dancing, up here for thinking.*'

He was beginning to slur his words, so he downed another mouthful of Miller.

'I'm telling you, James. We'll go on to big things! You wait and see!'

'Yeah. We'll see. Be big alright. Once I'm making out of it, that's all I care about. Hey – where's your bird tonight?'

'She's working till four in the morning.'

'Right. Give us another line of that.'

'Fire away, mate. Take as much as you want, lad.'

James snorted a big line.

'Shit!' he said, handing the rolled €50 note to John. 'That's good!'

'Yeah.'

John bent over, snorting a couple more big lines.

'Man!' he said, throwing his head back on the sofa. 'That is good! Yeah!'

'Listen till I ask ye. That girl – Lisa what's-her-name?'

'Yeah – Lisa. Lisa Webb. Yeah?'

'Yeah? The bleedin' head on you, man!'

James laughed.

'Yeah. Her. Any more hassle from her?'

'No, James. No. No way, man.'

'Listen – where does she live? Like, is she from Skerries or what? John! Are you listening to me?'

'Yeah? What? Whatcha say? Whatcha say? I can't make ye out!'

James lit another fag, straight from the last one.

'The girl, Lisa Webb. Does she live around Skerries, like? You want one?'

'Shit, James!! I don't feel right. Something's not right, man!'

'Shit. You're white as a ghost. Are you alright?'

'God, James. Me chest. I can't breathe! James! Me chest! Help me!'

John went to stand up but collapsed backwards, his right foot catching on the coffee table, sending the coke and the beers flying. He crashed back across the sofa.

'Shit, man! John! *John!* Are you ok? Shit, wake up, man. You're after taking too much coke. Wake the f**k up, will ye!'

'Help me, James. Ring a doctor . . . Help me . . . Ring Ca– . . . '

His eyes were rolling back in his head.

James pulled his phone out of his pocket and rang Darryl.

'Alright, James? Did you make the call?'

'No, no, shit, Darryl. It's John. I think he's after taking an overdose on the coke. He was at an all-nighter, and all day today. He just collapsed right in front of me. What'll I do, Darryl? I better ring an ambulance. Yeah?'

'Hey, James! Pull yourself together. You hear me? Now calm down. Feel his pulse. Is he dead or alive or what?'

'Ok.'

James bent over.

'Yeah. A very small pulse, Darryl. He looks awful. I think he's dying. What'll I do?'

There was a pause on the line. A deathly, eerie silence.

'Ah f**k him, James. . . Let him go. Ring no one. Don't want cops all over this. Where's his bird?'

'She won't be back till 4am.'

'Right. Now, listen to me. Did you get the cash?'

'No, but I know where he keeps it.'

'Right. Get the cash and the coke, clean up any fingerprints. Keep your head now, James. You hear me?'

'Yeah. I'm with ye.'

'Take our numbers out of his phone. You hear? Don't forget. Put the phone in his hand. Are you wearing a hoodie?'

'Yeah.'

'Put it up and walk out slowly, close the door and drive away.'

'But Darryl – the girl's address! I never got the f**king address!'

'Cop onto yourself, James! We don't need to touch the girl now that that fool's dead. It's over, James! Now get the stuff and get out now. Go! I'll call off the hit myself. Go!'

James cleaned up, took all of John's cash from the biscuit tin, plus all the remainder of John's coke. Putting up his hoodie, he quietly let himself out, closed the door and was gone into the night.

It was 8:50pm.

The clock ticked to 9:05pm.

John opened his eyes. His hands felt numb. He let out a fearful gasp and slowly sat up.

The room is in darkness. Light's turned off . . .

'James! James?'

Shit. Where's James gone?

The only light in the room was that of the open fire.

Slowly he stood up and stepped forward into the middle of the room.

'James! James!' he called out again. . . 'Anyone there . . .?'

He slowly dropped his gaze down, seeing the coffee table and coke and beer slopped all over the carpet.

*Shit, what the f**k happened to me?*

He went to bend down to pick up the coffee table but nothing happened.

What's going on? I can't seem to move my arms. Bloody hell!

His phone rang, making him jump with fright.

He turned back around slowly towards the sofa.

What's . . . Wha . . .the fu . . .?

There, slumped across the sofa, was his own lifeless body. His eyes open, foam trickling out the side of his mouth.

His phone in his lifeless hand ringing, stopping, then ringing again. Cara's name coming up each time. . .

What is this? My God, what's happening to me?

He tried to move his body but he now seemed unable. A deep sense of the most awful fear flooded his mind and heart, then seemed to engulf his very soul.

'O my God . . . Help me!!'

He tried to turn around but couldn't.

He felt something touch him from behind.

'What is it? Who's there?'

He turned his head and screamed in terror as he felt himself being slowly dragged away. . .

'No! No! Please! What's happening to me . . .? Help me, someone!!! Cara . . . Cara . . . I'm sorry . . . Cara, help me!. . .'

For we wrestle not against flesh and blood, but against principalities, against powers, against the rulers of the darkness of this world, against spiritual wickedness in high places.
Ephesians: 6.12

Dieses Buch wurde zwischen
Herbst 2007 und Sommer 2008 geschrieben.
Alle beschriebenen Personen und alle
Begebenheiten sind frei erfunden.

Die den Kapiteln vorangestellten Buchstabenfolgen
sind Albert Leblancs Gitarrenakkorde.

Kontakt:
david.bielmann@gmail.com

DAVID BIELMANN

FLUCHT EINES TOTEN

ROMAN

Verlag

Verlag und Autor danken herzlich für die Unterstützung:
Direktion für Erziehung, Kultur und Sport EKSD
ETAT DE FRIBOURG
STAAT FREIBURG

1. Auflage 2011

Umschlaggestaltung:
Fabienne Bielmann,
Graphic & Web Dimorph.ch
Satz und Lektorat:
WOA Verlag, Zürich
Druckpartner:
CPI books, Ulm
www.cpibooks.de

ISBN 978-3-9523657-2-4
www.woaverlag.ch

A Bùùm, dä stiit
ma gwennt si dra
ù niemer
fragt mù nüt derna
bys wan er kyyt

Franz Aebischer

Alle Kunst entsteht aus Angst vor dem Tod.

Hermann Hesse

Prolog

Die fackelnde Kerze erhellte die bereits etwas vergilbten Fotoabzüge, die ausgebreitet auf dem Tischtuch lagen. Die Abzüge waren atemberaubend – zumindest waren sie dies für den ergrauten Mann, der mit aufgewühlten Erinnerungen dasass. Doch trotz aller Wehmut, wie sie im Alter beim Schwelgen in vergangenen Zeiten aufzukommen droht, war er zufrieden. Er konnte sich in der äusserst erfüllenden Gewissheit wiegen, das Leben ausgekostet zu haben.

Nach abenteuerlichen und ruhelosen Jahren in der Fremde war er vor einigen Tagen in Rechthalten eingetroffen, wo er sich für unbestimmte Zeit niederzulassen gedachte. Nun, da seine Abenteuerlust allmählich nachliess, die Antike ihn nicht mehr wie früher begeisterte, war er bestrebt, sich endlich zur Ruhe zu setzen. Dies waren allerdings nicht die dringendsten Gründe für seine Ankunft in dem beschaulichen Dorfe. Er war gekommen, um einen jungen Mann kennenzulernen.

Diesen doch etwas verwegenen Entscheid hatte er sich nicht leicht gemacht. Sein plötzliches Auftauchen würde nach Erklärungen verlangen, würde berechtigten Anlass zu unangenehmen Fragen geben. Ob er die Kraft aufbringen konnte, sich diesen zu stellen? Das würde sich weisen. Vorerst waren es gewöhnliche Dinge zum Wesen seines Sohnes, die ihn brennend interessierten: Hatte er die Schönheit seiner Mutter, die Trinkgewohnheiten seines Vaters ererbt? War er glücklich, war er einsam?

Etwas müde ergriff er das edle Glas und roch daran. Der wohlbekannte Duft von würzigem Anis strömte durch seine Nase. Genüsslich bewegte er das Glas an seine Lippen und kippte es leicht, um sich einen Teil des Inhalts in den Mund laufen zu lassen. Einen Moment lang glitt der Absinth über seinen Gaumen, bevor er sich beseligend in seinem Körper ausbreitete.

Der Mann lehnte sich im Stuhl zurück. Er war in jenes Dorf gekommen, in dem er dereinst sterben würde.

Erstes Buch
Tod eines Lebenden

1. Am runden Fenster

Am / C / G / D
Am / Cm / G / D
Am / Cm / Gm / D
Am / Cm / Gm / Dm
Am

Eine Dunstwolke aus saurem Herrenschweiss und prägnantem Damenparfum, aus üblen Schnapsfahnen, ätzendem Friteusendampf und beissendem Rauch billiger Zigarren lag in der Luft. Sie hatte sich bereits in den Kleidern, den Haaren, ja sogar in der Haut der anwesenden Gäste eingenistet. Die frische Nachtluft, die durch ein offenes Fenster in den Raum strömte, vermochte den Gestank nicht zu verdrängen. Im Gegenteil – die Luft draussen war immer noch durchtränkt von Gülle, die am Nachmittag auf den naheliegenden Feldern verteilt worden war. Diese Unannehmlichkeiten schienen jedoch niemanden zu stören. Man lachte, diskutierte, atmete sorglos weiter.

In der Ecke residierte eine vornehm gekleidete Dame, die ihre besten Jahre sichtlich hinter sich gelassen hatte. Ein Stück ihres Rindsfilets verschwand eben durch ihre knallrot geschminkten Lippen, während ihrem nicht minder manierlichen Gatten ein Tropfen Château Margaux die Kehle hinunterrann. Gleich daneben, im dichten Qualm ihres eigenen Zigarrenrauchs, ereiferten sich vier Herren fortgeschrittenen Alters über einen Trumpf, der nicht gespielt worden war. Der Grauhaarige, dessen runder Buckel sich über die Tischplatte wölbte, wurde unverzüglich zum Sündenbock erkoren. Am nächsten Tisch schlürften zwei kürzlich volljährig gewordene Frauen nicht ohne Stolz an ihrem Wermut und unterhielten sich dabei lebhaft über den Monatsfluss, der bei der einen seit zwei Wochen ausblieb. Derweil trat der Metzger aus der Toilette und schnallte sich seinen Ledergürtel zu. Aufgrund seiner beharrlichen Magenprobleme hatte er den Beginn eines hitzigen Wortgefechts um den neuformierten Gemeinderat verpasst, das in seiner Runde tobte. Ein wenig abseits, sofern dies innerhalb des überfüllten Raumes überhaupt möglich war, studierte Karl, ein berüchtigtes Dorforiginal, die Inserate der *Freiburger Nachrichten* jenes Freitags, 9. Juni 1967. In der Mitte der Gaststube schliesslich – an der Stelle, an der die Alkoholfahnen am konzentriertesten und die Wortfetzen am lautesten umherschwirrten – legte ein Mann mit Helm und feinem Oberlippenbart der Kellnerin Mona schamlos den Arm um ihre Hüfte, nachdem sie ihm sein achtes Pastis serviert hatte.

Um den grossen Stammtisch scharte sich mindestens ein Dutzend uniformierter Männer. Im Grunde spielte sich an jenem Tisch dasselbe ab wie an den restlichen, allerdings in etwas forscherer Manier: Es wurden Speisen verschlungen, Gesöffe hinuntergestürzt, Jasskarten umhergeworfen, man prahlte mit Weibergeschichten, verfluchte den neuen Gemeinderat und fädelte krumme Geschäfte ein.

«Dieser – wie heisst dieser Stümper noch gleich?», knurrte ein beleibter Mann in Uniform, ehe seine Zähne den noch verbleibenden Knorpel von einem Hähnchenflügel abrissen. Dass ihm der Name eben entfallen war, schrieb er nicht etwa seiner Betrunkenheit oder seinem kümmerlichen Gedächtnis zu, sondern der Bedeutungslosigkeit des Angesprochenen. «Leblanc! Jetzt hab' ich es wieder. Dieser Leblanc soll uns noch etwas Warmes machen!»

«Ich hätte nichts dagegen», gurgelte sein Tischnachbar zwischen seinen Barthaaren hervor, die mit allerlei Alkoholika bestückt waren. «Obwohl mir dieser Leblanc immer noch nicht geheuer ist. Nach allem, was der hier schon geboten hat.»

«Leblanc!», brüllte der Hungrige dessen ungeachtet, bevor sich der Name des jungen Kochs wieder aus seinem Hirn fortstahl. «Wir nehmen noch etwas!»

«Die Küche hat schon zugemacht», liess der Wirt verlauten, dem es mit dem dritten Streichholz eben gelungen war, sich eine weitere Toscanelli anzuzünden.

Dies wollte man am Stammtisch nicht gelten lassen. «Komm schon, Walter, zur Feier des Tages. Noch eine letzte Bestellung!», tönte es.

Dem Wirt leuchtete ein, dass er an der Bande heute Abend noch einen schönen Batzen Geld verdienen konnte. Er stand auf und schlurfte in die Küche.

«Mittlerweile macht sich Leblanc doch gar nicht schlecht, finde ich», meinte ein anderer in der Männerrunde, dessen Blickrichtung nicht mehr exakt zu bestimmen war. Vorsichtig fügte er hinzu: «Wenn man nur daran denkt, wie schwierig es der Bursche früher hatte …»

«Von wem redest du?», fragte ihn der Beleibte.

«Eben, von Leblanc.»

«Schwierig?», empörte sich daraufhin ein glattrasierter, gepflegter junger Mann. «Wenn ihr mich fragt», begann er überlegen, «war Leblanc schon immer ein Nichtsnutz. Wir hatten es ja zu Hause auch nie einfach, gewiss nicht.» Dann hob sich seine Stimme, da er etwas lauter wurde. «Und trotzdem haben wir es zu etwas gebracht. Aber Leblanc …» Er sprach den Satz nicht zu Ende, lachte stattdessen nur kurz auf. «Ich könnte euch so einige Geschichten über ihn erzählen …»

Plötzlich beschlich ihn ein Gefühl von Mitleid, von Reue, als er sich diese Worte sagen hörte. In nüchternem Zustand spielte er sich nicht halb so hochmütig auf. Die erwartungsvollen Blicke, die von ihm verursacht wurden, drängten ihn nun aber doch, von einer schon länger zurückliegenden Begebenheit zu erzählen. Insgeheim erhoffte er sich damit, bei seinen älteren Kameraden Sympathien zu gewinnen. Er konnte noch gut ein paar mehr gebrauchen.

Als der Wirt wieder aus der Küche kam, hörte man dem Jüngling bereits zu oder tat zumindest so. Er berichtete, wie ihm vor vielen Jahren, noch zu Schulzeiten, der kleine Leblanc mit einem Säcklein Lakritzstangen über den Weg gelaufen war. Gemeinsam mit seinem älteren Bruder habe er sodann entschlossen, Leblanc die Stangen abzunehmen. «Der Mistkerl», wie er ihn despektierlich nannte, sei allerdings nach kurzer Verfolgung schnurstracks auf die Kirche zugesteuert und in dieser unauffindbar verschwunden. «Noch heute weiss ich nicht, wo er sich damals versteckt hat», versicherte er. «Wir hatten allerdings Geduld.»

Man versuchte, den Worten des Jünglings zu folgen. Dieser genoss es ausgiebig, im Mittelpunkt des Stammtisches zu stehen. Unterdessen machte Mona die Karten spielenden Herren auf den Kreuz König aufmerksam, der schon seit geraumer Zeit unter der Eckbank ruhte.

Kurz darauf donnerte ein Lachgewitter durch den Raum, sodass die elegante Dame in der Ecke vor Schreck mit dem Stück Fleisch, das an ihrer Gabel steckte, ihre säuberlich gefärbte Oberlippe touchierte. «Wie kann man sich nur so gehen lassen?», fragte sie sich gereizt. Sie schaute zu ihrem Gatten, der die ungezügelte Bande ebenfalls nicht goutierte. Dabei hatten sie sich doch auf ein gemütliches Abendessen gefreut. «Die Lakritze hatten wir uns dann aber verdient!», hörten sie einen jungen, hochmütigen Mann vergnügt ausstossen, wussten aber nicht, worum es bei dem Gelächter ging. Sie wollten es auch nicht wissen.

Die Uniformierten am Tisch, die der Anekdote gelauscht hatten, befanden die damalige Tat ihres jungen Kollegen eigentlich für ganz unverschämt. Trotzdem lachten sie alle herzhaft mit. Lediglich der Alte mit den dunklen Brillengläsern mochte sich an der geschlossenen Taktlosigkeit nicht beteiligen. Er war froh, diesen rüden Kreaturen künftig den Rücken kehren zu können. Nach seinem letzten Einsatz für den Verein hatte er sich heute noch zu einem gemeinsamen Wirtshausbesuch überreden lassen. Anstelle seines Abschieds wurde nun aber die Herabwürdigung eines unschuldigen und bedauernswerten Mitbürgers gefeiert. Als er aufstand und seinen unerträglich betrunkenen Kameraden einen letzten Gruss entsandte, wurde dies nicht einmal bemerkt. Hans Fahler verliess den Gasthof mit dem schwermütigen Gefühl, einen besseren Abgang verdient zu haben.

Die Völlerei am Stammtisch nahm indessen immer ausgelassenere Züge an.

«Eines muss man Leblanc aber lassen: Er verwechselt Zucker nicht mehr mit Salz und Essig nicht mehr mit Weisswein», lallte der Kommandant und spielte damit auf Missgeschicke des Kochs an, die einen gewissen Bekanntheitsgrad erlangt hatten. Der Kommandant war für seine erstklassigen Sprüche bekannt.

«Dafür Weiber mit Männern!», schrie derjenige mit dem feinen Oberlippenbart, der noch eben an Mona die Richtung seiner Gelüste eindeutig demonstriert hatte. Der Lärmpegel im Gasthof erreichte seinen Tageshöchstwert.

Durst hatte längst keiner mehr. Nichts jedoch lag den berauschten Männern in jenem Moment ferner, als mit dem Trinken aufzuhören. Ihr Dasein wurde durch nichts mehr getrübt. Ihr Denken, oder vielmehr ihr Instinkt, reichte gerade noch bis auf den Grund ihres Bierkruges, ihres Schnapsglases. Der Alkohol hatte ihnen den letzten Anstand, das letzte Quäntchen Scham geraubt. Selig vor lauter Trank begannen sie schliesslich, auf schmähliche Weise den Namen des Kochs zu skandieren.

Den übrigen Gästen wurde das Gelage nun doch allmählich zu masslos, weshalb sie nach und nach das Weite suchten. Nur die Gruppe in Überkleidern hatte es wiederum verpasst, das Feierabendbier bei demselben bewenden zu lassen. Mittlerweile debattierte auch der Metzger lauthals mit.

Und hinter der Küchentür stand ein hagerer, bleicher Mann. Ängstlich spähte er durch das runde Fenster, das in die Tür eingebaut war. Er kratzte sich nervös am Hinterkopf und schluckte tief. Das wilde Treiben in der Gaststube erfüllte ihn mit einer unendlichen Traurigkeit, denn sein Name war Albert Leblanc.

2. Weissweinsauce

Am / C
E / Am / E / Am

Wenige Stunden später befand sich Albert bereits wieder am gleichen Ort. Er umhüllte sich mit seiner fettigen Kochschürze und las den Tagesmenüplan durch, der am Kühlschrank hing. Eglifilet an einer Weissweinsauce, dazu frischer Spinat und Reis.

Seine Glieder waren schwer, denn für einen erholsamen Schlaf hatte die Zeit nicht ausgereicht. Der Blick durch das Küchentürfenster gestaltete sich nun jedoch um einiges sympathischer, als dies bis weit in die Nacht hinein der Fall gewesen war.

Mit Grausen dachte er an den letzten Abend zurück, als zu fortgeschrittener Stunde noch die lokale Feuerwehr aufgekreuzt war und ihm zum wiederholten Mal den wohlverdienten Feierabend stahl. Und nicht nur das. Nach einer anstrengenden Atemschutzübung hatten die Kerle ihre Köpfe mit einem Gesöff nach dem anderen bereichert, woraus schliesslich wieder einmal Beschimpfungen der übleren Sorte resultierten.

Ja, man behandelte ihn zuweilen wie ein Tier, wie Dreck. Vor allem gestern, so schien ihm, waren die trinkseligen Feuerwehrmänner frei von jeglichem Gewissen gewesen. Sie hatten ihn regelrecht verängstigt.

«Hast du genügend Kräuter in die Sauce gemischt?» Die scharfe Stimme des Wirts liess Albert zusammenzucken. Wortlos reichte Albert ihm die Pfanne. Der Wirt tauchte seinen grossen Zeigefinger in die Weissweinsauce ein, führte ihn in den Mund und zog ihn schnalzend wieder heraus. «Gar nicht übel, Junge», lautete sein Verdikt.

Die Milde überraschte Albert. Da waren schon ganz andere Donnerwetter auf ihn niedergehagelt. Er vermutete, dass sein Meister zur Abwechslung einen guten Tag erwischt oder abermals seine Beruhigungsmittel geschluckt hatte.

So sehr ihn die ausbleibende Rüge erleichterte, so unbegreiflich war es ihm, dass er immer noch ständig «Junge» genannt wurde. Mit siebenundzwanzig Jahren! Da hatte man doch ein wenig mehr Respekt verdient. Vor allem wenn er bedachte, wie uneigennützig er zuletzt im Gasthof schuftete. Er leistete Überstunden, opferte freie Tage, er war dem Wirt unentbehrlich geworden.

Gleichgültig begann Albert Spinat zu waschen. In den nachfolgenden Stunden würde er mit den nötigen Zutaten verschiedene Gerichte zubereiten, und er würde dies ohne jegliche Leidenschaft tun. Warum sollte er auch? Kochte er gut, erhielten die Kellnerinnen ein dankendes Trinkgeld, der Meister ein anerkennendes Lob – kochte er hingegen schlecht, was inzwischen kaum mehr vorkam, packte man die missratenen Gerichte noch Jahre später genüsslich aus, um sich daran zu belustigen.

Albert marinierte die Eglifilets mit Salz, Pfeffer und Zitronensaft. Aus dem Radio ertönte ein aktueller Gassenhauer, in dem eine traurige Stimme beklagte, dass es heute keine Milch gab.

3. Der Sonnenuntergang

Em
Bm / A / G / Em
Bm / A / G / Em

Bei Anbruch der Abenddämmerung marschierte Albert erschöpft nach Hause. Er war froh, heute bei Zeiten in sein kleines Haus, das abgeschieden am Waldrand stand, zu gelangen. Es stank immer noch nach Gülle. Albert konnte Gülle nicht ausstehen.

Der nun bevorstehende freie Abend löste in Albert zwar keine Euphorie, aber doch eine gewisse Erleichterung aus. Das Paradoxe an seinem unglücklichen Leben war, dass er, obwohl er sich angenehmen menschlichen Kontakt so sehr wünschte, im Alleinsein die grösste Zufriedenheit fand. Er war in eine Sackgasse geraten, aus der er nicht mehr herausfand, witterte er doch hinter jeder Ecke Hohn, hinter jedem Mitbürger einen Spötter. So hatte er begonnen, Menschen zu meiden.

Zu Hause angekommen, stellte er sich unter die Dusche und wusch sich in Rekordzeit den vergangenen Tag ab. Er versuchte jeweils, seinen dünnen Gliedern das entsetzlich rasch erkaltende Wasser so kurz wie möglich zuzumuten. Kaltes Wasser hasste er wie der Teufel das geweihte. In seinem abgelegenen alten Haus hatte er sich allerdings mit der unbefriedigenden Wasserversorgung abfinden müssen. Er sah darüber hinweg, wenn er dafür abseits in Ruhe hausen konnte. Und dies konnte er, seit er sich das Haus am Rande des Buchholzes vor gut zwei Jahren zu einem Spottpreis ersteigert hatte. Zum Missfallen des Verkäufers war er damals der einzige Interessent gewesen.

Nachdem er sich eine weisse Unterhose übergestreift hatte, legte er sein etwas stumpf gewordenes Rasiermesser an. Eigentlich hätte er sich gerne hinter einem dichten Gesichtsfell versteckt. Als Junggeselle sah er sich jedoch in der Pflicht, eine gewisse Gepflegtheit zu unterhalten. Mit seinem spärlichen Bartwuchs hätte er allzu haarigen Ambitionen wohl ohnehin nicht gerecht werden können.

So war Albert sowohl in seinem Äusseren wie auch in seinem Auftreten ein unscheinbares, unauffälliges Geschöpf. Sein Seitenscheitel sass stets tadellos, exakt in rechtem Winkel zum Haaransatz – die Damenwelt liess sich davon aber keinerlei begeistern. Andererseits machte sich auch niemand über seine etwas gar zu gross geratene Nase lustig. Dafür war sie dann doch wieder zu wenig markant.

Als ihn sein Ebenbild im Spiegel ansah, erschrak er. Er starrte in die Augen eines jungen, traurigen Mannes. Je länger er diesen jedoch betrachtete, umso stärker wurde sein Gefühl, einen verbitterten, entseelten Greisen vor sich zu haben. Der Blick in den Spiegel wurde ihm unheimlich. *Sieh nur in mein Gesicht. Du siehst, mein Lächeln ist fehl am Platz. Schau näher, die Spuren meiner Tränen sind leicht zu verfolgen. Aussen trage ich eine Maske, innen verblasst meine Hoffnung.*

Es kam zwar gelegentlich vor, dass vor dem Schlaf aus Enttäuschung einige Tränen in sein Kissen tropften. Aber ob diese Tränen seinen Blick um Jahre hatten altern lassen können?

«Was ist nur aus dir geworden?», fragte er sich murmelnd und erschrak beinahe beim Vernehmen seiner eigenen Stimme. Sie war ihm so vertraut wie die Stimme eines Fremden.

Der mächtige Klang eines E-Moll-Akkords durchbrach die ländliche Idylle. Albert sass nun draussen auf der Holzbank, die sich auf einer kleinen Veranda befand, um sich einem der wenigen schönen Dingen im Leben zu widmen. Soeben hatte er das tägliche Gitarrenspiel mit seinem bevorzugten Akkord begonnen. Er stützte die Beine auf dem Holzgeländer der Veranda ab, seine Augen richteten sich gen Westen zur untergehenden Sonne.

In jenen kostbaren Momenten, in denen er zu Hause an seiner geliebten Gitarre zupfen konnte, fand er ein wenig Trost. Die Gitarre war sozusagen sein einziger Freund – nur ihr konnte er seine Wünsche offenbaren, seine Empfindungen mitteilen. Zuletzt spielte er fast nur noch traurige Lieder.

Mittlerweile hielt er sich für einen ziemlich untalentierten Spieler, und noch schlechter stufte er seine Fähigkeiten als Sänger ein. Obwohl er keinen Besuch zu fürchten hatte, getraute er sich auch in den eigenen vier Wänden nicht mehr, zu singen. Er schämte sich beim Klang seiner Stimme vor sich selbst.

Heute, und das war aussergewöhnlich, verging Albert sogar die Lust, auf der Gitarre zu spielen. Als er sie an das Geländer stellte, vibrierten ihre Saiten noch eine Weile disharmonisch weiter. Er stand auf und begab sich in die Stube, um eine Schallplatte auf den Teller zu legen. Sollten doch andere für die Musik sorgen.

Die Nadel senkte sich, verursachte ein kurzes Kratzen, ein Knacken, das sich dann aber umgehend in einen treibenden Rhythmus verwandelte. Ein schriller Schrei schoss aus den Boxen, dann setzte die durchdringende Hammondorgel ein. Albert liess sich wieder auf die Bank fallen.

Er nahm einen Schluck Absinth, dem er zuvor mit Wasser seine Trübheit, ja seine Trinkbarkeit verpasst hatte. Er fühlte die angenehme Wärme in seinem Magen und liess dem ersten Schluck noch einen zweiten, grösseren folgen.

Doch, vielleicht besass er neben der Gitarre noch einen zweiten Freund: den Schnaps. Im Unterschied zum Wirt etwa trank er allerdings nie während der Arbeit, trank nie bei Mona an der Bar und schon gar nicht am Stammtisch. Albert trank ausschliesslich daheim, allein.

Obwohl er im Gasthof zur Genüge beobachten konnte, wie das teuflische Wasser seine Jünger verführte, sie knebelte und ruinierte, hatte auch er vor einiger Zeit angefangen, sich diesem Übel hinzugeben. Seit der Wirt die Unart pflegte, ihn für zusätzliche Leistungen mit Schnaps zu entlöhnen, hatte das Laster bei ihm seinen Lauf genommen. Es war ja auch nicht an ihm, nicht zu trinken, sagte er sich dann manchmal. Wem sonst, wenn nicht ihm, musste man den täglichen Tropfen gönnen? Er, der nichts und niemanden hatte, der kaum lebte, sondern bloss existierte. Alle anderen hätten wesentlich mehr

Gründe gehabt, nicht zu trinken. Albert war ein Trinker, der sich das Trinken verdient hatte.

Die Schwäche für Absinth führte er nachsichtig gegenüber sich selber auf seine jurassischen Wurzeln zurück, denn seine früheste Kindheit hatte er irgendwo im westlichen Val de Travers verbracht. Es war vermutlich eine glückliche Kindheit gewesen, die durch unglückliche Begebenheiten jäh beendet worden war. Viele Jahre lebte er nun schon im freiburgischen Senseoberland – so lange, dass sich seine früheste Vergangenheit aus dem Bewusstsein der Dorfbewohner weitgehend gelöst hatte. Der letzte Buchstabe seines Vornamens wurde längst betont.

Er verabreichte sich einen weiteren Schluck Absinth, der bereits eine gewisse Wirkung zu erzielen begann. Albert war allerdings Realist genug, um den euphorisierenden Effekt von Alkohol zu durchschauen und so wieder abzuschwächen. Das Glas Absinth konnte ihm zwar den Abend ein wenig erträglicher machen, morgen aber würde ihn der flaue Alltag wieder einholen. Aus einem unglücklichen Leben konnten auch vielgerühmte Spirituosen keine Wunderdinge verrichten.

Gleichwohl jagte er den restlichen Inhalt des Glases durch seine Kehle. Er wandte den Blick nicht vom Horizont ab, konnte der Sonne förmlich zusehen, wie sie unterging.

Wie sie verschwand und das Land der Dunkelheit überliess.

Begleitet wurden die Bilder von der tiefen, trüben Stimme aus der Stube. *Der Mörder erwachte vor Morgengrauen.* In diesem Augenblick kamen in Alberts Kopf von neuem Gedanken auf, die er schon länger mit sich herumgetragen hatte. Gedanken, die ihn bisher stets beklemmt hatten.

Heute nicht. Heute schienen sie ihm vielmehr eine erlösende Wirkung auszuüben.

Albert war zufrieden und gab sich ganz der Stimme aus der Stube hin. Er hatte eben entschieden, dem bösen Treiben noch diese Woche ein Ende zu setzen.

4. Sonntagmorgen

Am / Asus2 / Am / Asus2 / Am / Asus2 / Am

Am Sonntagmorgen herrschte in der Gaststube für gewöhnlich eine aussergewöhnliche Ruhe. Es war die Zeit, in der Trinker ihren Rausch ausschliefen, Kartenspieler alle Karten ruhen liessen, Fromme sich dem Heiland widmeten und Karl mutterseelenallein an der Bar sass.

Von seinen zahlreichen Aufenthalten in der Gaststube war Karl derjenige am Sonntagmorgen einer der liebsten, da sich Mona dem Gespräch mit ihm nicht entziehen konnte. Mona ihrerseits begehrte den Sonntagmorgen aus dem gleichen Grund umso weniger. Zumindest blieben sowohl Karls Sprüche wie auch seine Blicke noch über der Gürtellinie, da er mit eisernem Willen vor dem Mittag keinen Alkohol trank.

Albert marschierte pfeifend den Karrweg hinauf und gelangte nahezu auf die Anhöhe des Fofenhubels, einem von Naturfreunden, Romantikern oder Heimlichrauchern gleichermassen geschätzten Aussichtspunkt. Er war etwas müde, da er vergangene Nacht kaum geschlafen hatte. Sein Gemütszustand hob sich heute jedoch von seinem üblichen Wert ab.

Über den rund tausend Seelen von Rechthalten hatte sich bereits ein strahlender, veilchenblauer Himmel geöffnet, der sich keiner trübenden Wolke annahm. Die Sonne kletterte wieder hinter den Hügeln empor und leuchtete, so schien es Albert, so hell wie nie zuvor. Die Luft war derart klar, dass man den Gämsen auf dem Schwyberg beim Fressen hätte zusehen können, wenn man denn gewollt hätte.

Die Strasse führte Albert schliesslich hinab in den Kern des Dorfes, das sich an einem Hang ausdehnte. Er stiess die schwere Tür des Gasthofs auf und grüsste freundlich den Meister. Mona konnte ihm gar den Ansatz eines steifen Lächelns entlocken. Dann verschwand er in der Küche.

Albert Leblanc bekochte nun schon seit einer Ewigkeit

Tag für Tag die aufkreuzenden Gäste. So zumindest empfand er die Jahre, die sich seit seiner Anstellung im Gasthof von Rechthalten hingezogen hatten. Seine Beschäftigung als Koch war aber keineswegs die Erfüllung eines lange gehegten Herzenswunsches gewesen. Eher zufällig hatte es ihn damals ins Gastgewerbe verschlagen, das seine Dienste bis heute beanspruchte. Die Freundschaft zwischen seinem Pflegevater und dem Wirt hatte seinen Werdegang nicht unwesentlich beeinflusst.

Noch drei Tage. Dann würde er das nächste Mal frei haben. Dann gedachte er, seine gestern gefassten Absichten zur Tat zu machen.

Während der Arbeit sann er darüber nach, wie er am besten vorgehen sollte. Mit einem Schuss vielleicht? Die Vorstellung war ihm zunächst nicht unsympathisch. Allerdings, den Schuss würde er wohl schon selber abfeuern müssen. Ob er denn auch wirklich treffen würde? Er hatte ja keinerlei Übung im Umgang mit Waffen. Sie machten ihm sogar Angst, spätestens seit dem Militärdienst, wo er nach vier Wochen entlassen worden war. Gut möglich also, dass er den Schuss nicht wunschgemäss abfeuern würde. Nein, mit Schiesseisen sollte er vielleicht doch nicht hantieren.

Allmählich kamen in ihm doch wieder Zweifel auf. Die Sache gestaltete sich vermutlich, wie so vieles im Leben, in der Vorstellung etwas einfacher als in der Ausführung. Einmal aber musste doch auch er Erfolg haben, ermutigte er sich. Danach musste ihm nichts mehr gelingen.

Ein junges Paar hatte sich inzwischen eingefunden. Albert kannte den schwarzhaarigen Verführer, der sich weit über den Tisch lehnte und der glücklich aussehenden Begleitung die Hand reichte. Sehnsüchtig verfolgte Albert durch sein rundes Fenster die gegenseitige Zuneigung der beiden.

Dies tat er oft, wenn schöne Frauen zum Essen ausgeführt wurden. Dabei fühlte er sich stets ausgeschlossen. Ausgeschlossen von den schönen Seiten des Lebens. Manchmal stellte er sich vor, wie es wäre, wenn er den Frauen gegenübersitzen würde. Diese Träumereien sorgten bei ihm regelmässig für erhöhten Puls, feuchte Hände und angebrannte Zwiebeln.

In letzter Zeit war ihm sogar nachgesagt worden, Männer den Frauen vorzuziehen. Gerne hätte er jene Gerüchte erstickt, sie ein für alle Mal aus dem Weg geräumt, doch dazu brauchte es Taten. Taten, die allein nicht zu bewerkstelligen waren.

Der Gottesdienst war zu Ende. Mit Leichtigkeit setzten sich weitere Leute zusammen an einen Tisch, tranken und unterhielten sich mühelos gemeinsam, lachten mit einem ungeheuren Selbstverständnis. Die geselligen Gruppen entfachten in Albert jeweils ein unangenehmes, in letzter Zeit ständig stärker werdendes Gefühl, das sich aus Trauer, Neid und Hass zusammensetzte. Von Enttäuschungen hätte Albert nämlich ein Lied singen können. Sogar viele Lieder. Aber singen wollte er ja nicht mehr.

5. Fünfundsiebzig Kieselsteine

Em / Em / Em / Em
Em / Em / Em
Em / Em
D7

Albert wippte auf seinem Schaukelstuhl und starrte auf die Wanduhr. Das Zifferblatt zeigte zehn nach elf. Sofern er sich auf seine Rechenkünste und seinen am Nachmittag erdachten Plan verlassen konnte, hatte er noch fünfundsiebzig Stunden zu leben. Musste er noch leben. Viertausendfünfhundert Minuten, errechnete er sich nach einer knapp zweiminütigen Denkpause, nun also noch gut viertausendvierhundertachtundneunzig Minuten. Für die exakte Ermittlung der ihm noch verbleibenden Sekunden fehlte ihm dann doch die Geduld. Einige tausend Sekunden würden es noch sein, vielleicht hunderttausend? Die Vorstellung war ihm zu abstrakt, sodass er seine ablaufende Lebenszeit wieder in der Stundeneinheit betrachtete. Noch fünfundsiebzig Stunden.

Schaufelte er jeweils etwa fünfundsiebzig Erbsen neben den Kaninchenrücken und den Kartoffelstockberg in die Teller? Oder kannte er etwa fünfundsiebzig verschiedene Gitarrenakkorde? Die Verbildlichungen befriedigten Albert nicht. Er unterbrach das beruhigende Schaukeln auf seinem Stuhl, stand auf und ging nach draussen.

Als er wenig später in die Wohnstube zurückkehrte, hatten sich seine Hosensäcke mit fünfundsiebzig Kieselsteinen gefüllt. Nun legte er diese säuberlich nebeneinander auf den Tisch, auf dem hier und dort noch eingetrocknete Absinthtropfen klebten. Dann setzte er sich wieder.

Gewiss würde er bis zum Tod noch knapp zwanzig Stunden im Schlaf verbringen. Viele Menschen erachteten den Schlaf als notwendiges Übel, als Zeitverschwendung. Ganz anders Albert. Ihm war das nächtliche Aussetzen aus dem aktiven Leben jeweils sehr genehm. Dem ewigen Schlaf konnte er also entspannt entgegenblicken.

Allerdings, konnte er im ewigen Schlaf noch träumen? Träume ermöglichten es Albert gelegentlich, der unliebsamen Wirklichkeit zu entfliehen. Auf diese Weise hatte er bereits auf einer Bühne gestanden, um mit seiner Gitarre Leute zu unterhalten, hatte sich schon mit Freunden getroffen, und einmal, da hatte er sogar eine Frau geküsst … Träume, die der Wirklichkeit nicht einmal ähnelten. Wozu aber brauchte es nach dem Tod noch Träume, wenn es dann auch keine Wirklichkeit mehr gab? Doch, der Tod war eine gute Sache, die einzig richtige.

An ein Leben nach dem Tod glaubte Albert nicht, er tat dies als religiösen oder abergläubischen Unfug ab. Wie sollte einem reglosen, toten Körper noch etwas Lebendiges entschweben? Bestimmt würde bald ein Studierter kommen und all jene, die auf eine Wiedergeburt hoffen, eines Besseren belehren.

Der Minutenzeiger näherte sich während Alberts philosophischen Betrachtungen langsam dem Stundenzeiger. Bald würde er ihn wieder einholen und gemeinsam mit ihm himmelwärts deuten.

Nun war es der gleichmässige Rhythmus des Sekundenpendels, dem sich Alberts Aufmerksamkeit nicht mehr entziehen konnte. Mit erbarmungsloser Beständigkeit schaukelte das Pendel von links nach rechts nach links nach rechts, und jede Bewegung verkürzte sein Leben um eine Sekunde. Dies brauchte ihn jedoch nicht zu besorgen, es ging ja jedem Menschen auf der ganzen Welt gleich. Links nach rechts nach links nach rechts. Nur wusste wohl kaum jemand, welche Sekunde der eigenen Lebensuhr gerade schlug. Albert wusste es, weil er es so wollte.

Eine schwarze Spinne krabbelte über seine neusten Schallplatten, die auf dem grauen, staubigen Teppich verstreut lagen. Die langen, fein behaarten Beinchen trippelten über einen

Schriftzug in kryptischen Lettern – *im Land der Dunkelheit wird das Schiff der Sonne angetrieben vom dankbaren Tod* – und dann weiter über ein Vielzahl von Köpfen, die hinter einem farbig angezogenen Quartett versammelt waren. Albert beobachtete, wie die Spinne auf einer Trommel eine kurze Pause einlegte, und dann ihren Rumpf, der etwa die Grösse eines Hemdknopfes erreichte, über gelbe Blumen bewegte.

Spinnen faszinierten Albert. Er hatte einmal gehört, dass die Erde mit einer dicken Schicht aus Insekten überzogen wäre, gäbe es keine Spinnen. Sie schufen ausserdem Netze von beeindruckender Schönheit, von eigenartiger Präzision – und gehörten dennoch zu den unbeliebtesten Geschöpfen überhaupt. Es war Albert unverständlich, dass sich Menschen vor diesen harmlosen Krabbeltieren ekeln oder gar fürchten konnten. Er hatte noch nie eine Spinne getötet und ebenso selten Spinnengewebe aus den Winkeln seiner Balken entfernt. Aus diesem Grund wäre es den meisten Leuten unter Alberts Dach wohl etwas unheimlich zumute gewesen. Aber dazu sollte es wohl nie kommen.

Albert versuchte, den Rhythmus seines Schaukelns demjenigen des Pendels anzugleichen. Dabei überlegte er sich, ob er in seinem sich zu Ende neigenden Leben noch etwas Aussergewöhnliches unternehmen wollte.

Es fiel ihm nichts ein, und eigentlich war er darüber sogar etwas erleichtert. Seit seinem Entschluss, den er während des Sonnenuntergangs getroffen hatte, befasste er sich bereits derart stark mit dem Tod, dass die noch bevorstehende Zeit ihn kaum mehr kümmerte. Was interessierte ihn seine Zukunft, die in Kürze gänzlich Vergangenheit sein würde? Überhaupt war es nie eine besondere Eigenschaft von ihm gewesen, sich Ziele zu setzen. Vielmehr hatte er dahingelebt und versucht, dies auf möglichst erträgliche Weise zu tun.

Um nicht aufzufallen, musste er noch drei Tage zur Arbeit gehen. Um keinen Verdacht zu erregen, musste er seine letzten Tage so alltäglich wie möglich gestalten. Er würde noch ein paar Lieder auf seiner Gitarre spielen, sich einige Gläser Absinth gönnen, aber sonst? Das Leben hatte ihm nichts mehr zu bieten. Er öffnete das Fenster und schleuderte einen Kieselstein in die Dunkelheit.

Plötzlich aber blitzte ein Gedanke durch seinen Kopf, der sein Blut schlagartig in Wallung brachte.

Es gab da etwas, was dem Leben noch zu entlocken war. Etwas, an dessen Erfüllung Albert gar nie richtig zu glauben gewagt hatte. Er stand auf, machte einige ziellose Schritte durch seine karg eingerichtete Stube und kratzte sich am Hinterkopf. Er hatte nicht mehr ewig Zeit, nicht einmal mehr vierundsiebzig Stunden.

Albert Leblanc hatte in seinem ganzen Leben noch nie eine nackte Frau zu Gesicht bekommen.

6. Mona

Am / G
Am / G / C / D
Am / Em
Am / Em / D

Vor dem Gasthof begegnete Albert einem älteren, buckligen Mann. «Bist du noch nicht an der Arbeit, Junge?», wurde Albert in einem unüberhörbar verächtlichen Ton gefragt.

«Nein, ich beginne immer um neun», antwortete er beherrscht.

«Schön muss man es haben», meinte der Mann mit dem Buckel seufzend.

«Bald. Bald werde ich es schön haben», murmelte Albert, eher zu sich als zu seinem Pflegevater.

Seit dieser aufgrund anhaltender Rückenbeschwerden den Bauernhof hatte aufgeben müssen, sass er beständig in der Gaststube und gab sich dem Kartenspiel hin. Albert kam damit nicht umhin, ihn beinahe täglich zu erblicken. Heute mochte er sich von ihm allerdings nicht ärgern lassen.

Albert hatte in seinem Kopf noch einmal verschiedenste Methoden durchgespielt, mit denen er unter sein Leben einen Schlussstrich ziehen konnte, und sie ihrer Tauglichkeit nach beurteilt.

Mit einem Sturz von der Galternbrücke hätte er wahrlich nichts dem Zufall überlassen. Doch dachte er an die wackelige Hängebrücke zurück, die noch vor drei Jahren über dem Galterngraben geschaukelt hatte, wurde ihm unwohl. Der Gang über die wankende Unterlage hatte in ihm stets Unbehagen, ja gar eine heillose Höhenangst ausgelöst. Den Sprung in den Tod schloss er also aus.

Die Idee, sich zu ertränken, hatte er schleunigst wieder verworfen. Natürlich, der Schwarzsee oder die Saane hätten ihn, einen kümmerlichen Schwimmer, kaum lebendig wieder ausgespuckt – allein der Gedanke an die unmenschlich tiefen Temperaturen jener Gewässer liess ihm aber das Blut in den Adern gefrieren.

Auch die Chancen, sich totzutrinken, hatte er anfänglich für intakt befunden. Die Vorstellung, sich langsam und schmerzlos zu betäuben und schliesslich zu entschlafen, war ihm sogar von allen die angenehmste gewesen. Er hatte sie bereits liebgewonnen, hatte sich mit seinem ganzen Schnapsvorrat ins Bett legen sehen, hatte dabei eine Kerze auf seinem Nachttischchen aufflackern lassen, auf der Gitarre sein eigenes Abschiedslied angestimmt und nicht mehr aufgehört, zu trinken … Bis ihm eingefallen war, dass er bereits unzählige Male so viel getrunken hatte, wie er nur konnte.

Albert hatte bereits befürchtet, das nächste Wochenende zu überleben, als ihn verschiedene Ereignisse der letzten Tage doch allmählich zu einem Plan inspirierten. Ein Plan, der sich schliesslich doch nicht so sehr vom romantischen Trinkertod unterschied.

Absinth. Die gute Laune des Wirts. Seine Beruhigungstabletten. Die Feuerwehrmänner. Deren anfänglich noch gesitteten Gespräche. Rauchvergiftung. Um seinen Tod auch wirklich zu gewährleisten, brauchte es mehrere Methoden, respektive deren geschickte Kombination. Wie fahrlässig es gewesen wäre, sich nur auf die eine Methode zu verlassen! Ein todsicherer Plan.

Inzwischen war Albert restlos davon überzeugt, sich und sein Haus in Schutt und Asche zu verwandeln. Es sollte ihm recht sein, wenn nach seinem Tod niemand mehr sein armseliges Obdach würde betreten können. Niemand brauchte zu wissen, dass sich an seinem Tisch nur ein Stuhl befand, dass in seinem Geschirrschrank nur ein Glas stand. Auch seine nicht vorhandene Abneigung gegenüber Spinnen und seine Sammlung von vielerorts verpönten Platten durften ruhig Geheimnisse bleiben, die er mit ins Grab nehmen würde. Das Feuer in seinen vier Wänden würde also nicht nur ihn, sondern auch seine Spuren auslöschen. Zudem konnte er mit seiner Aktion die Feuerwehrmänner noch ein wenig ärgern. Die sollten ruhig auch einmal anderes löschen als ihren Durst.

Weiter liess sich mit dem Brand verhindern, dass man seinen Leichnam mitnehmen, anstarren und studieren würde. Denn käme es zu einer Untersuchung, würde man ihn bestimmt seiner Kleider entledigen, sich dann etwa gar noch über ihn lustig machen. Er stellte sich weiter seine Aufbahrung in der Totenkapelle vor, wo er den neugierigen Blicken der ganzen Dorfbevölkerung ausgeliefert sein würde. Sogar mit kaltem Wasser würde man ihn dann bespritzen! Ihm graute. Nein, er musste nicht nur tot sein, er musste zu Staub gemacht werden.

Dachte er an seine Nacktheit, wurde er unweigerlich an eine Idee erinnert, die ihn gestern Abend doch in erhebliche Aufregung versetzt hatte.

Was die Erfahrung mit Frauen betraf, hinkte Albert seinen Altersgenossen meilenweit hinterher. Nicht wenige siebenundzwanzigjährige Männer in der Region hatten zu der Zeit bereits den Bund fürs Leben geschlossen, sogar schon für Nachwuchs gesorgt. Andere waren verlobt oder unterhielten immerhin eine Liebschaft. Die wenigen, die noch übrig blieben, konnten wohl zumindest das eine oder andere Erlebnis verbuchen. Umso schmählicher fühlte sich Albert, der sich in der Welt der Frauen noch mit jungfräulichen Augen bewegte.

Es war ja keineswegs so, dass er sich vom anderen Geschlecht nicht angezogen fühlte. Sehr wohl vermochten charmante, hübsche Frauen ihn und seine Aufmerksamkeit zu erregen. Richtig erfreuen konnten sie ihn aber noch nie. Vielmehr lähmte ihn der Kontakt mit Frauen, sie waren für ihn untrennbar mit Angst und Scham verbunden. Fünfundsechzig Stunden vor seinem Tod stand für ihn aber fest, dass ihm noch eine entblösste Frau vor die Augen kommen musste.

Natürlich waren die Frauen an warmen Sommertagen wie heute etwas leichter bekleidet, geizten nicht mir Verlockungen, sondern liessen die Herzen der Ästheten höher schlagen. Albert mochte sich mit solchen Andeutungen aber nicht mehr zufrieden geben. Im Gegenteil. Der tiefe Ausschnitt, mit dem Mona heute zur Arbeit erschien, bekräftigte ihn in seinem Vorhaben zusätzlich.

Es verstand sich für ihn von selbst, dass sein Unterfangen ohne jegliche Gewalt über die Bühne gebracht werden musste. Gewalt war ihm ebenso fremd wie Damenhaut, kennenlernen wollte er nur letzteres. Ein Abenteuer auf Bezahlung entsprach ebenfalls nicht seinen Vorstellungen. Das hätte er ja schon längst tun können. Er wollte sein Bedürfnis niemandem mitteilen, durfte dabei von niemandem gesehen werden. Er hatte nicht vor, seinem an Peinlichkeiten reichen Leben noch ein weiteres Kapitel hinzuzufügen.

Wohl oder übel musste er also einer Frau nachstellen, so unmoralisch ihm das auch vorkam. Einmal aber, so sagte er sich, durfte doch auch er sich eine anrüchige Tat leisten. Allzu lange würde er damit nicht mehr zuwarten können, denn wieder hatte sich sein ihm noch verbleibendes Leben über Nacht um einen beträchtlichen Bruchteil verkürzt, sein Hosensack erheblich an Gewicht verloren.

Albert hatte sich bereits für ein Opfer entschieden. Eines, das er schon mehrmals ausgezogen hatte, allerdings nur kraft seiner Gedanken.

Mona verdiente ihr Brot seit ein paar Monaten als Kellnerin im Gasthof. Und Brot verdienen, das musste sie, sowohl um sich selber wie auch ihren Ehemann über Wasser zu halten. Franz, ein heilloser Angeber, hatte aufgrund verschiedener Machenschaften bereits einmal für ein halbes Jahr hinter Gittern gesessen. Seitdem hatte er keine Arbeit mehr und war darüber gar nicht einmal unglücklich. Seine überflüssigen Kräfte entluden sich in den täglichen Liegestützen, in der Erziehung seines jungen Hundes und in der Begattung von Mona. Für ein eifersüchtiges Wesen wie Franz übte Mona den falschen Beruf aus. Hin und wieder schlug er sie, wenn sie nicht pünktlich nach Feierabend bei ihm auftauchte.

Mona führte also eine unglückliche Ehe, zu der sie als junges und naives Mädchen überrumpelt worden war. Die unbeschwerten Züge in ihrem Gesicht wichen inzwischen zunehmend nachdenklichen. Dies machte sie allerdings nicht minder attraktiv. Die schönen braunen Haare, die ihr auf die Brust hinabfielen, strahlten trotz Monas sechsunddreissig Jahren noch Jugendlichkeit aus.

Obwohl Albert und Mona täglich unter dem gleichen Dach verkehrten, kannten sie einander kaum. Alberts Reich war die Küche, Monas die Gaststube. So hatten die beiden trotz der räumlichen Nähe wenig miteinander zu tun. Albert brachte Mona Ehrfurcht entgegen, sie begegnete ihm liebenswerterweise mit Freundlichkeit.

Ihre vor kurzem gemachte, eigentlich belanglose Aussage, sie freue sich nach einem arbeitsreichen Tag jeweils auf eine erfrischende Dusche, war für Albert von einschneidender Wirkung gewesen. Umso mehr, wenn er sich nun vorstellte, diesem Ereignis beizuwohnen.

Ich dachte, dass Liebe nur in Märchen existiert. Sie ist für andere gedacht, nicht für mich. Meine Träume wurden von Enttäuschung verfolgt. Wenn ich Sonne brauchte, erhielt ich Regen. Dann sah ich ihr …

7. Amboss & Franz

Am / F / Am / F

Spannung, Angst und Erregung begleiteten Albert Leblanc, als die Tür des Gasthofs um zweiundzwanzig Uhr hinter ihm ins Schloss fiel. Der helle Mondschein, der durch die Strassen zog und sich mit der Nacht zu einem Nebel vermischte, beunruhigte Albert. Sein Vorhaben wäre auch bei vollkommener Dunkelheit delikat genug gewesen. Das Pfarrhaus und die Kirche, die sich vor ihm in jenem nächtlichen Nebel reckten, erinnerten ihn irgendwie an riesige Grabsteine. Albert kramte in seinem Hosensack nach einem Kieselstein und liess diesen in einen Wasserschacht fallen. Noch war er nicht in Eile, denn Mona würde sich erst gegen Mitternacht zur Heimkehr aufmachen.

Mona bewohnte nahe dem Unteren Schloss den ersten Stock eines schmucken Hauses, lebte also nicht in unmittelbarer Nähe von Albert. Ungeachtet dessen trat er vorerst seinen üblichen Nachhauseweg an. Er hatte sich dazu zwei Überlegungen gemacht. Zum einen war es noch zu früh, um sorglos von seinen alltäglichen Gepflogenheiten abzuweichen. Gewiss wären diejenigen Leute bereits neugierig geworden, die ihn jetzt auf dem Weg ins Unterdorf gesehen hätten. Er musste Geduld bewahren. Zum anderen bot ihm ein kurzer Abstecher nach Hause die Gelegenheit, mit ein paar kräftigen Schlücken Absinth seine Nervosität zu zähmen.

In der Tat wirkte sich die kleine Alkoholzufuhr etwas beruhigend aus. Nun war er bereit. Bereit für die verwegenste Tat seines Lebens. Der bevorstehende Tod hatte ihn mit einer nicht für möglich gehaltenen Kühnheit ausgestattet. Dennoch mied er auf seiner Expedition das Dorfzentrum und nahm einige Umwege in Kauf. So bewegte er sich über Wiesen und Felder, auf denen er lediglich einer Vogelscheuche und schlafenden Kühen begegnete.

Nun stand es vor ihm. Das Haus, in dem Mona lebte, liebte und duschte. Noch dauerte es rund eine Stunde, bis sie hier eintreffen würde. Albert blieb also genügend Zeit, um das Badezimmer ausfindig zu machen. Etwas ungelenk schlich er der Hausmauer entlang. Zu nervös war er, um elegant über die Gartenplatten zu gleiten. Beim Vorbeitappen an den Fenstern duckte er sich.

Vielleicht war der Entscheid, Mona aufzulauern, doch nicht allzu glücklich gewesen. Bereits zweifelte er an seiner Unternehmung. Zumindest hatte er sich die Sache etwas leichter vorgestellt.

Er gelangte in einen kleinen, duftenden Garten.

An der hinteren Hausmauer, die ihm von der Strasse aus noch verborgen geblieben war, fiel ihm ein Fenster im ersten Stock ins Auge. Das Fenster war offen, was Albert an einem Sommerabend wie diesem nicht überraschte. Das Schimmern des Mondlichts wurde von der Fensterscheibe nicht gespiegelt, sondern gebrochen reflektiert. Es musste sich also um das Badezimmerfenster handeln, beurteilte Albert, auf dessen Stirn sich inzwischen dicke Schweissperlen gebildet hatten.

An einem herunterhängenden Geäst glänzte eine reife dunkelrote Kirsche. Albert schnappte sie sich geistesabwesend und schluckte sie ohne zu zerkauen und samt Stein.

Innerhalb der Mauern, um die Albert schlich, stand in diesem Moment Franz mit angespannten Oberarmmuskeln vor dem Spiegel und begutachtete, ob seine Liegestützen Früchte getragen hatten. Sie taten es.

Albert hatte sich nun in den Schatten eines stattlichen Baumes begeben, der mitten im Garten stand. Er dachte kurz nach, dann musste er sich missmutig eingestehen, dass sich das Hochsteigen auf den Baum durchaus lohnen würde. Zur Einsicht war es sogar notwendig. Zudem würde die dichte Baumkrone ein überaus günstiges Versteck abgeben. Hatte er eigentlich schon jemals einen Baum bestiegen? Auch das nicht. Er hatte dem Beklettern von Bäumen nie einen Sinn abgewinnen können. Nun, in diesem Augenblick konnte er.

Er schaute in die Höhe, wo er innerhalb der prächtig blühenden Baumkrone einen dicken Ast entdeckte. Wenn er sich lang machte, fehlte ihm nur ein lausig kleines Stück, um sich daran hochziehen zu können. Sicherheitshalber schnürte er die Schuhsenkel noch etwas fester, hielt die Luft an und setzte den rechten Fuss auf einen hervorstehenden Auswuchs des Baumes.

Als er sein Gewicht auf den aufgestützten Fuss verlagerte und sich in die Höhe stemmen wollte, unterlief ihm ein folgenschweres Missgeschick. Die glatte Fusssohle des Halbschuhs rutschte ab, was in der nächtlichen Stille für erschreckend viel Lärm sorgte. Alberts Stirn faltete sich vor Entsetzen. Sie sollte sich für eine Weile nicht mehr glätten.

Bestürzt musste er mitverfolgen, wie unter schallendem Gebell ein sehr unansehnlicher Hund um die Ecke hervorpreschte. Der stimmgewaltige Kläffer schien nicht mit Humor gesegnet zu sein. Die Entschlossenheit, mit der er auf den erstarrt dastehenden Albert zusteuerte, liess keine Hoffnung zu. In Kürze würden sich die spitzen Zähne, die aus der triefenden Schnauze ragten, in irgendein Stück Fleisch Alberts bohren.

Albert schmiegte sich an den Baum, als erwarte er von ihm ausreichend Schutz, schlang die Arme über seinen Kopf und wartete. Wartete auf seinen Tod, der nun doch etwas gar früh eintreffen würde.

Alberts Tod liess allerdings auf sich warten. Das wilde Gebell war plötzlich verstummt und in ein klagendes Wimmern übergegangen.

Endlich traute sich Albert, um den Baumstamm herum zu spähen. Und was er sah, beglückte ihn.

Der Sturmlauf der Bestie war von einer Kette gestoppt worden, deren Glieder wohl zu sprengen gedroht hatten. Der junge Boxerhund hatte offenbar eben gelernt, wie schmerzhaft sich das stramme Halsband bei Nichtbeachten der Kette in sein Fell schnitt. Das Ende seines Anfalls musste ihm jedenfalls zugesetzt haben, denn der Fremde im Garten schien ihm nicht mehr die dringendste Angelegenheit zu sein.

Albert atmete tief durch. Er wollte zwar sterben, aber gewiss nicht zerfetzt werden. Und zuerst hatte er ja noch vor, sich seinen letzten Wunsch zu erfüllen.

«Was ist denn los, Amboss, warum bloss dieses Geheul?» Franz erkundigte sich durch ein Fenster nach seinem Liebling, woraufhin dieser weinerlich aufjaulte. «Ja Amboss, ich komme ja schon! Was bist du nur für ein Angsthase!», brüllte Franz.

Albert hatte keine Zeit, sich über den etwas sonderbaren Hundenamen zu wundern. Erneut startete er einen Versuch, den Baum zu bezwingen, doch seine Schuhe rutschten wie Seife am Baumstamm ab. Verzweiflung befiel ihn, denn zur Flucht war es wohl zu spät. Vielleicht klappte es barfuss. Rasch schlüpfte er aus den Schuhen und entledigte sich seiner Socken. Wohin damit? In der Eile warf Albert die Schuhe samt Socken in das nächstgelegene Gebüsch. Sogleich ärgerte er sich darüber. Zumindest aber fielen die Sachen im Moment niemandem auf.

Tatsächlich fanden seine nackten, schweissnassen Füsse einen ungleich besseren Halt auf der Baumrinde. Ein spitzer Holzsplitter drang in Alberts grossen linken Zeh – nur mit Mühe konnte er den Schmerzensschrei in seiner Kehle behalten. Gleich würde er den rettenden Ast erreichen, über den er in der Krone des Baumes untertauchen konnte.

8. Theater

Am / F / G / D7

Mona ging bedächtigen Schrittes die Strasse hinunter. Mehr als einmal war sie heute ins Schwitzen geraten, sodass sich unter ihren Armen die Ansätze von kleinen dunklen Ringen auf dem weinroten Oberteil abzeichneten. Sie fühlte sich unwohl in ihrer Haut.

«Guten Abend, Mona.»

Mona erschrak ob des freundlichen Grusses, der scheinbar dem Nichts entsprungen war.

«– Guten Abend», konnte sie erst antworten, als der Mann bereits an ihr vorbeimarschiert war. Er trug einen schwarzen Hut, der einen dunklen Schatten auf sein Gesicht warf. Darunter kräuselten ein paar graue Haarfetzen hervor.

Mona kannte den älteren Mann, jedoch nicht mit Namen. Er kam oft zum Abendessen in den Gasthof. Letzten Freitag hatte er wieder einmal mit der Feuerwehr am Stammtisch gesessen, wobei er ihr gerade durch seine Unauffälligkeit angenehm aufgefallen war. Sie wusste ausserdem von ihm, dass er häufig ausgedehnte Spaziergänge unternahm. Aber nachts?

Normalerweise war zu dieser Uhrzeit keine Seele im Dorf anzutreffen, schon gar nicht werktags. Doch wen kannte Mona denn hier schon? Manchmal bildete sie sich ein, durch ihren geselligen Beruf schon beinahe das ganze Dorf zu kennen. Im Grunde aber kannte sie hier gar niemanden. Wer waren schon die Stammtischprediger, die sich anderntags zu Hause um Frau und Kind kümmerten? Wer waren die Trinker, die am nächsten Tag wieder zu Sinnen kamen? Wer waren die sich vornehm gebenden Geniesser des Sonntagmenus, die sich unter der Woche irgendwo abrackerten? Es kam ihr vor, als ob im Gasthof alle Theater spielen würden. Auf der Bühne der Gaststube waren sie alle Schauspieler, die ihr wahres Gesicht zu verbergen suchten.

Während sie sich ihrem Zuhause näherte, steckte sie sich eine Zigarette zwischen ihre dezent gefärbten Lippen.

Nein, sie kannte auch diejenigen Gäste nicht, die mehrmals in der Woche bei ihr aufkreuzten. Nicht einmal Karl, dieser alte Kauz, mit dem sie immerhin jeden Sonntagmorgen in Zweisamkeit verbrachte. Auch Albert kannte sie nicht, ihren verschlossenen, verklemmten Koch. Eigentlich schade, fand sie, denn in ihm schlummerte durchaus ein gewisser Charme. Er tat ihr leid, man ging nicht immer besonders herzlich mit ihm um.

Und Franz? Ihn kannte sie wohl. Vielleicht, dachte sie, wäre es besser gewesen, gerade ihn nicht kennengelernt zu haben.

9. Der Baum der Einsicht

Am / F / Am / F
Am / F / G / D7
Am / F / G / D7
Am / F / Am

Albert sass auf einem dicken Ast, umgeben von der Pracht eines üppig bestückten Apfelbaumes. Sein Angstschweiss war so ausgeprägt, dass er über das Gesicht bis zum Hals hinunterrann. Er atmete kaum mehr, sondern gewährte seinen Lungenflügeln nur langsam und lautlos das Nötigste an Sauerstoff.

Franz kniete sich hin und tätschelte seinen immer noch etwas benommen wirkenden Hund. Dann bewegte sich sein grimmiger Blick flüchtig durch den Garten, wobei er verständlicherweise nur die begehbare Grünfläche prüfte. Auch der eigentlich gerissene Franz fasste nicht den Gedanken, dass sich in jenem Augenblick ein Eindringling auf dem Apfelbaum hätte festklammern können, der seine Ehefrau nackt sehen wollte. Dann widmete er sich wieder ganz Amboss.

Albert wagte keine Bewegung, obwohl ihn seine eingenommene Stellung immer mehr danach drängte. Er betete. Zum ersten Mal seit vielen Jahren.

Als er für eine Weile kein Geräusch mehr aus dem Garten vernahm, riskierte er einen Blick nach unten. Sowohl der Hund wie auch sein Herr waren verschwunden.

Sein Herz begann, wieder in etwas gemässigterem Rhythmus zu beben. Er überlegte sich, wer von den beiden, Amboss oder Franz, ihn im Falle einer direkten Begegnung wohl übler zugerichtet hätte.

Mit dem Ärmel seines Hemdes wischte er sich die Schweissperlen aus dem Gesicht. Auch er hätte jetzt eine Dusche vertragen können, doch die war zuerst anderen vorbehalten. Er bewegte sich so, dass sich ihm zwischen Blättern, Äpfeln und

Ästen hindurch eine glänzende Sicht auf das offene Fenster des Badezimmers bot.

Er wartete.

In welch miserable Umstände ihn seine Gier nach ein bisschen nackter Haut nur getrieben hatte! Und wenn Mona heute etwa ohne zu duschen ins Bett fallen oder nach dem Betreten des Badezimmers das Fenster zumachen würde? Albert mochte gar nicht an derartigen Jammer denken.

Er wartete weiter.

«Was macht der Köter in der Stube?» Es war Monas überraschend harsche Stimme, die durch das offene Fenster auch im Garten zu vernehmen war.

«Er hat sich wieder mal gefürchtet. Hat gebellt und gejault. Hat wohl die ganze Nachbarschaft geweckt.» Franz klang enttäuscht über das unzulängliche Verhalten seines Hundes.

«Wovor soll sich der denn fürchten?»

«Vor einem Marder, einem Fuchs, vor der Dunkelheit, was weiss ich!»

«Ich möchte, dass das Viech wieder nach draussen geht, Franz.»

«Nun sei mal nicht so streng. Amboss tut doch hier niemandem was!»

«Ich gehe jetzt ins Bad. Wenn ich zurückkomme, möchte ich den Köter nicht mehr hier drinnen sehen, bitte Franz.»

«Gib mir zuerst einen Kuss!»

«Später vielleicht.»

Mona konnte es nicht leiden, wenn sie nach einem arbeitsreichen Tag den Hund im Wohnzimmer vorfand. Das Tier war zwar stubenrein, aber gegenüber Hundehaaren und Hundespeichel auf dem Sofa hegte sie tiefe Abneigung. Zudem schleppte Amboss dauernd Zecken, vollgepumpt mit Blut, mit nach drinnen. Mona nahm es mit der Sauberkeit um einiges genauer als Amboss und Franz. Davon abgesehen war ihr beim besten Willen unverständlich, dass jemand einen Boxerhund schön finden konnte.

In der Hoffnung, dem Köter heute nicht mehr begegnen zu müssen, verschwand sie im Bad und schloss erschöpft die Tür ab. Endlich hatte sie Ruhe. Zum ersten Mal heute.

«Warum tust du dir das Ganze bloss an?», fragte sie sich leise. Sie nahm die Blockseife und wusch sich damit die Hände, durch die heute eine Menge Geld geflossen war. Über das Trinkgeld konnte sie sich erneut nicht beklagen. Dann tupfte sie sich mit einem Stück Watte sanft die Farbe von den Lippen.

Als sich Mona ihres weinroten Oberteils entledigte, bemerkte sie, dass ihre Fingernägel wieder etwas rau geworden waren. Sie griff zur Nagelfeile und bearbeitete säuberlich die Nägel all ihrer Finger. Ein angenehm warmer Hauch der Junimilde flog ihr über den blanken Rücken. Mona bekam Gänsehaut.

10. E-Moll-Septakkord mit None

Em9

Als Albert die Geschehnisse im Badezimmer mitverfolgte, vergass er für einen kurzen Augenblick, dass er auf den Höhen eines Baumes stand. Er vergass für einige Sekunden sämtliche Enttäuschungen, die er in seinem Leben so zahlreich erfahren hatte. Für einen ihm ewig scheinenden Moment vergass er sogar seinen Wunsch, zu sterben. Aufgewühlt pflückte er sich einen runden, makellosen Apfel und biss gierig in dessen Fruchtfleisch.

Ein E-Moll-Septakkord mit None versprühte für Albert eine eigenartige Schönheit, träumte und wunderte sich, barg Geheimnisse, war ahnungslos und trotzdem zuversichtlich.

11. Das Muttermal

Am / C / Dsus2 / F
Em / Am / Em / Am

«Albert, wie siehst du denn aus?», entfuhr es Mona.

Er schwieg.

«Was ist bloss mit dir passiert, sag schon!», löcherte sie weiter und zeigte mit ihrem gepflegten Zeigefinger auf seine mit üblen Schürfungen versehene Backe. Er stand nun direkt vor Mona und kämpfte gegen die aufkommende, hinterlistige Nervosität.

Alberts spannende Nachtaktion war nicht reibungslos vonstatten gegangen, wenngleich er doch glaubte, unentdeckt geblieben zu sein. Bei seinem Sturz vom Apfelbaum hatte seine linke Backe allerdings die raue Oberfläche eines Astes gestreift.

Als er sich heute Morgen etwas genauer im Spiegel betrachtet hatte, wäre er am liebsten gar nicht zu seinem letzten Arbeitstag erschienen. Sein Plan jedoch sah dies vor, ausserdem wollte er seinen entjungferten Augen die Gelegenheit geben, sich von Mona, Wunder der Natur, zu verabschieden.

«Ich habe …», begann Albert. Sein Stottern verflüchtigte sich aber plötzlich und schlug in ein etwas gar zu schnelles Sprechen um. «Ich habe auf einem Baum schöne Äpfel gesehen und als ich mir einen holen wollte, verlor ich den Halt und fiel.»

Sein Tonfall erinnerte Mona irgendwie an denjenigen eines Schülers, der demütig ein Gedicht vorträgt. Ausserdem überlegte sie sich, ob Albert tatsächlich spätabends oder frühmorgens auf Bäume stieg, um Äpfel zu pflücken. Sie wollte ihn aber nicht weiter mit Fragen belästigen. Der Arme sah genug gezeichnet aus. «Ach Albert, du bist mir einer. Hast du die Schürfung desinfiziert?», fragte sie stattdessen.

Er verneinte.

«Das solltest du aber. Warte.»

Albert wunderte sich über Monas Fürsorge.

Sie hielt eine rote Serviette in der Hand, auf die sie einen Tropfen Kirsch fallen liess, der den Stoff sofort durchtränkte. Es brannte entsetzlich, als der Kirsch in die Poren seiner linken Gesichtshälfte drang. Als er jedoch spürte, wie Monas warme Hand kurz seine Haut berührte, wurde der Schmerz augenblicklich unterbunden. Der Kontakt durchblitzte seinen Körper vom Seitenscheitel bis in die Spitze seines grossen Zehs, in dem noch immer ein arglistiger Holzsplitter steckte. Ob Mona ihn etwa absichtlich berührt hatte? Unsinn. Ihm wurde klar, dass er wieder in die triste Wirklichkeit zurückkehren musste. In die bald endende Wirklichkeit.

«Ihr beide, ich habe euch nicht angestellt, damit ihr einander im Gesicht herumfummelt!»

Da war sie also wieder, die Wirklichkeit.

«Du meine Güte, wie sieht der denn aus?», fragte der Wirt mit unverständlicher Miene, ohne allerdings die Antwort abzuwarten. «An die Arbeit, Junge!»

Albert bedauerte, dass der Gang in die Küche die Gesellschaft von Mona beendete. Mona fiel auf, dass Albert auch noch leicht hinkte.

Dankbar nahm er zur Kenntnis, dass er an seinem letzten Tag im Gasthof frische Morcheln zubereiten durfte. Ein erdiger Duft breitete sich in der Küche aus, als er die Morcheln zu waschen begann, die angeblich ein Rentner bei Sonnenaufgang am Senseufer gesammelt hatte. Er liebte es heute besonders, mit seinen Fingern über die Strukturen des bräunlichen Huts, über den glatten hellen Stiel zu fahren. Hin und wieder gönnte er seinem Gaumen eine Kostprobe. Am besten schmeckten ihm Morcheln roh, in ihrer reinen, ungeschminkten Eigenart.

Morcheln gehörten seit seiner Beschäftigung als Koch zu Alberts liebsten Speisen. Heute aber, heute vermochten sie ihn wie nie zuvor zu beglücken. Im Wissen, sie ein letztes Mal geniessen zu können, schienen ihm seine Sinne um einiges schärfer zu sein als an Tagen inmitten des Lebens.

Beinahe versäumte Albert durch das Entzücken, in das er geraten war, ein heute unbedingt zu erledigendes Vorhaben. Er musste an die Tabletten kommen, die ihm morgen gemeinsam mit Alkohol und giftigen Gasen den Lebensgeist rauben sollten. Wo er diese auffinden würde, wusste er nahezu mit Überzeugung.

Sein erster Arbeitstag im Gasthof war ihm noch so präsent wie jener Frühlingsmorgen, an dem er seine Gitarre aus dem Müllcontainer gerettet hatte. «Und dieses Schranktürchen hier, das geht dich nichts an. Du sollst dich also nicht daran vergreifen, Junge.» So lauteten damals die mahnenden Worte des Meisters, als dieser Albert zum ersten Mal durch die Küche führte. Über all die Jahre hatte sich Albert nie getraut, gegen dieses Gebot zu verstossen. Es hatte ihn auch nie danach verlangt. Ihm war jedoch nicht entgangen, dass sich der Meister nach dem Schliessen des Törchens oft eine Tablette in den Mund warf und diese mit einem Schluck Hahnenwasser hinunterspülte. Nun stand Albert also vor dem verbotenen Schranktürchen, das etwas oberhalb der Küchenkombination angebracht war. Ein überraschendes Auftauchen des Meisters konnte er praktisch ausschliessen, da dieser eben in der Gaststube Platz genommen hatte, um gemeinsam mit seinen Stammkunden Karten auf den Tisch zu werfen.

Die Scharniere quietschten schrill auf. An der Innenseite des Türchens prangte ein irgendwo ausgeschnittenes Bild, das den bis dahin letzten Schweizer General zeigte. Weiter entdeckte er Zigarren, Pastillen gegen Mundgeruch, ein Sackmesser, grüne Plastikhandschuhe, eine alte Postkarte von Rechthalten, und schliesslich drei Gläser, gefüllt mit Tabletten. Die mussten es sein.

Es war Valium.

Albert liess hastig eines der Gläser in seinem Hosensack verschwinden, in dem noch achtunddreissig Kieselsteine lagen.

Am stärksten wurde seine Aufmerksamkeit aber auf etwas anderes gelenkt. Im obersten Regal lag eine kleine Truhe, die dunkelblau schimmerte. Die Truhe übte eine eigenartige Faszination auf Albert aus, wahrscheinlich deshalb, weil er neben dem Valium eher unspektakuläre Gegenstände angetroffen hatte. War es etwa doch die Truhe, die den vom Meister geforderten Abstand zum Schrank begründete?

«So, wie geht es meinem Koch?»

Albert machte eine derart unkontrollierte Bewegung, dass ihm ein herzliches und zugleich entschuldigendes Lächeln entgegensah.

«Tut mir leid», sagte Mona, und blickte dabei immer noch anzüglich durch den schmalen Spalt zwischen Tür und Türrahmen, «ich wollte mich nur nach deiner Backe erkundigen.»

«Es – ist alles in Ordnung», murmelte Albert, der seinen Schreck nicht verbergen konnte.

«Schön, dann war meine Behandlung also nicht umsonst ...», freute sich Mona augenzwinkernd und verschwand wieder.

«Oh nein, das war sie nicht», dachte sich Albert. Rasch schloss er die Schranktür, beschämt, von Mona ertappt worden zu sein. Tatsächlich ging ihn der Inhalt des Schranks nichts an. Mit dem Stehlen der Tabletten sollte sein Quantum an Unrecht erfüllt sein.

Mona hatte ihn «meinen Koch» genannt. So persönlich hatte sie ihn noch nie angesprochen.

Er wusste, dass er nicht zu viel Wert darauf legen durfte. Trotzdem fand er es schön, zumindest in Worten kurz in ihrem Besitz gewesen zu sein. Mona hatte sich jedoch bestimmt nicht im Entferntesten so viele Überlegungen zu ihrer Wortwahl gemacht, wie er es nun tat. Oder vielleicht doch?

So seltsam es ihm auch vorkam, irgendwie fühlte er sich Mona verbunden, seit er sie gestern Nacht beobachtet hatte. Er war so tief in ihre Privatsphäre vorgedrungen, wie er es noch nie bei einem Menschen getan hatte – und wie es bei

Mona bestimmt auch noch nicht viele getan hatten. Das Muttermal, das er gesehen hatte, war wohl nur einigen wenigen Männern bekannt. Er gehörte jetzt einer kleinen, exklusiven Gruppe an. Albert genoss diese Gedanken reichlich. Sein ganz persönliches Geheimnis, das er nun mit sich trug, erfüllte ihn mit Stolz.

Durch das Küchenfenster erspähte er, wie sich Karl von Monas schwungvollen Bewegungen beim Tischdecken ablenken liess, dabei hatte es noch nicht einmal zwölf geschlagen. Täglich wanderten in der Gaststube männliche Blicke hinter Mona her, und in noch so manchen Männerfantasien dürfte die nackte Mona die Hauptrolle bekleidet haben. Er hatte also etwas erreicht, wovon andere Männer ebenfalls träumten, wonach andere ebenso trachteten. Doch weder für ihren Ehemann noch für irgendjemand anderen hatte sich Mona entblösst, sondern nur für ihn. Mona hatte, wenn auch für kurze Zeit, ganz ihm gehört.

Keine Frage, die letzte Nacht hatte in Alberts Denken, in seiner Sicht der Dinge etwas verändert. Er verspürte plötzlich eine ihm eigentlich fremde Selbstsicherheit, ja fast schon ein Gefühl der Überlegenheit.

Ein Ehepaar betrat die Gaststube. Es war gekommen, um sich ein Kalbsfilet an der von Albert mit viel Liebe zubereiteten Morchelsauce schmecken zu lassen.

12. Heisses Wasser

Am
Em
Am
Em9

Albert sass an seinem Küchentisch und tat sich schwer. Er wollte die grössere Pause am Nachmittag nutzen, um einige verabschiedende Worte an Mona niederzuschreiben.

Er befand zwar, dass er seiner Nachwelt nichts schuldig war, doch wollte er im Dorf für Gewissheit sorgen. Die Leute durften ruhig wissen, dass er seinem Leben selbst ein Ende gesetzt haben würde – oder besser, dass sie ihn mit ihrer Rücksichtslosigkeit dazu getrieben hatten. Durch seinen selbstgewollten Tod würde bei manchen Personen die Reue aufkommen, was Albert durchaus begrüsste.

An seinen Pflegevater mochte er keinen Abschiedsbrief schreiben. Die Kunde seines Freitods sollte die letzte Botschaft an ihn sein, und sie würde deutlich genug daherkommen. Auch hatte er keine Lust, sich noch persönlich an den Meister zu wenden, der ihn stets nur ausgenutzt hatte. Kein Gruss war auch ein Gruss. Und sonst? Bei jemand anderem stellte sich die Frage nach einem Abschiedsbrief gar nicht. Bis eben auf Mona.

Schon eine Weile hatte der Füllfederhalter in Alberts Hand das Papier nicht mehr berührt. Stattdessen schwebte er durch die Nacht, wurde getragen von den sanften Klängen eines E-Moll-Septakkords mit None, gelangte schwerelos durch das offene Fenster, bestaunte die Wäsche, die da lag, näherte sich dann dem Muttermal, das immer grösser wurde und erreichte endlich das herausquellende Wasser, das herrlich heisse Wasser …

Ein Blick auf die Uhr machte ihm klar, dass er in Kürze zu seiner letzten abendlichen Schicht im Gasthof anzutreten hatte und in zweiunddreissig Stunden nicht mehr an Mona denken musste. Denken konnte.

13. 1939

Dm
C
B
F
Dm
C
Gm

Zum letzten Mal band sich Albert die Kochschürze, die ihm auch nach all den Jahren immer noch eigenartig fremd war, um die Hüfte. Mona war gerade damit beschäftigt, die halbvollen Gläser der Kartenspieler mit Vully nachzufüllen.

Da der Vorrat an Kartoffeln in der Küche demnächst auszugehen drohte, wollte Albert noch einmal für Nachschub sorgen. Über eine steile Steintreppe mit abgerundeten Stufen stieg er in den alten Keller des Gasthofs hinab.

Er knipste die Glühbirne an. Die Umrisse innerhalb des Gewölbes wurden spärlich erkennbar. Da wurde Albert von einer schmerzlichen Wehmut überfallen – wenn er am Gasthof je irgendetwas gemocht hatte, dann den dunklen Keller. Im Unterschied zur hektischen Gaststube oder zur Küche, die ständig nach Arbeit verlangte, strahlte der Keller angenehme Ruhe aus. Es herrschte Grabesstille.

Albert entschied, gerade heute nicht zu eilen, sondern seinen letzten Aufenthalt da unten zu geniessen. Er liess den modrigen Duft des Kellers in seine Nasenflügel strömen. Er mochte diesen Duft, aus dem er denjenigen von Korken und Zedernholz herausfiltern konnte. Beim Anblick der verschiedenen Flaschen, die in den Nischen ruhten, meinte er zudem gar, eine fruchtige Weinnote erriechen zu können. Dies entsprang aber wohl eher seiner lebhaften Einbildung.

Albert war alles andere als ein Weinkenner. Zwar wusste er mittlerweile Rotwein von Weisswein blindlings zu unterscheiden und auch die gängigsten Weinsorten wie Dôle oder Vully kannte er. Erlesenere Flaschen hatte er sich aber nie gegönnt. Doch trotz oder gerade wegen seiner Ahnungslosigkeit faszinierte ihn der edle Rebensaft. Er nahm sich für einmal Zeit, den Weinbestand etwas näher zu betrachten. Immerhin war der Gasthof für sein reichhaltiges Weinsortiment bekannt. Albert erinnerte sich an zwei städtische Herren, angeblich Professoren, die gelegentlich die Gaststube aufsuchten und sich stets voll des Lobes über die aufgetischten Flaschen äusserten.

Reihenweise Fendant, daneben elsässischer Pinot noir, Beaujolais und Tessiner Merlot. Das Weinlager präsentierte sich zwar recht ansehnlich, doch würden dies kaum die Flaschen sein, die den Weinkeller zu dem machten, was er war. Cabernet Sauvignon, Oeil de Perdrix und Rioja, auch diese Tropfen schienen Albert nicht des Meisters Stolz zu sein.

Er ging einige Schritte weiter und kam zu einem Regal, das durchwegs verschiedene Weinflaschen beherbergte. Sie wurden von einer dicken Staubhülle umgeben, sodass Albert die Etiketten im ohnehin schwach flackernden Licht kaum ausmachen konnte. Châteuneuf du Pape, Jahrgang 1948, konnte er entziffern, Château d'Yquem oder Château Lafite Rothschild. Nie hatte er von solchen Weinsorten gehört, doch die wohlklingenden Namen sprachen für sich.

Albert entstaubte eine weitere Flasche, indem er mit den Fingern vorsichtig über ihre Etikette fuhr. Barolo Mirafiore Piemonte, konnte er der Etikette entnehmen, und etwas weiter unten die vier Ziffern 1939.

Berührt starrte er auf die Flasche. Er hatte einen Wein seines Jahrgangs entdeckt, einen Tropfen, der ebenso viele Jahre zählte wie er.

Er staunte darüber, wie Flüssigkeiten aus entfernten Ländern jahrzehntelang aufbewahrt wurden, nur um sie dereinst innerhalb eines nichtigen Bruchteils ihrer Lagerzeit zu verputzen. Kurzerhand beschloss er, den Altersgenossen sein Ei-gen zu nennen. Er nahm die Flasche vom Regal und füllte den freien Platz, der dadurch entstand, bewusst nicht auf.

Bevor Albert wieder an die Arbeit ging, erinnerte er sich seiner eigentlichen Aufgabe, die er im Keller zu erledigen hatte. Im hinteren Teil des Raumes schnürte er einen vollen Sack auf, legte den 1939er vorsichtig zu den Kartoffeln und beförderte die Last mit Mühe auf seinen Buckel.

Als Albert bereits einen Fuss auf die erste Stufe gesetzt hatte, erblickte er neben der Treppe einige ihm wohlbekannte Flaschen.

Es war Absinth.

Die Vereinbarung, dass ihn die regelmässige Flasche für seine Überstunden entschädigte, war durchaus nicht gegen seinen Willen getroffen worden. Er war der grünen Fee längst verfallen und mochte nicht mehr auf ihre Gefälligkeiten verzichten. Der Meister hingegen lachte sich ob seiner Einsparungen wohl hinterrücks ins Fäustchen. Albert war sich sicher, dass der Meister die Flaschen einem gutmütigen Schnapsbrenner für wenig Geld abluchste.

Er stellte den prallen Kartoffelsack kurz ab und legte neben die Flasche Wein auch noch eine Flasche Absinth. Zwar lagerte in seinem Schrank noch ein ordentlicher Vorrat davon, doch wollte er sicherstellen, dass ihm morgen nicht plötzlich auf halbem Weg in den Tod der Schnaps ausgehen konnte. Sollte er dann doch nicht alles, was er besass, in sich schütten müssen, würde der im Keller fehlende Absinth zumindest noch den Meister ergrimmen. Albert grinste gezwungen.

Er ergriff eine weitere Flasche, entkorkte sie und setzte zu einem kräftigen Schluck an. Dann stellte er sie wieder zu den anderen, noch vollen, knipste das Licht aus und überliess all den Trank der Dunkelheit.

Die beiden ergatterten Flaschen legte Albert gleich auf den äusseren Sims des Küchenfensters. Er beabsichtigte, sie bei Antritt des Nachhauseweges von aussen abzuholen.

Die Gewissheit, nun die letzten Kartoffeln seines Lebens zu schälen, setzte ihm unerwarteterweise zu. Warum nur? Er war doch unbeschreiblich glücklich, morgen nicht mehr genötigt zu sein, in dieser stinkenden Bude aufzukreuzen, nie wieder «Junge» genannt zu werden, nicht mehr als Dummkopf vom Dienst amten zu müssen. Warum also drohte eine gefährliche Melancholie ihn einzunehmen? Doch nicht aus Freude zur Arbeit?

Mit aller Kraft stritt Albert die immer stärker werdende Zuneigung zu Mona ab, kämpfte vehement gegen jene Gedanken an, die für die Vollstreckung seines Todesurteils höchst hinderlich waren.

Es gelang ihm nicht.

Er musste sich eingestehen, dass ihm der Abschied von seiner Kellnerin schwer zu schaffen machte. Ganz gleich, wie gross oder klein die Entfernung zwischen Mona und ihm war – sie stand ihm von allen Menschen am nächsten. Allein dies machte sie zu etwas Besonderem.

Wie würde er sich heute von ihr verabschieden? Wie würden sie heute auseinandergehen? Für sie würde sein Gang nach Hause ein gewöhnlicher, alltäglicher Abschied sein, für ihn bedeutete er Abschied für immer. An manchen Abenden hatte er ihr mit leiser Stimme «gute Nacht» gesagt, und war sie gerade beschäftigt gewesen, hatte er sich jeweils wortlos aus dem Gasthof geschlichen. Zu grösseren Wortwechseln war es bei Feierabend nie gekommen. Stumm wollte er aber nicht von ihr gehen, obwohl es möglicherweise das beste gewesen wäre.

Die Zeit war unerbittlich dahingeschmolzen, er hatte mechanisch Kartoffeln geschält, geraffelt und gebraten, Mona servierte den Gästen bereits seine Freiburger Rösti. Ob sie denn auch wirklich geniessbar war, erfuhr er nicht mehr.

Die viel zu wenigen Sekunden, mit denen ihn Mona in der Küche noch beehrte, kostete Albert unersättlich aus. Sekunden, die sein Herz erwärmten, sich nach Ablauf aber sogleich zu Eis verwandelten. Es waren Sekunden, in denen Mona allmählich aus seinem Leben trat, sich verflüchtigte, sich auflöste. Er vermehrte die Sekunden, indem er ihre Worte erwiderte und sie zum Sprechen brachte. Verlängerte die Sekunden, indem er seine Bewegungen verlangsamte. Liess die Sekunden stillstehen, indem er träumte.

14. Gute Nacht

Gm / Fm
Gm / Dm

Albert hatte seine Pfannen heute um einiges gründlicher als üblich gewaschen. Die Küche und alle verwendeten Utensilien glänzten vor Sauberkeit. Er entledigte sich für immer seiner Schürze und stülpte sie zum letzten Mal über den rostigen Haken. Er hatte aufgehört zu träumen. Er hatte Feierabend.

Wie er dies in seiner nun endenden Kochlaufbahn unzählige Male getan hatte, blickte er auch jetzt wieder durch sein rundes Küchenfenster in die Gaststube. Karl thronte auf seinem Barhocker, in der linken Hand hielt er ein Glas Cynar, mit der rechten fuhr er geduldig über die Zeitungsspalten, um keine Zeile zu überspringen. Der Meister hob gerade den Stapel Karten ab, den Alberts Pflegevater gemischt hatte, und Mona wurde von den beiden Männern in den schmutzigen Überkleidern in die Ecke gerufen.

Der Zeitpunkt zum Gehen war jetzt alles andere als günstig. Mona würde es nicht einmal bemerken, wenn er sie nun verlassen würde. «Was darf ich servieren?», fragte Mona, und Albert beobachtete, wie sie sich anschliessend zur Zapfsäule hinbewegte, zwei Stangen auffüllte und den beiden Durstigen den Gerstensaft auftischte. Dann kehrte sie hinter die Bar zurück, die sich gleich neben der Küchentür befand. Sie begann, Kaffeetassen zu spülen, an deren Innenseiten sich die eingetrockneten Rückstände bereits verkrustet hatten.

Albert konnte sich nicht entschliessen, Mona auf ewig zu verlassen.

Nun wäre der passende Moment gekommen, um ihr lebwohl zu sagen, um sich die letzten gemeinsamen Sekunden mit ihr zu erbeuten.

Er blieb noch.

Schaute ihr lieber zu, schaute ihr zu, wie sie die Tassen ins Wasser tauchte, wie sie diese mit einem Schwamm abwusch. Hörte das Plätschern von Wasser und das Glitschen von Seife. Schaute ihr zu, wie sie Gläser ins Wasser tauchte und diese abwusch, das Plätschern von Wasser und das Glitschen von Seife …

Plötzlich zeichneten Alberts Augen auf, dass Mona sich ihnen rasant näherte.

«Geht es dir nicht gut?», fragte sie und sah ihn durch das Türfenster an. Die Gesichter der beiden wurden nur noch durch die dünne Glasscheibe getrennt.

«Es – geht mir gut», stammelte Albert, dem es eben ein wenig schwindlig geworden war.

«Willst du nicht nach Hause gehen?»

Es entstand eine entsetzlich lange Pause.

«Doch», sagte Albert.

Mona öffnete die Küchentür, so dass sie sich nun ganz gegenüberstanden. «Der Sturz vom Baum scheint dir nicht gut getan zu haben, nicht wahr?», fragte sie mit etwas besorgtem Blick.

«Es geht schon. Danke für die … liebe Pflege, Mona», brachte Albert über die Lippen.

«Gern geschehen. Hör mal, wir sollten mal ein Glas zusammen trinken!»

«– Ja, das sollten wir eigentlich tun.»

«Wir finden sicher bald Zeit dafür. Geniess den freien Tag morgen.» Albert spürte, dass sich das Gespräch und somit das atemberaubende Kapitel Mona zu Ende neigte. Fieberhaft suchte er nach einem Thema, das er hätte ansprechen können, um dem Kapitel noch eine Seite, ein Satz, ein paar Buchstaben hinzuzufügen.

«Gute Nacht, Albert», waren schliesslich die Worte, die ihn ins Elend stürzten.

«Auf Wiedersehen, Mona», konnte Albert noch mit erstickter Stimme von sich geben. Dann brach er mit langsamen Schritten auf. Mona schaute ihm noch kurz nach.

«Ach, Albert! Die Sandalen stehen dir gut!» Albert drehte sich noch einmal um und sah, wie Mona lächelte.

15. Die Melodie des Lebens

Em9

A / Em / Bm / A
A / Em / Bm / A / G
Em / Bm / Em / Bm
G / A / E / Dsus2
Dm

Eine Träne tropfte in das halbleere Glas und vermischte sich mit dem puren Absinth. Albert führte das Glas an seine Lippen und trank den restlichen Inhalt samt Träne leer.

Der von ihm gewollte Tod, der in sechsundzwanzig Stunden eintreffen sollte, war gar nicht mehr präsent. Sein Tod hatte die Allgegenwart in seinem Kopf verloren, war hinter den Abschied von Mona zurückgetreten. Aber es konnte ja nicht bloss von einem Abschied die Rede sein. Für ihn war Mona nun eigentlich gestorben, sie war tot. Hätte er denn nicht alles dafür gegeben, um dies zu verhindern? Sein Leben, seinen Tod?

Es war drückend warm. Der prächtige Sommerabend wirkte erfunden, verlogen. Albert brauchte nun Hilfe, die Hilfe seiner beiden besten Freunde. Die Flasche Schnaps hatte sich bereits zu ihm gesellt, nun setzte sich auch die Gitarre auf seinen Schoss, um ihm Trost zu spenden. Zumindest waren seine Freunde da, wenn er sie brauchte.

Im Moment war er allerdings nicht im Stande, die Gitarre zum Spielen zu benützen. Er drehte die Gitarre so, dass ihr Hals auf den sichtbar werdenden Mond zielte, legte seine Arme um ihren Körper und drückte sie fest an sich. Er schloss die Augen und verharrte einige Minuten in dieser innigen Haltung.

Er wusste, dass er sich mit dieser Geste, zu der es ihn in jenen qualvollen Momenten hinriss, der Lächerlichkeit preisgab. Gegenwärtig war er jedoch für Nähe jeglicher Art dankbar.

Die tröstende Umarmung tat ihm gut. Allmählich stieg ihm wieder ins Bewusstsein, dass er morgen verschwinden würde, und mit ihm auch die Trauer und der Schmerz. Es hatte keinen Sinn, seine letzten Stunden dem Leid zu widmen, das morgen vorüber sein würde.

Das neuerliche Vorausblicken auf den Tod erleichterte Albert. Er nahm sich nun vor, die ihm verbleibende Zeit noch erträglich, oder soweit möglich gar angenehm zu gestalten. Er beschloss, noch heute mit seiner Gitarre das nahe Löhlimoos zu besuchen und dort ein paar Hymnen an die Nacht anzustimmen. Morgen würde er ausschlafen, am Nachmittag nach Freiburg fahren, vielleicht eine Weile durch die Unterstadt spazieren und sich dort in einem schmucken Restaurant eine ausgiebige Henkersmahlzeit gönnen. Dann konnte er abends in Würde sterben.

Er schenkte sich noch einen Schluck ein, und eben wollte er sich über den nunmehr komfortablen Besitz von Absinth zufrieden schätzen, als er das Ärgernis bemerkte. Die Flasche Absinth, der er eindeutig die geringere Bedeutung zumass, und der 1939er Barolo mussten noch immer auf dem Fenstersims des Gasthofs stehen.

Albert vertröstete sich auf später. Er konnte nach seinem Ausflug ins Löhlimoos noch kurz beim Gasthof vorbeigehen, um die Flaschen abzuholen. Er machte sich bereit.

Bis auf seine eigenen Schritte war kein Geräusch zu vernehmen. Er trug seine Gitarre unter dem Arm, da sie über kein Band verfügte, das er über seine Schulter hätte spannen können. Über abgelegene Karrwege würde er in einer Viertelstunde das Löhlimoos erreichen.

Schon oft hatte er sich des Nachts in jenes Moos begeben, da sich zu dieser Zeit mit Sicherheit keine Menschenseele darin aufhielt. Die Leute fürchteten sich zu später Stunde im Moos, niemand sonst kam auf die kühne Idee, dieses bei Dunkelheit aufzusuchen. Unangenehme Gesellschaft hatte Albert also noch nie angetroffen. Völlige Einsamkeit herrschte innerhalb des sumpfigen Gebiets aber keineswegs. Das Quaken der Wasserfrösche, dazu das Gurgeln der Erdkröten oder das Zirpen der Grillen ertönte gerade nachts am ausgeprägtesten. Gelegentlich knackten zudem Äste, die unter dem Gewicht von Wildschweinen zerbrachen.

Albert hatte den Feldweg mittlerweile verlassen, bog quer über die bereits taunasse Wiese ab und gelangte schliesslich an die Stelle, an der sich ein schmaler Pfad durch das Dickicht zu schlängeln begann. Es brauchte immer wieder eine ordentliche Portion Mut, sich in das scheinbare Nichts zu stürzen. Durch das verwachsene Gesträuch fand selbst das Mondlicht keinen Eingang, es war finster wie in einem Grab. Einen Mann, der nicht einmal den Tod fürchtete, mussten derartige Umstände aber kalt lassen.

Endlich erreichte er die Lichtung, den bei Nacht menschenfernsten Fleck des ganzen Dorfes.

Heute wirkte der Ort wie ausgestorben. Der Mondschein glänzte auf der Oberfläche des kleinen, lieblichen Sees, der von einem dichten Gehölzgürtel umgeben war. Es kam Albert vor, als würde sich das merkwürdig ruhig liegende Gewässer in der klaren Sommernacht nicht zu bewegen wagen, als würden sich die Nachttiere heute in ihren Gemächern verstecken.

Er setzte sich auf einen Baumstumpf am Ufer, ergriff einen E-Moll-Akkord und zupfte langsam jede Saite nacheinander an. Da kitzelte ihn etwas auf seinem rechten Handrücken – doch noch ein Lebenszeichen. Eine Spinne, der die Schwingungen der Saiten wohl nicht gut bekamen, war aus dem Schallloch der Gitarre gekrabbelt. Albert legte seine Hand auf die moosbewachsene Erde, um die Spinne davoneilen zu lassen. Glücklicherweise war er sich an schlagartig auftauchende Spinnen gewöhnt.

Als er nun so dasass, das romantische Gewässer überblickte und bedächtig seinen eigenen Tönen lauschte, kam er auf die Idee, hier und jetzt ein Lied für Mona zu komponieren. Er wollte zwar nicht in seinen Wunden stochern, doch schien ihm, dass er die leidvollsten Augenblicke überstanden hatte. Der unerträgliche Schmerz war in der Erwartung des baldigen Todes erträglich geworden. Er würde Mona eine Melodie widmen, die so noch nie und nirgends erklungen war.

Alle guten Lieder beginnen mit einem Moll-Akkord. Dies zumindest war Alberts Meinung, und sie war bis dahin durch nichts zu erschüttern gewesen. Alle seine Lieder hatte er mit Moll-Akkorden begonnen, immer und immer wieder nach der gleichen Masche, ohne daran die geringsten Zweifel zu hegen. Dies allerdings, das musste er zugeben, mit eher mässigem Erfolg. Einige seiner bisher komponierten Lieder waren durchschnittlich, andere vermochten dieses Niveau nicht zu erreichen.

Albert prüfte einige Akkordfolgen, die ihn jedoch nicht zufrieden stellten. Sie waren ihm stets zu düster. Seine jetzige Trauer durfte auf seine grossen Gefühle für Mona keinen Schatten werfen.

Möglicherweise befand sich Mona gerade auf dem Nachhauseweg, überlegte sich Albert. Seine Augen ruhten auf dem See, in dem sich der Mond spiegelte.

Wiederum umspielten Albert die Klänge eines E-Moll-Septakkords mit None, lullten ihn ein und schickten ihn auf eine wunderliche Reise. Eine Reise ins akustische Paradies.

Sorglos flog Albert durch einen klaren, warmen A-Dur-Akkord. Atmete den süssen Duft ein, der von ihm ausging. Betastete seine Geschmeidigkeit. Vermischte sich mit seiner Harmonie – da nahm die Geborgenheit plötzlich ein Ende. Albert fand sich im Nebel eines E-Moll-Akkords wieder. Das Eindringen in diesen kam ihm unwirklich vor, so, als würde er durch ein Fenster in die Vergangenheit schweben. Seine Bewegungen wurden schwerfälliger, doch schien ihm eine unbändige Kraft unter die Arme zu greifen, die ihn trotz der schattenhaften Umgebung zuversichtlich stimmte. Sodann wurde er von einem Sog erfasst, einem wunderbaren und schmerzhaften zugleich – er tauchte ein in das Reich eines B-Moll-Akkords, das von Wehmut beherrscht wurde. Albert wurde hin- und hergerissen, mit verwegener Geschwindigkeit vom Himmel in die Hölle geworfen und wieder zurück, er trauerte und vergoss Freudentränen, war erfüllt von Leid und Hoffnung, verstarb und wurde geboren.

Endlich konnte er dem Sog entkommen, bestieg eine Anhöhe und erblickte aus der Ferne die unendlichen Farben. Die Farben verschiedener Dur-Akkorde schimmerten in unerhörter Pracht, flossen ineinander, fügten sich zusammen zu einem von allen Übeln erlösten Ort.

Albert rang nach Luft. Noch sass er eine Weile da, bewegungslos, fassungslos.

Er hatte sie.

Es war eine Melodie, die seiner bescheidenen Meinung nach sein gesamtes, über Jahre hinweg gereiftes musikalisches Streben verkümmern liess, ja alle seine bisher ausgedachten Melodien auslöschte, da sie nicht mehr dazu taugten, jemals wieder gespielt zu werden.

Für Sekunden – vielleicht waren es auch Jahre – war Albert aus seiner Versagerhaut geschlüpft, hatte gar nicht mehr gespielt, hatte sich nur noch zugehört, hatte sich nicht einmal geschämt, zu singen.

Die Begeisterung ob seinem doch vorhandenen Talent steigerte sich nun unaufhaltsam. Er, der zu nichts fähige Albert Leblanc – aufgewachsen ohne Eltern, ohne Freunde und Gefährten – hatte auf seiner klapprigen, auch schon bereits totgesagten, mit rostigen Saiten bestückten Gitarre ein Meisterwerk erschaffen. Und es gehörte allein ihm, und er schenkte es allein Mona.

Gerührt betrachtete er die Gitarre, die er in seinen Armen hielt. Es war eine spanische Flamencogitarre, die allerdings laut einem etwas bekleckerten Aufkleber in Japan hergestellt worden war. Ihr Resonanzkörper war mit einigen Beulen versehen, kreuzweise angebrachte Klebestreifen deckten gar ein kleines Loch zu. Zusätzlich wurde die Holzplatte, die als Rückseite des Körpers fungierte, von einem feinen Spalt geteilt, der Albert stets daran mahnte, behutsam mit dem Instrument umzugehen. Und statt mit Nylon-, wie es sich für ein Exemplar ihrer Art gehört hätte, war die Gitarre mit Stahlsaiten bespannt. Als Albert noch ein blutiger Anfänger war, hatten sich die Saiten jeweils tief in seine Finger eingeschnitten. Mittlerweile verfügten seine Fingerkuppen aber über genügend Hornhaut, um schmerzlos über die Saiten zu gleiten. Nur beim sechsten Bund der tiefen Basssaite musste er vorsichtig sein. Da hatte sich nämlich die Umwicklung des Stahldrahts gelöst und ragte nun scharf wie eine Nadelspitze aus der Saite. Albert hatte sich von Beginn weg daran gewöhnt, die Saite an jener Stelle nicht zu benützen.

Ohne seine Gitarre hätte er sein Leben wohl schon früher beendet, dachte sich Albert. Wie oft sie ihn ermutigt, aufgebaut, gestärkt hatte! Allerdings hatte sie früher auch immer wieder Anlass zu Streit gegeben. Seine Pflegeeltern hatten nämlich das Geklimper nicht ausstehen können, und hätte sich Albert nicht zur Wehr gesetzt, die Gitarre wäre längst zum Einheizen des Kaminofens verwendet worden.

Die Grundlagen des Gitarrenspiels hatte sich Albert mit einer erstaunlichen Leichtigkeit selbst beigebracht. Er war damals, kurz nach dem Fund der Gitarre, in der Schulbibliothek auf ein kleines vergilbtes Büchlein gestossen, das die Griffbilder der wichtigsten Gitarrenakkorde enthielt. Es hatte ihm wenig Mühe und viel Freude bereitet, sich diese anzueignen, und kurz darauf war er bereits im Stande gewesen, Lieder aus dem Radio nachzuspielen. Bald hatte er eifrig begonnen, eigene Melodien zu kreieren und eine Zeitlang hatte er fest daran geglaubt, dereinst als berühmter Gitarrenspieler gefeiert und verehrt zu werden. Es hatte sich bei ihm die kurzlebige Überzeugung eingestellt, dass ihm doch eine einzigartige Fähigkeit verliehen worden war. Aber dann zogen die Jahre vorbei, die

Erwartungen wurden grösser, die Fortschritte kleiner, ausserordentliche Kompositionen blieben aus. Und heute nun, als er schon mit einem Bein im Grabe stand, gelang ihm der nicht mehr erwartete musikalische Geniestreich.

Er hatte ein eigentlich nicht zu realisierendes Unterfangen auf eindrückliche Weise fertiggebracht: Er hatte die Empfindungen, die Mona in ihm geweckt hatte, zu Musik verwandelt. In seinem Freudentaumel beging er beinahe den Frevel, in seinem Lied die noch makellosere Schönheit als in Mona zu sehen.

Albert glaubte, seinen Seelenfrieden gefunden zu haben. Wenn er seine Zuneigung zu Mona schon nicht ausleben konnte, hatte er es zumindest vollbracht, sie in einem Lied kundzutun.

Die Sache hatte allerdings einen Haken. Morgen würde er sterben, und mit ihm auch die verehrende Melodie. Er, Albert, war es nicht wert, der Welt erhalten zu bleiben. Sein Lied allerdings war es mit Sicherheit. Der Gedanke, dass dieses für immer verloren gehen würde, war ihm unangenehm.

Er musste es irgendwie verewigen. Auf irgend eine Weise liess sich Musik ja aufnehmen, so, wie es auf seinen Schallplatten auch gemacht worden war, doch wusste er darüber nichts Genaueres. Hingegen war ihm bekannt, dass grosse Komponisten ihre Stücke jeweils zu Papier brachten. Noten konnte er aber weder lesen noch schreiben. Albert hoffte, die Angelegenheit morgen, nach einem langen und verstandschärfenden Schlaf, lösen zu können.

Er verliess das Moos, holte die beiden Flaschen vom Fenstersims des Gasthofs ab und begab sich nach Hause. Auf dem ganzen Heimweg schwirrte ihm die unbeschreibliche Melodie durch den Kopf – die Melodie seines Lebens.

16. Der Traum

Am / E
Am / E

A / Em / Bm / A
A / Em / Bm / A

B7

In seiner letzten Nacht hatte Albert einen Traum. Er träumte von seiner eigenen Beerdigung. Er lag im Sarg, der im Vorderteil der Kirche aufgebahrt war, die Hände ineinander gelegt auf seinem Bauch. Der Sarg war offen, und – dies war das Merkwürdige und zugleich Unheimliche an seinem Traum – Albert, eigentlich tot, war bei Bewusstsein und konnte den Gottesdienst vom Sarg aus mitverfolgen.

Die Kirche war gut besetzt, sehr gut sogar, soweit er dies überblicken konnte. In der ersten Reihe zu seiner Linken sassen seine leiblichen Eltern und sein Bruder Gustav. Sie weinten. In der rechten Frontreihe entdeckte er Mona. Auch sie weinte. Dahinter sassen erstaunlich viele Leute, deren Gesichter er allerdings nicht erkennen konnte. Hie und da vernahm Albert aber auch aus den entfernteren Teilen des Kirchenschiffs ein Schluchzen.

Plötzlich ertönte das Orgelspiel. Aus den Orgelpfeifen drang ein wunderbarer Klang. Es war die Melodie, die er am Tag vor seinem Ableben ersonnen hatte. Die unsterbliche Melodie. Der langhaarige, praktisch nackte Mann, der an einem Kreuz hing, begann seinen Kopf im Takt zu bewegen, doch wurde dies von niemandem bemerkt.

Dann packten zwei dunkel gekleidete Totengräber den Sargdeckel und legten ihn auf den Sarg, in dem der entsetzte Albert lag. Er versuchte, dies mit den Beinen zu verhindern, versuchte zu schreien – vergeblich. Sein Körper verharrte in Starre, zu Bewegungen unfähig. Sein Mund liess sich nicht öffnen. Der Deckel schloss sich, seine Leiche wurde der vollkommenen Finsternis, der absoluten Stille überlassen.

Da erwachte Albert, seine Hände waren ineinander gelegt auf seinem Bauch. Mit rasendem Puls schnellte er in die Höhe. Um den Traum endgültig als Traum zu entlarven, versuchte er, einen leisen Ton von sich zu geben. Es gelang, und Albert fühlte sich wie ein Idiot. Er liess sich wieder auf die Matratze fallen und dachte eine Weile nach.

Der Traum hatte ihn zutiefst beunruhigt. War etwa nach dem Tod doch nicht alles aus und vorbei? Würde das Elend gar noch grösser werden? Albert hatte sich mit Vorstellungen dieser Art nie auseinandergesetzt.

Ja, eingeschüchtert hatte ihn der Traum, zugleich war er von ihm auch beeindruckt. Seine Familie, an die er sich gar nicht zu erinnern vermochte, war aufgetaucht. Der Traum hatte sie wirklicher erscheinen lassen, als seine Gedanken es je hatten tun können. Ob die Gestalten aus dem Traum seinem Vater, seiner Mutter, Gustav etwa ähnelten?

An seiner Beerdigung würden sie leider mit Bestimmtheit nicht anwesend sein. Sie konnten ja nicht. Wer aber würde da sein? Gab es denn neben dem Pfarrer und dem Totengräber tatsächlich welche, die kommen würden? Albert musste sich eingestehen, dass ihn die Antworten auf seine etwas makabren Fragen ungemein interessierten. In diesem Augenblick erst wurde ihm klar, dass er bei seiner Beerdigung zum ersten Mal im Mittelpunkt eines Geschehens stehen würde. Leute, auch wenn es nicht viele sein mochten, würden seinetwegen in die Kirche gehen und zum Gedenken seiner eine Stunde ihres Lebens opfern. Er rechnete sich das Datum seiner Beerdigung aus. Womöglich fand sie am Samstag statt. Allenfalls am Montag. Von den Gedanken zu seiner Abdankungsfeier konnte er sich nur schwer trennen.

Als er neben dem Bett die Gitarre stehen sah, stutzte er einen Moment, dann packte ihn das Entsetzen.

Schleunigst schnappte er sich das Instrument, setzte sich und spielte. Zumindest die Akkorde hatte er noch. Das nützte ihm allerdings wenig. Die Akkorde waren ja nur das blanke Gerippe, die Knochen, denen Fleisch und Blut fehlte. Es war das Lied mitsamt seiner einzigartigen Melodie, mit all seinen Feinheiten, das ihn gestern Abend derart berauscht hatte. Das Lied, dessen plötzliches Verschwinden ihm gestern noch unvorstellbar schien – es war weg! Gestorben. Albert war bestürzt.

Immer wieder schlug Albert die Akkorde an, zupfte die Saiten in verschiedensten Reihenfolgen und Geschwindigkeiten, erdachte sich abermals darüber passende Melodien aus. Erfolglos.

Ob die Melodie doch nicht so unwiderstehlich war, wie er im Löhlimoos noch geglaubt hatte? Er war gestern doch in eine recht eigenartige Verfassung geraten – hatte ihm diese etwa einen Streich gespielt? Er konnte es nicht ausschliessen.

Dennoch verbrachte er den restlichen Morgen mit unzähligen Versuchen, das verlorene Lied wieder zurückzuergattern. Und mochten seine Bemühungen nur dazu dienen, das Lied noch einmal in seinem Leben zu hören. Er wollte es wieder haben. Er wollte in dessen Besitz sterben.

17. Der Brief

Am / Em / F / G
Am / Em / F / G

Das heisse Wasser strömte über seinen Körper, floss über die geschlossenen Augenlider, plätscherte über die geöffneten Lippen, passierte die unbehaarte Brust und durchnässte die weisse Unterhose – bis es jäh erkaltete.

Die nackte Mona. Albert kratzte sich heftig am Hinterkopf. In einem Anflug von Übermut hatte er sein Geheimnis gestern wie einen Pokal in die Höhe gestemmt, hatte sich bereits für einen Frauenheld gehalten. Die Tatsache, dass sich Mona für einen Augenblick nur ihm offenbart hatte – nein, der naive Glaube daran – hatte ihn noch vor wenigen Stunden entzückt. Wie leicht ihn solch entrückte Gedanken verführt hatten!

Nun sah er plötzlich ein, dass er nie einen gemeinsamen Moment mit Mona erlebt hatte. Sie hatte sich ihm nicht offenbart, sondern lediglich, im Glauben allein zu sein, geduscht. Vor den Augen eines scheusslichen Spanners. Seine Aktion im Unterdorf war nur von ihm wahrgenommen worden, kein Mensch nahm daran Anteil, also hatte sie auch keinen Wert.

Sein Gesicht verdüsterte sich weiter, als er den angefangenen Abschiedsbrief noch einmal durchlas.

Liebe Mona,

du bist die einzige Person auf Erden, vor der ich mich verabschieden möchte.
Du hast mich von Beginn weg ernst genommen, hast dich nie an den Gemeinheiten beteiligt.
Du hast mir die schönsten Augenblicke meines Lebens beschert.
Dafür danke ich dir von Herzen.

Die bisher zu Papier gebrachten Worte waren nichts als Zeugnis seines jämmerlichen und unerfüllten Lebens, konstatierte er verbittert. Wie erniedrigend es war, sich bei einer Person für ausgebliebene Gemeinheiten zu bedanken. Wie trostlos, im Nachstellen einer Frau die höchste Erfüllung gefunden zu haben.

Sein Erlebnis im Garten von Mona verblasste weiter, wenn er bedachte, was ein glückliches Menschenleben noch alles hergegeben hätte. Was hatte er nicht alles versäumt! War er denn nicht auch ein gewöhnlicher Mann, der Anspruch darauf gehabt hätte, eine Frau nicht nur anzuschauen? Sie gelegentlich zu einem Kalbsfilet an Morchelsauce einzuladen? Mit ihr glücklich zu sein? Die Begeisterung über sein Abenteuer erlosch und wich einer immer grösser werdenden Sehnsucht.

Mona war verheiratet.

Sie würde sich nicht mehr auf andere Liebschaften einlassen. Schon gar nicht auf einen zehn Jahre jüngeren Verlierer. Einen Lüstling.

Albert vollendete den Abschiedsbrief.

> *Wenn du diese Worte liest, bin ich schon nicht mehr da. Das Leben hat es nicht gut gemeint mit mir, darum gehe ich.*
> *Ich wünsche dir alles Liebe und hoffe, dass du ein erfülltes Leben verbringst.*
> *Vielleicht könntest du von Zeit zu Zeit eine Rose auf mein Grab legen? Das wäre schön.*
>
> *Lebwohl, Mona*
>
> *Dein Koch*
> *Albert Leblanc*

Eine Viertelstunde später stand er vor dem Postschalter.

Zu seinem Missfallen kam er nicht umhin, mit dem Postbeamten in Kontakt zu treten, denn selbstverständlich besass Albert keine Briefmarken.

«Einen schönen guten Tag, junger Mann!» Der Postbeamte näherte sich ihm langsam. Ein Lächeln lag auf seinen Lippen.

«Guten Tag», grüsste Albert. Er hatte vor, das ihm unangenehme Zusammentreffen schleunigst hinter sich zu bringen.

«Das sieht mir aber übel aus.» Der Postbeamte deutete mit einer entwürdigenden Kopfbewegung auf Alberts Gesicht.

«Beim Apfelpflücken», antwortete Albert rasch. Ihm war gar nicht mehr bewusst gewesen, mit welch entstelltem Gesicht er sich im Dorf zeigte.

Der Postbeamte versuchte nicht einmal, sein Lachen zu unterdrücken. «Was kann ich für dich tun?», fragte er dann seinen nervösen Kunden.

«Ich möchte gerne diesen Brief frankieren.» Albert legte das Couvert auf die Theke und wurde von Scham ergriffen. Er hatte sich das Aufgeben des Briefes etwas diskreter vorgestellt.

«Gerne.» Der Postbeamte musterte Alberts Brief.

«Mona Gutmann», sagte er plötzlich mit lauter Stimme, so dass Albert zusammenzuckte. «Eine gute Frau …», meinte er und nickte Albert dabei anerkennend zu.

In Albert kam Wut auf. Wut auf die wenig vertrauliche Art des bald in Rente gehenden Mannes. Noch mehr ärgerte ihn aber die Bemerkung zu Mona. «Das ist sie», entgegnete er knapp, als wollte er Mona wieder an sich reissen.

Ein blondes, sommerlich gekleidetes Mädchen – es musste um die zwanzig Jahre zählen – betrat die Post und wartete hinter Albert, wodurch sich seine Anspannung nicht verringerte. Er kannte das Mädchen, das samstagabends oft in der Gaststube ein Wermut bestellte.

Wiederum studierte der Postbeamte stirnrunzelnd Alberts Antlitz.

«Sag mal, täusche ich mich, oder bist du der Koch des Gasthofs?»

Was war nur in diesen taktlosen Menschen gefahren? «Das bin ich», antwortete Albert knapp.

«Und du nimmst dir die Mühe, zur Post zu kommen und der Kellnerin des Gasthofs einen Brief zu schicken?» Es waren Worte, die der Beamte nicht aussprach, doch Albert konnte sie seinem Blick entnehmen. Er kratzte sich am Hinterkopf.

«Möchtest du gleich einen ganzen Bogen Briefmarken kaufen? Es gibt da eine neue Serie mit Steinbockmotiven, die ist ganz hübsch. Und Briefmarken kann man ja immer gebrauchen.»

«Nein, ich möchte nur eine Briefmarke.» Albert hörte, wie das Mädchen hinter ihm ungeduldig von einer Ecke in die andere ging.

«Schau mal, die sind wirklich ganz hübsch, die sind auch allerorts …»

«Dann geben Sie mir halt so einen Bogen», zischte Albert verzweifelt. Im Grunde hätte er sein ganzes Vermögen für Briefmarken ausgeben können, oder für Bleistiftspitzer oder Toilettenbürsten. Morgen würde er Geld genauso wenig mehr brauchen wie alles andere, es machte keinen Unterschied.

«Vielen Dank, junger Mann, ich wünsche einen schönen Tag.» Der Postbeamte war sichtlich zufrieden.

«Adieu.»

Beim Hinausgehen lächelte das Mädchen Albert mitleidig zu.

Gleich neben der Post befand sich die Bank, an der Albert nun auf seinem Rückweg vorbeikam. Spontan trat er ein.

Er steuerte auf den Schalter zu, hinter dem eine Frau mit etwas hochgeratener Bienenstockfrisur auf Kundschaft wartete.

«Guten Tag!»

«Guten Tag.»

«Was kann ich für Sie tun?» Die Frau mittleren Alters war

ihm gleich um einiges sympathischer als der unverschämte Postangestellte.

«Ich möchte gerne meinen Kontostand wissen.»

Die nette Frau verschwand und liess Albert kurz warten. Er drehte sich um und hoffte, dass er diesmal seine Geschäfte ohne hinter ihm wartende Kunden erledigen konnte.

«Auf ihrem Konto befinden sich momentan 3187 Franken und 55 Rappen», teilte ihm die Frau Augenblicke später mit.

Donnerwetter! Der Betrag überstieg Alberts Erwartungen bei weitem.

«Gut. Dann geben Sie mir doch die 3187 Franken.»

Die Frau hinter der Glasscheibe versuchte, ihre Überraschung für sich zu behalten, was ihr beinahe gelang.

«Und die 55 Rappen, möchten Sie die auch abheben?»

Albert verliess die Bank mit 3187 Franken und 55 Rappen im Hosensack. Natürlich beabsichtigte er nicht, seine Ersparnisse nun noch zu verjubeln. Wofür auch? Doch immerhin hatte er eben verhindert, dass sein Vermögen nach seinem Tod in falsche Hände geraten würde. Womöglich hätte sich dann etwa ein eigennütziger Beamter, wie etwa der Postangestellte einer war, daran erfreut. Oder sein Stiefvater, Gipfel der Unverschämtheit, hätte letzten Endes noch das Erbe beansprucht. Albert war erleichtert.

Heute Abend allerdings, in der Unterstadt, da würde er es sich für einmal richtig gut gehen lassen. Vorspeisen, vielleicht eine scharfe, delikate Suppe, oder ein exotisches Teigwarengericht, dazu ein kräftiger, harmonischer Wein, danach Kaffee, Schnaps, vielleicht noch ein Erdbeereis … Er begann sich darauf zu freuen.

So viel Geld würde er aber auch da beim besten Willen nicht ausgeben können. Vielleicht konnte er einem Obdachlosen einen unvergesslichen Tag bereiten. Der Einfall vergnügte ihn.

Ein Hungergefühl machte sich nun bei Albert bemerkbar, er hatte heute noch nichts gegessen. Ohnehin kam er auf seinem Weg nach Hause noch an einem Laden vorbei. Auf dem

Land liessen sich die wichtigen Geschäfte alle in einem ziemlich kleinen Kern erledigen.

An seinen freien Tagen hatte Albert jeweils keine Lust, sich warme Speisen zuzubereiten. Dies war auch heute nicht anders. Er liess sich im Laden ein Pfund Schwarzbrot reichen und schnappte sich ein Paar Landjäger. Dies musste ihm als Mittagsimbiss genügen. Mit allzu vollem Magen wollte er am Abend nicht an sein Abschiedsmahl herangehen. Da Albert heute nicht knauserig sein musste, erlaubte er sich aber, ein Säcklein Lakritzstangen zu kaufen. Er suchte das Süssigkeitenregal auf, wo er mit einer vornehm gekleideten Dame zusammenstiess, die ihre besten Jahre sichtlich hinter sich gelassen hatte. Die ihm bekannten, mit zu viel Wimperntusche umrahmten Augen sahen ihm gereizt entgegen.

Er bezahlte seine Sachen und schämte sich beinahe, von seinem Vermögen im Hosensack nur einen Franken und dreissig Rappen locker zu machen.

Beim Verlassen des Ladens begegnete Albert ein glattrasierter und gepflegter Mann, seinerseits Mitglied der örtlichen Feuerwehr. Sie sahen sich kurz an.

«Hallo.»

«Hallo.»

Albert meinte, eine gewisse Verlegenheit im Gesicht des Grüssenden auszumachen.

18. Sommerwein

Em9

A / Em / Bm / A
A / Em / Bm / A / G
Em / Bm / Em / Bm
G / A / E / Dsus2

G / Am

Es war schwül. Albert sass auf seiner Holzbank und schob sich abwechslungsweise ein Stück Brot und einen Happen Landjäger in den Mund.

Was er vor vier Tagen an gleicher Stelle beschlossen hatte, galt es heute bereits zu verwirklichen. Noch am Sonntag schien ihm seine Hinrichtung weit weg, beinahe eine Utopie, ein Wunschdenken zu sein. Nun trennten ihn nur noch gute zwölf Stunden davon, wenn denn alles nach Plan laufen würde. Und sein Plan überzeugte.

Vielleicht kam ihm die Zeit seit seinem Beschluss so kurz vor, weil sich in den letzten Tagen doch einiges ereignet hatte. Albert hatte zum ersten Mal in seinem Leben eine Frau ohne Kleider gesehen, war dabei beinahe von einem Hund zerrissen worden, war von einem Baum gefallen, hatte mit Mona kokettiert und ihr einen Brief geschrieben, ein hinreissendes Lied komponiert und wieder verloren, Wein, Absinth und Tabletten gestohlen und schliesslich sein ganzes Bankkonto geplündert. Sie waren abenteuerlich, die letzten Tage, das war nicht zu bestreiten. Allerdings waren sie ja gerade deshalb abenteuerlich, weil Alberts Ende nahte, und darum sollten es auch die letzen bleiben.

Die Gitarre mochte er nicht mehr zur Hand nehmen, um seinem verlorenen Lied nachzujagen. Zu ernüchternd war es, wenn statt der gesuchten himmlischen Melodie bloss wieder eine irdische erklang. So wollte er seinen letzten Tag nicht verbringen.

Tatenlos blickte Albert über die Felder, die sich vor ihm erstreckten. Bald war es an der Zeit, die letzte kalte Dusche über sich ergehen zu lassen und nach Freiburg aufzubrechen.

Da geschah etwas äusserst Seltenes. Albert konnte von seiner Holzbank aus am Horizont eine Gestalt erkennen. Sie ging auf dem Weg, der zu seinem Haus führte und bewegte sich langsam auf ihn zu.

Die Annäherung war Albert nicht geheuer. Hatte er seinen Abschiedsbrief etwa zu früh zur Post gebracht? Ob sich der Postbeamte nicht an das Briefgeheimnis gehalten hatte? Zuzutrauen wäre es ihm gewesen, diesem Schelm, aber er durfte doch nicht einfach … Würde man ihn nun etwa holen und in ein Irrenhaus einsperren? Albert zog für einen kurzen Moment in Betracht, davonzurennen, in den Wald zu flüchten, sich irgendwo zu verstecken, doch erschien ihm dies mit jedem Schritt, den die Gestalt machte, sinnloser.

Plötzlich wusste er, wem der unverkennbare Gang und die zarten Umrisse gehörten.

Panik ergriff ihn. Er stand auf. Ein Brief konnte doch nicht am gleichen Tag, an dem er aufgegeben worden war, schon empfangen werden, das war doch ausgeschlossen! Er versuchte, ruhig Blut zu bewahren, nahm sich vor, die Geschichte mit dem Abschiedsbrief falls nötig als Versehen, als riesiges Missverständnis abzutun, und im nächsten Augenblick sah er wieder ein, wie unglaubwürdig, ja lächerlich derartige Ausreden klingen würden.

Was auch immer Mona dazu veranlasst hatte, bei ihm aufzukreuzen, er konnte sie doch nicht bei sich in seinem schäbigen Haus empfangen! Konnte ihr nichts anbieten, hatte nur Hahnenwasser und Schnaps, hatte nicht einmal zwei Gläser! Und seine mit Spinnweben verzierte Wohnstube konnte er doch keiner Frau zumuten, schon gar nicht einer, die ihm gefiel. Zudem hatte er auch den restlichen Haushalt seit Sonntag seinem bevorstehenden Tod entsprechend geführt.

Vielleicht konnte er Monas Einfall in sein Heim irgendwie verhindern, denn glücklicherweise verhielt sich das Wetter heute so, wie man es an einem Junitag erwartete.

Aus der Lebhaftigkeit in Monas Gesicht, die er schon von Weitem ausmachen konnte, schloss Albert, dass sie den Abschiedsbrief noch nicht bekommen hatte.

«Hey!», rief sie munter, als nur noch einige Meter zwischen ihr und Albert lagen.

«Hallo, Mona.»

«Ich habe mir überlegt, na ja – ich habe mir gedacht, ich könnte dich einfach mal besuchen kommen.» Albert fiel auf, dass auch Mona nervös wirkte. Dies machte sie für ihn noch liebenswürdiger.

«Das ist – schön von dir», stammelte Albert.

«Albert, das ist für dich.» Sie reichte ihm ein Glas, das eine weisse Paste enthielt. «Mein Hausmittel, damit dein Gesicht bald wieder schön ist», fügte sie scheu lächelnd hinzu.

«Oh – Mona, das ist nett, danke, vielen Dank.» Trotz seiner Verwirrung war Albert bewegt und versuchte, ihr seine Freude mitzuteilen. Es war ihm fremd, gegenüber anderen Menschen in Überschwänglichkeit zu verfallen.

Mona ging die Treppe zur Veranda hoch.

«Weisst du, Albert», begann sie, «Franz – das ist mein Mann – er spielt auch an meinen freien Tagen lieber mit seinem Hund als mit mir.» Mona bemerkte, dass sie sich etwas unglücklich ausgedrückt hatte. «Als mit mir etwas zu unternehmen», verbesserte sie sich und grinste verlegen.

Albert wusste nicht, wie er auf Monas Missmut zu reagieren hatte. Er masste sich nicht an, Franz in ihrer Gegenwart herabzusetzen, war sich jedoch nicht sicher, ob sie genau das von ihm erwartet hätte. «Das ist nicht sehr nett von ihm», sagte er schliesslich. Die unangenehme Stille hatte er gerade noch durchbrechen können, errötete aber dennoch ob seinem wenig originellen Kommentar.

«Franz macht sich Sorgen, weil sich der Hund seit zwei

Tagen irgendwie seltsam verhält. Bellt nicht mehr richtig, rennt nicht mehr umher. Aber das interessiert uns beide ja nicht!» Ihr Lächeln versteckte sie rasch hinter der hochfahrenden Hand, weckte damit erneut ein verbindendes Gefühl in Albert.

«Ich war bei der Post, wie du heute morgen!», sagte sie plötzlich.

Albert schluckte.

«Der Postbeamte hat mir von dir erzählt. Das ist ein richtiges Waschweib, nicht wahr?»

«Das ist er, ja», antwortete Albert, dessen Verunsicherung wieder wuchs.

«Eigenartig – eigentlich bin ich durch ihn auf die Idee gekommen, dir mein Mittel zu bringen», gab Mona zu.

«Ach so. Ihr habt also über mich gesprochen?», forschte Albert vorsichtig nach.

«Nun ja – ein bisschen schon. Genau genommen hat er mich nach dir gefragt.»

Albert ärgerte sich wiederum, aber es schien, dass auf den Postbeamten doch mehr Verlass war als zunächst befürchtet. Er mochte aber nicht mehr über ihn reden. Nicht an seinem letzten Nachmittag, nicht mit Mona. «Wusstest du denn – wo ich zu Hause bin?», fragte er.

«Nicht genau. Nur ungefähr. Ich habe mich erkundigt ...» Mona sagte dies in beinahe entschuldigendem Ton. Dann schaute sie sich in der Gegend um. «Du hast es wirklich sehr schön hier», sagte sie nahezu bewundernd, wobei ihr Blick über die blühende Wiesenlandschaft wanderte.

«Mir gefällt es hier jedenfalls wunderbar», entgegnete Albert. «Möchtest du dich vielleicht – setzen?» Er vermutete, dass diese Frage bereits etwas früher hätte fallen müssen.

«Oh ja, gerne!» Mona setzte sich auf die kleine Holzbank, der einer Person reichlich, zweien aber etwas knapp Platz bot. Albert blieb daneben stehen, ahnungslos, welche Reaktion nun am angebrachtesten war.

«Komm, setz dich doch auch!», forderte ihn Mona auf.

«Ich hole mir rasch einen Stuhl.»

«Denkst du nicht, dass wir da beide Platz haben, Albert?» Sie bewegte sich noch etwas weiter an den Rand der Bank. Schüchtern nahm Albert neben ihr Platz.

«Ich – bin auf deinen Besuch nicht vorbereitet, Mona. Habe nichts Rechtes zu trinken im Haus und schon eine Weile nicht mehr aufgeräumt.»

«Aber Albert, ich habe dich ja auch unangemeldet überfallen, mach dir also nichts draus», beschwichtigte Mona. «Und ausserdem, ich bin mir von zu Hause gewohnt, dass nicht alles glänzt.»

«Vielleicht – finde ich ja trotzdem etwas zu trinken für dich», hoffte Albert.

«Gerne. Mir ist alles recht!»

«Ich habe Wasser, Absinth und – Wein.»

Mona schmunzelte, wurde aber gleich wieder ernst. Sie wandte sich Albert zu und senkte ihren Kopf leicht, sodass ihr beidseits feine Strähnen ins Gesicht fielen. Ihre tiefgrünen Augen blitzten ähnlich verschmitzt wie gestern Abend, als sie ihn durch das Küchenfenster angeschaut hatte. «Wollen wir uns eine Flasche Wein gönnen?», fragte sie.

Albert jubelte innerlich. Er hatte sich genau diese Antwort gewünscht und verschwand durch die Haustür. Er wusste nun auch, wie das Problem um das fehlende zweite Trinkgefäss zu lösen war. In seinem Haus gab es nämlich doch noch ein zweites Glas. Es befand sich im Badezimmer und enthielt seine Zahnbürste.

Kurze Zeit später setzte sich Albert wieder neben Mona auf die Bank. Er hatte in aller Eile sämtliche Zahnpastaspuren vom einen und jegliche Absinthrückstände vom anderen Glas entfernt. So hektisch hatte er sich seinen letzten Nachmittag eigentlich nicht vorgestellt. Es war allerdings eine aufregende Hektik. Neben den beiden Gläsern brachte er einen Zapfenzieher und eine verstaubte Flasche Wein mit nach draussen.

«Albert», begann Mona zurückhaltend, als sie auf die Etikette des Weins schielte. «Bist du dir sicher, dass du diese Flasche öffnen möchtest?»

«Warum meinst du?», fragte Albert mit gespielter Selbstverständlichkeit, hoffte aber, dass der 39er Barolo Mona nicht bekannt vorkommen würde.

«Wie alt der ist. Sieht mir nach einem besonderen Tropfen aus», staunte Mona.

«Umso besser», entgegnete Albert, der sich neben Mona allmählich wohler fühlte. «Du kommst mich ja auch nicht jeden Tag besuchen.» Er klemmte die Flasche zwischen seine Knie und versuchte, das Spiralgewinde des Zapfenziehers in den Kork zu drehen. Er hatte wenig Übung darin, und die Präsenz Monas machte die Aufgabe nicht einfacher.

Er errötete erneut, als er zum zweiten Male scheiterte.

«Kann ich dir helfen?», fragte Mona mit einem milden Lächeln. «Das Flaschenöffnen ist ja sozusagen mein Beruf …»

Der Korken sprang mit einem dumpfen Knall aus dem Flaschenhals.

«Darf ich dir dafür einmal zusehen, wie du deine Morchelsauce zubereitest?», fragte sie.

«Ach. Ist nichts Aussergewöhnliches.»

«Den Leuten schmeckt sie immer ausgezeichnet.»

«Tatsächlich?»

«Ja, gerade gestern hat man sie wieder gelobt.»

Die Komplimente erheiterten Albert, doch wollte er Mona keine Versprechen abgeben, die er nicht mehr erfüllen konnte.

«Trinken wir doch erst einmal einen Schluck!» Albert ergriff die Flasche und füllte die beiden Gläser, die nicht ganz dem Charakter des vortrefflichen Weins entsprachen.

«Zum Wohl.»

«Zum Wohl, Albert.»

Die zusammenstossenden Gläser klirrten stumpf.

«Schön, dass du da bist, Mona.» Albert hatte seinen ganzen Mut zusammengerafft. Wahrlich freute er sich über den unerwarteten Besuch von Mona und dachte dankerfüllt an den Postbeamten, der wohl seinen Beitrag zu dieser freudigen Überraschung geleistet hatte. Mit Mona einen Tropfen Wein, Jahrgang 1939, auf seiner Veranda zu trinken, kam ihm wie ein spätes Geschenk des Lebens vor.

«Ich bin auch froh, hier sitzen zu können», beteuerte Mona beinahe gerührt. «Weisst du», begann sie zögernd, «es ist nicht immer leicht mit Franz.»

Albert schaute sie verwundert an. Sie erwiderte seinen Blick nicht, dachte kurz nach und fuhr dann fort. «Ich schufte im Gasthof, scheffle Geld nach Hause, und er lässt sich bedienen und ist mir dafür nicht einmal dankbar», platzte es aus ihr heraus. Auf einmal klang Mona geknickt. Albert spürte, dass es ihr Mühe bereitete, über ihren Mann zu sprechen. Ihre Sorglosigkeit war verflogen und zum ersten Mal realisierte er, dass auch ihre fröhliche Fassade bröckeln konnte. Es befriedigte ihn jedoch, dass Mona gerade ihm Dinge aus ihrem Privatleben preisgab. Sie wandte sich ihm nun wieder zu und sagte: «Vielleicht sollten wir beide einmal zusammen in die Ferien fahren.»

Albert starrte sie ungläubig an.

«Also – Franz und ich, meine ich.» Mona bemerkte das Missverständnis, das sie verursacht hatte. Sie versuchte, dieses zu überspielen. «Aber daraus wird wohl nichts. Wir können uns Reisen nicht leisten. Mein Einkommen brauchen wir zum Leben, und Franz verdient ja nichts.» Sie klang traurig.

«Aber warum denn nicht?»

«Er findet keine Arbeit mehr.»

Albert ging nicht weiter darauf ein.

«Hast du schon einmal von Matala gehört?», fragte Mona plötzlich, und ihre Augen erhellten sich wieder.

«Nein. Was ist das?»

«Das ist ein Dorf, Albert.» Mona lachte. «Ein kleines Fischerdorf auf einer griechischen Insel. Es soll wunderschön sein dort. Irgendwann einmal möchte ich dort hingehen.»

«Ach so», sagte Albert leise. Er kannte sich mit fremden Ländern nicht aus, hatte in seinem Leben noch nie einen Fuss über die Landesgrenzen gesetzt. Es war ihm unangenehm, über Reiseziele, überhaupt über Zukünftiges zu sprechen.

«Aber was soll's. Jeder Mensch hat wohl seine Probleme. Und jeder muss damit irgendwie fertig werden.» Mona klang wieder optimistischer.

Endlich liess es das Gespräch zu, einen weiteren Schluck Wein zu kosten.

«Ist schon aussergewöhnlich, einen so alten Tropfen zu trinken. Achtundzwanzig Jahre sind eine lange Zeit», sinnierte sie.

Albert bestätigte dies.

Der Wein schmeckte den beiden ausgezeichnet, wohl eher aus Ehrfurcht vor seinem Alter als seines Wohlgeschmacks wegen. Auch im Schatten der Veranda glühte ihre Haut, während sie gemeinsam auf der kleinen Bank sassen und sich über dieses und jenes unterhielten. Der 39er Barolo war noch zu drei Viertel voll.

«Ich möchte dir auch etwas schenken, Mona.» Alberts Bemerkung kam etwas überraschend.

«Etwas schenken, mir?» Mona blickte ihn erstaunt an.

«Ja, warte einen Augenblick.»

Als Albert wieder zurückkam, reichte er ihr ein Buch.

Mona war leicht irritiert. Was sollte sie nur mit einem Buch anfangen? Sie hatte keine Zeit, keine Geduld, um Bücher zu lesen. Aus Anstand schlug sie den unbeschriebenen Buchdeckel auf und begann zu blättern. Ein Satz sprang ihr in die Augen: *Es war ihre Insel.*

«Du musst es aber nicht jetzt lesen, Mona. Bücher sollte man lesen, wenn man allein ist.» Albert schien nervös zu sein.

«Da hast du recht, Albert.» Sie schloss das Buch. «Warum schenkst du mir gerade dieses Buch?»

«Das Buch wird dir helfen, dein Fernweh zu lindern.»

Mona bezweifelte dies, bedankte sich aber dennoch artig.

Albert schenkte nach. Die Flasche war noch halb voll.

«Sag mal Albert, du spielst Gitarre?» Mona sah nun das Instrument, das am Geländer der Veranda lehnte.

«Ja, ein bisschen», antwortete er zaghaft. Ob dies Mona beeindrucken würde? Er war ein wenig stolz, sich als Gitarrenspieler ausgeben zu können. Allerdings begann er gleich zu ahnen, was nun kommen musste. Er fürchtete sich vor Monas Frage.

Die Frage kam prompt.

«Ich weiss nicht, Mona … ich bin kein guter Spieler», wich er aus.

«Komm schon Albert, ich liebe Gitarrenmusik!»

Warum hatte er bloss die Gitarre draussen liegen gelassen? Er sträubte sich dagegen, Mona etwas vorzuspielen, zugleich reizte es ihn aber, ihr zu imponieren.

Langsam nahm er die Gitarre zur Hand. Nun war es zu spät. Er musste spielen. Etwas Aussergewöhnliches, irgendetwas, egal was.

Er setzte sich auf das Geländer der Veranda, während Mona ihm gegenüber gespannt auf den ersten Saitenanschlag wartete. Sein Puls pochte. Er brachte die Gitarre in Stellung und sah noch einmal zu Mona. Sie führte das Glas, in dem normalerweise Alberts Zahnbürste stand, an ihre vollen, weinroten Lippen und trank.

Sie blickte ihn an.

Er blickte sie an.

Ihre Blicke näherten sich, steuerten geradewegs aufeinander zu, trafen sich in der Mitte, kollidierten –

Da war sie wieder.

Albert reichte Mona mit einem E-Moll-Septakkord mit None die Hand, entführte sie, vergötterte sie … Dazu summte er, denn das Lied hatte keine Worte. Es brauchte sie nicht. Die Melodie sprach ihre eigene Sprache, die durch Worte nur ihrer Klarheit beraubt worden wäre.

Die verlorene Melodie.

Mona war aufgewühlt. Noch nie hatte sie ein schöneres Lied gehört.

Beide versanken sie nun in der Herrlichkeit der Melodie, doch gerade dies vereinigte sie. Sie hörten ein Lied, das nur ihnen beiden gehörte, das nur für sie beide bestimmt war.

Als das Lied verstummte, hallte es noch lange, scheinbar unaufhörlich, in ihren Ohren nach.

Albert konnte es kaum fassen, dass ihm die exakte Tonfolge wieder eingefallen war, und noch weniger, dass er sich getraut hatte, vor Mona zu singen. Mona ihrerseits war verzaubert – selbst ohne zu wissen, dass sie dem Lied als Inspirationsquelle gedient hatte, dass das Lied vor wenigen Stunden ihretwegen entstanden war. Sprachlos sassen sie sich noch eine Weile gegenüber.

«Das war – wunderschön, Albert.»

«Danke.»

Dann blieben beide wieder stumm. Die Rückkehr ins Diesseits vollzog sich nur schleppend.

«Was ist das für ein Lied?», fragte Mona endlich.

«Wie – wie meinst du das?»

«Woher kennst du dieses Lied?»

«Das – das hab' ich selber erfunden.» Albert wusste, wie unglaubhaft sich das anhörte. Es war ihm ja selbst schleierhaft, wie ein kleiner Versager seiner Sorte zu dieser grossen Melodie gekommen war. Und es war eine grosse Melodie, das wusste er spätestens jetzt mit Bestimmtheit.

«Du machst Scherze, nicht wahr?»

«Nein. Neinnein, Mona, ich habe die Melodie gestern Abend komponiert», stotterte er.

Mona sagte nichts und grübelte, ob sie ihm glauben sollte. Nach einer Weile tat sie es. Versuchte es zumindest.

«Du bist – du bist unglaublich, Albert. Niemand im Dorf weiss, dass du Gitarre spielst, und du komponierst hier in deinem Garten solch märchenhafte Musik!» Mona war voller Bewunderung.

Albert wusste darauf nichts mehr zu entgegnen. Musste er auch nicht. Still sass er da und genoss die Genugtuung. An seinem letzten Tag wurde er gewürdigt, erhielt endlich Anerkennung, und dies aus dem zarten Munde von Mona. Jener Moment entschädigte so manche bittere Stunde, die er erduldet hatte. Linderte so manchen Schmerz, der ihm widerfahren war. Er würde nun doch mit einer gewissen Würde dahinscheiden können.

An seinem letzten Nachmittag verbrachte Albert mit Wein, Mona und Gitarre die schönsten Stunden seines Lebens. Doch auch diese waren nicht für die Ewigkeit bestimmt, auch diese mussten bald ihr jähes Ende finden.

Erdbeeren, Kirschen und der Kuss eines Engels. Mein Sommerwein ist wirklich aus all diesen Dingen. Ein Lied, das ich nur für sie gespielt hatte. Meine Augen wurden schwer, und meine Lippen konnten nicht sprechen. Ich versuchte aufzustehen, aber konnte meine Füsse nicht finden. Sie beruhigte mich auf eine unbekannte Weise. Dann gab sie mir mehr Sommerwein. Als ich aufwachte, schien die Sonne in meinen Augen.

Der 39er Barolo war fast leer.

19. Das Grabkreuz

Am / E / Am / Dm / Am / E / Am
Dm / A / Dm / G / Dm / A / Dm

Mona war weg, für immer.

Natürlich hätte Albert noch beschliessen können, weiter zu leben. Er war ja nicht dazu verpflichtet, zu sterben, war niemandem seinen Tod schuldig – ausser sich selbst.

Den hinterhältigen Spielzug des Schicksals hatte er nämlich durchschaut, hatte erkannt, dass das Ereignis Mona bloss ein weiterer Streich war, den das Leben mit ihm zu spielen gedachte. Indem ihm auf verführerische Weise ein starkes Gefühl beigebracht wurde, sollten sich nämlich nur seine Leidensgrenzen erweitern. In Zukunft würde sich der Schmerz noch tiefer in sein Herz bohren können. Albert spürte, wie ebendieser Prozess bereits in Gang gebracht worden war. Er musste ihn aufhalten, musste das bösartige Spiel beenden, durfte der Zukunft keine Zukunft geben. Er zog es vor, gefühlsstumpf im Grab zu liegen, statt Mona und Franz bei deren Abfahrt in den Süden zuzuwinken.

Ausserdem – würde er sich heute Abend nicht das Leben nehmen, hätte er morgens bereits wieder in den Gasthof zur Arbeit gehen müssen. Im tristen Alltagssumpf versinken, den er verdammte.

Die Stunden mit Mona waren wie im Fluge zerronnen. Den geplanten Ausflug nach Freiburg musste Albert streichen, wollte er heute noch sterben. Ein bisschen wurmte es ihn schon, nie mehr durch die malerischen Gässchen der Unterstadt flanieren, nie mehr dem Rauschen der Saane lauschen zu können. Auch das letzte Abendessen war ihm wegen Monas längerem Besuch abhanden gekommen. Er nahm es ihr nicht übel.

In der näheren Umgebung, wo man ihn kennen konnte, mochte er sich nicht allein in ein Wirtshaus begeben. Dann würde er halt heute nichts mehr essen. Zu viele Speisen hätten sich ohnehin unvorteilhaft auf einen ehrgeizigen Alkoholkonsum ausgewirkt.

Und seine Melodie, die er aus der Vergessenheit zurückgeholt hatte? Nun, er hatte sie dem liebsten aller Menschen vorgespielt. Mona würde sie in ihrem Herzen tragen und behüten.

Nur Mona und er hatten die Melodie also je gehört. Zwei Personen in der ganzen Geschichte der Menschheit, des Universums, ja der Zeit. Der Gedanke gefiel ihm so ausserordentlich, dass er sich nicht mehr wünschte, die Melodie der ganzen Nachwelt zu hinterlassen.

Was aber sollte aus seiner Gitarre werden? Musste er sie wirklich in Holzkohle verwandeln? Albert machte ein besorgtes Gesicht. Am Leben seiner Gitarre lag ihm mehr als an seinem eigenen. Doch wem konnte die Gitarre in die Finger kommen, wenn er sie vom Feuer verschonen würde? Albert überlegte sich, ob er sie Mona anvertrauen sollte.

Nein, entschied er, vermutlich würde Franz mit seinen dreckigen Fingern auch noch die Gitarre anfassen. Er entschloss sich zum Kompromiss, die Gitarre zu vergraben.

In seiner kleinen Werkstatt suchte er nach einem geeigneten Hilfsmittel. Die Werkstatt befand sich ebenfalls in seinem Haus, war jedoch nicht mit dem Wohnteil verbunden. Albert hatte sie praktisch nie betreten, da sie ihn an seine handwerkliche Unfähigkeit erinnerte. Er wusste lediglich, dass der vormalige Besitzer des Hauses darin etliche Arbeitsgeräte hinterlassen hatte.

Zwischen einer abgewetzten Sense und einer Leiter mit dürren Sprossen fand Albert einen Spaten.

Eine mühselige halbe Stunde später stoppte er seine Bemühungen. Am Waldrand, wo die Erde nicht so trocken war wie unmittelbar neben dem Haus, hatte er eine ordentliche Senke ausgegraben. Er blickte auf den Erdhaufen, in dem sich einige Würmer ringelten. Da schüttelte er den Kopf. Der feuchten

Erde konnte er seine Gitarre nicht anvertrauen. Während dem Schaufeln war ihm ein besserer Bestattungsort eingefallen.

Er setzte sich wieder auf die Bank und trank einen Schluck Absinth aus dem Zahnpastaglas. Monas Lippenstift klebte noch an dessen Aussenseite. Er führte seinen Mund exakt an diese Stelle. Dann nahm er ein Messer zur Hand und ritzte seinen Namen und seine Lebensdauer in den Rücken des Gitarrenkorpus:

ALBERT LEBLANC
1939-1967

Er setzte ein gequältes Lächeln auf. Er würde seine Gitarre mit ins Grab nehmen. Zumindest beinahe. Sie sollte mit dem Hals voran in die Erde gesteckt werden und sein Grab zieren, als Grabkreuz auf dem Friedhof von Rechthalten. War er vielleicht als Lebender niemandem aufgefallen, sein Grab würde gewiss die Blicke auf sich ziehen.

Die Sonne ging langsam unter.

20. Requiem

Am / F / E
Am / F / E
Am / F / H

Die Zeit war gekommen, um Abschied zu nehmen. Abschied von seiner geliebten Gitarre, die ihm über all die Jahre eine treue Lebensstütze war. Dass er die Gitarre weder zerstören noch begraben musste und sie künftig in der Erde stecken sollte, zu der auch er sich bald verwandeln würde, machte die Trennung erträglicher.

Mühe bereitete ihm allerdings der Umstand, dass er in den nächsten Minuten das letzte Mal auf der Gitarre spielen konnte. Das letzte Lied, die letzte Melodie, den letzen Ton anstimmen musste.

Albert verabschiedete sich von einigen Akkorden, die ihn stets begleitet hatten, entfachte zum letzten Mal das Rätsel eines *A7*, die Leichtfüssigkeit eines D-Dur, die Hoffnung eines *vorgehaltenen A*, die Bosheit eines E-Moll und sog noch einmal sämtliche Geheimnisse der Akkorde in sich auf. Er zupfte jeweils langsam Saite für Saite an, genoss jeden einzelnen Ton. Die Vielfalt an Stimmungen, in die er sich mit seinen Klängen versetzte, machte ihn etwas trunken.

Es war dunkler geworden.

Die Basssaite vibrierte, während Albert sie beim sechsten Bund auf das Griffbrett drückte. Aus seinem Finger rann ein Tropfen Blut. Er liess die Saite ausklingen, ohne den Finger, in den die herausragende Spitze des Stahldrahts eingedrungen war, wegzubewegen.

Nun herrschte komplette Ruhe.

Dann flog ein E-Moll-Septakkord mit None über die Wiese, die sich vor Albert in der Dämmerung verlor. Er hatte sich entschieden, seine musikalische Regsamkeit mit Monas Melodie ehrenvoll zu beenden.

Er schloss die Augen. Seine Finger linkerhand ergriffen die Saiten an den entsprechenden Stellen, sodass sich das Blut seines triefenden Fingers auf dem Griffbrett verteilte. Seine Stimme setzte ein, die jetzt aber eher wie ein Wehklagen klang. Dann erhob er sich, stieg die kleine Verandatreppe hinab und ging saitenzupfend, immer noch Monas Melodie, einige kraftlose Schritte über die Wiese.

Plötzlich senkte sich sein Oberkörper nach vorne, bis er auf die Knie fiel.

In diesem Moment veränderte sich sein Gitarrenspiel.

Der lachende, unbesorgte A-Dur wich einem zerreissenden A-Moll-Akkord. Dann schleuderte Albert zwei weitere tonnenschwere Akkorde in die Mondnacht hinaus. Dazu sang, schrie er. So laut, wie er es in seinem endenden Leben noch nie getan.

Wäre Alberts Stimme einem nächtlichen Vagabunden zu Ohren gekommen, sie hätte ihn bis auf die Knochen erschüttert. Wie ein Verrückter drosch Albert dazu in einem bedrohlichen, schleppenden Rhythmus auf die Saiten ein. Bei jedem Saitenanschlag warf er seinen Kopf aus dem Nacken nach vorne, die Haare flogen, ungeachtet der Seitenscheitel, wirr durch die Luft. Tiefe Furchen zierten seine Stirn, sein Gesicht nahm die wildesten Züge an. Albert war zu diesem Zeitpunkt der Welt entrückt.

Doch er war quicklebendig.

Es war eine weitere unsterbliche Melodie von Albert. Und doch war sie sterblich, denn mit ihm würde auch sie die Welt auf immer verlassen. Es war Alberts Todesmelodie, sein Requiem. Es war gut. Teuflisch gut.

Die gespielten Tonfolgen waren von solcher Ergriffenheit, dass sich Albert erschöpft hinsetzen musste.

Er hatte seine eigenen Todesklänge als Schlussteil zu Monas Melodie zelebriert und dieser damit die Krone aufgesetzt. Erst jetzt war sein Lied, sein Opus Magnum, vollendet.

Albert nahm die Gitarre, entfernte sich etwas vom Haus und stützte sie an eine Buche. Durch die Saiten flocht er einen Zettel, auf dem in krakeliger Schrift geschrieben stand:

Im Leben wart ihr mir nicht gut gesinnt.
Möget mir im Tod meinen letzten Wunsch erfüllen.
Die Gitarre soll mein Grabkreuz sein
und euch an einen Unglücklichen erinnern.

Wenn der Wind nächste Woche über den Friedhof von Rechthalten fegen würde, sollten die Klänge seiner Gitarre durch die Grabsteinreihen schleichen. Albert bekam Gänsehaut.

Er betrat kurz sein Haus, legte eine seiner Unterhosen auf den Gaskochherd und kehrte wieder auf die Veranda zurück. Er ging ans Geländer, kratzte seinen letzten Kieselstein aus der Hosentasche und schnippte ihn ins Gras. Dann setzte er sich. Die letzte Stunde des Albert Leblanc hatte geschlagen.

An seinen Gläsern hielt er sich fest. Die linke Hand umfasste das Schnapsglas, die rechte das Zahnbürstenglas, beide randvoll mit Absinth gefüllt. Durch das Glas konnte er seine blutverschmierten Finger sehen – trübendes Wasser hatte im Absinth heute nämlich nichts verloren, sein Plan verlangte die Zufuhr von purem Schnaps. Heute war das Trinken nicht Genuss, heute war es Arbeit, eigentlich ein Handwerk, ein Todeshandwerk. Der nackte Absinth schmeckte Albert denn auch nicht besonders. Womöglich konnte der Tod sogar einem Lebensmüden nicht schmecken.

Albert war nicht einmal ein besonders talentierter Trinker. Er trank zwar fleissig, stürzte sich regelmässig in einen Rausch, doch gegenüber gestandenen Säufern wie etwa Karl war er ein bescheidener Schlucker. Er setzte ein Glas an und ekelte sich dabei beinahe vor seinem alltäglichen Gesöff. Konnte er in seinem Glas bereits den Tod riechen? Sein Hals war wie zugeschnürt, jeder Tropfen musste sich mühsam durch die Kehle kämpfen. Möglicherweise lag dies auch daran, dass er seit

Mittag nichts mehr gegessen hatte. Er durfte wohl nicht zu viel wollen, nichts überstürzen, musste behäbig, doch unentwegt an seinen Gläsern nippen.

Schliesslich erlaubte er sich doch, etwas Wasser in den Absinth zu giessen. Er leerte die beiden noch beinahe vollen Gläser bis zur Hälfte aus. Absinth hätte er genug gehabt, um die ganze Feuerwehr zu bezechen. Zu sparen brauchte er nicht mehr, das Wort hatte für ihn jegliche Bedeutung verloren.

Nach der Wasserzufuhr nahm er einen kräftigeren Schluck und verabreichte sich dazu die erste Tablette Valium.

Es war erbärmlich, unbemerkt, in aller Stille dahinzuraffen. Vielleicht würde ihm etwas Musik die Kraft geben, den letzten Weg zu gehen? Geknickten Hauptes begab er sich in die Stube und liess die Schallplatte rotieren, die auf dem Teller lag. Es war immer noch die gleiche wie letzten Sonntag – Albert war in dieser ereignisreichen Woche gar nicht mehr dazugekommen, Musik zu hören. Er rückte den Arm des Plattenspielers etwas einwärts.

Kannst du dir vorstellen, was sein wird? So grenzenlos und frei. Verzweifelt angewiesen auf eines Fremden Hand, in einem verzweifelten Land. Es schmerzt, dich zu befreien, du wirst mir nie folgen. Das ist das Ende, schöner Freund. Das ist das Ende, mein einziger Freund, das Ende.

Albert nahm einen weiteren Schluck und musste sich seine nicht optimale Trinkverfassung eingestehen. Er tat, was sich tun liess und versuchte, den fehlenden Alkohol mit umso mehr Valium zu kompensieren. Er warf sich fünf Tabletten auf einmal in den Rachen, trank wiederum, warf zwei weitere Tabletten gleich ins Glas und versuchte, zu trinken, zu trinken, zu trinken …

21. *Und der weisse Ritter spricht rückwärts*

ALBERT LEBLANG stand auf den Gitarren, und trotzdem ist er keine dreissig geworden, war ein grosser Musiker, hat ein unglaublich gutes Lied gemacht, ein perfektes Lied gemacht, das beste, war ein Genie und niemand hat es bemerkt, o Genie, der Herr ehre dein Ego, bin jetzt aber betrunken, und Mona ist weg, meine Mona, und mir ist schwindlig, sehr schwindlig, die Liebe ist Sieger, stets rege ist sie bei Leid, bald sterbe ich, noch ein Valium, *das hilft dir auf deinem Weg, hilft dir an deinem Todestag*, wann kann ich endlich sterben, will ich eigentlich überhaupt wirklich sterben, habe mit Mona Wein getrunken, bald
wird es schwarz, völlig schwarz, für immer schwarz,
sollte ich ins Haus gehen, kann ich noch gehen
ich sollte jetzt wohl ins Haus gehen und die
Kochplatte anmachen sicher ist sicher
Mona liebt Franz die Platte ist an
ist voll an und ich torkle und
bin müde und schwindlig
und lege michaufs Bett
wo ich schlafen kann
schlafen und ruhen
schlafen lebwohl
Mona schlafen
entschlafen
sterben
Mona
Em
D

22. *Ein sehr eigenartiger Mann*

Mona wurde von einem Lied aus dem Radio sanft aus ihren Träumen gerissen.

Er war ein sehr eigenartiger Mann.
Er lebte ganz allein in einem Haus,
in einem Raum, in sich selbst.
Ein sehr eigenartiger Mann.

Es war dunkel, also immer noch Nacht. Sie lag nicht in ihrem Bett, wie es sonst üblich war, wenn sie aufwachte, sondern im Wohnzimmer auf dem Sofa. Einen kurzen Augenblick verstand sie nicht, dann fiel ihr ein, dass sie am Abend sehr müde und nachdenklich gewesen war. Sie hatte sich schliesslich nicht neben Franz ins Bett legen mögen. Sie hatte vor dem Schlafen nicht einmal geduscht.

Er hatte keine Freunde,
er sprach nur selten,
er war nicht wie sie –
nein, er war ein eigenartiger Mann.

Er starb letzten Freitag.
Er drehte das Gas an und schlief ein,
mit geschlossenen Fenstern,
und wachte nie mehr auf,

in seiner stillen Welt, in seinem kleinen Haus.

23. Das Lebensfeuer

Es brannte lichterloh.

Die Flammen hatten sich rapide entfacht, sich von der Kochplatte ausgehend der Küchenkombination entlang über den Kachelofen und eine klapprige Kommode ins Wohnzimmer geschlängelt, wo sie Schallplatten in flüssiges Plastik verwandelten, leere und volle Flaschen Schnaps bersten liessen, die Vorhänge hinauf zu klettern begannen. Die unsägliche Hitze löste Spinnweben samt Spinnen kaltblütig auf, die Pendel der Wanduhr fielen in Flammen zu Boden, Spiegel zersprangen, der Schaukelstuhl knackte, die Zahnbürste verschwand.

Die Flammen erreichten das Schlafzimmer, tanzten über den karierten Teppich, ergriffen den Holzschrank, vertilgten die darin sich aufstapelnden Kleider. Immer schneller dehnte sich das Inferno aus, nahm Nachttischchen und Bett in Beschlag, frass sich mühelos durch Leintuch und Kissen.

Plötzlich näherte sich dem brennenden Haus ein Mann. Er hinkte ein wenig, bewegte sich etwas starr, und trotzdem kam er mit beeindruckender Schnelligkeit dahergerannt. Entsetzt eilte er um das Haus, von dem nun schon ein beträchtlicher Teil in Flammen stand.

«Albert!», schrie der Mann, «hörst du mich?» Die Antwort blieb aus. Er schnappte sich einen Stein und warf ihn gegen das geschwärzte Fenster, hinter dem sich Alberts Schlafzimmer befand. Scheiben klirrten.

«Albert! Bist du da drin?», schrie er weiter und versuchte, durch die zerbrochene Fensterscheibe einen Blick zu erhaschen. Wiederum klang ihm nur das Knistern und Knattern des Feuers entgegen.

Der Mann kratzte sich verzweifelt am Hinterkopf und schaute mit zuckenden Kopfbewegungen umher, um sich zu vergewissern, ob nicht doch vielleicht schon Hilfe im Anmarsch war. Doch ganz Rechthalten hatte zu diesem Zeitpunkt nicht die geringste Ahnung, welche Tragödie sich in der Einsamkeit nahe des Buchholzes abspielte. Und sich noch abspielen sollte.

In der Not fällte der Mann einen leichtfertigen Entschluss – es war nicht sein erster, wohl aber sein schwerwiegendster. Wagemutig betrat er die Veranda, schrie weiter nach Albert, trommelte mit den Fäusten gegen die Haustür, bis er bemerkte, dass diese gar nicht verschlossen war.

Da geschah das Unglück. Unter lautem Krachen und Knallen fiel das Dach, das auch die Veranda überdeckte, in sich zusammen. Der Mann hatte keine Chance, den brennenden Balken zu entfliehen. Er wurde von der herabstürzenden Masse erschlagen und begraben.

24. Der Dachboden

H
Hell
heiss
die Hölle
überall Feuer
sehr heiss, ist das
der Tod, immer näher
das Feuer, glühend heiss,
wo kann ich hin, wo kann ich
raus, durch das Feuer, Flammen
überall, Hilfe, ich brauche sofort Hilfe,
unerträglich heiss, ich muss hier raus, ich
werde verbrennen, verrecken, da muss ich raus,
endlich raus, brauche kühles, kaltes, eiskaltes Wasser.

Albert stand am Waldrand und übergab sich. Neben einer Unmenge giftigem Gas spuckte sein Magen elf aufgelöste Valium-Tabletten, drei Deziliter Absinth, acht Deziliter Wasser, einige Tropfen Rotwein sowie drei zersetzte Lakritzstangen neben die Buche, an der er sich mit beiden Armen abgestützt hielt. Als seine Kräfte erneut schwanden, sackte er zusammen, rappelte sich wieder etwas hoch, während er von heftigen Hustenanfällen geplagt wurde. Stumpfsinnig starrte er auf das brennende Haus. Die wütenden Flammen arbeiteten sich bereits zum Dachgebälk hoch.

Das Auftauchen eines schreienden Mannes nahm er emotionslos zur Kenntnis. Hinter der Buche sah er zu, wie der Mann aufgeregt um das Haus brauste und unentwegt nach ihm rief. Albert wunderte sich nicht darüber. Die Panik des Mannes veranlasste ihn nicht dazu, sein Versteck zu verlassen. Im Gegenteil – irgendein dumpfer Instinkt befahl ihm, lautlos hinter der Buche zu verharren.

Nachdem der Eindringling unter dem einstürzenden Vordach verschwunden war, blieb Albert noch eine Weile im

Gehölz stehen, wobei er unberührt registrierte, dass sein Haus komplett abfackelte.

Plötzlich kehrte bei Albert die Fähigkeit, Entsetzen zu empfinden, schlagartig zurück. Er preschte zwischen den Bäumen hervor, fiel in ein kleines Erdloch, entstieg diesem gleich wieder und blickte in die alles vernichtenden Flammen. Ein Mann lag unter den Trümmern seines brennenden Hauses, er brauchte Hilfe! Ein Mann, der ihn aus dem tödlichen Feuer hatte retten wollen! Er musste losrennen und Hilfe holen, den Arzt und die Feuerwehr rufen! In einem Dämmerzustand jagte Albert so schnell er konnte ins Dorf.

Frühmorgens um zwanzig nach zwei erreichte er mit rauchgefärbten Kleidern und ebenso geschwärztem Kopf den Platz neben dem Gasthof. Er atmete schwer und blieb verwirrt stehen. Was nun? Wohin nun? Er versuchte, mit seinem eben erst dem Delirium entwichenen Kopf klare Gedanken zu fassen, die Geschehnisse zu sortieren: Sein Haus brannte. Ein Mann hatte das Haus betreten. Das Haus war eingestürzt. Es befand sich also ein Mann in den Trümmern seines brennenden Hauses …

Der Mann musste tot sein! Erschlagen, erstickt, verbrannt, jedenfalls tot. Wie nur sollte er dies jemandem weismachen? Jeder halbwegs vernünftige Mensch würde ihm seine Geschichte nicht abnehmen. Gerade ihm würde man nichts glauben. Albert wurde von einer Furcht erfasst, als ihm bewusst wurde, wie sinnlos der eben zurückgelegte Spurt war.

Nun wurde ihm unbegreiflich, dass er sich ausgerechnet ins Dorf begeben hatte. Er musste auf der Stelle verschwinden, bevor man nach ihm suchen würde. In seiner Ratlosigkeit irrte er auf ein Gebäude zu, das sich unweit vor ihm erhob. Es war das Schulhaus.

An der nördlichen Fassade des Schulhauses war ein kleiner Fahrradunterstand angebracht. Tagsüber stellten Schulkinder hier ihre Fahrräder ab, tauschten Briefchen aus oder erledigten andere verbotene Geschäfte. Albert stahl sich unter das

Schutzdach, welches das Mondlicht etwas fernhielt und liess sich in einer Ecke nieder.

Erst jetzt spürte er den scharfen Schmerz in seinem linken Oberarm.

Es sah abscheulich aus. Der Stoff seines Hemdes klebte auf der verbrannten Haut. Albert versuchte, den Stoff vom Arm zu trennen, doch wurde ihm vor Schmerz und noch mehr vor Ekel übel. Er presste den Arm an die kühle Steinmauer.

Vom Unterstand aus hatte er den Stützpunkt der Feuerwehr im Auge, und etwas beruhigt stellte er fest, dass der von ihm verursachte Brand offenbar noch unentdeckt geblieben war. Nach einer allfälligen Alarmierung der Feuerwehr würden sich die Hilfskräfte aber auf dem Platz unmittelbar vor ihm treffen. Sein Versteck konnte ihm also nur für begrenzte Zeit als Versteck dienen. Ausserdem durfte er hier auf keinen Fall einschlafen, wollte er nicht in wenigen Stunden für verängstigte Schulkinder sorgen.

Inzwischen fehlte ihm der Mut, den Dorfkern wieder zu verlassen. Erneut hätte er sich an vielen Häusern vorbeischleichen müssen, das erschien ihm zu gefährlich. Zudem wusste er auch nicht, wo er hingehen konnte. Er hatte ja kein Zuhause mehr. In den Wald? Ins Löhlimoos? Auch da konnten sich bereits im Morgengrauen Spaziergänger aufhalten. Ausserdem war er sehr müde. Und betrunken.

Er wagte sich wieder ans Mondlicht und begutachtete die Fensterreihe des ersten Stocks.

Albert wurde nervös. Er traute dem unerwarteten Glück nicht, das ihn nun erwartete. Und doch war eines der Fenster etwas oberhalb des Unterstandes zweifelsfrei offen. Befand er sich einmal im Innern des Schulhauses, überlegte er, konnte er sich auf dem Dachboden verschanzen.

Er erinnerte sich an seine Schulzeit. Selten, nur ganz selten waren damals von Zeit zu Zeit Schüler beauftragt worden, um abkömmliche Materialien auf dem Dachboden zu verstauen. Und wenn es einen denn einmal traf, hatte man den Aufenthalt in dem dunklen Speicher immer so kurz wie möglich gestaltet. Ansonsten hatte er nie rege Verwendung gefunden. Der ideale Ort also, um eine Zeitlang unbemerkt zu verweilen.

Albert musste nur den Unterstand hochklettern, um das geöffnete Fenster zu erreichen. Mittlerweile hatte er ja erste Erfahrungen im Klettern gesammelt, ausserdem war er heute bereits barfuss. Nur sein Arm, der vor kurzem von Flammen beleckt worden war, würde ihm Mühe bereiten.

Er hob sich mit Hilfe des Abflussrohrs in die Höhe, wo er sich gleich an der Dachrinne festhalten und hochziehen konnte. Er spürte, wie sich das Blut in seinem Kopf sammelte. Trotz stilwidrigster Bewegungen schaffte er es, die Dachplatte des Unterstandes zu erklimmen. Sein Arm verursachte dabei Höllenqualen.

Er schlüpfte durch den Fensterrahmen hindurch und landete in der Toilette, wo er sofort eiskaltes Wasser über seinen Oberarm fliessen liess. Ein Schrei entglitt ihm. Er musste vorsichtiger sein, hielt etwas Toilettenpapier unter den Wasserhahn und betupfte sachte seine Brandwunde. Dann wickelte er einige Lagen nasses Papier um seine kaum vorhandenen Oberarmmuskeln.

Als er schliesslich im Halbdunkel sein Antlitz im Spiegel sah, zuckte er zusammen. Sogar seine Zähne waren pechschwarz. Zudem war seine Kopfhaut auf der linken Seite teilweise fast blank. Offenbar hatten die Flammen einige Büschel von seinen Haaren verschlungen. Er sah zum Fürchten aus. Rasch rubbelte er sich das Gröbste an Russ von seinem Kopf ab.

Sein letzter Tag war längst zu Ende gegangen. Sein vermeintlich letzter Tag war schon zu gestern geworden, und heute, da lebte Albert Leblanc immer noch. Ohne sich darüber weiter den nun etwas saubereren Kopf zu zerbrechen verliess er die Toilette und stieg kraftlos die Stufen zum Dachboden hoch.

25. Hans Fahler

Wo war er? Wie war ihm geschehen?

Erst nach Augenblicken der Ungewissheit wurde Albert klar, dass er sich weder im Himmel noch in der Hölle, sondern auf dem Dachboden des örtlichen Schulhauses befand. Er hatte sich des Nachts in das hinterste Kämmerchen verkrochen, das auch für ein bescheidenes Mannsbild wie Albert nur geduckt zu betreten war.

Durch eine kleine Dachluke verdichtete sich das einfallende Tageslicht zu einem hellen Kegel. Albert musste also für einige Stunden geschlafen haben.

Ein schreckliches Bild schoss ihm durch den Kopf.

Die Holzdielen knarrten, als er seinen Oberkörper etwas aufrichtete. Dies gelang ihm nicht ganz, die starken Schmerzen am Oberarm hinderten ihn daran. Ausserdem litt er unter entsetzlichem Durst, sein Mund war trocken wie der Humor von Karl. Er legte den dröhnenden Kopf in seine Hände.

Mit brutaler Wucht wurde ihm langsam die Tragweite seiner letztnächtlichen Untat bewusst. Er hatte seinen Versuch, aus dem Leben zu scheiden, auf unfassbare Weise vermasselt. Sein Haus war zerstört, sein ganzes Hab und Gut weg, und das eigentliche Ziel der Aktion, sein Tod, war ausgeblieben. Die Ausführung des vermeintlich genialen Todesplanes war desaströs gewesen, hatte sich gar zur grössten nur auszudenkenden Katastrophe ausgeweitet.

Hätte er doch bloss mehr getrunken, noch mehr Valium geschluckt! Was war nur in ihn gefahren, so halbherzig zur Sache zu gehen? Hätte er sich doch besser in den Galterngraben geworfen, sich erschossen oder ertränkt!

Warum nur liess Gott ihn nicht sterben? Nichts gönnte ihm der Allgütige, nicht einmal den Tod. War denn sogar der Tod zuviel verlangt? Das Sterben konnte ihm doch nicht noch schwieriger als das Leben gemacht werden. Albert wurde von Krämpfen geschüttelt.

Als er sein Taschentuch aus dem Hosensack zog und dieses auswickelte, ertönte ein dumpfes Geräusch. Albert blickte zu Boden und entdeckte auf einer Holzlatte verwundert den Kieselstein.

Er hob ihn auf und steckte ihn in sein ledernes Portemonnaie, das den Brand überlebt hatte. Darin befand sich seit gestern kein Geld mehr, aber immerhin noch sein Ausweis, ein Gitarrenplektrum und ein weisser Knopf, der ihm einmal von einem Hemd abgefallen war.

Die Kirchturmglocke vermeldete die Mittagszeit.

Gebückt verliess er das kleine Kämmerchen, kämpfte sich durch das herumliegende Gerümpel und gelangte in den grösseren Teil des Dachbodens. Er setzte sich auf einen kleinen, bemalten Stuhl. Er haderte weiter, mit dem Schicksal, der Welt und sich selbst. Ob er damit nur vom schrecklichen Bild ablenken wollte, das immer wieder vor seinem inneren Auge auftauchte? Es war das Bild des Hans Fahler, Veteran der Rechthaltner Feuerwehr, der unter einem brennenden Dach begraben wird. Dazu erinnerte sich Albert an den erschütternden Schrei, welcher der gute Mann einen kleinen Augenblick vor dem Einsturz ausgestossen hatte. Albert wusste, dass Hans mit grösster Wahrscheinlichkeit tot war. Ihm fröstelte.

Warum nur liess Gott Hans nicht am Leben? Sein Tod diente Albert als weiterer Beweis für Gottes Ungerechtigkeit.

Langsam schritt er durch den dunklen Dachboden. Überall standen Kisten, Pulte oder gebastelter Plunder, den die Welt nicht brauchte. In der Höhe thronte auf einem dicken Querbalken ein ausgestopfter Mäusebussard. Er sah bedrohlich lebendig aus. Nahe der Treppe, die nach unten führte, erblickte Albert den übergrossen Rechenschieber, den er noch aus seiner Schulzeit kannte. Daneben stand ein aus Holz angefertigtes, klappriges Glücksrad. Albert näherte sich den entdeckten Objekten.

Er drehte am Rad, das nur schleppend in Schwung kam. «Bei welcher Zahl das Rad stillsteht, ist reines Glück», dachte er. Albert setzte das Rad ein weiteres Mal in Bewegung. Eines war klar, das Glücksrad konnte nur dann bei der gewünschten Zahl stehen bleiben, wenn man es drehte. Und wenn man es mehrmals drehte, erhöhten sich die Chancen.

Albert grübelte unaufhörlich. Immer wieder sah er Abrisse des geschehenen Dramas. Hans hatte zahllose Male nach ihm gerufen. Hatte ihm helfen wollen. Hatte schliesslich gar das brennende Haus betreten wollen und dies mit dem Leben bezahlt. Albert hätte seinen Tod verhindern können.

Immer eindeutiger musste Albert die Schuld am Tod von Hans Fahler auf sich nehmen. Hatte er ihn also getötet? Sein Gesicht erstarrte.

Nein, er war doch kein Mörder! Nie im Leben hatte er den Tod von Hans Fahler gewollt, er bedauerte ihn zutiefst. Er konnte ja auch keinen Nutzen aus seinem Tod ziehen.

Er ging einige Schritte weiter und gelangte zu einer grossen, ausgerollten Landkarte. Sie hing an einer blauen Schnur und schaukelte schwach in der Luft. Es war die Schweizer Karte, die seinerzeit des Öfteren im Geografieunterricht verwendet worden war.

Viel von der Welt hatte er in seinem Leben nicht gesehen, musste er sich eingestehen, nicht einmal im eigenen Land war er kundig. In der Westschweiz, ja, da hatte er mit ein paar wenigen Dörfern Bekanntschaft gemacht. Weiter konnte er sich an die Eigentümlichkeiten einiger Kinderheime im Bernbiet sowie einer Kaserne in der Innerschweiz erinnern, zu mehr reichten seine Ortskenntnisse nicht aus. Das Tessin hätte ihn einmal noch gereizt, ganz zu schweigen vom Meer. Dieses war ihm aber immer unerreichbar weit weg vorgekommen. Es befand sich ja nicht einmal auf der Karte, die er gerade studierte.

In einer Ecke stiess er auf einen Haufen verschiedenster Kleider. Seidene Blusen, schicke Damenröcke, karierte Hemden, schwere Mäntel, pralle Jacken, ein Ledergilet und ganze Herrenanzüge lagen wild durcheinander da. Unwillkürlich liess sich Albert auf der ausgebreiteten Kleidersammlung nieder. Er streckte seine Glieder und genoss die Traulichkeit. Nachdem er die Nacht auf den harten Holzdielen verbracht hatte, war ihm das Einnisten in die lauschige Unterlage eine regelrechte Wohltat.

Selten hatte er sich so geborgen gefühlt. Beinahe schien ihm, dass jedes einzelne Kleidungsstück noch ein paar Rückstände menschlicher Wärme enthielt. Er deckte sich mit den Kleidern zu.

Albert hatte noch nicht zu Kräften zurückgefunden. Sein Körper verlangte nach Wasser, nach Schlaf – immerhin hatte er sich noch vor wenigen Stunden mit dem Tod duelliert, ihn schliesslich gebändigt. Im Nu schloss er die Augen und fiel in einen unruhigen Schlaf.

26. Die Verkündung

Der Klang einer kleinen Glocke eilte durch die belebten Strassen, über die blühenden Felder, in die gemächlichen Stuben von Rechthalten. Verglichen mit den mächtigen Glocken, die zu jeder Viertelstunde schlugen und täglich entschieden zur Heiligen Messe aufforderten, tönte die kleine Glocke viel sanfter, lieblicher. Dennoch fürchteten sich die Leute gerade vor ihr, denn ihr zarter, nahezu graziöser Klang stand in erheblichem Gegensatz zur Botschaft, die sie jeweils verkündete. Es war das Sterbeglöckchen.

Der schlaftrunkene Albert entfernte den modrig riechenden Rock von seinem Gesicht und horchte genau. Kein Zweifel, er konnte das Sterbeglöckchen läuten hören.

Nun hatte er also die Gewissheit. Hans Fahler war tot. Umgekommen beim Selbstmordversuch des Albert Leblanc.

Albert wurde übel, zudem war er zu erschöpft, um weiter nachzudenken. Er nickte wieder ein. Es sorgte ihn nicht, dass nur wenige Meter unter ihm der Unterricht wieder aufgenommen wurde. Die Müdigkeit war stärker als die Befürchtung, aufgefunden zu werden.

Eine gute halbe Stunde später knarrte die Holztreppe, die zum Estrich hoch führte. Die immer lauter werdenden Schritte rissen Albert nicht aus dem Schlaf. Regungslos blieb er eingemummt im Kleiderhaufen liegen.

Der Junge atmete schwer. Die Kiste, in der sich mehrere Dutzend Rechenbücher türmten, machte ihm ausserordentlich zu schaffen. Er musste erneut eine Pause einlegen und stellte die schwere Last auf einer Stufe ab.

Ausgerechnet ihn hatte es getroffen! Er, der schon genug unter nächtlichen Albträumen litt. Ehrfürchtig blickte er den Estrich hoch, von dem ihn nur noch wenige Stufen trennten. Das nun bei ihm aufkommende Gefühl glich demjenigen eines unerfahrenen Bergwanderers, der sich während seiner letzen Rast zum finalen, gefährlichen Aufstieg bereit macht.

Ein stechender Blick musterte ihn. Der Junge zuckte zusammen. Er konnte nur hoffen, dass der Raubvogel auf dem Balken nicht echt war.

Der Junge schickte sich an, die letzte Etappe zu bewältigen. Ein muffiger Gestank flog ihm zu. Er hatte ihn so ähnlich erwartet, er wusste, wie es auf Dachböden roch. Doch da war noch etwas anderes in der Luft. Es erinnerte ihn an den Geruch, der am Sonntagmorgen zuweilen aus dem Schlafzimmer seines Vaters strömte. Er hasste diesen Geruch.

Endlich hatte er den Dachboden erreicht, wo er die Kiste sogleich auf die Dielen fallen liess. Eine dicke Staubwolke wirbelte durch die Luft. Wo genau die Kiste hingehörte, wusste er nicht. Darum sollten sich andere scheren, dachte er erleichtert.

Da liess ihn etwas aufhorchen. War da nicht ein Geräusch? Er meinte, ein gleichmässiges, schweres Röcheln zu hören. War er nicht allein auf dem Dachboden? Gab es hier oben doch lebendige Tiere, oder – noch schlimmer – gar einen Verbrecher, einen Mörder? Fragen, die in Sekundenschnelle durch das unbedarfte, aber neugierige Hirn des Drittklässlers schossen.

War es nur die Höllenangst des Jungen, die den Kleiderhaufen in der hinteren Ecke in Bewegung brachte? Obwohl er das Bedürfnis hatte, den Dachboden schleunigst wieder zu verlassen, zog ihn eine eigenartige Kraft zu den zuckenden Kleidern hin.

Als der Blick des Kleinen über die verschiedenen Kleidungsstücke schweifte, verkrampfte sich plötzlich sein Gesicht. Es drückte ein Entsetzen aus, das tief aus seinem Inneren drang. Er öffnete den Mund, versuchte zu schreien, doch konnte er vor Schauder keinen Ton von sich geben. Der grausige Anblick lähmte ihn derart, dass er einen Moment lang nichts anderes tun konnte, als sich zu fürchten.

Er hatte einen schwarzen Fuss entdeckt, der unter einem weissen Leintuch hervorschaute. Der Fuss mutete animalisch an, und doch gehörte er zweifelsfrei einem Menschen.

Nun endlich gelang es dem Jungen, einen schwachen Schrei zu entfesseln und seine kurzen Beine wieder in Bewegung zu setzen. Ohne sich umzudrehen liess er den Kleiderhaufen hinter sich, fegte über die Holzdielen, hetzte die Treppe hinunter und erreichte schliesslich das Klassenzimmer, wo sein vor Furcht gezeichnetes Gesicht unter seinen Mitschülern für Heiterkeit sorgte.

27. Des Feuerwehrmanns Klagen

Ein angebrochenes Zehneretui Toscanelli lag auf dem Holztisch, über dem sich die Rauchschwaden in den verschiedensten Beschaffenheiten walzten. Wortlos sogen die alten Herren an den Zigarren, um aus ihren Lungen trübe Luft japsen zu können. Ihre Zungen bewahrten sie mit spritzigem Weisswein vor dem Austrocknen.

Karl hatte die Gunst der Stunde erkannt und der schluchzenden Mona den Arm über die Schulter gelegt. Sie liess ihn ausnahmsweise gewähren. Eigentlich hatte sie sich ja sogar erhofft, im Gasthof den Trost zu erhalten, der ihr zu Hause verwehrt worden war.

Der Stammtisch war wiederum der uniformierten Schar vorbehalten. So manches alteingesessene Vereinsmitglied hatte im Laufe der Jahre gar einen Stammstuhl für sich in Anspruch genommen, so dass sich dem Wirt auch heute ein altbekanntes Bild bot: Der Kommandant fürstlich an der schmalen Kante der Tischplatte, der alte Leo neben seinem Sohn, Heinrich in der diagonal gegenüberliegenden Ecke seines langjährigen Erzfeindes Herbert, auf der Fensterseite die Armeenostalgiker, ihnen gegenüber zwei passionierte Fischer sowie des einen Schwager. Dazwischen zwei Grüppchen, die sich aus weniger zwingenden Gründen zusammengetan hatten.

Einer aber fehlte.

Wie hatte sich die Stimmung im Vergleich zum letzten Beizenbesuch gewandelt! Die Mannen waren ruhig. Sie waren geschafft und erschlagen. Niemand traute sich, etwas in die Runde zu werfen. Zu sehr war jeder mit sich selbst beschäftigt, um zu begreifen, was vorgefallen war. Jeder einzelne brachte die Geschehnisse des letzten Samstagabends mit denjenigen der vergangenen Nacht in Verbindung, ohne dies jedoch auszusprechen. Dazu gab es auch keine Notwendigkeit. Jeder konnte sich in die Gedanken seines Tischnachbarn versetzen, sie waren mit den eigenen identisch.

Obwohl vor der Eingangstür des Gasthofs seit wenigen Stunden eine Schiefertafel mit kreidener Aufschrift «Heute Ruhetag» stand, hatte sich ein Teil der üblichen Gäste in der Gaststube eingefunden.

«Ich versteh' das nicht, warum nur?» Das erstickte Klagen Monas veranlasste Karl dazu, ihr sanft den Nacken zu kraulen. Sie sass zusammengesunken auf einem Stuhl, die Ellbogen auf den Tisch gestützt, das Gesicht in den Handinnenflächen vergraben.

«Ich versteh' das einfach nicht», schluchzte sie immer wieder. An der Tragödie konnten jedoch keine Zweifel mehr aufkommen.

Ein Angehöriger des Stammtischs, der für seinen ungewöhnlichen Appetit bekannt war, hielt die Stille nicht mehr aus. Er räusperte sich, blickte den Wirt an und begann zaghaft: «Vielleicht – würde es uns ganz gut tun, wenn wir etwas in den Magen bekommen könnten.»

Mit versteinerter Miene hob der Wirt seinen Kopf, den er zuvor für geraume Zeit dem Aschenbecher zugewandt hatte. Wie ein Schlag hatte ihn heute Morgen der Anblick des abgebrannten Hauses getroffen, als er ans Buchholz marschiert war, um seinen nicht auftauchenden Koch persönlich aus den Federn zu reissen. «Begreifst du denn nicht», antwortete er konsterniert, «heute gibt es nichts zu essen. Auch morgen und übermorgen nicht.»

Der Hungrige bemerkte nun, dass seine Frage alles andere als taktvoll gewesen war. Er war beileibe nicht der einzige, der sich nun ein kräftiges Mahl gewünscht hätte, doch nüchtern besass auch ein hartgesottener Feuerwehrmann ein gewisses Einfühlungsvermögen.

Der Rohling mit dem Doppelkinn versuchte, seinen Lapsus wieder gutzumachen. «Der gute Kamerad wird uns fehlen. Gott hab ihn selig», sprach er in etwas gar heiterem Ton.

Der Knall eines zerspringenden Glases liess alle vor

Schreck zusammenfahren. Die bis dahin tatenlos dasitzenden Männer drehten sich eiligst zur Quelle des Lärms um.

«Und jetzt nennst du ihn plötzlich den guten Kameraden?», warf Mona dem verdutzten Feuerwehrmann forsch zu. Sie war mittlerweile aufgestanden. «Hast du ihn nicht vor einer Woche noch wie ein Tier, ja wie Dreck behandelt?»

Sie erhielt keine Antwort.

«Du bist mitschuldig an seinem Tod!» Die Herzlichkeit, die für gewöhnlich von Mona ausging, hatte sich verloren. Aus ihr sprach nun der pure Hass. Sie ging ein paar Schritte um den Stammtisch.

«Du auch!», schrie sie den Kommandanten an, an dessen Schläfe eine Ader angeschwollen war. «Du hast nie gemerkt, dass alle nur aus Anstand über deine lausigen Sprüche lachen, nicht wahr?» Sprachlos nahm der Kommandant die Erniedrigung hin.

«Komm schon, Mona, das bringt jetzt auch nichts mehr.» Karl bemühte sich, die brodelnde Stimmung etwas zu entspannen.

«Von dir möchte ich im Moment nichts hören, Karl. Du hast schon getrunken», antwortete Mona bestimmt.

Sie ging weiter zum Träger des feinen Schnurrbarts und setzte ihre Abrechnung fort. Wäre ihm bewusst gewesen, wie erbost Mona sein konnte, hätte er sich gewiss nie an ihr vergriffen, dachte er bei sich. Sie liess es nicht aus, auch seinen Stolz zu kränken: «Vor Flegeln wie dir ekeln sich die Frauen.»

Mona knöpfte sich den nächsten vor, der ihr unangenehm in Erinnerung geblieben war: «Jetzt zu dir, du verzogenes Bürschchen …» Mona leuchteten hochrote Backen entgegen. «Wie fühlt es sich an, einen netten, aufrichtigen Mann in den Tod getrieben zu haben?» Erneut liess sie die mächtigen Worte durch eine Pause wirken. «Was wohl dein Vater dazu sagen wird?» Mona deutete mit einer Kopfbewegung auf einen ebenfalls rotbäckigen Mann in Uniform.

«Ihr seid alle mitschuldig an seinem Tod!» Ihre Stimme überschlug sich. «Ihr alle!»

Nun stürmte sie entschlossen an den Tisch, an dem sich der Wirt und sein Gegenüber im dichten Zigarrenqualm zu verstecken schienen. Vor den beiden blieb sie stehen und musterte sie abschätzigen Blickes.

«Und ihr seid die Hauptschuldigen, dass es soweit gekommen ist. Schämt euch.» Mona sprach die Worte nun leise, doch waren sie für alle Anwesenden gut verständlich. Blitzartig ergriff sie ein Weinglas und goss dessen Inhalt dem Buckligen ins Gesicht. Er schrie auf und rieb sich die Augen: «Du Kuh! Bist du wahnsinnig?»

Noch bevor sich der Begossene erholt hatte, schnappte sich Mona ein zweites Glas und überschüttete auch den Wirt mit Weisswein.

«Du unverschämtes Weib, du wirst mich morgen noch kennenlernen!», schnauzte er, schäumend vor Wut.

«Ich werde morgen nicht kommen. Und übermorgen auch nicht!» Mona knallte die Eingangstür hinter sich zu und überliess die Männer ihrer Scham.

28. Das Sonnenblumenröckchen

Die Gedanken erschütterten Albert.

Musste die Leiche von Hans Fahler nicht völlig verkohlt und somit unkenntlich geworden sein? Hatte er sich nicht mit einem Brief für immer von Mona verabschiedet und sie über sein bevorstehendes Ableben aufgeklärt? Stand nicht neben den Trümmern seines Hauses sein Grabkreuz bereit? Bereit, um in die Erde gesteckt zu werden, in der seine sterblichen Überreste verwesen sollten?

Ein kalter Schauer jagte Albert über den Rücken. Er fragte sich noch einmal, ob er heute tatsächlich das Sterbeglöckchen vernommen hatte. Er war versucht, die Schläge als Täuschung seiner aufgewühlten Sinne zu überführen, doch konnte er sie allzu genau aus seiner Erinnerung abrufen.

Das Sterbeglöckchen hatte also geschlagen. Und es musste ihm, Albert Leblanc, gegolten haben.

Ihm schwindelte. Fest stand eigentlich nur, dass ein Bürger von Rechthalten gestorben war. Immer deutlicher aber schien es Albert, dass er der einzige war, der wirklich wusste, um wen es sich bei dem Toten handelte. Die Geschichte kam ihm allerdings noch reichlich unglaubwürdig, wie aus einem schlechten Roman vor.

Als sich Albert aus der Kleidersammlung erhob, bemerkte er erleichtert die Dunkelheit, die draussen bereits wieder eingekehrt war. Er hatte den ganzen Tag ohne Wasser verbracht. Nun war die Luft rein, um der Durststrecke ein Ende zu setzen.

Er ging zur Treppe und lauschte. Absolute Stille. Dennoch schlich er auf Zehenspitzen weiter und schwankte langsam die Stufen hinunter. Wiederum durfte er auf keinen Fall das Licht anmachen. Er tastete sich voran und spürte, dass ihm allmählich die Kraft ausging.

Endlich erreichte er die Toilette, über die er letzte Nacht in das Schulhaus gelangt war, stürzte sich zum Wasserhahn und lechzte wie ein dürstendes Pferd nach dem Wasser, das stramm herausquoll.

Wahrhaftig fühlte er sich durch die Flüssigkeit, die er in grossen Mengen in sich hatte laufen lassen, wieder lebendiger. Das Spiegelbild hingegen zeigte immer noch das zerzauste und geschwärzte Wesen, das knapp dem Feuertod entkommen war. Seine überaus unansehnliche Erscheinung missfiel ihm zutiefst. Er musste unverzüglich aus dieser hässlichen Hülle schlüpfen, musste raus aus den kümmerlichen Kleidern, musste sich reinwaschen, um wieder Mensch zu werden.

Albert entblösste sich und betrachtete seinen linken Oberarm. Die Wunde sah widerlich aus. Blasen hatten sich gebildet, zudem klebten überall zerschlissene Streifen Toilettenpapier. Der brennende Schmerz, gepaart mit dem üblen Anblick liess Albert in Schweiss ausbrechen.

Die Flammen, die sein gemütliches Haus verschluckten, loderten in seinen Gedanken.

Da hielt Albert seinen Kopf unter das kalte Wasser, liess seinen ganzen Körper überströmen mit kaltem Wasser, gierte richtiggehend nach kaltem Wasser. Unentwegt begann er, den Russ von seiner Haut zu reiben, schrubbte wie ein Rasender mit Seife sein Gesicht, seinen Rumpf, seine Arme und Beine ab, und mit jeder Entfernung von Schmutz erlangte er ein Stück seiner Würde zurück.

Nach dem energischen Waschakt konnte sich Albert wieder sehen lassen. Seine bleiche Haut war wieder zum Vorschein gekommen, lediglich unter seinen Nägeln, zwischen seinen Fingern und an seinen Zähnen hafteten noch Rückstände des Brandes.

Erheblichere Schwierigkeiten bereitete es ihm, seiner entstellten Frisur wieder ein Mindestmass an Ordnung zu verpassen. Allerdings konnte er feststellen, dass er mit unwahrscheinlichem Glück (er wusste nicht recht, ob er dieses Wort gebrauchen sollte) davongekommen war. Das Feuer war knapp nicht bis zur Kopfhaut vorgedrungen, sondern hatte ihm lediglich einige Haarbüschel verglüht. Durch geschicktes Verrücken seines Scheitels gelang es ihm, das Gewirr auf seinem Kopf halbwegs zu kaschieren.

Hastig raffte er seine Kleider zusammen und begab sich splitternackt wieder auf den Dachboden. Als er die Treppe hinter sich gelassen hatte, blieb er stehen. Er musterte eine mit Büchern überfüllte Kiste.

Die Kiste lag unmittelbar vor dem Glücksrad, an dem er heute Mittag gedreht hatte. Sie war ihm vorher nicht aufgefallen. Albert hätte schwören können, dass sich die Kiste bei seinem heutigen Rundgang im Estrich noch nicht an jener Stelle befunden hatte.

Ein mulmiges Gefühl überkam ihn. Offenbar war heute Nachmittag jemand den Dachboden hinaufgestiegen, während er unter den Kleidern begraben geschlafen hatte.

Vielleicht war man nun bereits im Anmarsch, um ihn, den Störenfried, auf dem Estrich des Schulhauses zu schnappen? Möglicherweise hatte er jetzt noch die Gelegenheit, zu fliehen.

Albert wurde unruhig. Unter keinen Umständen wollte er lebendig aufgefunden werden. Und für einen weiteren Versuch, sein Leben wegzuwerfen, fehlte ihm im Augenblick der Mut. Noch fehlte er ihm. Die folgenschwere letzte Nacht war noch nicht verdaut, zu tief sass das Debakel. Hier zu bleiben war ihm aber zu riskant.

Ausser Frage stand, dass sich Albert erst einmal wieder bekleiden musste. An Kleidern mangelte es ihm auf dem Dachboden ja freilich nicht.

Er knüpfte sich ein rot-schwarz kariertes Hemd zu und verstaute dieses in einer dunklen Hose. Seine Halbschuhe, die immer noch im Garten von Mona liegen mussten, fanden respektablen Ersatz. Weiter schlüpfte er in ein Ledergilet, das ihm den Hauch eines verwegenen Abenteurers verlieh. Der schwarze Mantel, den er sich über die Schultern warf, war eines Toten würdig. Abschliessend setzte er sich einen Hut auf, den er sich tief ins Gesicht zog. Seine neue Garderobe war komplett.

Aus seiner geschwärzten Hose zog er mit spitzen Fingern sein Portemonnaie und liess es in den Mantel gleiten, die Überreste seiner alten Kleider vergrub er tief unter den herumliegenden Stoffen, wo man sie so schnell nicht finden würde.

Es gab allerdings noch ein Teil, welches liegenzulassen ihm widerstrebte. Ein aufreizend kurzes Röckchen, bestückt mit hübschen Sonnenblumen, verschwand ebenfalls in der Innentasche seines Mantels.

Bevor er sich aus dem Staub machte, traf er noch ein interessantes Objekt an. Hinter einer Wand aus übereinandergestapelten Pulten verbarg sich ein Harmonium.

In den turbulenten letzten Stunden war an Musik nicht zu denken gewesen. Obwohl er kein Tasteninstrument beherrschte, trat er nun unversehens in die Schöpfpedale und betätigte damit das Gebläse. Ein schauderhaft unharmonischer Klang erfüllte den Dachboden, als Albert mit beiden Händen in die Tasten griff.

Einige Misstöne später aber wusste Albert, welche Tasten er zu benützen hatte und welche nicht. Da erklang es wieder – sein Lied, das er mit seinen letzten Gitarrenanschlägen vollendet hatte. Zwar bevorzugte er die Gitarre, doch das Lied klang auch auf dem Harmonium aussergewöhnlich. Die Melodie war so gut, dass sie auf jedem beliebigen Instrument der Welt wirkte, befand Albert stolz.

Es war schon wieder Mitternacht. Er konnte flüchten. Früher oder später musste er hier ohnehin weg. Ein letztes Mal sah er sich auf dem Dachboden um und verliess diesen über die knarrende Treppe.

29. Vieille Prune

Bis dahin machte das Haus nicht den Eindruck, bewohnt zu sein. Alberts Anspannung löste sich dadurch aber noch keineswegs. Leise betrat er einen Raum, den er bereits im hereinschimmernden Mondlicht als Küche ausmachen konnte. Sofort kannte er den vertrauten Geruch. Es war der Geruch von frischen Pilzen. Er zog die Vorhänge zu, um das Licht anmachen zu können.

Prüfend sah er sich um. Einen Moment lang fixierte er den Kochherd. Böse Erinnerungen wurden wach.

Nachdem er auch in der Wohnstube und im Badezimmer niemanden angetroffen hatte, gelangte er in den ersten Stock hinauf.

Das erste Zimmer enthielt einen Tisch und eine Kommode, die Albert nicht weiter interessierten. Eine weitere Toilette sowie das nächste Zimmer, in dem ein Büchergestell einsam an der Wand stand, liessen Albert vorerst ebenfalls kalt.

Er passierte den Gang und näherte sich dem hintersten Zimmer. Die Tür war halb geöffnet. Hinter ihr konnte er nichts als Dunkelheit erkennen. Er spitzte die Ohren.

Totenstille.

Noch zögerte er. Im Kopf hatte er alle ihm nur möglich scheinenden Hergänge durchgespielt. Sein Gesicht glühte. Leise zog er seinen schweren Mantel aus.

Endlich konnte er sich überwinden und drückte auf den Lichtschalter.

Das Bett stand in der Mitte des Zimmers, in dem alle Fensterläden geschlossen waren. Es war leer. Albert trat ein und wusste nicht, ob er erleichtert sein sollte.

Ein Paar gebrauchte Socken lag auf dem Teppichboden, am Griff des Holzschranks hing ein braunes Hemd. Durch ein gekipptes Fenster strömte etwas Luft in das Zimmer, das alles andere als ausgestorben wirkte. Nach Leben suchte er aber vergebens.

Ohne sich weiter umzusehen verliess Albert das Zimmer. Er hatte Hunger.

Auf einem grosszügig gepolsterten Fauteuil hatte er es sich gemütlich gemacht, genoss ein Stück vom nicht mehr ganz frischen Brot, und liess sich die fein geschnittenen Tranchen Greyerzerkäse schmecken. Seit den Valiumpillen hatte Albert nichts mehr gegessen.

Er erlaubte sich, seine Füsse auf das Tischchen vor ihm zu legen, auf dem eine Vase mit schönen Blumen stand. Albert war kein Blumenkenner, doch glaubte er, dass die Vase Nelken enthielt. Vielleicht konnte ein kräftiges Getränk noch etwas zur Traulichkeit beitragen. Albert erhob sich und inspizierte die Wohnwand.

Hinter einem breiten Türchen eröffnete sich Albert eine aussergewöhnliche Spirituosensammlung. Erheitert begutachtete er eine Flasche nach der anderen. Dabei stiess er plötzlich auf einen namhaften Tropfen.

Absinth.

Albert wunderte sich über die gemachte Entdeckung, umso mehr, als die Flasche mit exakt der gleichen Etikette versehen war wie diejenige, die er jeweils vom Meister bekommen hatte. Diejenige, die ihn eigentlich hätte umbringen sollen.

Er spürte wieder eine leichte Übelkeit in sich aufkommen. Möglicherweise hatte die lebensgefährliche Mischung, die er gestern eingenommen hatte, doch einen Teil von ihm getötet. Zumindest schien sich seine Liebe zum Absinth abgekühlt zu haben. Ausgerechnet zum Absinth, der ihn, den Einsamen, so treu begleitet hatte. Albert hoffte, dass die Beziehung wieder ins Lot zu kriegen war. Momentan wurde ihm aber bereits beim Gedanken an das Anisextrakt schlecht.

Er entschied sich schliesslich für einen Vieille Prune. Aus der Küche holte er sich ein Glas, ein wohlgeformtes, vorzügliches Schnapsglas. Er liess das bräunliche Getränk in das Glas tröpfeln, bis es zu zwei Dritteln voll war. Warum er sich wohl nie ein so schönes Glas geleistet hatte? Es war ihm schlichtweg nie in den Sinn gekommen. Erst beim unerwarteten Besuch von Mona war ihm die Hässlichkeit seines üblichen Glases aufgefallen.

Albert stiess im Stillen auf sich selber an. Auf sich und sein Leben. Plötzlich lachte er, immer noch nicht wissend, was in seinem Kopf eigentlich vorgehen sollte. Er hielt das schöne Schnapsglas auf Augenhöhe, sodass sich sein Gesicht darin spiegelte. Seine Frisur liess zwar noch alle Wünsche offen, doch im übrigen sah Albert einen nicht unattraktiven, jungen Mann. Ob er in seinem Gesicht gar einen Anflug von Zufriedenheit ausmachen konnte?

Er machte das Radio an und drehte den Lautstärkeregler auf die kleinstmögliche Stufe. Ein schönes, aber trauriges Lied erklang. *Gestern waren alle meine Probleme noch so weit weg. Jetzt sind sie da. Plötzlich bin ich nicht einmal mehr die Hälfte des Mannes, der ich einmal war. Ich bin gar nicht mehr. Ein Schatten hängt über mir. Der Tod. Jetzt brauche ich einen Ort, an dem ich mich verstecken kann. Ich sehne mich nach gestern.*

Trotz der Melancholie fühlte er sich wohl in der fremden Stube. Eigenartigerweise hatte er in seinem früheren Wohnzimmer nie solche Geborgenheit empfunden.

Was Mona wohl zurzeit tat, was sie wohl dachte?

Albert nahm einen weiteren Schluck, der ihm aber sogleich etwas weniger mundete. Das Glas offenbarte ihm nun seinen traurigen Blick, der von tiefen Furchen umrahmt wurde.

Ein Geräusch riss ihn aus seinen Grübeleien.

Es kam aus dem hinteren Teil des Erdgeschosses, den er sich vorhin nur flüchtig besehen hatte. Sein Herz begann wieder stärker zu pochen. Hatte er sich etwa eine Spur zu selbstherrlich aufgeführt? Er blieb regungslos auf seinem Sessel kleben und wartete.

Schritte kamen näher. Oder waren es nicht Schritte? Zumindest nicht menschliche? Sondern viel eher der kaum hörbare, leichte Gang eines Tieres?

Freudig nahm Albert die kleine Katze zur Kenntnis, die in die Wohnstube stolzierte, ohne sich die geringste Verwunderung über den Fremden anmerken zu lassen. Sie ging geradewegs auf Albert zu, sprang auf den Sessel und legte sich unmittelbar neben ihn hin.

Das Zutrauen, das ihm die Katze entgegenbrachte, überraschte Albert. Gerade zu ihm, der mit Tieren nie etwas hatte anfangen können. Ob er sie berühren durfte? Zögernd bewegte er seine Hand zur Katze hin, strich ihr erst sachte über das Fell und kraulte ihr dann liebevoll den Bauch.

Er genehmigte sich noch einen Tropfen Vieille Prune und kostete die Wärme aus, die von der Katze auf ihn überging.

30. Der Verstorbene ruht in der Totenkapelle

Albert lag regungslos im kalten Wasser. Seine Lippen waren bereits blau, seine Haut gezeichnet. Die Wanne war randvoll. Von draussen strahlte die prächtige Morgensonne, klang das fröhliche Vogelgezwitscher ins Badezimmer herein.

Sein Leben lang hatte er noch nie in einer Badewanne gelegen. Einerseits aus Abscheu vor kaltem Wasser, andererseits aus Mangel an Gelegenheiten dazu. Heute Morgen schien ihm ein kühles Bad aber das Richtige zu sein, um die Heilung seines Armes voranzutreiben.

Er hatte sich nicht einmal gesträubt, in die Badewanne zu steigen. Seitdem er nur knapp dem Inferno entwichen, sein Körper gar mit beissenden Flammen in Kontakt getreten war, hatte sich seine Auffassung von Kälte gewandelt. Auf einmal empfand er kaltes Wasser als ungemein erfrischend und belebend.

Mit lautem Geplätscher erhob er sich aus der Wanne. Seine Zähne hatten nun doch zu klappern begonnen. Für heute war genug.

Über dem Waschbecken stutzte er seine Nägel und entfernte dabei die letzten Russreste. Zudem ragte der Holzsplitter in seinem grossen Zeh nun so weit heraus, dass er ihn endlich aussondern konnte. Nun erinnerten nur noch die dunklen Zähne an seinen Aufenthalt im Feuer. Es ekelte ihn etwas, eine fremde Zahnbürste zu benützen. Er tat es trotzdem, denn die Zähne, die wie abgestorbene Wucherungen in seinem Mund steckten, ekelten ihn noch mehr.

Albert vernahm in der Richtung des Hauseingangs ein Geräusch. Zuerst ein Rascheln, dann ein dumpfer Aufschlag.

Auf dieses Geräusch hatte er gewartet. Trotz der Aufregung, die ihn nun befiel, versuchte er ruhig zu bleiben. Mit weissen Zähnen schritt er zur Tür und bückte sich, um die Tageszeitung aufzuheben, die durch den schmalen Türschlitz ins Innere des Hauses geworfen worden war.

Ohne bereits einen Blick auf sie zu werfen, legte er die Zeitung auf den Küchentisch.

In der Wohnstube schnappte er sich die Flasche Vieille Prune und das schöne Schnapsglas und kehrte in die Küche zurück. Er setzte sich. Es war früh, um Alkohol zu trinken, das wusste Albert. Doch möglicherweise würde er nicht anders können.

Er entfaltete die *Freiburger Nachrichten*, versehen mit dem Datum 17. Juni 1967, adressiert an Hans Fahler, Schwarzseestrasse 37 in 1718 Rechthalten.

Das Weltgeschehen interessierte ihn nicht, jedenfalls heute nicht. Nach kurzem Überfliegen der Titelseite blätterte er weiter.

Bereits die dritte Seite warf ihm ein trostloses Bild entgegen. Das Bild zeigte einen Waldrand, vor dem ein Haufen aus Trümmern und Schutt in zaghaftem Rauch stand. Albert hielt sich niedergeschlagen die Hände vor den Mund. Von seinem Obdach war wirklich kaum etwas übrig geblieben. Das Feuer hatte erbarmungslos gewütet.

Dann betrachtete er sehr genau den angrenzenden Wald. Konnte er zwischen den straffen Stämmen der Buchen nicht einen kleinen Gegenstand ausmachen? Tränen begannen sich zu bilden. Es musste sie sein – seine Gitarre. Mit dem Daumen fuhr er sanft über die Stelle des Bildes, an der er die Gitarre vermutete. Vieles hätte er jetzt getan, um sie in seine Arme nehmen zu können. Ob sie sich immer noch am Waldrand befand? Wohl kaum. Ohnehin war es für ihn ausgeschlossen, sein ehemaliges Haus aufzusuchen. Oder vielleicht nachts?

«Tödlicher Brand in Rechthalten» lautete die Überschrift oberhalb des Bildes. Die Vermutung hatte sich also bewahrheitet, sein missglücktes Unternehmen hatte einen Tod verursacht. Doch wen hielt man für den Toten? Albert las weiter.

In der Nacht von Donnerstag auf Freitag zerstörte ein Brand ein kleines Wohnhaus nahe des Buchholzes in Rechthalten. Ein Mann wurde dabei tödlich verletzt.

Ein Einwohner von Rechthalten hat am Freitag Morgen den Brand am Waldrand entdeckt und kurz darauf, um 9:45 Uhr, die Feuerwehr alarmiert. Als die rasch ausgerückte Feuerwehr von Rechthalten am Unglücksort eintraf, konnte sie kaum mehr etwas retten. «Wo kein Feuer mehr ist, kann auch kein Feuer gelöscht werden», erklärte der Kommandant der lokalen Feuerwehr gegenüber den Freiburger Nachrichten. Das Holzhaus sei zu diesem Zeitpunkt schon praktisch abgebrannt gewesen.

Einen grausigen Fund machten die Löschtruppen schliesslich bei den Aufräumarbeiten. Unter den Trümmern des Hauses wurde die verkohlte Leiche eines Menschen gefunden. Laut dem örtlichen Wachtmeister handelt es sich dabei um einen Mann.

Der genaue Ablauf des Dramas sei nun aber noch Gegenstand von Untersuchungen. Ein Gewaltverbrechen könne ausgeschlossen werden.

Der Berichterstattung konnte Albert nichts entnehmen, was ihn überrascht hätte.

Seine Gedanken waren nun bei Hans Fahler. Wie der arme Teufel wohl hatte sterben müssen? Albert wünschte sich, dass ihm beim Einsturz des Hauses gleich das Genick gebrochen worden war. Er hatte es nicht verdient, einen erbärmlichen Tod in den Flammen zu sterben. Albert wusste, dass ihm darüber bis ans Ende seiner Tage die Ungewissheit bleiben würde. Sie war bedrückend.

Er blätterte weiter und gelangte zu Seite fünf. Seine Augen überflogen die Seite.

Albert musste sich zurücklehnen, musste sich am Hinterkopf kratzen. Die beiden mächtigen Wörter schossen wie Kugeln auf ihn ein. Dann gaben die Wörter ihre strenge Formation auf, zerlegten sich in schemenhafte Buchstaben, krochen unter grellem Ächzen über den mattweissen Grund, bewegten sich immer schneller, drehten sich, bogen sich gerade, verwandelten sich in spitze Nägel, die in seine Netzhaut, in seine Stirn eingeschlagen wurden und ein Kribbeln hinter seiner Schädeldecke verursachten …

Obwohl ihm beim Anblick der beklemmenden Seite bereits schwindelte, leerte er das Glas in einem Zug.

Was Albert entdeckt hatte, entsprach eigentlich nichts anderem als seinen kühnen Erwartungen. Allerdings warf ihn auch das Eintreffen von Erwartetem in tiefste Ungläubigkeit, denn wer konnte schon von sich behaupten, seine eigene Todesanzeige in der Zeitung erblickt zu haben?

Unter einem schwarzen Kreuz, umrahmt von dicken Balken, las Albert:

†

Schmerzerfüllt teilen wir allen Freunden und Bekannten mit,
dass es Gott dem Allmächtigen gefallen hat,

Albert Leblanc

zu sich in die ewige Heimat zu berufen. Er starb nach
mühevollem Leben, wohlversehen mit den Heiligen
Sakramenten, im jungen Alter von 27 Jahren.

Der Beerdigungsgottesdienst findet statt am
Montag, 19. Juni um 9:30 Uhr in der Pfarrkirche zu Rechthalten.

In Trauer: Sein Pflegevater Bernhard Brülhart, Dorf, Rechthalten

R.I.P.

Der Verstorbene ruht in der Totenkapelle zu Rechthalten.

Diese Anzeige gilt als Einladung zur Beerdigung.
Leidzirkulare werden keine versandt.

Albert war also nicht mehr. Die Welt hatte ihn für tot erklärt. Dabei hielt er sich weder in der Totenkapelle noch in der ewigen Heimat auf, sondern ganz leibhaftig im Haus des tatsächlich Verstorbenen.

Gleich daneben prangte eine andere Anzeige, die ebenfalls ihm galt:

†

Der allseits beliebte Gasthof in Rechthalten gibt mit tiefem Bedauern Kenntnis vom Hinschied seines treuen Arbeiters und geschätzten Kollegen

Albert Leblanc
Koch

Die Beerdigung findet am Montag, 19. Juni
um 9:30 Uhr in der Pfarrkirche zu Rechthalten statt.

Albert vermutete, dass die Anzeige Werbezwecken dienen sollte. Dass der Wirt ihn als «geschätzten Kollegen» bezeichnete, kam ihm wie ein schlechter Witz vor. Oder ob vielleicht Mona dahintersteckte?

Es war die dritte Anzeige, die ihm zusetzte, ihn erschütterte, sich schmerzhaft, wohltuend in seine Eingeweide frass. Freude, Verzweiflung, Stolz und Entsetzen eroberten wechselweise sein Gemüt. Tränen kullerten aus seinen Augen, rannen über seine Wangen, tropften auf die Zeitung. Die lieben Worte kamen für Albert derart überraschend, dass sie seinen Körper durchschüttelten. Immer wieder las er durch die Tränen hindurch Monas persönliche Abschiedsworte:

†

Mona Gutmann weint und trauert um
ihren lieben Freund und Koch

Albert Leblanc

Gäbe es bloss mehr solcher Menschen,
wie der liebe Verstorbene einer war.
Möge er im Tod die Erfüllung finden,
die ihm im Leben verwehrt blieb.

Was hatte er bloss getan? Was hatte er sich nur dabei gedacht? Bis dahin war ihm dieser Gedanke überheblich vorgekommen, doch nun wurde ihm bewusst, dass er Mona mit seiner Untat Leid und Schmerz zugefügt hatte. Der Gedanke war ihm unerträglich. Die Anzeige war jedoch Beweis genug dafür, dass Mona um ihn trauerte. Wie konnte er seine Dummheit nur gutmachen, rückgängig machen?
Es konnte es nicht, dafür war es zu spät.

Er war für tot erklärt worden, Hans Fahler war tatsächlich tot, und nun war er auch noch in dessen Haus eingebrochen. Nein, sein Tod liess sich nicht mehr annullieren.

Für den Rest des Tages blieb das Türchen des Schnapsschrankes offen. Im Suff dachte Albert an Mona, Hans und seinen eigenen Tod. Seinen wirklichen Tod.

31. Alchemie

Albert setzte sich an den Küchentisch, um ein Stück Brot hinunterzuwürgen. Nur vage konnte er sich an den gestrigen Tag erinnern. Er war heute Morgen auf dem Boden des Schlafzimmers aufgewacht. Ob er sich direkt auf den Teppich gelegt hatte oder vom Bett gefallen war, konnte er nicht bestimmen.

Die Samstagzeitung lag immer noch offen auf dem Tisch. So traurig die Todesanzeige, die Mona verfasst hatte, auch war – sie war ihm eine ungeheure Genugtuung. Mona wurde von vielen begehrt, nicht nur von ihm. Ihre Worte hatten Gewicht. Die gewiss etwas ungewöhnliche Anzeige rehabilitierte ihn, den kleinen, dummen Albert Leblanc. All die Leute, die ihm nie etwas zugetraut hatten, konnten nun staunend feststellen, dass ausgerechnet die gute, schöne Mona Sympathien für ihn empfand. Empfunden hatte. Albert war ihr dafür unendlich dankbar.

Zerstreut blätterte er eine Seite weiter. Werbungen und Inserate, dicht aneinandergedrängt. Heute um viertel nach acht im Kino Eden. Hotel der toten Gäste. Spannung bis zum Siedepunkt. Albert seufzte und überlegte sich, ob er sich nicht auch in einem seltsamen Film befand. Sein Leben würde gewiss Stoff dafür bieten. Bestattungen und Leichentransporte in Düdingen. Tag und Nacht. Särge und Kränze auf Lager. Die hatten mittlerweile wohl auch schon Hans Fahler eine neue Bleibe beschafft. Damensommerrock zum Preis von sieben Franken neunzig, derzeit in der Lausannegasse erhältlich. Waschbar, trocknet rasch, kann gebügelt werden, ausserdem ist er schwer entflammbar. Was damit wohl gemeint war? Albert erinnerte sich an den kleinen Rock, den er in die Innentasche seines Mantels gestopft hatte. Nur wer Toscanelli raucht, weiss, wie bekömmlich sie sind. Verloren am Feldschiessen in Giffers, automatische Herrenarmbanduhr. 14 Wochen trächtiges Mutterschwein zu verkaufen, dritter Wurf, sowie ein Mutterschwein zum Schlachten. Das Restaurant de la Grenette sucht per sofort oder nach Übereinkunft ein junges Mädchen für die Lingerie, einen Kellner und einen Kochlehrling. Warum hatte er eigentlich nie in Betracht gezogen, das Restaurant zu wechseln? Krampfadern und geschwollene Beine verhindern Sie mit elastischen Strümpfen in bester Qualität. Ärztlich empfohlen, unsere Krampfadernstrümpfe. Wie verrückt die Welt geworden war. Das Inserat kam ihm wie ein Hohn vor. Grosses Waldfest im Brügiwald Rechthalten. In seinem Dorf würde man am Abend vor seiner Beerdigung also feiern.

Alberts Kopf dröhnte. Er nahm sich vor, den heutigen Tag nüchterner zu gestalten. Vielleicht würde er im Haus von Hans Fahler irgendeinen sinnvolleren Zeitvertrieb finden.

Er betrachtete das schwarzweisse Bild, das über dem Küchentisch hing. Es zeigte vier Menschen, vermutlich eine vierköpfige Familie. Der junge Mann trug einen exakten Seitenscheitel und lächelte schüchtern in die Kamera. Albert zweifelte, doch glaubte er, im Gesicht des schmächtigen Mannes den jungen Hans Fahler zu erkennen. Die Frau neben ihm war recht hübsch. Nur ihre markante Nase wollte nicht ganz zu ihrer ansonsten zierlichen Gestalt passen. Die beiden Jungen zu den Füssen des Paares schienen praktisch gleich alt zu sein. Sie sassen auf dem Boden und lachten, als ob der Ernst des Lebens nicht auf sie warten würde.

Albert stand auf und gelangte über ein Wendeltreppchen ins Untergeschoss. Es war ein seltsames Gefühl, sich in einem fremden Haus so ungeniert wie in seinem eigenen zu bewegen. Er erreichte einen schmalen, finsteren Gang. Nur aus einem Türspalt drang ein wenig Licht.

Und wiederum hörte Albert unerwartete Geräusche. Sie kamen aus dem Raum mit der leicht geöffneten Tür, dem nun Alberts volle Aufmerksam galt. Erschrocken blieb er stehen und horchte. Aus verschiedenen Lauten konnte er das Schnurren der Katze herausfiltern. Doch da war noch etwas. Etwas Lebendiges. Ein hohes, beständiges Piepen gellte in seinen Ohren. Dazu kam ein unregelmässiges Klopfen, Schlagen, Hämmern. Langsam und möglichst lautlos näherte sich Albert der Tür.

Endlich konnte er durch den Spalt spähen.

Die Feststellung, dass er im Keller, den er nun betrat, kein menschliches Wesen antraf, entspannte ihn. Und dennoch erschrak ihn der Anblick des dramatischen Schauspiels, das sich ihm bot. Die Katze schlug mit ihren Pfoten unentwegt gegen eine kleine Käfigfalle, stiess sie umher, liess sie auf den Kopf stürzen, um sie dann wieder gewaltsam auf ihren Holzuntersatz zu drehen. Gelegentlich drangen ihre Zähne zwischen die feinen Gitterverstrebungen der Falle. Innerhalb der Käfigfalle befand sich eine zitternde, völlig verängstigte kleine Spitzmaus. Welch entsetzliche Folter sie durchleben musste – eingeschlossen ohne Nahrung, ohne Aussicht auf Überleben, und dennoch froh, nicht in der todbringenden Freiheit zu sein.

Albert führte die Katze aus dem Keller, schloss die Tür und hob den Käfig auf. Immer noch piepste das Mäuschen aufgeregt, und Albert bemerkte, dass die Furcht des kleinen Nagetiers durch sein Hinzutreten nicht kleiner geworden war. Verständlich. Er stieg auf einen dreibeinigen Hocker, klappte das kleine Fenster auf, das sich oben an der Kellermauer befand und stellte die Käfigfalle im Freien ab.

Die Falle schnappte auf und das Mäuschen sprang mit einem kessen Satz in die Freiheit. Wieviel Zeit ihm wohl da draussen noch bleiben würde? Gewiss lauerten bereits die nächsten Gefahren. Er versuchte, dem Mäuschen noch hinterher zu sehen, da entdeckte er plötzlich nur wenige Meter vor ihm eine Frau. Behäbig pflückte sie das Unkraut, das sich in ihrem Garten angesammelt hatte. Es musste sich um eine Nachbarin von Hans handeln. Rasch schloss Albert das Fenster.

Schlagartig war er wieder daran erinnert worden, dass seine Zeit da draussen bereits abgelaufen war.

Er bemerkte nun, in welch sonderbare Kammer des Hauses er geraten war. Was er sah, versetzte ihn in Staunen.

An der dem Fenster gegenüberliegenden Mauer präsentierte sich ihm eine Apparatur, ähnlich einem Ofen. Sie war mit einem Rohr versehen, das in einen metallenen Kessel führte. Ein Brennkessel? Daneben lag ein grosser Glasballon in einem Holzverschlag, umgeben von unzähligen leeren Flaschen. Albert roch den starken, beissenden Geruch.

War Hans Fahler etwa eine Art Alchemist gewesen, der hier, verborgen unter der Erdoberfläche, tüftelte und experimentierte? Albert wusste ja nur allzu gut, zu was Menschen in der Abgeschiedenheit fähig waren. Die Herstellung des Lebenselixiers oder des Steins der Weisen dürfte Hans da unten allerdings nicht gelungen sein, bedauerte Albert. Der Gedanke veranlasste ihn dazu, rasch in sein Portemonnaie zu sehen. Er war immer noch da, der letzte Kieselstein, den er im Schulhaus fast verloren hätte.

Albert schaute sich noch ein wenig um, doch schwand seine Neugierde allmählich. Er verliess den Keller und stieg hoch in den ersten Stock. Noch einmal besah er sich das Zimmer mit dem Büchergestell. «Ein allzu spektakuläres Leben wird dieser Hans wohl nicht geführt haben», dachte Albert. Er fühlte sich zuweilen an sein eigenes Haus erinnert. Einige Heimatschmöker lagen zuvorderst im Gestell. Dahinter ein Buch über den letzten Weltkrieg. Albert ergriff es und blätterte es in Windeseile durch. Kriegsberichte hatten ihn nie interessiert. Das Leben bot genug Elend, er brauchte es nicht noch in konzentrierter Form. Die Enzyklopädie über nachtaktive Tiere liess er unberührt, ebenso den abgegriffenen Handatlas und die Sagen des klassischen Altertums.

Mit einem Holzgriffel öffnete Albert eine Deckentür, aus der sich eine Klapptreppe nach unten ziehen liess.

Der Dachboden von Hans Fahler wies bei weitem weniger Entdeckungspotential als derjenige des Schulhauses auf. Der übliche Kram häufte sich hier an. Gebündelte Zeitungen, ein alter Schlafsack, verschiedene Hüte, eine Trommel. Etwas seltsamer mutete da schon der schwarze Koffer an, der etwa ein Dutzend dunkle Sonnenbrillen sowie ein ekliges Glasauge enthielt. Albert prüfte vorsichtig mit seinem Finger, ob es sich dabei nicht doch um ein echtes handelte. Dann besah er sich das Foto, das in einem silbernen Rahmen auf dem Boden lag. Wieder Hans Fahler, bereits etwas älter. Die Frau an seiner Seite jedoch war nicht mehr die gleiche, das erkannte Albert an ihrem südlichen Teint. Zwei Frauen also. Nun ja, Hans musste selber wissen, was er tat, sein Liebesleben ging Albert nichts an. Er wandte sich ab und erblickte, an einen alten Stuhl gestellt, ein Gewehr.

Vorsichtig ergriff Albert das Schiesseisen und sah es sich genauer an.

Hätte er sich nicht eine Menge Kummer ersparen können, wenn er, anstelle seiner dämlichen Brandentfachung, sich eine Ladung Schrot in den Kopf gejagt hätte? Er hielt sich den Lauf an die Schläfe. Was konnte dabei schon schief gehen? Würde man etwa Hans Fahler beerdigen wollen, wenn man ihn, Albert, erschossen hier auf dem Dachboden auffinden würde? Die Überlegung belustigte Albert, obwohl Scherze im Moment nicht angebracht waren. Es war jedoch unwahrscheinlich, dass die Waffe geladen war. Oder war sie es zufälligerweise, versehentlich doch?

Alberts Stirn war inzwischen schweissnass. Sollte er einfach abdrücken und sein Leben dem Gewehr, dem Schicksal in die Hände geben? Wollte er wirklich auf diese Weise herausfinden, ob die Waffe geladen war? Herausfinden konnte er so allerdings nur, dass sie nicht geladen war.

Er legte den Finger an den Abzug. Seine Hand zitterte. Er schloss die Augen.

Seine Angst war zu gross. Er nahm den Lauf weg von seiner Stirn und zielte gegen die Decke. Dann betätigte er den Abzug.

Der Schuss blieb wie erwartet aus.

Er ärgerte sich über seine unüberlegte Handlung. Nicht

auszudenken, in welche Misere er sich mit einem krachenden Schuss inmitten des Dorfes erneut geritten hätte. Er stellte das Gewehr zurück an seinen Platz und war froh, den beklemmenden Ort verlassen zu können.

32. Die edle Kunst des Dichtens

Heute Ruhetag. Immer noch wurde die Kundschaft mit dem abweisenden Schild vor der Eingangstür vom Gasthof ferngehalten.

In der Gaststube sassen sich zwei in die Jahre gekommene Männer gegenüber. Sie hatten ihren gewohnten Tisch eingenommen und zogen an ihren Zigarren.

Bernhard Brülhart sah sich in der Pflicht, einen Lebenslauf des Verstorbenen zu schreiben. Walter Niederhäusern, sein langjähriger Freund, sollte ihm dabei behilflich sein.

Walter entkorkte die Flasche Absinth, die er eben in seinem Keller geholt hatte. Verwundert stellte er fest, dass sie nicht ganz aufgefüllt war. Klagen wollte er jedoch nicht. Er konnte sich glücklich schätzen, fast umsonst an das kostbare Getränk zu gelangen. Derweil hatte Bernhard mit dem Bleistift bereits einige kaum lesbare Schwünge zu Papier gebracht.

«Wann wurde er geboren?», fragte Walter.

«1939.»

«Wann genau?»

Bernhard zuckte mit den Schultern.

«Lassen wir das halt. Ich weiss es auch nicht», seufzte Walter.

«Dann seine Kindheit», begann Bernhard. «Du weisst doch. Der Vater weg, der Bruder tot, die Mutter verrückt. Beim Vater wurde ja zuerst nur eine leichte Augenverletzung gemeldet, und dann war schliesslich doch alles viel schlimmer, und dann …»

«Jaja, ich kenne die Geschichte längst, Bernhard, noch besser als du», sagte Walter und dachte dabei an die Krankenpflegerin aus dem Süden, die massgeblichen Anteil am Verfall der Familie hatte. «Ausserdem muss ein Lebenslauf kurz gefasst werden.»

«Hast schon recht, alles muss nicht drin stehen.» So kritzelte Bernhard ein paar weitere Zeilen nieder. Der Beginn war allerdings wenig zufriedenstellend.

«In der Küche liegen noch ein paar alte Zeitungen herum», kam Walter in den Sinn, «vielleicht könnten wir von da einige schlaue Sätze kopieren.»

«Gute Idee.»

Wenig später sassen die beiden über den ausgebreiteten Zeitungen und feilten an ihrem Text.

«So, soweit hätten wir es. ‹Und dann kam er zu mir›», meinte Bernhard stolz. «Wie wäre es damit: ‹Bernhard Brülhart aus Rechthalten hatte die Güte, den Knaben auf seinem Hof aufzunehmen, wodurch er ihm eine überglückliche Jugend ermöglichte.›»

Der Wirt blickte ihn stirnrunzelnd an. «Das nimmt dir niemand ab, Bernhard. Damit machst du dich nur lächerlich», meinte er. «Du hast ja selber immer gesagt, dass du ihn dir als Hilfskraft auf den Hof geholt hattest.»

Nachdenklich strich Bernhard einige Wörter. Allzu gerne hätte er jene Sätze in der Zeitung gesehen. Er willigte aber zur Abänderung des Textes ein. Für die Schlussfassung war er dann ja schliesslich doch allein verantwortlich.

«Und nach der Schule hat er dann bei mir begonnen», fuhr Walter fort. «Vielleicht könnte man das so formulieren: ‹Im Gastgewerbe fand er einen liebevollen Meister, der ihn geduldig in die edle Kunst der Gastronomie einweihte.›» Er lächelte.

«Ha! Hör dir den an. Du bist wohl verrückt geworden!»

«Na gut. Machen wir ‹die edle Kunst› zum ‹Metier›, in Ordnung?», versuchte es Walter abermals, stiess aber wiederum auf Unverständnis.

Als sich der Pegel der Absinthflasche bereits der Etikette annäherte, konnten sich die beiden Trotzköpfe einigen.

33. Das Bild

Die Teigwaren an seiner Pilzsauce schmeckten köstlich, und der leichte Rotwein passte hervorragend dazu. Es hatte Albert sogar Freude bereitet, zu kochen. Niemand hatte ihn gedrängt, nichts ihn dazu gezwungen – es war herrlich, für einmal sein eigener Meister, sein eigener Gast zu sein.

Der Bilderrahmen, der über dem Tisch hing, war leer. Albert hatte das Familienfoto von Hans Fahler aus dem Rahmen getrennt. Weiter hatte er beschlossen, das Haus noch heute Abend zu verlassen. Er musste dies tun. Er musste es einfach tun.

Nach dem Mahl richtete er sich auf dem Stubensessel ein, den er bereits liebgewonnen hatte, und wartete geduldig den Sonnenuntergang ab. Die Katze lag auf seinem Bauch. Erst zaghaft, dann immer beherzter, drückte er die Katze an sich. Noch nie hatte sich Albert so innig mit einem Lebewesen abgegeben.

Als es schon eine Zeitlang dunkel war, legte er seinen Mantel um, setzte seinen Hut auf und zog los. Nun befand er sich wieder in der Welt draussen. In der Welt, in der er nicht mehr existieren durfte.

Bald schritt er durch ein eisernes Tor. Unter seinen Füssen knirschte der Kies, mit dem der ganze Hof belegt war.

Abertausende von Kieselsteinen.

Obwohl er sich nun mitten im Dorf befand, stieg in ihm ein ähnlich gelöstes Gefühl hoch wie bei seinen nächtlichen Besuchen des Löhlimooses. Auch hier trieb sich nachts niemand herum. Dennoch zog er seinen Hut tief ins Gesicht.

Die Klinke klemmte etwas, dann aber liess sich der Türflügel, von einem Knarren begleitet, langsam öffnen. Stickige Luft erwartete ihn. Die Wände atmeten den Duft des Todes. Er machte die Tür hinter sich wieder zu. Nun war er allein im Raum – ganz allein mit Hans Fahler.

Links und rechts vom aufgebahrten Sarg versuchten farbige Blumen, der Düsterkeit der Kapelle entgegenzutreten. Allerdings verschloss sich die Totenkapelle schon allein ihres Zweckes wegen dem farbigem Frohmut. Auf dem Sargdeckel stand ein Portraitbild. Es zeigte das Antlitz des Albert Leblanc, zirka in seinem fünfundzwanzigsten Lebensjahr. Bei diesem Anblick sträubten sich Alberts Nackenhaare.

«Es tut mir leid, lieber Hans», hauchte Albert in gequältem Flüsterton, «unendlich leid.» Es fiel ihm sogar schwer, die reumütigen Worte an einen Toten zu richten. «Es war – ein Unglück. Ich danke dir, danke dir für alles.»

Zusätzlich zu den Schuldgefühlen bedrückte Albert, dass Hans nicht würdig verabschiedet werden sollte. Dass man morgen nicht *ihm* die wohlverdiente letzte Ehre erweisen würde. Auch Hans, gerade er, hätte es verdient gehabt, als derjenige aufrichtige Mensch zu sterben, der er gewesen war. Albert konnte an diesem Umstand nichts ändern, doch wollte er zumindest symbolisch etwas dazu beitragen, dass das morgige Begräbnis auch ein Begräbnis von Hans sein würde.

Aus der Innentasche seines Mantels zog er zwischen Rockzipfeln ein Bild hervor. Es war das Bild der Familie Fahler. Albert wollte es dem Toten mit unter die Erde geben.

Er versuchte, das Bild durch den kleinen Spalt zwischen Sargunterteil und Sargdeckel zu schieben.

Statt durch den Schlitz zu gleiten, bog sich das Bild aber immer wieder. Konsterniert musste Albert feststellen, dass es so nicht in den Sarg gelangen konnte. Der Sargdeckel musste wohl oder übel ein kleines Stück angehoben werden.

Er konnte sich angenehmere Tätigkeiten vorstellen, als des Nachts einen besetzten Sarg zu öffnen. Doch war er dies Hans schuldig. Es war das Mindeste, was er noch für ihn tun konnte.

Albert bückte sich nach vorne und erfasste mit beiden Händen den Sargdeckel. Das Bild steckte mangels besseren Einfällen zwischen seinen Lippen. Ihm graute vor dem nächsten Schritt.

Mit aller Kraft drückte er den Deckel nach oben. Der Deckel war leichter als angenommen, sodass Albert den Sarg mit einem Ruck weit öffnete. Seine Lippen liessen das Bild ins Innere der Kiste fallen, wobei ein grässlicher Gestank aus dem Sarg direkt in Alberts Nase drang – er musste den Deckel unverzüglich fallen lassen. Der Sarg schloss sich mit einem lauten Knall.

Albert hustete und konnte nur mit Not verhindern, sich in der Totenkapelle zu übergeben. Er musste raus hier, sofort. Er stellte das umgekippte Portraitbild – sein eigenes! – wieder auf den Sarg und ergriff eiligst die Flucht.

34. Ehre seinem Andenken

Eine eigenartige Stimmung herrschte an jenem Morgen im Dorf Rechthalten. Im Laden grüsste man sich, doch liess man den kleinen Schwatz bleiben. Auf dem Feld verrichtete man wortlos die Arbeit, die ohnehin bald wieder unterbrochen werden musste. Und im Hotelrestaurant, das in den letzten Tagen einen Aufschwung erfahren hatte, verzichteten die Gäste auf unbekümmerte Scherze und erheiternde Kartenspiele. Stattdessen schlürften sie nachdenklich, in sich gekehrt an ihrem Kaffee. Es war heiss, drückend heiss, obwohl der Himmel etwas bedeckt war.

Nachdem das Glockengeläut verstummt war, wurde der Innenraum der Kirche von einer bedrückenden Stille erfüllt. Hin und wieder ertönte ein Räuspern, ein Husten, ein Hochziehen von Naseninhalt. Man scheute die Blicke anderer, atmete schwerer als üblich, schluckte etwas tiefer.

Im Rücken der anwesenden Leute, die sich nun erhoben, öffnete sich die Kirchentür. Es traten sechs kräftige Messdiener mit starren Mienen ein. Langsam gingen sie durch das Kirchenschiff, ein massives Gewicht drückte auf ihre Schultern. Von den Bänken, die sich links und rechts des Mittelganges hintereinander reihten, zielten betrübte, mit gespielter Zufälligkeit ausgeführte Blicke auf den vorbeiziehenden Sarg. Der Sarg wurde vorne schliesslich zwischen ein liebevoll hergerichtetes Sargbouquet und einen leuchtenden Strauss roter Rosen abgestellt.

Mit einer schwer verdaulichen, pompösen Trauermelodie erlöste der Organist die Gemeinschaft vom stillen Warten. Obwohl man die bevorstehende Stunde lieber gemieden hätte, war man froh, dass die Trauerfeier in Gang gebracht wurde.

Aus der Sakristei trat andächtig der rüstige Pfarrer, begleitet von zwei schlaksigen Messdienern. Er schritt zum Rednerpult und sprach, sich bekreuzigend: «Im Namen des Vaters und des Sohnes und des Heiligen Geistes.»

«Amen», erscholl es aus zahllosen Kehlen. Die Messe hatte begonnen.

Der Pfarrer ergriff wieder das Wort: «Wir haben uns heute versammelt, um uns zu verabschieden. Zu verabschieden von unserem lieben Mitchristen Albert Leblanc, der allzu früh, auf unglückliche Weise von uns gegangen ist.»

In der Tat hatte man sich heute in der Pfarrkirche von Rechthalten versammelt. Wer in den letzten Jahren regelmässig den Gasthof aufgesucht hatte, war erschienen, um dem schüchternen, manchmal etwas unbeholfenen, aber sympathischen Koch einen letzten Gruss zu entsenden. Niemand konnte von sich behaupten, den Dahingeschiedenen richtig gekannt zu haben. Und dennoch fühlte jeder einzelne Bürger, dass dieser Tage ein Stück Dorfgeist gestorben war. Albert Leblanc hatte mittlerweile zum Inventar von Rechthalten gehört.

«Wir alle wollen dem lieben Verstorbenen heute die letzte Ehre erweisen und gemeinsam trauern um einen achtbaren Menschen, Mitbürger und Freund.»

Die Eingangstür öffnete sich. Ein stattlicher Mann stahl sich etwas verlegen in die Kirche und setzte sich in die hinterste Reihe neben den Gemeindepräsidenten. Es war der Metzger.

«Wie war man überrascht und schockiert, als die Sterbeglocke vergangenen Freitag verkündete, unser liebe Albert sei vom Vergelter alles Guten abberufen worden. Die Trauerkunde verbreitete sich wie ein Lauffeuer durch unser Dorf.»

Der Postbeamte biss sich auf die Lippen. Die letzten Worte des Pfarrers schienen ihm nicht besonders sorgfältig gewählt zu sein.

«Die Pfarrei Rechthalten trägt mit Albert Leblanc einen jungen Mann zu Grabe, der es verdient, dass man einige Worte über sein Leben und Wirken verliert.» Der Pfarrer hatte vorerst genug gesprochen. Er setzte sich, nachdem die Messdiener seinen Umhang über die gepolsterte Stuhllehne gestrafft hatten.

Zur Überraschung aller trat nun ein Mann ans Pult, dem man alles andere zutraute, nicht jedoch eine Grabrede. Es war

Karl, der im Gehen einen beschriebenen Zettel entfaltete. Er blickte kurz über den Rand seiner ausnahmsweise getragenen Brille in die Menge und begann zu lesen: «Albert wurde 1939 als zweiter Sohn des Jean und der Marie Leblanc in Môtiers, nahe der Grenze zu Frankreich, geboren. Auf einem schönen Gut verlebte er unbeschwert und glücklich seine ersten Lebensjahre, bis die Familie jäh von Unglücksfällen heimgesucht wurde. Nach Kriegsausbruch wurde der Vater einberufen, um an der Grenze seine vaterländischen Pflichten zu erfüllen. Er kehrte nie von seinem Einsatz zurück. Kurz darauf fiel Gustav, der ältere der beiden Knaben, beim Spielen mit Albert ins Güllenloch und verschied. Die Mutter, die nun mit Albert allein gelassen war, konnte die schrecklichen Ereignisse nicht verkraften. Man sah sich genötigt, sie in die Nervenheilanstalt einzuweisen, womit bedauerlicherweise ihre mütterliche Aufgabe entfallen musste. Der kleine Albert wuchs in der Folge in verschiedenen Heimen auf, und gelangte schliesslich, in der Blüte seiner Kindheit, nach Rechthalten, wo Bernhard Brülhart ... »

Karl stutzte.

«... den Knaben auf seinem Hof aufnahm. Nach seiner obligatorischen Schulzeit fand er im Gastgewerbe einen Wirt – bei dem er das Kochen erlernen konnte.»

Bernhard und Walter tauschten verständnislose Blicke.

«Bereits in seinem siebenundzwanzigsten Lebensjahr ist er in die Ewigkeit erhoben worden. Ehre seinem Andenken, Friede seiner Seele – der Herr habe ihn selig.»

Er faltete das Blatt zusammen. Dann sagte er noch: «Albert, ich werde dich vermissen. Wir alle werden dich vermissen. Auf Wiedersehen.»

Die Gemeinde hatte sich die traurige Lebensgeschichte von Albert bedrückt angehört. Den meisten war bis dahin gar nicht bewusst gewesen, welch schwere Schicksalsschläge der arme Albert hatte hinnehmen müssen. Viele der regelmässigen Wirtshausbesucher haderten mit sich selbst. Bedauerten, dass man nie ein freundliches Wort mit dem Verstorbenen gewechselt hatte. Bereuten, dass man ihm nicht hin und wieder ein Zeichen der Dazugehörigkeit gespendet hatte. Ein Lob für die exquisite Morchelsauce hätte das Menü jeweils auch nicht teurer gemacht. Jetzt war es zu spät.

Karl begab sich wieder an seinen Platz. Die Frau mit Bienenstockfrisur, die neben ihm sass, versuchte ihre Fassung wieder zu erlangen. Hätte sie nicht etwas ahnen müssen? Der von Karl einfühlsam vorgetragene Nachruf hatte nicht nur sie zu Tränen gerührt.

Es war der Gemischte Chor, der für die Fortsetzung der Trauerfeier sorgte. Die musikalische Überleitung kam den Trauernden gerade recht, um Alberts bedauerlichen Werdegang etwas verdauen zu können. Der Chor auf der Empore sang erstmals eine Sequenz der neu einstudierten Totenmesse. Als an der letzten Probe angekündigt worden war, bereits die nächste Beerdigung mit der schwierigen, aber eindrücklichen Sequenz zu begleiten, hatten viele Chormitglieder den Kopf geschüttelt. Hinter vorgehaltener Hand hatte man die Eile des Dirigenten zu begründen gewusst: Dessen kränkelnde, aber zähe Mutter lag schon seit drei Wochen auf dem Sterbebett. Nun, unverhofft, war ihr Albert Leblanc drei Tage zuvorgekommen.

Eine vornehm gekleidete Dame, deren Stimme älter klang, als ihr lieb war, hielt ihr Vibrato am Ende der Strophe etwas zu lange aus. Eine Träne hatte vorhin ihren Lidschatten leicht verschmiert. Im Sopran sang ein Mann mit feinem Oberlippenbart inbrünstig die lateinischen Worte, die nicht einmal der Pfarrer verstehen konnte. Den Chorkameraden des besagten Sängers schien es, dass dieser heute mit besonderem Eifer bei der Sache war.

Als der Gemischte Chor seine überaus gelungene Darbietung beendet hatte, vermeldete der Pfarrer: «Wir kommen nun, liebe Trauernde, zu den Fürbitten.»

Stille.

Nach einigen bangen Sekunden konnte die angespannte Trauergemeinde eine braunhaarige Frau erspähen, die sich langsam nach vorne bewegte. Sie schien kraftlos zu sein. Ihr Blick war leer.

Mit ihrer etwas eigenwilligen Todesanzeige in den Freiburger Nachrichten hatte sie im Dorf für einigen Gesprächsstoff gesorgt. Die schöne Mona und der biedere Albert? Das Staunen war gross gewesen, und die Leute fragten sich, wie gut die beiden sich wohl gekannt hatten. Umso mehr stieg nun die Spannung, die auch in der hintersten Reihe knisterte, als Mona sich aufmachte, das Wort zu ergreifen.

«Herr», begann sie mit erstickter Stimme, «gib uns die Kraft, den Schmerz, der durch den Hinschied Alberts entstanden ist, zu ertragen.»

«Wir bitten dich, erhöre uns.»

«Wir bitten dich, dass unsere Erinnerung an einen lieben und aussergewöhnlichen Menschen nie verblassen möge.» Monas Stimme fand langsam zu Kräften.

«Wir bitten dich, erhöre uns.»

«Herr, lass uns den schwer hinzunehmenden Abschied von Albert nur zu einem Abschied auf Zeit werden.»

«Wir bitten dich, erhöre uns.»

«Lass Albert im Tod seinen Frieden finden und schenke ihm ewiges Leben.»

«Wir bitten dich, erhöre uns.»

«Wir bitten dich, dass der Tod Alberts uns alle zu besseren Menschen machen wird.»

«Wir bitten dich, erhöre uns.»

Stille.

Vornehmlich die letzte Bitte hatte bei den Leuten tiefen Eindruck hinterlassen. Bei vielen wurden Erinnerungen an verschiedene Vorkommnisse wachgerufen, in denen Albert gescholten und genarrt wurde. Man hatte dabei entweder nichtstuend zugehört, mitgelacht oder gar mitgemacht. Alberts Tat nun hatte den unzähligen Sprüchen und Schelmereien nachträglich den Spass geraubt, mit dem diese grösstenteils versehen waren. Oder hatte man nur geglaubt, dass sie mit Spass versehen waren?

Die junge blonde Frau, deren aufreizendes Oberteil nicht ganz der Ernsthaftigkeit des Anlasses entsprach, grübelte derweil über die Vergänglichkeit nach. Menschen gehen, Menschen kommen. Im Grunde gab es nichts natürlicheres, und doch konnte einen beides erschüttern.

Fest in sich gekehrt nahm so mancher die Aufforderung des Pfarrers nicht auf Anhieb wahr, sich nun nach vorne zu begeben und dem Verstorbenen den letzten Segen zu erteilen.

Schleppend setzte sich die Trauergemeinde in Bewegung. Man ging zum Altar, tauchte den metallenen Stab in das geweihte Wasser und bespritzte den Sarg. Nach einer kurzen persönlichen Verabschiedung reichte man den Stab weiter – der Bäcker dem Forstwart, der Forstwart der Bäuerin, die Bäuerin dem Käser, dieser der Hebamme … Es dauerte seine Zeit, bis auch die Letzten an die Reihe kamen. Der Organist zog dabei noch einmal alle Register seines Könnens. Teile des Requiems, die der Gemischte Chor noch nicht eingeübt hatte, schossen aus den Orgelpfeifen. Ob sich der Organist nur die besonders ergreifenden Passagen für die heutige Beerdigung ausgesucht hatte?

Endlich stand Mona vor dem Sarg. Sie berührte mit ihrem Finger ihre Lippen und fuhr mit ihm über den Deckel. Unter Tränen konnte sie sich letztlich überwinden, Albert für immer zu verlassen.

Die sechs kräftigen Messdiener hoben den Sarg wieder auf ihre Schultern und marschierten nach draussen. Auf dem Kirchhof wartete die Musikgesellschaft, um den Trauermarsch zu begleiten. Erneut sahen sich die Anwesenden einer erstickenden Hitze ausgesetzt. Die Sonne wurde allerdings immer noch von grauen Wolkenschleiern verhüllt.

Das Trauerspiel begann. Die Musikanten bliesen in ihre Posaunen, Trompeten und Klarinetten, dass ihre Backen rot anliefen. Bei zweien wurden sie gar dunkelrot.

Albert Leblanc wurde zu Grabe getragen.

35. Im Kreis der Toten

Albert war gestorben als einsamster Mensch der Welt – nun lebte er noch einsamer weiter. Flüchtige Betrüger, Verbrecher, Mörder wurden immerhin gesucht. Ihn jedoch, ihn würde mit Sicherheit niemand suchen. Für die Leute existierte er nicht mehr. Er war nicht mehr. Dabei lebte er, lebte als Toter weiter. Er war kein Gauner, er war bloss ein lebendiger Toter. Und doch, oder gerade deswegen, musste er sich verstecken. Jedenfalls hier und jetzt noch.

Wie gerne er die Tränen von Mona weggeküsst hätte! Wie gerne er die Trauergemeinde in den Gasthof eingeladen hätte, um mit allen auf sein Leben anzustossen! Doch das war undenkbar.

Albert war einiges klar geworden. Erst durch seinen Tod hatten ihn die Leute zu schätzen gelernt. Erst sein Tod hatte ihn zum geachteten, anerkannten Bürger gemacht. Ohne seinen Tod aber wäre alles beim Alten geblieben, dachte er verbittert. Und würde er nun seinen Tod rückgängig machen – was ja durchaus in seiner Macht stand – hätten die Leute allen Grund gehabt, ihm wieder missmutig zu begegnen. Nein, es gab kein Zurück.

Es hatte seinen Tod gebraucht. Sterben mochte er im Moment nämlich nicht mehr. Das Trauern der Leute, die damit bekundete Wertschätzung, hatte in ihm ein kleines Feuer entfacht, das ihm lange Zeit gefehlt hatte. Das Lebensfeuer.

An der Wand konnte Albert die Umrisse eines Kreuzes ausmachen, an welches ein schauerlich lebendiger Jesus Christus genagelt war. Seit seiner Kindheit kam es ihm höchst sonderbar vor, überall – ob in Schlafzimmern oder Schulräumen, in Armeekasernen oder Kuhställen – Kruzifixe aufzuhängen. Noch mehr irritierte ihn aber, dass die höchst makabren Darstellungen von der Allgemeinheit gar nicht als solche wahrgenommen wurden.

Ob man dereinst die Wände mit Statuen des brennenden

Albert Leblanc schmücken würde? Beinahe musste er lachen. Eigentlich hatte er ja nichts Geringeres vollbracht als einst Jesus von Nazareth – er war von den Toten auferstanden.

Albert öffnete das Türchen und entstieg dem Beichtstuhl. Endlich konnte er seine Glieder wieder strecken. Knapp achtzehn Stunden hatte er in ungemütlichster Stellung verbracht. Die Mühen hatten sich allerdings gelohnt.

Fast alle, die er gekannt hatte, waren zur Messe gekommen. Und noch einige mehr. Nur einer hatte gefehlt: Hans Fahler. Ob man ihn wohl bald vermissen und suchen würde? Er war ja nun aus der Feuerwehr zurückgetreten und hatte sonst, so viel Albert wusste, kaum Kontakte unterhalten. Bestimmt würde sein Verschwinden vom örtlichen Landjäger kaum gelöst werden können, dessen war sich Albert sicher.

Obwohl er sachte über die Steinplatten des Kirchenschiffes ging, hallten seine Schritte bis hoch an die Deckenfresken. Er verliess die Kirche, eilte noch einmal ins Haus von Hans Fahler, ass und trank etwas und nahm den Atlas in seinen Besitz. Dann schlich er weiter durch das Oberdorf und erreichte den Fofenhubel. Rechthalten, sein Dorf, wog sich hinter ihm in die Nacht. Er lehnte sich kurz an das steinerne Kreuz, das da oben stand, und überblickte die zahlreichen Lichter, die ihm aus Nah und Fern entgegenschimmerten.

Vielleicht war er ja nun tatsächlich tot, überlegte sich Albert. War es vielleicht im Kreis der Toten üblich, das eigene Sterbeglöckchen schlagen zu hören, die eigene Todesanzeige zu lesen, an der eigenen Beerdigung teilzunehmen? Kannte er jetzt etwa die Antwort auf die Frage, was nach dem Tod ist? Die Gedanken ängstigten ihn.

War er für die Lebenden überhaupt noch wahrnehmbar? Seit seinem Tod war er niemandem mehr direkt begegnet. Nur der Katze von Hans Fahler – aber sagt man Katzen nicht einen sechsten Sinn nach? Sein Verstand sträubte sich gegen derartige Irrationalitäten. Er atmete, fühlte, dachte – er erfüllte alle Voraussetzungen, um zu leben.

Seine ganzen Habseligkeiten hatte er allerdings verloren. Mit nichts als einer unmenschlich guten Melodie im Kopf stand er da. *Wie fühlt es sich an, ohne Heim zu sein, wie ein völlig Unbekannter, wie ein rollender Stein?* Es fühlte sich ungeheuer an. Zugleich verspürte Albert ein nie dagewesenes Gefühl von Stärke. Wohin des Weges? Innerlich zerrissen zog er von dannen, um alsbald wie die Sonne hinter den Hügeln zu verschwinden.

Zweites Buch
Leben eines Toten

Once you're dead, your're made for life.

Jimi Hendrix

Und als ich ihn sah, stürzte ich zu seinen Füssen wie tot; da legte er seine Rechte auf mich und sprach: «Fürchte dich nicht. Ich bin es, der Erste und der Letzte und der Lebendige. Ein Toter bin ich gewesen, doch siehe: ich bin lebendig in alle Ewigkeit und halte die Schlüssel des Todes und der Unterwelt. Schreibe also auf, was du schautest und was ist und was hernach geschehen wird …»

Offenbarung des Johannes 1, 17-19

36. Auf der Flucht

Im Dunkel der Nacht rannte Albert Leblanc aus dem Dorf. Rannte, bis seine Kräfte schwanden, ging ein Stück, um sie wieder zu sammeln, um weiterrennen zu können. Bald watete er durch die ruhig fliessende Sense, trank, wusch sich die Erschöpfung aus dem Gesicht, überquerte den Flussgraben und drang ins Bernbiet ein. Häuser, Weiler und Dörfer umlief er in sicherer Distanz. Er bewegte sich bevorzugt über einsame Wiesen oder, als die Morgendämmerung wieder aufzog, durch Wälder. An einem Feld rastete er kurz, versteckte sich hinter Maispflanzen, riss einen der zähen Kolben ab, verdrückte ihn hastig. Dann setzte er seine Flucht unbeirrt fort, die idyllische Landschaft entzog sich dabei vollends seiner Aufmerksamkeit. So weit ihn die Beine trugen rannte er, und je weiter er sich von seinem Grab entfernte, umso stärker verbreitete sich in ihm das Bewusstsein, zu leben.

Völlig entkräftet stiess er am späten Nachmittag etwas unterhalb des Gantrischgipfels auf eine Berghütte, aus deren heruntergekommenem Zustand er schloss, dass sie nicht mehr rege benützt wurde. Der mühselige Aufstieg, das nunmehr recht kahle Gelände, die kühler gewordene Luft bestärkten zudem sein Gefühl, der Zivilisation weitgehend entflohen zu sein.

Es herrschte völlige Ruhe. Albert versuchte, durch ein Fenster in die Hütte zu spähen, doch ein gezogener Vorhang versperrte ihm die Sicht. Er ging ein paar Schritte weiter und blieb vor der Haustür stehen. Kraftlos legte er seine Hand auf die Türklinke, hoffte, gleich in ein weiches Bett fallen zu können.

Die Tür war verschlossen. Natürlich war sie verschlossen. Warum auch sollte der Eigentümer, falls er denn wirklich abwesend war, seine Berghütte, jeden Streuner einladend, einfach offen lassen?

Entmutigt umkreiste er die aus morschem Holz bestehen-de Hütte und gelangte vor einen weiteren, durch seinen mit Spinnweben bespannten Türrahmen etwas unscheinbaren Eingang.

Die sperrige Tür liess sich öffnen und Albert betrat eine kleine, leere Scheune. Es stank. Albert kümmerte sich nicht darum. Wie gross war seine Erleichterung, als er die einladende Heubühne erblickte, die über eine angestützte Leiter zu erreichen war. Umgehend fiel er ins Heu, wo ihn ein tiefer Schlaf übermannte, der ihn trotz der bissigen Kälte und der Ratte, die im Heu nistete, für ein paar Stunden aus dem prallen Leben nahm.

37. Im Reich der Natur

Ein quälendes Hungergefühl liess Albert schon in den frühen Morgenstunden die Heubühne hinuntersteigen.

Der Stall war mit Tierexkrementen übersät. Albert wusste nicht, ob er den Gestank Ziegen oder Kühen zuordnen sollte. Es war ihm im Grunde egal.

Als er sich zur Tür aufmachte, um einer Brise Bergluft Einzug zu gewähren, fiel ihm an der Seitenwand der Scheune, eingeengt zwischen zwei dicken Balken, eine kleine Schiebetür auf. Er hatte sie gestern übersehen, als es bereits dunkler war und das Verlangen nach Schlaf seine Sinne abgeschwächt haben musste.

Die Tür war mit geringem Kraftaufwand nicht zu bewegen. Das Holz hatte wohl im Laufe der Jahre ausgeprägte Verformungen erlitten. Albert stemmte sich gegen die Kante der Schiebetür, stiess sich erst mit den Händen, dann mit den Beinen am nahen Balken ab, um die Tür mit noch mehr Kraft auf die Seite drängen zu können. Seine Brandverletzung schmerzte wieder stärker.

Endlich erreichte der freigelegte Durchgang die Masse von Alberts schmalem Körper. Er blieb noch einen Augenblick stehen, bis sich sein Herzschlag wieder beruhigte.

Hinter der Schiebetür befand sich eine Feuerstelle, über der sich die breite Öffnung des Kamins bis an die Decke hochzog. Die Tür schien den Stall also mit der Wohnstube der Hütte zu verbinden. Über verkohltem Holz hing ein Gefäss an einer Halterung, wohl eine Messingpfanne. Daneben lag ein geflochtener Korb, der mit Holzscheiten gefüllt war. Gegenstände, für die sich Albert im Moment nicht näher interessierte, ganz im Gegensatz zu einem etwa auf Augenhöhe angebrachten Haken, an dem ein prächtiges Stück Speck hing.

Alberts Augen weiteten sich. Seit zwei Tagen war er nicht mehr in den Genuss einer ordentlichen Mahlzeit gekommen. Er roch am Stück. Es war geräuchert.

Hastig nahm er den Speck vom Haken und setzte sich an einen Tisch, der mit einem rot-weiss kariertes Plastiktischtuch belegt war. In der Tischschublade fand er ein Messer, das gerade scharf genug war, um sich durch das Fleisch zu kämpfen.

Während er den Speck verzehrte, betrachtete er das Hasenfell, das an die Wand gespannt war. Daneben ragte das stolze Geweih eines Steinbocks aus dem Holz. Dass sich nun zwischen den beiden Jagdtrophäen auch noch ein angenagelter Jesus Christus befand, hielt er für besonders makaber.

Albert wurde bewusst, dass seine Zähne gerade das Fleisch eines Tiers durchtrennten. Totes Fleisch eines toten Tiers. Er spürte, wie die Fleischfasern und Fettfädchen zwischen seinen Zähnen hängenblieben. Körper eines Lebewesens.

Er hatte genug gegessen. Er steckte das noch übrig gebliebene Stück Speck wieder an den Haken und begab sich ins Freie.

Inmitten einer herrlichen Berglandschaft, eingebettet zwischen Gantrisch und Ochsen, da stand er nun. Dahin hatte es ihn also auf seiner ziellosen Flucht verschlagen. Er entschied, einen kleinen Spaziergang zu unternehmen.

Etwas ausser Atem erreichte er das Joch, das sich zwischen den beiden Gipfeln hinzog. Wie ein Koloss erhob sich vor ihm der mächtige Stein, dessen Spitze gerade eine Wolke in zwei Stücke riss: Der Gantrisch, der dem Gebiet, in das Albert geflohen war, seinen Namen gab.

Albert spielte mit dem waghalsigen Gedanken, den Gipfel des Berges zu erklimmen. Sofort wurden seine Hände feucht. Dennoch verwarf er den Gedanken nicht schleunigst, wie dies eigentlich seiner Natur entsprochen hätte.

Natürlich würde ihn der Aufstieg eine gewaltige Überwindung kosten. Allerdings blieb ihm früher oder später nichts anderes übrig, als sich zu überwinden, sowohl um zu leben wie um zu sterben. Und wenn er denn leben, wirklich leben wollte – dann würde er Dinge tun müssen, an die er bis dahin nicht zu denken gewagt hatte.

Über den Grat näherte er sich wacker der letzten Erhebung. Er sprach sich leise Mut zu und bemühte sich, das Gefälle, das sich beidseits von ihm auftat, zu verachten.

Nun stand der eigentliche Aufstieg bevor. Meter um Meter schwang sich Albert empor, kam besser voran, als er es sich vorgestellt hatte, das ermutigte ihn weiter.

Eine steile Felsplatte, die nur mit Hilfe eines im Stein befestigten Seils zu bewältigen war, bremste dann aber seine Zuversicht. Anfänglich sträubte sich sein mit Speck gefüllter Magen gegen ein Fortschreiten, und doch zog er einen Abbruch nicht ernsthaft in Betracht. Er wollte nicht aufgeben, wollte sich unter allen Umständen der Herausforderung stellen, wollte den tödlichen Berg bezwingen.

Mit beiden Händen hielt er sich verkrampft am Seil fest. Langsam setzte er einen Fuss vor den anderen. Da wagte er einen Blick nach unten. Sofort bemerkte er, dass er einen unverzeihbaren Fehler begangen hatte.

Obwohl er stehenblieb, begann sich der Abgrund unter ihm zu bewegen. Die fernen Berge vervielfachten sich, der Horizont geriet in Schieflage. Albert schloss die Augen, um den Schwindelanfall nicht mit noch mehr Nahrung zu versorgen.

Als die ihn umgebenden Objekte wieder ihre übliche Form, ihre natürliche Anzahl erlangt hatten, stieg er weiter hoch und verbot sich einen weiteren Blick in die Tiefe. Nur noch wenige Meter. Mit beinahe beängstigender Zielstrebigkeit näherte er sich dem Gipfel. Nur noch wenige Schritte.

Dann kam er oben an und konnte es kaum glauben.

Die atemberaubende Aussicht war mit nichts aus seinem bisherigen Leben zu vergleichen. Still genoss er den Moment.

Ein seltsames, höchst gegensätzliches Gefühl kam in ihm auf, als er die gewonnenen Eindrücke zu verarbeiten suchte. Zwar fühlte er sich auf dem Gipfel unbeschreiblich allein, fühlte sich abgeschirmt, losgelöst von allen Menschen, Dörfern und Städten. Doch gerade diese Entrücktheit, in alles überragender Höhe, liess die Welt wieder greifbar werden, liess unermessliche Weiten zusammenschrumpfen.

Er versuchte sich zu orientieren. Besorgt schaute er nach Westen, in dessen Richtung er Rechthalten vermutete. Eine würdige Abschiedsfeier hatte man da für ihn veranstaltet. Er schluckte tief. Die traurigen Reaktionen auf seinen Tod hatten seine kühnsten Erwartungen übertroffen. Und nun durfte er sich in der Gegend auf Lebzeiten nicht mehr blicken lassen.

Zu seiner Rechten erstreckte sich das Schweizer Flachland. Jene endlos scheinende Fläche hingegen würde ihm offen stehen, sie lag vor ihm ausgebreitet wie ein riesiger grüner Teppich. Die ganze Welt würde er betreten und bereisen können – bis eben auf einen winzigen Fleck im Westen der Schweiz.

Hinter ihm richteten sich die schroffen Gipfel dicht aneinandergedrängt auf. Hügel und Berge schossen scheinbar bedenkenlos, jeder Vernunft spottend, aus dem Erdball. Und zuhinterst erhob sich majestätisch die schneebedeckte Alpenkette. Irgendwo hinter dieser Kette, da musste das Meer liegen.

Auf dem Rückweg zur Hütte entschied Albert, vorerst in den Bergen zu bleiben. Der Entschluss erleichterte ihn.

Im Verlaufe des sonnigen Tages begann sich dann aber der Hunger wieder bemerkbar zu machen, und mit ihm die Sorge über die künftige Nahrungsbeschaffung, die er bisher etwas naiv als Nebensache abgetan hatte. Nun aber, da er den Speck gänzlich verzehrt hatte, sah die Sache anders aus. Als er vor seiner Hütte stand und sich die karge Umgebung besah, kratzte er sich nachdenklich am Hinterkopf. Wie nur sollte es ihm hier gelingen, zu überleben? Er machte sich auf, die Nahrungsbestände der Natur zu erkunden.

Bald wurde ihm klar, dass sich auf jener Höhe nichts Essbares finden liess, zumindest nichts, das seine Existenz sichern konnte. Er musste sich einige Meter tiefer auf die Suche machen.

Eine Stunde später, als sich die Sonne bereits wieder neigte, setzte er sich entgeistert auf einen Holzstumpf und spähte in den Hut, den er wie einen Teller in der linken Hand hielt. Ein angeknabberter Steinpilz, sechs lausige Waldbeeren und ein schleimiger Wurm. Was für ein jämmerlicher Anblick.

Der Biss in eine Beere entstellte Alberts Gesicht. Bevor er sich den Hut wieder auf den Kopf setzte, flog dessen restlicher Inhalt in hohem Bogen durch die Luft.

Albert sah sich gezwungen, schon bald einen kleinen Abstecher in den nächstgelegenen Weiler zu machen. Beim gestrigen Aufstieg hatte er aus sicherer Entfernung eine kleine Häusersiedlung gesichtet, doch musste er zuerst die Nacht hereinbrechen lassen. Es war ihm zwar höchst unangenehm, sich menschlichen Wesen anzunähern – doch wo Menschen leben, gibt es auch Nahrung.

Albert lag im Heu und wartete.

War es denn rechtmässig, einen Bauern aufzusuchen und diesen auszurauben? Nein, natürlich war es das nicht. Aber hatte ein offiziell Verstorbener, der sich zu verstecken gezwungen war und kein Geld mehr besass, nicht doch eine gewisse Berechtigung dazu? Doch, versuchte er sich zu überzeugen, das Nötigste an Nahrung musste ihm doch zustehen. Man konnte ihn doch nicht einsam in den Bergen verenden lassen.

38. Kräuterschnaps

Die zweite Nacht in der Hütte war um einiges wärmer als die erste. Ohne die Heubühne in der Scheune nebenan verschmähen zu wollen, liess es sich im Schlaflager der Hütte doch komfortabler übernachten. Albert hatte sich wieder in seinen warmen Mantel verkrochen und war zusätzlich noch in den zuvor ausgeleerten Kartoffelsack geschlüpft, um der Kälte zu trotzen.

In der Ecke neben dem offenen Kamin häufte sich ein stattlicher Nahrungsvorrat, der Albert für einige Zeit versorgen sollte. Kartoffeln und Karotten, dazu Bohnen, Erbsen, Zwiebeln – Alberts Streifzug vorbei an einem üppigen Garten hatte sich mehr als gelohnt.

Die folgenden Tage verbrachte Albert am Gantrisch, ohne von einer Menschenseele gestört zu werden. Wie herrlich es war, niemandem etwas schuldig zu sein! Wie herrlich, keine Erwartungen erfüllen zu müssen! Viele Stunden döste Albert im Gras liegend vor sich hin und genoss das wunderbare Gefühl der Unabhängigkeit, der Zwanglosigkeit. Dabei pfiff er gelegentlich Melodien, die ihm gerade durch den Kopf gingen, beobachtete aus der Ferne Gämsen beim Fressen, atmete frische Bergluft. Den Gipfel des Berges, der laut einem Schild, das auf der Anhöhe stand, 2175 Meter aus der Erde ragte, bestieg er jeden Tag. Und wenn er jeweils auf das tieferliegende Wolkenmeer Ausschau hielt, fühlte er sich der Welt samt all seinen Menschen völlig entrückt.

Jetzt ist sie weg, und ich sitze auf dem Dach der Welt.

Auch heute – Albert wusste nicht mehr, welchen Wochentag man schrieb – sollte sich der Tag in der gewohnten Manier abspielen. Mit dem Kamm und einem Rasiermesser, die er im Haus vorgefunden hatte, machte er seine gewohnte, sorgfältige Morgentoilette. Dann begab er sich auf den Gipfel und erfreute sich an der Stille, die ihm noch vor seinem Tod derart überdrüssig geworden war. Die etwas unplanmässig verlaufe-nen Geschehnisse der letzten Woche hatten ihn gelehrt, das Alleinsein wieder zu schätzen. Vielleicht würde er irgendwann vergessen, dass ausser ihm noch andere Menschen existierten. Vielleicht würde er sich einmal als alleinigen Menschen auf der Erde betrachten, sich an niemanden mehr erinnern, niemanden mehr vermissen.

Albert sass auf einem Stein und summte leise sein Lied. Gut möglich, dass er sich getäuscht hatte, überlegte er. Das Lied seines Lebens – vielleicht war es noch gar nicht vollendet. Er lebte ja noch und konnte dem Lied, wann immer es ihm beliebte, weitere Teile hinzufügen. Ob er dies auch ohne Gitarre tun konnte?

Da der Proviant bereits wieder auszugehen drohte, erwog er, dem Weiler einen erneuten Besuch abzustatten. Gewiss bereitete es ihm Mühe, einen liebevoll gepflegten Garten, einen reichhaltigen Keller unverfroren zu plündern. Doch hatte er die Wahl? Es ging um das nackte Überleben. Und noch hatte er nicht vor, den gemütlichen Ort zu verlassen.

«Hallo.»

Die Stimme, die hinter seinem Rücken erklang, erschrak ihn dermassen, dass ihm ein Schrei entwich, seine Glieder unkontrolliert zappelten und er rückwärts von seinem Stein purzelte. Noch während er sich umdrehte, sausten zahllose Gedanken durch seinen Kopf, die sich an Abscheulichkeit übertrafen. Wusste man über alles Bescheid? War es ein Landjäger? Würde man ihn nun auf dem Dorfplatz von Rechthalten öffentlich enttöten, wiederbeleben, ihn danach auf alle Zeit ächten?

Dem stattlichen Herr mit der tiefen Stimme fiel, als er laut zu lachen begann, der Strohhalm aus der Mundecke. Er trug ein kariertes Hemd, eine kurze rote Hose und einen gelben Rucksack. «Es tut mir leid», entschuldigte er sich, immer noch lachend. «Wenn ich gewusst hätte, dass Sie gleich einen solchen Überschlag machen …»

Die Angst Alberts löste sich etwas, als er den breiten Berner Dialekt hörte. Gleichwohl schämte er sich über seine derart heftig gezeigte Erschrockenheit.

«Ein Narr, wer heute nicht in die Berge geht, nicht wahr?» Der Aufstieg hatte den Wanderer zwar ins Schwitzen gebracht, doch seinen Frohsinn schien die Erschöpfung nicht im mindesten zu gefährden.

«– Ja, so ist es.» Albert war zu verwirrt, um ein vernünftiges Gespräch zu führen. Er, der verstorbene Albert Leblanc, stand einem lebenden Menschen gegenüber!

Der Wanderer öffnete seinen Rucksack und entnahm diesem ein belegtes Brot, aus dem eine Tranche Käse und eine fein geschnittene Scheibe Ei herausragten. Als er herzhaft zubiss, entglitt dem Brot ein Stück Gurke und fiel zu Boden, ohne dass dies vom Speisenden bemerkt wurde. Auch Albert schien er nun gar nicht mehr wahrzunehmen, sein lautes Kauen deutete jedenfalls darauf hin.

Albert lief das Wasser im Mund zusammen. Von seinem geraubten Gemüse liess sich zwar leben, doch hätte er im Moment nur allzu gerne ein paar Kartoffeln gegen das schmackhaft aussehende Brot eingetauscht.

Nach der Mahlzeit griff der muntere Wanderer in seine Hemdtasche und zog einen Gegenstand hervor, der im Sonnenlicht glänzte. Es war ein Flachmann. Er entfernte den Deckel und füllte diesen auf. Als er bemerkte, dass ihm Albert dabei zusah, lächelte er. «Kräuterschnaps», sagte er stolz. «Ein Schluck gefällig?»

«Oh ja, gerne.» Albert hatte das gütige Angebot nicht erwartet, doch freute es ihn sehr. Der Wanderer reichte ihm den gefüllten Deckel. Albert trank ihn begierig leer.

«Vielen Dank. Sehr nett von Ihnen, wirklich», stammelte er.

«Nichts zu danken», entgegnete ihm der Wanderer und genehmigte sich nun seinerseits einen kräftigen Schluck.

Wortlos standen sie einen Moment lang nebeneinander und bestaunten die Aussicht.

«Ein herrlicher Tag heute, was?», begann der Wanderer

nun wieder, und Albert schien es, dass der durchaus liebenswürdige, schätzungsweise fünfzigjährige Mann bereits vorhin das Wetter gepriesen hatte.

«Ja, es ist so», antwortete Albert.

«So, jetzt will ich unseren Besuch hier oben aber noch verewigen.» Der Tatendrang des Wanderers war ungebrochen.

Albert war gar nie auf die Idee gekommen, dass der kleine Kasten auf dem Gipfel ein Buch enthalten könnte. Mit einem spitzbübischen Lächeln im Gesicht begann der Wanderer, eine leere Seite zu beschreiben.

«Wie ist Ihr Name?», wollte er plötzlich wissen und schaute ungeduldig zu Albert.

Darauf war dieser nicht vorbereitet. «Wie bitte?», fragte er nach, um Zeit zu gewinnen.

«Nun sagen Sie mir schon Ihren Namen!» Der Wanderer starrte ihn immer unruhiger an, seine Augen glänzten.

«Al – fred», erhielt er schliesslich zur Antwort, sodass er seinen Eintrag ins Gipfelbuch vervollständigen konnte.

39. Bergfreunde

Die Begegnung mit dem lebenslustigen Wanderer hatte Albert zunächst beunruhigt, dann aber auch ermutigt.

Weder der Berg, auf den er sich zurückgezogen hatte, noch die Hütte, in der er hauste, gehörten ihm. Der Berg war allen frei zugänglich – an warmen, klaren Sommertagen würden hier weitere Ausflügler auftauchen. Und das Freiburgerland, wo man schon bald seines Dreissigsten gedenken würde, lag doch in bedenklich wenigen Kilometern Entfernung.

Das Gipfeltreffen hatte ihm allerdings auch aufgezeigt, dass man ihn in den meisten Teilen der Welt wie einen ganz normalen Menschen behandeln würde.

Wie einen lebenden Menschen.

Die panische Angst davor, Leuten unter die Augen zu treten, war etwas gewichen. Albert sah ein, dass es für ihn auf dem Berg keine längerfristige Zukunft gab. Er konnte in der freien Natur ohne fremde Hilfe nicht überleben. Und ständig Bauern zu berauben, war ihm zuwider.

«Ein Kreuterschnepschen in Ehren liessen sich nicht verweren, die Bergfreunde Felix und Alfret.» Die schwungvoll ausgeführten Worte hatten Albert irgendwie aufgewühlt.

Die kommende Nacht war die letzte, die er in der Berghütte verbrachte.

40. Almosen für einen Toten

Immer noch abseits von allen Siedlungen umlief Albert Thun, kämpfte sich durch endlose Wälder, passierte das Entlebuch. Am dritten Tag nach seinem Abstieg vom Gantrisch schlenderte er durch die Strassen Luzerns und wagte sich erstmals wieder zaghaft unter die Leute. Derweil auf dem Land jeder Fremde Misstrauen verbreitet, lässt es sich in Städten ungleich besser in den Untergrund abtauchen. Wie dringend er aber etwas Geld benötigt hätte! Nur einen kleinen Teil seines Vermögens, nur ein paar Münzen! In der Altstadt sank er schliesslich zu Boden und erbettelte sich – mit zugeschnürtem Mantel und tief ins Gesicht gezogenem Hut – einen Franken dreissig. Welche Pein er dafür aber ertragen musste! Obwohl er von den Leuten wie ein normaler Bettler, wie ein heruntergekommener Landstreicher angestarrt wurde, stellte sich Albert laufend die Frage, ob sie ihn nicht wie einen Toten anstarrten. Sein anstrengender Marsch führte ihn dann, weiter dem Vierwaldstättersee entlang, nach Brunnen, wo eine etwas längere Erholung nötig war.

Trotz der Strapazen bevorzugte er stets, sich zu Fuss fortzubewegen. Auf die gelegentlich vorbeibrausende Eisenbahn verzichtete er gerne – jeder Schritt vermittelte ihm das wunderbare Gefühl, den Tod besiegt zu haben, vom Tode auferstanden zu sein. Er hätte sich die Fahrt ohnehin nicht leisten können, und schwarzfahren war zu gefährlich. Er durfte unter keinen Umständen mit dem Gesetz in Konflikt geraten.

Als er das Urner Reusstal hinter sich gelassen hatte, stand ihm dann noch das härteste Stück seiner Reise durch die Schweiz bevor: Die Überquerung des mächtigen Gotthardmassivs.

Wie viele Strassen muss ein toter Mann gehen, bis aus ihm wieder ein lebendiger wird?

Gewiss – die Reise war aufreibend, die Verpflegung wenig schmackhaft, die Schlafplätze eines Menschen unwürdig.

Doch Albert Leblanc lebte. Er hatte sich noch nie so lebendig, so frei gefühlt wie jetzt.

Endlich wichen die deutschen Ortstäfelchen den italienischen, was für einen beruhigenden Hauch von Fremde sorgte. Auch die Vegetation, die sich allmählich veränderte, verlieh Albert das entspannende Gefühl, sein Grab weit hinter sich gelassen zu haben. Er musste sich inzwischen im Süden befinden, und da war er ein völlig Unbekannter. Befand er sich schon im Tessin? Er wunderte sich über die doch recht niedrigen Temperaturen, als er entlang des Ticino durch die schattige Leventina zog.

41. Fussbad

Gut drei Wochen, nachdem Albert beigesetzt worden war, traf er müde aber zufrieden in Locarno ein. Was er da nun vorfand, entsprach gänzlich seinen Vorstellungen vom Süden.

Er hatte seinen schweren Mantel, der ihn in den letzten Nächten vor Kälte geschützt hatte, über den Arm gehängt. Unter natürlichen Bedingungen hatte er noch nie eine derartige Hitze verspürt. Nur in seinem brennenden Haus, da musste es noch ein paar Grad Celsius heisser gewesen sein.

Das grosse Hotel, an dem Albert vorbeiging, machte gewaltigen Eindruck auf ihn. Auf einer leichten Anhöhe erstrahlte ein imposantes Gebäude, das sogar der umgebenden Grünfläche Würde verlieh. Und trotzdem schienen Albert die rötlichen Mauern nicht zu prahlen, sondern sich vielmehr mit bescheidenem Stolz zu erheben. Er bestaunte das Hotel, ganz ohne danach zu drängen, je eine Nacht darin zu verbringen. Zu stark unterschied sich diese Welt von derjenigen, die ihm bis dahin zugänglich gewesen war. Nach den letzten Tagen war es sich Albert erst recht gewohnt, in Demut zu leben.

Er zog weiter durch malerische Gassen und gelangte schliesslich an den See. An einem kleinen gepflasterten Plätzchen, das direkt am Ufer lag, setzte er sich hin und blickte über die sanften Wellen, die das Gewässer schlug.

Er hatte es geschafft. Seine Füsse hatten ihn aus der Westschweiz in den Süden getragen.

Irgendwo dort hinten, hinter den grünen Hügeln, da kannte man ihn. Da kannte man seine unrühmliche Vergangenheit, seine tragische Geschichte. Hier jedoch, hier wusste niemand etwas über ihn – weder dass er tot war, noch dass er lebte. Er konnte durchatmen.

Er entblösste seine Füsse. Schuhe und Socken waren ihm mittlerweile wie angewachsen vorgekommen. Der Marsch hatte seine Füsse stark in Mitleidenschaft gezogen, sie waren völlig verrunzelt, an den Fersen sprangen Blasen hervor. Er tauchte seine Füsse in den See.

Dann begutachtete er seine Wunde am Arm. Die Heilung verlief gut, doch weg waren die Schmerzen noch nicht.

Trotz der Erleichterung darüber, sich nun im fernen Tessin eingefunden zu haben, musste er weiterhin Acht geben. Es schien ihm vernünftig zu sein, den Namen Albert Leblanc nicht mehr zu gebrauchen, ja nie wieder auszusprechen. Albert Leblanc war tot, ein neuer Name musste her. Zudem kam er wohl nicht umhin, sein Äusseres etwas zu verändern. Mantel, Ledergilet und Hut hatten bereits das ihre dazu beigetragen, und gewiss würde ihm die glühende Sonne bald eine ungewöhnliche Bräune verabreichen. Er nahm sich weiter vor, bezüglich Frisur und Rasur nicht mehr allzu exakt zu sein. Frauen hatte er ja selbst mit einem ordentlichen Mass an Eitelkeit keineswegs von sich überzeugen können. Vielleicht war es ja gerade ein gewisser Ausdruck von Wildheit, an dem es ihm bis dahin ermangelt hatte? Das etwas verwegene Ledergilet stand ihm ja durchaus gut. Es konnte also womöglich nicht schaden, einen etwas unfügsameren Eindruck zu hinterlassen. Jedenfalls was die Haarpflege betraf.

Vielleicht konnte er es mit der Vorsicht aber auch übertreiben, zumal er sich hier neugierigen Blicken viel weniger ausgeliefert fühlte als etwa noch in Luzern. War es die ihm fremde Sprache der Leute, die ihn neben der geografischen Distanz in Sicherheit wiegen liess? Oder sorgten das milde Klima, die Palmen, der blaue See für die beruhigende Exotik? Es war wohl die Summe von allem.

Es wurde dunkler. Immer noch spazierten Fussgänger den See entlang und bewegten sich dabei nur wenige Meter an Albert vorbei. In der Tat kümmerte er sie nicht. Für sie war Albert weder tot noch mittellos, weder Jungfrau noch Gitarrenspieler.

Er war für sie nichts als ein junger Mann, der am Ufer des Lago Maggiore die Füsse badete.

42. Der Handel

Albert spürte den warmen Sonnenschein auf seiner Stirn. Einen Moment lang hielt er die Augen noch geschlossen, lauschte dem Kreischen der Möwen und den Wellen, die sich betulich gegen die Ufersteine warfen. Erstmals konnte er die südliche Morgenluft riechen, die nach Kastanienbäumen, Fisch und Lavendel duftete. Dann stand er auf.

Auf einer Bank am Ufer des bereits wieder strahlend blauen Sees hatte er die Nacht verbracht. Sein schwarzer Mantel hatte ihm erstmals nicht als Wärmespender, sondern als Kopfkissen gedient. In der sommerlichen Milde von Locarno nächtigte es sich draussen bedeutend angenehmer als in nördlicheren Regionen. Er entfernte sich etwas vom See, um sich im Ortskern umzusehen.

Er streifte vorbei an unzähligen Strassencafés und Eisständen. «Festival internazionale del film» las er auf einem Tuch, das über die Strasse gespannt war. Die Ankündigung behagte ihm nicht. Ob der idyllische Ort hier etwa Leute aus aller Welt, oder schlimmer, aus dem ganzen Land anzog? Er hoffte, dass das Fest lediglich ein erfolgloser Versuch des Städtchens war, sich Bekanntheit zu verschaffen.

Albert überquerte einen grossen, mit Kopfsteinpflaster bestückten Platz und bog in eine kleine Strasse ein, in die sich kaum Leute verirrt hatten. Verschiedene Läden, die sein Interesse nicht zu wecken vermochten, zogen an ihm vorbei.

An einer Tür prangte ein Schild mit der Aufschrift «Antiquario». Ohne zu zögern trat Albert ein.

Schnell fiel ihm auf, dass es kaum etwas gab, das man in diesem Geschäft nicht hätte kaufen können. Silberbesteck, Lavalampen, Badetücher, Tonkrüge, Krawatten, Bratpfannen, Grammophone, Wörterbücher, Gummienten, Muttergottesstatuen, Plastikblumen – ohne erkennbare Ordnung türmte sich hier alles Erdenkliche auf den rappelvollen Regalen.

Albert schaute sich eine Ansichtskarte etwas genauer an.

Sie zeigte eine sehr schöne Seepromenade vor einer schmucken Häuserreihe. In der Ecke der Karte stand in eleganter Schrift «Ascona» geschrieben.

Er betrat den hinteren Teil des Antiquariats.

«Buongiorno!» Albert erschrak, als plötzlich zwischen zwei Regalen ein kleiner, spärlich behaarter Mann zum Vorschein kam, aus dessen Mund ihm ein goldener Stockzahn entgegenblitzte.

«Posso aiutare?» Der Mann schien freundlich zu sein, doch verstand Albert seine Sprache nicht.

«Kann ich Ihnen helfen?», fragte der Mann, offenbar der Inhaber des Antiquariats, nun in gebrochenem Deutsch.

Albert musste sich erst einmal kräftig räuspern, um einen Laut durch seine Kehle drücken zu können. Wieder hatte er einige Tage nicht gesprochen.

«Hm, haben Sie hier auch – Instrumente?»

«Oh ja, signor.» Der Mann lächelte. «Vorne liegt ein Akkordeon, hier sehen Sie eine Blockflöte und dort ein Triangel.» Er zeigte auf ein kleines Gestell. Albert konnte die besagten Instrumente im Chaos nicht ausfindig machen. «Weiter gibt es im Lager eine Geige und eine Balalaika.»

Ein derart wildes Gestikulieren hatte Albert der kleinen Erscheinung gar nicht zugetraut.

«Und dann hätte ich noch eine Gitarre …»

Albert horchte auf.

« …die allerdings kaum mehr spielbar ist.»

«Könnten Sie sie mir zeigen?» In seiner Ungeduld sprach Albert beinahe ebenso schnell wie der kleine Mann.

«Kommen Sie!»

Albert folgte ihm durch einen engen Gang und hatte Mühe, nichts von den Regalen zu stossen.

«Ecco, das ist sie.»

Ein derart schönes Exemplar hatte Albert nicht erwartet. Die Gitarrendecke war aussen schwarz gefärbt und verlief in Richtung Schalloch in ein betörendes Weinrot.

«Der Hals war einmal vom Rumpf abgetrennt, ich habe die Teile wieder zusammengeleimt. Ich bin kein Gitarrenspieler, aber man sagt mir, dass das Ding Schrott sei, basta.»

Albert hatte ihm gar nicht richtig zugehört. «Sie ist wunderschön», murmelte er.

«Davvero?» Der Händler zog erstaunt die Brauen hoch.

Albert schlug die Saiten an – es klang katastrophal. Ihm war jedoch bewusst, dass die Gitarre noch nicht gestimmt war.

«Sehen Sie? Schrott!»

«Was müssen Sie dafür haben?», fragte Albert unbeirrt.

«Non lo so …», seufzte der Mann. «Geben Sie mir etwa zehn Franken, signor.»

«Ich – ich kann Ihnen leider kein Geld geben.» Albert schämte sich.

«Wie meinen Sie das, kein Geld?»

Albert hob den Mantel in die Höhe, den er in der südlichen Hitze eigentlich gar nicht mehr brauchte. «Wie wär's, wenn ich Ihnen diesen hier für die Gitarre geben würde?»

Der Mann schüttelte heftig, ungläubig den Kopf.

«In Begleitung noch – eines feinen Damenröckchens.» Albert zog als zusätzlichen Trumpf noch das Sonnenblumenröckchen aus der Tasche des Mantels.

«Mamma mia, Sie sind mir vielleicht ein komischer Kerl!», stiess der Mann aus. Er schien allerdings nachzudenken. «Na gut. Ich kenne eine Dame, die mir garantiert zehn Franken für diesen Rock hinblättert.» Er lachte auf seinem goldenen Stockzahn.

«Wenn das so ist, kann ich dann den Mantel behalten?», fragte Albert vorsichtig.

Der Händler sah ihn entgeistert an. «Wissen Sie was? Sie wären ein guter Verkäufer. Wenn ich mal tot bin, können Sie meinen Laden übernehmen und hier drinnen für etwas mehr Platz sorgen.» Ein seltsam lautes Lachen scholl Albert entgegen. «Aber nun nehmen Sie die Gitarre und den Mantel und gehen Sie.»

«Haben Sie vielen Dank, signor.» Am liebsten hätte Albert den kleinen Mann auf dessen hohe Stirn geküsst. Bevor er das Antiquariat verliess, drehte er sich noch einmal um und fragte: «Können Sie mir sagen, wo Ascona liegt?»

«Ascona?» Wieder lachte der gütige Mann heiser und streckte schliesslich seinen Arm aus. «Gehen Sie eine halbe Stunde in diese Richtung!»

43. Der Menschensohn

A7

D

Asus2

Em

Em9

A / Em / Bm / A

A / Em / Bm / A / G

Em / Bm / Em / Em

G / A / E / Dsus2

Am / F / E

Am / F / E

Am / F / H

A7 / Em / Bm / Asus2

Roccos kräftige Wurstfinger ergriffen das Bierglas, das vor ihm auf dem runden Tischchen stand. Sein oben freigiebig geöffnetes Hemd gab den Blick auf seine pechschwarzen, gekräuselten Brusthaare preis, in denen sich sogar sein wulstiges Goldkettchen verstecken konnte.

Neben ihm sass Nico, der sich mit der Hand durch seine fettige Mähne strich. Er hatte kürzere Haare als etwa Rocco, dafür klebten besonders dichte, rötliche Koteletten auf seinen Wangen.

Toni schliesslich, der schmächtigste im Bunde, trug auch an heissen Sommertagen wie diesem jeweils eine lange, schwarze Hose. Die meisten seiner dunklen Haare waren ebenfalls lang – bis auf die Fransen, die seine Stirn zierten und knapp oberhalb seiner Rehaugen endeten.

Die drei jungen Kameraden hatten sich auf der Terrasse

ihres Stammlokals, direkt an der Seepromenade von Ascona, getroffen, um später gemeinsam um die Häuser zu ziehen.

«Ciao ragazzi!» Ein weiterer junger Mann mit hellen Locken, rasiertem Gesicht und verwaschenen Jeans setzte sich zu der Runde. Er sah geschafft aus. Die Rockband – zumindest nannte sie sich so – war komplett.

«Hallo Bob.» Seine Freunde begrüssten ihn.

«Mann, bin ich kaputt», seufzte Bob und lieh sich vorab einen Schluck von Nicos Bier. Dieser schaute ihn missmutig an.

«Bring mir bitte auch ein Bier, Giulia. Ein grosses», rief Bob dem Mädchen zu, das hinter der Bar über einem Kreuzworträtsel brütete.

«Und, woran seid ihr gerade?», fragte Bob, der trotz seines Arbeitspensums noch immer über mehr Energie verfügte als seine drei Kollegen zusammen.

«Eigentlich haben wir gerade über gar nichts gesprochen, Bob», erklärte Rocco.

«Ach kommt schon, was ist denn los mit euch?» Bob konnte es nicht leiden, wenn seine Kollegen still vor sich hin dösten.

«Wir sind bloss etwas müde und geniessen unser erstes Bier. Wir werden dann schon noch in Fahrt kommen», beschwichtigte Toni.

«Ihr seid müde?» Bob lächelte. «Habt ihr etwa heute ein Lied geschrieben?»

Toni nahm einen Schluck Bier, Nico zog an seiner Zigarette und Rocco blickte ernst dem Schiff nach, das über den See ritt.

Bob wusste, was das zu bedeuten hatte. «Also gut. Habt ihr heute zumindest geübt?», fragte Bob.

Niemand wollte das Wort ergreifen.

«Nun ja, Bob», begann Rocco dann, «ich war heute am Strand, weil – », er versuchte, den Blick von Bob zu meiden, «weil Toni und Nico auch da waren.»

Enttäuscht musste Bob feststellen, dass die Band heute wieder keinen Schritt vorangekommen war. «Hat sich jemand von euch zumindest ein paar Gedanken über einen Bandnamen gemacht, oder habt ihr den ganzen Tag nur Weibern hinterhergeschaut?», fragte er weiter.

Schweigen.

Plötzlich platzte es aus Nico heraus: «Du hättest sie heute sehen sollen, Bob, sie hatte …»

«Lass das, Nico», unterbrach ihn Toni und versuchte damit, Bobs Ärger in Grenzen zu halten.

«Seht ihr, Freunde.» Bob holte zu einer längeren Rede aus, während er einen nach dem anderen eindringlich ansah. «So kann das nicht weitergehen. Von euch muss einfach mehr kommen. Ich schufte jeden Tag im Restaurant, mir fehlt im Moment die Zeit, um die Band weiterzubringen. Oder hat jemand von euch Lust, mich mal bei der Arbeit abzulösen?»

Schweigen.

«Ihr jedoch, ihr habt die Zeit. Nutzt sie aus! Wenn wir erst mal ein paar Lieder auf Lager haben, ich meine richtig gute Lieder, dann müsst ihr den Frauen nicht mehr hinterherrennen, dann braucht ihr nur euer Hotelzimmer zu öffnen …»

Bob war nicht der Mensch, der seinem Ärger ungehalten Luft verschaffte. Vielmehr hatte er ein besonderes Talent dafür, seinen Kumpeln wirksam ins Gewissen zu reden.

«Bob hat recht», pflichtete Toni seinem Freund bei. «Niemand von uns will sein Leben lang jeden Montag arbeiten gehen.»

Nico und Rocco nickten.

Bob hatte mittlerweile sein grosses Bier erhalten. Sie stiessen auf ihren bevorstehenden Durchbruch an und blickten sich beherzt in die Augen – jeder der vier meinte zu spüren, dass sich in jenem Moment gerade ein Wendepunkt in ihrer Laufbahn ereignete. Wenn ihre Erfolgsgeschichte dereinst niedergeschrieben werden sollte, würde man die vergangenen Minuten in allen Einzelheiten darstellen.

Nach dieser beinahe verschwörerischen Versöhnung ging es am Tisch der vier lockerer zu. Man scherzte und lachte, trank ein weiteres Bier und noch eines, und Nico konnte doch noch seine heute Nachmittag am Strand gemachten Eindrücke schildern.

«Hey Leute, seht euch bloss diesen Landstreicher an.» Rocco machte die anderen auf eine seltsame Gestalt aufmerksam, die sich langsam dem Seeufer näherte.

Die paar abstehenden, Unerschrockenheit ausdrückenden Haarbüschel passten irgendwie nicht zur ansonsten höchst anständigen Frisur. Die tiefen Furchen unter den Augen wirkten neben den im Übrigen jugendlichen Gesichtszügen fast unheimlich. Und während er bedächtig wie ein Chorknabe voranschritt, erinnerte sein Ledergilet an einen tollkühnen Westernhelden. Es war schwierig, die höchst unterschiedlichen Empfindungen, die der Unbekannte weckte, miteinander in Einklang zu bringen. Der seltsame junge Mann, der ausserdem eine Gitarre in seiner Hand hielt, belustigte, faszinierte, verängstigte die vier selbsternannten Musiker.

Er setzte sich auf eine Bank, die ihm eine schöne Sicht über den See bot. Das Lokal der Band und die Bank wurde nur durch die Strandpromenade getrennt.

Die Spannung von Bob, Nico, Rocco und Toni entlud sich etwas, als der Zigeuner, wenn es denn einer war, scheinbar ziellos einzelne Akkorde zupfte.

«Toni, vielleicht gibt dir der Kerl ja ein paar Nachhilfestunden», witzelte Bob.

Toni allerdings wusste nicht, ob er Bobs Äusserung für einen Scherz halten sollte. Er traute dem eigenartigen Fremden nach wie vor alles und nichts zu.

Seine Kollegen hingegen gaben sich mehr und mehr wieder ihren Gesprächen, ihren Getränken hin, und nahmen gar nicht zur Kenntnis, dass die wenig aufregenden Klänge, die eben noch von der Bank her zu hören waren, verstummten.

Doch dann nahm der Fremde sein Gitarrenspiel wieder auf, und es veränderte sich schlagartig. Bob, Nico, Rocco und Toni hörten hinter sich eine mächtige Melodie. Da wandten sie sich um, die Töne zu hören, die ihnen entgegenflogen. Und wie sie sich umgewandt hatten, hörten sie sieben glänzende Akkorde, und inmitten der Akkorde sahen sie einen, gleich einem Menschensohn, angetan mit wallendem Ledergilet und einer über die Schultern gehängten Gitarre. Sein Haupt aber und seine Haare zuckten, und aus seinem Munde ging ein leises, aber scharfes Pfeifen, und sein Antlitz war, wie wenn die Sonne am Horizont aufgeht.

44. Via Borgo

Am / G / C / G
Am / G / C / G

«Vater. Ich möchte dir Natan vorstellen. Er ist neu hier, sucht Unterkunft und Arbeit.» Bob verwies auf den jungen Mann, der ihn ins Restaurant an der Via Borgo begleitet hatte.

«Bene. Und was hat das mit mir zu tun?», fragte der etwas rundliche Mann hinter der Bar skeptisch.

«Er hat sich bereit erklärt, mich zumindest am Morgen zeitweise zu vertreten», antwortete Bob.

«Ach, so ist das», bemerkte der Vater von Bob mit gespielter Erleuchtung. Er musterte den Fremden mit der Gitarre. «Du spielst doch nicht etwa Gitarre, oder?» Die Idiotie seiner Frage wurde ihm schon während dem Aussprechen der Worte bewusst. Gegen den Musikgeschmack der Jungen, insbesondere gegen denjenigen seines Sohnes, hatte er nämlich gewisse Vorbehalte.

«Doch – aber nur ein bisschen», antwortete der junge Mann eingeschüchtert.

«Hast du bereits irgendwelche Erfahrungen im Gastgewerbe gemacht?», wurde er weiter gefragt.

«Ja – ich habe etwa zehn Jahre in einem Gasthof gearbeitet.» Albert hätte die Worte am liebsten rückgängig gemacht. Er wollte so wenig wie möglich über seine Vergangenheit preisgeben. Hätte er sich doch bloss als ehemaliger Melker oder Mechaniker oder Mäusefänger vorgestellt! Andererseits konnte auch ein Lügengerüst immer wackeliger werden, je höher man es aufbaute. Das Fundament dieses Lügengerüsts hatte er mit seinem neuen Namen bereits gelegt.

«Gut. Wenn du gewillt bist, zu arbeiten, dann bist du willkommen!» Der Besitzer des Restaurants sprach nun in etwas freundlicherem Ton und reichte Albert seine kräftige Hand. «Mein Name ist Paolo. Komm, setz dich erst einmal.»

So setzte sich Albert mit Paolo und Bob an den Tisch, um

die Anstellung zu besprechen. Er erfuhr, dass man ihn jeweils am Morgen als Kellner brauche. Reich würde er dabei nicht werden, räumte Paolo ein, jedoch konnte man ihm ein kleines Zimmerchen unter dem Dach des Restaurants anbieten. Albert war damit vollumfänglich zufrieden.

«Wo hast du eigentlich dein restliches Gepäck?» Paolo wunderte sich, als er bemerkte, dass Albert lediglich mit einer Gitarre in der Hand aufgekreuzt war.

«Ich – ich bin noch ohne grösseres Gepäck unterwegs. Ich werde es mir nachschicken lassen.» Albert lächelte, fühlte sich aber äusserst unwohl in seiner Haut. Erst recht, als er den beiden über die Arbeit in seinem früheren Gasthof im Neuenburger Jura berichtete. Ihm war in der Not nichts besseres eingefallen. Natürlich hätte er sich lieber als Äthiopier ausgegeben. Dazu fehlte ihm aber das entsprechende Erscheinungsbild ebenso wie die erforderlichen Sprach- und Ortskenntnisse. Und doch hielt er jede Lüge für besser als die Wahrheit. Jede Erdichtung war besser als das Eingeständnis, kürzlich verstorben zu sein.

«Roberto, zeig unserer neuen Arbeitskraft doch sein Zimmer!», beauftragte Paolo seinen Sohn.

Albert folgte Bob. Über schmale Stufen gelangten die beiden ins Obergeschoss des Restaurants.

«So, da wären wir», sagte Bob etwas ausser Atem. «Ganz schön anstrengend, da hochzukommen, was?»

«Na ja – ich habe schon Anstrengenderes gemacht», antwortete Albert.

«Wenn du etwas brauchst, dann sag es mir.»

«Danke, Roberto.»

«Kein Problem. Aber nenn mich bitte nicht so.» Bob lächelte, obwohl seine Bitte ernstgemeint war. «Gute Nacht, Natan, wir sehen uns morgen!»

«Gute Nacht.»

Die Tür schloss sich. Albert legte sich auf sein Bett.

Sein Bett!

Er konnte es kaum fassen, dass er unter so glücklichen

Umständen bereits eine feste Bleibe hatte finden können. Noch vor zwei Stunden hatte er sich darauf eingestellt, wiederum einsam auf einer harten Holzbank zu schlafen. Und nun kannte er vier Musiker, konnte sich schon morgen ein paar Batzen verdienen und logierte in einem gemütlichen kleinen Zimmer eines Restaurants. Die Leute, die er bisher kennengelernt hatte, schienen alle in Ordnung zu sein. Er schloss die Augen, seine Mundwinkel hoben sich leicht nach oben.

45. Athanatos

Em9

A / Em / Bm / A
A / Em / Bm / A / G
Em / Bm / Em / Em
G / A / E / Dsus2
Dm

Am / F / E
Am / F / E
Am / F / H

A7 / Em / Bm / Asus2
A

Die ersten Takte der Gitarreneinleitung durchdrangen die stickige Luft des Proberaums. Umgehend sorgten sie für Seligkeit, in welche die ganze Band eintauchte, versank.

Zum himmlischen Zupfen von Albert gesellte sich nun die erdige Stimme Bobs. Die von Bob benützten Worte konnte Albert nicht verstehen, doch verleibten sie sich geradezu in sein Lied ein. Bob schien ein gutes Gefühl für Text und Rhythmus zu haben. Sein sehnsüchtiger Gesang war genau das, wonach das Lied verlangt hatte. Albert und Bob harmonierten bereits ungeheuer gut. Toni, Nico und Rocco hörten den beiden andächtig zu.

Dann begannen die Mauern zu vibrieren. Aus den Verstärkern dröhnte eine Wucht, die den fünf Musikern tief in ihren Innereien wühlte. Es waren die Akkorde von Toni, die schwer wie Stahl wummerten – der todverkündende Mittelteil hielt Einkehr. Unterlegt wurde Tonis heftige Gitarrenwand von Roccos Bass, dessen dicke Saiten in den untersten noch hörbaren Regionen donnerten. Dazu schlug Nico auf seine

Kessel, als ob es kein Morgen gäbe. Und über allem thronte die götterhafte Stimme von Bob, der Alberts Melodie mit unerhörter Leidenschaft hinausschrie.

Das apokalyptische Gewitter verstummte und ging wieder in Alberts akustisches Gitarrenspiel über. Bobs Gesang wurde wieder sanfter, leiser, verlor aber nichts von seinem Charisma. Albert zupfte ein letztes Mal an seinen Saiten und liess diese ausklingen, bis komplette Stille herrschte.

Niemand getraute sich, dieser Stille ein Ende zu setzen. Welche Worte wären jetzt schon angebracht gewesen? Es brauchte keine Worte. Erschlagen blickte man sich an, wohlwissend, was man eben vollbracht hatte. Jedes einzelne Gruppenmitglied wurde von Stolz erfüllt. Stolz, die vergangenen Minuten miterlebt zu haben, ja sogar Teil des Geschehens gewesen zu sein. Und mittendrin – seine neue Gitarre in den Händen haltend – stand Albert, der den Triumph schweigend genoss. Es war ihm nicht entgangen, in welch heilige Ekstase er die Band versetzt hatte.

Endlich legte man die Instrumente ab.

Heute würde man keinen Ton mehr spielen. Niemand wollte die durch Alberts Lied entfachte Magie, die immer noch durch den Proberaum schwebte, in irgendeiner Weise antasten.

Noch am See hatte man gestern den eigentümlichen Fremden, der auf den Namen Natan hörte, zur nächsten Bandprobe eingeladen, zu der er heute auch prompt erschienen war. Mit fieberhafter Aufregung hatte man sich sogleich an das Lied gewagt, das die Einladung Alberts begründete. Der Rest war bereits jetzt eine Legende, wenn auch vorerst nur innerhalb der Gruppe.

Obwohl es sich wie ein ausgefallener Schwindel anhörte, hatten die vier Albert sofort geglaubt, dass das Lied seiner Feder entsprungen war. Dafür hatten sie ein schlagendes Argument: Hätte das Lied nicht von diesem eigenbrötlerischen Sonderling gestammt, wäre es ihnen längst zu Ohren gekommen.

Die Gruppe verschob sich nach der Probe in ein nahegelegenes Grotto, um gemeinsam auf die kommende Zeit anzustossen. Noch wollte keiner mit seinen trunkenen Gedanken allein sein. Auch Albert war dabei. Er hatte sich nach der Probe bereits verabschieden wollen, doch beharrte die Band darauf, dass er sie noch begleite. Bob, Nico, Rocco und Toni betrachteten ihn bereits als neues Bandmitglied.

An einem Steintisch unter wuchernden Traubenstöcken erfuhr Albert allerhand über seine neuen Kollegen. So erzählte Bob, dass er seit dem Tag, an dem er in Besitz eines Radios gekommen war, Sänger werden wollte, doch mit seinem Wunsch stets nur belächelt wurde. Die Beschäftigung bei seinem Vater im Restaurant betrachtete er nur als vorübergehende Lösung. Der nachdenkliche Toni studierte Klassische Altertumswissenschaften, wusste allerdings nicht recht, ob er damit nur seinen Eltern oder auch sich selbst einen Gefallen tat. Irgendwie passte es zu Toni, der ein grosses Kreuz um den Hals trug, sich mit toten Kulturen zu beschäftigen, dachte sich Albert. Nico war einst Bademeister im örtlichen Freibad gewesen, bevor ihm dann aufgrund seiner etwas unvorteilhaften Postur ein ansehnlicherer vorgezogen wurde. Dies zumindest war seine Version der Absetzung. Und aus Rocco sollte es ursprünglich einen Seemann geben, doch hatte er bemerkt, dass er fern von zu Hause unter entsetzlichem Heimweh litt.

Albert hatte während den kurzen Lebensschilderungen den Eindruck, dass die vier, obwohl ihnen das Glück nicht gerade hold war, das Leben mit einer gesunden Portion Humor betrachteten.

Natan beschrieb sich schliesslich als früheren Koch, der sich in den Süden abgesetzt hatte, nachdem ihm der Alltag leid geworden war. Wiederum versuchte er, möglichst wenige Lügen aufzutischen, möglichst viel zu verschweigen.

«Natan! Auf uns!» Rocco hatte bereits wieder eine Runde Bier bestellt.

«Auf … wie heisst eure Band denn eigentlich?» Albert blickte in ratlose Gesichter.

«Hör mal, Natan. Unsere Band ist auch deine Band. Wir möchten, dass du dazugehörst», eröffnete ihm Bob.

Vier Augenpaare blickten Albert beinahe bittend an.

Er fühlte sich geschmeichelt. Die Frage überraschte ihn jedoch nicht. Er hatte sie sogar früher oder später erwartet.

«Na ja», antwortete Albert zaghaft, «ich würde schon gerne öfter mit euch Musik machen.»

Die Zukunft war der Band damit gesichert. So zumindest fassten Bob, Nico, Rocco und Toni die Worte Alberts auf. Jeder der vier malte sich aus, was ein Beitritt dieses Genies in die Band bedeuten würde.

«Auf … unsere Band?» Albert, dem das Schweigen unangenehm wurde, erhob sein Glas, um die vier aus ihren Träumereien zu reissen. Jetzt erst begannen sie, ihre Freude kund zu tun. Sie lachten und prosteten sich zu. Die Zuversicht funkelte regelrecht in ihren Augen.

«Wie wär's, wenn wir uns *Athanatos* nennen würden?», warf Toni plötzlich in die Runde.

«Klingt nicht schlecht – doch was bedeutet die Scheisse?», fragte Nico in seiner gewohnt unverblümten Manier.

«Das ist griechisch. Es bedeutet *unsterblich*.»

Die übrigen Mitglieder liessen den Namen auf sich einwirken.

«Ja. Das ist gut.» Rocco äusserte sich als erster. «Das könnte zu uns passen», fügte er ernst hinzu.

«Ich mag den Namen auch», vermeldete Bob etwas überraschend. Bob war mit Sicherheit derjenige, der am schwierigsten zufrieden zu stellen war. «Was meinst du, Natan?» Auch Alberts Meinung war also gefragt.

«Mir gefällt der Name ausgezeichnet», sagte er, und tatsächlich stimmte ihn Tonis Namensvorschlag heiter.

«Dann taufe ich uns auf den Namen *Athanatos*!» Nico tauchte seine Finger in Bobs Glas und bespritzte seine Kollegen mit Bier. Alle lachten, auch Bob rang sich dazu durch.

«Auf *Athanatos*!» Eine weitere Runde ging in Bestellung.

Toni war glücklich. Erstmals hatte er das Gefühl, sich für das richtige Studium entschieden zu haben.

«Sag mal, Natan. Hast du noch mehr solche Lieder auf Lager?», wollte Rocco plötzlich wissen.

Es war eine Frage, die Albert irritierte. Darüber hatte er sich noch gar keine Gedanken gemacht, und unversehens wurde ihm bewusst, dass er bis anhin erst *ein* richtig gutes Lied geschrieben hatte. Natürlich würde man weitere Lieder von ihm erwarten, alles andere wäre einer Beleidigung gleichgekommen. Doch die Erwartungen, die man nun an ihn stellen musste, waren hoch. Unendlich hoch. Er hatte sie selbst zu verantworten.

«Ich – ich habe viele Ideen im Kopf. Allerdings sind diese noch nicht ausgereift. Und wie sieht es bei euch aus?» Erneut wollte Albert schleunigst von sich ablenken.

«Wir befinden uns momentan in einem kreativen Loch», erklärte Nico. Die anderen ergötzten sich an seiner Antwort, denn gerade Nico war alles andere als ein begnadeter Komponist. Er beachtete die Flachsereien nicht und fuhr fort: «Doch nun ist unser Warten vorbei. Unsere Zeit ist gekommen.»

Etwas angetrunken verliess man schliesslich das Grotto und trat den Heimweg an.

Heute konnte Albert nicht sofort einschlafen. Er dachte an seine vier ersten Kameraden. Insbesondere Toni hatte er bereits näher kennengelernt. Toni hatte ihn heute abgeholt und ihn in den Keller von Roccos Zuhause begleitet, wo sich der Proberaum befand. Er war ihm sofort sympathisch gewesen.

Die unterschiedlichen Lebensgeschichten, die er sich dann nach der Probe aufmerksam angehört hatte, beeindruckten und berührten ihn. Eigentlich unterschied sich sein Leben – sein früheres – gar nicht so stark von demjenigen seiner neuen Bandkollegen. Sie alle warteten auf bessere Zeiten, keiner von ihnen liess sich als besonderer Held bezeichnen. Auch mit Frauengeschichten brüsteten sie sich nicht. Konnten sie es nicht? Im Grunde trugen sie alle die Züge eines Versagers. Eines Versagers, wie Albert einer war. Oder war er etwa bereits kein Versager mehr?

Eines aber unterschied die vier von Albert: sie waren auf ihre Weise glücklich. Und heute, da hatte er an diesem Glück teilhaben können.

46. Trinkgeld

D / C / G
D / F / G
D / – / E

Es war neun Uhr zwanzig. Albert stand allein hinter der rustikalen Holztheke und wartete auf Kundschaft. Das Restaurant war leer. Er nutzte die ihm dadurch gewährte Pause, um die beiden Aperitifgläser zu spülen, aus denen vorhin zwei krawattierte Herren Campari getrunken hatten.

Albert mochte seine Arbeit als Kellner auf Anhieb. Sie war ihm nicht völlig fremd, und doch unterschied sie sich ausreichend von seiner früheren Tätigkeit.

Man war nett zu ihm. Die Leute hatten im Allgemeinen Verständnis dafür, dass er ihrer Sprache nicht mächtig war. Einige brachten ihm gelegentlich sogar ein paar Wörter bei.

Seine Hauptaufgabe bestand darin, den Gästen Kaffee und frisches Morgengebäck zu servieren. Er freute sich über jedes dankende Wort, über jeden anerkennenden Blick. Manchmal erhielt er Trinkgeld.

Als sein Blick wieder durch das Restaurant flog, bemerkte er, dass nun jemand an einem Tisch sass. Merkwürdig, dachte er verwundert, er hatte gar niemanden kommen gehört.

Sie war blond. Albert näherte sich ihr, grüsste freundlich und fragte sie schon beinahe routiniert: «Was darf ich servieren?» Sie las in einer Frauenzeitschrift und liess sich von Albert nicht ablenken. Ohne den Kopf zu heben sagte sie mit jugendlicher Stimme: «Ein Wermut bitte.»

Erblasst kehrte Albert ihr den Rücken zu.

47. Leichenblässe

C7

Das Klingeln des Telefons riss Bob aus seinem essentiellen Schlaf. Erst hoffte er, dass das widerliche Geräusch bald wieder verstummen würde. Als sich dieses unaufhörlich hinzog, vermutete er, dass der Anruf doch von Bedeutung sein könnte. Vielleicht gab es ja Neuigkeiten für *Athanatos*. Vielleicht würde er es noch bereuen, einfach liegen geblieben zu sein. Widerwillig entfernte er seine warme Bettdecke, torkelte zur Kommode und hob den Hörer ab.

«Bob! Das hat aber lange gedauert!» Bereits jetzt bereute Bob, bereute, aufgestanden zu sein. Sein Vater war am Apparat.

«Ja», presste Bob heraus.

«Du musst unbedingt ins Restaurant kommen. Natan hat sich hinlegen müssen. Er war bleich wie ein Toter. D'accordo?»

«Ja.» Langsam legte er den Hörer wieder auf die Gabel und wankte ins Bad.

Mit schleppenden Armbewegungen strich er mit der Zahnbürste über seine Zähne, seine Knie drohten einzuknicken. Er schloss den Toilettendeckel und setzte sich darauf.

Bob war müde. Es war dies eine Folge seines nunmehr unermüdlichen Bestrebens, ein anständiges Lied zu schreiben, dem er sich oft bis tief in die Nacht hinein hingab. Die Band brauchte einfach mehr Lieder, haderte er, mehr gute Lieder. Lieder, die sich auch neben demjenigen von Natan nicht bloss wie ein zufälliges Zusammentreffen von Tönen anhörten.

So zuversichtlich ihn Natan auch auf baldige erste Erfolge von *Athanatos* stimmte – ganz in seinem Innern kränkte es ihn, plötzlich nicht mehr als führender Kopf der Band betrachtet zu werden. Natürlich würde er dies gegenüber Nico, Rocco und Toni nie zugeben, schon gar nicht gegenüber Natan. Es galt nun, die Kreativität, die er seiner Meinung nach durchaus besass, zu beweisen, um nicht vollends in den Schatten von Natan zu geraten.

Etwas schleierhaft war ihm allerdings, weshalb ein derart mirakulöser Musiker wie Natan – und das musste er zweifellos sein – bisher nur ein einziges Lied zustande gebracht hatte. Warum schüttelte er nicht noch weitere Lieder aus dem Ärmel? Konnte er nicht, wollte er gar nicht, oder stellte er einfach unheimlich hohe Ansprüche an sich?

Oder war es etwa möglich, dass sich Natans ganze Fantasie, seine ganze Schöpfungskraft über Jahre hinweg angestaut hatte, und endlich in Form eines einzigen übermächtigen Liedes, einer gewaltigen Eruption gleich, explodierte?

48. Aus einem toten Buch

E / C / A / G
A / G / C / D

Langsam gewöhnte sich Albert an Gesichter, die ihm bekannten ähnelten – ihm bekannten aus seinem früheren Leben. Nachdem ihn anfänglich doch einige Begegnungen in Schrecken versetzt hatten, musste er sich zur eigenen Beruhigung vor Augen führen, dass auch im Tessin blonde Mädchen verkehrten, die Wermut tranken, dass wohl auf der ganzen Welt Toscanelli-Raucher oder Angeber mit feinen Schnurrbärten anzutreffen waren. Allerdings zuckte er immer noch zusammen, wenn am Restaurant vorbeischlendernde Leute einen Dialekt sprachen, den er in die Nähe des Freiburgerlandes situierte.

Am frühen Nachmittag war sein tägliches Arbeitspensum jeweils schon zu Ende. Dann tauchte für gewöhnlich Bob auf, um ihn abzulösen. Es konnte aber auch vorkommen, dass Albert nach dem Eintreffen von Bob noch eine Weile blieb, um auszuhelfen. Es machte ihm nichts aus.

In seiner Freizeit traf sich Albert gelegentlich mit Toni, der ihm die bisherigen Lieder von *Athanatos* beibrachte. Albert fand die Lieder zwar nett, wenngleich etwas gefühllos. Einige erinnerten ihn an eigene Stücke, die er Jahre vor seinem Tod geschrieben hatte. Es war durchaus üblich, dass die beiden ein bestehendes Musikstück etwas abänderten. Toni erwies sich fraglos als talentierter Gitarrist und hatte den Drang, vermehrt düsterere Töne in die Lieder einfliessen zu lassen. Alberts Requiem hatte ihn massgeblich beeinflusst – er hielt es für das beste, was bis dato mit einer Gitarre angestellt worden war. Albert hingegen gestaltete seine Einstreuungen in die Lieder weniger melancholisch. Er hatte in seinem Leben zu viele E-Moll-, zu wenige D-Dur-Akkorde gespielt.

Und wenn er allein war, dann beschäftigte ihn Roccos

Frage nach weiteren Kompositionen. Er bemühte sich oft, ein zweites Lied zu schreiben, ein Lied, das seinem ersten einigermassen das Wasser hätte reichen können. Er musste jedoch ernüchtert feststellen, dass er weit davon entfernt war. Immer stärker befürchtete er, dass ihm kein weiteres Meisterwerk mehr gelingen sollte, so schwer dies auch zu begreifen war. Denn schliesslich hatte er seine grossen Melodien in den aufwühlendsten Momenten seines Lebens geschrieben: im Angesicht des Todes. In diese Lage konnte er, wollte er sich nicht wieder versetzen.

Heute stattete er Toni wieder einen Besuch ab. Durch ein Gittertor, das den eisernen Zaun unterbrach, beschritt er das etwas betrüblich anmutende Anwesen, trat ein und traf ihn schreibend an einem Marmortisch an. Trotz herrlichem Sommerwetter hatte sich Toni in ein dunkles Zimmer verkrochen, in dem nur ein sechsarmiger Kronleuchter ein wenig Licht spendete. Links und rechts von seinem Notizblock stapelten sich Bücher, die schon Jahre, Jahrzehnte auf dem Buckel haben mussten.

«Schreibst du einen neuen Liedtext?», fragte Albert nicht ganz ernsthaft.

«Nein, leider nicht. Ich habe mir heute sogar vorgenommen, die Gitarre nicht anzufassen. Ein Haufen Arbeit erwartet mich noch. Studentische Pflichten.» Toni lächelte verlegen.

«Ach so. Dann will ich dich in deinem Fleiss nicht stören.»

«Kein Problem, setz dich doch.»

Albert nahm die Aufforderung an und besah sich das Bild, auf dem vier dürre Männer hoch zu Pferd, bewaffnet mit Pfeil und Bogen, vorangaloppierten.

«Worüber schreibst du denn?», erkundigte er sich dann, da er sich nicht recht vorstellen konnte, was den alten Schmökern zu entnehmen war.

«Ich schreibe eine Arbeit über Epikur», erklärte Toni.

«Wo ist das?»

«Nein, das ist kein Ort. Das ist ein antiker Philosoph»,

antwortete Toni nachsichtig und überblickte kurz das aufgeschlagene Buch. «Der hat Sachen geschrieben wie: ‹solange wir sind, ist der Tod nicht da, und sobald er da ist, sind wir nicht mehr.› Welch bahnbrechende Erkenntnis, nicht wahr?» Er lachte, und Albert lachte mit ihm, um seine Verwirrung zu verbergen.

«Damit könnten wir doch tatsächlich einen Liedtext schreiben, was meinst du?», schlug Toni zu Alberts Überraschung vor.

Albert überlegte. «Warum eigentlich nicht? Aber vielleicht – könnten wir den Text etwas abändern?»

«Klar.»

49. Die Zeit ist nahe

Em
E

«Natan, ich muss mit dir reden», sagte Bob ohne Grusswort. Sein an sich braungebranntes Gesicht war farblos und kontrastierte nicht wie üblich mit seinen hellen Locken. Seine zuckenden, hastigen Bewegungen verrieten Nervosität. Etwas Aussergewöhnliches musste vorgefallen sein, denn Bob stürmte bereits am Morgen ins Restaurant.

«Ich komme gleich.» Albert servierte einer älteren Dame ihren Minzentee und überlegte sich mit Kummer, was das seltsame Auftreten von Bob wohl zu bedeuten hatte.

«Setz dich kurz, Natan», forderte ihn Bob auf.

Albert setzte sich.

«Nico hat mich gestern spät noch angerufen», begann Bob mit ungewohnt angespannten Gesichtszügen.

Alberts Puls wurde schneller. Die Art und Weise, wie Bob sprach, gefiel ihm nicht.

«Ich hoffe, dass ich dich damit nicht allzu sehr überrumpeln werde», fuhr Bob ernst fort.

Albert konnte sich kaum vorstellen, dass ihn seine Vergangenheit hier bereits eingeholt hatte. Die Kunde seines Todes konnte sich doch unmöglich schon bis ins Tessin verbreitet haben!

Eine fünfköpfige Familie setzte sich an einen Tisch auf der Terrasse, die gleich an die von Fussgängern belebte Strasse grenzte.

«Bob, ich habe nicht mehr ewig Zeit, die Leute warten schon.» Hilflos versuchte Albert, der Tragödie auszuweichen, verwies auf den Tisch, an dem die Getränkekarten bereits wieder in den hölzernen Ständer gesteckt worden waren.

«*Wir* haben nicht mehr ewig Zeit, Natan.» Bob lächelte gequält.

«Ich verstehe nicht, Bob.» Albert ärgerte sich allmählich darüber, dass Bob ihn so lange hinhielt, ihn regelrecht folterte mit seinen gedehnten Mitteilungen. Sollte er ihm doch gleich seine Todesanzeige vor die Nase halten.

«Es ist so», begann Bob. «Nico hat den Wirt unseres Stammlokals am See angefragt, ob wir da nicht einmal auftreten könnten.»

Albert war ungemein erleichtert und beunruhigt zugleich.

«Er hat sofort eingewilligt.»

«Und wann soll dieser Auftritt stattfinden?»

«Nächsten Freitag.»

50. Das Bekenntnis

Em9

A / Em / Bm / A
A / Em / Bm / A / G
Em / Bm / Em / Em
G / A / E / Dsus2
Dm

Am / F / E
Am / F / E
Am / F / H

A7 / Em / Bm / Asus2
A / Em / Bm / -

Wilde Wüstenlandschaften, dürftig bewachsen mit riesigen Kakteen, in deren Schatten vereinzelt Ochsenschädel und andere Kadaver lagen, zierten grossflächig die Wände. Das dumpf glimmende Licht liess die Rauchschwaden sichtbar werden, die sich an der niederen, dunkel getönten Decke sammelten. Auf den mit rotem Leder überzogenen Ecksesseln, an der Bar oder stehend im breiten Gang, ertränkte man den Werktag, frönte dem Feierabend, freute sich auf das Wochenende, das eben angebrochen war. Viele liessen sich durch die Darbietung fünf lokaler Jungspunde nicht stören, sondern amüsierten sich weiter.

Das Lokal war nicht allzu geräumig, das Publikum überschaubar, und dennoch – es fühlte sich schrecklich an, auf dem kleinen Podium zu stehen und für alle hörbar die Saiten anzuschlagen.

Albert konnte den Schriftzug auf dem Glas lesen, das die schöne Schwarzhaarige gerade an ihre Lippen führte. Er konnte den Sonnenbrand auf dem Scheitel des flott gekämmten Strahlemannes erblicken – gar den Pickel, der aus dem linken Nasenflügel des hüftsteif Tanzenden drang. Die intime Nähe beängstigte ihn.

Als Auftretender gab er den Gästen ja die Erlaubnis, ihn zu mustern, ihn ohne Scham endlos lange Minuten anzustieren, ihn mit Blicken zu durchlöchern. Er fragte sich, wie viele Augen wohl gerade über seinen Körper wanderten.

Obwohl er sich etwas hinter Bob versteckt hielt, würde man das Zittern seiner Finger bemerken. Was noch? Hatte er seinen Hosenverschluss zugemacht? War sein Hemd nicht mit Flecken beschmiert? Trug er überhaupt eine Hose?

Die etwas schleppend daherkommenden Lieder von *Athanatos* hauten niemanden vom Barhocker. Als Albert in seiner Aufregung gar noch versehentlich eine Tonfolge spielte, die er versehentlich im vorletzten Lied nicht gespielt hatte, verringerte sich die Anzahl der aufmerksamen Zuhörer noch einmal. Albert wäre am liebsten im Erdboden …

Wäre er das wirklich? Im Erdboden, da hätte er ja eigentlich tatsächlich liegen sollen. Reglos, gefühllos, vermodernd in feuchter Erde, in Gesellschaft klebriger Würmer, tot, ganz und gar tot.

Nach jenen Gedanken zog es Albert doch vor, sich lebendig vor ein paar ihm unbekannten Leuten zu blamieren.

Zwei gelungene Lieder später wurde ihm allmählich bewusst, was er gerade tat – was überhaupt in den letzten Tagen alles geschehen war. All die überwältigenden Erlebnisse, die seit seinem Tod auf ihn zugekommen waren, hatte Albert noch nicht vollends realisieren können. Erlebte er hier gerade das einschneidendste? Er stand auf einer Bühne! Mit Leuten, vor Leuten!

Und dann kam das letzte Lied.

Als Albert an seinen Saiten zu zupfen begann, war ihm, als ob der Raum von einer sonderbaren Wehmut erfüllt würde, einer Wehmut, die sich augenblicklich in die Herzen der Besucher einnistete. Er sah, dass man vielerorts die Gespräche unterbrach und ernst wurde. Mehr noch, davon war Albert überzeugt – man sehnte sich. Sehnte sich nach dem Schönen, dem Vollkommenen, dem man allerdings noch nie begegnet war. Und dieses Unbekannte, nach dem man sich sehnte, erklang nun im ganzen Lokal, in den Köpfen aller Gäste. Aus Alberts Augen löste sich eine Träne. Es war sein öffentliches Liebesbekenntnis zu Mona, zum Leben.

Es folgte der erschütternde Mittelteil. Ein Glas zersprang am Boden, die Mienen versteinerten sich, ein kalter Windhauch zog durch die Wüste. *Solange ich bin, ist das Leben nicht da.* Natürlich konnten die Leute den Mittelteil nicht verstehen, nicht nachvollziehen. Und doch waren sie von seiner Intensität fasziniert. *Und sobald der Tod kommt, beginne ich zu leben.* Albert aber wurde von einer leisen Erleichterung befallen. Irgendwie verspürte er das seltsame Gefühl, den Leuten sein dunkles Geheimnis zu verraten.

Immer noch betroffen, vernahm man nun wieder die liebliche Melodie der Strophe. Zu Bobs Überraschung gesellte sich Albert plötzlich zu ihm ans Mikrophon und begleitete ihn mit der zweiten Stimme, verlieh dem Lied damit noch mehr Leben, als wollte er jedem einzelnen Zuhörer seine Auferstehung von den Toten verkünden.

Eben trieb die Strophe ihrem Höhepunkt entgegen, als es plötzlich still wurde.

Die Sicherung war durchgebrannt. Man hatte die Anlage etwas zu stark strapaziert. Die Stille dauerte noch eine Weile an. Der Auftritt war beendet.

Aus den hinteren Rängen hallte ein einsames Klatschen durch das Lokal, dem sich allmählich ein paar weitere Hände anschlossen. Der Applaus blieb verhalten.

Bob, Nico, Rocco und Toni waren irritiert. Der überschwängliche Jubel, der von ihnen erwartet wurde, kam nicht. Albert jedoch genoss den Moment. Er konnte die Antwort auf sein Lied in den eigenartig vertieft wirkenden Gesichtern ablesen. Die Musik, die aus den tiefsten Abgründen seiner Seele gesprochen hatte, erwärmte und erschütterte das Innenleben der Leute. Die herrschende Stille bestätigte ihm jedenfalls die Grösse seines Werkes. Sie war ihm wesentlich wertvoller als ein anständiger Pflichtbeifall. Es schien ihm fast, dass man ihm für einmal zugehört hatte und dabei versuchte, ihn zu verstehen.

Wortlos packten die fünf Musiker ihre Instrumente zusammen.

Der Chef brachte der Band fünf leere Krüge und einen Kübel Bier. «Lasst es euch schmecken», meinte er, «war gar nicht übel, für den ersten Auftritt.»

«Auf *Athanatos*!», sprach Bob.

Nico, Rocco und Toni erhoben nachdenklich ihre Gläser und genehmigten sich einen grossen Schluck.

«Lasst die Köpfe nicht hängen.» Albert versuchte, sein Glücksgefühl auf die anderen zu übertragen. «Wir waren gut», fügte er hinzu.

Die Stimmung heiterte sich schluckweise auf. Die spärlich geäusserten Beifallsbezeugungen und der Stromausfall hatten unmittelbar nach dem Auftritt etwas auf die Gemütslage der Band gedrückt. Nun aber machte sich nach und nach doch Zufriedenheit über die ansonsten geglückte Darbietung breit. Zudem hatten die fünf Musiker immer wieder den Eindruck, dass ihnen aus dem ganzen Lokal bewundernde Blicke entgegenflogen.

«Ich danke dir, Natan.» Das Quäntchen Alkohol hatte in Nico bereits eine gewisse Zutraulichkeit entfacht.

«Aber – wofür denn?», fragte Albert, obwohl er wusste, dass es um sein Lied ging.

«Für den Lebensgeist, den du uns eingehaucht hast», antwortete Nico.

Albert war ergriffen.

«Ohne dich wären wir nicht hier, verstehst du?», fuhr Nico fort.

Sie tranken weiter.

Albert entschied, seinen Kollegen als Dank für die herzliche Aufnahme in die Band eine weitere Runde zu spendieren. Er ging an der Bar vorbei und sah das schöne Mädchen mit den schwarzen Haaren. Da er seinen Schritt verlangsamte, konnte er zusehen, wie es jemanden küsste – es war ebenfalls ein Mädchen. Etwas verdutzt suchte er zunächst die Toilette auf.

Mit entleerter Blase begab er sich dann an die Bar. Sogleich fiel ihm auf, dass das Mädchen nun allein dasass.

Er wartete an der Theke, um die Bestellung aufzugeben, als sich ihm in seinem rechten Augenwinkel plötzlich etwas annäherte.

«Hallo Gitarrenheld.»

Albert blickte zaghaft in die unschuldigen Augen des Mädchens.

«Ich habe gerade meine letzte Zigarette geraucht. Hast du vielleicht noch welche?», fragte das Mädchen ungehemmt, aber durchaus nicht aufdringlich.

«Ich rauche keine Mary Long», gab Albert zur Antwort.

Einen kleinen Moment lang rang sie nach Worten, fing sich aber sofort wieder auf: «Ich rauche auch andere Marken.»

«Ich rauche gar nicht.» Es gelang Albert, eine ungewohnte Ruhe zu bewahren. Er fühlte sich nach seinem ersten Auftritt schon ein klein wenig wie ein berühmter Musiker.

«Ach so.» Das Mädchen klang enttäuscht.

«Es tut mir leid», sagte Albert, und leid tat es ihm tatsächlich. Höchst unsympathisch, ja beinahe arrogant war er dem Mädchen gegenüber aufgetreten, dabei hatte sie eigentlich eine gewinnende Art. Er wollte sein zunächst abweisendes Verhalten wieder gutmachen. «Ich kann dir höchstens noch ein Glas Caipirinha anbieten.»

Das Gesicht des Mädchens erhellte sich wieder, freudig, überrascht.

Albert bestellte zwei Caipirinha.

«Ich bin Lucia.»

«Ich heisse – Natan.»

«Ich habe euer Konzert mitverfolgt.»

«Ich weiss.»

Albert hatte zum ersten Mal in seinem Leben eine Frau im Ausgang kennengelernt. Dass sie um Jahre jünger sein mochte als er, störte ihn nicht. Er schaute ihr ins Gesicht – sah, wie sich ihre langen Wimpern wölbten, wie sie sich mit ihren zartgliedrigen Fingern durch die schwarzen Haare fuhr, wie sie den Trinkhalm zwischen ihre gespitzten Lippen steckte. Noch nie hatte er ein weibliches Gesicht so lange aus so kurzer Distanz erforschen können.

«Natan. Würdest du mich vielleicht nach Hause bringen?» Lucia sah ihn bittend und plötzlich etwas traurig an.

Albert schluckte.

51. Die norwegische Flöte

Asus2 / Csus2
Asus2 / Csus2 / Dsus2 / Em
Csus2 / Dsus2 / Em

Lucia führte Albert durch verwinkelte Gassen der Altstadt von Ascona, bis sie vor ihrer Wohnung Halt machte. Aus irgendeinem Grund hatte sich Albert flüchtig von seinen Freunden verabschiedet und die Gitarre bereits mitgenommen.

«Möchtest du noch kurz hereinkommen?», fragte sie in kindlicher Unschuld.

«Na gut.»

Albert betrat den kleinen Wohnraum.

«Setz dich doch», forderte Lucia ihn auf und verschwand durch eine Tür, «ich bin gleich wieder da.»

Albert sah sich im dunkel gehaltenen Raum um und bemerkte, dass dieser über gar keinen Stuhl verfügte. Also setzte er sich auf einen farbenprächtigen Teppich, der in der Mitte des Raumes lag.

Mit einer Flasche Wein in der Hand kam Lucia Augenblicke später zurück. Albert begutachtete die Etikette. Tessiner Merlot, Jahrgang 1949.

«Würdest du schon einmal die Flasche öffnen?», bat Lucia, reichte ihm einen Flaschenöffner und verschwand wieder. «Gleich bin ich soweit», versicherte sie ihm. Er entkorkte den Merlot und widmete seine Aufmerksamkeit einem kleinen Regal. Sofort entdeckte er das Instrument: eine auffallend schöne Blockflöte.

Endlich tauchte Lucia wieder auf, setzte sich ebenfalls auf den Teppich und stellte zwei Gläser zwischen sich und Albert. Er füllte die Gläser zur Hälfte – Paolo hatte vergangene Woche auf seinen etwas zu grosszügigen Ausschank hingewiesen.

«Wem gehört diese Flöte?» Albert zeigte mit dem Finger auf das Regal.

Lucia holte die Flöte und reichte sie Albert in die Hand. «Norwegisches Holz», bemerkte sie vieldeutig.

Zögernd betastete Albert die Flöte. «Sie ist sehr schön», bezeugte er. «Kannst du etwas spielen?»

«Klar. Möchtest du mich begleiten?» Sie sah ihn herausfordernd an.

Lucia begann zu spielen. Ihre Melodie war schlicht und schnörkellos, sodass Albert rasch dazu passende Akkorde aufspüren konnte. Die Klänge, welche die beiden ihren Instrumenten entlockten, fanden sich ohne Umschweife und verschmolzen ineinander.

Er wagte nicht, sie während dem gemeinsamen Spiel anzusehen. Vielmehr versuchte er, sich in die Melodie hineinzufühlen. Wie die Melodie wohl zustande gekommen war? Was wohl dahinter steckte? Das Flötenspiel von Lucia machte ihn stutzig – die wenigen Töne waren unheimlich fesselnd.

Endlich suchten sich die Blicke von Albert und Lucia, um gemeinsam den Schlusston anzustimmen, der langsam, nicht mehr enden wollend, verhallte.

Ohne über ihr Duett zu sprechen, tranken beide einen Schluck Wein.

«Möchtest du meinen Wein trinken, Natan?», fragte Lucia, nachdem man die Stille noch eine Weile genossen hatte. «Ich habe für heute genug getrunken.»

«Wenn ich dir damit einen Gefallen tue, gerne», antwortete Albert etwas überrascht.

Lucia reichte ihm das Glas. Aus einem Säckchen nahm sie etwas Tabak hervor, um sich eine Zigarette zu drehen.

«Du bist etwas schüchtern, was?» Sie lächelte verständnisvoll.

«Es geht so.» Alberts Hand bewegte sich an den Hinterkopf, senkte sich dann aber reflexartig wieder. Er musste sich diese seltsame Eigenart unbedingt abgewöhnen.

«Das letzte Lied, das ihr gespielt habt. Du hast es geschrieben, nicht wahr?»

«Warum meinst du?»

«Ich habe dich beobachtet.» Lucia fuhr sorgfältig mit ihrer Zunge über das Zigarettenpapier und klebte dieses zu. Sie zündete den Glimmstängel an.

«Hat es dir gefallen?», fragte Albert.

Lucia führte eine Kopfbewegung aus, die Albert nicht zu deuten verstand. «Wovon handelt das Lied? Ich meine, weshalb hast du es geschrieben?», wollte sie wissen und hauchte aufreizend langsam den Qualm aus ihrem Mund.

«Weisst du, dass sich dein Leben mit jedem Zug an deiner Zigarette um ein paar Sekunden verkürzt?», wich Albert aus.

«So ist es doch auch mit dem Wein. Mit jedem Schluck überspringst du ein paar Sekunden deines Lebens. Mit jedem Schluck näherst du dich schneller dem Tod», konterte Lucia sogleich.

«Tatsächlich?»

«Aber du rauchst ja nicht. Du kannst also ab und zu gut zwei Gläser Wein auf einmal vertragen.» Lucia grinste, und ihr Grinsen mutete Albert grotesk an.

«Vergiss es, Natan», meinte sie nach einer Pause, während der Albert über das Gesagte nachgegrübelt hatte, «am Ende kommt dann doch alles anders, nicht wahr?»

Allerdings, dachte sich Albert, und wusste nicht, weshalb sich ein unbekanntes Mädchen mit ihm über den Tod unterhielt. Er schwieg weiter.

«Ich fürchte mich nicht vor dem Tod», meinte sie nun gleichgültig. «Fürchtest du dich?»

Albert nahm einen Schluck Wein und sagte schliesslich: «Es sind Dinge geschehen, Lucia, die du nicht verstehen kannst. Sei mir nicht böse, aber ich möchte nicht darüber sprechen.»

«Es geht um eine Frau, nicht wahr?» Wieder änderte Lucia schlagartig das Gesprächsthema.

«Was meinst du?» Ihre Hartnäckigkeit verunsicherte Albert etwas. Zwar freute es ihn, dass sie sich offenbar für seine Vergangenheit interessierte – davon zu erzählen behagte ihm aber natürlich nicht.

«Dein Lied. In deinem Lied steckt eine Frau», wiederholte sie.

Albert antwortete nicht.

Es war bereits zwei Uhr morgens. Lucia stand auf und teilte Albert mit, dass sie nun ins Bett müsse. «Bald ist wieder Morgen, und ich muss früh aufstehen.» Sie lachte.

«Ich nicht. Ich habe morgen freigenommen», antwortete Albert.

Sie stand auf, betrat ein Zimmer und schloss die Tür hinter sich. Albert blieb sitzen und gönnte sich noch einen Schluck Wein aus dem Glas von Lucia. Die merkwürdige Bekanntschaft gab ihm Rätsel auf.

Die Tür öffnete sich noch einmal einen spaltbreit. Im Dunkel erschien Lucias Gestalt. «Lebwohl, Natan», säuselte sie leise und zog die Zimmertür wieder zu. Ob sich Albert nur einbildete, dass sie ihm noch einen Kuss zugeworfen hatte?

Albert bemerkte, wie müde und berauscht er eigentlich war. Er ging ins Bad, um sich den Kopf zu waschen.

52. Wie ein Vöglein ausgeflogen

D / C / G / D
D / C / G / D
Dm / G
Dm / Em

Als Albert erwachte, war ihm bitterkalt. Die Unterlage, auf der er geschlafen hatte, schien ihm zudem ungewöhnlich hart zu sein. Er öffnete die Augen und sah auf die weissen, quadratischen Fliesen, auf denen farbige Blumen wild durcheinander wucherten.

Albert fand sich in einem unbekannten Badezimmer wieder. Nach bangen Sekunden, in denen jegliche Rekonstruktionsversuche des gestrigen Abends scheiterten, dämmerte ihm, wie er hierher gekommen war. Aber natürlich – der grossartige Auftritt, sein Lied, das schwarzhaarige Mädchen, Lucia, das faszinierende Duett. Und als Lucia plötzlich schlafen gegangen war, hatte er sich ins Bad begeben und sich da spontan hingelegt. Ein aussergewöhnliches Ende eines aussergewöhnlichen Abends.

Die Sache war ihm nun aber etwas unangenehm. Er hoffte, schleunigst aus diesem Haus verschwinden zu können. Wenn er sich recht erinnern mochte, musste Lucia nun bei der Arbeit sein. Aber ob sie allein wohnte? Er hatte keine Lust darauf, im Wohnzimmer einen Fremden anzutreffen.

Vorsichtig öffnete Albert die Badezimmertür und spähte nach draussen. Er konnte kein Lebenszeichen erkennen. Leise schlich er aus dem Badezimmer und traf die Stube genau so an, wie er sie gestern verlassen hatte.

Zögernd bewegte er sich vor die Tür, durch die Lucia gestern verschwunden war, und klopfte an.

«Lucia», flüsterte er, «bist du noch da?»

Er erhielt keine Antwort.

Er war also allein in der Wohnung – wie ein Vöglein war das Mädchen ausgeflogen.

Der ausgebreitet daliegende Teppich vergegenwärtigte ihm die Stunden, die er mit Lucia verbracht hatte. Oder waren es doch nicht Stunden gewesen? Wie lange er wohl mit Lucia über das Leben, über den Tod gesprochen haben mochte? Er hatte Mühe, den verflossenen Abend in ein Zeitgewand zu kleiden.

Die Zigarette, die Lucia vor dem Schlafengehen noch gedreht hatte, lag im Aschenbecher. Gleich daneben stand ihr Feuerzeug. Sie hatte es heute Morgen wohl vergessen einzupacken. Weiter bemerkte Albert, dass er in seinem Weinglas noch einen ordentlichen Tropfen zurückgelassen hatte. Er nahm das Glas, hob es, um zu trinken, doch dann zögerte er. Langsam liess er das Glas wieder sinken. Stattdessen ergriff er Lucias Zigarette und roch daran, roch den starken Tabakgeschmack, der sich mit Verbranntem vermischte. Unsicher klemmte er den Zigarettenfilter zwischen seine Lippen und machte Feuer.

Ein lautes Husten befreite sich aus seinem Hals, als sich der Rauch einen Weg durch diesen erhaschen wollte. Er warf die Zigarette zurück in den Aschenbecher.

Auch die Flöte lag noch auf dem Teppich. Albert nahm sie erneut zur Hand und betrachtete sie. Ein wenig unterhalb des Mundstücks konnte er eine Schrift erkennen. «Lucia Pica» war da in das Holz eingeritzt. In das norwegische Holz.

53. Grappa

C / B# / A / G# / F / Em

Eben hatte sich Albert auf sein Bett gelegt, als jemand an seine Zimmertür hämmerte.

«Natan! Ich muss dir was erzählen!» Es war die sich überschlagende Stimme Bobs, die ihn aus seinem Schlummerzustand riss.

Obwohl ihm der Besuch nicht besonders genehm war, öffnete er die Tür. Er war müde, ausserdem hatte er sich gestern Abend etwas geschmacklos aus dem Staub gemacht.

«Tut mir leid, dass ich dich nicht ausschlafen lasse», begann Bob ausser Atem. Er führte sich ähnlich hektisch auf wie letzte Woche, als er Albert den bevorstehenden Auftritt angekündigt hatte.

«Was ist denn, Bob?» Albert versuchte, einen verschlafenen Eindruck zu hinterlassen.

«Als du gestern Abend schon weg warst, hat sich ein gewisser Herr zu uns an den Tisch gesellt …»

Bob war ja ein netter Kerl, doch seine dramaturgische Art, Neuigkeiten zu berichten, konnte einem ganz schön auf die Nerven gehen.

«Und?», fragte Albert knapp – nicht gewillt, in Bobs Stück die Rolle des Unwissenden, allmählich Staunenden zu übernehmen.

«Rate mal!», schlug Bob vor, obwohl er viel ungeduldiger auf seine Mitteilung wartete als Albert.

«Bob, sag es mir doch einfach.» Nun bemerkte auch Bob, dass Albert sich ein wenig ärgerte.

«Also. Es war – ein Journalist …» Bob liess sich das Wort, das Albert sogleich in Bestürzung versetzte, auf der Zunge zergehen.

«Ein – Journalist?» Albert bemühte sich, seine Beunruhigung dem beglückt abwartenden Bob vorzuenthalten.

«Na, was sagst du jetzt?» Bob hatte seine Augen, seinen Mund weit aufgerissen.

«Das ist aber eine Überraschung», entgegnete ihm Albert nüchtern.

«Es ist der Anbruch unserer Zeit! Wir werden uns heute Abend mit ihm treffen. Du hast doch nicht bereits etwas vor, oder?»

«Heute Abend …» Die Pause wurde länger und länger – zu lange, um noch irgendetwas Glaubwürdiges dazwischenkommen zu lassen.

«Es ist wichtig, dass alle dabei sind, Natan. Nächste Woche soll ein Artikel über uns erscheinen, dafür benötigt er natürlich ein paar Auskünfte – von allen. Stell dir vor, der will sogar ein Gruppenbild von uns machen!»

«Ein Bild? Mit unseren Gesichtern?» Albert wurde die Angelegenheit immer unheimlicher.

«Nein, mit unseren Füssen … Aber natürlich mit unseren Gesichtern!» Bob konnte Natans Unbehagen nicht begreifen. «Und weisst du, was das beste ist? Der Mann scheint überall Kontakte zu haben, kennt Leute in Luzern, Bern, ja in Italien! Er könnte sich sogar vorstellen, eine kleine Konzerttour für uns zu organisieren, ist das nicht wunderbar?» Damit besiegelte Bob Alberts Verzweiflung.

«Eine Tour.» Alberts Resignation fasste Bob in seiner Euphorie als glückliche Ungläubigkeit auf.

«Wir sehen uns um halb sieben bei Nico im Keller. Aber jetzt schlaf noch ein bisschen weiter!» Bob lachte und klopfte ihm auf die Schulter. «Bis später, mein Freund!»

«Bis später», sagte Albert leise. Bob rannte wie ein Verrückter die Treppe runter und hinterliess einen entgeisterten Albert.

Schmerzlich war ihm wieder aufgezeigt worden, wie schwer das Gewicht war, das nun sein Leben lang auf ihm lastete – das Gewicht seines eigenen Todes.

Ein Bild! Sein Gesicht durfte auf keinen Fall in irgendwelchen Zeitungen zu sehen sein. Überhaupt durften keine Bilder von ihm existieren, die seinen Tod widerlegten, sein Leben bezeugten.

Eine Tour! Niemand konnte ernsthaft von ihm verlangen, sich in der Nähe seines Grabes auf einer Bühne zu präsentieren, ausgeschlossen, undenkbar!

Dabei hätte er sich doch gerade in Gegenden, wo man ihn früher missachtet hatte, einen umjubelten Auftritt gewünscht. Er schloss die Augen und stand mit *Athanatos* auf der Bühne. Mona stand in der vordersten Reihe, wippte im Takt, war stolz auf ihn. Auf der Tanzfläche gab man sich ganz seinen Klängen hin, und am ganzen Waldfest sprach und staunte man über das verkannte Genie Albert Leblanc …

Wie herrlich es gewesen wäre, diese Anerkennung ausgiebig geniessen zu können! Nichts hätte ihn glücklicher gemacht, als endlich richtig geachtet zu werden – zu seinem tiefsten Leidwesen musste er aber gerade dieser Achtung tunlichst aus dem Weg gehen.

Albert verbarg sein Gesicht im Kissen und weinte. Er musste seine Freunde heute enttäuschen. Er konnte sich doch nicht einem sensationslustigen Journalisten ausliefern. Und wohl oder übel musste er seine Freunde nicht nur heute enttäuschen.

Er hörte nicht auf zu weinen.

Bittere Stunden später verliess er samt Gitarre das Restaurant durch den Hinterausgang. Für heute blieb ihm keine andere Wahl, als zu verschwinden, sich unauffindbar zu machen. Er entschied, zunächst den grünen Hügel emporzusteigen, der sich neben dem Städtchen Ascona erhob.

Über eine schroffe Treppe gelangte er stufenweise höher. Er ging an einer Kapelle vorbei, unter deren Dachgiebel ein Totenschädel in Stein gemeisselt war. Er stieg weiter hoch und machte auf einer Plattform kurz Halt. Die wunderbare Aussicht über den See konnte er aber nicht geniessen. Heute nicht.

Als er die Treppe hinter sich gelassen hatte, führte ihn

eine Strasse zu einer grossen Wiese. Er setzte sich neben eine Feuerstelle auf einen grossen, flachen Stein.

Auf seiner Gitarre zupfte Albert kurz die Flötenmelodie von Lucia. Bildete er sich nur ein, in ihrer Melodie eine unsägliche Verzweiflung ausmachen zu können? Zumindest enthielten die Töne Fragen, drückten Nachdenklichkeit aus. Und sie waren schön, sehr schön.

Lucia im Himmel mit Diamanten.

Er zog weiter und drang in einen Wald ein, es wurde kühler und dunkler. Nur vereinzelte Sonnenstrahlen fielen zwischen den dicken Stämmen, Ästen und Zweigen hindurch ein, durchdrangen, unterstützten die Melancholie des Waldes. Gedankenverloren ging Albert weiter, ohne zu wissen, wohin ihn seine Beine tragen würden.

Bereits aus einiger Entfernung erfasste er das einsam in einer Lichtung ruhende Haus. Er näherte sich dem irgendwie nackt wirkenden Gebäude, das trotz der bröckelnden Mauern aus altem, totem Stein nichts von seiner Anmut eingebüsst hatte. Ob es bewohnt war? Albert rang seinen Blick über die hohe, von Rissen durchzogene Frontseite und fühlte sich seltsam unbehaglich.

Er schritt die breite, flach abfallende Steintreppe entlang der Seitenwand hinab. Da sah er, dass der hintere Teil des wuchtigen Gebäudes aus einer Kirche bestand. Er ging an einem mit Gitter verschlossenen Torbogen vorbei, hinter dem sich offenbar eine Kapelle verbarg. Auf einem Tisch, wohl ein Altar, standen Kerzen. Brennende Kerzen, obwohl die ausgestorbene Gegend den Eindruck erweckte, schon seit längerer Zeit von keiner Seele mehr durchstreift worden zu sein. Albert fragte sich, ob sich hinter der Kirche noch ein Friedhof erstreckte. Ihm schauderte.

Er schickte sich an, den Hügel wieder zu verlassen, ihn ohne Umwege zu überqueren, um sich noch weiter von Ascona zu entfernen.

Am Fusse des Monte Verità erreichte er eine Siedlung, in

der er den Abend zu verbringen gedachte. Hier würde man ihn um halb sieben kaum suchen kommen. Gebrochenen Mutes hielt er Ausschau nach einer Gaststätte, in der er seinen Kummer etwas ertränken konnte. Er wurde rasch fündig.

Trotz Sonnenschein mied Albert die einladende Terrasse, setzte sich lieber in eine Ecke der traditionell eingerichteten Gaststube. Gäste waren kaum anwesend, worüber er sich aber nicht wunderte. Er hatte gelernt, dass man sich im Süden zu anderen Zeiten an den Essenstisch begab.

Nach drei Stangen, die er in Windeseile hinuntergekippt hatte, winkte er den Kellner zu sich.

«Bringen Sie mir nun drei Grappa, wenn Sie so gut sein wollen», gab Albert ausdruckslos von sich.

Der junge Kellner mit den etwas gross geratenen Schneidezähnen stiess ein kurzes, hohes Lachen aus. Als er bemerkte, dass sich der leere Blick des Gastes nicht veränderte, fragte er unsicher: «Sie scherzen, oder?»

Albert überflog die Getränkekarte und sagte schliesslich, bereits etwas angeheitert: «Ja, das tu ich. Geben Sie mir lieber nur einen Grappa. Dazu einen Vieille Prune und einen Ouzo.»

Irgendwie fühlte sich Albert wohl in der Rolle des Frustsäufers. Warum denn auch nicht? Was hätte er denn nun anderes tun sollen, als zu trinken? Ein Mann weint bei Sorgen nicht, sagte er zu sich, er trinkt. Sein Äusseres passte jedenfalls hervorragend zu einem gebrochenen, niedergeschlagenen Trinker. Er hatte seine Federn heute nicht gekämmt und sich seit seiner Ankunft im Tessin nicht mehr rasiert.

Sollte er sich etwa doch noch umbringen? Er stiess stockend die Luft aus.

Auf seinem Tisch lag eine Zeitschrift. «Der Sonntag» stand da in schwarzer Frakturschrift auf gelbem Grund. Albert blätterte darin.

Erwecken Sie die Galle ihrer Leber, forderte ein Werbeinserat auf, Sie fühlen sich dann viel frischer. In Apotheken und Drogerien Fr. 2.35 und die vorteilhafte Familienpackung

Fr. 5.45. Die Familienpackung wäre wohl das richtige für ihn gewesen, dachte Albert verbittert. Madame, für seinen Geburtstag …? Schenken Sie ihm einen Feldstecher! Auch diese Anzeige schmerzte Albert. Sie erinnerte ihn an seine einsamen Geburtstage, an Mona – Madame Mona. Unangenehmer Fussgeruch. Der antiseptische Fusspuder saugt übermässige Schweissabsonderung auf, lindert Reizungen und tilgt üblen Geruch. Kaputt und doch nicht kaputt sind Herrenhemden, wenn Kragen und Manschetten zerfranst sind. Vertrauen Sie Ihre defekten Hemden unserem Reparatur Service an! Ob die auch defekte Herzen reparieren konnten, fragte sich Albert zynisch. Ein Mädchen, dem ein paar Zähne im Mund fehlten, blickte ihn an. Die Zähne, die ihr jetzt wachsen, sollen ein Leben lang halten. Ein Leben lang. Ein Leblanc. Albert schmunzelte leise. Wie definiert man schon ein Leben? Restlos enthaart, jetzt bequem, spur- und schmerzlos mit klinisch anerkannter Dauerwirkung. Beseitigt garantiert wurzeltief in nur drei Minuten Damenbart, hässliche Bein- und Körperhaare restlos. Albert schüttelte den Kopf. Zum Glück gibt's Bier, stand auf der letzen Seite.

Albert wusste nicht, wie lange die drei gefüllten Schnapsgläser schon vor ihm standen. Er schnappte sich den Vieille Prune und stürzte ihn in einem Zug in den Schlund. Es kribbelte in seinem Bauch.

Die Eingangstür quietschte. *Es wird schwer, es wird schwer, es wird ein schwerer Regen fallen.*

Nun ergriff Albert das Gläschen, aus dem der fruchtige Duft des Grappas strömte. Dieser Tropfen war ihm zu schade, um ihn in nur einem Schluck zu vertilgen. Lieber teilte er den Grappa in kleine, ganz viele Schlücke ein. Bei Halbzeit gab er das langsame, genussvolle Trinken wieder auf, denn nichts sprach ja dagegen, noch mehr Grappa zu bestellen.

Albert hatte eben das Glas geleert, als er eine Stimme vernahm, die zu laut war, um jemand anderen in der Stube anzusprechen. Die Stimme galt zweifellos ihm.

«Ich glaub's nicht!», hörte Albert die Stimme sagen. «Komm' ich in den Süden, geh' in ein Wirtshaus, und wen seh' ich da? Den guten alten Albert Leblanc!»

Alberts Angetrunkenheit war auf der Stelle weg.

54. Schwerer Regen

Em
Em
Em / G / A
Em / G / D

Ohne zu bezahlen hatte sich Albert aus dem Gasthaus gestürzt. Er war kreidebleich, torkelte, zitterte. Das Entsetzen, das ihn beim Vernehmen der ekelhaften Worte heimgesucht hatte, war nicht zu beschreiben.

Wie von Sinnen rannte er davon. Der Regenschauer, der inzwischen eingesetzt hatte, kümmerte ihn nicht. Er bemerkte ihn gar nicht. Er wollte nichts, als diesen grässlichen Ort verlassen.

Etwas ausserhalb des Dorfes begann er, bei sich nähernden Fahrzeugen den Daumen hochzuhalten. Die Wagen preschten allerdings allesamt herzlos an ihm vorbei, schleuderten ihm noch das Regenwasser entgegen, das sich auf der Strasse in Pfützen angesammelt hatte. Wenn gerade kein Fahrzeug in Sicht war, rannte Albert weiter, rannte so schnell er konnte, als wollte er die Zeit einholen, sie überholen, um die Begegnung rückgängig zu machen.

Ein weiterer Versuch, mitgenommen zu werden, begann vielversprechend. Der bullige Lastwagen verlangsamte seine Fahrt. Er fuhr schleppend an Albert vorbei, kam aber wenige Meter hinter ihm zum Stillstand.

Albert eilte hin und öffnete die Tür zum Beifahrersitz. Eine scharfe Schweisswolke quoll aus der Fahrerkabine.

«Wohin soll's gehen, junger Mann?» Der Lastwagenfahrer trug ein dünnes Unterleibchen, hatte einen breiten Kopf und glänzend weisse Zähne. Albert meinte, dem Gesicht etwas Freundliches, Wohlwollendes entnehmen zu können.

«Ich möchte gerne ans Meer», antwortete Albert bittend.

Der Lastwagenfahrer konnte sich kaum mehr erholen vor

Lachen. Er lachte noch, als die beiden bereits einige Kilometer ihres weiten Weges in den Süden zurückgelegt hatten.

Wir werden uns wieder sehen. Ich weiss nicht wo, ich weiss nicht wann. Aber ich weiss, dass wir uns eines Tages wieder sehen werden. Eines Tages, wenn der blaue Himmel die dunklen Wolken verdrängt. Eines sonnigen Tages.

55. Das Rauschen des Meeres

Em / Bm / C / D
Em / Bm / C / D / Dsus2

Die Lastwagenfahrt war für Albert der Beginn einer längeren Reise. Gut zweihundert Kilometer später konnte er zum ersten Mal in seinem Leben das Rauschen des Meeres hören. Er war in Genua angekommen.

Dort hielt es ihn aber nicht lange, als er sich die Karte von Europa in seinem Atlas genauer ansah. Er musste weiter, musste noch grössere Weiten zwischen sich und seine Vergangenheit schaffen.

Mehrere Tage verbrachte Albert auf hoher See. In Genua hatte er einen Dampfer genommen, um bald darauf erstmals seinen Fuss auf einen anderen Kontinent aufzusetzen. In Tunis kaufte er sich ein paar Briefmarken und schrieb seinen ehemaligen Bandkollegen einen Brief. Schrieb ihnen, dass sonderbare Umstände ihn dazu gezwungen hatten, das Tessin zu verlassen. Entschuldigte sich für seinen plötzlichen Ausstieg. Teilte Rocco mit, dass er seine Begeisterung für die Seefahrt nun verstehen konnte. Dankte ihnen für die schöne Zeit. Wünschte ihnen alles Gute.

Ausserdem hatte er mit dem leichtsinnigen Gedanken gespielt, mit Mona brieflich zu verkehren. Glücklicherweise obsiegte die Vernunft.

Albert wusste, wohin ihn seine Reise führen sollte. Er schiffte sich wieder ein, um in östlicher Richtung über das Mittelmeer zu gleiten. Auf dem Dampfer reiste er mit Leuten verschiedenster Herkunft, die ihn allesamt nicht beunruhigten. Er fühlte sich unerkannt. Er liebte die geschlossene Gesellschaft auf dem Wasser, wo niemand unerwarteterweise an Bord auftauchen konnte. Meist sass er an der Reling, liess den Wind durch seine Haare fliegen und blickte über die unermessliche Weite des Meeres. Am meisten aber genoss er die unendlich scheinende Entfernung zu Leuten, die den Namen Albert Leblanc je gehört hatten.

Dennoch mied er den Kontakt zu seinen Mitreisenden, spielte kaum Gitarre, und wenn, dann nur in seiner engen Kabine. Strengstens hütete er sich allerdings davor, sein Lied anzustimmen.

Gelegentlich fragte er sich, was wohl Bob, Rocco, Nico und Toni nun mit seinem Lied anstellen würden. Im Grunde waren sie ja nicht berechtigt, es ohne ihn weiterhin zu spielen. Er war der alleinige Urheber, der Schöpfer des Liedes. Andererseits interessierte es ihn natürlich, ob eine mittelmässig begabte Gruppe mit dem Lied Erfolg haben konnte. Gegönnt hätte er den vieren den Erfolg alleweil. Da er sich aber irgendwie vor der Verbreitung seines Werks fürchtete, zögerte er, es ihnen zu schenken.

Über die Begegnung mit seinem früheren Armeegenossen mochte er nicht mehr nachdenken. Nüchtern betrachtet durfte er wohl annehmen, dass der Mann aus Muotathal nie etwas über seinen Tod erfahren hatte. Und doch hatte ihm die Begegnung einen Schrecken ohnegleichen eingejagt, dem er rückblickend aber durchaus auch Gutes abgewinnen konnte. Ihm war klar geworden, dass sein Weiterleben als Toter in der Schweiz früher oder später aufgeflogen wäre.

Manchmal, und immer häufiger, dachte er an Mona. Ob sie immer noch servierte, mit Franz lebte, abends duschte? Bereits in das Buch hineingeschaut hatte, Rosen auf sein Grab legte? Ob Mona immer noch die gleiche bezaubernde Frau war?

Es waren entsetzliche Fragen.

Auf dem Seeweg gelangte er schliesslich über Piräus an den Hafen der kretischen Hauptstadt Iraklio. Endlich strandete er also auf derjenigen Insel, auf der er für eine Weile heimisch werden wollte. Die Karte in seinem Atlas zeigte eine lang gestreckte Insel, die Albert, fernab vom europäischen, asiatischen und afrikanischen Festland wie ein eigenes, abgeriegeltes Reich vorkam.

Albert hatte jedoch nicht vor, im nördlichen Iraklio zu bleiben. Es zog ihn umgehend an die Südküste. Wiederum per Anhalter – ein rüstiger Mann mit wucherndem Bart gab sich diesmal die Güte – drang er ins Innere der Insel vor. Mit einem Kaninchentransporter fuhren sie über die hüglige Landschaft, über karge und trockene Landstriche, vorbei an Ziegen- und Schafherden, Olivenhainen und Weinreben. Albert wurde bis nach Festos gebracht. Da endete nämlich die holprige Strasse.

Festos war eine Siedlung auf einer Anhöhe, die aus der weitläufigen Ebene strebte. Zumindest nahm Albert an, dass es sich um eine frühere Siedlung handelte, davon zeugten die noch erhaltenen Ruinen. Wann man hier wohl gelebt hatte? Vor hunderten oder gar tausenden Jahren? Die unverwüstlichen Mauern und Säulen, die trotz des Untergangs ihrer Kultur bis heute Bestand hatten, beeindruckten Albert.

Er schaute über das weite Land. Täuschte er sich, oder konnte er in der Ferne bereits eine Schlaufe des blauen Meeres erspähen? Beglückt, aber angespannt trat er zu Fuss die vorerst letzte Etappe seiner Reise an. Er hoffte, noch vor Sonnenuntergang in der Bucht von Matala einzutreffen.

56. Alberts Vermächtnis

Em9

A / Em / Bm / A
A / Em / Bm / A / G
Em / Bm / Em / Em
G / A / E / Dsus2

Im Schatten der Arkade sass sie und schlürfte an ihrem Kaffee. Das Treiben auf dem grossen Platz vor ihr bot ihr zwar reichlich Unterhaltung, konnte die immer wiederkehrenden Gedanken aber nicht verdrängen.

Ob Franz ihr gefolgt war? Die Ruchlosigkeit, die sie ihm mittlerweile zutraute, regte ihre Vorstellungskraft auf beängstigende Weise an. Doch eigentlich hielt sie ihn für zu wenig schlau, sie hier aufspüren zu können.

Es hatte sich vieles verändert. Mona hatte begonnen, ihr Leben wieder in die Hand zu nehmen, versuchte nun, ihr verloren gegangenes Glück zurückzuerlangen. *Eines Tages, wenn der blaue Himmel die dunklen Wolken verdrängt. Eines sonnigen Tages.*

Als der Köter in einer ohnehin schon schwierigen Zeit mit einem unbekannten Herrenschuh im Wohnzimmer aufgekreuzt war, hatte sie abermals Schläge von ihrem Gatten erhalten. Es sollten die letzten gewesen sein. Am nächsten Morgen war sie zur üblichen Zeit aus dem Haus gegangen, allerdings nicht, um wieder im Gasthof zu bedienen. Stattdessen hatte sie das Dorf ohne Ankündigung verlassen. So, wie Albert es auch getan hatte.

Gelegentlich kämpfte sie gegen das schlechte Gewissen, gerade jetzt das Leben geniessen zu wollen, zumal sie dies auch noch auf Alberts Kosten tat. Sie war aus allen Wolken gefallen, als sie einige Tage nach seiner Beerdigung im Buch blätterte, das er ihr geschenkt hatte, und zwischen den Seiten die Geldscheine entdeckte. Stolze 3180 Franken waren es gewesen, die er ihr vererbt hatte.

Alberts Vermächtnis hatte ihr aufgezeigt, dass seine Tat keine Kurzschlussreaktion, sondern bereits länger geplant gewesen war. Mona wusste nicht, ob diese Erkenntnis sie trösten oder noch mehr schmerzen sollte.

Weshalb ihr der Tod von Albert derart zugesetzt hatte, war Mona noch nicht ganz klar. Vielleicht, weil ihr wieder einmal die eigene Sterblichkeit bewusst geworden war? Oder gar, weil sie sich in gewisser Weise mitverantwortlich fühlte? Oft grübelte sie darüber nach, ob sie seinen Tod irgendwie hätte verhindern können. Der Abschiedsbrief und das Erbe bezeugten doch, dass sie auf ihn eine besondere Wirkung ausgeübt haben musste. Womöglich hatte er mit dem Buch verzweifelt versucht, ihr einen leisen Hinweis auf seine bevorstehende Tat zu geben. Und was hatte die Verletzung in seinem Gesicht, mit der er einen Tag vor dem Tod zur Arbeit erschienen war, wirklich mit seinem Unglücklichsein zu tun gehabt?

In den Tagen nach Alberts Tod war Mona von einer Ohnmacht ergriffen worden, aus der sie sich erst jetzt langsam wieder befreien konnte. Sie musste lernen, die brennenden Fragen unbeantwortet zu lassen.

Nun sass sie hier im Süden, gab das Geld eines Toten aus, ohne sich mit der herannahenden Zeit abzumühen. Sie steckte sich eine Zigarette in den Mund und lehnte sich zurück. Es war sonderbar und reizend zugleich, ganz allein in fremde Gegenden einzutauchen.

Plötzlich stutzte sie.

Ihr Puls beschleunigte sich. Woher nur kam die liebliche Melodie? Mona hörte genau hin. Sie war sich nicht sicher, ob das Lied im Radio gespielt wurde oder ob gerade irgendwo um die Ecke ein Auftritt stattfand. Sie fühlte sich gleich ähnlich beglückt wie damals, als sie das Lied zum ersten Mal gehört hatte. Diesmal aber mischte sich der Wonne ein beklemmendes Gefühl bei.

Es war das Lied.

Das Lied, das Albert ihr an seinem letzten Lebenstag vorgespielt hatte. Sie versuchte, sich das Unglaubhafte zu erklären. «Ich habe die Melodie gestern Abend komponiert.» Mona hörte die Worte Alberts, als ob er sie eben erst gesprochen hätte. Damit durfte, musste Mona doch davon ausgehen, dass das Lied nirgends hatte verewigt werden können. Oder hatte Albert auch die Bewahrung seines Liedes exakt geplant? Die Umstände seines Todes wurden ihr immer unheimlicher.

Mit dem Gedanken, dass sie die alleinige Hüterin seines Liedes hätte sein müssen, hatte sie sich bisher nicht näher auseinandergesetzt. Nun stellte sich womöglich heraus, dass Albert das Lied an seinem letzten Tag noch mindestens einer anderen Person vorgespielt hatte. Doch wem nur? War Albert vielleicht Mitglied einer Musikgruppe gewesen? Dann hätte er sich also regelmässig mit Freunden getroffen, um gemeinsam zu musizieren? Das konnte sich Mona nicht vorstellen. Er hätte ihr bestimmt davon erzählt. Zudem hatte sie an seiner Beerdigung keine Trauernden entdeckt, die ihr als Alberts mögliche Musikkollegen in Frage zu kommen schienen.

Vielleicht deutete ja gerade dieses Fernbleiben auf einen Streit innerhalb der Gruppe hin? Auf einen handfesten Streit, aus dem Alberts Gesichtswunde resultierte?

Schliesslich beschäftigte sich Mona mit der Wahrscheinlichkeit, dass zwei Menschen unabhängig voneinander die gleiche Melodie komponieren konnten. Theoretisch war dies durchaus möglich, überlegte sie, denn Lieder bestehen ja lediglich aus Tönen, die von jedem Menschen jederzeit hervorzubringen sind. Ähnlich, wie sich wohl kaum ein alleiniger Erfinder des Rades bestimmen lässt, konnte es doch auch mehrere Komponisten geben, die zufälligerweise das gleiche musikalische Werk schufen. Angesichts der grossen Anzahl Lieder, die auf der ganzen Welt täglich komponiert wurden, waren gelegentliche Übereinstimmungen doch nicht zu verhindern.

Doch Mona befriedigte diese Erklärung nicht. Warum sollte ausgerechnet Alberts Lied, das ihr damals wie heute derart eigenartig, unvergleichlich schien, einen exakten Doppelgänger besitzen?

Monas Zigarette lag am Boden und gab einen letzten dünnen Rauchfaden von sich.

Später spazierte Mona durch ein Gässchen etwas abseits des Ortes. Sie wollte allein sein, allein mit sich und ihren Gedanken. Eine unangenehme, aber denkbar einfache Lösung hatte sich inzwischen noch angeboten: Albert war ebenso ein Schwindler gewesen, wie Franz einer war.

Nein, das war eine zu böse Unterstellung. Aber möglicherweise hatte Albert sie einfach beeindrucken wollen und sich dann als Urheber eines nicht sonderlich bekannten Liedes ausgegeben, das er auf einer Platte besass. Es war eine Vorstellung, die Mona enttäuschte. Ihre Gutgläubigkeit spielte ihr aber immer wieder Streiche.

Je länger sie nun über Albert nachdachte, umso stärker beschäftigte sie die Frage, ob sie gar nicht in erster Linie um den Verlust des Menschen Albert getrauert hatte. Sie hatte ihn kaum gekannt, dies war ihr durch das Hören des Liedes wieder deutlich bewusst geworden. Sie hatte gewissermassen um einen Fremden getrauert. Ob ihre Trauer lediglich eine innere Auflehnung gegen die Ungerechtigkeit auf Erden war? Oder tat sie Albert nun doch allzu unrecht? Denn andererseits konnte sie nicht verleugnen, dass sie ihn gemocht hatte – sie hatte mit ihm den schönsten Nachmittag seit längerer Zeit verbracht. Er hatte ihr Stunden vor seinem Tod angedeutet, dass er ein ganz besonderer Mensch war.

57. Unter leuchtendem Firmament

G / Em / C / G
G / Am / C / G
G / Em / C / G
G / Am / D
D / D7 / G / D
G / C / G / D

Es war bereits dunkel.

Was Albert am Strand wohl erwarten würde? Er ging mittlerweile durch ein Tal, an dessen Ende sich sein Ziel befinden musste. Die Chancen, sich nun noch zu verlaufen, waren gering. Behilflich war ihm dabei auch das leuchtende Firmament, das sich spektakulär über ihm wölbte. Es schien ihm, dass er noch nie so viele Sterne auf einmal gesehen hatte.

Von Weitem erblickte er einige Lichter. Ob es sich bei diesem recht ausgestorben wirkenden Ort tatsächlich um Matala handelte? Albert begann zu zweifeln.

Plötzlich vernahm er ein Durcheinander von verschiedenen Lauten. Es waren Stimmen und – er ging einige Schritte weiter – Stimmen, Gesang und Gitarren, die sich mit dem Rauschen des Meeres vermischten. *Denn noch dreht sich das Rad, und wer weiss, welche Zahl es am Ende zeigen wird. Der Verlierer von heute wird der Gewinner von morgen sein, denn es kommen andere Zeiten.*

Unsicher betrat er den breiten Sandstrand und erspähte die Umrisse von Gestalten. Im feinen Sand, um mehrere flackernde Lagerfeuer, da sassen sie. Einige der offenbar eher jungen Leute zupften an ihren Gitarren, andere klopften dazu rhythmisch auf ihre Trommeln oder bliesen in ihre Mundharmonikas. Man sang, trank, lachte, Paare lagen sich in den Armen, liebkosten sich, sorglos, beglückt. Es waren beeindruckende Szenen, die sich vor den Augen des staunenden Albert abspielten.

«Da ist jemand!», hörte er eine Stimme rufen. «Ein Neuer!»

Er erschrak.

Sofort erhob sich eine der Gestalten und kam geradewegs auf ihn zu. Die Gestalt schien gross und stark zu sein. Ein Wilder! Nun wurde auch dessen imposante Haarpracht erkennbar. Albert konnte nicht bestimmen, welche Haare aus der Kopfhaut sprossen, welche bereits dem Bart angehörten.

Augenblicke später hatte Albert im Kreis der hier Versammelten Platz genommen. Links von ihm sass Gunnar, der riesige Norweger, der ihn in nordisch gefärbtem Deutsch freundlich empfangen hatte. Das Mädchen zu seiner Rechten – sie hatte sich als Alice aus Australien vorgestellt – reichte ihm zur Begrüssung ein Glas Wein.

Etwas nervös liess er seinen Blick noch einmal durch die Runde schweifen, die aus bunt oder spärlich bekleideten Zeitgenossen bestand. Seine Anspannung löste sich.

Mittlerweile hatte man das Musizieren, das durch seine Ankunft kurz unterbrochen worden war, wieder aufgenommen.

Während Albert die ungetrübte Stimmung genoss, streckten ihm zwei weitere Nachtschwärmer, José aus Portugal und Pete aus Schottland, die Hand entgegen. Sie boten ihm umgehend eine kleine Pfeife an, aus der ein süsslicher Duft stieg. Albert zog nur leicht daran, wurde aber gleich etwas schwindlig. Schwindlig und glücklich.

Die kleinen violetten Fische rennen lachend durch deine Finger, deinen Leib, deinen Geist.

Hatte Albert je ein derartiges Gemeinschaftsgefühl erlebt? Hatte er sich je so dazugehörig gefühlt?

In seiner Seligkeit entging ihm beinahe, dass sich Gunnar vor ihm erhoben hatte. «Du möchtest wohl hier übernachten?», fragte er mit einer sanften Stimme, die seiner Postur spottete.

«Ja – so hab ich mir das eigentlich vorgestellt», antwortete Albert, obwohl er seit seiner Ankunft nicht mehr an die kommende Nacht gedacht hatte.

«Komm, ich zeige dir deine Höhle!» Albert verstand nicht. Was hatte Gunnar gesagt? Er folgte ihm.

Sie gingen noch einige Meter über den Sand, bis sich vor ihnen ein steil ansteigender Fels aufrichtete. Über eine kleine Kuppe kletterte Gunnar in die Höhe – der nicht mehr gänzlich standfeste Albert hatte Mühe, ihm zu folgen. Wo zum Teufel führte man ihn nur hin?

«Da.» Gunnar blieb stehen und zeigte auf ein schmales Loch, das ins Innere des Felsens führte. «Hier kannst du einziehen.» Damit entfernte sich Gunnar.

Albert fragte sich, ob man ihn etwa wieder zum Narren machen wollte.

Dann aber hörte er Geräusche, die ebenfalls aus dem Fels zu kommen schienen. Etwas missmutig schlüpfte er durch den Felseingang. Im Inneren musste er sich ducken, um sich nicht den Kopf an der Steindecke anzuschlagen. Er legte sich hin und bemerkte, dass die Höhle gerade über die Masse verfügte, die es seinem Körper erlaubten, sich zu strecken. Das musste reichen. Er wunderte sich über die recht sonderbaren Gepflogenheiten dieses Stammes.

Er konnte es kaum abwarten, den Ort samt Leuten und deren Lebensformen auszukundschaften. Erschöpft, aber voller Zuversicht vertröstete er sich auf morgen.

58. Matala

Am
D
Am
D

Als Albert im Frühlicht aus seiner Höhle schlüpfte, den abschüssigen Fels hinunterkraxelte und den Sandstrand erreichte, da verstand er.

Verstand, weshalb Mona von dem Ort gesprochen hatte, weshalb Menschen aus aller Welt ihn aufsuchten und weshalb eine unbestimmte Gewalt ihn nicht hatte sterben lassen. Allein die Sicht über das türkisfarbene Meer, aus dem in der Ferne beinahe unglaubhaft ein markant beschaffener Fels ragte, war es wert gewesen, den Tod zu verschieben.

Der breite Sandstrand befand sich in einer Bucht, eingeschlossen zwischen zwei Felsnasen, die sich beide ins Meer streckten und zum Wasser hin abfielen. Der Fels, der sich rechts von ihm aufbäumte, war mit kleineren und grösseren Löchern ausgestattet. Es mussten dies alles Eingänge zu Höhlen sein. Und eine der Höhlen, inmitten dieser atemberaubenden Kulisse, war ihm gestern spät zugeteilt worden. Albert bekam Gänsehaut.

Das eigentliche Dorf, etwas abseits der Höhlen, bestand aus wenigen kleinen weissen Hütten und Tavernen. Das also war Matala, das zu seinem vorübergehenden Domizil werden sollte.

Albert schlenderte den Strand entlang. Einige hatten draussen genächtigt und schliefen noch, eingemummt in zerschlissene Schlafsäcke. An den Bäumen hingen ebensolche Kleider. Er schaute den geschmeidig schwappenden Wellen zu. Gelegentlich grüssten ihn wildfremde Leute freundlich. Das war er sich so nicht gewohnt. Noch gab sein nach vorne geneigter Hut aber nur einen kleinen Teil seines Gesichts preis, dessen

Erscheinung sich in den letzten Wochen durch zunehmenden Bartwuchs weiter verändert hatte. Er setzte sich in den Sand, der bereits wieder erwärmt wurde.

Natürlich wäre es Zufall gewesen, wenn er Mona hier gleich begegnet wäre. Vielleicht war sie schon da gewesen, vielleicht kam sie noch – vielleicht kam sie gar nie. Doch ebenso gross wie die Hoffnung, dass Mona eines Tages hier eintreffen würde, war die Ungewissheit, ob er ihr dann tatsächlich vor die Augen treten wollte. Auf jeden Fall hatte er vor, zu warten.

«Und, gut geschlafen?» Gunnar hatte sich erstaunlich lautlos in Alberts Nähe geschlichen.

«Ja – wie ein Stein.»

«Hast du Hunger?»

«Es geht so.»

«Ich zeige dir, wo es etwas zu essen gibt.»

Sie begaben sich zu dem Platz, der sich noch am ehesten Dorfkern nennen liess, und betraten den kleinen Laden. Hier gab es Brot, Feta, Wein, Raki.

«Das ist Natan Natos, er ist gestern hier angekommen», sagte Gunnar zu der älteren Frau hinter der Theke. Sie schenkte Albert einen warmen Blick. Als er die Büchse auf dem Tresen musterte, erklärte Gunnar: «Hast du wenig Geld, erhältst du auch für wenig etwas. Hast du aber viel Geld, musst du mehr bezahlen.»

Albert staunte.

«Hast du Geld?», fragte ihn Gunnar.

Albert kramte in seinen Hosentaschen und stiess auf einige Münzen in verschiedenen Währungen.

Die beiden verliessen den Laden und teilten sich draussen ein knuspriges Brötchen. An einem sprudelnden Wasserhahn gleich daneben säuberte sich ein ziemlich wild aussehendes Paar Zähne, Hände und Gesicht.

Gegen Mittag ass man gemeinsam am Strand. Ein Feuer loderte wieder, an dem der morgendliche Fang eines einheimischen Fischers gegrillt wurde. Albert, als früherer Koch eigentlich mit allerlei Speisen vertraut, kostete zum ersten Mal Tintenfisch und Seeigel. Es schmeckte ihm.

Nach dem Essen tummelten sich viele der hier Lebenden im Meer, einige, um sich zu waschen, andere, um sich zu vergnügen. Albert wagte sich bis zur Hüfte ins Wasser. Es war angenehm warm.

Als er später im Sand sitzend wieder über die Wellen blickte, gesellte sich eine junge zierliche Frau zu ihm, die sich als Sophie aus Frankreich ausgab.

«Warst du schon einmal da drüben?», fragte Albert und deutete auf die Insel vor der Küste.

Sophie verneinte. «Es sind übrigens zwei Inseln. Von hier aus wird man getäuscht.»

Albert hörte ihr interessiert zu.

«Sie heissen Paximadia-Inseln», erklärte sie.

«Paximadia», wiederholte Albert. Allein der Name klang in seinen Ohren schon geheimnisvoll. «Wie weit ist es bis dahin?», wollte er wissen.

«Keine Ahnung. Ich kenne niemanden, der rübergeschwommen und wieder zurückgekehrt ist.»

«Kennst du jemanden, der rübergeschwommen ist?», fragte er etwas besorgt.

«Nein.»

Sie lachten beide.

«Du scheinst schon eine ganze Weile hier zu sein», sagte Albert und schaute sie fragend an.

«Ich bin seit zwei oder drei Monaten hier, ich weiss es nicht so genau. Für mich gibt es hier weder Wochentag noch Uhrzeit.»

«Und was treibst du die ganze Zeit?»

«Ich lebe.» Sophie lächelte vielsagend.

Abends hatte man sich im Café Mermaid eingefunden.

Über Kerzen und Kerosinlampen unterhielt man sich in verschiedenen Sprachen, wobei die im Vokabular fehlenden Ausdrücke mit Händen, Gesten oder Geräuschen wiedergegeben wurden. Man trank Raki und Retsina, die einen mehr, die anderen weniger, während im Hintergrund leise traditionelle Musik lief.

Auch Albert, der mittlerweile nur noch sein Ledergilet und seine über den Knien abgeschnittene Hose trug, hatte sich unter die Gäste gemischt. Von Brian, einem Nordamerikaner mit intellektueller Hornbrille, erfuhr er allerhand über die Höhlen von Matala.

«Bereits in prähistorischer Zeit wurden die Nischen in den weichen Kalkstein gehauen und dienten den Urbewohnern als Schlafplatz und Herdstelle», wusste Brian zu erzählen.

Albert nahm einen Schluck Retsina und betrachtete die bemalte Frontseite des Cafés. Eine Meerjungfrau mit langen Haaren und ausgeprägten Rundungen zierte die Wand. Etwas oberhalb schaute eine Sonne mit lachendem Mund und weit aufgerissenen Augen auf sie herab. Die Meerjungfrau jedoch wandte ihren Blick einer Pflanze zu, die Albert nicht kannte.

«Die Römer nutzten die Höhlen in der Folge als Grabstätten.»

«Als Grabstätten?» Albert schüttelte es beim Gedanken, dass in seiner Höhle der Tod gehaust haben könnte.

«Ja. Aber das ist eine Ewigkeit her. Der Verwesungsgestank dürfte mittlerweile ausgezogen sein.» Er lachte kurz auf. «Und dann kamen die Sechziger, und mit ihnen die Aussteiger, Kriegsverweigerer, Nonkonformisten, Sinnsuchenden, um hier die Erfüllung zu finden.»

Wieder nahm Albert einen Schluck Retsina. Inzwischen hatten sich einige der Gäste zum Tanz zusammengetan.

«Ach. Warst du eigentlich schon am Roten Strand?», fragte Brian plötzlich.

Albert schüttelte den Kopf.

«Den solltest du dir nicht entgehen lassen.» Das Gesicht von Alberts ansonsten sehr seriös wirkendem Gesprächspartner nahm leicht verschmitzte Züge an.

Weitere Gäste setzten sich an den Tisch zu Albert und Brian. Wie selbstverständlich tranken, sprachen und lachten sie gemeinsam. Man war glücklich, stiess an auf nichts.

Heute ist das Leben, ein Morgen wird es nicht geben.

59. Roter Strand

B7
E
B7

Bereits kurz nach Sonnenaufgang, als sich die meisten noch in ihren Höhlen wanden, brach Albert auf. Von Neuem beeindruckte ihn die Sicht auf Paximadia.

Die Anhöhe, die gegenüber dem Höhlenfelsen ins Meer hineinstach, musste er nun überqueren. Er hatte sich von Brian den Weg erklären lassen. Ein kaum erkennbarer Pfad kämpfte sich zwischen dürren Büschen und Geröll den Berg hoch. Albert ging barfuss. Langsam gewöhnten sich seine Füsse an den steten Kontakt mit der Natur. Von Weitem sah er eine grosse runde Verformung des Felsgesteins, die ihn an einen brüllenden Löwenkopf erinnerte.

Oben auf der Kuppe blieb er plötzlich stehen. Da war jemand.

Ein Mann sass da, allein inmitten der steinigen Landschaft. Er hielt seinen nackten Oberkörper übertrieben aufrecht, seine Füsse lagen jeweils auf dem gegenüberliegenden Oberschenkel. Um seine Hüfte hatte er ein gelbes Tuch gewickelt. Albert musste an diesem Sonderling vorbeigehen, um an den Roten Strand zu gelangen.

«Hallo», grüsste Albert, wie er bis jetzt alle Leute hier gegrüsst hatte.

Der bärtige Mann bewegte nur kaum merklich den Kopf.

«Kann ich dir irgendwie helfen?», fragte Albert.

«Niemand kann mir helfen», antwortete ihm der Mann.

«Und – was tust du hier oben genau?»

«Ich bin den Weg der Entselbstung gegangen.»

«?»

«Ich habe den Schmerz, den Durst, die Müdigkeit überwunden, habe den Sinn von allen Vorstellungen leergedacht.»

Da Albert sich dazu nicht äussern konnte, fuhr der Mann mit seinen Erklärungen fort. Er artikulierte sie eigenartig stumpf, melodielos.

«Ich habe mein Ich verlassen und verharre nun im Nicht-Ich.»

«Und was bist du dann, wenn du nicht du bist?» Albert war froh, zumindest in der Lage zu sein, etwas zu fragen.

«Im Augenblick bin ich ein Stein», sagte der Mann. Er schien nicht an seiner Aussage zu zweifeln.

Albert musste die Lippen zusammenpressen. «Weisst du, was ich bin?», fragte er dann.

Er erhielt keine Antwort.

«Ich bin ein Toter.» Sprachs und liess den Stein wieder in Ruhe.

Bereits aus einiger Höhe sah er den rötlich glühenden Sand, der ihn unten am Strand erwartete.

Es war traumhaft. Die Strukturen der Felsnase, deren bisher verborgene Seite er nun erstmals sah, der Schaum heranzischender Wellen, der feinkörnige rote Sand – Albert war es, als stünde er vor einem riesigen abstrakten Gemälde.

Mit einem Freudenschrei stürzte er sich ungelenk ins Wasser, spritzte dieses wie ein Wilder umher, ruderte überschwänglich mit Armen und Beinen und liess sich dann vom Seegang treiben.

Erschrocken blickte er an den Strand. Zum Glück hatte ihn niemand beobachtet.

Nach der Abkühlung legte er sich in den roten Sand. Es war gestern wieder spät geworden, nun verspürte er doch eine leichte körperliche Schwäche. Kurz darauf schlummerte er ein.

Er träumte von Mona. Träumte, wie sie sich ihm bei ihrer Ankunft um den Hals warf, wie sie weinte vor Glück, wie sie dann zusammen am Strand spazierten. An einem etwas abseitigen Plätzchen legten sie sich zu Boden. Sie schmiegte sich eng an ihn, und gemeinsam schliefen sie ein …

Die funkelnden Wellen fordern dich auf, ihre weissen Lippen zu küssen. Und du siehst ihren braunen Körper durch das Türkis tanzen. Und ihre Fussspuren führen dich dahin, wo der Himmel das Meer liebt. Und wenn deine Finger sie finden, ertränkt sie dich in ihrem Körper.

Ein Lachen störte die traute Zweisamkeit. Albert erhob seinen Kopf etwas und öffnete ein Auge. Vor ihm sonnten sich nun einige Leute im Sand. Andere genossen die Erfrischung im Meer.

Er entdeckte José, den Pfeifenraucher, der im Wasser mit der Australierin Alice turtelte. Sie schienen sportlich zu sein. Vor ihm lagen drei weibliche Geschöpfe, eine davon war Sophie. Sie lag auf dem Bauch und bräunte sich. Dem Meer entstieg eine hünenhafte Gestalt, die ihn an einen Bären erinnerte. Es musste sich dabei um Gunnar handeln.

Albert erblickte Körper – weibliche Körper, männliche Körper, braungebrannte und bleiche, beleibte und schlanke, behaarte und geschmeidige. Nur eines war ihnen allen gemein. Sie waren ausnahmslos nackt.

60. Zeit

Em / C / D
Em / C / D
Am
Am / F
Am / G / D / Am

Ja, er hatte geträumt. Allerdings nicht den ganzen Tag. Wie hätte er denn dergleichen träumen können? Dazu boten ihm seine Erfahrungen eine zu dürftige Grundlage. Sie reichten nicht, um Fantasien, um Träume derart lebendig, derart vielfältig zu gestalten.

Ob er einen Hitzeschlag erlitten hatte? Oder ob die Pfeife von José seinen Bewusstseinshorizont derart erweitert hatte? Wenn ihm seine Wahrnehmung derartige Streiche spielen sollte, war er ein kranker Mann. Er fühlte sich jedoch gesund, kerngesund. Nein, er konnte nicht irren.

Nun plagte ihn das schlechte Gewissen. Er wusste nicht, wie lange er das Treiben am Roten Strand studiert hatte. Dabei war er doch allein mit der wenngleich auch gefürchteten Hoffnung, irgendwann auf Mona zu treffen, nach Matala gekommen. Er schloss mit sich den Pakt, den sündigen Strand nicht mehr aufzusuchen.

Albert gewöhnte sich daran, viel Zeit zu haben. Grenzenlos Zeit. Ungeregelte Zeit. Zeit, um den Meereswellen zuzusehen. Zeit, um seinem Gitarrenspiel zuzuhören. Zeit, um ein Glas Wasser zu trinken, um mit Leuten zu sprechen, um mit Leuten zu schweigen.

In den folgenden Tagen verbrachte Albert viele Stunden am naheliegenden Kommos Strand, wo er immerhin nackte Meeresschildkröten beobachtete, schöne Steine sammelte oder seine Schwimmkünste verbesserte. Weiter unternahm er ausgedehnte Spaziergänge, die ihn bis in verschlafene Dörfer des Hinterlandes führten. Einmal ging er an einem Feld vorbei, wo sich Einheimische bei der Traubenlese abmühten. Spontan packte er mit an, wofür ihm als Dank am Hof ein ausgiebiges kretisches Abendessen serviert wurde. Albert war überrascht und zugleich stolz darauf, eine brauchbare Hilfskraft abgegeben zu haben. Ausserdem begann er, sich für die Vergangenheit zu interessieren, besuchte das römische Odeon von Gortys und noch einmal die minoische Siedlung von Festos. Immer mehr faszinierten ihn die toten Überreste früherer Zeiten, die er in Gedanken wieder aufleben liess. Überdies hatte er eine spannende Tätigkeit in Angriff genommen, die ihm gar noch einen kleinen Verdienst einbrachte. Er fuhr jeweils am Morgen mit Fischern auf See, um ihnen beim Fang zu helfen. Die Abende verbrachte er meist in geselligen Runden am Strand oder im Café Mermaid. Und wenn ihn Sophie und ihre Freundinnen nachmittags aufforderten, sie zum Roten Strand zu begleiten, lehnte er dankend ab.

Albert Leblanc war glücklich. Glücklich wie nie zuvor.

Eines Abends, als er auf dem Weg zu seiner Höhle war, um sich schlafen zu legen, rief ihm eine wohlbekannte Stimme hinterher. Es war Gunnar.

«Natan, warte», bat er ihn.

Albert blieb stehen.

«Natan.» Gunnar war sichtlich bemüht, die richtigen Worte zu finden. «Ich will es kurz machen, sonst wird es zu schwer.»

«Was ist denn, Gunnar?», fragte ihn Albert etwas besorgt.

«Ich möchte mich von dir verabschieden.» Gunnar klang traurig. «Es ist Zeit für mich, zu gehen.»

«Wohin denn?»

«In meine Heimat.» Seine leuchtenden Augen verrieten, dass er sich trotz des schmerzlichen Abschieds von Matala darauf freute. «Da gehöre ich hin», sagte er.

«In die Heimat», flüsterte Albert, als die beiden sich kurz umarmten.

61. Heimat

Am6 / D / A / Gm
A / C / H / D
G# / D

C / G / F / C / G

Der Abzug von Gunnar nach Norwegen brachte Albert wieder ins Grübeln. Er dachte oft nach, meist nun über seine eigene Vergangenheit.

Die letzten Wochen hatten ihn zweifellos geprägt. Er hatte vieles gelernt. Hatte gelernt, die Welt zu bereisen, sich unter die Leute zu mischen, hatte endlich gelernt, das Leben zu schätzen.

Allerdings hatte er auch gelernt, dass er immer Albert Leblanc geblieben war. Natan Natos war lediglich ein Abziehbild von Albert. Natan hatte keine Vergangenheit, und es war ja gerade die Vergangenheit, die Albert zu dem gemacht hatte, der er nun war. Zwar konnte er im Umgang mit Menschen seine Vergangenheit verheimlichen, doch konnte er sich in seinem Innern nicht von ihr trennen. Zu ihm gehörte auch die Zeit vor seinem Tod.

Albert sass allein im Sand des Kommos-Strands und malte sich die Ankunft von Gunnar in seiner Heimat aus. Gewiss würde man ihn als verlorenen Sohn des Dorfes empfangen, ihn freudig wieder als einen der ihren willkommen heissen. Wie würde man wohl reagieren, wenn er plötzlich wieder in seiner Heimat aufkreuzen würde?

Eines stand fest, er würde nie wieder als normaler Bürger in Rechthalten leben können. Seine Heimat allerdings war weder Matala noch das Tessin oder der Jura – seine Heimat war Rechthalten, Freiburg – da, wo er aufgewachsen war, gescholten wurde, gestorben war. Er gehörte in jenes Dorf, das er nicht mehr betreten durfte. Das war gleichbedeutend mit dem Unheil, keine Heimat zu besitzen.

Dabei verspürte er allmählich das Bedürfnis, gerade auch die Leute zu Hause wissen zu lassen, dass er sich gewandelt hatte. Allzu gerne hätte er, der vom kleinen Jungen Leblanc zu einem Mann von Welt aufgestiegen war, im Gasthof von seinen Erlebnissen im Süden berichtet. Hätte den Gästen mit Freude Bilder gezeigt, auf denen er mit Männern und Frauen aus aller Welt lachte. Er hätte mit Vergnügen den Wein mit ihnen geteilt, bei dessen Herstellung er mitgeholfen hatte.

Er dachte an Karl, an den Fofenhubel und an den Metzger, an das Löhlimoos, sogar an seinen Pflegevater und an den Wirt. Ob sich im Dorf bereits etwas verändert hatte? Bestimmt. Vielleicht konnte er irgendwann einmal die Freiburger Nachrichten abonnieren, um sich zu unterrichten, was geschah, wer heiratete, wer verstarb.

Und jedes fremde Gesicht, das ich sehe, erinnert mich an zu Hause. Nach Hause, wohin meine Gedanken flüchten, wo meine Musik spielt, wo meine Liebe leise auf mich wartet.

Er fuhr mit der Innenfläche seiner Hand durch den Sand, so dass darin eine langgezogene Furche entstand. Ungefähr so verlief die Strasse durch Rechthalten. Sogleich kratzte er mehr Sand zusammen, formte daraus erst verschiedene Haufen, die nach und nach würfelähnliche Gestalt annahmen – den Gasthof, das Hotel, das Schulhaus und die Kirche.

Nun war sein Ehrgeiz entfacht. Alles, woran er sich erinnern konnte, versuchte er im Sand umzusetzen. Neben ein Haus im Unterdorf pflanzte er einen Apfelbaum, auf der Anhöhe oberhalb des Dorfes errichtete er ein Kreuz, die Senke südöstlich des Dorfkerns füllte er mit Wasser. Beinahe wähnte er sich dabei zurück in der Heimat.

Vier Stunden später stand er stolz vor seinem Werk, und sah, dass es gelungen war. Er hatte im Sand sein ganzes Dorf aufgebaut. Sogar sein Grab hatte er versucht nachzubilden.

Nachdenklich betrachtete er das Werk eine Weile. Jetzt fehlten nur noch die Menschen.

62. Zenit

Am
F#m
Am
F#m

«Findet ihr es nicht auch eigenartig, dass man auf der ganzen Welt nur von einer Sonne lebt? Egal, an welchen Fleck der Erde man sich begibt, überall wird man von der gleichen Sonne verfolgt», erzählte Albert ernst.

Britta und Frida blickten sich verständnislos an. «Denkst du nicht, dass vielmehr deine Gedanken etwas eigenartig sind, Natan?», flachste Britta. «Kein Mensch überlegt sich solche Dinge.»

Albert fuhr unbeirrt fort. «Denkt doch einmal nach. Egal wo und wann in der ganzen Geschichte der Erde ein Mensch gelebt hat, er hat die gleiche Sonne gesehen wie wir. Die Blicke jedes einzelnen Menschen haben bereits auf der Sonne geruht. Und die Sonne, die wir gerade sehen, kann jetzt, zur gleichen Zeit auch von Gunnar in Norwegen oder von euren Familien in Schweden erblickt werden. Ist das nicht unglaublich?»

«Bei uns ist es wahrscheinlich bewölkt», sagte Frida.

Albert gab es auf, seine Begeisterung für die seit Zeiten erdflankierende Sonne mit den beiden schwedischen Studentinnen teilen zu wollen.

«Spiel uns doch lieber etwas auf deiner Gitarre vor!», forderte Britta ihn auf.

«Na gut», gab Albert von sich. Im Grunde mochte er es, wenn man ihm beim Spielen zuhörte. Vor allem Frauen bezirzte er liebend gerne mit seinem Gitarrenspiel.

Noch einmal blickte er kurz zur Sonne, die sich bald dem Zenit näherte. Dann sah er wieder zu Britta und Frida, die sich in ihrem Aussehen erstaunlich ähnelten. Vielleicht lag dies auch nur an den blonden Haaren, die sie beide offen trugen.

Plötzlich stand er hastig auf, stammelte ein paar unverständliche Worte und fegte dann derart rasant über den Strand, dass der Sand in Wolken durch die Luft wirbelte.

«Er ist wirklich etwas verrückt.» Frida schüttelte den Kopf.

«Ich mag ihn trotzdem», meinte Britta, die Albert hinterherschaute und ihn bereits durch sein Höhlenloch schlüpfen sah.

Der Moment war eingetroffen, der Alberts Aufenthalt in Matala schlagartig veränderte. Der Moment, der Albert erbeben liess, ihn gleichzeitig über alle Massen erfreute und zutiefst verängstigte.

Sie war angekommen.

63. Der Begleiter

D / D7 / Dm
D7 / Dm / D
Dm / D / D7

Albert schielte vorsichtig durch das runde Loch seiner Höhle, von der aus er den gesamten Strand im Auge behalten konnte. Es war unverkennbar Mona.

Die Freude darüber, dass Franz nirgends zu sehen war, wich jäh der Ernüchterung, als er an ihrer Seite einen anderen Mann erblickte. Wer dieser grossgewachsene, ihm nicht bekannte Knilch bloss sein mochte? Es beruhigte Albert etwas, dass sich die beiden nicht wie ein verliebtes Paar hätschelten. Sie sprachen lediglich miteinander, ohne sich dabei zu berühren. Allerdings waren sie gemeinsam angekommen, und nun gingen sie gemeinsam in die entgegengesetzte Richtung der Höhlen über den Strand. Mona hatte kein Gepäck dabei, der Unbekannte hingegen schleppte mühelos einen grossen Sack auf dem Rücken. Ob er etwa nur ihr Gepäckträger war? Dazu hinterliess er einen etwas zu wohlhabenden Eindruck. Die beiden verschwanden im Café Mermaid.

Ich brauche dich, ich lüge nicht. Ohne deine Liebe werde ich bestimmt sterben. Oh Mona.

Es wurde dunkler.

Heute würde Albert nicht mehr nach draussen gehen, das stand fest. Es galt nun, erst die Lage abzuschätzen, nichts zu überstürzen. Immerhin rechnete sie doch eher nicht damit, hier einem anfangs Sommer zu Grabe getragenen Mann zu begegnen. Ob er Mona zutrauen konnte, ihm zu verzeihen, ihn zu verstehen und als immer noch Lebenden zu akzeptieren? Wenn nicht Mona, wem dann?

Fest stand also auch, dass er sie nicht weiterziehen lassen wollte, ohne sich ihr irgendwie angenähert zu haben.

64. Das gestohlene Lied

F / C / G
F / Am / G
F / C / G
F / C / G

Mona war immer noch eine Augenweide. Das starre Gesicht, mit dem sie noch zu seiner Beerdigung erschienen war, hatte wieder zu ursprünglicher Schönheit gefunden. Wann immer sie sich in Sichtweite seiner Höhle aufhielt, beobachtete Albert sie in geduckter Stellung. Beobachtete, wie sie einige Meter ins Meer hinaus watete, wie sie sich am Strand sonnte, wie sie ihr Eis kostete oder an einem Orangensaft nippte. Besonders angespannt schaute er hin, wenn sie sich mit ihrem immer noch anwesenden Begleiter zeigte – und das kam anwidernd oft vor. Wenn sich die beiden unterhielten, versuchte er jeweils angestrengt, zumindest einige Wortfetzen aufzunehmen. Es gelang ihm nicht.

Mona hauste im Café Mermaid. Sie hatte ja genug Geld, um sich ein Zimmer leisten zu können. Das konnte Albert recht sein. Er war erleichtert darüber, dass sie sich nicht in einer nahen Höhle eingerichtet hatte.

Heute nun sass Mona wieder am Strand, sogar ganz in seiner Nähe, und noch aufregender als ihr stilvoller Bikini war die Tatsache, dass sie allein war.

Entlang der Felsnase, in einer deren Höhlen sich Albert ein paar Meter höher kaum zu bewegen getraute, schritt sie ins Meer und liess sich in das erfrischende Nass fallen. Albert konnte sie nun nicht mehr sehen – sie war zu nahe bei ihm. Der Felsvorsprung vor seiner Höhle verdeckte ihm die Sicht. Er vernahm nur noch das sanfte Rieseln des Wassers, als Mona mit langsamen Zügen zu schwimmen begann.

Wenn er sich nun aus seiner Höhle gewagt und sich über den Vorsprung geworfen hätte, wäre er direkt neben Mona ins

Wasser eingetaucht. Hätte mit beiden Armen nach ihr greifen können, ihr die frohe Botschaft, sein Überleben, verkünden, mit ihr gemeinsam im Meer, im Glück baden können. Einen kleinen Augenblick dachte er daran, die halsbrecherische Idee zur Tat zu machen, konnte seinen Drang dann aber doch bändigen.

Fieberhaft griff er schliesslich zur Gitarre und stimmte das Lied an, das er Mona gewidmet hatte.

Sie watete an den Strand zurück. *Kannst du mich hören? Kannst du mich hören, wie ich das Lied zu dir singe? Halte die Ohren offen. Kannst du mich sehen?*

Albert wusste nicht, ob er sich nur einbildete, dass Mona kurz aufhorchte, den Kopf etwas zur Seite neigte – und sich schliesslich dessen ungeachtet wieder hinlegte. Ob sie zu weit weg war, das Meer zu laut rauschte? Oder ob sie sein Lied gar nicht in Erinnerung hatte?

Du kannst mich nicht sehen.

Zutiefst enttäuscht sass Albert später gitarreklimpernd an der Mauer innerhalb seiner Höhle, die Beine gestreckt und übereinandergelegt. Er überlegte sich, ob er das sehnlichst erwartete Zusammentreffen mit Mona nicht akustisch, mit einer berauschenden Melodie, vorwegnehmen konnte. Das Lied seines Lebens – immer noch fehlte ihm die Schlussstrophe. Konnte Musik aber überhaupt derart erlösend, ekstatisch sein, um dem Ereignis gerecht zu werden?

Er schloss die Augen.

Er schwelgte in seinen Träumen. Versuchte, sich das Wiedersehen mit Mona in allen Einzelheiten vorzustellen. Versuchte dann, alle noch so beiläufigen Gedanken in Töne zu verwandeln. Er schwelgte in seinem Gitarrenspiel …

Als er die Augen wieder aufmachte, fand er sich in seiner dunklen, von öden Felswänden beengten Höhle wieder, in der nur Platz für ihn allein vorhanden war.

Nur grosse Gefühle erzeugen grosse Musik, davon war

Albert überzeugt. Woher aber nimmt man die Gefühle, die demnach am Ursprung der Musik stehen? Bloss aus Fantasien? Nein, musste er feststellen, bloss mit Fantasie liessen sich nicht alle Gefühle herleiten, dies war ihm ausreichend aufgezeigt worden. Seine stärksten Gefühle gründeten vielmehr auf Erlebtem, auf Erfahrenem.

Da begriff Albert etwas. Die grenzenlose Sehnsucht nach Mona, nach Liebe und Leben hatte er in seinen vermeintlich letzten Stunden auf eindrückliche Manier vertonen können. Weil sie real war. Ebenso die Stimmung des nahenden Todes. Die Begegnung mit Mona war allerdings nur in seinen blanken Gedanken, in seinen entlegenen Fantasien gegenwärtig. Es war nicht möglich, sie zu vertonen – jedenfalls nicht so, wie sie es verdient hätte. Ausserdem konnte ihm keine Melodie der Welt die unbefriedigende Wirklichkeit ersetzen. Er begann, eine gewisse Abscheu für seine Gitarre zu empfinden.

Es krachte. Holzspäne flogen durch den Innenraum der Höhle. Die Gitarre lag zerschmettert auf dem Steinboden. Abermals krachte es. Die Gitarre zerfiel in zwei Teile – der Gitarrenhals wurde nur noch von den Saiten mit dem Korpus verbunden. Albert setzte seinen Fuss auf den Korpus und zerrte mit aller Kraft am Gitarrenhals. Saite um Saite gab nach und peitschte durch die Luft.

Albert betrachtete den Gitarrenkorpus. Die Rundungen erinnerten ihn irgendwie an Mona. Nun, eine Gitarre würde er bestimmt nicht noch einmal umarmen, so tief würde er sich nicht mehr herablassen. Er hatte jetzt anderes verdient. Besseres.

Verbittert schleuderte er den Korpus aus dem Höhlenloch. Er flog über den Felsvorsprung und klatschte auf die Meeresoberfläche.

65. Wandmalerei

Albert Leblanc war fahl. Seit Tagen hatte er nicht mehr richtig gegessen, obwohl er sich in seiner Höhle einen Vorrat an Hartbrot und Trinkwasser zugelegt hatte. Seine Höhle war zu seinem Refugium geworden. Er verliess sie nur noch nachts, nur noch in äusserster Not.

Seit ihrer Ankunft in Matala hatte er Mona bereits dreiunddreissig Mal erblickt. Auch hatte er erzürnt feststellen müssen, dass sich dieser abstossende Fremdling praktisch ununterbrochen an ihrer Seite aufhielt – insgesamt sechsundzwanzig Mal bisher.

Aus Langeweile hatte er begonnen, mit einem spitzen Stein die Innenwände seiner Höhle zu bekritzeln. Alle nur erdenklichen Dinge hatten ihre Verewigung im Sandstein gefunden. Erst hielt er Namen von Akkorden, dann ganze Akkordfolgen, oder – falls ihm die genauen Bezeichnungen nicht bekannt waren – Skizzen der Gitarrengriffbilder fest. Was hatte ihn nur für ein Teufel geritten, sein geliebtes Instrument zu zertrümmern? Zum Glück besass er noch den Gitarrenhals. So konnte er die Zeit mit dem Greifen von Akkorden totschlagen, wenn diese auch stumm blieben.

Mithilfe von eingeritzten Strichen zählte er akribisch, wie oft er Mona nun bereits mit und ohne Begleitung gesichtet hatte. Ausserdem zeichnete Albert. Zeichnete ein brennendes Haus, eine Frau mit Muttermal, Grabkreuze mit den Namen Hans Fahler und Natan Natos, versehen mit der Dauer ihrer Lebenszeit. In endlos langen Rechnungen ermittelte er ausserdem, wie lange er nun bereits am Leben war. Bald würde er eine Milliarde alt werden.

Eine Milliarde Sekunden.

Gestern um elf hatte er ziemlich genau achthundertachtundachtzig Millionen Sekunden lang gelebt. Ärgerlich, dass er seine genaue Geburtszeit nicht kannte. Heute Nachmittag hatte er sich ausserdem ausgerechnet, wie viele Sekunden sich

Mona bereits in Matala befand, und anschliessend das Resultat durch dreiunddreissig geteilt. Und nachts, da versuchte er, sich möglichst viele Sternbilder des leuchtenden Nachthimmels von Matala einzuprägen, um sie tags darauf an seine Höhlendecke skizzieren zu können.

66. *Form von intelligentem Leben*

Sind das die Sterne im Himmel, oder regnet es weit von hier, weit von jetzt? Wird es mich verbrennen, wenn ich die Sonne berühre? Bin ich wahrhaftig, wenn ich dich als das Einzige für mich wähle? Oh, wie ist mein Geist durcheinander. Müssen all ihre Züge mir vergönnt bleiben? Mein Herz brennt, aber mein Verstand ist kalt und taumelt.

Jede Bewegung ist in sechs Schritten vollendet. Und der siebte bringt die Rückkehr. Sieben ist die Zahl des jungen Lichts. Es ergibt sich, wenn man Dunkelheit um eins erhöht. Sonnenuntergang, Sonnenaufgang.

Keine Sonne scheint in meine Höhle. Ich fühle mich, wie ich in meinem Grab leben würde. Keine Sonne in meiner Höhle. Ich wünsche mir, beeile dich und rette mich. Heute lebe ich nicht. Vielleicht morgen, ich weiss es nicht.

Jede Bewegung ist in sechs Schritten vollendet. Und der siebte bringt die Rückkehr. Sieben ist die Zahl des jungen Lichts. Es ergibt sich, wenn man Dunkelheit um eins erhöht. Sonnenuntergang, Sonnenaufgang.

Lass mich neben deinem Feuer stehen. Ich habe nur einen brennenden Wunsch. Lass mich neben deinem Feuer stehen.

Jede Bewegung ist in sechs Schritten vollendet. Und der siebte bringt die Rückkehr. Sieben ist die Zahl des jungen Lichts. Es ergibt sich, wenn man Dunkelheit um eins erhöht. Sonnenuntergang, Sonnenaufgang.

Bin ich glücklich oder elend? Ein weinroter Schleier umhüllt meine Augen. Ich weiss nicht, ob jetzt Tag oder Nacht ist. Du hast mir meinen Verstand weggeblasen. Ist es morgen, oder einfach das Ende der Zeit?

Jede Bewegung ist in sechs Schritten vollendet. Und der siebte bringt die Rückkehr. Sieben ist die Zahl des jungen Lichts. Es ergibt sich, wenn man Dunkelheit um eins erhöht. Sonnenuntergang, Sonnenaufgang.

Ich bin in der Umlaufbahn um den dritten Planeten vom

Stern namens Sonne. Du meinst, dass dies die Erde ist? Es ist bekannt, dass es dort irgendeine Form von intelligentem Leben gibt. Ich denke, wir sollten einen Blick darauf werfen.

Sonnenuntergang, Sonnenaufgang.

67. Vangelis

Sonnenuntergang, Sonnenaufgang, Sonnenuntergang.

Möglicherweise war es die so eingetretene Abgestumpftheit seines Hirns, welche die Furcht vor dem Wiedersehen mit Mona allmählich abschwächte und zugleich eine gewisse Kühnheit in ihm entfesselte.

Als Mona und ihr Gefährte eines Abends am Strand sassen und sich dem Meer zugewandt hatten, verliess Albert seine Höhle.

«Ich bin sehr froh, dass ich hier sein kann, Vangelis», sagte Mona zu ihrem Begleiter, der offensichtlich Grieche war. «Es war heute wieder sehr interessant und … schön.»

«Ich möchte dir noch mehr zeigen, Mona», hauchte Vangelis.

«Gerne. Ich bin gespannt.» Mona lächelte.

«Du kennst doch die Paximadia-Inseln, oder?»

«Ja. Du hast mir ja bereits von ihnen erzählt.»

«Ich möchte morgen mit dir dahin gehen, Mona.»

Sie sah nicht allzu erfreut aus. «Du weisst doch, Vangelis – ich fürchte mich etwas auf dem Meer.»

«Morgen früh werde ich ein Boot organisieren, das uns zu den Inseln bringen wird.» Vangelis zeigte Entschlossenheit, ging gar nicht auf Monas Bedenken ein. Unmissverständlich fügte er noch hinzu: «Keine Seele werden wir dort antreffen. Dort herrscht noch so etwas wie das Paradies.»

Albert, der sich hinter einer Baumreihe versteckt hielt, fuhr sich durch die Nackenhaare. Er hatte genug gehört. Er raste vor Wut und Enttäuschung. Dieser Grieche war ihm mehr als ein dicker Dorn im Auge. Er war ihm zutiefst überdrüssig.

Als er wieder in seiner Höhle lag, hallten ihm die letzten Worte von Vangelis noch in den Ohren. «Keine Seele werden wir dort antreffen.» Da hatte er sich aber gewaltig geirrt, dachte sich Albert aufgeregt, begierig.

Plötzlich vernahm er zwei weibliche Stimmen. Es waren

die Stimmen von Britta und Frida, den beiden Schwedinnen.

«Hallo Hübscher», sagte die eine, «hast du jetzt vielleicht Lust, uns in deine Höhle reinzulassen?»

Albert hatte keine Lust.

68. Paximadia

Das Meer färbte sich allmählich heller, um schliesslich wieder das reine Türkisblau anzunehmen.

Vangelis hatte Mona im Café Mermaid abgeholt. Mona freute sich nun doch auf den Abstecher nach Paximadia. Zu verlockend ragten die Inseln aus dem Meer, um ihrer Anmut nicht zu erliegen.

Als sie das Boot erblickte, das nahe der linken Felsnase im Meer schaukelte, verflog ihr Kummer umgehend. Das Boot war recht gross und würde den beiden hinten auf dem Deck einen sicheren Sitzplatz bieten.

«Wir können einsteigen, der Bootsmann ist bereit.» Vangelis forderte Mona auf, über die leicht begehbare Felsplatte ins Boot zu steigen und reichte ihr dabei die Hand.

Als die beiden Platz genommen hatten, startete der Motor. Vangelis sah durch seine Sonnenbrille, wie die braunen Haare von Mona im Wind zu flattern begannen. Langsam entfernte sich der Sandstrand von Matala. Die Paximadia-Inseln, die von der Küste aus zum Greifen nah schienen, wurden aber nur unmerklich grösser.

«Wie lange bleiben wir auf der Insel?» Mona musste schreien, damit Vangelis sie hören konnte. Der dröhnende Motor und das Fauchen des Windes verhinderten ein normales Gespräch.

«Das Boot wird uns heute Abend wieder abholen kommen», anwortete Vangelis zufrieden.

«Heute Abend erst?» Mona war etwas irritiert.

«Ich habe für uns Brot, Tomaten, Oliven und Feta mitgenommen, dazu Wasser und Wein.» Vangelis zeigte mit einer selbstgefälligen Armbewegung auf den Korb, der vor seinen Füssen lag.

Ob Mona wirklich den ganzen Tag mit Vangelis auf einer einsamen Insel, umschlossen von den Tiefen des Meeres, verbringen wollte? Irgendwie war ihr doch etwas mulmig zu

Mute. Konnte sie ihm überhaupt trauen? Ihrem Gefühl nach schon, doch bereits allzu oft hätte sie sich gerade auf dieses Gefühl nicht verlassen dürfen. Was wollte sie mit ihm? Was wollte er mit ihr? Auf jeden Fall hatte sie vor, heute nichts zu überstürzen.

Plötzlich wurde es still.

Der Motor war ausgefallen. Mona blickte besorgt über das Bootsgeländer – die Distanz zur Küste war schon beträchtlich. Vangelis versuchte, sich zuversichtlich zu geben, war aber bereits etwas gereizt. Aus der Fahrerkabine vernahmen die beiden ein Klopfen.

«Keine Sorge, Mona, das wird schon wieder. Kleine Defekte sind auf See an der Tagesordnung.»

«Was versteht man unter kleinen Defekten?»

«Keine Ahnung, vielleicht ist ihm einfach das Benzin ausgegangen.»

Mona und Vangelis warteten einige Augenblicke, doch es tat sich nichts. Immer stärker gelangte das Boot in die Herrschaft des unruhig wippenden Meeres.

«Ich gehe mal zum Fahrer und schaue nach», sagte Vangelis plötzlich, seiner Ungeduld nachgebend. Er erhob sich und suchte die Fahrerkabine auf.

Gespannt wartete Mona auf dem Deck und hoffte, dass sich die Angelegenheit alsbald zum Guten wenden würde. Eigentlich verrückt, was sie hier alles erlebte, dachte sie. Noch im Frühjahr hatte sie Tag für Tag die Gäste eines Dorfgasthofs bedient und war abends neben dem Mann eingeschlafen, den sie bedauerlicherweise einmal geheiratet hatte. Und nun sass sie plötzlich mitten im Meer auf einem defekten Boot mit einem Griechen, dessen Bekanntschaft sie zufälligerweise auf einer längeren Reise gemacht hatte.

«Es scheint irgendein Problem mit dem Motor zu geben.» Vangelis holte sie aus ihren Gedanken. «Der Propeller funktioniert nicht mehr.»

Vangelis ging an Mona vorbei und betrat den hintersten

Teil des Bootes. Er ging auf die Knie, streckte seinen Kopf zwischen die Verstrebungen der Reling und blickte in die Tiefe.

«Ich kann nichts sehen», lautete sein verärgerter Kommentar. «Weder Propeller noch Motor.»

«Kann ich irgendwie helfen?», fragte Mona anstandshalber und gesellte sich zu ihm.

«Nein, Mona, lass nur.» Er stützte seine Arme auf die blaue Reling, um noch besser auf den Unterbau des Bootshecks sehen zu können. Mona setzte sich wieder.

Da wurde das Boot von einem plötzlichen Schub erfasst. Der Motor heulte laut auf und brachte das Gefährt schlagartig wieder in Bewegung. Mona wurde von ihrem Sitz geworfen, konnte sich aber an einem Seil festhalten, das am Geländer angebracht war.

Als sie sich wieder aufrappelte und ihren Kopf aufrichtete, bemerkte sie das Unglück. Die Reling an der Rückseite des Bootes hatte sich gelöst und war ins Meer gefallen – und mit ihr Vangelis. Mona erblickte ihn mit den Armen rudernd in den schäumenden Wellen. Sein Gesicht war verzerrt, aus seinem offenen Mund vermutete sie einen Hilferuf.

Das Unheil hatte sich im Nu ereignet, und für einen Augenblick kam sich Mona ohnmächtig vor. Dann erst schrie sie ihm nach, womit sich seine ungemütliche Lage aber keinen Deut verbesserte. Sie musste den Bootsmann verständigen! Vielleicht hatte dieser gar nicht bemerkt, was auf dem Deck vorgefallen war!

Sie eilte zur Kabine und drückte den Türgriff nach unten. Die Tür war verschlossen. Sie hämmerte an die Tür und spähte durch das runde Fenster, das Einsicht in die Kabine gestattete. Der Bootsmann hatte seinen Blick auf das Meer hinaus gerichtet und fuhr unbeirrt weiter. Er hatte eine weisse Kutte über die Schultern geworfen und trug einen grossen Hut, unter dem dunkle Haare hervorkräuselten. Vangelis musste nun schon in einiger Entfernung im Meer treiben, doch der Bootsmann hörte Mona nicht. Und je länger er sie nicht hörte, umso stärker wuchs in ihr der Eindruck, dass er sie gar nicht hören wollte.

Ihre Schläge gegen die Tür wurden schwächer. Das energische Trommeln verwandelte sich allmählich in ein schwaches, hoffnungsloses Klopfen.

Auf einmal, als der Motor wieder etwas leiser wurde, konnte Mona aus der Kabine ein Pfeifen vernehmen.

Sie hörte genau hin.

Die Töne klangen etwas schief, doch sie waren ihr wohlbekannt. Der Bootsmann pfiff das geheimnisvolle Lied, das sie nun schon zum vierten Mal zu Ohren bekam.

Und dann geschah das, was sich mit gesundem und urteilsfähigem Menschenverstand nicht erklären liess. Es war ein Anblick, der jedem noch so schicksalserprobten Erdenbürger durch Mark und Bein gegangen wäre. Ob je ein Wesen unter der Sonne von solcher Ungläubigkeit erfasst worden war, wie Mona in dem Moment, als der Bootsmann ihr kurz eine Gesichtshälfte zuwandte?

Eine Starre von Kopf bis Fuss ereilte sie, als sie in das bleiche, ausdrucksleere Antlitz des verstorbenen Albert Leblanc blickte.

69. Der verschlossene Garten

Mona hatte sich wieder hingesetzt. Nach einer langen Fahrt strandete das Boot an einer flach abfallenden Küste auf der westlicheren der beiden Paximadia-Inseln.

Nun endlich öffnete sich die Tür der Bootskabine. Aus der Kabine trat ein Mann, der Mona zwar anders in Erinnerung geblieben, jedoch zweifellos mit jenem identisch war, den sie gekannt hatte.

«Hallo, Mona», begrüsste Albert sie mit zittriger Stimme. Mona aber sass draussen und weinte. Wie sie nun weinte, beugte sich Albert über ihren niedergesunkenen Kopf und fragte: «Was weinst du, Mona?»

Sie antwortete nicht.

Albert liess sie noch eine Weile dasitzen, bis er ihr die Hand reichte. Mona nahm seine Hand und er führte sie vom Boot an den Strand. Eine Zeitlang gingen sie, ohne miteinander zu sprechen. An einer einsamen Stelle, die noch nie von Menschen betreten worden war, blieben sie stehen und schauten sich an. Albert zog sie an sich heran und drückte sie fest.

Sie liessen sich in den feinen Sand fallen. Sie waren allein, und vor ihnen lag nichts als das unbegrenzte Meer – es war ihre Insel. Gab es überhaupt noch anderes Land, andere Menschen?

Albert fand sich in einer herrlichen Welt wieder. In einer Welt, wo sich Bäume mit prallen Äpfeln brüsteten, wo ihn unbekannte Pilzarten mit wollüstigen Duftwogen betäubten, wo Bäche aus Wein wohltuend rauschten und Rosen ihre Knospen im Sekundentakt öffneten.

Mona war braun, die Sonne hatte sie verbrannt. Braun und schön. Alles an ihr war schön, es haftete ihr kein Makel an. Seine Linke lag unter ihrem Kopf, seine Rechte umfing sie. Albert war krank vor Liebe, und er hoffte, dass nichts die Liebe stören, die Liebe aufwecken würde. Noch süsser als der gemeinsame Wein war die Liebe. Albert gelangte in einen verschlossenen Garten, roch, kostete, verzehrte die kostbaren Früchte und Blüten. Wie süss sie in seinem Gaumen schmeckten!

70.

Em9 / A
A / Em / Bm / A
A / Em / Bm / A / G
Em / Bm / Em / Em
G / A / E / Dm
Am / F / E
Am / F / H
Em / D / C / D
Em / D / Cadd9 / D
Em / D / C / Dsus2
Em / A / Em
Dsus2
Em
Em
Em
Em
Dsus2

71. Die Verbannung

Die unwirklichen und flüchtigen Erinnerungen an jenen himmlischen Tag veranlassten Albert danach nicht etwa dazu, an den Geschehnissen zu zweifeln. Vielmehr unterstrichen sie für ihn die Eigenart der Stunden, die nur ihm und Mona gehört hatten. Erst später schöpfte er den niederschmetternden Verdacht, dass die Stunden nur von ihm so über alle Massen ausgekostet worden waren.

Am nächsten Morgen war Albert aufgewacht, müde, nackt und – allein. Er hatte Mona anschliessend gesucht. Sie überall gesucht. Sie nicht gefunden.

Schon für manchen mag die Welt zusammengebrochen sein. Bei Albert jedoch war es nicht die Welt, die zusammenbrach. Es war das Paradies. Entsprechend grösser war der Schmerz, der sich im Anschluss in seiner Seele niederliess.

Als er registriert hatte, dass nicht nur Mona, sondern auch das Boot verschwunden war, war ihm der Umfang der Katastrophe langsam bewusst geworden. Ohne grosse Hoffnung, die Küste Matalas lebend zu erreichen, war er daraufhin losgeschwommen. Matrosen hatten ihn später entkräftet an Bord ihres Schiffes gezogen.

Nun lebte Albert Leblanc also immer noch.

War jetzt der Zeitpunkt gekommen, sich endgültig umzubringen?

Nein. Den letzten Kieselstein, den er sorgfältig aufbewahrt hatte, trug er nun um seinen Hals, denn kein anderer Gegenstand bedeutete ihm mehr. Nie hatte er bedauert, letzten Juni nicht gestorben zu sein. Warum sollte er also jetzt, in jenen gewiss unsäglich trostlosen Tagen, die Hoffnung verlieren, wieder einmal glücklich zu sein?

All jene kläglichen und berauschenden Momente, die er erlebt hatte, würde er für immer mit sich tragen – in seinem Herzen, in seinem Lied. Das Lied seines Lebens nämlich war jetzt vollendet.

Ob er Mona böse war? Er konnte, durfte es nicht. Weshalb sie sich ihm aber so grenzenlos hingegeben hatte? Aus Angst, oder etwa doch aus einem Hauch von Liebe? Albert wusste es nicht.

Er würde dereinst – vielleicht in Wochen, vielleicht in Jahren – sich die Frage stellen, ob er denn Mona wirklich geliebt hatte. Er würde sich dann einreden, dass sie ihn damals, im Juni 1967, in seinem düstersten Lebensabschnitt, nur mit ihren weiblichen Waffen oder mit einer an sich nicht ausserordentlichen Zuwendung in ihren Bann gezogen hatte. Und wenn er sich dann schliesslich würde eingestehen können, dass er sie doch viel zu wenig gekannt hatte, um ihr derart verfallen zu sein, dann würde er versuchen, sie nicht mehr als einzige Frau auf Erden zu betrachten.

In einem nicht ganz unwesentlichen Punkt würde er ihr aber, gerade wenn er in vielen Jahren an sie zurückdenken mochte, stets mit Dank verbunden sein. Sie hatte ihm wohl einen frühen Tod erspart.

Epilog

Eine Dunstwolke aus saurem Männerschweiss und prägnantem Frauenparfum, aus üblen Bierfahnen, ätzendem Friteusendampf und beissendem Rauch von Zigaretten lag in der Luft. Sie hatte sich bereits in den Kleidern, den Haaren, ja sogar in der Haut der anwesenden Gäste eingenistet. Die frische Nachtluft, die durch ein offenes Fenster in den Raum strömte, vermochte das Gemisch aus ekligen Düften nicht zu verdrängen. Diese Unannehmlichkeiten schienen jedoch niemanden zu stören. Man lachte, diskutierte, atmete sorglos weiter.

In einer Ecke sass eine elegant gekleidete Frau, die ihre besten Jahre noch vor sich hatte. Ein Stück ihres Hirschmedaillons verschwand durch ihre diskret gefärbten Lippen, während ihrem nicht minder aufgeputzten Freund ein Tropfen australischer Shiraz die Kehle hinunterrann. Gleich daneben, im dichten Qualm ihres eigenen Parfums, ereiferten sich vier Frauen höheren Alters über eine Chance, die in Bedrängnis nicht verwertet worden war. Der Unparteiische, dessen Pfiff wieder einmal ausblieb, wurde unverzüglich zum Sündenbock erkoren. Am nächsten Tisch schlürften zwei kürzlich aus der Schule gekommene Mädchen an ihrem Martini und unterhielten sich dabei über die Sendung, die seit einer Woche nicht mehr ausgestrahlt wurde. Derweil trat der Kaufmann ein und befestigte sein Mobiltelefon wieder an seinem Gürtel. Aufgrund seiner stets etwas länger dauernden Ferngespräche hatte er den Beginn einer hitzigen Diskussion um den neuformierten Bundesrat verpasst, die in seiner Runde vonstatten ging. Ein wenig abseits überdies studierte ein junger Banker die Börsenkurse von einundzwanzig Uhr. In der Mitte der Gaststube schliesslich – an der Stelle, an der die Nerven am gespanntesten waren – legte ein Mann mit Hut und feinen Koteletten der Serviertochter die Hand auf den Rücken, nachdem sie ihm seinen dritten Wodka gebracht hatte.

Um den grossen Tisch, der im Zentrum stand, scharte sich

mindestens ein Dutzend Gäste. Im Grunde spielte sich an jenem Tisch dasselbe ab wie an den restlichen. Es wurde gegessen, getrunken, das Eishockeyspiel verfolgt, man bemängelte das Fernsehprogramm, politisierte ohne Einstimmigkeit und beklagte die Teuerung des Benzins. Aus Platzgründen hatte man sich eher zufällig an den gleichen Tisch gesetzt. So fanden sich Leute aus allen Dorfwinkeln, mit unterschiedlichsten Jahrgängen, Zivilständen und Trinkgewohnheiten zusammen. *Flügel der Sehnsucht tragen uns, wohin wir wollen. Flügel der Sehnsucht lassen uns in die Ewigkeit fliegen*, tönte es leise aus dem Radio.

«Kennt eigentlich jemand von euch Albert Leblanc?», fragte der ältere Mann mit dem langen ergrauten Bart zögerlich.

Die neben ihm sitzenden Burschen, bei denen ebenfalls erste Gesichtsbehaarung zu spriessen begann, schüttelten allesamt den Kopf. Sie widmeten sich ohnehin lieber dem Spiel, in dem es nach einer Verlängerung roch.

«Doch, ich habe schon von ihm gehört», sagte plötzlich ein Milchgesicht mit etwas längeren Haaren.

«Tatsächlich?» Der Alte hob überrascht die Brauen. «Kannst du mir von ihm erzählen?»

«Viel weiss ich nicht über ihn. Aber es ist eine verrückte Geschichte. Er war früher Koch, hier im Gasthof. Dann hat er sich plötzlich mitsamt seinem Haus in Brand gesetzt», begann der junge Mann.

«Was du nicht sagst! Und was passierte dann?», erkundigte sich der Alte.

«Was soll dann passiert sein, er war natürlich tot.» Er grinste zynisch. «Doch das Verrückte war sein letzter Wunsch. Seine Gitarre, die er wohl über alles geliebt hatte, sollte über seinem Sarg in die Erde gesteckt werden.»

Der Alte blickte ihn erwartungsvoll an, doch der Junge hatte seinen Blick bereits wieder auf das Eisfeld gerichtet.

«Ich danke dir.»

«Weshalb fragen Sie nach ihm?»

«Er war ein guter Freund von mir.»

«Ach so. Das tut mir leid.»

«Es muss dir nicht leid tun. Es ist lange her.»

Noch bevor das Spiel in der Landeshauptstadt beendet war, verliess der Alte den Gasthof.

Am Garten des Pfarrhauses machte er kurz Halt und pflückte an einem Blumenbeet eine Nelke, die bereits blühte. Es war dunkel und kalt.

Er betrat den mit Kieselsteinen bedeckten Platz. Früher noch hätte ihn der Gang, den er jetzt antrat, mit Anspannung, ja mit Grauen erfüllt. Heute nicht mehr.

Eine Weile ging er mit langsamen Schritten durch die Grabreihen, bis er auf einmal stehen blieb.

Da war es – das Grab.

Es war wahrlich ein aussergewöhnliches Grab. Der Gitarrenhals steckte in der Erde, auf dem Rücken des Korpus standen Name und Lebensdauer. Daneben war ein oval ausgeschnittenes Bild angebracht. Die Gitarre zierte das Grab, so, wie er es sich in Gedanken immer ausgemalt hatte. Nur eines entsprach so nicht seinen Vorstellungen: Die Gitarre war aus massivem Stein.

Er legte die Nelke, die er eben gepflückt hatte, auf das Grab. Da sah er, dass im Grabbeet einsam eine Rose lag.

Es war eine rote Rose.

Sie war etwas verwelkt, aber sie war da. Einen Moment lang blieb er noch, bis seine Kräfte langsam schwanden. Er war schwach, doch haderte er nicht. Dann bückte er sich, nahm die Rose und schritt überwältigt davon.